IN VIVO

A NOVEL BY

MILDRED SAVAGE

SIMON AND SCHUSTER

NEW YORK

TO MY HUSBAND

To me this is, in a sense, an historical novel, even though we are in only the second decade of the age of antibiotics. Today knowledge and tools in this phase of drug research are plentiful and sophisticated, but at the close of the Second World War, when a few men in a few laboratories—in universities, in research foundations, in industry—began to search for antibiotics, the techniques were crude and knowledge of the subject was almost nonexistent. In research this was a frontier, and these men were pioneers—as much as the men who, in another era, went west to open new territorial frontiers.

As with any historical novel, it has been necessary to go to the sources, and in this case the sources have been the men who lived the story—who were part of the search or who were able to observe it closely. More than a hundred persons—in industry, in universities, in government research—have contributed information. Many busy men gave me hours of their time in order to explain the sciences and the techniques involved. Many of them, in the interest of accuracy, took the trouble to dig out old records long since filed away. Many men who have since then done other important research have said, "Those were exciting days—*that* was a story, and it has never been told." I have tried to tell it as I heard it, with all the agonies and the ecstasies that were a part of it—and that will always be part of all research, as long as men continue the struggle to break through new frontiers.

I am grateful for the patience and the generous help of these men, and I have not modeled characters after any of them or after anyone described, referred to, or remembered by any of them.

—M. S.

PART ONE

APRIL 1946

DR. CLAUDE MORRISSEY, director of biochemistry at the Enright Drug and Chemical Company, was damned annoyed.

Striding into his office, he put his briefcase down on the desk and just stood a moment, still clutching the handle. "That damn fool, Cable," Morrissey said to himself. "Damn-fool crackpot idea."

Irritably, Morrissey began brushing away at the pocket of his tweed jacket, as though removing a speck of dust or lint. He had just come from a company meeting, and ordinarily after a company meeting he felt fine. Ordinarily he enjoyed a comfortable sense of having achieved a sound responsible position in life. Not today. To-day's meeting had been called to examine again, before the directors' meeting on Friday, this crackpot idea of Dr. Cable's that a drug could be discovered with curing properties that were beyond the imagination of any sensible research man.

When Dr. Morrissey first heard the idea, he had called upon the experience of twenty-four years at Enright and pronounced it unscientific. "What Dr. Cable hopes to stumble on is not a drug," he had said with a chuckle. "It's a witches' brew." When Dr. Harrup, the director of chemical research, heard it, he shook his head gloomily and said, "Impossible." When Mr. Brainard, the vice-president for production, heard it, he used a word that Dr. Morrissey would not repeat. Today the three men had gone to the meeting with a clear purpose—to "put the idea on the shelf," which was the Enright equivalent of sudden death, to block its getting to the board of directors. And right to the end, the meeting had gone even better than Morrissey had hoped. Everyone had opposed the idea. Ade Hale, the president, had picked it to pieces. Tom Cable had made a complete fool of himself. And then the meeting had ended —all wrong.

Morrissey's eyes swept across his desk, taking in the afternoon mail and the picture of Winifred, his wife, and then the handsome bookends that held three stout reference works on biochemistry. For eight years those bookends and books had stood there. He could remember the day he brought them in—May 4, 1938—the day after he had been appointed head of the department and had moved into this office.

Eight years next week, he thought. If he said it himself, in those eight years he had run an efficient department, a tight ship, without friction or dissension—until now. Damn it, he just didn't like this thing cropping up in his department. Not that anyone was blaming him—not yet—but you never knew when someone might start. At the board meeting they might ask embarrassing questions. Those directors were smart and they liked to let you know it.

His eyes went back to the picture of Winifred and he told himself that he ought to call her. He ran his hand over his close-cropped, white hair and picked up the telephone.

"It's over," he said, and reached across to close his office door.

"Well—?" she said. "How did it go?"

"I don't know—Tom Cable made an awful fool of himself. Yelled like a maniac. Walked out."

She gave a dry little laugh.

"Everyone was against it," Morrissey said. "You could see Ade Hale didn't cotton up to it at all."

"Then what are you worried about?"

"Because the thing is still alive. Right to the end I thought Hale would throw it out. But he didn't."

"Did he come right out and say it—that it would go to the board?"

"It's on the agenda. He didn't take it off."

Mentally he could see her frowning. He could picture her plunked down on the little seat in front of the telephone—her hard brown eyes riveted on it as though it were he—thoughtfully stroking her thumb over her colorless lined face. Often lately Morrissey had noticed that Winifred looked older than he did, an observation that both pleased and fretted him. There were times when he wished she were more attractive—and then other times he enjoyed reflecting that he had held on so firmly to his own youthful appearance.

"Well, if it is, it is," she said now.

"That's easy to say," he said, "but this is dangerous. Fantastic as that idea is, it just might look interesting to those directors. Someone is going to tell them that if we could actually find a drug like that, we'd make a fortune."

"You would."

"Well, then they just might be tempted to try it. And then you

10

know whose lap the problems will fall into. Mine. It'll be in my department."

He jiggled the handle of his briefcase and glanced out the window and saw Ade Hale heading for the fermentation building, walking as he always did, as though the whole place would blow up if he didn't get there in thirty seconds.

"Claude," she said, "tell me what happened. Tell me what *you* said."

"I washed my hands of any association with it. That's what was important."

"What did you *say?*"

"Well, I was brief. And I certainly didn't stoop to arguing with Cable. I told them the whole idea was unscientific."

"That's all?"

"I told them," he said, "that this was like looking for a needle in a haystack—when you don't know what the needle looks like or whether you're even in the right field—or whether there's even any needle there to be found at all—which I doubt."

"You said that at breakfast," she said dryly.

Now Morrissey saw Gil Brainard heading for the fermentation building, too, and he thought, Good—now Brainard will get Ade Hale alone and talk to him.

"Winifred, there's cocktails and dinner for the directors tomorrow night at the Inn and we're all going. Gil Brainard thinks it would be a good idea for some of us to do a little quiet talking against this then, if we can, before they get it on Friday at the meeting. A little insurance against anything going wrong." He hoped she would get her hair done, at least, but he hesitated to ask her to.

Through the glass partitions that separated the offices, Morrissey could see that nearly everyone was back from the meeting now. "Cable walked out, Winifred," he said. "I wish you could have seen him. My God, what a spectacle!"

"Well, he's that wild type, you know." He could swear she was smiling.

"He's a fool, you mean." Morrissey looked at Dr. Strong's office, which was where Cable would be, if he were still here. "I think he's left the plant altogether."

"He'll be back."

Well, if she was in one of those moods he wasn't going to stand here talking to her, letting her upset him even more. He had things to attend to—and he wanted to find out whether Tom Cable had walked out altogether. That, he felt, would be significant.

"I'll let you go now, Winifred," he said. "You probably have things to do." Then, "Uh—you might want to make an appointment to have your hair done—or something—for tomorrow night."

He hung up and with sharp annoyance he began to brush at his pocket again. If that fool, Cable, when he first got this idea, had gone through proper channels and come to him, Morrissey, as his immediate superior, Morrissey would have put a stop to it fast enough. But Tom Cable hadn't done that. He'd bypassed Morrissey and had gone straight to Will Caroline, the vice-president for research, and there was never any predicting what Will Caroline would do. And now the thing was getting out of hand. Eight years a perfect department and you got one rotten apple and this was what happened.

From the start he hadn't liked Tom Cable, Morrissey told himself. From the first day Cable came to Enright, nearly a year ago, Morrissey had predicted that there would be trouble. Several times he had mentioned it to Winifred. Only this morning at breakfast he had reminded her of that.

"I told you he was a troublemaker," he had said, as soon as she came to the table with her coffee. "He's too aggressive. He always reminds me of a bull—even if he's not squat or stocky."

"It's because of his father," Winifred had said, with that look of authority in her eyes. "His father died a failure."

"How do you know anything about his father?" He always wondered how Winifred found out these things.

"I've heard. His father was a person of considerable means once and then lost everything. Every dime!" She rolled it off her tongue, enjoying it. "He's compensating. It's very significant."

It didn't strike Claude Morrissey that this explained Tom Cable, but he never liked to argue with Winifred.

"Most companies wouldn't give a fellow like that a job," he said. "He's no good as part of a team. But leave it to Will Caroline."

"He's not the usual Enright type, I'll admit that." She almost smiled. Then her eyes narrowed over her coffee cup. "What've you really got against his idea, Claude?"

"It's no good. That's what I've got against it. It won't work. There's never been a drug like it."

12

"There's penicillin," she said.

"The whole field is too new."

"There's streptomycin," she said, as though she hadn't heard him.

"Streptomycin isn't even pure yet. They're having a very bad time with it."

"It's here," she said.

Angrily Morrissey looked up. "What this idiot has in mind," he said, "is one about twice as good as either penicillin or streptomycin. Oh, he admits antibiotics are so new that practically nothing is known about them. He's the first to admit that—tells you before you ask. He just doesn't think that should stop us."

He didn't want to talk about it. All he wanted to do was kill the idea today and then figure out a way to get rid of Tom Cable because Tom Cable spelled trouble. And it wasn't just this idea. It was in the laboratory, too. It was everything.

"And besides, I think there's something doing"—he cleared his throat—"between him and one of the technicians in the assay lab."

"Who?" Winifred's eyes snapped to attention.

Morrissey stirred his coffee. "I wouldn't know her name. But I know he's up to something."

He knew her name, all right. It was Midge Potter. Midge Potter, who had wide dark eyes and breasts like round melons and full swinging hips. The technician's coat that Midge Potter wore had less shape than this old flannel thing Winifred was wearing now, but when you looked at Midge all you thought was that there was nothing under it—nothing but the melon breasts and the round hips. Many times Dr. Morrissey had thought it might be wise to have Midge Potter transferred to another department, but the opportunity never seemed to arise. And now he was certain there was something between her and Dr. Cable.

He finished his coffee and stood up to go, letting out a little sigh as he thought of what was ahead of him today. "The man stirs up trouble the way a dog scratches up a bone," he said. "It's instinctive."

"Well, Claude," Winifred said, "just remember the old saw—if you can't beat them any other way, try laughing at them."

Dr. Morrissey didn't think it was funny. "The important thing is to disassociate myself from it," he said. "Because if by any horrible mischance they actually give this fool project a try, it'll be expensive before it's through—and then when it's failed, someone will have to be blamed. And they'll remember that it got started in my department." It wasn't funny at all.

Now, standing in his office, Morrissey told himself that he hadn't laughed occasionally during the meeting because Winifred had suggested it. He had laughed because the idea invited laughter. It deserved to be ridiculed.

He looked through the glass panels again and saw that Max Strong was still alone in his office, and he thought again that if Cable were around, he would certainly be in with Maxwell Strong, going over what had happened. Now, there was a friendship he would never understand—Cable and Maxwell Strong. Strong was a gentleman.

It comforted Dr. Morrissey to think that Cable had felt so thoroughly defeated that he had not only walked out of the meeting but had left the plant altogether—had crawled off like a whipped pup. And why wouldn't he, he thought, after the way we licked him? The only trouble was that after what they had done to that idea it should have died—and it hadn't.

TWO

Tom Cable sat on the steps in front of Max Strong's house and fiddled with a piece of rope. The day was still warm for late April but the sun was dropping, cutting a white streak on the water that a man couldn't look into, and now and then a small wind licked in off the bay. Over on the opposite shore he could see the familiar outlines of the Enright plant—the twin smokestacks, the storage tanks, the squat fermentation building, the research laboratories. From here, if he tried, he could pick out the windows of his own laboratory. He looked away and began to tie another knot in the rope.

Beside him, Max turned a page of the evening paper and settled back against the wide porch post. "Well, lots of news today," he said.

"What kind of news?"

"Human interest variety," Max said. "Lots of human interest today."

Tom Cable shifted about on the steps and moved over against the other porch post. He was a solidly built man of twenty-seven, of better than average height, with a bold-featured face and good-humored lines around his eyes and a look about him—in his face and body, and in the quick way he moved—of energy spilling over, impatient and uncurbed. Impatiently now, he yanked the rope into a knot while painful memories of this afternoon's meeting chased each other through his brain.

He remembered it all, from the uneasy tension in the dining room at lunch, when he began to suspect something was wrong, right up to the moment he closed the conference room door behind him. In his mind's ear, he could hear the click of the door and the incredulous silence on the other side while somewhere in the distance, faintly, a telephone rang.

"Here's a nice bit of human interest for you," Max said. "Woman in Tennessee chained her paraplegic husband to the bed because he wouldn't hand over his pension check. Seems she had a friendly mountain boy waiting to share it."

"Nice girl."

"Don't go away. I have a better one for you."

15

He could remember the exact moment when he knew that Will Caroline was letting him down.

"Ah, here it is," Max said. "Farmer chained his kid brother to his truck—the lad borrowed it without permission and cracked it up. Ordered him to haul it to the repair shop. Well, I suppose you can't blame the man—boy took it without permission, after all." Max was silent a moment, reading. Then he said, "Chains seem to be in the ascendancy this season—in the unending cycle of man's inhumanity to man."

Tom didn't bother to answer. He'd seen Max in this mood before. At best, Max Strong's opinion of mankind was not high, but it was usually at a point between his second and third drinks that it took such an abrupt downward turn that he felt compelled to express it. At those times, Tom knew, it was partly Max and partly the liquor talking. Today Max was sidling up to the subject for another reason.

"Fellow died. Pulled the truck a quarter of a mile in three days and died. Interesting way, isn't it, for a man to die in the United States of America—in the year 1946?"

"Okay, Max," Tom said. "Okay."

Max lowered the newspaper. "I'm only suggesting—"

"I know what you're trying to say, Max."

"I'm only saying that if the great men of Enright, with their remarkable vision, won't let you work to save mankind, you shouldn't let it bother you too much. Just remind yourself that it hasn't been firmly established that mankind is worth saving." Max tapped the newspaper. "You'll never find a drug to cure that, Tom!"

In spite of his soreness, Tom smiled. This cynicism that came so readily to Max's tongue never seemed to touch his slender, fine-featured face, and even now he looked only a little melancholy.

"That's not the drug I have in mind," Tom said evenly.

It wasn't the drug he had in mind, and yet, it seemed, to some men at Enright a drug to cure all the evil in the world would be no more farfetched than the one he was suggesting—another antibiotic, like penicillin or streptomycin, but one with a broader spectrum—one that would cure more diseases than either and some diseases that neither would touch. To him, the idea was so logical —even though he knew there was no proof. To nearly everyone else at Enright, it was madness.

Thoughtfully Tom untied the knot he had made and let his eyes travel across the lawn to the small cottage he rented from Max and Max's wife, Constance. Once these had been summer homes along the beach here, and many had small cottages on the grounds which had been guest houses or servants' quarters. Now this west shore of the bay was occupied the year round and most of the Enright officials lived here. Looking up the beach, Tom could see Will Caroline's house on the point of land near the lighthouse, and, farther off, Ade Hale's slate roof showing through the treetops. Looking in the other direction, he could pick out Morrissey's and Harrup's houses and then Gil Brainard's far down at the other end, just before the curved beach ended at Tollie's boat dock. He looked back across the water at the twin smokestacks on which ENRIGHT was painted vertically in bold black letters, and then at the research building, where the windows of his laboratory were catching the rosy glow of the late sun.

Only a few hours ago, he thought, he had stood there, in front of those windows, checking a streptomycin experiment, still thinking he could win. He remembered exactly the way a ray of the midday sun had struck a glass beaker and was refracted across the room past the streptomycin experiment in a Büchner funnel, past a row of bottles, and across the little sign that hung crooked on the wall —that little sign that had had special meaning for him when he first came to Enright and that had seemed to have a special meaning again today.

It was a small sign, black letters on a white ground, with a narrow black frame, and it read:

YOU CAN WALK WITH A WOODEN LEG
YOU CAN EAT WITH FALSE TEETH
BUT YOU CAN'T SEE WITH A GLASS EYE

The little sign had been hanging there, tilted a little in the same way, on the day almost a year ago when Tom had seen his laboratory for the first time, coming in with Mr. Caroline who had hired him. It wasn't the best-looking lab in the world, Tom had thought that day—nor the worst. The Enright plant was old and this was an old room, with pipes showing and dark counters and cabinets. Compared to some he'd seen, it was a small laboratory, but the light was good, with extra-large windows, and with a little planning he could make it efficient. The equipment was new and modern and that had pleased him. And then he had seen the little sign and that, foolishly, had pleased him more.

"We're short on space," Mr. Caroline had said without apology. He was a lean, rangy man of about fifty, with an easy relaxed way about him, who could keep you moving, Tom noticed, without making you feel hurried. "We can't give our research department as much room as we'd like to. But we'll give you good tools to get the job done."

At the door Tom had taken a departing look around and had noticed the little sign again. Just a simple little sign, hardly worth talking about, but on that day he had just returned from three years of war—three years of seeing life held cheap—and it had given him a clean feeling to find value placed again on something like a human eye. Then, seeing Mr. Caroline looking at him, he had smiled and said, "I like your sign," and Will Caroline had laughed and said, "I'm the sign man around here. It's given me a bad reputation. They say I've papered the walls of Enright with advice."

That was nearly a year ago. In the months since then Tom had looked at the little sign so many times that he no longer noticed it. But today after lunch, when he stopped in his laboratory to check the streptomycin experiment before going to the meeting, it had caught his eye again. Now, sitting on Max's steps, Tom remembered that he had told himself even then, as he and Max entered the laboratory, that the meeting was not going to go as smoothly as he had hoped. At lunch there had been that strained silence around him. Even men who were not directly involved had worn uneasy expressions. Even the waitress had said, "What'll it be, Dr. Cable?" as though she, too, knew it was going to be a bad day.

It had puzzled him at lunch, and in the laboratory he stood and looked idly out the window, thinking about it. Outside he could see the Enright barge getting ready to leave the dock. It was a long barge with three deep bins into which was dumped, day after day, the waste from penicillin and streptomycin production. When the bins were full, the barge moved down the bay to the open sea where it emptied its refuse into deep waters and then it returned.

"Wouldn't you think," he said, "that just seeing that barge pulling out every couple of days would convince these men that antibiotics are here to stay?"

He would feel a lot better, he told himself, if he knew what to

18

expect—if he had some idea what he was up against. And then he thought, Don't kid yourself, Cable—you know what you're up against.

He turned away and went into his office and came back with the thin folder of notes he'd prepared for the meeting and began to read through it.

"You getting worried?" Max said, watching him.

"No," Tom said. Then he grinned. "Hell, Max, I guess I'm like a fellow getting married. He knows this is the girl he wants and he's been champing at the bit thinking the day would never come—but now that it's here, he wishes he'd taken a little more time to get to know her better."

But he knew that a little more time wouldn't have helped a thing. Here in this folder was everything he had with which to argue his case—all that he or anyone else knew about antibiotics. Just a thimbleful of facts—too meager, he supposed, to be convincing to men who needed the safety of evidence in quantity. To him they were convincing and enough. They were enough long ago.

Abruptly, he closed the folder. Damn it! It was dangerous to want a thing too much. It made a coward of a man! He knew everything in these notes backwards and forwards—and going over them now was an act of fear.

"Tom," Max said, "you've got a fight on your hands. You might as well know it."

"So?" He went over to the experiment he'd come in to check.

"A helluva fight."

"I've been in fights before." Tom glanced around and smiled. "Max, five minutes before going into a fight isn't the time to admit you're worried. Not to anyone. Not even to yourself. Take it from an old fighter. It's one of the first rules of battle."

"That opinion is just a hangover from your misspent youth. With your gangster friend you tell me about. Angel—whatever his name was."

Tom grinned. "Angel wasn't a gangster. Just a borderline case."

But ducking down to look at the experiment, he told himself that he ought to use these last few minutes to think about the men that he knew would be opposing him and the arguments they would use and how they would operate. The core of the opposition, he supposed, was Dr. Morrissey. Not that Morrissey had said anything, but all week he had seen him talking to Dr. Harrup, to Gil Brainard —to anyone who would listen. And besides, Morrissey didn't work on antibiotics. He always told you that he was an industrial acids specialist and didn't touch antibiotics, intending it as a form of snobbery, a mark of company status, although Tom had never interpreted it that way.

"How does Morrissey operate at these meetings, Max?" he said. "I can't imagine him coming out in the open and fighting like a man."

"Tom, it's not just Morrissey," Max said. "I'm not sure anyone is for this—except you and me."

"Will Caroline is for it. He was all for it from the start."

"Did he tell you that?"

"Yes—he told me that!"

"That he was for it? Or only that he'd get you a hearing—that he'd get management to listen to what you had to say?"

"He said he was for it." Tom saw that the experiment was coming along all right and he straightened up. "Why? What's bothering you?"

"Because Will Caroline is for what Ade Hale is for. And do you know what Hale is for?"

"No, I don't know what Hale is for. I don't even know Hale except to say good-morning."

"Hale is for Enright. Hale is for what is good for Enright—for what will make money for Enright and keep on making money for Enright." Max looked at Tom and then, as though he had just realized it, he said, "Tom, have you ever been to a company meeting?"

Tom shrugged. "Hell, Max—you know how I am at meetings."

"Have you even been to *one?*"

"No." He grinned. "I've always considered myself a pretty ingenious fellow at avoiding them."

"How about a board meeting? You know anything about that?"

"How would I know anything about a board meeting? I never expected to have to go to a board meeting."

Max shook his head and then looked at his watch and stood up. "Come on," he said, "it's time to go."

Picking up his notes, Tom started for the door. Then the little sign caught his eye and for the first time in months he read it through:

YOU CAN WALK WITH A WOODEN LEG
YOU CAN EAT WITH FALSE TEETH
BUT YOU CAN'T SEE WITH A GLASS EYE

His eye lingered on the bottom line. And all at once the meaning changed and he read it with a new twist.

"Max, you've got that sign in your lab, too," he said. "You ever look at it?"

"It's been there as long as I have."

"That bottom line says everything that can be wrong with a place like this."

Max glanced at the sign, and the melancholy smile came to his face. "I think," he said, "you oversimplify."

Maybe, Tom thought. But to him, suddenly, that line summed up everything he was up against—that special blindness of men who saw only what could be proved—that pious, misdirected skepticism that looked at the uncertain and the unfamiliar and refused to see. But it was more than that. It's not just that they won't see, he told himself. They can't see. They were born with—or somewhere they traded vision for—a glass eye.

All along Tom had known there were men at Enright—as there were everywhere—with special blindness. Now he asked himself the more important question: how many other men were there here —as there had to be somewhere—with special sight?

They stood in the corridor that smelled of fermentation and of a dozen chemicals and waited for the elevator. On the wall beside the elevator door was one of Will Caroline's little black-framed signs that read: WORK CAREFULLY—THE LIFE ENRIGHT PENICILLIN SAVES MAY BE YOUR OWN! Tom read it and looked at another sign that read: QUALITY IS OUR BUSINESS!

The elevator came and Tom smiled as the door opened and he saw Midge Potter inside, twisting a lively black curl around her finger, carrying a rack of test tubes in her other hand. As he stepped into the elevator, she smiled at him with her dark liquid eyes that always astonished him because they retained so convincingly the look of the innocence she had long since discarded.

"Hello, Miss Potter," Tom said with a grin.

With her lovely eyes, Midge Potter indicated the rear of the elevator and Tom saw that Dr. Morrissey was here, too, and at that moment Morrissey looked up disapprovingly. In his department Morrissey didn't condone what he called "fraternization," and he was always on the alert to put out any little fires that might be kindling. But when he saw who it was, Morrissey's expression hardened from disapproval to something more, and Tom knew that he was not thinking now about fraternization.

Reflectively, Tom looked at Morrissey—at the handsome but vacuous face, the bright blue eyes, the white crew cut that gave him that old-young look. Many times he had thought that Morrissey had been born old in spirit and had worked, perhaps subconsciously, at retaining this youthful appearance to compensate. Then suddenly he realized how much, for the past week, he had been worrying about this man. And how pointlessly! In the first place, he told himself, he's not that formidable an opponent. And in the second place, you know you can expect nothing from him. You can't change him and you can't woo him. Write him off. If you have to count on Morrissey, you lose. If you win, it's without Morrissey.

He leaned over past Max to Midge Potter. "You're looking ravishing today, Miss Potter!" he said. Midge Potter rewarded him with a look of pure horror. He grinned, feeling much better.

A moment later, he stood in the doorway of the conference room, taking his first look inside.

It was a functional-looking room, like the rest of the plant, with walnut-paneled walls and heavy-framed windows that faced the bay. The only decorations, if they could be called that, were three portraits on each of the two side walls—the six former presidents of Enright. The fourth wall was covered with a green-tinted blackboard. On the conference table, at each place, were a white pad of paper, three yellow pencils and a black ashtray. Next to the table was a transcribing machine on a metal stand at which May Nelson, Ade Hale's secretary, was already seated. Tom looked around for Will Caroline and saw that he wasn't here yet.

Across the room, he watched Morrissey move about holding his briefcase as though it were a good-conduct medal, and stop to talk to a small man with thick eyeglasses who, Tom remembered, was Rosswell, the comptroller.

Tom ran his fingers along the edge of the manila folder. "If I'd known I'd be performing at one of these things," he muttered, "I'd have cased a few to get the lay of the terrain."

"I'll tell you what to expect," Max said. "Hashing, wrangling, hairsplitting. Everyone putting on a great performance to show Ade Hale what a great man he's got in him."

Tom looked at the long table and wondered where he ought to sit. Then he saw Dr. Harrup, the director of chemical research, coming in—Dr. Harrup who always seemed to have only half of his mind on the problem at hand, the other half turning in on himself, as though considering some private misery.

"What about your boss, Max?" Tom said. "Where does he stand on this?"

"You know Harrup. With Harrup, bellyaching is a way of life."

Harrup stood a moment near the door and then went over to Morrissey, who greeted him with a worried shake of his head, and Harrup responded in kind. But of the two, Tom knew, Harrup was the better scientist. At least he worked on antibiotics and kept up with the literature. With Harrup it was a question of heart. He just never expected anything to go right.

Probably, Tom decided, he ought to sit at a corner. If he was going to have to talk a long time, he wanted room to move around. He wondered what was keeping Will Caroline.

Then Gil Brainard came in and Tom shifted his attention to him. He hardly knew Brainard, who was in production, not research. While he watched him, Brainard lit a cigar, rocking a little on his heels, and drew a satisfied puff. He was a big man—a man, Tom thought, whose center of gravity seemed to be his middle. There were some men, he mused, who struck you as all head—and with some, especially with delicate ones like Morrissey, you remembered mostly their hands, usually busy—and some men always seemed to plop their whole weight down on their feet. With Brainard it was his middle. His stomach protruded a little and you would not be surprised to see him pat it, caress it a bit. Even with the cigar between his lips, Brainard seemed to be enjoying it with his stomach.

"Fine day for a meeting, Gil," he heard Morrissey greet him.

"Wonderful," Brainard agreed.

"Be nice if it's like this for the board meeting," Morrissey said.

Ade Hale came in and the little group seemed to come to attention. If you looked at Ade Hale and then at Gil Brainard, you realized that they were built alike, but there the similarity ended. There was nothing flabby about Hale, who moved as though he had a built-in boiler feeding him steam twenty-four hours a day. He had gray hair, with an unruly shock in front, sharp blue eyes, and when you'd been with him about two minutes you found yourself thinking that anything those eyes missed would have to be pretty well hidden.

Then at last Will Caroline came in, tall and lean, moving in that quick effortless way of his. As he passed in front of him, Will said, "Just play it by ear, Tom—and use your head."

Will Caroline took the seat on Ade Hale's right and Brainard took the one on the left, and the meeting began. A moment later Tom pushed back his chair and stood up and began to talk.

Now, leaning against Max's porch post, watching the water growing gray and busy, Tom Cable understood that he had counted too much on Will Caroline. He had waited too long and too expectantly for the help that never came, and now, more than anything else, he remembered his feelings in that instant when he knew it was not coming.

During the whole twenty minutes that Tom spoke, Ade Hale had sat back in his chair with his eyes half closed. Tom had heard that Hale listened this way. He wasn't a patient man, they said, but he'd listen as long as you kept your talk like a tight line, tied right to the point. And during the whole twenty minutes Will Caroline wrote steadily and unhurriedly on his white pad until, toward the end, Tom began to wonder what he was writing. If Will wanted a record of the meeting he could get it from May Nelson, who was taking down every word on her machine.

He found it unnerving to watch Will writing so steadily, and he looked away, letting his eyes take in the rest of his audience. He saw that the ash on Brainard's cigar burned long while he watched Ade Hale, covertly but carefully. He saw that Morrissey was hardly listening. He looked at Rosswell—how could you tell anything behind those thick glasses?—and then at Harrup who was running his finger back and forth, back and forth, over the handle of his briefcase. The smoke from Brainard's cigar mingled with that from Morrissey's pipe in a thin layer over the table. By the time he sat down, Tom wasn't sure that anyone at all had been listening to him.

When he finished, Ade Hale opened his eyes. "Dr. Cable," he said, "how much do you figure this will cost?"

"That would be hard to say at the start, Mr. Hale," Tom said. "This is a new field—all the techniques are new. Although they're being improved every day."

"Would a half-million dollars be a reasonable figure?"

Tom glanced over at Will Caroline, thinking that Will ought to handle this part—he knew more about costs—but Will Caroline was still writing on his pad. "I can't say whether half a million would do it or not," Tom said. "I don't know."

"What if we said three-quarters of a million?"

"At the start, sir, it would be hard to name any figure, responsibly. It would just be guessing."

Next to Ade Hale, Gil Brainard lit up a fresh cigar. "I'm just wondering Ade," he said. "I don't want to leap to conclusions before the facts are all in—although it's my impression that we've got them all now. That right, Dr. Cable?"

"You've got it all," Tom said.

Brainard examined his cigar. "It seems mighty little information to base a decision on," he said.

As Brainard turned to Morrissey, Tom looked at him carefully, seeing the start of bags under his eyes and the fleshiness at his jowls, the first hints of the looseness of age invading the big face and body. With a sharp look, Brainard was urging Morrissey to speak up, but Morrissey was watching Ade Hale. He's figuring what he'll say if Hale comes out for it, Tom thought—and what he'll say if Hale is against it—and how he'll put it if the worst happens and he has to speak his piece before he knows for sure where Hale stands.

Hale leaned forward on the table. "Getting back to costs, Dr. Cable. Would you say that a million would do it? I don't say we've got a million dollars to put into this, but would you say that a million would cover it?"

At last Will Caroline looked up from his pad. "There's no way of knowing, Ade," he said. "It's not likely to be cheap or easy. If it turned out to be, it would be the rarest kind of luck, and we shouldn't expect it—shouldn't play it that way."

Tom waited for him to go on—to give some arguments in favor of it, to say that it could be done, that it would be worth the effort. But Will Caroline had finished.

Brainard puffed his cigar. "It seems to me," he said, "that Dr. Cable can't talk costs because he just doesn't know enough." He paused and looked at Hale, trying to decide, as Morrissey was, where Hale stood on this. Then he said, "Dr. Cable—supposing we tacked on another half-million, just for the human element—human frailties of overoptimism and maybe a few blunders—what then?"

"Mr. Brainard," Tom said, "you know that in something like this there are no guarantees."

"Dr. Cable," Hale cut in, "is there any point at which you'd be sure of success?"

Tom looked at Will Caroline, who was still writing and hadn't even looked up at the question, and the first tug of disappointment went through him. He turned back to Hale. "I believe in this," he said. "I believe it can be done. I don't know about the cost."

"Then there is no figure, no matter how large, at which you'd be certain?"

"No, sir, there is not!"

Brainard made a little hopeless gesture with the hand that held the cigar. "Ade, this is like being at a horse race and having a tout nudge you and say, 'Put everything you've got on Number Six,' and when you ask why, he says, 'He looks good and besides I've got a real feeling about him.'"

Harrup smiled and Morrissey took his pipe out of his mouth and threw back his head and laughed heartily and put the pipe back into his mouth.

"Well, maybe that's the way it seems to you, Mr. Brainard," Tom said, "but that's not the way it is."

"Why isn't it?"

Tom told himself to calm down and to get off the defensive. "It's true that the research scientist and the gambler have a lot in common," he said. "They know the meaning of the calculated risk. Or —to put it your way, Mr. Brainard—they both play some pretty long shots. And sometimes it seems the line that separates them is very fine. But that line does exist."

"Good!" Brainard said. "I'm glad to hear it. What is it?"

"It's knowledge, Mr. Brainard."

"But that's the whole trouble." Brainard's smile broadened. "In this case knowledge is the missing ingredient. You don't know a damn thing about it. It's a blind gamble."

"It's not a blind gamble!" Tom said.

"It's a gamble, all right."

"But not blind!"

"A gamble, all the same. And I say we'd better remember that when you gamble, you bet only what you can afford to lose."

Morrissey's eyes twinkled, but Brainard's went over to Hale to see how he had taken this first firm thrust. He frowned a little and Tom thought, He's not sure yet.

Hale changed the subject. "Dr. Cable, what can you tell us about our competition? Who else is working on this?"

Will Caroline looked up, relaxed and undisturbed. "This is getting tight security, but I'd guess there are several companies working on it. And possibly some university people, too."

"You know, Dr. Cable?"

"No, sir, but there must be others. This is so logical that I can't believe the others wouldn't have thought of it."

With a small gesture Brainard signaled again to Morrissey to speak, and Morrissey pretended not to notice—so Brainard forced his hand.

"Dr. Cable," Brainard said, "do you understand that drugs are patented?"

"Yes, I know that drugs are patented."

"In that case . . . Claude"—Brainard turned back to Morrissey — "How would you feel about our chances—a little company like Enright—against giants like Lederle, or Parke-Davis or Merck? How would you feel in a patent race against, say, Merck?"

Morrissey puffed his pipe, gave his head a little shake, looked thoughtful, finally removed the pipe and said, "Don't like to think about it."

Watching him, Tom wondered how you could explain a man like Morrissey. How did he get this way? Had there ever, long ago, been half-brave efforts that had failed and frightened him? Had there ever been a spark? Or was he born this way? With a glass eye.

"Well, I don't like to think about it, either," Brainard said. "Because if these big companies pour a couple of million dollars into a totally unknown field and lose, it's not a disaster. But for us—"

"Gil," Max broke in, "this isn't a totally unknown field. We're working with antibiotics every day. You're producing them every day."

"We still don't know much," Brainard snapped. "Ade, I'm beginning to think this is not only a horse race—it's a race against champions—and all we know is that the stableboy says this horse ought to run. No record on any track, no trial time, you get no statistics on him and you can't look at him and you don't know how long the track is—and with that information, gentlemen, step up and place your bets!"

Morrissey laughed heartily and Harrup smiled at that one, too. Wearily Tom looked at Will Caroline, asking himself what he was waiting for. What was so important for him to be writing down? Then, without thinking, he leaned over and looked at Will Caroline's pad and a terrible sinking feeling stabbed through him. In that single quick glance Tom saw that Will Caroline had not written a single word! His pad was covered with pictures—lines—circles—odd figures. Will Caroline was doodling!

Stunned, staring at Will's pad, Tom heard Brainard say, "Now, it seems to me that if these giants are working on this, too, and any of them could put up five million dollars to our one million, that gives them five times the chance of getting there first."

Tom didn't bother to argue.

Brainard said, "Enright is a pygmy among giants. We can't compete with those fellows."

Still Tom didn't argue.

Ade Hale asked whether, apart from the race against the bigger companies, the project could succeed scientifically. Slowly Tom wrenched his eyes away from Will Caroline.

Brainard said, "We should hear from Dr. Morrissey and Dr. Harrup on that." He rested his hand on Morrissey's shoulder like a coach telling him to get in and fight.

Dr. Morrissey folded his hands and unfolded them. "As a scientist, I base my opinion on facts, not on dreams," he said. He cleared his throat. "Now, just consider the history of this sort of thing. Take penicillin. Pencillin hung around useless for years after Fleming discovered it because no one knew how to produce it or even how to get it reasonably pure. It took the backing of the United States government—unlimited funds—and six companies pooling their knowledge to finally develop it for human consumption. Some of us here know what a job that was because we were part of it."

Tom stared at Morrissey. This man, who hated antibiotics, wore a look on his face as though he, single-handed, had borne the terrible load.

28

"Now, that wasn't incompetence," Morrissey went on. "It was just plain lack of knowledge. Nobody knew how to proceed. And history is full of that kind of heartbreak."

Maybe there never was a spark, Tom thought. Maybe the only thing he was ever good at was playing according to the rules, and he could keep on playing if the rules didn't change too much.

"With penicillin the government spent more millions than we dare talk about," Morrissey went on. "And then we only managed to produce a limited amount, in a crude state, for the armed forces. Even with millions we didn't perfect it—we're still working on penicillin today—you know that."

"And we already had our product," Brainard put in. "We had the penicillin mold from Fleming. With what he's talking about"—Brainard jerked his head toward Tom—"first we've got to find this great antibiotic he's dreaming about—and then go through everything we went through with penicillin to develop it."

At last Tom found his voice again. "The obstacles aren't the same," he said. "We can use that knowledge from penicillin—and all we're learning now from Waksman and streptomycin—"

"Streptomycin!" Harrup put in gloomily. "Do you know how long Waksman worked on microbes before he hit on streptomycin? Eighteen years!"

"On the whole science!" Tom said. "He made it a science."

"I say this is risky business," Brainard said. "Pour in one million—two million—how much more? This could break us. At what point do we admit we've failed?"

"How can you talk failure before we even begin?" Tom demanded.

"When do you propose to talk about it—later? How much later? After we've failed? After we're broke?"

Angrily, Tom pushed back his chair and got to his feet.

Brainard leaned over the table toward him. "You fellows come in here with these hotshot ideas that may cost a couple of million dollars and maybe in the end there'll be something and maybe there won't—maybe just a nice piece of work with no practical results—"

"I don't believe it," Tom said heatedly. "I don't believe Enright is so impoverished that it can't undertake this research without a written guarantee!"

"You don't want to believe it! You don't like to talk about anything practical."

"Just bear in mind, Dr. Cable," Hale cut in, "we're not a research foundation. We're a business."

"Then you don't need scientists!" Tom's voice rose. "To play it safe, you don't need scientists! You can get along with hacks!"

Morrissey flushed crimson. He jerked his pipe from his mouth and spoke through tight lips. "To me this is looking for a needle in a haystack—when you don't know what the needle looks like—or whether you're in the right haystack—or even in the right field— or whether there's any needle to be found at all! Just because we have penicillin and streptomycin doesn't convince me that there have to be more antibiotics."

"My opinion," Harrup said, "is that we're having enough trouble with penicillin and streptomycin—getting them pure, ironing out the problems. My department—well—" His eyes shifted about uneasily. "We have our hands full. And at least with those two we know we've got a product."

"And on top of that," Morrissey chimed in again, "maybe somebody who can afford it has a crew ten times your size—and maybe they're combing the haystack with better equipment. Maybe by the time you see the needle, it'll be in someone else's hands. Besides, I don't think it will work at all."

That was when Tom began to lose control. He looked around him at the cautious worried faces—he looked at May Nelson's machine where all the arguments were being recorded for the board of directors—he looked at Will Caroline who was silent, doodling on his paper, who had not said a word in his defense—and suddenly something inside him snapped.

"If you're going to stick your heads in the sand, you're never going to make any progress! This safe, conservative, don't-try-anything-new approach isn't the scientific attitude. It's a psychological type!" He began to shout. "Why is everyone here so sure this can't be done? And, if it could, that *we* can't do it, that we shouldn't try? Why shouldn't we try? Just because we're small? This can be done, and nobody here has given a valid argument, financial or scientific, for crawling away from it and crying that we're licked before we begin!" He stopped. He strained for control. Then, in a quieter voice, he said, "Maybe Enright won't do it. Maybe you won't even try. But I'll tell you this. Somebody will!" He looked around the table. "Somebody will do it!"

Suddenly there was nothing more to say. He knew he should sit down again, but the thought of staying here any longer gagged him. For a moment he stood perfectly still, seeing them all staring at him, and then, with a fresh rush of rage, he strode toward the door.

"Ade—" Undisturbed, unimpressed, Brainard's voice cut into the shocked silence. "Ade—I wonder what you'd think of this approach—"

At the door, Tom stopped. He'd left his notes. The hell with them—Max would bring them.

"I won't give you any vague figures," Brainard said. "Maybe a half-million or a million—or two million—and even vaguer hopes. I'll give you a definite figure—one million dollars—and I'll make you a promise."

No, Tom decided, he'd get the notes. He started back, all eyes following him.

"Give me one million dollars for production," Brainard said, "and I'll lower your costs on every major product. I'll give you half again your profit. And that's a promise, not a dream. You tell that to the board and the stockholders—and they'll know what you're talking about."

Brainard smiled over at Hale, confident of his approval. May Nelson was taking it all down. Will Caroline was still doodling on his pad and he even seemed to be restraining a smile.

"Then in a couple of years we'll have some extra cash to let these boys play around with their bright ideas," Brainard said. "And maybe they'll hit on something and maybe they won't. And if they don't, we won't feel it so badly then. . . ."

Tom closed the door behind him. It clicked into place, and on the other side he could hear the shocked silence, and off somewhere in the distance, faintly, a telephone rang.

THREE

Now the warmth was gone from the sun, and sounds were softening and the smell of night was coming into the salt air. On the beach a lone gull unhurriedly walked a crooked circle, and Tom watched it a moment as it pecked at the sand and moved on, exploring, maybe, to see what else was around to interest it.

Some of the soreness was leaving him and he was beginning to think more logically. All right, he said to himself, what if you hadn't counted so much on Will Caroline? What if Will Caroline hadn't said at the start that he liked it, so that you didn't even ask where he would stand in a showdown—what then? Would you have done a better job? And if so, how?

Max folded his paper and stood up. "Come in for a drink, Tom," he said. "We could both use one."

Tom shook his head. As long as there was another day left before the board meeting to try to save this—one more day to try to think of a way, although he didn't honestly believe that he would —he wasn't going to booze it away. "When this is over," he said, "I'm going to hang one on that will make history."

Max didn't say that for all the hope there was, he might as well hang it on right now. He only wedged the paper under the porch rail so it wouldn't blow away and went into the house, and Tom got to his feet, too, and walked out to the concrete boardwalk that was built several feet above the beach. Standing at the edge, he looked down at the crusted sand that still bore the marks of winter— ragged seaweed and the footprints of dogs and birds.

In the end, he thought, a man was more the victim of his ideas than the master. An idea took hold of you and there was nothing you could do to shake it. It held you until it had had its share. Like landing a fish, he thought. The fish hooked on to your line and you felt it—more than just your hands felt it—and you had to play it along, at least until you had had a good look at it—and then you made up your mind to work to land it—or maybe you saw it was not so much of a fish after all—you were after bigger game—and you let it go.

Or, he thought, like a woman. A woman got on your mind and

into your blood, and whatever you did she stayed there, and you went back to her again and again—or else you found that she was not so much of a woman after all, and then you forgot her. And, he thought—like a woman, many times the ideas that were most difficult in the beginning were most worth the trouble in the end.

He saw Max coming out again and he started back to the porch. Max paused in the doorway and called something to Constance and then came out with a bottle of Scotch and some glasses. On the boardwalk a girl walked past, a long-legged, smart-looking girl with heavy, honey-blond hair. She wore slacks and walked with a long quick stride. Tom glanced at her and went up the steps and sat down, and the girl turned in to a house a few doors away.

"Good-looking girl," Max said.

"Friend of Will Caroline's," Tom said. "Maybe."

"What do you mean a friend of his—maybe?"

"He asked me about her the other day. When he first came here, there was a family named Welles living in that little cottage. Will saw a light there the other night and hadn't heard the place had been sold, so he wondered who was back. Seems there were two girls—little then—and one of them used to join him feeding placebos to dying fish. He'd like to see that one again but not so much the other one, so he asked if I knew who was living there."

"Sugar pills to dying fish!"

"That's what he said. Their names were Hope and Amity. Hope was a normal bratty kid but Amity was his pet—Ammie, he called her—and every time she found a sick animal or a fish dying on the beach she dragged it around to Will, and he gave her ointments and placebos. He'd like to see his little Amity again. But I think he's got Hope."

"Why Hope?"

"Did that girl look to you as though she'd care about sick fish?"

Max laughed. "I like that. Placebos to dying fish."

"It's a good story but not today." Already Tom's mind was off the girl and back to his own problems. He told himself to forget today's fiasco and think about the board meeting. At least he knew now what he was up against, and that was something. He knew he was alone and he knew the men who were against him and what could be expected of them. Then he began to think about the men who made up the board—the company men, Hale, Caroline, Brainard and Rosswell—and besides them, a retired admiral, a lawyer, a few businessmen, one man who was called a financial wizard and one man who had a seat on the exchange. Considering his audience, Tom could only think how hopeless was his position.

"How the hell do you explain antibiotic activity of microbes to businessmen, Max?" he said.

Max looked at him over his glass, and Tom knew he didn't bother to answer because, obviously, there was no answer.

"How the hell do you do it," Tom said again, "without boring the pants off them?"

Then Constance, a lovely, serene-looking girl with dark hair drawn tightly back, came out, pulling a sweater across her shoulders. "Bad time, Tom?" she said, sitting down on the step. "I am sorry."

"The problem is," Tom said, "how am I going to sell the idea to a board that's not made up of scientists when I can't sell it to men who are?"

Max poured a drink for Constance and slid one over to Tom, who let it sit, and refilled his own. "That's not the whole problem," he said.

"Today I had almost all scientists," Tom said. "They knew the language—they understood what I was saying, or could have if they'd wanted to—they're men who know that in research there's always something new. On Friday I get businessmen who don't even know the terminology. I'll practically have to give them a course in microbes and antibiotics before I can even begin to get to the point. That's the whole damn trouble."

"The whole damn trouble is the human race," Max said. He'd finished his second drink and was warming up to his favorite subject. "The whole damn trouble is that we call everyone human that's walking around on two legs, and then we expect them to behave that way. The term 'man' is used much too loosely."

Maybe, Tom thought, if I could find a few men who are for it, who believe in it—maybe some of the younger men—not so much prestige, but I could sell the idea of youth . . .

"Just consider the kind of person you'd like to call a man," Max said. "And then think about these fine fellows today—Brainard and Morrissey and Harrup. A little different, aren't they, from what you had in mind?"

"It's not a question of being different, Max. It's a question of being

34

blind." Tom bent down and picked up the rope again. "I've known people who were pretty different from what you've got in mind, but they weren't blind. They could see things pretty fast. You take when I worked at Angel's—" He paused, thinking back nearly ten years.

"Who's Angel?" Constance said.

"Constance, darling!" Max said. "You haven't heard about the legendary Angel? Where've you been all these months?"

"No," Constance said. "Who is he, Tom?"

"Angel Amati ran a dive in New Haven. I worked my way through Yale—through college and most of graduate school—by, among other things, playing a mean piano there, nightly. I was a great hit. They loved me."

"Tom, you never told me that!"

"Angel was a great man. If there was a straight way and a crooked way to do a thing and they were equally effective, Angel would do it the crooked way just to stay in practice."

Constance laughed.

"He wasn't great, of course. Just another guy trying to make ends meet the only way he understood," Tom said. "But at Angel's even the women knew more devious ways to operate than anyone at Enright ever heard of." Remembering, Tom smiled. "We were different —Angel and the girls and I—as different as people could be. I was just a green kid—at the start anyway. And we knew we were different. But we got along. They were tough and hard-boiled and certainly not smart—the girls, I mean—Angel was smart, in a way— but for their mental capacity, they weren't blind. They saw things. In fact, they didn't miss much. There was one little girl—very young and fresh-looking and more beguiling than the rest—and she couldn't wait to get her clothes off—so once, after she'd been there about a week, I said to her, 'Kitty, why don't you ease up a bit—try leaving something to the imagination?' And Kitty looked at me out of her big blue eyes that had already seen too much and she said, 'Baby, those guys ain't interested in imagination!' And she was right. She was even more popular with the customers than I was."

Constance smiled. "Strange, isn't it?"

"And that's the way it is at Enright," Tom said. "Those guys ain't interested in imagination." It was getting dark now and he ought to go home and think about which of the younger men might have a little imagination—enough to be interested in this. And he ought to figure out something to say to a bunch of businessmen who wouldn't know what he was talking about.

"You know, people like that fascinate me!" Constance said. "Oh, I know what they are—hard and tough and sometimes dirty and sometimes even vicious—but there's a quality about them that is totally strange to people like us. They live by their wits. It's something we never know—people like us—people at Enright."

"Especially people at Enright," Max said.

"You're right, Constance," Tom said. "I lived by my wits during those years, too." He smiled, reminiscing. "I learned from Angel. 'Try it, maybe it'll work,' Angel would say. 'And if it don't, try something else. All you can do is lose!'" He laughed and looked up from the rope. "Maybe I should remember that now."

Max drained his glass. "It's a splendid sentiment," he said. "Mr. Caroline should include it next time he makes up his signs."

"All I have to do is think about Angel and I begin to think of a few unsavory methods myself. You kind of slip into that devious frame of mind."

It was more than a frame of mind. A little thread of an idea was forming and, for the first time, he was thinking that maybe this was not impossible, after all. Starting with the premise that the board has to understand it, he said to himself. . . . It was more than a thread now—it was an idea that was growing and taking an unexpected shape. I wonder, he thought—I wonder how I could work this out.

And then he thought, Cable, you're at Enright now, not at Angel's. This is a different league, and what you're hatching is not for Enright. And then, But would it work—and could I get away with it? *So what if you lose?* Angel used to say. *You think you're the first loser of all time?*

"It must seem pale to you at Enright by comparison, Tom," Constance said. "There's no one like that at Enright."

"No, there's nobody like Angel at Enright."

And there's nobody like Angel on the board, either, he told himself—so go home and figure out something else. Go talk to the younger men. Go talk to "Pearly" Gates—that's the best place to begin. He looked up the boardwalk, barely making out Gates's small stucco house, tucked in next to Harrup's larger white one. Go now, he told himself, and if he's interested, ask him about George Weir and some of the others. And get Angel and his fancy footwork out of your head.

From Woodrow "Pearly" Gates's front porch, Tom could see Harrup next door pacing the floor in his living room. Feeding his ulcer, Tom thought and turned away. Pearly's wife opened the door.

Madeline Gates was a buxom, practical woman, a former nurse, with a direct manner of speaking. "Tom, I hope you've come for a bit of cheer!" she said, when she saw him. "I'd like nothing better than to make some small contribution to the cause."

Over Madeline's shoulder, Tom saw that George Weir and his wife were here, too. Gates and George Weir had been hired at Enright on the same day and had become close friends in spite of the fact that Madeline and the languid, auburn-haired Janet Weir had little in common.

"It's our night for dinner and bridge," Madeline said, "but don't let that bother you. Join us if you care to. Woodrow—"

Gates came out of the kitchen, carrying a bucket of ice. "Tom! Well!" he said. "Come on in!"

Tom had to smile at Pearly's determined cheerfulness. Gates was a sandy-haired man with a mildly blemished complexion, who was willing to be completely serious about the smallest problem and who felt it his duty, if you had a real problem, to try to be cheerful. Right now he was being very cheerful.

"What're you drinking, Tom?" Gates said.

"No thanks, Pearly—I don't want a drink."

"Come on, Tom, we're way ahead of you, boy!" George Weir called out. A dark-eyed, dark-haired man, handsome in spite of a chronic look of discontent, Weir gestured with his glass as Tom came into the living room. Sitting on the sofa, Janet uncurled her legs and smiled.

"How's everything, Tom?" Weir said.

Tom told himself that he might as well get out.

Then Madeline said, "Maybe a drink would be good for what ails you, Tom—or should I say for what is probably galling hell out of you?"

"Madeline, for God's sake—" Gates said.

"Well, I for one am sorry," Madeline said.

"Well, hell—I'm sorry, too," Gates said unhappily. "I am, Tom. I'd like to see you be able to do what you want."

37

"Is it anything you'd want to do, Pearly?"

Gates hesitated a moment and glanced at George Weir who was looking hard at the glass resting on his knee. "I think it might be interesting, Tom," Gates said.

"How interesting? Does the idea excite you?"

Thoughtfully, Gates sipped his drink. "I suppose there's a lot to be said for it—"

"Tom," George Weir said suddenly, "what're you beating a dead horse for?"

"This isn't dead!" Tom said. "This is going to the board on Friday."

"They could still block it, Tom," Gates said soberly, "and not bring it up on Friday."

Tom looked at Gates carefully. "You heard something, Pearly?"

"I just know how they operate. They're pretty sharp—some of them. It's no accident that they're where they are."

"Where are they?"

"They're at the top, Tom," George Weir said. "They're the top brass—and they're welded together—solid. And the board has known them all for a long time. And if you try to tell the board that the brass don't know what they're talking about, you know what'll happen? One, you won't get anywhere—and two, you're volunteering for the suicide squad, because when the smoke settles, very quietly you'll be liquidated."

"Well, I don't know that it's that bad," Gates said.

"Use your head, Tom," Weir said. "What're you cutting your own throat for?"

"I don't know what you're getting upset about, George," Janet said. "You're not involved."

"Tom—look at it this way," Gates said, troubled. "Now, Tom, I know this means a lot to you—but why don't you withdraw this before Friday—voluntarily?

"What!"

"Wait till there's more dope on it. There is damn little—" Then, seeing the look on Tom's face, Gates said, "Tom, you ought to wait until you have some chance of winning."

"I intend to win now!"

"After this afternoon! How?"

Madeline began to tap nervously on a table, and Tom leaned across it and said, "I'll tell you how, Pearly—"

Abruptly Madeline stood up. "Tom," she said sharply, heading for the kitchen. "Come in here and fix yourself whatever you're willing to drink."

"I don't want a drink." But Madeline signaled from the kitchen door and he stood a moment, puzzled, and then followed her.

"I think you should have a piece of information before you say another word," Madeline said, turning on the water in the sink. "I trust you won't use it to perpetrate a disaster. Now—how shall I put this indelicate matter delicately? Reach me that glass, will you? It matches the others and Woodrow will be upset if I don't use it."

Tom reached up to the top shelf and took down the glass.

"You wouldn't notice, of course, but Janet is wearing new pearls tonight. They're rather good. They cost well over a hundred dollars."

"I didn't notice."

"With two children, George cannot afford this sort of expenditure. George thinks they are simulated."

"Who knows better?"

"Here's your drink. Very mild to allow for clear thinking. Gil Brainard knows better."

Tom looked at Madeline Gates with admiration. "Remind me to marry you, Madeline."

"You do that. Shall we rejoin our fellow citizens?"

Tom put the drink down on the counter and followed Madeline's ample figure into the living room and said goodbye.

"Tom," Gates said, as he walked with him to the door, "if you see the board's against you, you might do better to let them turn you down gracefully. Don't get their backs up. They'll probably just say, 'Let's wait.'"

Tom closed the door behind him. No imagination this season—try us later—about a year later.

He walked back along the deserted boardwalk where lights in the houses shone behind drawn curtains. Night dampness had settled in and a night wind was pushing waves high onto the beach. No imagination today, he said to himself, and no recruits among the younger men—and where does that leave you? Exactly where you started, he said to himself.

For a while he walked aimlessly on the boardwalk and then he went home and got his car and drove into town, to the edge of the business district where new stores and office buildings crowded old houses. He stopped in front of an old apartment house where, on the fourth floor, Midge Potter's light was on and the radio blared.

A few minutes later, stretched out on Midge's sofa, he said, "It's a perfect example of synergism. You know what synergism is?"

"What I'm really an expert at is organic chemistry," Midge said.

"Synergism is one and one equals more than two. The total equals more than the sum of the parts. Wrong plus wrong repeated a hundred times equals right. Similarly, right plus right equals right, provided you can find a way to get it repeated a hundred times, which isn't easy."

"You're feeling pretty good tonight, huh?" Midge said. She came over and sat beside him and he put his arm around her.

"Tonight I am Diogenes—I'm going up and down the countryside looking for a man with imagination."

"What I like about you is how I always know what you're talking about."

Midge laughed and looked up at him with her big, dark, innocent-looking eyes, and Tom thought, not for the first time, that those eyes should be displayed to every young scientist, as part of his training, to prove that nothing should be accepted on superficial evidence alone, without further proof.

Midge patted the sofa, which she converted at night into her bed. "You want me to open this up?" she said.

"I'll do it in a little while." Wearily Tom leaned his head back and closed his eyes, pressing himself to answer the question that seemed to have no answer. "Midge," he said, "how would you explain the antibiotic activity of microbes to the board of directors?"

Midge laughed. "They don't know anything about it!" she said. "When they come in the lab looking around, you can see that they don't know anything!"

Fine, he thought. Great. He stood up and went to the window. You'd better turn up a little imagination in yourself, he thought—or nobody at all is going to understand you on Friday—half of them won't because they don't want to and the other half because they can't.

Then the little thread of an idea that he had pushed aside began to push back. He stood at the window, staring out at a branch of an old oak tree that crowded between the buildings, and at the sign on the corner drugstore, blinking on and off. If they have to understand it—he resumed his thinking where he had left off—if the only hope lies in their understanding it, you'll have to see that they do. You'll have to make it clear—and you'll have to do it fast. The little brainchild of a plan came roaring back, full grown.

He rushed out the door and down the three flights of steps to the street and walked twice around the block. Think, he said to himself —think about this very clearly and very hard. You made a damn fool of yourself today and what you're planning now could be twice as bad. Or—he argued back—it could turn the trick.

Slowly, he walked to the corner and stopped outside the drugstore. In a mirror in the window he caught a glimpse of his own reflection, frowning because this was a serious decision, and then half smiling because—oh, hell, it was so tempting! His divided mind made itself up and his face went into a broad grin. He went into the drugstore.

At least try something, Angel used to say. *Luck ain't lookin' for you.*

He stood in the telephone booth and called the Rockford Hospital where Sam Lewis, who had been his roommate at Yale, was a resident physician.

"Dr. Lewis is off duty," the girl said. "He's asleep."

"Wake him."

"Is this an emergency?"

"It's an emergency," Tom said and grinned. Sam was the one who'd written him that there were jobs here at Enright. He was partly responsible for this problem. At last Sam's voice came through the receiver—the voice of a man awakened out of a deep sleep. "Sam—" Tom shouted.

"Mmm?"

"Sam, you had a woman in the hospital lately with gonorrhea?"

"Dangerous," Sam mumbled. "Stay away from that."

"Wake up!" Tom shouted. "I have to find a woman who's had gonorrhea."

Sam let out an oath. "Get off the line and let me go back to sleep."

"I want one who was cured."

At last Sam was awake. "What in hell's the matter with you, Tom?"

"Answer me and you can go back to sleep. Have you cured a woman lately of gonorrhea?"

"Mmm."

"Good. How'd she look?"

"How do you think she looked? Like hell. She looked like a dog."

"Do you remember her name? You got any records where you could get her name? And her address?"

"Hang up like a good fellow, Tom, what do you say?" Sam begged. "I'll take care of what ails you tomorrow."

"Can you get her name and address?"

At last Sam sensed that he was serious. "How'd it go today?"

"It was a disaster. Will you get me that name, Sam?"

"Will first thing in the morning do?"

"It'll do."

He hurried back upstairs to Midge's apartment.

"Midge," he said, bursting into the room. "Our left flank is surrounded—our right flank is destroyed. We attack!" It was corn. Pure whole-kernel corn. But it made sense—like Will Caroline's signs.

From the sofa where she was lying on her stomach reading a magazine, Midge glanced up briefly and raised one lovely leg and crossed it behind the other, running her toes over her ankle. Then, at last, she acknowledged his return with that unblinking, wide-eyed look. "I wasn't expecting you back."

"Don't be coy with me." Tom laughed. "When did I ever fail you?"

"There's always a first time, I always say."

"Think of something better to always say."

Midge closed the magazine and propped herself up on one elbow. "Honest to God, I think you're crazy," she said. "It's my opinion."

"It's a good opinion. You're not alone." He whacked her bottom and jerked his head toward the sofa. "Haven't you got this thing open yet?"

Later he stood on the steps of his cottage, too wide-awake for sleep. Beside the steps was a small lilac that grew between two hemlocks that denied it its share of sunlight so that it grew slowly and blossomed late, and Tom looked down at it and then bent down and snapped off a small twig, the buds still brown and closed, and twisted it in his hand.

He thought about today's meeting and wondered whether even one man, privately, was asking himself any questions tonight or whether they were all still so sure—so sure that it couldn't be done.

And then, with sudden misgivings, he asked himself whether he was rushing into this. Maybe he should have waited, as Gates had urged, for more information—so that cautious men might be more easily convinced. But more information was what he wanted to discover—not borrow. In research you never began with proof. Hell, if you had the proof, if wasn't research any more. It was bricklaying.

Slowly, drawing in his elbows against the night chill, he walked out to the boardwalk, and in the dim light of the streetlamp he looked at the twig of the small late lilac that he twisted absent-mindedly between his fingers—at the half-brave, half-reluctant, brown-green clusters of leaves starting—and he thought, maybe with everything there is this moment. Maybe there is always this single suspended second, when eagerness and reluctance have equal weight and pull with the same force and some men go one way and some the other. And, he thought, maybe the way he goes is the difference between man and man.

FOUR

WATER STREET was a street that came to life at night. At ten o'clock in the morning while Tom drove along looking for No. 147, it was almost deserted. He passed a shabby grocery store and a place called The Golden Bar and then crept on past a dark slit of a window that advertised a tattoo artist. No. 147 was an old green building, the bottom floor of which was occupied by an establishment called Mary's Blue Heaven. Tom surveyed the building and then took his camera and a small package from the car. He tried the door to Mary's Blue Heaven and found it open. Behind the bar a sallow, tired-eyed woman was dragging a rag over the counter.

"Good morning, ma'am," Tom said. "I'm looking for Miss Mignon Custey."

Suspicion came into the empty eyes. "We open at noon, mister."

"Are you Mary?" The damp rag left a beady streak on the varnished bar. "Are you Mignon?"

"You're a real pest, all right."

Tom looked around The Blue Heaven at the blue walls, the blue curtains, the blue upright piano decorated with three buxom silver nudes with pink breasts. "Nice place you have here, ma'am," he said. "Reminds me of a place I used to work in in New Haven—Angel Amati's."

The tired eyes brightened. "You worked at Angel's?"

"I played the piano." He tinkled a few notes on the yellowed keys. "For years."

He was all right now. The woman jerked her head. "Mignon's on the top floor rear."

Mignon Custey, henna-haired, with bags under her eyes like suitcases, greeted him at the door in a sleazy black robe printed with Japanese lanterns. When Tom told her he'd come for a favor, she indicated instantly a readiness to oblige. When he asked if he might take her picture, she shrieked with laughter.

"My picture!" she said. "What do you want with my picture?"

"I'd heard that you were ill a few months ago, Mignon," Tom said, "but that you had fully recovered." Wariness narrowed Mignon's eyes and Tom gave her his warmest smile. "I heard that today you look wonderful—and now that I see you, I can see it's true."

"A-ah, go on!" Mignon screamed.

"I want to take your picture and use it as an example of a woman who had hard luck and rose above it. Would you have a picture of yourself then—for comparison—to show how wonderful you look today?"

Mignon was bedazzled. "Right here!" She pulled a couple of pictures out of a drawer. They were marvelous—she looked awful. She looked awful now.

Tom held out the package. "There's a white blouse in here and a black hair ribbon. Would you put them on?"

Mignon unwrapped the package and shrieked when she saw the tailored white blouse. "My God, you think I'm a schoolteacher or something?"

"In the interests of people who are suffering," Tom said soberly.

"Ah, well," Mignon said. "What'll it cost me?"

"I'll pay you, of course," Tom said. "For modeling."

Mignon was won. She disappeared into the bedroom and Tom set up the camera and opened a package of flash bulbs. Downstairs in Mary's, someone was playing the jukebox and the music screamed up, raspy, through the old building. Tom looked around the shabby apartment that smelled of stale cigarette smoke and dirt and age. Through the kitchen door he could see a bottle of gin and two bananas on a table. Downstairs the record stopped and started over again, and then Mignon came back, wearing the white blouse and a black satin skirt that strained over her bulging stomach and hips. The ribbon dangled in her hand.

Tom turned to her with a smile. "Brush your hair back and tie the ribbon in the back." She didn't look too bad, except for the bags under her eyes. He tilted the camera up a bit to eliminate the skirt. "Try to look as saintly as possible," he said.

"What are you—some kind of a preacher?"

"I expect to preach on this subject tomorrow." The bulb flashed. "May I take another?"

"Help yourself, if you know what I mean!" Mignon said, and screamed with laughter.

He took six pictures and Mignon looked disappointed when he told her he had finished.

"You're quite a guy," she said. "You're pretty cute."

Tom had spent too much time at Angel Amati's not to recognize an offer when he heard one. "I wish I could stay longer, Mignon," he said. "But I have to keep moving." He collected the used flashbulbs, paid her ten dollars and put the "before" pictures she had given him into his pocket. "You'll keep the blouse, I hope," he said.

"Who knows—maybe I'll even wear it sometime," Mignon said. "Just for laughs."

As he walked down the stairs the record in the jukebox ended and started over again.

A few minutes later Tom stopped at a stationery store, where he bought a large sheet of pale green cardboard and several sheets of construction paper, black, white and gray.

It was a little past eleven when he headed for the Woodcrest Cemetery.

Gil Brainard made his way down the length of the production room that morning, automatically looking around to let everyone know he had his eye on them. He passed the area where bottles of vitamin pills were being capped and saw a woman glance up and turn back to her machine. He stepped around a man washing the floor and stopped a minute to watch another woman who was filling tubes with veterinary ointments. It wasn't that she was slow—but she wasn't hurrying, either. This was one thing he'd change when he started revamping production here. These operations would be automatic and he wouldn't have to worry about these women, damn 'em, with their minds half on their jobs and half on their own troubles, their aches and pains and their brats. A lot they cared about production rates.

It didn't bother them that Ade Hale sat over there in his office going over production reports every time he turned around—or that he was always showing up in the plant, unexpected, unannounced, never at the same place at the same time. Well, Hale wasn't ever going to get the chance to say to Gil Brainard that things weren't right, even if he'd like to—even if he was always on the prowl, looking for something wrong.

Damn women—they gave you nothing but trouble. At the plant and, damn 'em, everywhere. His wife, his daughter, his wife's mother—goddamned meddlesome witch. For all she was dead, he

46

hated her still. If not for her, he'd handle Diana all right. The thought of his daughter only riled him more. She was home from college this week, and the week had been nothing but arguments, the latest of them this morning at breakfast. Well, today he had more important things on his mind, Brainard told himself, but he'd handle that girl yet—and when he said jump, she'd jump, the way her mother did—and when he told her to get rid of that tramp artist she'd picked up and to stay home nights, she'd get rid of the bum and by God she'd sit home—instead of walking out, leaving him telling Natalie to get her in line.

And Natalie had better do it or he would show both of them who was boss. Still, as Brainard moved on through the production room, unpleasant doubts gnawed at him. He could show Natalie any time he liked—and they both knew it—but Diana was another matter. And all because of Natalie's mother. If the old bitch hadn't left every dollar and stock and bond to Diana, he'd have a lot less trouble with that girl—damn it!

Brainard told himself he was edgy today. He ought to feel better. After yesterday's meeting he ought to feel great, but something nagged him—something he couldn't quite put his finger on. He stepped around another man washing this section of the floor. This washing the floor four times a day had been Will Caroline's idea and it was a good one. Not only did it keep the place clean but these slobs kept themselves cleaner for it, which was exactly what Will Caroline had predicted. It was a damn good idea and Brainard wished he'd thought of it himself.

He left the production room and headed for the research offices to find Morrissey and Harrup. He wanted to talk to them about this dinner for the directors tonight—to be sure they knew what he expected them to do, and that they intended to do it.

"Well, how's our boy, Cable, this morning?" he said, entering Morrissey's office.

Morrissey smiled that pleased, college-boy smile. "I'm afraid we were too much for Dr. Cable, Gil. He didn't show up today."

Brainard laughed. "I liked the way you handled yourself yesterday, Claude. Say the same thing tomorrow for the board—just that way."

Morrissey ran his hand over his white crew cut. "I didn't like Cable the day he walked in here," he said.

"Now, about tonight—" Brainard said. Then he saw Harrup in his own office and beckoned to him, and Harrup came in looking, as always, as though his ulcer was hurting.

"I liked your point yesterday, Neil," Brainard said. "We improve penicillin and streptomycin, we know what we're doing. Tell them that tomorrow. You're on solid ground—makes good common sense. Now, about tonight—"

Harrup nodded and then he said, "The thing that surprised me yesterday was Will Caroline. I had an idea he'd be for it, didn't you, Claude?"

"I thought so," Morrissey said.

Brainard laughed. "I'll tell you something about Will Caroline," he said. "Ade Hale brought Will Caroline here. When Ade Hale became vice-president, Will Caroline became director of research. When Hale became president, he made Will vice-president for research—and it was a job he could handle because Enright's always been a production company and there wasn't much research to worry about. Give him a couple of conscientious fellows like you two and what problems does he have?"

"That's true," Morrissey agreed.

"So Will Caroline says what Ade wants him to say. Ade Hale doesn't want problems from his own men, and Will Caroline doesn't give him any." Brainard broke the ash off his cigar. "Now, about those directors—" He'd buttered up these boys enough and he couldn't stay here all day. "Sometime between now and tomorrow Cable is going to figure out that his only chance is to get to a couple of those directors. I want to get to them first."

"I don't think he'd accomplish much even if he did reach them, Gil," Harrup said. "They wouldn't understand him. It takes a scientist to understand what he's trying to say."

Brainard looked at Harrup sharply. "Do you understand what he's trying to say?"

"Well—certainly I see what he's trying to say. Don't you?"

Brainard bit into his cigar. The uneasy feeling was nagging at his stomach again. He looked at Morrissey. "What about you? Do you get it, too, all of a sudden?"

"Well—" Morrissey took a minute to light his pipe, and Harrup said, "It's not all of a sudden, Gil. I've always understood it. I just don't think it'll work."

"That's it exactly, Gil," Morrissey said. "The problem isn't under-

48

standing it. The problem is doing it. But Neil's right—the board won't understand it."

Morrissey smiled and puffed his pipe, and Brainard had a wild impulse to grind the pipe into his face. "About tonight," he snapped. "Get there early. I want to talk to them, one or two at a time, while they're standing around drinking. If they're against the proposal before they even hear it, it'll make our job that much easier."

He walked back through the production room, stepping around a man washing the floor. His stomach was hurting badly and he wondered if he was getting an ulcer like Harrup. He paused and looked at a woman who was taking her own sweet time putting sealed tubes onto the belt that would carry them to be packaged. A million dollars would make a lot of changes around here.

At noon Tom pulled to a stop in front of the Woodcrest Cemetery. Out here the countryside was still back in winter, the brown trees barely brushed with copper. At the edge of the woods a blue jay flitted, looking a little drab, as though showing the wear of a hard winter. It flew low, staying close to the ground—a careful-seeming bird—as though it hadn't the heart to soar. Tom sat a minute and watched it and his thoughts worked around to Will Caroline.

He had had a warm affection for Will Caroline once, he told himself, and he supposed he would again when this was over, although it could not be quite the same. Probably Will had had his reasons for letting him down. Maybe he hadn't expected to have to fight the whole company. Maybe in the hard light of a showdown he decided he couldn't risk his own job. Well, at fifty, it wasn't easy to find a job. And then there was Callie. Callie was Will's first wife, but he was her third husband. Maybe Will had asked himself some questions privately—questions such as, if he pushed this and it failed and if it did cost him his job, then what about Callie? In a way you couldn't blame him, Tom thought, and he even smiled. Tom had always thought there was something great about Callie.

All the same, he thought, Will seemed damned pleased—he actually smiled—when Brainard said, "Give me that million." And then he thought, Oh hell—the guy was in too deep and Brainard was getting him off the hook. He was afraid of Hale or of losing his job or of losing Callie—what difference does it make? Fear is fear. And don't sit here all day analyzing it, because you've got too much

49

to do. He took a test tube and a teaspoon out of a box beside him on the seat, and picked up his camera and got out of the car. Maybe a man of twenty-seven had no right to judge a man of fifty, he thought as he walked toward the cemetery gate. Maybe at fifty you heard a different drummer. Maybe a man had no right to judge a man of any age just because he hadn't fought his battle for him.

For about ten minutes Tom wandered around and at last found what he was looking for—a family plot marked MILLER with a fresh, unmarked grave. He put down the camera and unwrapped the teaspoon and then, carefully, he raised a still-loose square of grass, feeling the cold in the ground, and scooped up a spoonful of earth and poured it into the test tube. "Thank you, Mr. Miller," he murmured. "And my apologies."

He put another spoonful of earth into the test tube, corked it and slid the square of grass back into place.

Behind him a voice said, "And what d'yer think yer doin'?"

Tom turned around, slipping the test tube of earth and the spoon into his pocket. "I missed the funeral day before yesterday," he said. "I was out of town."

"What was you doin' when I came up?" the attendant demanded.

Sadly Tom looked at the grave. "I'd have driven all night to make Mr. Miller's funeral. He was a friend when I needed him and you don't find many like that—"

"That's a fact, you don't," the attendant agreed.

Then Tom could see that his mind was working back to the other business. "So I came today as soon as I got home. I took a bit of earth from his grave—something to remember him by." Mr. Miller, he thought, what harm can these little lies do you now? He picked up the camera. "I wonder if I could ask you to take a picture of me next to the grave."

"Well—" Plainly the man's face said you met all kinds in this business. "I guess I could do that."

Tom took out the test tube and teaspoon. "I already have a teaspoon of the earth," he said, "so I won't take another. This is just for the picture."

"Mister," the man said, "I seen a lot of things around here, but ain't no one asked for a piece of the dirt before."

"It means a lot to me," Tom said.

He closed the cemetery gate behind him and walked back to his car. Near the car was a young maple tree just starting to put out leaves, still small and silvery green. And a little beyond the maple stood a single birch, its branches still bare, its white bark gleaming against the gray woods, as though it took more pride in the beauty it had always had than in anything new it might produce. And that's the way it is at Enright, Tom thought. He was pushing them to something new, but they didn't want it. They liked what they had.

At one o'clock Tom drove to the office of Dr. Edgar Bent, veterinarian, where he filled two more test tubes with dirt—one from the field where Dr. Bent buried animals, the other from the fenced run in the back yard next to the quarantine area. Then he went home to leave the tubes of earth he'd collected so far, each corked and labeled, and to develop the pictures. At two-thirty he took another test tube and headed for a tuberculosis hospital about forty miles away. He had one test tube left for tomorrow.

In the long, hot, noisy, windowless fermentation building, the massive tanks stood amidst mazes of pipes. Like columns of sentinels, they stood in two long rows—three sizes, three heights—the smallest ones higher than the ceiling of an ordinary room, the largest three times as high, rising to the top of the building. Each tank was surrounded by pipes; from several pipes, tails of steam hissed. Ade Hale closed the door behind him and walked down between the two rows. Back on his desk lay the transcript of yesterday's meeting. He had gone through it, sifting the valid arguments from the hysteria, and had about made up his mind. Now, to see whether it could be done, he was trying to talk himself out of his own position. Lining up Dr. Cable's arguments against those raised against him, he thought the lists were pretty much out of proportion. A very short list against a mighty long one.

He walked about halfway down the building, glancing out of habit at the control panel as he passed it. Then he turned and began to climb an iron stairway, coated against erosion from the steam, that led to the top of one of the highest tanks. On the first landing he paused, level with the tops of the smallest tanks, and climbed on to the second level and then stood at the top, his head almost touching the ceiling. In the entire plant, this was Ade Hale's favorite spot. Here, with the heat and the strong smell of fermentation and the roar of dozens of tails of hissing steam, he could think better than in the quiet of any office.

Closing his hand over the guardrail, he looked down at the tanks with their networks of pipes—pipes that fed them, pipes that controlled them, pipes that carried the broths from one to the other. Hale knew the function of every part of this equipment because he had designed most of it himself, before he was president, when he was still only a production engineer. For him this was the backbone of Enright. It was these tanks that made Enright what it was—and what it would be for a long time to come. Enright was a production company. It sold most of its products in bulk to other companies who manufactured the finished products and marketed them under their own labels, not Enright's. It was here in these fermentation tanks that Enright's roots were planted—solid roots that made it a solid company. Whenever Hale thought of progress for Enright, it was in terms of improved production techniques, with the research staff working toward that goal.

And yet, he told himself now, this idea that Cable had come up with was not a thing to turn your back on too quickly. A man could become too facile at saying no to what appeared impractical, imprudent, or just different from what he had in mind. But progress was inevitable. The trick was to know it when you saw it, even when its mask was not the one you were expecting.

Hale saw Will Caroline in the doorway, looking for him, and he went down the stairs and walked outside with him.

"We've got the money to spend, Will," Hale said after a few minutes. They both knew what they were going to talk about. "What it comes down to is deciding where it should go. Brainard's not exaggerating. With a million dollars he could add to the profits, substantially."

Will Caroline only nodded and kept walking and Hale smiled. That was one of the things that made Will a good man to talk to—he knew when you were looking for answers and when you were only thinking out loud.

"Another possibility would be to do more with finished products," Hale went on. "Make more vitamin pills, ointments, salves. Go in more for drugs in dosage form—not just in bulk. This new advertising agency we've taken on is pretty hot on that idea—" Hale smiled —"all set to make our name a household word."

"It's a possibility to consider," Will Caroline agreed.

"If we go after a share of that market, we'll get it," Hale said.

"How many producers of vitamin pills are there in the country, Ade?" Will Caroline said. "And of ointments—and salves?"

Hale nodded. "In the end, what've you got? Just what everyone else has. Nothing more." Hale smiled. "Kind of like a woman that you've gotten dressed and furred and jeweled and you look at her one day and say to yourself, What've I got? Toothpaste and ointment."

They passed the powerhouse, where pumps pulled salt water up from the bay to cool the fermentation tanks, and walked on.

After a moment Hale said, "That was a pretty emotional meeting yesterday, Will. They got something against Cable, personally?"

Will Caroline smiled. "There's no crime like disturbing the peace, Ade—especially when it's the peace of men's minds."

Hale looked up. "What about Cable? He's the youngest man you've got. And the newest. Does he know anything?"

"Progress is an ornery cuss," Will Caroline said, and grinned. "It doesn't recognize seniority."

"He was pretty much alone yesterday."

"In a thing like this, you don't get support quickly. It's new—unfamiliar—not many solid facts to go on. To most men it's unappealing."

"It's unappealing to me. And this was pretty strong opposition."

"With opposition you ask who," Will Caroline said. "And why."

Hale laughed. "You left your boy hanging pretty badly on the ropes yourself."

"Tom Cable won't stay on the ropes long. He'd never been to a meeting like that. Now he's been to one."

Will walked on, doing his best to hold back a smile. "Hell, Ade, that was a good meeting! Got everything out in the open." He looked down at the road and then he shook his head and his face went into a broad grin. "I was beginning to think Brainard would never get around to asking for that million for himself," he murmured.

Hale laughed and then his thoughts went back to this decision that had to be made. They stopped to let a truck go by, carrying drums of penicillin to a boxcar on the railroad siding, and then stepped across the tracks and walked over to the Enright dock. If Cable was right—if Enright could do it, find the drug, win the race against the others, get the patent—there was no question which was the best choice. There was no question, either, which was the most uncertain. He looked at Will Caroline. "We don't need it, Will. Enright will survive long beyond your time and mine without it."

"No, we don't need it. And there probably isn't a man in the company—or on the board—right now who thinks we do." Will Caroline smiled. "There probably isn't even a dissatisfied stockholder. We don't need it."

Idly Hale watched the truck backing up to the boxcar. "It'll be quite a departure for us—if we try it," he said.

"Ade, if we try this, it won't be just a departure. It'll be like walking into a peaceful countryside, where everything is quiet and contented, and dropping a bomb. And the house that will be closest to the explosion will be your own. You could blow it up—it could happen."

Hale laughed. "Whose side are you on?"

"Or you could blow up a gold mine." Will stopped. "Ade, you know I'm for this and I'm for it strong. But you have to decide, because you're the one who'll be responsible in the end. I'll run it and I'll get blamed if it doesn't work, but you'll get blamed more. And you heard yesterday what the chances are." Will paused and smiled. "Well, I think the chances are a little better than you heard yesterday."

"What about tomorrow, Will? You want to talk for it?"

"That depends on you. I'm not interested in selling this over your head. This will be a big project. It'll start small enough, but before we're through it will be big. You have to be for it or there's no point in starting at all. If you've decided against it, tell me now and I'll tell Tom Cable."

"It'd be the easiest way out."

"You're not in anything yet."

"No—" Ade Hale shook his head. "Let the board hear it—see if they want to go for it. They won't be easy to convince. Brainard has strong arguments, and more of them. And your own top men are behind him."

"My top men are very nervous about it."

"Too damned nervous. What's the matter with them? Is it beyond them? Can't they understand it?"

"They understand it too well," Will said. "They understand that if we try and fail, so much will have gone into it that everyone will be hurt."

54

Hale frowned, looking over at the truck that was starting to unload.

"Although," Will said thoughtfully, "I don't think they'd be that nervous if they were certain Cable was wrong. Then opposing this would be a much simpler thing. I think maybe they understand something else, too."

Hale turned around. "What's that?"

"Ade, supposing we don't try this—and it turns out Cable was right? And supposing someone else does it—not one of the giants, so they have a handy excuse—but another small company, no bigger than Enright? They understand what that means, too. They understand that for years they'll know they were at the pier—and that they missed the boat."

Later, walking back to his office, Will Caroline thought that if Ade decided to come out for this tomorrow, it would be an act of great courage—a greater act of courage for him than for Tom Cable—because Cable was a scientist, and for a scientist there was no stigma in failing for years. The failure only added glory to the success when it finally came. But Ade Hale was a businessman, and in business failure was not tolerated.

Besides, Will thought, Tom Cable believed in this totally. And Ade Hale did not.

Now it was dark and Tom stood on his porch, the frantic, half-antic day behind him. The water was quiet tonight. Small waves brushed the sand and slipped off with a quiet slush, heard only when there were no other sounds. Through a window of his cottage he could see the cardboard and the construction paper he had laid out on a table, and he told himself to go in and make the chart, since it was all that was left to be done, but he turned away and walked out to the boardwalk, thinking that he would do it in a little while—there was time.

Far down the beach, he could see the chain of lights on Tollie's dock and, across the water, the brighter lights of Enright, where the waterfront and the section around the fermentation building were always lighted. He began to walk up the boardwalk. It was that fermentation building, he thought, that held him here. Otherwise leaving Enright would be simple. The man didn't live who had fewer strings—and Enright could find another biochemist easily enough to replace him. But, although there were many laboratories where you might begin a search for a new antibiotic, in the end you couldn't produce it without fermentation, and for fermentation you needed those tanks—those huge, controlled, progressively larger tanks—and only a handful of companies had them. Far out, beyond Enright, where the bay went into the ocean, a foghorn called over the quiet water. He might as well go in and make the chart.

He thought of Mignon Custey and her pasty face and of Mary with her tired eyes and her Blue Heaven and her blue piano with the silver nude girls, and he remembered all the nights he had played the same kind of pianos at the same kind of places. He passed the house where the Welles girl lived and thought that she was in fact only a polished high-class version of the girls he had known then. He knew that type—cold, hard-eyed, disenchanted. They knew everything, they had seen everything, and they believed in nothing.

He turned and started back and then he walked past his house and kept walking, the length of the boardwalk, until he reached Tollie's. He went around the weather-beaten building past the dark boatshop, and into the restaurant for cigarettes. McCarthy, the old sailor who worked around the boats, was behind the counter, and Tom guessed that Tollie himself was driving for Enright tonight, meeting some director's plane or train.

"Hey, Dr. Cable," McCarthy greeted him. The restaurant was empty except for a couple in the second booth, a young girl wearing a high-necked red sweater and a man with a beard.

"Quiet night, McCarthy?" Tom said.

"Dead."

Tom dropped the coins into the cigarette machine, noticing that the girl in the booth had turned around to watch him. She was a striking girl—although very young, he saw—with black hair cut very short. She had deep blue eyes and she was watching him steadily, not looking away when she saw he had noticed. He picked up the cigarettes and left by the back door and followed the string of dim lights out onto the dock.

At the end of the lights he stopped and leaned on one of the thick dock posts and looked at the water, and feelings he had fought off all day began to close in on him. He felt tired and small and filled suddenly with the taste of defeat. Once again he asked himself whether he wanted to do it this way. Suddenly his plan seemed degrading and he had no taste for it.

He felt distaste for his plan and for all that made it necessary—for men like Brainard and Morrissey and, yes, Ade Hale, too. And yet he didn't suppose it was different anywhere else. Wherever you go, he thought, you will find the Brainards and the Morrisseys—whatever in fact they are—and the Ade Hales and, probably, the Will Carolines, too. The schemers and their stooges—the drivers and their driven. He thought that in the whole circle of the day this was the loneliest hour—the start of a lonely night.

But he knew it wasn't the hour. Many times this hour at the start of night, especially in spring, had stirred a passionate joy in him, a feeling almost of greatness, as though nothing could stop him. The smallness and aloneness were in the man, and the night only made them sharper. And there was nothing so alone as a man whose mind touched no other—a man possessed of an idea that had no takers—who, with his idea, had become an untouchable.

Then, through his weariness, he told himself stubbornly that that which is inherently right cannot be degraded.

And then he thought, Why this sudden reluctance—what are you afraid of? Not, he told himself, that the great chance might be lost this way, because the chance is already lost—or nearly so—and this is its only hope. And not that there will be those who will not approve of your method. You know already that almost no one will approve of you or of your method. You knew it yesterday. And that doesn't matter very much. Then what? he said to himself.

Below, the dark water lapped the weathered boards and he watched it. And then this feeling that had rushed over him so suddenly as suddenly left. He smiled, straightening up from the post, shaking his head at his own womanish misgivings. You're getting too squeamish in your old age, he told himself—too respectable. Why shouldn't you do it this way? Who will be injured? All that can happen is that they might laugh and say that you put on a sideshow. Well, if that is an injury, it is one you can bear. And if you have to go in tomorrow, not as a scientist, but as a huckster, you will have to do it. The question, my friend, is not whether this is quite nice. The question is whether this will work.

So go home and finish what you started. Go home and make up that chart. And stop worrying about your fine sensibilities. There will be time later for that, when there is nothing better to worry about.

He turned and started back down the dock to the boardwalk.

He was almost at the steps when he heard the tapping of heels on them, and he looked up and saw that it was the black-haired young girl who, a little while ago, had been sitting in the second booth.

The girl stopped as she came off the steps and looked down the dark pier. Then she saw him. "Dr. Cable—" she called, and came up to him. She was small and slim and she stood very straight, looking up at him. "I went to your house, looking for you tonight," she said. "Twice."

In the dim light, Tom saw that this was a remarkably good-looking girl. The gamine haircut was daringly short, and the blue eyes glowed with that terrible assurance of a very young girl who has just discovered her secret weapon—that she is beautiful.

"When you weren't there the second time, I hoped you'd gone for good," she said. "Although I was sorry not to have seen you first."

"Try me tomorrow," Tom said. "Maybe then I'll be gone for good."

"I hope so."

Curious and a little amused, Tom looked at the girl. He had never seen her before tonight, he thought—she was striking enough so that he wouldn't have forgotten her. Or maybe he would—these kids changed fast.

She leaned against the rail, studying him, and when he looked at her, she looked back undisturbed, like a young conqueror who expected to win. "So this is what you're like," she said.

Tom smiled. "Honey, does your mother know you run around talking to strange men like this?"

"My mother knows very little about me. And my father even less —which is all to the good, don't you think?"

"Well, I don't know about that—"

"And you're not so strange."

"Well," Tom said, "now that you've found me, why were you looking for me?"

The girl tilted her head. "You don't know who I am, do you?"

"Now we're getting somewhere," Tom said.

"It's just that Enright is such a tight little island—you know, so really insular. I'm Diana Brainard."

58

The water lapped the piles of the pier. "Well," Tom said. "Hello, Diana."

They faced each other in the dim light of the small bulb under which they stood, and then Diana Brainard said, "Now let's go somewhere and talk." She motioned to the roped-off stairs that led to the lower dock. "Let's sit on those steps and talk."

"Tollie's replacing the rail," Tom said. "That's why it's roped off."

She tossed her head. "Well, let's duck under the rope and sit there anyway."

He couldn't hold it against her that Gil Brainard was her father, Tom told himself, but neither did he want to stay here talking to her. He took her arm and started walking toward the boardwalk. "Ordinarily it would be very nice, Diana," he said, "but not tonight."

She walked beside him for a moment without speaking. Then she gave him a cool steady look and said, "I hope you lose tomorrow, Dr. Cable."

Tom smiled without answering.

Diana Brainard stopped walking and stood in front of him. "Don't you know what will happen if you win?"

"What happened to your bearded friend, Diana?" Tom said.

"Then you did notice me before!" She was the young conqueror again. She was young Alexander with his great Macedonian armies that would never lose.

"Of course I noticed you—you were the only ones in the place."

She laughed. Then she said, "Dr. Cable, the reason I hope you lose tomorrow is not the one you are thinking. It's because if you win, they will destroy you at Enright."

Tom glanced at her, thinking that it was hard to believe this was Gil Brainard's daughter.

"At Enright they destroy anything that's noble or great," Diana said with a strange intensity. "They don't even understand it. At Enright they understand one thing—profit. They don't want greatness there! They want profits." At the steps she stopped and looked up at him. "Take your idea, Dr. Cable, and run with it—before they give you what you want, and you stay with them and trade your life for it. Run while you still can."

He had almost forgotten what this fire of the very young was like, Tom thought. He tried not to seem amused. "Where would you suggest I go?"

"Go to some outpost of civilization where learning is still respected for its own sake. Take it to a research foundation."

Smiling, Tom led her up the steps. "You may be right, Diana," he said. "But I still have work to do tonight and I don't want to talk about this particular subject, so let me take you back to your bearded friend."

"Adam? I sent him home."

"Why did you send Adam home?"

"Because I wanted to talk to you," she said. "Will you buy me a drink, Dr. Cable? You can drink to your victory tomorrow, and I will drink to your defeat—so you can have a greater victory later."

Tom kept walking. "They won't serve you," he said. "You're too young."

"They do serve me, Dr. Cable," she said.

So she was older than she looked. "Diana, I don't want to drink tonight," he said. "Shall I take you home?"

At her door she said, "How about that drink tomorrow night, Dr. Cable? If you lose, I'll buy them. And if you win, I'll buy them anyway. Because either way you're going to suffer."

He laughed. "Either way, honey, I probably won't be in condition to be with a nice girl like you."

"Better still," she said, and the blue eyes laughed. "I'll wait for you. And if you don't come, I'll blame it on your condition and try to forgive you."

Half an hour later, in his living room, Tom spread out a newspaper on the table and measured the cardboard and figured and then sketched a small scarecrow-like figure. He folded the paper several times and traced the pattern and cut, making a row of figures, seeing that the third figure cut across Mr. Miller's death notice —Mr. Miller, whom he had never seen and about whom he knew almost nothing.

He traced the series of figures onto the different-colored sheets of construction paper he had bought this morning—the black, the white and the gray—and then he sat down to cut out the paper dolls and paste them in rows onto the green cardboard sheet.

In an oak-paneled private dining room at the Tides Inn, Gil Brainard said, "To be perfectly honest, I wouldn't say it's any crazier than a lot of other projects they work on in research foundations. Would you, Claude?"

"No," Morrissey said, after a moment's reflection. "I don't suppose it's really worse than a lot of them."

Brainard jiggled his drink. He was standing in a corner talking to two carefully selected directors—Palmerton, a pink-faced, white-haired man with silver-rimmed eyeglasses, whose wife had inherited a large block of Enright stock, and a pale, dark-haired man named Bodenhof, who, though still under forty, was known as an investment genius.

"It's different at the foundations," Brainard said. "They don't care about practical affairs."

Out of the corner of his eye he saw that Callie Caroline was moving this way and that both Palmerton and Bodenhof had glanced over at her, and he thought you always knew when Callie was around. There was always that little stir.

"And another thing those foundations don't care about is money," Brainard said. "And there's a good reason why they don't."

Palmerton frowned. "Why's that?"

"Because of where it comes from. Because most of their money was put up by people who are dead."

Morrissey puffed his pipe. "Makes a difference, all right!"

"You know what happens," Brainard said with a smile. "A fellow realizes he's getting on—gets to thinking maybe a couple things he did weren't what they should have been—so he decides to dress up the record a little, and he sets up a big grant to a foundation. Kinda buys his way into heaven." Brainard laughed. Then he said, "With that kind of money the foundations can afford to let dreamers like this Dr. Cable fool around for years."

"It's a different situation from business, obviously," Palmerton said.

"Although," Bodenhof put in, "they do have their successes."

"That's true." A quick appraisal told Brainard that this new fellow, Bodenhof, might be tougher than some of the others. "With enough time and enough money they do turn up something—once in a while. And I admit it adds up to progress. But progress is a slow expensive job. And my question is, does that kind of thing belong at Enright?"

"Hardly seems so," Palmerton said soberly.

"When you come right down to it, progress isn't paid for by the living," Brainard said. He chuckled. "It's paid for by the dying."

Morrissey sipped his martini. "Never thought of it quite that way, but you're right, Gil."

Brainard liked the reaction he was getting here. They weren't saying much but they were getting the point. He signaled the waiter for more drinks, and then he saw that Callie had moved closer.

Glancing over at her, Brainard thought that if anyone else, including Natalie—who was better looking—had turned up tonight wearing anything as plain as that black thing Callie had on, she'd have looked like nothing at all. But Callie made everyone else look a little shabby. It had always been like that with Callie. It wasn't that she was especially beautiful—she'd never been that—and Brainard had known Callie a long time, since long before Will Caroline ever saw her. She was tall and a little scrawny and she just parted her dark hair in the middle and let it hang. And it wasn't that long cigarette holder she carried—nor that damned emerald the size of a horse's tooth that she had from her first husband and had worn all these years on a chain as though she couldn't be bothered doing anything about it. It was just something about Callie—part of that not-giving-a-damn attitude that she converted into style.

Now Brainard had an uneasy feeling that she was going to join this carefully cornered group, and he looked away, hoping to discourage her. Callie had a way of upsetting things.

"Now, I say," he said, "that before a business indulges in this kind of lunacy, it had better have a pretty favorable tax situation. You start that stuff too soon and you won't be much use to anyone—to yourself, to the stockholders or to society." Uneasily he saw that Callie was coming up to them. "In business, I always say, solvency first and charity afterwards. Then both are done right. Reverse the order and neither is done right."

"Makes sense," Palmerton remarked.

Now Callie was here, and Brainard sighed as the two men turned to her. She greeted Palmerton and then turned to Bodenhof and said, "Carl, it's mighty fine to see you again!"

"How're you, Cal?" Bodenhof bent over to kiss her. Brainard didn't even know that Bodenhof knew Callie.

"What've you bought lately?" Callie said.

Well, that was a great question, Brainard thought, and then he realized that Bodenhof understood it.

"One small Braque—wonderful."

Then Palmerton said, "Gil, here, just came up with an interesting analysis, Callie."

"I heard it. I was eavesdropping." Callie wielded the cigarette holder and gave Brainard a smile. "Would you carry it one step farther, Gil—and say, then, that the foundation for progress turns out to be superstition?"

Brainard looked at her warily. "How do you figure that?"

"Buying your way into heaven does seem rather a superstition." Callie turned to Bodenhof. "What do you say, Carl? Is it any different from a sacrifice to make rain?"

Bodenhof smiled. "I'd give it the same label, Cal."

"And if all progress must come from research foundations—and if those foundations are supported by—" Callie spread her hands and smiled. "Then in progress, superstition is footing the bill."

"Interesting thought, all right," Morrissey said.

"Isn't it? But then progress has always been a tantalizing subject," Callie said. "It can be so capricious. Sometimes it doesn't even take anything new. All the ingredients are there. And suddenly somebody just puts them together right and there you are. A giant step forward. Lovely progress." Callie laughed. "Lovely rewards."

Smiling serenely, Callie moved away.

When she was out of earshot Brainard resumed, but in a carefully lowered voice. "You know, this young fellow, Cable, is all right. We don't have anything against him." Then Neil Harrup came up with Admiral Sutherland, and Brainard spoke a little louder. "Although I suspect he thinks stockholder and profit are dirty words. His reaction to a question about dividends would be 'Why bother about a little thing like that?' "

"He made quite a scene at a meeting yesterday," Harrup said.

"Probably do it again tomorrow." Brainard laughed. "Consider yourself warned. Ask Dr. Morrissey about him—Cable's in his department."

"Well, I don't work with him much," Morrissey said quickly. "I have a young assistant, Dr. Gates, who works more with antibiotics. So much of that is still guesswork—not the systematic research I like. And I find the older I get, the less patience I have for another man's blunders. It's a character weakness, I admit," he said with a bright smile. "But this Dr. Gates is a good-natured young fellow and we let him do most of the work on penicillin and streptomycin."

"What does Dr. Cable do?" Bodenhof said.

"Oh, he works on them a little, too," Morrissey said. He flicked at the pocket of his suit.

"Don't misunderstand me about Dr. Cable," Brainard said to Bodenhof. "These young research men are all like that—and that's all right. We don't want them thinking too much about profit. If they did, they wouldn't be thinking about their own work and that's what we're paying them for. But they have to be kept in the laboratory. We can't have them making policy or we'll be out begging for charity ourselves. Give them their way and we'll be papering the walls with our stock certificates." Then he laughed and added, "Instead of Will Caroline's signs."

He was glad to see they looked sober and rather worried, especially Palmerton, who, after all, controlled a large block of stock.

FIVE

T HE SIX FORMER PRESIDENTS looked down from
the walnut-paneled walls, and the black ashtrays and white pads
and yellow pencils were on the long table. Today there were new
faces, but otherwise it was all the same. Except, Tom thought, that
last time he had come in thinking he had support. Today he knew
he was alone. Seeing Will Caroline now, for the first time since
Wednesday, Tom glanced at him briefly and looked away. When
you had had so much faith in a man, it hurt—more than you liked
to admit—to learn you had been wrong.

He had taken the same place as before, at the foot of the table,
near the blackboard, and now he sat studying the unfamiliar faces.
Just to his right were Morrissey and Harrup and Tom understood
well enough what he saw in their faces. And he recognized the predatory look that Gil Brainard was wearing. But among the new ones
—the men he had never seen before—no man was yet a hero or a
coward, a friend or an enemy; no man was a man to write off or a
man to be counted.

His eyes moved slowly around the table, skipped past Gil Brainard, and then, with a new curiosity, went back to Brainard's face
while he searched briefly for some hint of the gamine, something
that once could have passed for fiery idealism, but all he saw was
the heavy jowls, the watchful eyes, the lips clamped over a cigar.
He looked on, past Ade Hale and then again at Will Caroline, who
was watching him with an easy, relaxed smile. Tom's eyes dropped
to his briefcase. Carefully he slipped out his folder of notes from
among the test tubes of earth.

"I'd like you to hear about this from Dr. Cable first," Ade Hale
said to the board. "There are a number of arguments against it, and
when Dr. Cable is through, we'll go over them. This isn't a simple
problem—you'll ask a lot of questions that can't be answered. That's
part of the problem." He looked at Will Caroline. "Anything you
want to say about this, Will, before we begin?"

Will Caroline smiled. "Dr. Cable can talk about it better than I
can."

"All right, Dr. Cable," Hale said, "let's get started."

Calmly, Tom got to his feet and held up the manila folder. "This

65

is about all the information available today on antibiotics," he began. He flipped through the notes and closed the folder and put it down. "It's not much."

He saw Morrissey and Harrup glance at each other and Morrissey roll his eyes ceilingward.

"So I've brought in some demonstration material," Tom went on, "to help illustrate the points I want to make."

"This lack of information is one of the things that worry us," Hale said to the directors. "Mr. Brainard feels it's a strong argument against it."

"The strongest," Brainard said.

Tom reached into his briefcase. "I have some Petri dishes"—he took out five small glass dishes—"and some test tubes containing soil." He took out the five test tubes of earth that he had collected.

He started to make his way around the table. The cold formality of the room today was upsetting, and for a moment Tom had a sinking feeling that this was not so good an idea as he had hoped, but it was too late now to turn back.

He put a Petri dish on the table between Morrissey and Harrup. "To a scientist," he said, "it's a thing of beauty to see all the pieces of a problem fit together perfectly—nothing missing and nothing left over. He has the instincts of a perfect housekeeper. A place for everything and everything in its place."

He paused to read the labels on the test tubes. "And it's possible for him to be satisfied because the natural world is in order. When it seems not to be in order, it is not the natural world that falls short of perfection but man's knowledge and understanding of it."

Standing between Morrissey and Harrup, Tom selected the test tube containing the earth taken from Mr. Miller's grave. He looked at the faces that were becoming a little less strange. Two seats away, one man, fairly young and rather homely, was watching him with clever black eyes that seemed to be saying, I suspect this is at least half a gag but I'll wait and see, and Tom remembered that this was Bodenhof, the one they called a financial wizard. He uncorked the test tube and poured the earth into the Petri dish.

"Over the centuries," Tom went on, "this sense of the orderliness of the natural world has increased as new pieces have been found that fit into the puzzle. Usually these pieces are discovered very far apart—both in time and in place—and the connections between them are worked out very slowly. For example—" He moved

66

around the table and put down another Petri dish between Bodenhof and the admiral. He glanced at Ade Hale and wondered whether he would let him go on to the end. He saw Brainard mash out a half-smoked cigar.

"For example," he went on, "over the centuries, students of medicine named and became familiar with a long list of diseases to which man fell victim—and for years this list remained a fairly random thing, without much classification. Then a classification was made. In Denmark a bacteriologist named Gram discovered that the cultures of some disease germs could be stained a beautiful color and that others could not. With some cultures the dye just washed off. And on that basis, Dr. Gram classified all known disease germs into two groups. Those that took the stain became known as gram-positive—those that didn't take it were called gram-negative."

Tom stole another look around, wondering whether they were following him. He emptied one of the test tubes he had filled at the veterinarian's into the Petri dish and glanced down at the admiral who was frowning at the dish and then the other way at Bodenhof who was still watching with bright clever eyes.

He moved on. "Of course, a man sick in bed doesn't care whether the germ that's making him sick can or cannot be colored. This was one of those bits of information that were known but didn't have much practical value. As recently as three years ago, this was still true." He saw Brainard yank the wrapper off another cigar. Brainard, he observed, was edgy today. "We had the lists, gram-positive, gram-negative, but we couldn't relate them to much. Then along came penicillin, discovered in England, developed in the United States. It was magic—a wonder drug. It cured diseases that no medicine had touched before. Every known disease was tested to see whether penicillin would cure it. And a lot of them it did. And a lot it didn't."

Brainard spoke up. "Ade—Enright was working on penicillin long before Dr. Cable ever came here. I don't think he has to tell us about penicillin."

Morrissey took the pipe out of his mouth and was going to laugh, but thought better of it and smiled instead. Hale looked at Tom questioningly and tapped the table.

Then Will Caroline said, "What're you driving at, Tom? That penicillin hits the gram-positive diseases?"

"Partly. More, too."

"It seems related to the problem, Ade."

"It seems pertinent," Hale agreed. "Let's keep it that way, Dr. Cable."

"Yes, sir." Surprised, Tom looked at Will Caroline, and then he hurried on before these men lost the thread he was trying to develop.

"Then, a few years later, in New Jersey, Dr. Waksman discovered streptomycin and tests were made again to see what diseases streptomycin would cure. When they were finished, it was found that penicillin was most effective against gram-positive diseases and that streptomycin was most effective against gram-negative diseases. Now, that's one of those beautiful satisfying connections—the wonderful fitting together of the pieces—"

"Ade—" Brainard started and then seemed to hesitate as though wondering whether to interrupt again and then went on. "We know all this. We all know that penicillin hits the gram-positive and streptomycin hits the gram-negative."

"I don't know it," Bodenhof said. Bodenhof wasn't just a face any more. He was becoming an individual and important.

Brainard's fingers pressed the table, and Tom saw the deep teethmarks in the cigar butts in his ashtray and he thought, He's worried —he's as worried as I am. He walked past Hale and Caroline and stopped between Brainard and Palmerton, a cold-looking man whose face showed no reaction whatsoever. He emptied the tube from the dog run. He had two tubes left, the one that he had filled at the tuberculosis sanitarium and the last one that he had filled this morning in front of an Enright building. He emptied them into Petri dishes between the last two pairs of directors and returned to his place.

From his briefcase he took the photographs of Mignon Custey. "Before I show you these pictures," he said, "I want to call your attention to Mr. Brainard's statement, 'Penicillin hits the gram-positive and streptomycin hits the gram-negative.'"

Brainard's face said he didn't like being dragged into the speech. "I think everyone heard me, Dr. Cable."

"Sir," Tom said to Hale, "may we ask Dr. Morrissey and Dr. Harrup to confirm the statement?"

"It's correct," Morrissey said crisply. "Penicillin hits the positive, streptomycin the negative."

68

"Dr. Harrup?"

Harrup nodded and shrugged and muttered, "With one or two exceptions."

Tom beamed at Harrup. "Now—my pictures. Two pictures of a Miss Custey—one taken six months ago, when the woman was obviously sick. The other I took myself yesterday—she has been cured." He passed the pictures around the table. When they came back, he took a moment to stand them on the chalk tray of the blackboard.

He turned around. "Miss Custey had gonorrhea."

A few of the directors winced. Palmerton looked at Brainard and began to play, a little impatiently, with his yellow pencil.

"Gonorrhea is a gram-negative disease," Tom said. "Gram-negative. Until now an almost incurable disease. But Miss Custey was cured in a short time because she was treated with penicillin."

He waited a moment.

Bodenhof leaned forward. "You just said penicillin hits the positive." Bodenhof had caught the point and had given it to the rest.

Tom nodded. "Mr. Brainard said penicillin hits the positive and streptomycin hits the negative, and Dr. Morrissey repeated it, but Dr. Harrup added the most important fact of all. Dr. Harrup said, 'With one or two exceptions.' Penicillin does hit the positive—but it jumps the fence twice and hits very hard at two gram-negative diseases. Two exceptions. Gonorrhea is one of them."

Then he said casually, "The other exception is a meningitis."

They were all listening carefully now.

"I'd hoped to bring a similar picture of a man recovered from meningitis," he told them, "but he died. It's possible that he had a doctor who still refuses to prescribe penicillin because he doesn't believe anything that new and different can be good. At any rate, the man died three days ago and he was buried, for religious reasons, on the same day, without embalming. His name was Miller. Yesterday I took two teaspoons of earth from Mr. Miller's grave."

At almost the same instant, a half-dozen pairs of eyes looked uneasily at the Petri dishes.

"And I brought in that earth today—"

Kaiser, the lawyer, took out his handkerchief and wiped his hands. Palmerton's yellow pencil stopped in midair.

"It's the earth in the dish between Dr. Morrissey and Dr. Harrup."

All eyes flew to that dish. And then, with almost simultaneous second thoughts, to their own. Palmerton's pencil moved slowly, eraser end pointed, to the dish near him, and he daintily, carefully, inched it away.

"I have a picture here of myself at Mr. Miller's grave, taking the dirt. It was snapped by an obliging cemetery attendant."

Ade Hale's fingers were tapping the table again and he was looking at Will Caroline.

Tom told himself it was imperative to go on quickly to something else. He seized the cardboard chart, almost knocking it over. "My next exhibit is a chart, bearing the legend of one of the oldest scourges of man—tuberculosis."

He rested the chart against the blackboard. Slowly their eyes came away from the Petri dishes.

"The top row"—he pointed—"has one hundred black figures, representing a hundred tuberculosis patients in hospitals before the discovery of streptomycin. One hundred sick patients.

"In the second row, there are twenty-five black figures. This is the number out of every hundred who still have not been cured—even now—with streptomycin. Twenty-five percent still have tuberculosis."

He pointed to the third row. "These gray figures represent questionable recoveries. Again twenty-five figures. Twenty-five per cent probably, but not certainly, have been cured with streptomycin."

Then he pointed to the bottom line—twice as long as the other two. "These white figures represent patients who have been cured. They are out of the hospitals, walking around, leading normal lives. Fifty white figures. Twice as many as the other two. This is how hard streptomycin hits t.b.—a sickness hardly touched before by any other drug—and not touched by penicillin." He leaned forward on the table. "Tuberculosis is a gram-positive disease."

This time nobody had to explain it. Hale's fingers stopped tapping and Tom knew he had a reprieve.

"T.b. is the jump that streptomycin makes into the gram-positive. But here on the wrong side of the fence is where it hits the hardest and against the most stubborn of diseases. Now, remember—in the natural world there are no mistakes. The natural world is in order. If each of these drugs jumps the fence—penicillin twice and streptomycin once—then we have to say that, much as we like the tidiness of the relationship of these drugs to gram-positive and

70

gram-negative, we must say that relationship is interesting but not absolute.

"From there it's only one step further to conclude that other antibiotics, still unknown, will jump, too. Antibiotics can be found that will do even more than penicillin and streptomycin—that will hit both gram-positive and gram-negative alike. And such a drug would be important and valuable because a doctor can't always make an early diagnosis. Not every doctor can get a culture test. Not every doctor will. Penicillin and streptomycin are called wonder drugs, but they're limited. There are still diseases that neither will cure. Think of the wonder of a drug that would cure diseases not touched by either of these—a broad-spectrum antibiotic that would hit twice as many and more—"

Brainard couldn't hold himself in. "Pretty rare breed of cat!"

"No!" Tom retorted. "I don't think so!"

"I think so!"

"Dr. Morrissey and Dr. Harrup don't think so," Tom said.

Brainard whirled on Morrissey and Harrup as though they had betrayed him, and they looked up, stunned.

"Look at them!" Tom said. "When I told you that the Petri dish between them contains earth taken from the grave of a man who died three days ago of meningitis, you all looked alarmed. You're wondering what's in the other dishes, the ones near you. Some of you moved them away. But Dr. Harrup and Dr. Morrissey aren't alarmed. They haven't pushed their dish away—they haven't touched it. It's right where I put it."

Bodenhof's pale face went into a broad smile. Tom hoped Bodenhof had a lot of stock.

"And yet, in two days, germs would have had time to spread around—a few of them would have gotten up to the surface. It would seem, then, that Dr. Harrup and Dr. Morrissey ought to be alarmed. Why aren't they? Because they know there's no danger. They know that disease germs introduced into the earth don't live. There are no more meningitis germs in that Petri dish than in any other sample of earth taken anywhere. And the reason disease germs don't live in the earth is that the soil is full of other microbes that are unfriendly to them and kill them."

"Well, now," Morrissey said. "There could be other reasons—other factors involved."

"No!" Tom cried. "This is the factor involved! If you introduce disease germs into normal soil, they are destroyed—promptly—while the normal microbe population of the soil lives. But—if you sterilize that soil first, so that you kill its normal population, and then introduce disease germs into it—then those disease germs thrive—they flourish—they grow luxuriantly!"

"Has that been proved?" Bodenhof said.

"Yes, sir, it has! Many times. I could repeat it for you here. Dr. René Dubos at the Rockefeller Institute has done detailed work in this field. Dr. Waksman has been studying it for years. The microbes in the soil kill these germs as part of their natural life function. They produce a substance that the disease germs don't tolerate. It's as simple as that." Tom paused and leaned over the table, gripping the edge. "That microbe killing is called antibiotic action. That substance that does the killing is called an antibiotic. An antibiotic isn't anything rare and mysterious. It's produced every day, naturally, by living microorganisms—by little bugs—and those little bugs are all around us, everywhere."

He straightened up. "And more than anywhere else, they're in the soil. The soil is teeming with them. In any one of these dishes there is a population at least equal to the population of a large city. Just as complex and just as busy. Microbes performing all kinds of functions—decaying, fermenting, killing each other, helping each other—and among all those things that the different microbes are doing, some of them are producing substances that kill disease germs—human diseases—animal diseases—plant diseases."

He stopped for a minute. He looked at the men sitting soberly around the table. "Are you wondering what's in the other dishes? Yours, sir"—he looked at the admiral and then at Bodenhof—"was taken from the grave of a recently buried rabid dog."

The admiral looked at the dish as though it contained the dog, still barking and foaming at the mouth, but Bodenhof grinned. Bodenhof, Tom decided, he had.

"Yours, Mr. Brainard and Mr. Palmerton, was taken from a fenced-in run at the same dog hospital—from the quarantined section where the dogs twice a day are let out briefly to relieve themselves. My apologies, gentlemen, I know it's unpleasant." Palmerton's pencil moved the Petri dish farther away. "And yours, sir"—Tom turned to Kaiser, the lawyer—"came from the area immediately over the dry well of the septic tank at the tuberculosis sanitarium."

Palmerton's pencil went again to the Petri dish, and then he hesitated because the dish was already in the center of the table and he couldn't push it farther without pushing it toward the admiral who already had a rabid dog. Instead, Palmerton moved his chair back a few inches.

"Of course that tank is buried," Tom said, "but everyone knows that the earthworms plow the soil steadily and that eventually some of those germs would have made their way to the surface if they had remained alive. But there is no great concentration of germs in any of those dishes, in spite of the areas from which I took them.

"Gentlemen, all disease-producing germs of animals and plants eventually end up in the soil—through excreta or the burial of diseased bodies. And yet the germs are not in the soil. Why?"

He was gripping the table again, and he made himself straighten up and ease up a bit. "That final dish—the one between Mr. Hoffman and Mr. Northrup—came from the front yard of our newest building, built this year on what was, until then, pastureland. For a hundred years it had been pastureland. All kinds of cattle grazed there, performing every animal function—healthy cattle, diseased cattle, dying cattle. And before that, wild animals roamed it for centuries. Why, then, isn't that land reeking with disease? Why doesn't every man at Enright get sick when he passes it? Because all those germs that found their way into the soil are no longer there!

"Consider the centuries that men and animals have existed on this planet. The mind can't conceive of the total amount of disease germs that have found their way into the soil. Then why isn't the whole earth a vast pesthole of bodies and disease so that, with every step a man takes, he churns up another deadly cloud? Because countless armies of microbes are in the earth, performing their natural functions, and among those functions the antibiotic function —killing disease-producing germs."

He stopped and the room was very quiet. He was almost through and he had only to ask the question. "With all those disease germs reaching the soil," he said, "with all the disease germs being destroyed every day—is it logical to suppose that penicillin and streptomycin are our only antibiotics? Or is it more logical to say that

73

we've hardly begun?"

He had finished, and now they were starting to tear his arguments apart. Brainard spoke his piece about the risk involved and about how expensive such a project would be. Morrissey and Harrup began to talk about how small were the chances of success.

For a while Tom hardly heard them. Like a runner who cannot stop abruptly at the finish of a race but must run himself out, his own words and arguments kept going through his head. Then, gradually, he began to listen to the discussion.

"Let me ask you one question," he heard Bodenhof say. "If we have, in this room now, in these dishes, a microbe population equal to the population of about five major cities—that can kill germs of meningitis and rabies and t.b. and God knows what else—why should this be such a long, expensive undertaking?"

Morrissey tapped his pipe on the table. "You have to find the one microbe out of millions that will kill germs, not only in the soil but in a test tube," he said. "And not only in a test tube but in the human body. And at the same time not kill the body itself. And then you have to find a way to separate that antibiotic from hundreds of other substances produced along with it—and you don't know what the substance is and you don't know what the hundreds of other things are. If you can do all that, you're lucky—mighty lucky."

"It's kind of like getting the right man for a big job," Will Caroline said. "You know he exists, but it's not always so easy to find him."

"They've found plenty of antibiotics already, in laboratories, that will kill the germs," Brainard said. "Only they kill the patient, too. This isn't my field—I don't claim to be anything but a production man—but even I hear about them."

"We've had germ-killing disinfectants for years," Will Caroline said. "You can scrub a room with them, but you can't give them to a human being."

"This is an awfully complicated problem." This was Harrup doing his bit for the cause. "Already we're hearing reports of side effects of penicillin. A few people have gone into shock—even died. With streptomycin there have been reports of eighth-nerve damage causing deafness, loss of balance."

"Of course a man dying of t.b. will risk deafness," Will Caroline said.

Gradually Tom realized that Will Caroline wasn't backing off today. Until now he had kept his eyes away from Will, and now, puzzled, he looked at him. Today Will wasn't doodling. His pencil lay across the unmarked pad, and he was leaning forward a little, eyes alert, with an air about him, in his own easy way, of a man prepared to do battle.

"The fact to keep in mind," Brainard said, "is that we're running a business, not a research foundation. And we're making money that way."

"I wonder whether that isn't dangerous thinking," Will Caroline said.

"What's that? To make money?"

"No—for us to always say we're running a business, not a research foundation."

"The question is," Brainard said, "how much can we afford to change our attitude?"

"Or is it," Will Caroline said, "how much can we afford not to?"

"Well, it's not worth changing for this! This is a shot in the dark!"

"All research is a shot in the dark," Will Caroline said. "If there's a light for you to see where you're shooting, someone put it there, and the research has been done. The light doesn't move by itself!"

Will Caroline hitched his chair and looked for a second at Brainard and then at the other men around the table. "In all progress the next step beyond established knowledge is in the dark, and one man has to see the way to go. One man with cat eyes sees the trail and takes it and inches that light forward. And while he does, the faint-hearted sit around and wait until it's a little brighter. Then, afterward, they see, too—by his light—and go rushing in to pick up what gain they can. But he went first. He blazed the trail. And if there are rewards, he is entitled to them."

Now Bodenhof glanced at something high on the blackboard wall and was about to speak when Brainard cut in again.

"What if there are no rewards?" he burst out. "People who try to blaze trails sometimes end up dead." He motioned angrily with his cigar, and the ash fell off onto the table. "Progress! I'll show you progress that isn't a shot in the dark. Give me that million to stream-line production, and I'll show you progress that'll look mighty good on a balance sheet—progress that'll spell dividends within a year."

"It's a good point," Will Caroline said agreeably. "And there's only one thing about it that bothers me. I keep asking myself whether maybe in the long run we wouldn't be outsmarting ourselves." He paused a moment, gathering attention. "I'm just wondering whether we wouldn't be like those old-timers improving their buggies and their saddles, while a couple of people who had the courage and the imagination were in a shack somewhere, putting together an automobile."

Bodenhof sat back in his chair, looking carefully at Will Caroline.

"Not even big buggy makers," Will Caroline said, with a smile. "Just little fellows in a shack."

Bodenhof jerked his head toward the blackboard. "You're the sign man around here, Will. Are those yours?"

Tom turned to look at the signs he hadn't seen from where he was sitting. There, high over the blackboard, were two signs— black letters on a white ground, with narrow black frames. One read:

WHATEVER CURIOSITY THE ORDER OF
THINGS HAS AWAKENED IN OUR MINDS,
THE ORDER OF THINGS CAN SATISFY.

The other one read:

MORE SERVANTS WAIT ON MAN
THAN HE'LL TAKE NOTICE OF.

At the bottom of each: EMERSON. On Wednesday there had been no signs in this room.

"As you say," Will Caroline said, "I'm the sign man around here."

Tom was still looking at the signs when he heard Bodenhof say, "You're for it, Will?"

He was still staring at them when he heard Will Caroline say, "I am for it, sir."

Slowly Tom turned around. You would never admit how much you cared when you had had faith in a man and you thought he had let you down—or how good it could be to find you were wrong!

A little later the board took a coffee break, and Tom gathered up his notes to leave. He was through here. They would talk some more and if they needed him, which wasn't likely, they would send for him. On his way out, he passed Ade Hale, standing to one side, talking to Will Caroline.

Hale looked up as he passed. "That was quite a performance, Dr. Cable," he said.

"Yes, sir," Tom said, a little embarrassed. Then he said, "Sir, a friend of mine, who is a doctor, once described, step by step, an operation he had performed. It was full of unpleasant physical and biological details. Parts of it were pretty bloody. But when he got through and said the patient lived, it all seemed all right."

Will Caroline grinned and Tom moved on. Then he heard Hale say, "You were right, Will—he doesn't stay on the ropes long. I don't know that I'd want too many like him around. We couldn't stand it."

"Don't need too many," Will Caroline said. "One or two is enough!"

"Doesn't he ever have any doubts?"

"I would say, Ade, that like all men, he has many."

Out in the corridor, Tom shook his head. Every young scientist, he told himself, at the start of his career, should be shown Midge Potter's eyes to convince him, once and for all, never to accept anything on superficial evidence without demanding further proof. It was a thing some men never seemed to learn.

For a few minutes before rejoining the directors after lunch, Will Caroline was alone in his office. It was going to pass. He knew now that it would. They would talk some more this afternoon, but in the end they would do what, just before lunch, Hale had asked them to do. They would set up a relatively small sum to get started and see what happened.

Reflectively, Will Caroline leaned back in his chair. How did you explain a thing like this? he thought. A little ember of an idea came along, and how did you explain either the way it set fire to men's imaginations or the different ways it made them burn? Tom Cable, for instance, was like a man who'd had a vision. With him, it was more than reason now—it was mixed with passion, and nothing and no man could talk him out of it. And Ade Hale was—maybe not caught, but neither could he ignore it, because he could see in a cold, realistic way that it could be important and that it could revolutionize his company.

"The list of reasons why Enright should not do this is a very long one," Hale had said. "Unquestionably it's a gamble. And a new field about which very little is known. You've heard what we're up against. This is a race in the dark and Columbus sailing into the unknown, and it's David against Goliath, too, because we're just a small company and some very big companies are probably already in the race and, possibly, ahead of us. It's a long and discouraging list—enough to convince us to let this alone. We have a business to run—an obligation to cling to our sanity for ourselves and for the stockholders."

The room had grown quiet and for a moment Hale, too, had remained silent as though considering whether to go on. Then he said, "On the pro side the list is short. One reason." They were listening carefully and Hale leaned forward on the table. "Somewhere, somebody is going to do this and win one hell of a prize. Let's not turn our backs on it. Let's at least get into the race."

So Hale was not caught—he was still objective about it. But neither was he free—he was sniffing the bait.

And what of himself, Will Caroline thought, who could not ignore it, either? What were his reasons—how could he explain his own fire? He smiled at himself and his eyes went to a little sign on the wall—between the window and the file cabinet—and he read:

ALL THE FACTS IN NATURAL HISTORY, TAKEN BY THEMSELVES, HAVE NO VALUE, BUT ARE BARREN LIKE A SINGLE SEX. BUT MARRY IT TO HUMAN HISTORY AND IT IS FULL OF LIFE.

EMERSON

SIX

I T WAS RAINING when Tom came home. He lit
a fire in the fireplace and put a bottle of Scotch on the floor beside
him and stretched out on the sofa, letting the sudden tiredness run
through him—the tiredness that he knew was part of the letting
down, now that it was over.

Outside a car slushed along the shore road and he watched the
rain-streaked window next to the fireplace light up in the beam of the
headlights and go black again. In a little while, he told himself, if
the rain let up, he'd go down to Tollie's for something to eat. And
if it didn't let up, he would just stay here and, probably, get quite
drunk, which wasn't such a bad idea either. He lay still, thinking
that victory never had quite the flavor a man had expected.

After a while another car came along and he could hear the tires
on the wet pavement. He poured another drink and decided against
going to Tollie's.

Then he was surprised to hear a step on the porch and a quick
tap on the door and more surprised to see the door open and Diana
Brainard come in. He put down the bottle and got off the sofa.
"Well—" he said, and grinned. "Hello, Diana."

Diana closed the door quickly behind her. She was wearing a
short yellow slicker, the kind you saw around the boats on stormy
days, and narrow slacks and, with her cropped hair hidden under the
yellow hat, she looked like a small fair-featured boy. She pulled off
the hat and ran her hand through her short black hair. "I've been
thinking about you today," she said.

"Well, now," Tom said. "Haven't you anything better to do than
that?"

"I didn't really expect to find you here." She moved into the
room, unsnapping her slicker, and Tom could see drops of rain
glistening on it and on her face. "I thought you'd be out celebrating
your great victory. Why aren't you? Why aren't you out carousing
wildly?"

"Maybe it's the rain," Tom said.

She looked at him. "That's not the reason."

"No."

He took the wet coat, and Diana went over and stood a minute

79

at the fire. Then she sat on the floor and pulled off her sneakers and put them on the hearth. "Do you mind? They're soaked," she said. Watching her, Tom grinned and wondered what she had in mind coming here and then thought that he had a pretty good idea what she had in mind coming here. He bent down and put another log on the fire and reached for the Japanese sword that he used as a poker.

Behind him, Diana said, "I've been thinking all day about you— and about how strange all this is."

"Why strange?"

"Because," she said. "Think of all those men—all those scientists —who go over there to Enright every day—the chemists and the bio-chemists and all the rest of them. The same dreary men to the same dreary place—doing the same dreary work. And—"

Tom smiled and glanced around at her. "Why do you think it's dreary?"

"Well, isn't it?"

"No. It's very exciting."

"That's the point exactly," she said. "That you can think so!"

Thoughtfully, Tom stirred the fire, wondering where she picked up some of her ideas. He could see her slender ankles below where her slacks ended, and her toes touching the hearth, and he could smell the rain in her hair. He put down the poker and stood up.

"What do you think?" Diana said. "Do I have a better chance of getting a drink tonight?"

"Are you really old enough?" He picked up the bottle off the floor.

"Why, Dr. Cable, I'm twenty-one. All of me."

"You must forgive me, Diana. To my ancient eyes you don't look it."

"I'm retarded," she said, and laughed.

He poured her a drink and another for himself. Then he went over and sat on the sofa and looked at her. She had turned a little and was sitting with her back against a chair, looking at him, her blue eyes dark in the firelight.

"It does bother me that you've gotten your way," she said. "It makes you so vulnerable. And they're so rapacious." She sipped her drink, her eyes smiling at him over the glass. "But what I've really been wondering about all day is you—and how and why you are as you are."

"Ho!" Tom laughed. "That's a real waste of time."

"I keep asking myself how these things happen as they do. There are two dozen scientists working at Enright all under the same conditions, all in the same situation. Out of the whole lot of them, all the others just go dragging along from day to day, like so many gray rats. And you are different. You have thought of this wonderful exciting idea! All day I've been asking myself why."

Tom laughed. "Diana, you know I didn't think of this!"

"Of course you did."

"I didn't, Diana. Everyone knows about antibiotics today—penicillin and streptomycin. You know that." Maybe she was older than she looked, he thought, but she seemed to have a bad case of hero worship that ought to be cured. "The truth is that this whole idea has been kicking around for centuries, just waiting for someone to pick it up."

"Which idea?"

"That a mold—which is where antibiotics come from—can cure human infections. The Chinese knew it twenty-five hundred years ago. They used moldy soybean curd to cure skin infections." He smiled at her. "If there's anything remarkable about this, Diana, it's not that we have stumbled over this idea at last. It's that it took so long."

Diana laughed. "There's quite a difference between what you're talking about and a moldy soybean curd!"

"Yes, there's a difference, but that moldy curd was a clue—and not the only one. Now that our eyes are open at last, we're finding that there were clues everywhere."

"Where everywhere?"

"Well—the Mayans, for one. For years they used a fungus to cure infections. Now a Mexican scholar suggests that the fungus was making penicillin."

"And was it?"

"We don't know that it wasn't." Tom grinned. "Of course, it's embarrassing to admit that it might have been. We wouldn't like to think that something that good was hanging around for centuries in primitive cultures before we stumbled onto it with our great scientific attitudes."

Thoughtfully Diana clasped her arms around her knees. Tom eased a little lower on the sofa, watching her, wondering whether she was really as old as she claimed or whether she was a precocious teen-ager telling a white lie. The blue eyes looked squarely into his.

"But that's folk medicine," she said. "And folk medicine is full of superstitions—and most of them are worthless."

"But these molds have turned up in so many places. In parts of Yugoslavia families keep bread in the cellar where it's damp to grow a mold and then use the mold to treat infections. In Brazil the Indians have used molds for generations."

For a moment Tom stopped talking, thinking about this. Even admitting that hindsight was always wiser, it could still astonish him that all these clues had been ignored. And yet, he supposed, in another age, in another scientific climate, he would have not seen them, either.

A log settled into the ashes and the fire flared, and he looked at Diana as her face and hair picked up the glow and the blue eyes shone. Or maybe, he thought, it wasn't this fire but the one inside her that made them that way. Silently he watched her, telling himself that what he was suddenly feeling was the liquor—the liquor and no dinner. But she was a remarkably appealing girl. He advised himself to keep talking.

"So you see, Diana," he said, and then sipped his drink, still looking at her, "there was water, water everywhere and no one took a drink."

She stood up and moved about the room in her bare feet. "Why not?" she said. "Why do you suppose they didn't?"

"Probably because no one was looking for those clues. Our eyes can be prejudiced—see only what we're looking for. More than fifty years ago a British physicist actually watched an antibiotic work and wrote about it without knowing what he'd seen."

Diana came over now and sat down again on the floor, this time near him, leaning back against the sofa. Her hair, still damp at the back of her neck, brushed against his hand. She looked at him and said, "How could he do that?"

Tom told himself that he had better answer her, even though he doubted that she wanted to know—answer her or keep talking about something else.

"He was growing bacteria in some test tubes," he said, "and at first the liquid in them was cloudy, which meant that the bacteria were growing, and then—" He downed the rest of his Scotch and looked at her. This is ridiculous, he told himself.

"And then?"

"He had left the test tubes uncovered," he said, "and a few days later, in two of them he noticed little tufts of mold on the surface of the liquid. And in another few days the mold had grown so that it covered the whole surface. And when that happened—"

Diana had turned and was resting her chin on her arm on the sofa, listening to him with wide-eyed fascination. "And it grew and grew," she said. "And then what happened?"

"Then, when the whole surface was covered with mold, the bacteria underneath it died. The liquid wasn't cloudy any more. It had become clear again."

"Somebody," Diana murmured, "ate up all my porridge."

"Exactly." Tom looked at her, surprised. "Only they didn't know about antibiotics then, and they thought that the bacteria died because the mold cut off the oxygen. But what actually happened was that the mold fought a battle for survival against the bacteria and the mold won. It was microbial warfare—a classic example— and for years nobody realized it. So you see"—he moved his hand an inch and toyed with a wisp of her black hair—"you don't have to think we scientists are so mistreated. We're not as smart as we think we are!"

"I think you are very smart indeed," Diana said softly, looking at him in the same way.

"Don't look at me that way, Diana." Tom grinned. "That's not good for a man!"

"And I think you are quite remarkable."

Outside the wind threw a gust of rain against the window, and Diana wiggled her toes and rubbed one slender bare foot against the other. She smiled a little, and Tom told himself that on a rainy night with a fire and a drink and . . . all the ingredients were here and stranger things had happened. Carefully he moved around her and stood up and went over to pour himself another drink. When he looked around again she was watching him, half amused, as though she knew, too, that this little thread was forming between them and that he was backing away from it. He walked to the window and looked out. On the beach the waves were climbing almost to the breakwater, warning that it would probably storm all night. When he looked back, she was still watching him.

"Were they penicillin?" she said. "The Chinese or the Mayan or any of them?"

"More likely his great-great-grandfather George, a million times removed."

"What!"

"These little bugs keep changing all the time in their fight for survival—in the war that never ends."

"Why do you keep saying that"—she laughed—"as though they were people actually fighting a war?"

"They are like that. They do actually fight a war. They fight for survival. Some of them are allies and help each other. And some wage constant warfare—chemical warfare, as though we used poison gas—and fight to try to destroy each other. And they never stop working on their weapons because the one who develops the best weapon—the best antibiotic—is the one who wins—for a while, anyway. Only his enemies don't fall down dead in a mass disaster. They use their wits. They mutate. They make subtle little changes to try to get around this antibiotic that's getting the upper hand, so they can live. And some of them succeed. By means of these little changes, they develop resistance to the antibiotic so that it doesn't work on them any more—and they can survive. Then the others begin to make changes, too, in their weapons, to counterattack. And these changes aren't just temporary—they're mutations and all their offsprings will have them. So probably in the twenty-five hundred years since the Chinese first used that mold, some strain of bug mutated over and over to meet changing conditions—and somewhere along the line it began to make penicillin. They're diabolically clever, these fellows."

He glanced down at her. Her toes were pink in the firelight and he looked at her slim ankles and then at her small sneakers on the hearth and he thought incongruously that he wished she would put them on.

She laughed. "Really, I love the way you think about them as people."

"No, I don't think about them as people." Tom grinned. "They're going to give me a lot more trouble than people do."

"But you do talk about them that way—instead of just something for people to use."

"Microbes aren't just something for people to use. They're a whole separate society. They live off us as much as we live off them. They thrive on man's waste—they decay our dead bodies. It's all part of the delicate balance of nature that they use us and we use them."

She shuddered. And then she laughed and said, "That's me. I'm a mutation. Because I'm not like my father or my mother. I'm really not, you know, in case you hadn't noticed."

"I noticed."

"Good," she said. "I'm glad you noticed. Only I'm not really a mutation, because my grandmother did it. She was the one who was clever. I spent lots of time with her. She was a great rebel."

"And are you a great rebel?"

"Of course. Can't you tell?"

It was all right now, and he went back to the sofa. Diana rested her chin on her arm again to look up at him. "You don't seem very elated over your great victory."

"Maybe I'm not a good winner."

She smiled.

"I'm not a good loser, either," he said. "Maybe, on second thought, that's the explanation. Maybe something warns me that if I'm not prepared to be magnificent in defeat, I shouldn't crow too much in victory. If I'd lost today, I'd have behaved very badly."

Her eyes laughed. "And have you been lying here all night thinking that magnificent thought?"

"Diana," he said, "it's no real victory. Not in any final sense. It's like a major battle in which you've won only the beachhead."

"You didn't feel that way last night."

"In any battle," Tom said, "while the fight is going on, you keep your mind on that battle only—on that little strip of land that's at stake. You don't think very much beyond it. But then, when the fighting is over and you've won, and you're sitting around at night —probably done in and spent—on your precious bit of land, then you know that it's nothing by itself—it's only a beachhead on which you can dig in, from which you can launch a much more desperate fight. What you've won is the opportunity to shed blood."

And you knew, too, he thought suddenly, that you couldn't lose the fight that was still to come, or you would be pushed back into the sea. You were here now and there was no escape.

Diana moved up and sat on the sofa, quite close to him. "Were you done in and spent?"

"And getting very drunk."

For a moment she sat up straight, and Tom knew she was thinking over what he had said about the battle. He sipped his drink, watching her.

"I think," she said, "that even knowing that, you should allow yourself the pleasure of this victory."

"Do you?" His hand moved toward her hair.

"Mmm."

He smiled. "Victory is a capricious creature, Diana." He touched the strand of hair that fell over her forehead. "Did you ever consider that, of all their goddesses, the Greeks gave wings to Victory?"

"Only to Victory?"

"Other Greek goddesses," he said, "are beautiful or amiable. Or radiant—like you." His hand moved to her face. "But Victory has wings. Maybe it was because they understood that Victory is a creature of motion. She never stands still—and if you try to hold her still, you lose her. Victory is never the end of something. It's always a beginning."

Diana's wide blue eyes searched his face, and Tom knew that he could move his hand only a few inches and there would be no protest and she would be in his arms, and he thought that he wouldn't exactly mind. But he suspected that she was too young—and there were rules about these things.

Abruptly he stood up and went over and picked up her shoes and brought them back to her. "You're right, Diana," he said. "Put on your shoes and we'll go out and celebrate this victory—whatever she may turn out to be."

Maybe she was just a nice little girl, but she thought he was great for all the wrong reasons, and she had ideas. And he wasn't going to stay here any longer to find out what they were or how long he could hold out against them.

PART TWO

JUNE –
NOVEMBER 1946

Gil Brainard felt as though every nerve in his body had been scraped raw. Pacing the floor of his office, a burned-out cigar in his mouth, he could feel his stomach beginning to bother him and his shirt going damp with perspiration in the mounting June heat. For two months this thing had been dragging its tail while Will Caroline figured and fussed, but now it was getting started. Brainard stopped at the window and stared at the research building. Now the fellow they'd been waiting for had arrived—the mycologist who did the fancy things with these microbes that they hoped were going to serve them up their witch's brew. He'd shown up this morning and he was over there now—setting up his laboratory—and the horse race was on.

Brainard dug his teeth into the dead cigar, getting the taste of the stale juices, and flung it into the wastebasket. Then, hearing someone at his door, he got hold of himself and sat at his desk as the door opened and Morrissey looked in.

"Well," Brainard said, "I hear they've blown the bugle—they tell me they're off and running."

Morrissey came into the room, carrying an armful of journals, his college-boy face wearing a worried look.

"Step up and place your bets, gentlemen," Brainard said.

"Have you seen him yet?"

"Who's that?" Brainard said. He knew who, all right, but there was a tug of pleasure in refusing to understand.

"Derrick," Morrissey said. "The new man—Dr. Derrick."

"Why should I bother to see Dr. Derrick? His work is a long way from mine. And I don't think it's ever going to get to me."

"I talked to him, Gil," Morrissey said. "Listen, do you know what that man's experience is? It's only with molds—growing them, classifying them. He doesn't know anything special about antibiotics at all!"

"Who does?" Brainard snapped. "He doesn't now and he won't when he's through."

His stomach was acting up again, and he worked his hand over his middle and let it lie there. Maybe, he thought, he ought to cut down a little with Janet. Maybe he'd do that—he was getting tired of her anyway. Maybe he'd just knock off with Janet altogether. Still, she had her points—he massaged his stomach—and maybe it wasn't that at all.

He could feel the damp blotches spreading on his shirt. Then he saw that the sun had come around and was pouring into the room, and he went over and yanked at the cord to lower the blind. The blind dropped an inch and stuck. He yanked again and it didn't give and he glared at it and then turned and focused his hatred on Morrissey.

"What've you got there, Claude?" he said, looking at the journals in Morrissey's lap. He was probably carrying that stuff around so he'd look good if any new people around here happened to look at him.

Almost reluctantly, Morrissey opened the top journal and let it slip shut again. "These are just a few things on antibiotics," he said. "This may be a long way from your department, Gil, but it's awfully close to mine. As soon as Dr. Derrick grows those cultures, they come to us for the real work." Morrissey got a little authority into his voice. "And since Dr. Derrick doesn't seem to know much— and I don't know that Cable does, either, for all his noise—I guess I'll have to keep ahead of every little thing."

Brainard laughed. Keep ahead of every little thing! Who did he think he was kidding? If there was one thing about antibiotics in those journals, Morrissey would learn something.

"Just last night I was telling Winifred," Morrissey said, "it's not easy to locate this stuff."

"And what'd Winifred say to that?" What could Winifred say? She'd probably wiped his nose, like she always did, and told him to quit sniveling—it'd be all right.

"There's precious little on it." Then the little flash of spirit collapsed and Morrissey shook his head. "I don't know what more we could have done to stop this, Gil."

Brainard came back and leaned over his desk. "Claude, were you at that board meeting or weren't you?"

"Oh, yes."

"And did you happen to notice that Hale railroaded this through —or were you off picking daisies somewhere?"

Morrissey puffed his pipe, and it annoyed Brainard that this needling didn't seem to bother him. Morrissey said, "Railroaded it through is right."

"All right, then—Will Caroline got to him and sold him a bill of goods." Morrissey looked up, surprised, and Brainard said impatiently, "Well, what did you think happened, for God's sake? It wasn't any accident that Hale didn't care beans about this one day and then two days later was jamming it through a board meeting. Will Caroline used that day in between to do some pretty fancy talking."

Brainard took out a fresh cigar and bit into it. "Now all we can do is wait until Hale begins to be sorry he saw it that way. Then, at the right time, we'll make our move and we'll knock it out."

Morrissey looked up hopefully. "How do you propose to do that, Gil?"

He didn't know yet how he proposed to do it, but he intended to think of something. "I'll decide when I see how this goes."

"Well—" Morrissey said, dispiritedly, and stood up to leave. "If there's anything I can do—"

When Morrissey had gone, Brainard went back to the window and yanked again at the cord. Damn it, he should have had that money—not Will Caroline. He was a better man than Will Caroline would ever be. And he was a more valuable man around here. This was a production company and he was production boss and he was good. In this company, it was Gil Brainard—not Will Caroline —who was the Number Two man, right next to the top, right next to Ade Hale. And, by God, he would still be Number Two man when this was over.

He yanked once more at the cord, and the blind went up instead of down and he jerked it again and the cord broke. He felt a strange satisfaction at seeing it dangling in his hand. Then he threw it down. The hell with it. And the hell with Will Caroline. Maybe Will had won that first round, but that's all it was—just the first round. And before this fight was over, Brainard told himself, he was going to hit Will Caroline so hard he would never get up again.

He reached into his pocket for a soda mint and put it into his mouth. If this project were good for the company, he told himself, he'd be the first to back it. But it wasn't good for the company. His stomach was hurting badly now, and the soda mint didn't help much.

The mycology laboratory on the third floor was empty except for a refrigerator, a constant-temperature oven and an assortment of glass equipment—Petri dishes, a few racks of test tubes, pipettes and flasks.

Charlie Derrick, a six-foot-four-inch beanpole, walked slowly around the room, pausing now and then to measure certain areas with his eye, and then came back and sat on the edge of the counter. At his elbow, his assistant, John Dominick, a shy, dark-eyed young man, stood like a new recruit, waiting for instructions.

"Well, sir," Charlie Derrick said with a smile, after he'd finished deciding how to set up his work, "ah guess you and ah'll be seein' a lot of each other. Now, what do they call you—John?"

"No, sir." John Dominick blushed. He was very young, just out of college, and this was his first job. "They call me Nick."

"Where are you from, Nick?"

"Wisconsin."

"Ah'm from Mississippi—originally, that is," Derrick said. "Now —we're goin' into mass production here, Nick. We're goin' to set up an assembly line—start here, move around the room, step by step —end up right there—just short of where we began."

Derrick took three small envelopes out of his pocket. "Ah just brought these soil samples up with me from New York. We'll get them started today an' by the time we're ready for them, they'll be ready for us." He carried over a rack of test tubes that he'd sterilized earlier. "You got yourself all set here, Nick—a place to live and everything?"

"Yes, sir. I'm at the Y for now, sir."

"Well, ah'm kinda campin' out too, for now." That sent his thoughts to Kate. "Ah'm waitin' for my wife to come up and find a place. She's an actress—" Derrick fell silent. In the two months that they'd known about this, Kate had found a hundred reasons to put off coming here to find a house.

"Where are you living meanwhile, sir?"

"Ah moved into the hotel for a week or so." Derrick got his mind back on the soil samples. He opened one of the packages and measured some soil and then some water into a test tube. "You know the water's sterilized," he said while he worked. "We don't want any outside visitors here. Just the microorganisms that are in the soil. We'll use a bit at this concentration and then dilute it down a couple of times to bring out other microbes. Ah have the proportions written out for you."

"Yes, sir," Nick said with concentrated respect.

Derrick smiled. The boy was nervous but he guessed he'd relax after a while. Then through the glass partition he saw Dr. Morrissey and Dr. Harrup walking past, and he looked after them a moment. Following his glance, Nick said, "A lot of people around here aren't too crazy about this, Dr. Derrick. I heard before in the cafeteria when I was having coffee."

"Can't please 'em all," Derrick said amiably.

Now that he was here, he knew, Kate would come soon because their being apart was so unthinkable, but still he wondered whether he'd done the right thing, taking this job, knowing how she felt about moving up here. Was it fair to take her away from New York —to ask her to give up her own career, small though it was—so that he could do what he wanted? He saw Nick watching him, wondering why he was shaking the test tube so long, and he smiled a little sheepishly.

"They watched a minute and moved on," Nick said.

"Who's that?"

"Dr. Morrissey and Dr. Harrup. Why do you suppose they're down on this?"

Derrick smiled. "Ah suppose some people kinda like to go lookin' for trouble," he said, "like me. An' some folks like to stay home by the fire. Just cut out different, that's all." Then he said, "Didn't you know when you took the job that this was a pretty uncertain thing, Nick?"

For the first time the boy smiled. "Oh, sure, I knew," he said, and Charlie Derrick felt better about him.

"O.K., sir," Derrick said. "Let's get on with our evil business here. Just hand me one of those Petri dishes, from the right side of that counter—you see, ah've already got them fixed up with agar." He pointed to the thin layer of colorless jellylike substance that covered the dish. "That agar's fixed up with nutrients we hope these bugs are goin' to like—so they'll be obligin' and grow."

"What's the formula, sir?"

"Well, ah've got two formulas here. These dishes here are fixed with one recipe and those over there to the left are fixed up with a different diet. Ah've got that written down for you, too." He handed Nick the paper on which he had written the formulas. "Now, we're goin' to dilute every sample three times and put all three dilutions into both formulas. An' we hope they're goin' to like something we do to them." He grinned. "An' if they don't, we'll have to try something else."

With a pipette, Derrick transferred a bit of the soil solution to the agar plate. "Just swoosh it around to get it all over the dish—pour off the excess—and put on the cover. Now, boy, in a few minutes ah'm goin' over to Mr. Caroline's office, so just let me set up this record book and show you how to keep it, an' then you can take over."

Derrick reached for the notebook that he had left on the counter. At lunchtime, he'd decided, he'd call Kate and tell her to come up here and stay with him at the hotel until they found a house. She could get her mother to come over to stay with the children. It wasn't right to leave Kate in New York, fretting—she never did well by herself, she was too used to leaning on him—and she was trying hard to behave well about this.

Actually, he thought, she had never said that she wouldn't come —not even that first night when he told her about this job and she had stared at him with her wide brown eyes, looking like a bewildered schoolgirl, the way she always did when she was troubled.

"Oh, Charlie!" she had gasped, running her fingers across her bangs in that frantic gesture she had. "Do we have to?"

"No, we don't have to."

"You've got a good job here and we're settled and everything's fine—" And then, "But you want to—don't you?"

"Yes, I want to—but we don't have to decide tonight." Maybe that was when he should have said it didn't matter. Only it did matter. He still wasn't sure why—maybe it was only a hunger for adventure left over from younger days—but this was something he wanted to get in on, and it did matter.

A week later, Kate said, "Charlie, do you have to do this? I mean is something in you just bursting to do this?"

He hadn't wanted to go that far. He had said, "I don't have to do anything, Kate, except let them know one way or the other—soon."

She had waited another few days for him to say they wouldn't go, and then, when he didn't say it, she had called her mother to tell her. He had heard her tell her mother that he was a great man and that this was something he simply had to do.

In a way she was playacting, and he knew it. Sometimes he thought she was always playacting—always working at a thing until she achieved a heightened sense of emotion—always with a sense of fate—of inevitability. Now he wondered whether, knowing that the words were spoken in an emotional moment of self-sacrifice and that later she would regret them, he had done right in accepting that emotion as an attitude that would continue.

Sitting at the counter, Derrick wrapped his long legs around the stool and gave a little sigh. Sometimes he wondered what would happen when Kate woke up and realized that he wasn't a great man, but just an ordinary guy like anyone else. Sometimes he wished that, just once, she would say, "You lazy lout, I don't know what I ever saw in you." Charlie Derrick smiled at himself. Sometimes a fellow didn't know when he was well off.

He opened the record book. "Now, right at the start, Nick, every soil sample gets a number, and the number goes into the record book—along with the date, the place the sample came from and the type of soil it is. That first sample is Number One. And remember —every sample gets three dilutions, every dilution goes into two formulas. We've got three soil samples here—we're going to have eighteen plates."

He picked up the Petri dish he had just plated and reached for a red crayon. "This dish is Sample One, Dilution One, Recipe A. We mark it 1-1-A. Mark the dish and not the cover. Covers can get mixed up. From now on everything we do with any culture from this dish has to get that number—with more figures added as we do more work—every piece of equipment we use, every Petri dish, every test tube. That's important, Nick. We need these numbers to keep things straight. An' we need the information"—he smiled—"to try to learn something about all this."

Derrick stood up to go over to Mr. Caroline's office. "We're going to keep a permanent record of everything, Nick—even the cultures that don't look promisin'. We might want to go back to them later."

Nick nodded and then he said, "Excuse me, sir, but why would we go back to something that wasn't promising?"

"Well, Nick—when you don't know much about somethin', you're a mite uneasy about sayin' it's no good. An' right now"—Derrick smiled—"well—ah'd be speakin' less than the truth if ah told you we really know much for sure about what we're doin'."

"All right, Dr. Derrick," Will Caroline said in his office a few minutes later. "You want soil samples. What kind?"

"All kinds, sir. Loam, clay, mud, rotting vegetation." Charlie Derrick leaned forward. "Ah believe, sir, that right now, when we don't know much about it, the best thing we can do is try to examine a large variety—both to find something and to learn something. Ah'd like all kinds—and from all different locations."

Will Caroline eased down a little in his chair, studying Derrick while they talked, trying to decide how much fiber lay behind this mild, easygoing exterior. "You mean mountains, valleys, riverbeds?"

"Yes, sir," Derrick said. "Farms, cities, woods—for the time bein'. An' from all different areas, too. From everywhere."

Will Caroline smiled. "You couldn't narrow that down a bit?"

"Sir, ah'd be mighty pleased to," Derrick said soberly. "But we just don't know enough yet to intelligently favor one area over another."

Will Caroline nodded and then his eyes went to the open door as he saw Gil Brainard walk past in the corridor. For a minute Will Caroline stopped talking and looked after him, thinking that a man never revealed his feelings so much as when he was trying to conceal them. Brainard had walked past at his usual pace—with the usual cigar in his mouth, at the usual angle—and yet there were those little telltale signals that you couldn't give a name to, that said Brainard was sore as a boil this morning.

"Of course, sir," Derrick was saying, "ah intend to watch our results an' try to find some reason for changin' that statement, but it's my opinion that we ought to look at everything—now at the start—when we know so little."

For a moment Will Caroline found himself studying Derrick carefully again. Derrick seemed to want it clearly understood that he didn't know much, and yet the thought didn't seem to disturb him. Will straightened up a little in his chair. "In that case," he said cheerfully, "we'd better work out some ways to get them."

"Ah was wonderin', sir, if the company employs any salesmen."

"Some—not many. But that's a good idea."

"An' if anyone in the company is goin' on a trip—"

"We'll put a sign on the bulletin board," Will Caroline said. "We'll ask everyone in the company who is taking a trip to dig us some dirt."

"Ah expect, sir, we ought to do that real soon."

"We'll do it now." Will Caroline pressed a button on his desk and his secretary came in. "We need a sign, Jeannie—for the bulletin board."

"No little black frame?"

"No frame." Will Caroline jotted down a few lines and looked back at Derrick. "I don't suppose people will want to carry around a lot of dirt in their luggage. Think they could mail it in?"

"We ought to provide packages for that purpose, sir. A kind of envelope—sturdy enough not to break."

"Right. We'll tell them to get their packages from us before they leave." Will Caroline thought a moment. "We'd better make this easy. A man on vacation won't do it unless it's easy. Easy to fill— and easy to mail." He took a piece of paper and started to fold it. "Now, if we make them up this way—got a scissors handy, Jeannie?"

Jeannie stepped back into her office, and Will Caroline noticed Brainard go past again and just barely pause to glance into his office.

"The envelopes could be smaller, sir." Derrick leaned over the desk. "A teaspoon of soil is enough."

"Fine. Sure that's enough?"

"Yes, sir. There are about a million microorganisms in a teaspoon of soil, sir," Derrick said. "Ah expect ah'll pick about a hundred out of each—more or less—at the start, anyway."

Will Caroline looked up. "A hundred? From every sample?"

"More or less, sir. Later, after we know more, ah expect we'll cut down."

Will Caroline tapped the folded paper on his palm. "Dr. Derrick, let me get this straight. This morning you plated three soil samples. From that you're going to pick out three hundred microbe cultures to work on?"

"We'll do that on Friday, sir," Derrick said. "By then they'll be growing all over the agar plates. We'll pick out each culture we want and grow it separately, by itself, on nutrient agar in a test tube, to get a pure culture. Then we'll transfer that pure culture to some fermentation broth in a larger test tube and grow it some more. Then we'll test it to see if it's making an antibiotic."

Thoughtfully, Will Caroline looked at Derrick. "Now, let me go over that again. On Friday morning you're going to have up to three hundred test tubes fixed with nutrient agar—"

"Yes, sir."

"And then next week you're going to have three hundred larger test tubes with fermentation broth—"

"Six hundred test tubes with broth, sir. At the start ah'd like to put each culture into two different fermentation broths—two different formulas. You see, these little bugs are sensitive, an' although we know a fair amount about growin' them, they can be mighty stubborn about makin' an antibiotic. An'—ah don't mean to repeat myself, sir, but you know—we don't know too much about that." He looked up. "So, if you don't mind, ah'd like to put them into two broths at the start."

"No—no!" Will Caroline said quickly. "I don't mind!"

"Then after we've let them grow enough," Derrick said, "we'll test them against gram-positive and gram-negative test organisms on agar plates to see which ones are making an antibiotic."

"Six hundred agar plates?"

"More or less, sir."

"Dr. Derrick," Will Caroline said, "out of all of these test tubes and all these test organisms and all these agar plates, what do you expect to find—from these three samples alone?"

"Ah expect, sir, that we'll hit about a fifty per cent average. That is, fifty per cent will show evidence of antibiotic action against test organisms. Of course, you understand, it's most unlikely that any of them will be any good. That's a pretty long shot. It doesn't mean they'll cure human diseases—or be fit to give to a man. It just means they can stop the growth of another microorganism."

Will Caroline sat back in his chair. "All that from three samples. And you want us to get you all kinds of samples sent in from all over the country."

"No, sir," Derrick said. "From all over the world."

And everyone agreed that the real work came after Dr. Derrick had finished his part and the cultures were turned over to the biochemists! Thoughtfully, Will Caroline's eyes went to an envelope on his desk, which contained the resumés of a biochemist and of a chemist he'd been thinking of hiring, if they would come. They were good men and they would add strength to the staff. Maybe, he thought, he'd better do that right away. But then, on second thought, maybe he shouldn't. Maybe now, when the only thing that seemed certain was that they knew next to nothing, he'd do better not to waste his money.

Then Jeannie was back with the scissors and said, "Is the sign ready?" He handed her the memo for the sign. "Earth for what, Mr. Caroline?" she said.

"For microbes. How's this package look, Jeannie? Easy enough?" He held up the envelope. "Maybe we ought to make them up in a little kit. Easier to carry—and not so likely to get lost." He trimmed the flap. "Ten in a kit."

"Mr. Caroline, maybe I could finish that envelope," Jeannie said, glancing toward the corridor. "Mr. Brainard's walked by three times in the last ten minutes. He's going to think we're in here cutting out paper dolls."

Will Caroline grinned. "You're getting too smart for me, Jeannie. You watch out or I'll put you in charge of something—make you work."

After Charlie Derrick had gone, Will Caroline leaned back in his chair, mentally reviewing their conversation and thinking that he was glad no one else had heard it. Although, he supposed, the facts would leak out before long. If a blind man was driving a car, word would get around that something was wrong.

Once again Will glanced at the resumés of the chemist and the biochemist. Then he picked up a letter on his desk from the company he'd written to about mice and reached for the telephone to call Callie—more because he felt like talking to her than because it couldn't keep.

"I have to run into New York one day next week, Cal," he said. "Buy some mice."

"Mice! Well!"

"Very special inbred white mice—very expensive—mice a man could be a snob about if he had a mind to."

"Darling," Callie said, "you don't have to coax me. There's nothing I'd rather shop for than mice."

"Would Thursday do?"

"Thursday's fine," Callie said. "How's it going, Will?"

He laughed. "This is going to be one hell of a mess for a while, Cal."

He hung up and put aside the chemist's and the biochemist's folders and reached for three others—the resumés of three pharmacologists. He needed a man to direct the testing on mice, and he wanted one who would also be able to handle the testing on higher animals, which required more training. He had narrowed the choice down to these three men, and now he decided to have them come in for interviews and settle that first—and sit on the other decision for a while.

"Right here, sir." Charlie Derrick held up a Petri dish for Gil Brainard to see. "We plated this on Monday, and this is what grew in four days."

Brainard moved up to the counter. He'd put off coming in here until today, and now, taking a quick look around, he saw that Derrick had himself pretty well organized—a lot of glass equipment lined up, all very orderly, some of it already in use. Over in the corner his kid helper was fooling around with some dirt in a test tube. On this counter where Derrick was working Brainard counted eighteen Petri dishes. "You do all these on Monday?" he said.

"Yes, sir," Derrick said. "We plated these from three soil samples."

Looking at the dish in Derrick's hand, Brainard saw that it was a jungle of growth. Across the upper quarter was a heavy pale-green mold, underlaid with white, bordered by a deep-green ring. Along the right edge were clusters of small orange specks, and below them a fuzzy black chain snaked across to a pink snaillike mass on the other side. At the bottom was a growth that resembled a puff of cotton and, next to it, a sprinkling of bright yellow pinheads.

"Now, sir"—Derrick pointed with a pencil—"that black fuzz is common bread mold. We don't want that. And this one—this spotty one, heah—is a germ—we won't bother with that one, either. And there are a few more types we don't want."

Brainard glanced at the other Petri dishes, which varied considerably in appearance. Some were peppered with pale dots, some were even more heavily overgrown than the one Derrick was holding. Thoughtfully he drew out a cigar from his breast pocket. "Still leaves a fair amount, though, doesn't it?" he said.

"It does, sir," Derrick said. "Ah expect that for a while we'll be pickin' a fair amount from every sample."

"That what you call it—picking?"

"Yes, sir." Derrick struck a flame in a Bunsen burner and said, "Let me have a rack of those test tubes, Nick."

The assistant brought over a rack of test tubes—dozens of test tubes—each with a wad of cotton stuffed in its mouth, each tube containing about an inch of agar, jelled on a slant.

While he waited, Brainard took a sharp, sidelong glance at Derrick. He'd looked this fellow over the first day in the dining room, and it hadn't taken long to see what he was—an ineffectual, mild-mannered man, just the sort you'd expect Will Caroline to hire. A nice boy. Thirty, maybe, or a little more, but still a nice boy—the kind you'd call a nice boy for another ten years. Now, talking to him, he didn't see anything to make him change his opinion. A nice methodical boy in a white coat—with a neat laboratory—a clerk with a Ph.D. degree.

Derrick sat on a stool. "Excuse me, sir," he said. "Ah can do this better sittin' down." Adjusting the Bunsen burner, he picked up a loop-tipped needle and held the loop in the flame until it was red-hot. Then he brought the needle over to the Petri dish and carefully picked out a bit of bright yellow growth. Working quickly, he flamed the mouth of a test tube, transferred the yellow speck onto the nutrient agar in the tube, flamed the mouth again and restuffed it with cotton.

He placed the tube in an empty rack and looked up at Brainard. "That's pickin' one, sir. We pick 'em out of the dish where they're all together and grow each culture alone for a few more days."

Brainard looked at the rack of test tubes. There must be damn near a hundred tubes in that rack—and there were two more racks just like it on the next counter. "You planning to use all those test tubes—for these few dishes?"

"That's right, sir."

"*Three* soil samples?"

"For the time bein' we're goin' to pick a large number from each sample," Derrick said. "Later we'll probably cut down a bit."

Brainard could feel his anger rising at Derrick's attitude. These research people were all alike. They acted as though there were unlimited funds—all the money in the world and all the time—just for them. "What's going to happen later," he asked sharply, "to make you cut down?"

"Ah expect we'll learn more about them, sir. Ah expect later the evidence will begin to tell us things."

Later! How much later did this Derrick think it was going to get? How long did he think he was going to fool around—learning his business at Enright's expense? "And what do you think you'll cut back to—later?" Brainard said. "Fifty, maybe, from each one?"

"Possibly, sir," Derrick said soberly.

Leaving, Gil Brainard stopped outside the laboratory and took another look through the glass door at Derrick, patiently picking the cultures and transferring them to agar slants. Later in the day he walked past again and saw that he was still at it. On his way home at five o'clock he passed the bulletin board and saw the sign asking any employees going on a trip to get a kit of envelopes from Will Caroline and send in dirt. Brainard could feel all the soreness of the past two months churning up in him again.

It was a hot sticky day, and as he drove out of the parking lot, his irritation climbing, all he could think of was those hundreds of test tubes and that fool Derrick picking, picking—not even knowing what he was looking for. Goddam it! Brainard said to himself, if I was spending that money, I'd sure as hell know what I was doing! And that spineless jellyfish was just pouring it down the drain— not caring a rap whether he used up twice as much as was necessary or three times or ten times as much. It was enough to make a man sick.

Turning off the bridge, Brainard drove west into the sun, which only made him hotter. He could feel his collar scraping the back of his neck. He pulled down his tie and opened his shirt while his thoughts worked around to Will Caroline. For the hundredth time he wondered what Will Caroline had pulled that day—between those two meetings. By Christ, he'd give a lot to know! Those quiet ones crossed you up every time, damn 'em. They were weaklings and they knew it. And they worked out some pretty low tricks to make up for it. Like with Callie. Suddenly Brainard's mind worked back to an older scar. Callie had come to visit Natalie Brainard and Will Caroline had met her, and in less than a month he had married her. The whole thing had taken three weeks, start to finish, and Callie wasn't easy to get—nobody knew that better than Brainard. For years Callie had been coming to visit Natalie, and even between marriages, when it should have been easy to get, it wasn't available. Yet she'd gone for Will Caroline. And had stuck to him now for nearly ten years.

By the time Brainard reached home, a tight cramp gripped his stomach. He found Natalie and Diana on the screened terrace. Diana, still wearing a bathing suit, had obviously just come in. Natalie was lounging on a chaise with a drink in her hand.

"How many's that?" Brainard snapped at her, flinging down his jacket and tie.

"Just my first, dear," Natalie said.

Brainard snorted and went to the bar to fix himself a drink. He could feel Natalie watching him. "You looking at something?" he said, and felt a tug of pleasure at seeing her lower her eyes. She wouldn't say anything now, by God. He finished his drink in two gulps and poured another and stood looking out at the bay. The day was still hot and there was no cooling breeze coming in off the water. His skin felt raw and irritated under his wilted shirt.

"That project," he said after a while, "is the worst mess I ever saw in my life." Turning, he saw that Natalie had finished her drink and he knew she wanted to get up for another, but she sat still with her hand tight on the glass. "There isn't a man over there who knows what he's doing. Or cares."

Natalie drained off the melted ice, squeezing the last drop out of her drink.

"There'll be six months of steady, expensive bungling before they accomplish a damn thing."

"You talk as though in the end it might work," Natalie said.

He stared at her. "You only think that because you're an idiot."

Natalie's hand tightened on the empty glass. From behind a magazine, Diana said, "Answer him back."

Angrily, Brainard whipped about. "You keep out of this!"

Diana turned a page of the magazine, but Brainard knew she wasn't reading it. This was just an act—one of the tricks she'd learned from the old woman. He could feel his blood pounding and his control slipping away. Even knowing that he would lose, as he always did with her, he snatched the magazine out of her hand and threw it down on the bar. "When I talk to you, you look at me and you listen."

"Gladly," Diana said. "What did you want to say?"

But Brainard only stared at her in frustration and turned back to Natalie who was staring at the melting ice in her glass. He moved away from the bar.

"Not only is that project not going to work," he said. "It's going to be the most colossal failure Enright ever saw."

"How do you know?" Diana said.

"Because I can see how they're blundering, that's how!"

"How's Dr. Cable getting along?" Diana said. "What's he doing?"

"He's not doing a damn thing—just sitting around on his can. And when he does do something, it won't amount to much."

Natalie got up and moved quietly to the bar.

"This is going to be six months nobody will forget in a hurry." Brainard gave a short laugh. "How could it succeed? It's a maniac project with a fool at the head of it."

At the bar, Natalie said, "I don't think Will Caroline is such a fool."

Brainard looked at her sharply. Not for the first time he wondered whether only his own plans had been upset when Callie suddenly married Will Caroline. No, he thought, she wouldn't dare! Besides, she wasn't that interested. She hadn't been for years—unless, for years, she'd been nipping at sex on the side. No—the only thing Natalie was interested in nipping at was a bottle, and it was beginning to show, too. She had her drink now, and took a quick sip. He went over and took the glass from her and poured it into the bar sink.

Diana stood up and walked out of the room. Brainard, drenched in perspiration, looked after her, wanting to stop her and knowing that he could not. And then Derrick and his damned test tubes were in his mind again, and anger pushed him so hard he couldn't be still.

"I made that money," he burst out. "I built up those profits—it was my efficiency—my bullwork—my know-how!" He paced about the room, throwing a look at Natalie, daring her to speak. His blood pounded as she stood silently watching him, and suddenly he felt that urge again. Brainard had never struck Natalie—he had never struck any woman—and yet he wanted to. In his reveries he had struck her hard and had tasted pleasure in it. His hand felt heavy at his side. It shot across his mind that he should restrain himself, and even while he thought it, control burned out, and fury mounted in him. He rushed out of the room and up the stairs.

He took a cool shower and lay down on his bed. His thoughts knifed deeper still. This project was small enough now, he knew— a mess of Petri dishes and test tubes didn't amount to much—but if it survived in spite of the blunders, it wouldn't stand still. And if it did survive—and it grew and became important—then what? Then Will Caroline's importance would rise with it—and that rise would be paid for with company funds.

He closed his eyes and put his hand over his stomach. What it boiled down to, he told himself, was that company money, not ability, was going to determine who would be stronger in the company—he or Will Caroline. For the first time Brainard admitted this fear to himself. He had never expected his power at Enright to be threatened. He was production manager—he had more ability—he was heir apparent to Hale and everyone knew it. But now Will Caroline was going to climb. And with money that he, Brainard, had earned. And his own hands were tied.

His stomach was burning badly now and his head ached. He covered his eyes and told himself that the defeat of this project could not be left to blunders and chance. Somehow it would have to be stopped. Somehow he would have to find a way.

On Wednesday, Charlie Derrick began to transfer bits of the pure cultures grown on agar slants to larger test tubes containing nutrient broths, made up largely of varying amounts of proteins, carbohydrates, salts and vitamins. "We're putting each culture into two different broths," he explained when Brainard asked him about the six hundred test tubes. "An' hopin' it'll do something in one or the other."

The larger test tubes were put into the constant-temperature oven, set for 37° C. In the oven were shelves that shook the test tubes continually to increase the circulation of oxygen and speed the multiplication of the microbes in the broths.

On Thursday Will Caroline went into New York and bought some C-strain inbred white mice—mice that were identical in every way so that there would be as few as possible individual differences to consider in the testing. The mice weighed twenty grams apiece. They were sold by the box, a hundred to a box. Will ordered two hundred mice and told the laboratory that he would notify them when to make shipment. The mice cost twenty cents apiece.

Lying under the bow of the old boat he and Max had bought, Tom peered up at the automatic starter that refused to start. Overhead the sky was taking on the paleness of the end of the day, and off to the east, if he looked, he could see the long fingers of clouds banked, as though waiting for the pink glow that would be the last touch of color before night.

From the upper dock he could hear the familiar noises of people beginning to come in from their boats, noises that were always a little louder, a little thicker, on Saturday than during the week. Idly

Tom glanced out at the water. Off the end of the dock his own boat, a twenty-foot sloop, rode at its mooring, the sails lowered and tied. Ordinarily on a day like this he would have been out on the water, too. But today the thought of sailing had only seemed an extension of the idleness that all week had oppressed him, and instead he had spent the day here, working with Max on this beat-up old powerboat that Max had insisted they must buy and which, for a month now, at odd moments, they had been repairing.

Beside him on the landing, Max said, "Let's wind up for today, Tom," and dropped his tools into the metal box. Then Tom heard him say, "Hello, Callie," and he knew that Callie Caroline must have seen them on her way in from her boat and come down to the lower landing to talk. He eased himself down the boat and climbed out.

"What're you two up to?" Callie said, coming up to them.

"Fixing up this old boat, Cal," Max said.

"What for?"

"Fell in love with it," Max said.

"Oh, well, then—" Callie said.

Max laughed and nodded toward Tom. "The real reason, Cal, is this madman here. He thrashes about these days as though he'd lost his wits. He wants to get to work and he has to wait for Derrick's microbes, which can't be hurried."

Tom picked up a rag and rubbed at the grease on his hands while, inside, he felt the restlessness churning up again.

"So we bought this old wreck for him to fix," Max said. "He's good at this sort of thing and it keeps him quiet."

"Don't listen to him, Cal," Tom said. "He's past his third drink—there's no telling what he'll say."

"All day long he's in and out of Derrick's lab," Max said. "And there's nothing he can do there. He can't make those microbes grow any faster. Just watches and stews."

Tom laughed, rummaged in the tool kit for the flask and saw that it was half empty, which was the reason Max was running on like this. Still, for all his exaggerating, Tom knew that what he said was true. "Drink, Cal?" he said. "Find you a glass somewhere."

Callie shook her head, and Tom unscrewed the top of the flask and took a drink. He didn't feel like going home, but neither was there any point in hanging around here much longer. Maybe, he thought, he'd drive into town and see if Midge was home. But he didn't feel like doing that, either.

Then he noticed Callie watching someone on the upper dock. He looked up and saw Diana walking slowly along the rail, with the same young man—the one with the beard—that she had been with that night in Tollie's restaurant. The man wore a grayish T-shirt and rolled-up faded jeans. He was bigger than Tom remembered him, and he moved a little too gracefully for a big man, walking as though he had nowhere to go and forever to get there. Since that night Tom had seen Diana with him often, usually at a distance, usually out in her little red-sailed boat. Tom knew the boat by its bright red sail, and he knew the man by his chin.

"That's a fine-looking fellow she's got there," Max said, following Callie's glance, too.

"He's an artist," Callie said. "Part of that ménage up the bay there—that art group that sort of hangs around, boozing and laying and doing a bit of work now and then—such as it is."

Diana came along the upper dock, wearing a white bathing suit and a blue shirt that matched her marvelous blue eyes, set off now by a deep tan. The blue eyes stayed on the bearded young man, and Tom looked at him again, too. It was a good beard, but it surrounded a soft petulant mouth—a better beard, Tom thought, than a man.

"How'd she get mixed up with this character?" he said.

"He does seem a bit unkempt, doesn't he?" Callie said. "But then, you have to understand about Diana—although frankly I'm not always sure that I do."

"Understand what?" Tom said.

Diana moved on, only looking away from her companion long enough to wave as she passed.

"What do you have to understand about her?" Tom said again.

"Tom, I've known Diana since she was born," Callie said, "and I'm still not sure. You know, she was brought up partly by her grandmother—Natalie's mother. The old lady hated Gil and tried very hard to get Natalie to leave him. When she failed, she turned to Diana and trained her very carefully in the gentle art of resistance —rebellion—whatever you want to call it. She wanted to be sure that Diana would be free of the kind of authority to which Natalie submitted so willingly."

"I've heard that story before," Max said. "It seems out of character—Gil letting that kind of sabotage go on under his nose."

"My guess is that Gil didn't interfere," Callie said, "because he figured the grandmother would leave Diana her money if he played his cards right. And she did. The old lady put a lot of time and effort into Diana, and then she was so pleased with her own handiwork that she left her every cent. It worked exactly as Gil had planned—although I suspect that he has regretted it more than once."

Looking after Diana, Tom watched the movement of her slender ankles and remembered the way they had slanted out of her slacks that night, stretched toward his fireplace.

"I'll bet that beard sponges off her," Callie said. "He looks the type."

Tom uncorked the flask again. "How do you mean, sponges?"

"I think that she keeps him. I think she passes out cash to him—regularly."

The flask stopped short of Tom's lips. "What for?"

"Darling," Callie said, puzzled, "have I touched a nerve?"

Tom took a drink from the bottle. "Hell, no—but why would she do that?"

"I suspect she fancies herself a patron of the arts," Callie said.

"She makes me nervous," Max said, closing the lid of the toolbox. "And I couldn't say why. She's so—intense, maybe—I don't know." He shrugged. "Well, let's get out of here."

Still looking down the dock, Callie gave a little sigh. "It always seems to me," she said, "that to Diana life is a spectator sport." Then she smiled a little and added as a kind of afterthought, "Although I'll admit she's quite a rooter."

Puzzled, Tom looked at Callie, expecting her to explain, but Callie only shook her head and said, "I'm going now."

"You coming, Tom?" Max moved to go, too.

"No," Tom said. "You go ahead. I'm going to stay awhile."

A little later Tom stood alone at the end of the dock. The bay was taking on evening quiet now. At their moorings the boats barely moved, and the shadows of masts slanted across the light and dark patches of water. It was going to be a nice night, he thought, and he ought to call Midge and take her out to dinner—drive along the shore with the top of his car down. But he stood still and thought again that he didn't want to. There was no one he wanted to be with tonight. There were times when your mind simply refused to touch another—when nothing pleased you—and this was one of those times.

This restlessness was strange to him, and yet, he thought, it was something he had known before. It reminded him of summer nights when he was younger—much younger—and he used to feel this same kind of yearning for something he couldn't give a name to then. Now, looking back on it, he understood. He knew that then it had been a girl he wanted. Out on the water the sails of boats that were still out seemed to be standing still against the evening haze. The pink glow had reached the fingers of clouds and soon would be gone. Now he could understand what he had felt then, he thought, and he could understand what he felt now, too. He wanted to get to work. And the feeling of waiting for one and wanting, and the feeling of waiting for the other and wanting were not dissimilar.

And then it was all dark, and a party was starting up on one of the boats. The voices rose and glasses rattled and someone heaved a beer can out into the water. The radio played the old Tommy Dorsey recording of "Marie" and somebody on the boat yelled, "Oi, Marie—oi, Marie."

Tom moved across the dock. Below, the water was black in the shadow of the dock and you couldn't see the bottom, although you could see the yellow-white barnacles far down on the posts. He watched the water move against a post and climb up it a few inches and recede and climb up again, and he turned away and started back down the dock. As he passed the boat where they were having the party, a girl said, "But, honey, my name isn't Marie—it's Sondra." He walked a little faster.

At the steps he stopped, deciding whether to go into Tollie's for a drink or find someone to take out or just go home. Then, as he moved up the lighted stairs, he heard someone call his name and he recognized Diana's voice. He looked into the darkness and saw her then, sitting on a low mass of rocks that humped up on the beach at the water's edge.

"I've been waiting for you," she said as he came up to her. "I thought you'd never come in from out there."

He saw that she had been home and changed into slacks and a sweater. "You should have come on out," he said. "You could have heard a fine rendition of 'Oi, Marie.'"

"I heard it from here." She laughed and he felt better already. "I wouldn't think of disturbing a dedicated man when he's thinking or brooding." She sat hugging her knees and tossed her head back and smiled up at him. "You see, I understand dedicated people very well. You should see more of me—I'd be good for you."

Tom smiled and put his foot on the rock. "You overrate me, Diana. It's not dedication. Just a bad case of congenital impatience. What happened to the beard?"

"You mean Adam?"

"That his name?"

"Not really. But he's a primitive and he thinks he should have a primitive name."

"And are you bound to Adam, Diana?" Tom said, restraining a smile. "To Adam who is not Adam?"

"Of course not! I'm not bound to anyone. Nor is Adam. We're both free!"

In a way, Tom thought, a little amused, Diana was dedicated, too—although he wasn't entirely sure to what.

"Adam's a great artist," Diana said. "The public will never appreciate him or understand him. When they do, I'll know that he has compromised, even if I haven't seen it yet in his work."

"Does that necessarily follow?"

"Of course."

Puzzled, Tom looked at Diana and wondered whether she was really supporting Adam, as Callie suspected. He started to ask her and then told himself it was none of his business and climbed up on the rock beside her. Thoughtfully he ran his finger along a crevice where moss grew. Then he said, "Diana, are you Adam's patron?"

Diana tugged at a strand of her black hair and looked up at him. "Yes," she said.

Troubled, Tom smiled at her. "You shouldn't do that, Diana—give money to Adam."

"Why not?" She laughed.

"Because a man shouldn't take money from a woman."

"Oh, don't be silly!"

"Especially one as young as you—and as pretty."

"Somebody has to support genius!"

"Do you believe that Adam is a genius?"

"Yes," Diana said defiantly. "I do."

Tom told himself to drop it. He shifted a little on the rock and looked down at the dark water.

After a moment Diana turned and looked up at him again. "My father says you're bungling terribly over there," she said.

"We've hardly begun."

"But he says you can't possibly succeed."

"Well, he's not alone. But then there are those of us on the other side, too."

"With all that bungling, how can you be so confident?"

"Nobody's bungling anything," Tom said. "They're just getting squared away."

"But how do you know that?"

Tom smiled and his eye traveled across the top of the rock that was as bright and smooth as granite in the moonlight. Then he looked down to the water where, below the surface, he could see small shells encrusted on the rock and long dark threads of rockweeds swirling with the waves like a woman's hair.

He turned back to Diana and saw her watching him, and suddenly, without warning, something went through him and he remembered that it had happened just this way—sharply and without warning—the last time he was with her.

He smiled and reached for her hand and said, "Diana, look down there—do you see how different the rock looks down below—different from up here where we're sitting? Let that be a lesson to you."

"All right," she said. "What kind of a lesson?"

"Up here, where it's above the surface, where we can see it, where it's lit by the moon, the rock seems innocent and harmless. But down there, below the surface of the water, it's half hidden and it has strange unfriendly-looking things attached to it—and it looks dark and ominous."

She looked up at him and he reached over and touched her hair. "And many things are like that, Diana. They only look ominous so long as you can't see them clearly." He smiled down at her. "Later this project will look better."

Down below, a wave hit the rock. The water splashed up into three deep hollows and didn't drain as the wave receded but stayed, looking like three mountain pools in a descending series—the lower two black, the upper one shallowly reflecting the moon.

Slowly Tom looked back at Diana. He felt his throat tighten and his hand tighten over hers, and then leave her hand and go to her throat, and he said to himself, Stop now—while you still can—if you still can. Don't kiss her—don't kiss her just because you're restless tonight—just because you were lonely and she's here and close and there's a moon. Because this girl is too serious—about everything. Behind that lovely laugh and that gay manner and those eyes that are practically a lethal weapon in themselves, there is something deadly serious—and you had better be careful. It's not just a question of playing the gentleman, he said to himself—it's a question of self-defense.

Another wave spilled over the lower rocks, and the moon wiggled in the pool. Tom drew back his hand. "On the other hand," he said with a grin, "I can think of some things that, the more of them you see and the better the light, the worse they look—so I guess it's not much of a lesson after all. Are we going out somewhere tonight, Diana?"

"Are we?"

He stood up. "I'll walk you home, and I'll go home and change and come back for you."

"Can you do that?" she said. "Wouldn't that be a compromise—coming to our house—with him there?"

Tom laughed. "Diana, I see your father nearly every day and we're quite civil to each other."

"But how can you be!"

"Just because two people have a difference of opinion doesn't mean that they're enemies for life! At Enright nobody ever agrees with anyone else all the time. I'll take you home and I'll call for you unblushingly."

He held out his hand to help her off the rock, but he could see that she didn't understand and that she was a little disappointed in him.

On Monday morning, Derrick began the tests on the first broths to learn which microbes were producing antibiotics. On a counter he lined up six hundred Petri dishes thinly coated with nutrient agar, and Nick, working with a pointed instrument, streaked two horizontal lines on each dish—one line of gram-positive test organisms and one line of gram-negative test organisms. Then Derrick followed and, on each test plate, streaked a vertical line from a broth, cutting across the first two.

Today the agar was colorless and clear, but overnight both the test germs and the microbes from the broth would grow, and where they grew the agar would be cloudy. In the morning three cloudy lines would be visible in the clear agar.

If the microbe in the broth was not producing an antibiotic, all three lines would be solid.

But where there was an effective antibiotic present, it would not permit growth of test germs near it, and one or both of the test organism lines would be broken. If the antibiotic was active against the gram-positive organisms, there would be a break in the gram-positive line. If it was active against the gram-negative organisms, there would be a break in the gram-negative line. If it was active against both, both lines would be broken.

The area where growth was stopped, where the agar remained clear, was known as the area or zone of inhibition.

When Brainard came into Derrick's laboratory that morning, Nick had streaked about fifty agar plates with test germs and Derrick was following up, streaking the broth lines across them.

Brainard watched while they streaked another twenty-five dishes and then he left, furious. There you have it, he thought. That's what it's going to be like. Dishes all over the place—test tubes all over the place—and the two of them sitting there, plowing their way through five hundred test plates left to do.

Angrily, he strode over to the production building and walked through the first floor—looking around to make sure that everyone was working—went up the stairs to the second floor and yanked open the door. Entering the penicillin room, he saw at once that one of the conveyor belts had been stopped. Lined up on the belt were vials of penicillin, which meant that the checkers had picked up one with faulty weight. In the glass-enclosed sterile area, two girls were working on the problem. Brainard's anger shot higher.

And that was another thing, he thought. That belt should stop automatically, the instant the weight was a milligram off. Then they'd spot the error in a second and they wouldn't have to wait while these damn women spent half the day weighing bottles to find it.

With forced good humor, he said to one of the women, "What's the trouble, Thelma?"

"This line was a little light, Mr. Brainard," the woman said. "It just happened. The last check a minute ago was all right."

Brainard gave her a smile. "They don't get past you very long, eh, Thelma?"

"No, sir, Mr. Brainard."

They always said it had just happened. Always. Brainard walked on. What with testing for net weight and for the dimensions and thickness and strength of the bottles and for the time it took them to drain empty and for just about every other damn thing you could think of—in production alone, excluding chemical and biochemical testing, there were sixty-seven different tests—it was a wonder they ever got anything out. If you didn't keep at these women, you'd get a pile-up you'd never get through. A lot they cared about production rate. Not them. They had other things on their minds.

Brainard closed the production room door behind him and stopped in the empty gray hall. For a moment he just stood there, numb with rage. He leaned against the wall and closed his eyes. Six hundred test tubes—six hundred agar plates—twelve hundred damned streaks of test organisms. And it was only the beginning. For months he would have to put up with this—for months nothing but confusion—not just what he'd seen these past two weeks—it would be these past two weeks multiplied a thousand times. At every step there would be mistakes—blunders—chaos. And there wasn't a thing he could do about it. Behind his closed eyes he could feel his head throbbing.

Then, slowly, Brainard's mind began to clear. He opened his eyes and for several minutes he stared at the steps. All at once, he saw this problem in a new light. Of course it would be a wild six months, he told himself. Of course there would be mistakes and confusion. But the thing to do was to take advantage of it—and make every mistake work for him. The thing to do was to watch for that confusion everywhere—and not just see it but use it.

Thoughtfully Brainard took out a cigar as he walked down the steps. He would have to figure out exactly how to go about this. It would take careful planning and a certain amount of discretion. Timing—that was important. Planning and timing.

He went back to the research building to look for Morrissey and found him coming out of the assay laboratory. "Claude, I want to talk to you."

"I'm on my way to a meeting in five minutes," Morrissey grumbled. "All we do these days is go to meetings. Neil and I were just saying since this Derrick came we can't get a thing done."

Brainard walked down the corridor with him. "What do you talk about at all those meetings?"

"Will Caroline's deploying his army." Morrissey snickered. "We talk about who's going to do what and how and why. I tell you, Gil, there isn't a man here knows what he's doing. No idea of the proper method—just a lot of ideas." They came up to the mycology laboratory and Morrissey looked in at Derrick. "What's your opinion of this fellow?"

"I like him!" Brainard said heartily. "I like him very much!"

"You're mighty cheerful today."

"Claude"—Brainard put a hand on Morrissey's shoulder—"just look at this fellow. He's sitting in there with that kid helper, and he's got six hundred goddam test tubes, and today he's testing every one of 'em on six hundred agar plates against twelve hundred streaks of test organisms. All from three pieces of dirt. And he's already started more. And he's asking for all the dirt he can get. You saw the notice. Any kind—from anywhere. Well, there's one helluva lot of dirt in this world. Is this joker going to examine it all?"

Morrissey chewed at the stem of his pipe and thought about that.

"Have you talked to him?" Brainard said.

"Well, I see him at these meetings. He's a mild enough fellow—although I can't say I like him. I get the feeling sometimes that he's not entirely sincere, if you know what I mean."

"He's a molly," Brainard said flatly. "In the next couple of months, Claude, there could be quite a backlog of dirt around here."

"Probably will be," Morrissey said gloomily.

"And quite a pile-up of dishes and cultures and test tubes. And God knows what else."

"No doubt about it."

"You go anywhere, you be sure to send them dirt, Claude. Send them plenty of dirt."

"Why?" Morrissey said resentfully.

Brainard laughed. Half the time he wondered how Morrissey found his way home at night. "Claude, when people don't know what they're doing, they make a helluva lot of blunders."

"Oh, it's my bet they're blundering already," Morrissey said. "Probably find out in a couple of months everything they're doing is wrong."

"Mmm-hmm." Thoughtfully Brainard chewed his cigar. "Every mistake costs money, Claude. Now, if this were a research foundation, we'd say it was normal. At Enright it's not going to be normal."

Enright was going to have to pay for all those blunders, Brainard told himself. An hour ago that idea would have made him sick, but now— He almost laughed out loud when he thought how he had let this worry him. Now, for the first time in months, he felt completely relaxed. He tilted the cigar to a confident angle while his mind worked around the problem, just looking it over. He would know when he hit on the right method—there was time.

EIGHT

T HE MAN IN FRONT OF HIM, whose name was Dr. Cahill, was discussing his experience as a pharmacologist, and although Will Caroline knew he was probably going to hire him, the idea did not particularly please him and he didn't want to decide now.

In the first place Will had one more applicant coming in this afternoon—Dr. Mills—although from the start he hadn't hoped for much from Dr. Mills. Yesterday Will had talked to and eliminated the first man, a poor-spirited fellow named Dr. Barter. He had wanted Mills to come yesterday, too, thinking that he would interview Cahill last, since he was probably the one he would hire, but Mills had wired asking, without explanation, to come on Tuesday instead. The wire had only increased his already strong doubts about Dr. Mills, but it was reason enough now to postpone the decision on Dr. Cahill.

And in the second place, right now Will Caroline wanted to get down to Derrick's laboratory. By now Derrick had thousands of Petri dishes and agar-slant test tubes and nutrient-broth test tubes lined up around his laboratory—all with microbes at various stages of incubation—and an inordinate interest in the procedure seemed to have developed among Enright personnel on all levels. Rosswell, the comptroller, who had never before betrayed the slightest scientific curiosity, but who could get very nervous over figures, walked past Derrick's laboratory regularly. Brainard was in there every day. Even Ade Hale dropped in more often than Will would have expected. And today the interest curve would rise sharply, because Derrick was getting his first results and everyone would be curious to see exactly what came out of all that work. Will Caroline was curious himself.

"Of course, I'd expect a great deal of autonomy," Dr. Cahill was saying. "I'd expect to set up my laboratory the way I want it."

"You're going to have to set it up, Dr. Cahill," Will Caroline said with a smile. "All we have now is a small mouse colony next to the assay lab where we do the routine testing on our batches of penicillin and streptomycin. Our assay people take care of it and run the tests. Not even inbred mice. But we've ordered C-strain mice for this new laboratory."

117

"Ordinarily I'd expect to order the equipment myself," Cahill said. "And to train my own men to do things my way."

It wasn't what he asked that was exasperating—it was the way he asked it. Will Caroline glanced over at the resumé that Dr. Cahill had submitted earlier. Cahill had worked at a good research foundation and had taught at two major universities and undoubtedly he was the best of the three applicants. Barter was out—and for experience, Mills just couldn't compare. And besides, Will had other doubts about Mills, who had held only one position—a teaching job for a year at a small college which he had resigned this past June, apparently because of some difficulty, because it had not been to go to another position. But then, Mills could afford to resign over any little difficulty—he was a member of an old and very wealthy New York family. Will frowned. The last thing he wanted around here was a soft-spined playboy who'd chosen the academic life because it was harmless. And he wasn't sure he wanted Cahill either, whom he was probably going to hire. Maybe he ought to take Cahill out to lunch and try to get a better, more relaxed picture of him.

"The new mouse colony couldn't be anywhere near the other, you understand," Dr. Cahill said almost primly. "We'll be using pathogenic organisms."

Will sighed. There was so much the record didn't show. "I have to leave you for a few minutes, Dr. Cahill," he said. "But if you can wait for me, we'll go out to lunch—have a drink and talk some more."

"I'm not a drinking man, sir," Dr. Cahill said.

"Well, we'll just have lunch then," Will said easily. "Stay right here if you like." Why did a certain type of man always put it that way? he asked himself. Why didn't he just say, "I don't drink"?

He looked into Jeannie's office to tell her where he would be and went over to Derrick's laboratory.

At about that time, two boxes of white mice, a hundred to a box, were delivered to the Enright freight room, shipped in error by the laboratory that was to hold them until notified. The arrival of mice at Enright was not unusual and the receiving department, as it always did when mice arrived, telephoned the assay laboratory. Joe Fry, a technician, was dispatched to take care of them.

118

Arriving in the freight room, Joe Fry, a knotty-muscled young man who looked like a prizefighter, inspected the mice and telephoned to Dr. Gates's office. "I got two hundred mice here," he said, "and they ain't like the others. Do I unpack 'em or no?"

A few questions about the shipping labels made it clear to Gates that these were not routine mice for his laboratory but the special mice that Will Caroline had ordered. He telephoned to Will Caroline's office, but Will had left for Derrick's laboratory. Jeannie promised to tell him about the mice as soon as he returned.

"They're Mr. Caroline's mice," Gates told Joe Fry. "Take them up to Room 42 on the fourth floor—the equipment for them is in there. And, Joe—be careful. Those are expensive mice."

"Dr. Gates," Joe Fry said, "you know I'm good with mice."

In Room 42 Joe Fry found all the equipment for the mice. There were three dozen glass jars, fifteen inches high, on the center counter, each with a wire mesh top, and next to each jar was a water bottle with a glass drinking tube in its cover. On the floor was a large carton of sawdust. As Joe Fry had said, he was good with mice. He covered the bottoms of the jars with sawdust, filled the bottles with water, and put ten mice into each jar. He screwed on the wire covers and placed an inverted water bottle over each, with the glass tube, from which the mice could drink, extending down into the jar. Having settled the mice into their new quarters, Joe Fry went downstairs to the other mouse laboratory to get some pellets of food. He stopped to tell Dr. Gates what he was doing, stopped for a few words with Midge Potter as long as Dr. Morrissey wasn't around, took a minute for a quick smoke in the men's room and then started back to the mice.

As Will Caroline walked down the corridor to Derrick's laboratory, he passed Rosswell and the chief accountant traveling north past the laboratory and then came up behind the chief janitor and his assistant traveling south. "Ain't that crazy son of a bitch having himself a big time?" the janitor remarked, and Will Caroline decided that now curiosity around here had run the gamut.

Inside the laboratory, Charlie Derrick showed him a few good-sized zones of inhibition and then said, "Mr. Caroline, ah've been wondering about numbering them."

Will Caroline looked at the Petri dish in his hand. "Isn't this the number right here?"

"That's our lab identification number for the soil sample and everything we did to it up through the broths. But those numbers are complicated and they're going to get pretty long after a while."

At that moment Will Caroline became aware of a slight disturbance down the corridor. He glanced up and saw nothing and looked back at the Petri dish in his hand that was marked 3-1-B-56-A. Derrick was right. It was an unwieldy identification.

"These numbers are all right while the biochemists are just lookin' them over, pickin' out the ones to work on," Derrick said. "An' maybe all right when they're just gettin' started. But when they get serious about 'em with a lot of people workin' on 'em and talkin' about 'em—well, sir, this is just too much of a number."

"What did you have in mind?" Will Caroline said.

"Just EA 1, for Enright Antibiotic Number One, and then EA 2 and so on, if that's all right with you, sir. Just for the ones that look good."

"Well—" Will Caroline thought a minute. "That seems as good as anything—" Then before he could say more, he looked up and saw Jeannie in the corridor running toward him. Immediately behind her was Joe Fry—and right behind Joe Fry a chunky, redheaded young man whom Will Caroline had never seen before. A cursory glance might have suggested to a stranger that Fry was chasing Jeannie down the corridor and the redheaded fellow chasing Fry, but Will Caroline doubted that that was the case. He moved toward the door.

"Mr. Caroline—" Jeannie called. Along the corridor a few heads appeared quickly in doorways. "Mr. Caroline," Jeannie gasped, still several yards away, "your mice are drowning!"

Will Caroline knew he couldn't have heard correctly, but the announcement produced several more heads in doorways. The janitor turned and came back with a look on his face that said this show was getting better all the time. If nothing else had improved around here these past two weeks, Will Caroline's capacity to smell trouble had strengthened considerably, and he decided that this crisis, whatever it turned out to be, should be faced in the relative privacy of Derrick's laboratory. Instead of going forth gallantly to meet bad news, he held his ground.

Joe Fry shot past Jeannie, stopped abruptly in the doorway, and babbled incoherently about pellets and water bottles. "And then

I come back," he said, "and a hundred and fifty mice are drowning —drowning like flies."

He had heard correctly, after all. Then the redheaded young fellow grabbed Fry's arm and said, "Buddy, are you taking me to your mice or do I hire a damned guide?"

Fry turned and stared, and raced off down the corridor with the redheaded young man close behind.

Along the corridor the men thought that Joe Fry had gone berserk. The news spread quickly. As Dr. Morrissey was coming out of Mr. Brainard's office, he was told that someone in his department had gone out of his head. Word reached the production area that someone in research had slipped his trolley at last. It was nothing more than they had expected. In all quarters work stopped instantly while waves of the curious converged on the fourth floor of the research building.

Outside the new mouse laboratory, a large spellbound audience had collected, which included Dr. Morrissey and Dr. Weir and several technicians.

The redheaded young man arrived and pushed through the crowd. "Kee-rist!" he said.

In two dozen glass jars, two hundred mice, frantically treading water with their pink paws, had achieved a state of hysteria. They knocked into each other. They climbed over each other. They slammed against the sides of the jars. They squealed.

The redheaded man rushed across the room. "O.K., fellows," he said, while he seized two jars and carried them to the sink and poured out the water. "Time to get out of the drink."

He raced back for two more jars, and then, seeing Joe Fry standing paralyzed, he said with considerable authority, "Bring them over and dump out the water."

Like a man in a trance, Joe Fry picked up a jar and promptly dropped it, and ten terrified squealing mice scurried in every direction away from the shattered glass. "Kee-rist!" the redheaded fellow yelled. A couple of mice darted behind the carton of sawdust and he dove to retrieve them. Another mouse shot across the floor, slammed into the carton, reeled and made straight for Dr. Morrissey, who was standing just inside the door.

"Pick it up!" the young man yelled while he groped behind the carton. Morrissey paled. "Grab it!" the young man yelled. Morrissey's mouth worked but nothing came out. "Then watch out, damn it!" The young man snatched up the mouse as Morrissey moved his foot. "Easy now, fella," he said soothingly to the mouse. "It was only a dip—you're back on dry land."

Pushing his way into the room, Will Caroline picked up two jars, and then Dr. Gates, who had just arrived, did the same. In a few minutes it was all over and two hundred wet unnerved mice were safe in dry jars. For another minute the crowd remained, with pained looks on their faces, and then, reluctantly, they dispersed.

The redheaded young man took out a handkerchief and wiped his hands. "Kee-rist!" he commented again, shaking his head at the mice, which were floundering about in the jars, still excited. Then, calmly, he said to Joe Fry, "You didn't fire-polish the tips."

Fry looked puzzled.

"The tip." He picked up an empty water bottle and pointed to the glass tube. "You have to fire-polish the tip down to a dropper so the water comes out a drop at a time. This way, as soon as the first mouse went for a drink, the whole bottle let go."

He hung his wet handkerchief over a pipe and walked back to look at the mice, which were still scurrying about, knocking into each other. "You've got too many in a jar," he said to Fry. "These are sensitive mice. Five's the best number—or six is O.K. I made a study of this once—with five or six they keep each other warm, but there's a minimum of activity. If the activity curve goes up, they start trampling each other. You ought to move a couple out of each jar. You know how to fire-polish the tips or you want me to show you before I go?"

"I can do it," Fry said.

"O.K." The redheaded young man grinned.

Then suddenly Jeannie recovered the gift of speech. "Mr. Caroline," she whispered, "that's Dr. Mills."

Will Caroline stared.

"Dr. Patrick Henry Mills," Jeannie said. "He was in my office when Joe Fry came running in about the mice. Dr. Cahill's still over there."

A broad smile spread over Will Caroline's face as he looked again at the redheaded hero of the rescue operation, and he thought that it was indeed an ill wind that carried no good. And then, that there was always so much a record didn't show.

"Here's Mr. Caroline now, Dr. Mills," Jeannie said.

Patrick Henry Mills turned, a wide smile on his freckled face, and held out his hand. "I appreciate your seeing me today instead of yesterday," he said. "I got married yesterday."

Will Caroline sat against a counter and folded his arms. He might lose a couple of mice here, but he had himself a pharmacologist. For the first time today he felt fine.

Later, back in Derrick's laboratory, Will Caroline said, "About those cultures that are going on for more work, Charlie. Don't number that first one Number One."

"No, sir?" Derrick said.

"We'll call it EA 50. And the second one will be EA 206. The third one is 139." He handed Derrick the slip of paper on which he had written ten numbers, and Derrick gave a quick nod and smiled. Will Caroline realized suddenly that Derrick understood more than he let on.

"We'll have to be careful about duplication, Mr. Caroline."

"We'll be careful."

Back in his own office, Will Caroline prepared a key and marked off the numbers he had given Derrick. The key was in numerical order and he locked it in his desk. When you were taming a wild horse, he told himself, you couldn't help being thrown now and then, but there was no need to keep a public count on how many times it happened.

Then he took a card out of his pocket on which, last night at home, he had copied a quotation, and he wrote out an order for one of his signs.

" 'It would be unsound fancy,' " he wrote, " 'to expect that things which have never yet been done—can be done—except by means which have never yet been tried.'—Francis Bacon."

That evening, lounging on the open deck before dinner, Will said, "Cal, do you remember how it was when we first tried to produce penicillin—and we had no idea at all how to go about it?"

"Of course I remember," Callie said.

There was still a smell of heat from the sand, but the sun had moved behind the house and here on the deck it was shaded and cool. Will put his feet up on the low stone wall and sipped his bourbon.

"Remember when good men were seriously trying to grow penicillin on the surface of milk bottles?" He smiled. It seemed inconceivable now. "But in the whole country there weren't enough milk bottles to produce even a fraction of what was needed? And do you remember what that first penicillin looked like when we finally produced it in tanks?"

Now that it was pure at last, penicillin was white, but that early stuff had looked like brown mud—and that mud had been scarcer than gold, and more precious.

"That mud gave me some bad moments," Callie said. "Whenever I thought of injecting it into human beings, I shuddered."

"It was the best we could do at the time. And the impurities didn't hurt anyone. Men are alive today because of that penicillin, who would otherwise be dead."

Callie took his empty glass over to the table to refill it, and Will looked after her, seeing how her pale yellow dress contrasted with her deep tan and her dark hair, and how slim she looked—too thin, maybe, for some men, but she suited him. Everything about her suited him.

From the table, Callie looked at him. "I'm trying to decide," she said, "whether you're pleased about getting started or not. You look these days like the cat who ate the canary but then wasn't sure he liked canaries."

Will laughed. "Maybe that's because I know what we're getting into. This time I know we're flying by the seat of our pants."

"But still," Callie said, "this time you know a little more."

"A little—but not much." His thoughts went back to the problem that, for two weeks, had been bothering him. "Right now, at the start, the problem isn't only what to do but how much and when. How big should this program be? How big now—how big later?"

Callie came back with his drink and sat on the edge of his chair.

"At best a lot of money will go down the drain on mistakes," he said. "We're going to go down a lot of dead-end streets—we're going to run up against dozens of stone walls, the same as with penicillin. If I know that—and I do know it—how much should I spend being wrong? It's a question of judgment, not science. Maybe at the start we should stay small—follow only a few dead-end streets at a time."

"If you're too careful, you'll still be warming up when the race is over," Callie said.

Will Caroline smiled because that was the kind of answer he would expect from Callie. Restraint was not in her nature.

"But then who am I to talk?" Callie laughed. "Look at all the messes I got myself into by starting to run before I knew what I was doing." She was referring to her two earlier marriages. "Still, I married you faster than either of the other two—so maybe it's not caution that's important. Maybe after a while you get lucky. Or maybe out of enough mistakes you learn something. And if that's so, Will, you might as well give it all you've got." Callie smiled because she had arrived reasonably at the conclusion that by temperament she found attractive.

"That's one way to look at it," Will Caroline admitted. "But in a thing like this, our men don't draw only on their own experience. We could spend millions getting nowhere, and then suddenly someone a thousand miles away could turn up a single scrap of information that would unlock the closed door that we'd been banging against for months. If that happened, it'd be nice to have all that money we'd wasted getting nowhere."

"But you might find that key yourself, in your own back yard, if you had enough men—enough good men—looking for it."

"Yes, we could—as well as anyone else."

"At any rate, darling, whichever way you decide, you must be very firm in stating that obviously it's the only logical decision." Callie laughed. "And if nobody else knows anything either, they can't prove you're wrong."

"No," Will Caroline agreed. "There's no right or wrong in this until the end. If we win, we were right. If we lose, we were wrong. No in-between."

Thoughtfully Callie sipped her drink. "I think if you're going to do it at all, you must have the courage to do enough."

"And the courage, too, not to panic and try to do too much."

But Callie was having none of that. She knew now where she stood. "Will—did you ever see anyone win a race who wouldn't run it?"

Will Caroline took his feet off the wall and reached for his wife's hand. "Cal," he said, "you're good to come home to."

"Of course, darling," Callie said. "I mean to be."

Still, he thought, her ideas made as much sense as any others. At this stage everything was only opinion, anyway—nobody could back up what he said with experience or with proof.

"How do you know?" Brainard said, leaning across his desk while he considered this piece of news that Morrissey had brought him.

"Derrick told Gates. Some of these cultures have to go to Gates very soon for more testing. Derrick told him that first they'd have one number and then later, if they were any good, they'd get a simpler number. Now, I ask you—how can we prepare reports properly if a culture has a number and then suddenly that's not the number?"

"Well, Claude," Brainard said, leaning back in his chair, "the numbers aren't going to make a hell of a lot of difference—nothing's going to amount to much, anyway."

"And the new numbers not even in order," Morrissey complained.

"Nothing about this is in order—why should the numbers be in order?" Brainard laughed. "Just get them plenty of dirt, Claude—just give them enough rope." Then he realized what Morrissey had said. "Why not in order?"

"I don't know why not—I just know it's going to be damned confusing and—"

Brainard waved his hand to silence Morrissey. Suddenly he had understood what Morrissey was saying, even if Morrissey did not, and he wanted to think. An idea had just occurred to him, and the minute it hit him he knew it was a very good idea. He worked his cigar over to the other side of his mouth.

"Claude," he said after a minute, "get interested in this."

"I'm interested, all right."

"Get more interested. You ought to want to know everything that's going on." For another moment Brainard examined his idea, although he didn't have to, to know it was good. "You ought to keep a record, Claude—a very careful, very complete, day-by-day record."

"That's Will Caroline's job. He's directing this. We do our reports and turn them over to him."

"You keep a record too, Claude. Or better still—make an extra copy of every report and give it to me. Anything that happens in your department, write it down and give it to me. I'll keep the record."

He was on the right track now, Brainard thought, and he knew it. Carefully he considered the problem. It might be a good idea to have a couple more of these boys give him reports, too. Morrissey

126

couldn't see everything. Not Morrissey. Enough rope, he said to himself, with a smile. But that wasn't all he wanted—not just to give them enough rope. The idea was to see that the rope ended up around the right necks. This would take a little thought, he told himself, but there was no hurry. Things weren't going to straighten out around here in a couple of days.

Tom came into his laboratory and set a rack of test tubes down on the center counter—ten test tubes, cotton-corked, each about half filled with a muddy-looking broth. "Moose," he said to his technician, "we go to work."

At the sink where he was scrubbing glass equipment, Moose Daniels looked around. He was a very large young man, blond and blunt-featured, whose bulk seemed even greater in his baggy white laboratory uniform. His arms extended like mountain ranges out of the short sleeves, and his neck rose out of the open collar like a thick post. Carefully he put down a glass flask and reached for a towel. "What've we got here?" he said.

"The cold plunge, Moose."

"How's that?"

"Our first ten cultures. Brace yourself, boy. These ten little bastards mean to give us trouble."

"O.K." Moose came over to the counter, and on his big arm a neat tattoo that read "Sweetie" rippled as he picked up one of the test tubes. "Dr. Weir was looking for you. Kinda chewing himself up, it seemed to me."

"Already?" Tom smiled. Some men, it seemed, couldn't wait to start worrying. Long before anything went wrong, they got going at it—as though in training for the big disaster, as though wanting to be sure they'd do a good job of it when things did go wrong and there was something to worry about.

"He said he'd be back," Moose said. "So where do we begin?"

"We don't really get going until tomorrow. Today we only send samples of these broths to Dr. Gates for a couple of tests." Tom rolled up the sleeves of his white laboratory coat. "Eat, drink and live dangerously tonight, Moose. From tomorrow on—we work."

"I'll do that," Moose said.

"You get those half-inch test tubes autoclaved?"

Moose nodded and went to get them, and while he waited Tom glanced out the window, scanning the bay. It was a hot summer morning with the sweet settled smell of July in the air—an almost ridiculously sleepy kind of day on which to be getting started, he thought. The water was still except where a little powerboat skitted back and forth like a frantic bug. Then, just coming into view, he saw what he was looking for—the small red sail, drifting lazily across the bay, blood-bright in the sunlight. Every day this week she had been out, earlier than she used to come—and alone, without the beard.

Moose was back with the sterilized test tubes. "What are we gonna learn from him?" he said. "From Dr. Gates?"

Tom looked at the muddy broths. "Anything he can tell us will help—and at the start it won't be much." He picked up a test tube of broth, careful not to disturb the wad of cotton in its mouth. "Right now this is just a mess of junk, Moose. There are probably about a hundred different substances in here—all mixed up—and we know almost nothing about any of them. All we know is that, mixed in with all that stuff, there's a little bit of some kind of antibiotic—along with the microbe that's making it. That's it—end of story. That's what we know."

"Well," Moose said, "that's quite a lot."

Tom shook the test tube, and in the broth muddy globules stirred about. "There's probably about one drop of antibiotic in here."

"In the whole test tube?"

Tom nodded. "So first we have to grow more—enough to work on. And that doesn't mean just nursing along the microbe in this broth to turn out a few drops of antibiotic. It means working out a special broth in which this particular microbe will step up production and make more antibiotic—a lot more—than it's making now. Then, after we've done that, we have to isolate the antibiotic—separate it from all the other junk."

"All that other stuff?"

"All the stuff we'll use to make it grow—and all the stuff the microbe will be producing along with it. While you and I were in the army, Moose, they did this with penicillin. It took four years."

"Four years! To do what?"

"To find a way to grow enough of it and to get it absolutely pure —separate it from the hundred other things so there was nothing left but penicillin."

"Four years?"

"And at least half a dozen companies were working on it. One culture." Tom put back the test tube. "We've got ten cultures right here.

129

And there are plenty more where these came from. And every week Dr. Derrick will be turning out a couple of hundred more. You getting the picture?"

Moose grinned. "Well—I can see what Dr. Weir is chewing himself up about."

"Now—back to Dr. Gates. We hope he'll tell us two things— whether the antibiotic is active enough to bother with, and whether it's new. We'll have enough to do without wasting time on something that won't cure much. And right now all our tests are pretty crude. But Gates will test every broth against five or six disease germs—both gram-positive and gram-negative—to see how many of them the antibiotic will knock out. If it won't do much, we'll toss it out."

"Right—I'm for that," Moose said.

"And another one we don't want to work on," Tom said, "is an antibiotic we've already got."

"One we've already got! Why do *anything* with one we've already got?"

"How would we know?"

Moose scratched his chin and looked puzzled.

"Hell, Moose"—Tom jerked his head toward the rack of broths— "that stuff could be anything. You can't tell just looking at them. Any one of them—or all ten of them—could be streptomycin. Or some antibiotic that somebody has already isolated—worked his tail off on it—and then found out it was toxic—like streptothricin."

"Thricin? That's one I don't know. Streptothricin?"

"It's an early one that Waksman found. It's pure poison. But very common—turns up all the time. Against germs in a test tube it looks great—knocks 'em out like flies. When you put it in mice, it cures them and for a couple of days they're fine, and then—boom—they die from the antibiotic, not the disease."

"Always?" Moose said.

"Every time. It's a delayed toxicity—but a real Sunday punch. So if we've got some streptothricin here—or some streptomycin or some other known—we want to find it out now. We don't want to waste months finding streptomycin all over again."

"And he can tell this—Gates?" Moose said.

"He'll try," Tom said. "He has germs in which he's been developing resistance to the known antibiotics. If he tests a broth against streptomycin-resistant germs and it won't touch them, we'll assume

130

that antibiotic is streptomycin and we won't work on it. Same thing for the others."

Then Moose jerked his thumb and the "Sweetie" on his arm jumped and he said, "Here's Dr. Weir back."

George Weir's usually handsome face was flushed, and he looked angry and resentful as he stopped at the far end of the counter. "I think we ought to talk about this, Tom," he said.

"Get labels on the test tubes that are going to Gates," Tom said to Moose and then went down to where Weir was waiting. "All right, George—shoot. What do you want to talk about?"

Through the window, he saw the little red sail going past again.

"Well—hell!" Weir burst out. "I guess there's enough about this lousy deal to talk about!"

Weir was a man who angered quickly and resented many things. If anything, he seemed more angry now than worried. Although, Tom thought, if he was sore about having to work on the project, it was because he was afraid of it and was worried—so in the end it was the same thing.

Then suddenly the flush drained out of Weir's face and he said, "Oh, Christ!" and Tom, following Weir's eyes, saw Ade Hale coming into the laboratory.

"Christ, he's not wasting any time checking up on us!" Weir muttered.

"Dr. Cable—" Hale nodded. "Dr. Weir." He came up to the counter and looked at Tom's rack of test tubes, and Moose moved out of the way. "These the cultures you picked?" Hale said.

"Yes, sir."

"What made you decide on these?"

Maybe Hale hadn't wasted any time getting here, but neither did he waste time with unnecessary questions—and that was something. Tom selected a test tube from the rack. "This one here did the best job of killing germs on Dr. Derrick's test plates," he said. "It left a very large clear area in the gram-positive line."

"You figure that makes it the best antibiotic?" Hale said.

"Only possibly one of the more potent."

"Why possibly—if it did the best job?"

"It could have left the largest clear area because there was more antibiotic in there," Tom said. "A higher concentration. This might be a microbe that just naturally produces a lot of antibiotic. Not necessarily more potent—just more of it."

Over Hale's shoulder, Tom could see George Weir scowling.

"And would that make it better in your opinion, Dr. Cable?" Hale said.

"At this stage, we can't say that any one is better or even good," Tom said. "The most potent antibiotic in the world is worthless if it's toxic—and it's too early to test for toxicity."

Hale's eyes stayed on him the whole time he spoke, and Tom thought that there was something almost aggressive in the way he listened. And yet you knew that if you said it all this time, you would never have to tell him this again—and when you stopped short of the whole story, the eyes told you to finish it. Tom was about to continue when Hale turned to Weir.

"What about you, Dr. Weir?" he said. "You pick them that way, too?"

"Yes, sir," Weir said quickly, and then as quickly hedged. "For the time being, at any rate."

"What do you mean, for the time being?" Hale said calmly.

A little flush returned to Weir's face. "Only that we'll be doing extensive work on these, sir," he said smoothly, "and I'm sure that we'll find evidence to either support our present theory on methods of selection or guide us to a new theory."

Tom leaned against the counter and folded his arms, wondering what Weir thought he was accomplishing with this dodge.

"And your present theory is to select the most potent?"

"Yes, sir."

"Or the most productive?"

"Yes, sir."

"Which?"

Weir jerked his hand. "Well—either, sir. That is, it's one or the other."

Abruptly Hale turned back to Tom. The blue eyes were calm and noncommittal, but Tom knew that Hale wasn't satisfied and he didn't blame him. He'd come for information—not a glib runaround.

"That about cover it, Dr. Cable?" Ade Hale said.

"No, sir. It's possible that a big area of inhibition doesn't mean either of those things. The antibiotic may not be any more potent—and the microbe may not be any more productive. It could be that the broth just happened to be right for this particular microbe."

Hale's eyes registered interest.

132

"You know how sensitive these microbes are," Tom said. "If they don't get the right diet, they don't produce. The broth might be giving them everything they need to grow and multiply—and they'll grow and multiply very well—and still make very little antibiotic. Like this one." Tom picked up another test tube which contained a particularly thick cloudy broth. "You see how turbid this broth is— you can see that the microbe has been growing like crazy—but it hasn't produced much antibiotic, so far."

Behind Hale, Tom could see Weir signaling to him furiously to keep quiet. Hale said, "Why'd you take it, then?"

"To see whether I can coax it to make more. These bugs are temperamental. It's possible to take a microbe and use the same broth in which it's not doing much, and just vary one ingredient—go from corn to soybean or add more nitrogen or more carbon—and that one ingredient might be the precursor that the microbe needs to make an antibiotic, and when it gets it, it might take off and produce a great deal of antibiotic. Go from a famine to a feast. It's possible that the broth Dr. Derrick used just happened to contain the right precursor for the first one and didn't have the precursor that this bug needs. It could be just that and nothing more."

"You've got a lot of ifs and maybes there, Dr. Cable. A lot of unanswered questions."

"Yes, sir. They're questions we can't answer yet."

"You think you could overlook a good one because it didn't do much on Dr. Derrick's plates?"

"We could, sir."

"You talk to Derrick about it?"

"He's using some pretty general broths, and we both feel the microbe would do something in one of them."

"Then why are you bothering with that one?"

"To see if we're wrong, sir."

"Could you pass one up right here? Throw it out because it didn't seem to make much—just because you didn't happen to hit on the precursor?"

"It's possible," Tom said. "But we're starting with five basic broths, and every culture will go into all five of them. Then, depending on the results, we'll work out variations on those five and try them all again—and then make changes in those variations and try them all again. Within reason we'll give them every chance to produce."

Now Weir was furious. The flush was creeping up his face again and rage sat in his eyes. Tom looked back at Hale and saw that he was satisfied now and was ready to leave. And then suddenly Tom himself was not satisfied. Suddenly he wanted to be sure that Hale understood what was going to happen here. He wanted Hale to realize later, when things began to go wrong, that they had to go wrong before they got right. For the life of this project suddenly it seemed important that Hale understand that clearly—before the trouble began.

"Mr. Hale," he said, walking with him to the door, "with this whole thing—not just selecting the cultures, but everything—there has to be a certain process of self-education, because nobody knows much about any of it. There's no certainty yet about anything we're doing."

"I've got the idea, Dr. Cable," Hale said. "You've made it clear."

But Hale didn't seem to find the idea particularly disturbing, and as Tom stood in the open doorway watching him stride down the corridor, it occurred to him that maybe more than anything else Hale had come to find out what kind of man he had here—one who was going to give him straight answers or one who was not.

He closed the door and turned back to Weir. "All right, George," he said. "What's eating you?"

"You crazy or something, Tom?" Weir burst out.

Tom went back to the center counter and motioned to Moose. "Let's get a cubic centimeter of each broth into one of the small test tubes to go to Gates," he said.

Weir came over to the counter. "Next time, Tom, you tell Hale what *you* don't know, not what *I* don't know."

"O.K., George." Tom flamed the pipette and the mouth of the test tube and transferred a cubic centimeter of broth, flamed the tubes again, stuffed in the cotton and checked the labels. "George," he said, "you can't fool a man like Ade Hale."

"You don't knock yourself out telling the president how much you don't know," Weir said, still very angry.

Tom put the test tube back into the rack. "George, how long do you think it's going to take Hale to find out? A day, maybe. Half a day."

"You don't tell a guy you're playing eeny-meeny-miney-mo with his money!"

"You do if that's what you're doing," Tom said. "Anyway, he knew it when he came in here."

"A-ah—" Angrily Weir turned away.

"George, you stood there eating yourself up because I talked about precursors. Don't you think he already knew about precursors? He's a chemical engineer. He went through penicillin and they sure as hell had a precursor problem with penicillin."

"With management you tell them what you have to and no more."

Tom sighed, wondering why he bothered to argue. "George, Hale wasn't born yesterday. He's seen a tough problem before. He might as well know it's tough and he won't expect a miracle next week. Because we can't hand him a miracle next week."

Weir looked at him, furious, and without another word he stormed out of the room.

"You want me to take these down to Dr. Gates when I'm through?" Moose said.

"No, I'll do it," Tom said. "I want to talk to him."

Midge Potter looked up when Tom entered the assay laboratory.

"Roll up your sleeves, Miss Potter," he said. "Spit on your hands. Your days of leaning on your shovel are over."

"Something I can do for you?" Midge said.

"Plenty!"

"Honest to God, you're crazy!"

"Where's Dr. Gates?"

"He's down having coffee with Dr. Weir," Midge said. "Of the two I don't know who's in worse shape. You want to leave that?"

"No, I want to talk about it. What's the matter with Dr. Gates?"

Midge Potter shrugged. "Off his feed, I guess." Then she flashed him a quick look and said, "Ah, you know—"

Yes, Tom thought, he knew and Midge knew and probably everyone else around here knew, too. Then he saw Gates coming back, and he set down the test tubes and nodded to them as Gates came through the door.

"The first ten, Pearly," he said. "Will you let me know if we've got any old friends among them?"

"Hello, Tom." Gates managed a halfhearted smile. His eyes went to the rack of test tubes, lingered a moment and then came back, and Tom thought that there was a difference between Gates and

George Weir. Weir blamed his lack of knowledge on everyone else and was mad at the world, but Gates was just plain worried—as only Gates could worry.

"All I want to know now is whether it's new or a known, Pearly," Tom said. "And how active it seems to be."

Gates sighed and then nodded. "I'll do my best, Tom—but I don't know—I can't be sure—"

"Well, Pearly, you're not alone—nobody's sure of anything yet."

Gates brightened a little and Tom held out the rack of test tubes. "O.K., girls, go get your tests and behave yourselves."

Gates smiled. "You figure they're female, Tom?"

"Pearly," Tom said, "they've got to be. Look at all the trouble they're causing."

Gates laughed and Tom thought that he had never seen a man who could change moods so suddenly and so completely as Pearly Gates.

But he knew that as soon as he left, Gates would remember all the things he had to worry about, and if he didn't, someone would come in to remind him—George Weir or somebody else.

The trouble here, Tom thought as he walked down the corridor, was that everyone knew too well how little they knew. Usually when a man started a job he had at least the illusion that he knew what he was doing—and by the time he recognized the enormity of his initial ignorance, he had picked up a little knowledge to lean on. But this time there were no such illusions.

He went upstairs to Max's office and dropped into a chair. "You know the old platitude, Max?" he said, after a while. "That when a man knows nothing—knowing that he knows nothing is the beginning of wisdom?"

"As a matter of principle, I'm opposed to all platitudes," Max said. "Otherwise I might be tempted to buy that one."

"Today I'm not so sure," Tom said. "In this case it might be better if they could believe that they know more than they do."

"They'd only be kidding themselves."

"Still—until they begin to learn something, it might help. The illusion of knowing—even if they didn't—" Tom shrugged. "It'd save them from a lot of misery like what they're going through today—be a kind of shield."

Max turned and smiled. "Hell, Tom," he said, "what illusion isn't—

136

against something? Why else would people go to all the trouble of having them?"

Gates turned off the motor and sat a minute in his car, feeling almost too tired to get out and go into the house. Beside him on the seat was his briefcase, a handsome soft leather one that Madeline had given him, and on top of it a few journals he had brought home to read. The librarian had brought him the journals this morning, but he'd hardly found time today to even open them.

It had been one of those days. After Tom left, George had brought in his cultures too, and although the tests were simple enough, Gates had not trained a technician yet in these techniques and he had done them himself. Not that he minded. He preferred to do them himself—at first, anyway—to be certain that, within the bounds of this horribly limited knowledge, he was doing everything he could for the biochemists. They were in for a hard enough time— the odds on this project were terrible. Really terrible.

Glancing next door, Gates saw that Neil Harrup hadn't come home yet. He wondered if anything was wrong, because he was late himself tonight. At four-thirty he had opened the journals at last and had stayed awhile, trying to read them. By the time he left, the corridors were almost empty, and they were completely deserted when, reluctantly, he had walked back again to get the journals to take home. At first he had thought that he wouldn't bring them tonight— he was just so tired he felt he couldn't bear it—and then he had decided that he'd better.

One of the troubles today, he thought wearily, had been Dr. Morrissey, who had interrupted him a dozen times to discuss the most insignificant details. Ordinarily Gates managed to put up with Morrissey's fussiness—it was something he could understand. His own father, who had been a high-school teacher, had been that way, a martinet who had harped on small details and insisted that everything be perfect. Gates could remember the first time he had overheard some students joking about his father. It was in the locker room, and he had sat there hidden—shocked and humiliated—until slowly it came over him that honor demanded that he show himself. And then, even while he was bracing himself to do it, his determination crumbled before the realization that he simply could not inflict on another person such embarrassment as his presence would cause. He had remained silent and hidden—and for days afterward, as a kind of penance, he had tried to accept his father's nagging with better grace. When it happened again a year later in the cafeteria, he had been less mortified and his penance had been longer.

So Gates could understand Dr. Morrissey and get along with him. But today Morrissey had been particularly nervous and difficult, with endless questions—mostly about Gates's reports. A dozen times Morrissey had reminded him that every detail must be entered. Gates had resented this because he had always prided himself on his reports and he didn't think Morrissey should be worried about them or take up his time today when he had so much to do. He supposed his resentment had showed—although he hoped not too much.

He would have trained Miss Potter to do some of that work, but Morrissey wanted to transfer her and Gates wasn't happy about that, either. Even though she had only a high-school diploma and the new technicians they would hire would probably have bachelor of science degrees, still Miss Potter was a natural. She worked fast and learned quickly, and Gates didn't know what Morrissey had against her. He supposed he shouldn't argue with him on a small point like that—or maybe he should. He liked having Miss Potter in the laboratory. She was always cheerful and agreeable—and it raised your spirits, sometimes, just to look at her.

Next door Elaine Harrup came out to hang up her bathing suit, and Gates noticed that her hair was a little brassier than usual. Madeline referred to Elaine as a slick bitch, but Gates had always thought she was pleasant enough. Sometimes Madeline formed these opinions and there was no talking her out of them. Then he saw his two little girls, aged eight and six, still in their bathing suits, taking their showers at the side of the house. He noticed that they had left the latticed gate open and thought that he would have to speak to them about that. Not that there was anything so wrong with it, but they could be seen from the road, and it seemed that taking a shower, even with your bathing suit on, ought to be private. He could see the little river of water running down to the drain and the little ridge of sand that had formed at the edge.

"Hurry up, Barbara—Veronica," he heard Madeline call from an upstairs window. "You know your father likes you to be dressed

138

when he comes home." Then she saw him and said, "Oh, you're here."

Gates picked up the journals and the briefcase and got out of the car and started around the house to the front door that faced the boardwalk. This was a hangover from childhood. His father had always insisted that a gentleman entered his home by his front door and that he wore a tie and a jacket in his living room and at dinner. This latter bit of nonsense Madeline refused to tolerate in hot weather, but Gates still entered his house each evening by the front door.

In the house he put down his briefcase and the journals and went into the living room.

"I'll be right down, Woodrow," Madeline called. "Hurry up, girls. You know your father's home. Peter—"

There was no answer from his ten-year-old son.

"Woodrow, is Peter there?"

"No," he said. "I don't see him."

"What's the matter?" Madeline said instantly.

"Nothing."

"I can tell by your voice—I'll be down in two minutes. Woodrow, don't drink a martini. It's too hot. Fix yourself a long cold drink."

For a minute Gates just stood there in the living room. He saw that a cabinet door was open and went over and closed it. Then he took out a bottle of bourbon and poured some into a glass and sat down in his chair, the one that Madeline insisted was his—a huge, comfortable man's chair with a wide ottoman. Outside he heard his son taking a shower.

"Good heavens," Madeline said from the stairs, "take off your jacket. It's so hot."

"Peter's here now. What do you want him for?"

"Woodrow, what is wrong?" Madeline demanded.

"I don't know, Madeline," he said. "I'm just awfully tired tonight. Maybe I'm coming down with something."

"Woodrow, can't you feel how hot it's getting? Now, take off your jacket, and give it to me and your tie, too—and open your collar." Expertly she ran her hand along his face. "You're not coming down with anything. You're just tired. Get your feet up and relax for a few minutes."

She took the bourbon and went into the kitchen, and then Gates heard the screen door slam and Peter's voice in the kitchen, and Madeline said, "Peter, fix a charcoal fire in the barbecue. Your father's terribly tired tonight."

Then she came in with another drink for him, a tall one this time with plenty of ice and a tray of crackers. Gates sipped the drink gratefully. He felt so tired he didn't care if he never stood up again.

"Eat something," Madeline ordered. "Have some cheese and crackers. Now, what did you do today that wore you out so?"

"Nothing special. Well, the biochemists got their first cultures today and I set up a few tests on them, that's all."

"Did you do it yourself?"

He nodded.

"Why didn't you train your voluptuous answer-to-every-man's-prayer to do this little chore?"

"Morrissey's thinking of transferring her."

"Why? The light too blinding for his aging eyes?"

"Oh, Madeline—"

"Don't kid yourself, Woodrow. These pious ones are the ones to watch out for. Well, now, I'm certainly delighted that you're in the swim at last. Tell me what you did. What are you testing for?"

"Really, Madeline, I'd just as soon not talk about it. I'm awfully tired tonight." Then, seeing her face, he said, "It's not much right now. I've got those resistant organisms, you know—for the known antibiotics—and I test the culture we want to identify against them. If my test organism is resistant to streptomycin and if the antibiotic kills it, then the antibiotic isn't streptomycin. Otherwise—if my test organism resists the antibiotic—we'll assume that the antibiotic is streptomycin, and they won't work on it."

"But what if it's one that streptomycin wouldn't touch anyway? Streptomycin doesn't cure everything."

Gates took a long drink and put his head back. "Oh, I test for that first. I do a spectrum of organisms—not complete, of course—to see what the unidentified antibiotic is active against—what it will cure. I test it against five or six pathogenic organisms that haven't been made resistant to anything. That's another way of telling whether it's a known one. We know what streptomycin will do and we know what streptothricin will do—and the few other antibiotics that are known but not used in medicine because they're toxic. So if the culture behaves just like streptomycin, we say this is probably streptomycin."

140

"Well, then—fine! You've got a double check."

Gates raised his head. "Oh, Madeline, all these tests are so crude! All the techniques are so rough! I wish I had a half-dozen more tests I could do to be sure."

"Woodrow, you're worrying about this unnecessarily."

"Madeline, how resistant is resistant?" he cried. "How do I know? I don't know anything for certain. These organisms are supposed to be resistant. They've been exposed to small amounts of streptomycin—or some other antibiotic—and then to larger and larger amounts until supposedly they've built up resistance against it. How do I know whether my test organisms have become as resistant as I think they have? They can mutate in so many different ways. How do I know for certain what one has done? It's supposed to be resistant against a certain amount of streptomycin, but how do I know how much antibiotic is in that little bit of broth they bring me? And how do I know how potent it is? I test it to see whether it's active— I try to find out for them whether it's new or a known. I don't want them working on something for months and have it turn out to be streptomycin—or some other one that's known and isn't any good! I don't know—I do my best. I hope I give them the right dope but I can't be sure."

Madeline studied him carefully. "Woodrow, do you really have that much feeling against this project?"

"I'm not against it and I'm not for it. I don't feel anything. I just like to know what I'm doing."

Madeline sat down on the ottoman. "Woodrow, you're a very careful, accurate bacteriologist. You'll tell them as much as anyone could tell them now."

"Or what if it seems to be the streptomycin or another known and I tell them that and they throw it out? And what if it isn't a known? What if I tell them to throw out one that's new—and that's very good? . . . If there is such a thing!"

"Could that happen?"

"These tests are so crude, anything could happen."

"Woodrow," Madeline said firmly. "You are worrying too soon. Wait until something goes wrong before you go to pieces. Now, finish your drink and put on a cool shirt. I know you've had a hard day, and I'm sorry but I've invited people to dinner."

"Oh, Madeline, I wish you hadn't."

"I know—and I am sorry. If I'd known what a heavy work load

you had today, I wouldn't have done it. But, Woodrow, it's Charlie Derrick and his wife. She's finally moved up here and she's miserable. I do think they need help, Woodrow. And she's quite nice. But she's awfully unhappy and I think we ought to be nice to them."

"You're right, Madeline. Of course we should. Why's she unhappy?"

"I don't know, but she just seems lost. She's a wide-eyed little thing, but rather overwhelmed and, for the present, wretchedly unhappy. They've found a house two blocks in—a little away from Janet and George."

"Oh? By the way, Madeline, George was asking me again about a house on the boardwalk. You know—Janet. George wondered about that Welles house—the one down near Max Strong. She's that tall, blond girl. She only uses the place once in a while. You haven't noticed whether she's been up here lately, have you?"

"I haven't seen her, but I haven't been looking. Janet has wanted to live on the boardwalk for years. It's nothing to worry about."

"I don't know why she feels that way, but she considers it a mark of status. She resents living inland and it worries George. It's too bad for him to have that on his mind now."

"Well, perhaps Gil Brainard could pick her up one of the fourteen-room shacks."

"Madeline, I wish you wouldn't talk that way." Gates finished his drink and stood up. "Well, I'll go change and come down and give you a hand. Did you ask them over tonight, too—Janet and George?"

"No, I just asked the Derricks. Her name is Kate."

"Maybe we should give George a ring and tell them to come over —he's pretty low about this new work."

"He'll recover, Woodrow. Now, go upstairs and put on a cool shirt."

On the steps he stopped and looked back. "I don't suppose you could arrange to handle two more? It might cheer George up a bit."

"There simply wouldn't be enough."

It wasn't that she minded two extra people, Madeline thought, but she wasn't going to have George Weir come over, full of anger and gloom, and upset Woodrow again, now that she had cheered him up.

A few minutes later while she was in the kitchen making a salad, she heard him coming down the stairs. His step was lighter and when he didn't come straight into the kitchen, she knew he was all right again. Then a moment later he was opening the door and saying cordially, "Well, Charlie, come on in. Good to see you!" And greeting Kate in that almost courtly way he'd learned from his father —one of the few good things he had from him, as far as Madeline was concerned. She put the salad into the refrigerator and wiped her hands. She wished Woodrow wouldn't get so depressed over these things. She wished he didn't show it so.

In the small strip of mirror over the ugly varnished chest, Janet Weir studied her reflection and examined her lipstick while she wondered what he had in mind today, staying on afterwards like this. Usually he got out in a hurry. She lit a cigarette and sipped the drink he'd given her, and looked around the room. This place was a dump. He called it a fishing and hunting cabin. Fishing and hunting, my foot, she thought. It wasn't any outdoor sport he kept it for, and he'd better get it fixed up a little if he expected her to keep coming here.

Thoughtfully she looked at the closed bathroom door and wondered whether this would be the time to mention that solid-gold bracelet. He hadn't bought her anything in three months, not since the pearls. What did he think she was, anyway? She could hear him moving around in there and the water running, and then he came out and went over and poured himself another drink.

"It's hot in here this time of year, Gil," she complained.

"I'll put in air conditioning," he said.

She sat still, not bothering to answer, and he sat down opposite her, across the narrow room.

"Your husband's getting started on this new thing, I hear," he said.

She shrugged.

"I can see you're interested."

"If you're just going to sit and be sarcastic, why don't we go?" she said. "Why should I be interested? What's it to me?"

Brainard looked at her and laughed.

"You know what that project means to me?" she said. "It means he's twice as hard to get along with as before. Every night now he comes home and takes a drink and looks around for something to complain about. He's got it down to a routine. The only changes are who does he pick on—me or the kids—and does he yell half the night or do we get the silent treatment."

She looked at Brainard and saw he'd settled down and was going to talk awhile, and she nodded to her empty glass on the table. "Give me another drink, Gil," she said. If he got up and did it, she'd ask for the bracelet. If he told her to get her own, she would wait. She glanced at him and lit another cigarette. "It's like he's got a permanent hangover," she said. "Everything gets on his nerves and he gets on my nerves."

"Maybe you ought to talk it over with him more," Brainard said, without moving. "Find out what he's doing."

"I know all I want to know about what he's doing." She examined her coral nail polish. It matched her lipstick and it was a good color with her red hair. "I'm not interested. He's always had a mean streak that came out once in a while. I'd go upstairs and lock the door or I'd go to a movie or I'd argue if I felt like it. He's always figuring how he got a raw deal somewhere so I'd let him blow off steam. But now it's all the time, so don't tell me I should be interested. I'm not looking for trouble, and I don't care what they're doing at Enright because I don't think they're going to come up with anything. Are you going to get me a drink, Gil?"

He got to his feet.

She watched him go over to the bar. "I figure who's so great at Enright," she said, "that they're going to find some great drug? Tom Cable? Max Strong? The new people—Derrick? Mills? I'm not even sure I'd want to take a drug they found—that's what I think of them. I don't think I'd want a doctor who'd give it to me."

She flicked her coral nail against her cigarette and looked very carefully at Brainard because it had not escaped her that he was watching her much more carefully than he had for several months, and if she knew the reason, it would help to make up her mind definitely about mentioning the bracelet.

He handed her the drink and sat down opposite her again. "You like some good advice?" he said.

"What kind of advice?"

He lit a cigar, taking his time before he answered her. Then he said, "You ought to tell your husband to keep himself a record of this."

"Why?"

"A record for himself—not the one he turns in to Morrissey or Caroline. He ought to keep a record of everything he does—and he ought to compare it to everything the others do—especially Cable."

144

"Why?" she said again.

He sat on the sofa, looking at her, and for a moment she thought he wasn't going to tell her why. She shrugged. If he didn't want to tell her, he didn't have to. The whole thing was nothing to her. Sometimes she wondered why she'd been crazy enough to marry a scientist, anyway—you couldn't talk to them—there was nothing to say. And George Weir wasn't much any other way either.

Then Brainard said, "Think about what'll happen when this thing blows up and you'll see why." He took the cigar out of his mouth and gestured with it. "When something like this fails, there's a standard procedure. First you decide on a couple of fellows you can blame and you fire them. You don't fire everyone—just a few fall guys to show the board and the stockholders that you're taking care of the weak spots in your organization. So how do you decide who goes and who stays? It depends on who can be made to look bad— or good—without too much trouble."

"What do you mean by that, Gil?" She was becoming interested.

"Look—this thing is going to fail—so in the end who accomplished what isn't going to matter. Cable worked overtime every day this week. Who cares? When you fail, nobody's impressed that you worked your ass off to do it. With a failure, all that the Monday morning quarterbacks care about are a couple of reasons that sound like the right ones, even if they're not. Nobody gives a damn what the real reasons were. Then everyone's busy looking out for his own skin—making sure his own stock hasn't gone down. So a couple are going to die and the rest are going to live and the ones who live will be the ones who manage to look good. And there's nothing looks better to a committee or a board than an impressive set of records."

She wondered whether to believe him. She didn't really trust him, and she couldn't see where that was so important. "What for?" she said. "Who's going to read them?"

"Nobody's going to read them! Does anyone ask if spilled milk was Grade A? All they see is the mess. As long as he's got good records—a lot of stuff in there—the company figures this is probably a good man—systematic, conscientious—and they'll keep him." He waved his cigar and ashes fell off and he brushed them off his lap.

"On the other hand, take Cable," he went on. "Knocking himself out. They have to grow those cultures for a week in the broths— while he's incubating the first batch, he's started the second. Understand he's thinking of starting a third. He and his technician running

145

around like a couple of stud dogs with every bitch in the neighborhood in heat. Don't know where to turn first. And for what? Who cares how much it takes to fail? You tell your husband to take it a little easier and spend some time on his records, and he'll look a lot better than Cable in the end."

Thoughtfully Janet looked at Brainard. She doubted that it was her interest alone that was keeping him here—just having a drink and talking about George. She knew him better than that. Undoubtedly he was after something—in which case she could hold out for the solid-gold bracelet—maybe she could even hold out for two or three, which was what she really wanted. They looked better and she liked to hear them jingling against each other.

"I'll see what I can do, Gil," she said. "But I don't know—"

Brainard stood up to leave. "Have him keep himself a good complete record, Janet. You type it up for him. Make an extra copy and bring it to me and I'll look it over for you—I'll tell you if it's O.K. or if he ought to be doing something more."

Confidently, Janet crushed out her cigarette and stood up, too. She could deliver those records, all right. It was only a matter of deciding how much they were worth to him.

The night was mild and the water against his ankles was warm as Tom walked barefoot at the edge of the beach, thinking back through this first week's work. Out on the bay the beacon of the lighthouse blinked like a toy lamp, and the foghorn sounded a muted call in the quiet night. That was always the same foghorn out there year round, he thought—but this soft bleating sound on a still summer evening was no kin to the harsh melancholy cry of winter. Although, Tom knew, it wasn't the horn that changed.

He moved along, thinking not so much about the work, which was nothing yet, but about the men. Not since the army, he thought, had he been so aware of the differences between men or of the different ways they showed them. One man, like Derrick, was almost too easygoing so that you wondered whether there was any anger in him to stir up at all—while another man, like George Weir, had more than his share of anger, always ready to boil over. Or a man like Will Caroline went along seemingly undisturbed by all the unexpected problems that came up—while another, like Gates, hadn't had any problems yet but worried anyway—and wasn't the only one.

It was strange, Tom thought—some of them were men he had thought he knew well, but now they showed qualities he had not seen before—both good and bad. But a man's behavior was never a random thing. A man reacted according to all that he was—all that he had been and done, and thought and felt, and hoped for. Like debris that lay quiet at the bottom of a pond—that you didn't see until a storm churned it up to the surface. With these men, he supposed, it had all always been there—all the little strengths and weaknesses that were beginning to show themselves now—and would show themselves even more, probably, along with others in the months to come. And yet, not that much had happened until now—and the trouble so far was not in the project but in themselves and in the private meanings they had given it.

Tom came to a sand castle that Max's children had left on the beach, and stepped around it, although in an hour the tide would take it anyway, and then drew up opposite his cottage. He was about to walk on when he saw a figure on the porch, indistinct in the pale light from the streetlamp. He moved closer and then saw that it was Diana.

She was sitting on the wide rail of the porch, with her head back against the round post, sitting perfectly still, waiting for him. He walked across the beach toward the steps, and then she saw him and turned her head.

"What were you doing down there?" she said as he came along the walk.

"Just walking on the beach."

"You looked lonely down there—"

He laughed. "I'm not lonely."

She sat with her hands in her lap, still leaning back against the post, turning her head toward him as he came onto the porch. "You always seem rather lonely to me."

Tom leaned a hand on the post. "Maybe loneliness is like beauty, Diana," he said, "and is in the eye of the beholder." The foghorn sounded and he looked toward the blinking beacon and then back at her. "Just as some people think a foghorn is the loneliest sound in the world."

"It is," she said. "It is a lonely sound."

"I knew a man once who said that to him a foghorn sounded like the cry of all the forgotten people of the world—a cry to which everyone had grown so indifferent that they no longer heard it."

147

"How awful!"

Tom smiled. "Me, I like foghorns, boat whistles, train whistles—you know, faraway places I always wanted to go to and all that. Only I don't want to go so much any more."

"Why not?"

"I don't know why not."

"You know."

"Yes," he said. "I guess I know. Do you want to come inside, Diana?"

In his cottage Diana waited while he turned on a light, and then she went over and sat on the floor near the fireplace where she had sat the other time. "I waited for you to come to see me," she said. "But then—well, you know about the mountain—the one Mohammed was involved with."

"You caught me at a bad time," Tom said. "I've been busy." It was the truth but not all of it. Every day these past two weeks he had thought about Diana and watched for her little red-sailed boat from his laboratory—and looked to see whether she was alone. And every evening he had thought of calling her—he had thought of it tonight —and then he had thought better of it.

He turned on another light, and a moth that had squeezed in somewhere flitted over to it. On the floor Diana reached for the Japanese sword that he used as a poker. "Did you get this in a battle somewhere?" she said, turning it in her hand to examine it.

"No," he said, watching her. "I won it in a poker game in Hongkong." She was disappointed as he had known she would be, and she put it down. "I'm not much of a collector of souvenirs, Diana," he said.

"You kept it as a souvenir of a poker game."

"It's a less offensive memory."

"Poker! It's so shabby!"

Tom sat on the sofa, placing a little distance between them, and looked thoughtfully at her—studying the bright-eyed look and the glow she gave off—remembering suddenly that Callie had said that day on the dock that to Diana life was a spectator sport. Callie had never explained it, and now, more than ever, Tom wondered what she had meant. Callie had said, too, that day that she was her grandmother's handiwork, as Diana herself had told him, and Tom tried to remember what Callie had said about that.

148

"Diana," he said after a minute, "what was your grandmother like—the one you spent so much time with?"

"Oh, she was a great rebel, I told you that. She was against all kinds of things that other people just take for granted. And she tried to make me into something because my mother was a disappointment to her." She tilted her head. "Why do you want to know?"

"No reason."

"My mother never stands up for anything. She gives in to my father disgustingly—and then she drinks to forget how weak she is. She drinks too much. My grandmother wanted me to think for myself—to be sure that I'd think as she did and not as my father does—or my mother."

Tom smiled, because once you let a person think for himself, there could be no assurance of the shape the thoughts would take—but the blue eyes were bright with a passionate conviction, and he decided against pointing out the fallacy in the grandmother's reasoning.

"You know what he's like," Diana said. "He likes to think that when he speaks the whole world—his whole world—jumps. With one exception, of course. Ade Hale. When Ade Hale speaks, my father jumps—which would be a refreshing twist except that there's not much to be said for Ade Hale, either. They're two of a kind. Anyway, I stand up to him every chance I get. I think that if you're going to stand against things that are wrong, you must resist wrong wherever you find it. You can't suddenly fight if you never have—then it's too late."

"Well, I don't know," Tom said. "You keep hearing stories about those little fellows who retreat and retreat until they're pressed too far—then suddenly they turn and become tigers."

"You don't really believe that!"

"No. I'm just teasing you."

"You fought for what you wanted. Only you fought the wrong battle—in the wrong place."

"Why is it wrong"—he smiled—"if they're letting me do the work I want?"

"That's not the point." Diana leaned toward him, looking up at him, and mentally Tom reviewed all his reasons for keeping this distance between them. "The point is," she said, "that they're only letting you do it for the money they hope to make. And they'll push you and use you and sacrifice you if they have to—as long as it spells profit."

"Well—I guess if they push me a little, it won't kill me." Tom smiled. He wasn't really listening to her. The moth came back and buzzed around the light and then flew over to the fireplace where its pale wings blended with the gray fieldstones. Tom watched the moth and then let his eyes travel down the stones to the sword in the log basket and then back to Diana. It had been a long time since he had known a girl like this, he thought—and longer still since he had wanted a girl in just this way—the girl coming first and then the wanting. Usually it was the other way around. When he looked at Diana now, he saw that she was watching him, smiling a little as though she knew what was going on in his mind. And then, while his eyes stayed on her, she stood up and came and sat beside him, a little distance away. He reached his hand over to her hair.

"Well, I don't think they should be allowed to push you," she said softly. "I think that in a world where almost nobody cares about anything noble and great, the few people who do should be special. The great scientists—like you—should be protected."

"My sweet Diana," Tom said. He touched her throat and smiled. "You run on too much."

"Of course I don't care about the poor excuses that most of them are at Enright—they don't matter."

"Some of them are pretty good."

"I mean the wonderful ones—the dedicated ones—who really have a great purpose. Everyone who can think knows that they should be separated from the grubby moneylenders—"

"Diana, it's not all black or white like that."

"It's black enough," she said. "And white enough, too."

Thoughtfully, Tom looked at her. A moment ago he had been considering making mild love to Diana. Now he drew his hand away from her face. It wasn't that he was no longer tempted—nor that he thought he would be rebuffed; he was pretty sure that he would not be rebuffed. It was just that, with the image she had formed of him—the way she idealized him—he would feel like an impostor. And this was the feeling, he realized now, that had kept him away from her these past two weeks.

"Diana," he said, "I'd like nothing better than to let you go on thinking a scientist—and particularly this scientist—is a Galahad on a white horse who can do no wrong."

150

Tom shook his head and looked away from Diana, back at the fireplace where the moth, with single-minded purpose, was making its way down the stones. How could he bring this girl down to earth, he asked himself, so that he could proceed from there? The moth dropped onto the log basket and came up against the sword, and Tom looked at the sword, too—the trophy of several skillfully executed hands of poker—and then suddenly he grinned.

"What we really are, Diana," he said, "the whole lot of us, is just a bunch of educated gamblers."

Diana laughed, which was better than when she was so serious.

"And we're a pretty tough breed, so if they push us a little, we can take it. And we should be smart enough to counterattack if we have to. A scientist needs freedom to work—but not pampering."

"But you should be pampered!"

"I don't want to be pampered!"

"But certain people are special and they should be taken care of —so they can rise above materialism and bourgeois problems and live for their goals!"

Tom gave a silent little whistle. This girl was really flying. "Well, just watch a scientist in a good bourgeois poker game sometime, Diana—like the one in which I won my sword, which took place in a den in Hongkong"—he embellished the truth a little—"and was continuous for three days and three nights—and you'll see he can have some very materialistic goals. Did you know that scientists are the best poker players in the world?"

"Oh, Tom!" She laughed. Her face said that she didn't believe it.

"It's the truth!" he said. "You can take my word for it. I know a great biologist—a really creative thinker—who'll stay up all night in a good poker game. And I had a chemistry professor at Yale who was a genius and a spectacular poker player. And do you know why they're so good at it? There are reasons—as there are for everything."

"What are the reasons?" She said it as though she hoped they would not be convincing.

He closed his hand over hers. "I'll give you a scholarly analysis of this," he said. "For one thing, they're familiar with the law of probability—they know the probability of filling a flush, drawing an inside straight. And they're used to observing details—they're analytical. All these things are very important in poker." He glanced over at her. "And—most important—they're not overly concerned with failure. They know that most of what they do will end in failure. They know that they're not going to win every pot—and they know that one big pot can make up for ninety-nine that they lost—and they can coast through the failures with an air—with a certain flamboyant flair." He grinned at her. "They're used to thinking this way because everything they do is a gamble."

Now there was quite a blaze burning in the vivid blue eyes, and Tom suspected that he had not convinced her that scientists were like other men and could be counted among the fallible and the sinners.

"Is that how you feel?" she said.

Almost without meaning to, he reached out and touched her hair again, and something turned over in him and he wondered why he was talking so much.

"Is it?" she said again.

"Is what?" His fingers moved along the clean line of her throat.

"Do you feel that the work you're doing now will end in failure?"

"No," he said. He closed the space between them. "No, I—"

A faint voice of caution whispered again that there were reasons why he should not do this. Then the whisper died and his arms closed about her while his lips found her hair and he touched her face and turned it up to his.

"Why did it take you so long?" she said softly.

"What?"

"Why did it take you so long to do this?"

He smiled without answering, and the moth began to beat against the lamp again and Tom turned off the light.

After she had gone, after he had walked with her to her car and come back into the house, Tom wondered a little at himself. Why was he so eager to change her—to do away with her illusions? Why shouldn't she keep them? What harm did they do? He picked up the poker and looked at it and tossed it back into the basket. She was at an age that did well with illusions. He walked to the door and looked out. And besides, he liked her that way.

Far out on the water the lights of a ship crept toward the blinking beacon, and the foghorn called—and the call could be a soft and innocent summer sound or a harsh winter warning, and to one man it was the loneliest sound in the world and to another it was faraway places you didn't want to go to so much any more because what you wanted most was right here—and which was an image unaltered by private meanings? To each man the meanings were different, depending on all that he had been and wanted to be and was. And to each woman, too. And he had not felt this way for too long a time.

TEN

FERMENTATION was an ancient art but a young science. You knew about cheese and about yeast for bread. And about beer. For centuries beermaking had been an art passed along from beermaster to son to beermaster. With beer, you took the mash —which was the broth—and inoculated it with yeast—which was the microbe—and while the yeast grew and multiplied, it converted sugar to alcohol. Then you filtered off the yeast and you had Schlitz or Rheingold or Löwenbräu.

But with these unknown microbes it was different. You inoculated a broth with the unknown microbe and waited six days while the microbe grew and multiplied and converted something to something. And maybe that something turned out to be a decent amount of antibiotic—and maybe it was a hundred other things you didn't care about. So you began the great game of blindman's buff—the hunt for the precursor. You varied the broths a little and incubated the microbes in them for another six days and sent them to assay to learn whether there was more antibiotic now than before. And you varied them a little more and waited again. And varied again and waited again. And meanwhile, through all the working and all the waiting, you groped for answers and searched the assay reports for meanings.

Frowning, Tom read through the latest report for the third time. "Moose, there's too much—" He searched for the word to describe what he was beginning to feel about this. "There's too much garbage in this deal."

In a corner of the laboratory Moose grunted agreement. He had just finished mixing a broth in a ten-gallon glass bucket, and now he was starting to measure out small quantities into the glass flasks in which they incubated the microbes.

"Three weeks ago we had ten cultures," Tom said. "One was streptomycin and two weren't active enough. We began fooling around with broths for the other seven—and we're still fooling around with them."

He had put each of those seven cultures into all five of the original broths and had incubated them in the constant-temperature room—three days in shake flasks and three days more in stir pots—

and then he had sent them to Gates—thirty-five samples—to find out which broths were best suited to each microbe. Then, working with the two best for each, week after week he had experimented with small changes in the ingredients in an effort to increase the antibiotic yield. Today he would work out still further variations and begin to incubate those first cultures for the fourth time.

It was beginning to bother him. He wanted to move on. He had never been famous for his patience, and there was too much waste here—wasted motion and wasted time. By now, he thought, he should have found a few clues in these reports. He should have seen some correlation. He should have begun to draw a few conclusions that would enable him to cut away some of that waste. And, so far, he had not.

"Last time," he said, going over what he already knew, "we got some improvement in one—that one that looked good from the start—but nothing to brag about in the rest. Two of them are real deadbeats—grow in anything but won't produce." He looked up. "I'm tempted to chuck them all—all but that one."

"Say the word," Moose said cheerfully. "I'll be glad to do the honors."

For a minute, Tom considered the possibility. The second batch of cultures that he had started, while waiting out the week for the first, was shaping up in about the same way. Now today he was starting this third batch—another ten. From the little that he'd learned these past few weeks, he had worked out two more basic broths—so that today these new cultures were going into seven instead of five—and he supposed that was some progress, but not enough—not the kind he was looking for. It was mechanics, not insight.

"No," he said, "I guess we'd better try again—give them one more chance."

"Ah, might as well," Moose agreed. "See if we can wake 'em up."

Moose had the flasks ready now, each half filled with broth, and was putting them onto a cart to wheel them to the autoclave room to be sterilized before being inoculated with the new cultures.

Tom slipped the report into the pocket of his lab coat and went over to give him a hand. "I don't know whether I hope they come to life or not," he said.

"Why's that?"

"If one that's been stubborn suddenly catches fire and starts producing like crazy, I'll feel uneasy about having almost thrown it out. On the other hand, if they all still just plod along—all but that one—and just eke out a living, I'm not going to feel like fooling around with them much longer."

At the autoclave room they slid the racks, with the flasks on them, off the cart and onto a shelf in the room and closed the door. Then they stepped across the hall to the constant-temperature room, where the warm moist air was heavy with the sweet malt smell of fermentation.

Here, on one side of the room, the broths were in shake flasks, tightly capped, agitated by moving shelves to circulate oxygen through them. On the other side of the room there were larger stir pots, standing in water troughs. In the stir pots automatic stirrers agitated the broths, and through these stirrers sterilized air was blown in, giving the microbes a fresh supply of oxygen. At this stage, fermentation activity generated so much heat that the water troughs were necessary for temperature control.

Today cultures from Tom's second batch were in the stir pots, and at this stage they could be doing big things. Or, with all that activity, they could be producing nothing.

"These will be finished this afternoon, Moose," he said, looking at them. "Take them out and get samples to assay."

For another minute he looked at the thick broths. Then he turned away. You couldn't tell anything from looking. They could be thick as pea soup and give you next to no antibiotic at all.

"There's too damn much mileage, Moose," he said as they walked back to the laboratory. "We have to find a way to cut it."

Only how can you cut, he said to himself irritably, until you have some idea of what to cut and why?

In his office he opened the report again, and then he took out the earlier reports on these cultures and compared them. For a long time he studied them without seeing a thing that he hadn't seen before, and his dissatisfaction mounted. It was like being lost in a maze, he thought. You knew there was a way out—there was always a way out—but you couldn't find it.

He stood up and went over to the window. Like being in a maze, he thought. And in a maze there are two ways to find your way out. You can be patient and methodical—and explore every path in turn, follow it to its dead end and eliminate it when you find it leads nowhere. And that's what we're doing now.

Or—Tom ran his pencil thoughtfully along a groove in the varnished windowsill—provided the maze has design and is not a random thing—and nature is never a random thing—the other way is to find the key.

He moved the reports to the wide windowsill and stood looking down at them. "Come on," he said softly. "Come on—talk to me."

There was something here he ought to be seeing—he was certain of it—and he was missing it.

"Here she comes," Elaine Harrup said.

At the bathroom sink, Neil Harrup drank down the bicarbonate of soda and stood a moment, letting it settle his stomach. Through the mirror he could see his wife at her dressing table in the bedroom— see her yellow hair and her droopy breasts and skinny shoulders under her robe. "Here who comes?" he said.

"Diana—going to Cable's again."

"How do you know she's going to Cable's?"

"Who else does she know at that end of the beach?"

"I suppose she could know any number of people," he said.

The wide mouth—that wide, intrusive mouth—curled. "Name two," she said. She reached for the telephone and lit a cigarette, and Harrup sighed. He wished she wouldn't smoke so much in here. At night the room always smelled of stale smoke and it disturbed his sleep.

"We're going up to that camp on Sunday," Elaine told him while she dialed. "There was a letter today from Marcia and they've made some bunk changes and I don't like the people they've put her in with. They can do that with somebody else's kid, not mine." The mouth that proclaimed her jurisdiction over everyone else's affairs set in a straight line and she leaned forward and looked up the road. "She's going to miss Cable—he's out walking on the beach."

Harrup examined his face in the mirror. He didn't feel at all well, and he wished they were not going out tonight. He didn't look well either, he decided.

He heard a click on the telephone and then Elaine said, "Winifred, are you near the window? All right—quick—look out and see if little Diana drives by." She smoked her cigarette, and her mouth —that mouth that could swallow Jonah—looked hungry. "Ah-ha!" she said. "Well, where do you think she's going? She's there every night. . . . Winifred, if she goes to his place every night, who's chasing whom? . . . Well, it's damn near every night now."

She hung up. "And," she said, "what little Diana goes after, little Diana gets."

"I ought to go downstairs for some milk," Harrup said.

"Oh, my God," she said. "What's got you upset now?"

"Nothing," he said. "Nothing."

"I'm getting damned sick of your stomach," she said. "Well, just you be on your feet on Sunday to go up to that camp."

Harrup turned on the faucet. "I don't know why she has to go to camp anyway," he said, "with a perfectly good beach here."

"Now, don't start that again," she said. She applied mascara and held an eyelash curler to her eye. "She makes contacts. She adjusts socially. She learns to work with a group."

"What did you ever do with a group?"

She moved the weapon to her other eye. "You're deadly tonight, all right."

Harrup burped and felt relief.

"Oh, my God," she said again. "I've never put in a summer like this in my life. Just because you don't like that project, there's no living with you or your stomach."

"You're right. I don't like it."

"Why?" the mouth—all of it—demanded. "Just tell me why you can't make the best of it like any sensible, well-adjusted person."

"It's disorderly, that's why." He burped again. "It's not my idea of research. Good research is logical and systematic and based on facts. And this is illogical and there are no facts." Just thinking about it made him feel worse. "And if you want the truth, I'd like to get as far away from it as possible."

"What!"

"And stay away."

"You know what the trouble with you is," she told him. "You're neurotic. I used to see hundreds of cases like you. You're a type."

Harrup tried not to listen. Elaine had been a social worker, and whenever she went professional on him, he tried not to hear her, although it wasn't easy.

"Now, let me tell you something," she said. "As long as Enright is working on this, you're going to work on it and you're not getting far away. You've only been chemical director for six years, so don't get any idea that you've had it. Do you know Max Strong would love to have your job? Why should he be satisfied to be assistant director if he can get director? I know that type . . . he'd like to be president. Well, if he ever gets to be director, it'll be when you get to be vice-president. And not before. So don't think you're going to back away from this and let him take over by default—just because it gives you a stomach-ache!"

"I'm going down for some milk," he said.

"Well, if you're going by, just look out the window and see if Cable's walking on the beach."

"He probably is," he said. "He's always out walking on the beach."

"Well, he walks instead of getting an ulcer," she said, and went to the other window herself. "Where is he? I don't see him. Do you see him?"

"No, I don't see him," he said.

"Maybe he went back—maybe she won't miss him after all!" The mouth that could swallow Jonah went into a vicious smile. "I think on our way we'll just drive by there and see."

A week later, with another report in his pocket, Tom sat at lunch with Gates and Weir and a chemist named Brewer Wentner, who was five feet six inches tall and weighed well over two hundred pounds and had six children.

"There seemed to be a little improvement this time, Tom," Gates said, trying to be cheerful.

The report was on the first batch of cultures again, and the one that Tom had liked from the start still looked good but the others hadn't improved enough and the two deadbeats were still deadbeats. "Nothing to celebrate, Pearly," he said.

Weir gave his order to the waitress and turned around. "There never is," he said.

"Well, I think any improvement is encouraging," Gates said. "It shows you're on the right track."

"I don't know," Tom said. "At best a really talented bighearted microbe gives you antibiotic in such dilute solution. And most of them are so miserly that I'm beginning to wonder if they're worth bothering with. I'm tempted to dump a couple of these girls—pour 'em down the drain, get 'em out of my life."

"How can you do that?" Weir said. "You're not sure they can't do better."

"What'll it be, Dr. Wentner?" the waitress said.

"Just bring me the low-calorie grass, sweetheart. I'm down to two hundred and thirty pounds. I can't spoil it now." Wentner turned back. "Your attitude toward your bugs is influenced by the sad fact that you're a bachelor, Tom," he said. "You treat them like you do your woman. A bachelor of your years becomes cynical. Try once or twice to stir her up, and if she's not interested, get her out of your life."

Tom laughed. "With women I'm the soul of patience, Brew."

"Who ever had this much trouble with women?" Weir scowled.

"Now, sometimes a woman is interested," Wentner said. "She's merely unwilling because you haven't treated her properly. That's the wisdom of a married man with six children. It's all in how you treat them."

"You're right, Brew," Tom said. "I have to admit it. And that's the rub."

He knew it. He knew that a lot depended on the way you treated them, but with each new assay report his dissatisfaction was increasing, and before he fooled around with more broths for these cultures he wanted to do some thinking. This was Friday. He decided to put off working on them again until Monday morning. He would take all his notes home over the weekend—and all the reports—and go through everything again from the beginning. Maybe he would see something that he hadn't seen before.

After dinner Tom sat at the desk in his living room, which was covered with notes, memos, journals, formulas for fermentation broths, unpaid bills, and a postcard from his old roommate, Sam Lewis, who was in Boston now. The card recommended a new nurse at the hospital whose name was Lois. Tom tossed it on top of a pile of bills and pushed everything aside. He opened his notebook and spread out the assay reports and began, step by step, to go over it all again.

"Come on," he said softly, looking at the notes. "Open up. Tell me something."

Around midnight he stopped working and went outside and stood on the porch. It was a soft summer night with just a trace of the coolness that came into the air in August. The days were still hot, but at night you felt the first little hints that told you summer was moving along. After a moment he lit a cigarette and walked out to the boardwalk.

It's August, he said to himself, and you haven't learned enough. Time is passing. It's six months since you started looking into this—and five since you first talked about it to Will Caroline—and four since they voted to go ahead with it—and almost two since Derrick plated his first samples—and a month that you've been fooling around with broths for the first cultures. Time goes by quickly in this business, and you haven't taken a single giant step forward yet.

Throw them out—stop fooling around, he said to himself. Except for that one that looks good, throw them all out. And on Monday, get down to business on that one—move on to the real work, which is getting that antibiotic out of the junk.

And then he wondered whether this urge to throw them out was growing stronger in him every week out of conviction or out of weakness—out of his own impatience. There were no arguments based on facts for deciding that it was time to stop working on them. It was only a feeling—not science deciding, but intuition—and he asked himself whether that was enough.

He flicked his cigarette into the sand and went back into the house. He gathered up the notes and took them into the bedroom.

"Open up," he said again. "Come on—come on."

In the morning when he awoke, he remembered the Monday morning meeting. Every Monday morning now they all met in the small conference room on the research office corridor—everyone involved in the project—and they talked and reviewed what they had done, and talked and tried to decide whether anyone had learned anything, and talked and talked and talked. To Tom, a morning in a meeting was a morning wasted.

Now, if he decided to go on with these cultures, he wouldn't get to figure the new variations until Monday afternoon, and it would be Tuesday before Moose mixed the broths and three more days would be lost. Damn it, he had a block against that Monday morning meeting—he never remembered to plan for it. He decided to eliminate the two deadbeats, and while he drank his coffee he worked out variations for the other five. Then he thought that, even getting these changes to Moose early Monday morning, it would be ten days from today before he would know any more than he knew now. He went into the bedroom and got dressed and went over to Enright to do it himself today.

Walking down the deserted corridor, Tom passed the constant-temperature room where he could hear the machines shaking the flasks and came up to Derrick's laboratory where, in a corner near the door, he could see a pile of Will Caroline's little brown envelopes in which people had sent in soil samples. There was a good-sized stack of them there, waiting to be plated, and Tom wondered who had sent them and where they had come from.

Glancing in through the glass panel, Tom thought that Derrick ran a good lab here—turned out a lot of work in a small area—and he walked on. Then he stopped and went back and looked again. Slowly his eyes moved around the room. He saw the rows of Petri dishes on which Derrick had plated soil samples. He saw the test tubes of agar slants, hundreds of them, on which Derrick first grew the pure cultures. He saw the constant-temperature oven in which there were several hundred more cultures growing in broths. He saw the refrigerator where Derrick stored the cultures until the biochemists took them. Here in this room, he thought, in every stage of development, there were thousands and thousands of cultures. And, from the soil still in those envelopes, there would be thousands more.

Thoughtfully Tom looked at the refrigerator, where there were hundreds of cultures he could take at any time, and then he left and walked on to his own laboratory. He mixed the broths and put them into the autoclave, and while he waited for them to cool before inoculating them, he went back to the mycology laboratory again. The answer to their search, the one microbe they were looking for—and all they needed was one—could be anywhere in there—in any one of the test tubes, on any one of the Petri dishes, or in any one of the soil samples still lying there in an envelope waiting to be plated. Or it could be in none of them.

"I feel like one of those characters in a melodrama," he said a few hours later to Max, "locked in a room with a bomb. He's looking for it frantically—he's sure he's searched every inch—and he knows it's there—and yet he can't find it."

They were sitting on the lower dock, where Tom had come after he'd finished at Enright to wait for Diana. With time to kill he had been fussing with the old boat, still tied at the lower dock. Max and Constance had come along, on their way out for a late sail, and had stopped to talk.

"Still can't see daylight?" Max said.

162

"Nothing new." Tom looked around the bay for Diana's red sail without seeing it. It would be another hour before the first boats began to come in, and in the middle of a warm sleepy afternoon the dock was almost as quiet as Enright had been this morning. Off the end of the dock McCarthy, the maintenance man, was working on a boat. On shore a girl was painting, partly hidden by her easel. Otherwise the dock appeared to be deserted.

"You notice Derrick's lab lately, Max?" he said.

"Notice what?"

"He's got quite an assembly line going—thousands of cultures coming along."

"Make you nervous?"

"No—well—only that it makes me think all the more that it's time to chuck the old ones—except for that one that looks good—and move on."

"Do it, then."

"I don't have anything to back up the decision. No reason. It's just a feeling—"

"Do it anyway. Find the reason later."

Constance settled against a post and turned toward the sun. "It just isn't safe to let two Enright people get together any more," she said. "You're grounded for the day wherever the collision takes place."

"Constance, darling," Max said, "you're a long-suffering girl of great virtue."

"I know, darling," Constance said serenely. "Give me a cushion out of that duffel and let me practice my virtue in comfort."

Max pulled a canvas cushion out of the duffel bag they were carrying to the boat. Then he said, "There's that girl again."

"What girl?"

"That friend of Will Caroline's—maybe. Remember the placebo story? Will liked one and not the other. What were their names?"

"Oh, her. Welles—Hope and Amity," Tom said without looking around. Maybe, he thought, throwing them out first and finding the reason later made as much sense as anything else.

"That's a good-looking girl, Tom. You ought to go find out for Will which one she is."

"She's the wrong one, I'm pretty sure. Anyway, he's probably found out for himself by now."

"She must be an artist," Constance said. "She's painting some-

163

thing out on the bay. Do you suppose she's painting Enright?"

"Why would anyone paint Enright?" Max said. "Constance, don't you think that's a pretty good-looking girl? You're blind, Tom."

Tom laughed. "She's not my type. She knows too much for me."

"You ever talk to her?"

Tom scanned the bay again for Diana's boat and then, without interest, he glanced around at the Welles girl. From where he sat, the easel hid her face, but he could see the sun striking gold lights on her brownish blond hair. He looked away. "Max," he said, "I've worked since I was eleven. I've waited on tables and played a piano in high-class dives and low-class dives and I've seen too many dames who knew too much. They knew everything. That type bores me. I want a girl who can still be surprised now and then. It's refreshing. If she has to sin, let it be on the side of innocence. O.K.?"

Max looked at him carefully. "Tom, you're not getting serious about that little Brainard girl?"

"No—" Tom laughed. "She just thinks I'm a great man for all the wrong reasons."

But even while he said it, he took another quick look at the bay, and he thought that the Welles girl there on the beach could be Aphrodite rising out of the sea, and there would be no room for her with him now and he knew it.

"O.K.—but you're wrong." Then Max said, "You know, Tom, I don't know much about microbes—I can't help you until you're ready to get out the antibiotic—but I'd probably figure them a lot like people—most of them pretty crummy and damn few you could expect much from. That'd be my attitude."

Max looked out along the dock for a minute, and Tom saw that he was watching a man on a cabin cruiser tied nearby at the upper dock. Then Max motioned toward the boat and said, "Look there, Tom—on that big white boat. There's a classic example of what I mean. The heavy man standing with a glass in his hand—red face —see him? His name is Harry Pack. Take a look at him. The red face is the result of uninterrupted drinking. He never keeps his mouth shut for long, so any minute now you'll get the full impact of his remarkable personality. He's mean—loud—crude. He's so egocentric, he's practically a clinical case."

Suddenly, as though on cue, from Harry Pack's boat came a loud voice. "Now, goddammit, see here . . ." A burst of foul oaths followed.

"He has a fat son who is his near equal for charm."

A plump, petulant-looking boy of about ten stepped hurriedly off the boat and stood looking resentfully at his father, who went into the galley and slammed the door.

"When I first came to Enright," Max said, "while I was waiting for Constance to decide to marry me, I lived next door to this splendid fellow."

"Oh, I remember him!" Constance said. "He was a great favorite of yours!"

"Indeed he was. He had a modest income then. During the war he made money and now he's rich."

Suddenly Harry Pack's voice cut into the silence again, loud and angry. "Now, what the hell's going on here?" he demanded. "Who's that?"

Looking around, Tom saw that another young boy, carrying a fishing pole and a bucket, had apparently come in from the end of the dock and had somehow become involved with Pack and son.

"He don't believe it's your boat," young Pack whined. "Says if it's my father's boat, how come I can't even go on it?"

For a few seconds there was an unnatural silence. Then, bottle in hand, Harry Pack stepped off the boat. The boy read a threat in his manner and his eyes widened uncertainly.

"I din't do nothin', mister," he said.

With his free hand Harry Pack seized the boy's shirt, while he took a quick look up and down the dock to be sure no one was around. "Listen, you little dock rat—"

Quickly Tom stood up and Constance said, "Oh, Max!"

"Boy," Pack said, "you need a little lesson." He pressed forward and the boy tried to twist out of his grasp. "Now, first you apologize to my boy!"

"I din't do nothin'!"

"I say you apologize. And then you get off this dock and stay off. You little bastards are dirtyin' up this place—"

"Hey, cut that out!" Tom called. The rail was closer than the stairs, and in a few steps he reached it and climbed over, with Max a step behind him.

Startled that he had an audience, Harry Pack whipped about, and the boy took advantage of the moment to twist away and race for shore. Stunned, Pack stared at Tom and Max. Then, with a grunt of rage, he heaved himself onto his boat and disappeared below.

Slowly Tom walked with Max to the steps, noticing as he did that the Welles girl had come onto the dock too and was walking back to shore with the boy, talking to him.

Back on the lower level where Constance was waiting, Max opened the duffel bag and pulled out a flask and some cups and poured three drinks. Tom took out a cigarette and saw that it was his last one. He smoked it down to an inch before he threw it into the water.

A moment later Harry Pack stepped off his boat and, with his son hurrying along behind, strode toward shore. At the steps he met McCarthy, who had come in from the boat he was working on.

"I tell you, McCarthy," Pack said, "it's a crime when a decent citizen can't come out on an afternoon with his boy—"

McCarthy grunted and looked uncomfortable.

Pack put an arm around his shoulder. "Speedy, you know it and I know it—the goddam trouble is there ain't many of us left."

"You see what I mean?" Max said. "There's an example of an egg that's so rotten that no amount of doctoring can fix him up. Think about this, Tom. Harry Pack is loaded with money—big success— big wheel at the country club. He has a handsome house, big car, big boat—he travels all over on business. Now, all those ingredients, supposedly, should turn even an extremely ugly duckling into something of a swan, and this guy is untouched. He's still a crumb."

Tom looked at Max, knowing that he was only half serious in relating this to microbes—but he was coming awfully close to what Tom had been feeling.

Then Constance gasped and said, "Oh, no! He's not starting again!"

Harry Pack had gone into Tollie's and come out again, and now he was walking toward the Welles girl, who, to Tom's surprise, had turned her easel around and had found herself a model to paint— the young fisherman, who seemed to be enjoying himself enormously.

"Sister," Pack called, while he was still a few feet away, "how'd you like to paint a good-looking boy instead of that brat?"

The Welles girl looked up. "I've already started," she said.

"I mean to pay you, sister," Pack said. "I want it—I pay."

"No, thank you," Miss Welles said.

"Well, how about when you're done, then? How about after you've knocked off this one?"

166

"I won't be around here."

"Well—" Pack said. "Maybe some other time."

She didn't answer, and the boy, seeing that he was not going to be replaced and sensing that this constituted a victory, grinned and started to whistle, terribly off key.

Instantly Harry Pack snapped around. "Don't get fresh with me, kid!"

The boy stopped whistling, puckered up his lips uncertainly to continue, and then, seeing that Miss Welles was getting to work again, he straightened his mouth. Miss Welles smiled and gave her model a quick wink. "You can whistle!" she said.

The boy's face went into a wide grin and he whistled terribly.

"Sister, I'm not through with you," Pack said, his face going very red.

Without pausing in her work, Miss Welles said, "I am through with you."

"Tom," Max said as he stood up and held out a hand to Constance, "go ask that girl if she ever fed a placebo to a dying fish!"

After they had gone, while he sat alone on the dock, waiting for Diana to come in, Tom looked over again at the Welles girl, who was preoccupied now with her model. Of course Max was right, he thought—she had to be Amity. He had known it when he saw her on the dock with the boy. And then he thought that for a few minutes today there had been a flash of that wonderful quality that Will Caroline had remembered—but what about the rest of the time? What had happened, he wondered, to change her so much from the little girl who had been Will Caroline's pet?

Then his thoughts went to where they always did these days—to the microbes—and he mulled over what Max, half facetiously, had suggested. Maybe that was it, he thought. Maybe with these bugs you could fool around forever—and some of them, no matter what you did, would still be no good. They would still be crumbs. I wonder—he thought—I wonder if that's it.

A heavy tree branch stretched across the window of the small conference room and beyond it you could see the pipes around the fermentation building and the thin tails of steam that rose up from them.

Sitting in the Monday morning meeting, growing restless as he always did when it had dragged on for more than half an hour, Tom

167

shifted about and glanced down the table at Will Caroline, who each week sat through these meetings as he was sitting now, eased down a little in his chair, relaxed and attentive, while he let every man have his say. Sometimes Tom wondered where Will found the patience to listen this way. They talked so much—and there wasn't that much to say.

Every week it was the same, he thought. They talked and talked —always about the literature—always about what had already been done—by somebody else. They never talked about what they had observed themselves or deduced themselves—or about an idea that one of them had thought of himself, that he'd like to test, that might be right or that might be wrong. They talked only about what others had observed and deduced, only about ideas that someone else had thought of and handed down to them, all tested and tried—a neat package of facts—in the literature. About those things they talked lovingly, caressing each little fact that could be depended upon. Their thinking was dead, Tom thought. It was retrospective and sterile, and every Monday morning they came in here and performed the same ritual—the ritual of the adoration of the past.

"I've been reviewing the work of the past month," Dr. Morrissey was saying, "and there are some procedures that seem pretty irregular."

"What kind of procedures, Claude?" Will Caroline said.

"We haven't made the kind of progress I'd like to see," Morrissey said, "and there are several things that bother me . . ."

Tom stopped listening. He was sitting in his usual place, in a corner and back a little from the table so he could move around. In his lap was the assay report that Gates had given him just before the meeting. The report was on the cultures from his second batch, and, just as before, two looked promising and the rest uninteresting. Now Tom asked himself what he was going to do about them, knowing that what he wanted to do was throw them all out—all except those two.

"Obviously we're having precursor problems," Morrissey was saying.

"That seems to be a real problem," Harrup agreed. "And it's important."

"Now, here's a case where there are too many irregularities," Morrissey said. "I don't know whether these irregularities are the result

168

of ignorance—or of something else. But I think we ought to review what we do know, while we're all here, and find out."

"Might be sound," Harrup said. "Get it all on the table."

Tom sighed. Nobody respected the literature any more than he did or followed it more closely. But there wasn't that much of it—and you could read it anywhere, anytime. You didn't have to sit here every Monday morning rehashing the same old stuff, as though the barren soil would yield something new if only you raked it over enough!

He fingered the report in his lap and then he opened it and began to read it through again.

"I want to bring together the facts we're sure of," Morrissey said, "and establish some rules—standard rules for everyone. Now, the first thing I question is the sloppy mass-production approach with these broths. I want a custom-made broth worked out for each culture."

Abruptly Tom looked up from the assay report. "What kind of custom-made broth?" he said. "What do you mean?"

"I mean that each microbe would do its best job in its own particular broth. That's an established fact. Don't you agree, Dr. Derrick?"

"Well, sir," Derrick said slowly, "in theory, yes, but—"

Morrissey held up a hand. "Just let me finish, Dr. Derrick. Now, then—it follows logically that each culture should be getting that broth—carefully tailored to its individual needs."

"We're doing that," Tom said. "We're making changes every week to try to find the individual needs."

"But not enough."

"Not enough! It's more than enough."

"I want more individual work on each, Dr. Cable. Much more work."

Tom closed the report in his lap and put it on the table. "I think we're fussing too much now," he said. "I think if the culture still isn't doing much after three or four weeks, we shouldn't waste any more time on it."

"Maybe you just haven't hit on the right broth yet," Harrup said. "How do you know?"

"The fault, Dr. Cable," Morrissey said, "may not be with the microbe—but with you." He took out his pipe and put it into his mouth and sat back as though to say the discussion was finished.

Stubbornly Tom shook his head. "We should give them a fair chance, but if they don't do much we should forget about them—throw them out and move on and see what we can do with some others."

Morrissey was becoming upset and he showed it as he fussed with his pipe, filling it and tamping the tobacco. "Well, this is ridiculous. The one established fact we have—the only thing we're sure of—is the importance of the precursor—and you want to ignore it."

"I'm not ignoring it!" Tom said. "But we've only got so much lab space and only so many technicians—and the constant-temperature room holds only so many flasks and stir pots—and someplace the work reaches a point of diminishing return. At some point you have to say this is enough."

Morrissey turned to Harrup. "What do you say to this, Neil?"

"Very risky—with no new information. I'd say we have to be a lot surer about what we're doing than we are now."

"George?" Morrissey turned to Weir.

"For the present I'm working everything very thoroughly," Weir said. "It seems the only safe thing to do—until we know more."

"Of course it's the only safe thing to do," Morrissey said. "It's the only rational, scientific approach."

The only rational scientific approach—the only safe thing to do. Safe for what? Tom looked at the sober faces around him, and then suddenly he thought, No, not *what*—*whom*. Safe for *whom*. Because that's the way they're thinking. Not like men planning to win! They don't expect to win. They expect to lose, and every step they take is evidence for some future jury that will judge them—and they won't make a move that can't be justified with good solid accepted facts. Then, later if anyone tries to blame them, they'll bring out the literature to prove that, at the time, their decisions were the logical ones. They won't do anything unless the literature serves them up a reason that satisfies everyone—all around—one hundred per cent. They have to be sure—even if they're wrong.

He began to get mad. "We can't just sit around here waiting for the literature to give us the word," he said, "like some religious sect. When everything is in the literature, we won't be doing this. It'll all be done."

"Well, let's not start that again," Morrissey said.

"We can't just play it safe!" Tom's voice rose. "We have to take some chances. We must have the courage to make some decisions for ourselves—"

"A decision must be based on facts," Morrissey said.

"Not always! Sometimes you don't have the facts. Sometimes you have to decide on intuition."

And then he thought, You must have the courage to take a chance. All right—then take it. Don't just talk about it. Take it.

Morrissey fussed with his pipe, trying to appear calm, but under his ear a muscle fluttered. "Will," he said, "Dr. Cable puts on a good performance—and maybe we should remind him that he's a biochemist, not a football coach giving a pep talk—but there isn't one word in the literature to back up this notion. When he can bring me written evidence in a reputable journal, I'll sanction this in my department—and not until."

"I go along with that," Harrup said. "That's certainly reasonable."

Hasn't it ever occurred to them, Tom thought, that everything in the literature had to have a start somewhere—that the literature has been built up out of thousands of little pieces—and that every one of those pieces had to have a beginning? Every little piece had to be seen firsthand—for the first time—or deduced for the first time—and thought about for the first time—and tried and tested and proved. For all of it there had to be a first time—when it wasn't read in a journal but was observed directly, excitedly, somewhere, by someone in his own laboratory.

He looked at the assay report and he knew that he had decided. He had decided before the meeting but now he was sure. "The cultures in this report have had three chances," he said. "I'm through with them—all but two."

"Oh, no," Morrissey said.

"Well, now," Will Caroline said calmly, "let's just look at it this way. Are you satisfied in your own mind, Tom, that they've had enough?"

"They had five original broths and enough variations to convince me it's a waste of time to work on them any longer. Even if you squeezed a little out of them, getting them pure would be like Madame Curie working through tons of pitch for an infinitesimally small amount."

"But that amount was worth it," Harrup said.

171

"The antibiotic problem is not the same as the radium problem."

"You'd like to think that," Harrup said. "But you don't know. You're not sure."

"Well, it's not in the literature, if that's what you mean," Tom said.

"That's exactly what we mean," Morrissey said.

"The literature is a foundation to build on—not an altar at which to worship!"

"It seems to me," Will Caroline put in easily, "that right now, when we're just beginning and when we aren't really sure of anything, it might be a good idea to give every man his head a little. Dr. Weir is working his over carefully. Let's give Dr. Cable a chance to do it his way. When we begin to learn more, we can talk it over again. We have all the original cultures and a record of everything that's been done, so if he throws something out, it's not lost to us forever."

The muscle under Morrissey's ear twitched again. "In that case, I will not be responsible."

"That's fair enough," Will Caroline said.

"Then who is going to be responsible?"

"I'm responsible," Tom said. "I'm doing it. I'm responsible."

"I hardly think that would satisfy the company—or the board," Morrissey snapped. "Will, I want this made very clear to the company and to the board."

"I'm responsible, Claude," Will Caroline said good-naturedly. "The board knows that. But we can tell them again."

Afterward, when the meeting was over, Tom sat in his office with the new report in front of him.

"Come on, girls," he said with a smile. "Talk to me!" But he didn't say it the same as before. In an offstage whisper they had talked, and he thought maybe that was their only message.

He took out the records of the two cultures that he liked and worked out new broths for them. And out of this batch, that was all he was going to do. He'd picked up some new cultures this morning and he was going to push them through. And next week he was going to pick up some more. And out of the first batch, he decided, he was going to take the one he liked and start to purify it.

He walked into his laboratory, and without a pang he poured the rest of the broths down the drain.

With beer you filtered off the yeast mycelium and you had a clear broth which was the beer, and you sterilized it and bottled it and that was the end.

With this you filtered off the mycelium and you had a clear broth and that was the beginning. "From now on, Moose," Tom said, "we look at it this way. There's only one thing in there that we know anything about, and that's the antibiotic. There's only one thing in there we can measure, and that's the antibiotic. And there's only one thing we want—the antibiotic. The antibiotic is X. Everything else is an impurity. From now on, everything we do is designed to isolate X—to get rid of everything else—and separate out that little bit of antibiotic."

He handed the broth to Moose. "O.K., filter off the mycelium in a Büchner funnel and let's go. From now on, its number is EA 50."

ELEVEN

"C AL," Will Caroline said, "have you ever thought that there are men who are afraid of that which is simple?"

Callie looked around from the stone wall of the open deck where she was standing. "I was just noticing how much earlier the boats are starting back—the bay is almost empty." Then she said, "Do you mean that some men mistrust anything simple—that they feel there must be more to it than meets the eye?"

"I don't know," Will said. "I'm not sure whether I mean that—or something else. But lately, I've noticed that some men seem to resent anything simple. For some reason simplicity disturbs them. I ran into it today—twice—so I've been thinking about it."

Callie came over and sat near him. "I suppose it's a question of a man's makeup, Will. Some men back away from anything complex."

"That's easier to understand."

"Yes," she agreed. "And more common, I'm sure."

"I used to think it was a natural human urge to want to simplify, to see relationships that made sense—likenesses in things that seemed different. I used to think that this was common to all men. Now I'm beginning to think that's not necessarily so." Will paused a moment while the somewhat disorganized thoughts he'd had about this during the day went through his mind. "We had our Monday morning meeting today—with all the usual differences of opinion."

"But that doesn't bother you, does it?" Callie said.

"No—on the whole I think all that give and take is healthy," he said. "But today I realized that there's a deep philosophical difference behind these arguments."

"Just one?"

Will laughed. "There are probably as many philosophies in that room on a Monday morning as there are men. But this one has me thinking. Lately Tom Cable has been arguing for less work on each culture because we don't know much, and the others have been arguing for more work for the same reason. Today I realized that Tom is, in effect, saying, 'Let's keep it simple until we know enough to complicate it,' and the others have been saying, 'Let's keep it complicated until we know enough to simplify it.' This makes for quite a difference."

"Quite a difference," Callie agreed.

"All along I've been wondering about this gulf that I see developing. Here's a group of men—and on the whole they come to this project pretty much equal. Similar backgrounds, similar training —they've all been with it the same length of time—they share all the information. You'd think they would begin to find some small areas of agreement. But they don't—they go farther and farther apart. Of course, there's an age difference. Harrup and Morrissey are older. Maybe Tom Cable is young and foolish. But then, Tom's arguments appeal to me and I'm not young." He grinned. "Only foolish, maybe."

"Darling"—Callie touched his face affectionately—"you could never be foolish. Go on. Some like it simple and some like it complicated—and you are sitting here wondering what sinister motives are lurking behind the difference."

"That's right, Cal. Why do they want to keep it complicated? Is it because they can't see the possibilities of simplifying? Is there a blind spot there? Or is it that their minds grasp complexity more easily, so they feel no need to simplify as some men do?"

"Oh, that's being awfully charitable, Will."

He laughed. "But isn't it possible that the blind spot is on the other side? Maybe Tom is trying to oversimplify."

Callie thought a minute. "It's possible—I suppose. But oversimplifying is a form of evasion, and it doesn't seem that Tom would have reached that stage yet."

"That's my feeling," Will Caroline said. "Besides—there's more to my story. Let me tell you what happened this afternoon. Tom began to purify his first antibiotic, and you know Ade likes to know what's happening—see what's going on—so I went down there with him. Tom was just starting to purify with a technique called solvent extraction. Cal, did I ever tell you about our colored cook back in Virginia when I was a boy—her name was Hester?"

"Oh, I think you've mentioned her. Why?"

"Well, Hester used to make soap—not for us, for herself. She used to save all the cooking grease and fats in a big tin. And then when she had enough, she'd make her soap."

"Will, what does this have to do with Tom's solvent extraction?"

175

"I'm working up to it. Well, once I went into the kitchen to watch, and first Hester melted down her grease and then she poured in a bucket of water."

"Water—for soap?" Callie said. "Why?"

"That was my question, and Hester said that she had to get the salt out of the grease—the salt would spoil the soap—and that adding water would do it. Well, obviously, it wasn't just a matter of washing it off—the salt was all mixed up in that grease—so I asked her how that was accomplished. And she said—now listen to this, Cal—"

"I'm listening," Callie said. "I'm spellbound."

"She said, 'Salt jes' go in the water—that's all. This grease an' water don't stay mixed up. The water sink down on the bottom an' the salt's in it—an' that's all.' Well, now I know what happened. First, grease isn't soluble in water, so grease and water don't stay mixed. Water is heavier and settles to the bottom. Second, salt is more soluble in water than it is in grease, so although it was already in grease, when Hester added water, the salt left the grease and went into the water—and as the water settled to the bottom, the salt went with it and the grease was free of it. Then she could proceed with making some pretty good soap. Now, back to solvent extraction. Actually I've known about this technique for years— it's used to purify penicillin—but today, watching Tom use it on a small scale in his lab, I suddenly realized that this was just what Hester did when she began to make soap!"

Callie burst out laughing. "Will, that's lovely! How?"

"Well, the fermentation broths are run in water, and Tom used a solvent that isn't soluble in water—just as Hester's grease wasn't soluble in water. Today he used butyl alcohol—and he mixed it up with the broth that contained the antibiotic. But they didn't stay mixed—just as Hester's grease and water didn't stay mixed—and in a little while the broth settled to the bottom, because it's heavier, and the butyl alcohol was on the top. Tom was hoping that the antibiotic would be more soluble in the butyl alcohol than in the broth, because then, like Hester's salt, it would leave the broth and go into the alcohol. And he hoped that not too many impurities would go into the alcohol with it. He drained out the broth into one flask and the butyl alcohol into another and sent samples of both to assay to find out whether it worked—whether the antibiotic went into the alcohol or stayed in the broth."

"Darling!" Callie laughed. "Obviously we should send for Hester at once. She may have a great store of this kind of knowledge!"

Will smiled. "Sometimes I wonder how much more we know that we don't know we know. Of course, Tom's technique is a little more complicated. He has to add an acid or a base to combine with the antibiotic to make the salt so that it will work—and then he has to get the antibiotic out of the alcohol, back into clear water. Hester didn't want her salt back, and he does want his antibiotic. But that's not hard and the idea is the same. Well, by the time I'd thought of how Hester had used solvent extraction for years, Morrissey had come in, too. He was still sore about the meeting and complaining about going ahead like this before anyone knew what they were doing—and I could see he was upsetting Ade—so I broke in and told them about Hester."

"And—?"

"Ade thought it was a good story. He laughed and said it was good to know something about this was simple. But Morrissey didn't like it. Later, I told Harrup and he didn't like it either."

Callie laughed. "Well, really, Will—how would you feel if you had a Ph.D. degree and learned that Hester had known what you know all along?"

"So then I was right back where I was in the morning—after the meeting—asking myself why they wanted it to be complex. Why does it upset them to think that even one little step about it might be simple?"

"I don't know, Will," Callie said. "I suppose there could be any number of reasons. Maybe it makes them feel more important if they think they're struggling with something terribly complicated."

"Gives them a sense of their own value from the size of the problem?"

"Something like that."

"Or do they want to be sure that management understands how complicated it is? Or do they even know what they're doing? Maybe they really believe that every step of the way has to be complex."

Will was silent a minute, thinking about it. Looking across the bay, he remembered that last night, as they had sat down to dinner, he'd looked over at Enright and had noticed the lights. Every year, he thought, it was when he looked up before dinner one night and saw that the lights were already on that he realized that summer was ending.

177

"Even with Tom," he said, "you could ask whether his decision is independent of all other factors. Summer is almost over—time is passing and he feels it." He looked back at Callie. "A man is so much more than the moment, Cal. What really decides? His head? His heart? Memories—endurance—his energy of the moment? How do you know what goes on inside a man that weights the scales? The least complicated part of a man is his conscious thinking. If he tries, he can usually find arguments to back up almost any decision. Logic is simple compared to the things that are beyond thinking—blood, humor, passion. Tom says we should have the courage to make a decision without all the facts, but couldn't the others say we should have the courage not to decide until we have enough facts—that we should keep our heads? You see, you can argue it either way."

"Yes, you can, Will, with logic—but not with that blood and passion—"

"But even there I could ask, Do I lean to Tom because I, too, would like to think there are at least a few things about it that might be simple? Maybe with both of us the simplicity isn't in the nature of the work but only in some ancient yearning in ourselves."

She didn't answer, and Will's thoughts moved on. After a moment he said, "Sometimes I think that men today are contemptuous of nothing so much as simplicity. Philosophers don't talk about simple truths any more. They develop complicated systems—and the systems become more important than what they embrace. Men dwell on words—and semantics becomes more important than what a man has to say." He paused. The tide was going out and he could hear the water slushing off the rocks below. "There's a lesson there in Hester and her soap," he said. "Man becomes sophisticated and divorces himself from simplicity. He outsmarts himself. He loses sight of the things he knows naturally and instinctively, and he has to learn them over again, intellectually."

He turned and smiled at her. "Sometimes I wonder how much he gains, Cal—and how much he loses."

From the window of the bedroom, late that afternoon, Ade Hale looked out at his young wife coming across the beach, moving at a leisurely pace, with the children trailing behind her. While he watched, the boy Jonathan, who was three, dropped a shovel in the sand, bent over to retrieve it and spilled a pail of shells he was carrying. Hale watched a minute, knowing what would happen. The boy began to pick up the shells, and the girl Ann, who was five and thin and brown and long-boned like Helen, walked back to help him, and Helen stopped and waited.

Ade Hale gave his head an amused shake and turned away. He didn't have the patience to stand here while the shells were gathered up. If he'd been with the boy, he would have told him to come along, that the shells would be there in the morning. But Helen, with the patience so characteristic of her and so necessary, he knew, to live with him, would wait until Jon had finished, without even urging him to hurry.

Hale walked across the plainly decorated bedroom with its extra-wide double bed, into his dressing room. In this big house most of the rooms were furnished rather luxuriously, but his own study and his dressing room and the bedroom he shared with Helen were almost Spartan, which was more to his taste. He had bought this house, which was larger than he wanted, because it was alone, around the bend, without neighbors. The only house that could be seen from here was the tip of Will Caroline's out on the point.

In his dressing room, Hale found the slacks and the baggy sweat-shirt that Helen laid out for him each evening. He had no idea where she kept them or how many he had or when they were replaced. He only knew that every evening they were there—and in the winter a bulky sweater was with them.

On his dresser was a picture of Helen that she had given him six years ago, just before they were married. She was twenty-five then and on the way, she always said, to being an old maid. If anything, she looked younger and lovelier now—although most men, he knew, would consider Helen quite plain, which was their loss. She was even-featured, with brown hair and eyes, a tall, thin, gentle girl whom no one had noticed until he came along, and when he married her, everyone had been astonished. Ade Hale could not have cared less. He had known what he wanted—and he wanted Helen. In a world where most people were mixed up, she seemed peculiarly to have retained her sanity and serenity. She was a lot like Will Caroline, and there were people who didn't notice Will either—at least not right away—but in their quiet way they were both absolutely dependable and sane. And if there was one thing Ade Hale was thoroughly sick of by the time he became president of Enright, it was people who talked a good game and had nothing to back it up.

He finished changing and looked out the window again, and then he heard Helen turning the children over to the maid and, a moment later, coming up the stairs.

Her skin was warm from the sun as she came over to kiss him. She was wearing a two-piece bathing suit, and she reached around and unbuttoned the top and began to take it off. "I'll shower and dress, Ade, and be right with you."

Lying on the bed, he heard her go into her bathroom and turn on the shower and move back into her dressing room.

"Helen—" She came to the door. "Come out and talk to me for a few minutes," he said.

Drawing on a white silk robe, she came across the room and sat on the bed. Faintly through the closed door of her bathroom he could hear water running in the shower. He touched her warm skin under the loose silk robe. "You're so young," he said. "Next to me, you're very young."

She smiled. "There's no difference between us, Ade. You know that."

Her skin was young, and the slender lines of her body, and her breasts were young, a little fuller since she'd had children but still small and firm and young.

"A generation is thirty years, Helen," he said, "according to people who figure these things. And that's something more than the difference between you and me—but not much more."

"That's all right for people who like to figure those things," she said, "but not for you and me."

Smiling down at him, she put a hand under his head, and for a moment he looked at her without speaking. She was calm and quiet and young, he thought, and she was as passionate as he was and she loved him totally and unquestioningly. Whatever he was to her—lover, companion, father substitute—he was all of it, and she loved him fiercely and beyond anything else in the world. "You're part of a different age," he said. "And you'll live through a different age."

"Ade," she teased, "are you planning to leave me for an older woman?"

He laughed. Then he said, "A generation is thirty years, and a century is a hundred years—but how do you measure an age? History gives pat names to its ages—the age of reason, the age of electricity—now the atomic age. But when does an age begin? When

180

everyone knows about it—or when one man begins to think about it—or when a few people begin to believe in it? When does an age become an age?"

"Does it matter when it gets a name? Why do you care?"

"I don't. I only care how long it takes to be born once it's conceived. Births can be painful"—he reached for her hand—"and drugs—and my company—are pushing into a new age—and we don't know enough—and it hurts."

She sat quietly on the bed, listening without comment because no comment was necessary as long as she listened.

"How long," he said, "from the brink, when you know next to nothing, to the heart of an age when you know almost everything and it gets a name and a place in history? The path from ignorance to knowledge can be one of the longest and bloodiest trails in the world."

"You're not satisfied with the way it's going?" she said.

"We're ignorant—and I don't like ignorance. And the ignorance breeds inefficiency, and I don't like inefficiency. And I sense mediocrity in some of our people and I have no use for a half-baked job."

"Still—in the beginning you thought it was worth a try."

"I still think it's worth a try—for a while. But I'm completely objective about it and I'll stay that way. If things don't straighten out —we can survive without it. I won't let it get in the way of my business."

She understood him and she loved him for what he was. It wouldn't occur to her to object to his statement. He wasn't a sentimental man and she wouldn't try to feed him sentimentality.

"I'm a businessman," he said. "By my own choice. As long as this makes sense, I'll stick to it. When it stops making sense, I'll stop and it will stop. This isn't a crusade, and I'm not a martyr."

"Was it only because you felt the age was at hand that you decided to try?"

"It was the only reason for deciding—there wasn't any other. And my sense of history is strong enough so that I'd rather have tried reasonably and failed than have passed it by altogether. I'm not that frightened a man."

"You're not in any sense a frightened man, Ade."

He smiled at her and drew her hand to his lips. "But I have a sense of impermanence, too. Just because we're in the wave sweeping up on the shore doesn't mean we're touched by the hand of

God and chosen to ride the crest. We could be drowned, too, and I won't let that happen. In everything else we do, we stop and appraise our results regularly—and we'll appraise this, too. And when it doesn't add up, we'll stop."

"Is that what you're thinking, Ade—that you'll have to decide to give it up?"

She touched his face and he closed his hand over hers. "I can't know that yet—there are too many factors involved—too little information—competition—time. Time costs money and ours is limited. I never expected results so soon—but we're caught in a trap of ignorance. We're wallowing in it."

She bent over him and his hand left hers and went to her narrow waist and moved up her young body and he drew her down to him.

"Yes," he said, feeling her warm against him, and her arms around him and her young breasts against him. "You're right. I think that's the decision I'll have to make. I don't really believe we can do it. And I'm only willing for a little while to try."

TWELVE

HERE ARE PERSONALITIES and institutions—or segments of institutions—which are totally unsuited to each other. Occasionally an early recognition of the incompatibility by both parties results in quick divorce. In other cases, the recognition is one-sided. The more energetic of the parties plunges on about his business with never a sideward glance, while the other grows tense, understanding that an explosion is inevitable, and hoping that when it comes it will not be too messy. Such was the situation that existed between the two research directors of Enright and Dr. Patrick Henry Mills.

There was simply nothing in the experience of Drs. Morrissey and Harrup to prepare them for Dr. Mills. Although technically he would probably have fallen under Dr. Morrissey's jurisdiction, Dr. Morrissey didn't wish to press the claim. Dr. Harrup never made the claim. By default it evolved that Dr. Mills reported directly to Mr. Caroline.

But it wasn't only the ruling hierarchy who felt his impact. Mills affected everyone who worked with him in one of two ways, both extreme. People considered him either the worst thing that had ever happened to them or one of the best. His first technician, Miss Setall, a serious-minded young woman just graduated from college, resigned in tears, convinced that he was crazy. He talked to himself. All day long he said, "Kee-rist!" and "Hell—goddam—*shoo!*" He talked to the mice. He addressed himself continually to his superiors, which would not have been so bad if only they had been present. They were not. At the smallest provocation he would stand in his laboratory, in the presence of only Miss Setall and the white mice, and yell, "Mr. Caroline, I quit. I quit, Mr. Caroline." It was a disillusioning experience for Miss Setall. She was replaced by Miss Watterling, who was not much happier.

It was generally conceded that Mills's spectacular entrance at Enright was an omen—an omniscient finger pointing to the future, warning of what to expect. "It's uncanny," Will Caroline said to Callie about a week after Mills had reported for work. "There was that wild hysterical setting that he had nothing whatever to do with. And yet it was inevitable that mice be drowning or running loose or

183

that something equally unbelievable be happening at the exact moment that Mills arrived. It just couldn't be that he could walk in on a quiet normal morning and ask for a job like anyone else. With Mills, it just couldn't happen that way."

"Darling," Callie said, "have you seen his wife?"

"Not yet."

"I have. I spoke to her on the beach the other day. She's just as unbelievable. She looks like a Girl Scout who probably has earned about eighty-seven merit badges. At first I could hardly believe that this was his wife. But when you talk to her you begin to understand. She looks like a Campfire Girl and she has a mind like Madame de Staël."

"That fits," Will Caroline said. "That's about what I'd expect."

"Darling," Callie said, "it was a stroke of genius to hire him."

On a Friday morning in early September, Pearly Gates was feeling particularly depressed, and the reason for his depression was Miss Potter. He hadn't started to train Miss Potter in these new techniques, because Dr. Morrissey was still thinking of transferring her. But while he waited for Morrissey's decision, Gates reached a decision himself; namely, that he didn't want a change—he wanted Miss Potter. He had almost, but not quite, decided to take a stand on the issue. Meanwhile a conflict raged within him, with feelings of persecution on one hand and guilt on the other. He was miserable.

Unenthusiastically that morning, he checked the results of the resistant-organism and bacterial-spectrum tests that he had set up the day before on some new cultures. One culture was streptothricin and the others were active only against gram-positive organisms.

Recording the results, Gates sighed. This was another thing that bothered him. Every culture that had hit both gram-positive and gram-negative organisms on Derrick's plates had turned out to be streptomycin or streptothricin. Those two were becoming as thick as flies around a dead fish, but every other culture he had tested had been active only against gram-positive organisms. Not a single culture had turned up that was active against gram-negative alone —not a single new culture had turned up that was active against both. Gates didn't like to be unfair, but there certainly didn't seem to be any new broad-spectrum antibiotic, as Tom Cable had predicted there would be.

Turning to a rack of broths that George Weir had left earlier this morning, Gates looked at Miss Potter, tempted to call her over and show her right now how to do the test. Then he thought better of it. Dr. Morrissey would be pretty upset, and Gates still wasn't sure that he should make an issue of Miss Potter, much as he wanted to.

He saw that it was ten o'clock. "I'm going down for coffee, Miss Potter," he said. "When Dr. Weir comes, tell him I'll meet him down there."

"O.K.," Miss Potter said cheerfully.

"Tell him I'm sorry I couldn't wait for him," Gates said.

"Ah—I guess he'll find it himself O.K.," Miss Potter said. "I seen him do it once or twice before."

In the cafeteria Gates spotted Mills's red hair, and saw Derrick sitting with him and went over to join them.

"Ah'd feel a lot better if we were gettin' samples from more places," Derrick was saying as Gates came up to the table. "Ah'd like to get 'em from all over an' make a study of areas and types of soil and climate and see if ah can learn anything. An' besides, ah believe that then we'd get a greater variety of cultures. Now we're gettin' some things over and over."

"We're getting streptomycin and streptothricin over and over," Gates said.

"They're mighty common," Derrick agreed.

"And a couple of others, too," Gates said. "And they all just hit the gram-positive. Doesn't it kind of bother you, Charlie, that they all just hit the gram-positive?"

"Well," Derrick said easily, "ah figure it doesn't have to stay that way. That's another reason ah'd like to get samples from more places."

"I don't know," Gates said gloomily. "Everything that hits both turns out to be streptomycin or streptothricin. And for gram-positive we already have penicillin—"

"I need a new technician," Mills said, looking up from the journal he was reading. "Miss Watterling is as bad as Miss Setall. She thinks I'm crazy. I don't know why."

"You scare hell out of 'em, Pat," Derrick said.

"My wife understands me, why shouldn't my technician?" Mills said. "Pearly, you ought to give me Miss Potter. I'll bet she doesn't scare easily."

"Why not give me Miss Potter, Pearly?" Derrick said. "An' ah'll send Nick down to Pat. Nick's pretty tough, Pat."

Dejected, Gates stirred his coffee and changed the subject away from Miss Potter. "One that would hit gram-negative would be valuable," he said. "They're reserving streptomycin almost exclusively for t.b. now because resistance to it develops so quickly. They want to use it where it counts. There's a real need for something that's good against gram-negative. But when these cultures all just hit gram-positive and we have penicillin, I don't know—you're competing against something that's too good."

"Well—*shoo!*" Mills said. "There are troubles with penicillin, too. Resistance. Allergies. There are real allergies to penicillin. People take it—go into shock—die, even."

"But it's pretty rare," Gates said. "And on the whole penicillin's damn good."

"Well, now, there's a fine attitude," Mills said. "What about those poor devils who are allergic? Sir, I say they have a right to a medicine that won't send 'em into shock. Anything less is undemocratic."

Derrick laughed and even Gates smiled a little. "Ah believe something is bound to turn up sooner or later," Derrick said.

"*Shoo*, Pearly! You've got to have faith!" Mills said. "Like me. My faith is boundless. I always expect my mice to live. And I tell 'em so. Fellas, I tell 'em, you're going to be heroes. When I have to sacrifice 'em, I tell 'em they're heroes already. Only this morning I announced to the entire company present—of mice, that is—that they were all heroes. Well, hell, why not?"

"Is that when Miss Watterling blew up?" Derrick said.

"Broke a test tube full of lethal germs that we're nursing along against the day you fellows send us some work. I'll probably die of a wasting affliction, the way Miss Watterling breaks test tubes full of galloping diseases. Damn place reeks of formaldehyde from cleaning up the mess. I told my wife I'd probably fall in love with Miss Watterling, and she said, 'Happy landing.' But I think Miss Watterling will leave me."

"Mills, you're mad as a hatter," Derrick said.

"Right."

"Ah'd still feel better," Derrick said again, "if ah could figure a way to get a bigger variety of samples. They're coming mostly from New England and New York and New Jersey. An' the salesmen go down as far as Washington and into the Midwest. But ah'd like to get 'em from all over—the west, the south, the whole country. And from other parts of the world."

"I suppose that might make a difference," Gates said. He was feeling a little better.

"Why don't you go on that honeymoon you talked your poor wife out of, Pat?" Derrick said. "Take her around the world and stop every couple of miles and dig me some dirt."

"Well, shoo, whyn't you tell me? I would have." Mills drank his coffee and continued reading his journal.

"It might not make any difference. Ah mean, when we find a good one, it might come from our own front yard, but ah sure would like to get 'em more from all over—"

Mills had put down his journal and was looking hard at Derrick. "Charlie," he said, "how fussy you going to be about that dirt?"

"Well—hell—shoo!" Derrick grinned. "Ah'm not the fussy type, man."

"I mean would you mind a little good Oregon dirt if it happened to be mixed with a little Utah dirt and a little old Ohio dirt?"

"Ah'll tell you, Pat," Derrick said. "For a study ah'd need 'em separate. But what we're after isn't a study but an antibiotic. You find me any little ole mixed-up dirt with a good broad-spectrum antibiotic in it and ah'll just keep that culture producin' and multiplyin' and ah won't even ask where it came from."

Mills closed the magazine. "O.K., then—let's go get some! Let's go to New York tonight after work—let's all go—and get some dirt. Go phone Kate and tell her to be ready to leave at five-thirty. Pearly, go phone Madeline. We'll stay at our place. It's all closed up and covered with bed sheets, but what the hell?"

"What all did you have in mind, Pat?" Derrick said easily.

"We go to New York tonight, get up early tomorrow morning and go down to the warehouse district—and every time we see a truck from out West or down South—anywhere except New England— we'll scrape some dirt off the mudguard. Hell—shoo—we'll get you more dirt than you ever saw."

"Mills, you're nuts," Gates said.

"Why not?" Mills said. "Why not? We'll get dirt from every state of the union—piles of dirt! You know how much dirt there is in New York? Whole damn country sends dirt to New York. What do you say—you coming?"

"Ah do believe," Derrick said reflectively, "that we'd do as well at the Lincoln Tunnel. On the Jersey side."

Mills's face lit up with admiration. "I do believe we would!"

"They all come that way and stop to pay a toll," Derrick said soberly.

"Right! Ho-ho! Hundreds of trucks with their dirty mudguards, lined up to pay tolls—be the greatest single dirt collection of all time."

"It would be a hell of a variety of dirt," Gates agreed, suddenly getting into the mood. "By golly, we ought to do it!"

"Hell, we're going to do it! Only thing we're waiting for is your wives." Mills stood up. "Time to feed the mice. Steady, Miss Watterling, steady, now. Here I come. Tomorrow morning it's the Lincoln Tunnel—on the Jersey side. Action, that's what we need around here—action!"

With buoyant spirits and quickened step, Gates returned to his laboratory. In the doorway he paused and looked at Miss Potter. Action, he said to himself, that's what we need around here—action! "Dr. Morrissey," he muttered in a low voice, echoing Mills, "the hell damn with you!"

Miss Potter looked up, startled.

"Miss Potter," Gates said firmly. "Come over here. It's time you learned how to do this. If you can leave what you're doing, that is."

"This'll keep," Miss Potter said. "What's been keeping you?"

"I beg your pardon, Miss Potter?"

"You took long enough getting around to letting me in on it."

"I wanted to be sure of the techniques myself, Miss Potter." Gates moved a rack of test tubes into position. "These test tubes contain gram-positive disease germs—that other rack contains gram-negative."

"Dr. Gates," Miss Potter said, "did you go for coffee or did you take a quick snort in the men's room?"

"Pay attention, Miss Potter—"

"Don't worry, I got it. These are positive—those are negative."

"And here are samples of the broths we're testing for Dr. Weir —to learn whether the microbe is producing any more antibiotic than before." Gates struck a flame in the Bunsen burner and selected a test tube from Weir's rack. "Using all our sterile techniques, Miss Potter, we take one cubic centimeter of Dr. Weir's broth, and we dilute it in one hundred cubic centimeters of sterile water. And from that solution we remove one cubic centimeter and put it into a test tube of gram-positive germs. Have you got that?"

He wondered whether they really ought to go to New York tonight. In a way it was a hell of an idea, but still— He'd better decide because if they were going, he ought to let Madeline know.

"Next, we dilute the one-hundred-c.c. solution down to two hundred c.c. and out of that we take one c.c., and put it into the next test tube of germs. Then dilute from two hundred c.c. down to three hundred c.c. and put one c.c. out of that into the third tube. We continue this procedure for ten test tubes, and by the tenth tube we have a tenfold dilution, so that the antibiotic is ten times as weak in the tenth test tube as in the first. The first is ten times as strong as the last. That is the technique, Miss Potter."

"So then what? What do we do with it then?"

"We incubate these test tubes overnight, and in the morning some of them will be clear, which will mean that, in them, the antibiotic is working. And some of the test tubes will be turbid, which will mean that, in them, the antibiotic is not working and the germs are multiplying. In some of these the antibiotic will be too diluted to be effective, so it won't inhibit the growth of the germs. This particular antibiotic, in the last broth that Dr. Weir used, inhibited growth in only the first three tubes. If we have only three clear tubes again tomorrow, he will know that his new broth didn't produce any more antibiotic than the old one. But if we should have four clear tubes or five—or more—then he'll know he's had some improvement."

"What if all ten are clear?" Miss Potter said.

"Then Dr. Weir would be very happy. And we would go on with further dilutions. We always dilute to the point where it fails to inhibit the growth. We call that point the M.I.C. We always go on to the M.I.C., Miss Potter."

"What's that mean? M.I.C.?"

"Minimum inhibitory concentration."

"M.I.C.," she repeated. She would forget what it stood for, he knew, but she would remember what to do and what to call it. "O.K.," she said. "Let's get on with the rest."

"That's all there is for now," he said.

"That's all?"

"Yes."

"That's all!" she said. "That's all! And this is what it took you more'n a month to learn before you could show me?"

Dr. Gates cleared his throat and said, "Excuse me, Miss Potter. I have to phone my wife. We're going to New York tonight."

On Saturday morning Mills and Derrick and Gates went through the Lincoln Tunnel just before seven o'clock. On the New Jersey side they parked the car, and with Mills carrying a small case of envelopes, they walked back to the entrance. There they separated, each placing himself between two lanes of the traffic approaching the tunnel. In a little while a truck with California license plates came along, and Mills ran up and scraped some dirt off the mudguard into an envelope and slipped it into his pocket. A few minutes later, Gates scraped the mudguard of a truck from Alabama and at the same time Derrick was working on one from Michigan.

Inside one of the toll booths a tunnel employee looked out just in time to see a fellow go up to a trailer truck and bend down and scrape something off the mudguard. Then, farther down in the next lane, he saw another fellow doing the same thing. Then a third—the place was crawling with them. He flicked his light from green to red and walked to the next booth. "Myron," he said, "we got a couple of nuts for a change. Three of them."

He moved along between the first and second lanes of traffic until he reached Mills, who was working on a truck from Oklahoma. He watched. The fellow just scraped some dirt off the mudguard into an envelope, sealed the envelope and put it into his pocket. He waited for him to do something else. He didn't. He just straightened up and took out another envelope.

The tunnel attendant said, "All right, buddy—"

"Excuse me," Mills said. "There's one from New Mexico. I don't want to miss that."

The tunnel attendant blinked. "What are you—some kind of nut?" he said when Mills came back.

"We're just scraping a little dirt off the mudguards," Mills said.

The attendant pushed back his hat. "You some kind of society—for clean mudguards—or something?"

"This is for scientific research," Mills told him, keeping an eye on the traffic.

"Buddy, whatever kind of a nut you are, just knock it off."

"Sir, let me introduce myself." Mills pumped the attendant's hand. "My name is Dr. Mills and I'm collecting dirt samples for scientific research—for a study of the inhibitory effects of soil microorganisms on pathogenic organisms invading the human host and the chemotherapeutic advantages to that host derived therefrom."

"I think," the attendant said, "I better call the chief."

During the next half hour, the traffic increased, the noise of grinding gears and honking horns increased, the morning dampness burned off, and heat rose up from the concrete road. Under the anxious eyes of the attendant, Mills and Derrick and Gates continued to scrape mudguards.

At eight-thirty, a screaming siren announced the arrival of a Port of New York Authority deputy chief of police, accompanied by a lieutenant and a patrolman. At precisely the same moment an old wreck of a car in the first lane broke down. There was a grinding noise as the driver made a futile attempt to start it, and then the door opened and a remarkable-looking female stepped out. Her hair, bleached almost white, hung to her elbows. She wore white pancake makeup, purple eye shadow, no lipstick, a black turtleneck sweater and black stockings. She looked ready to die.

The deputy chief of police looked at the walking death and then at the trio scraping mudguards, hesitated a moment, and decided that the nuts ought to be attended to first. "O.K., mister, you had your fun. Let's go," he said.

"How do you do, sir?" Mills said.

"Mister, what do you think you're doin'?" the deputy chief said, looking at the scraper and the envelope.

"We're scraping dirt samples off mudguards," Mills explained. Then Derrick came up. "Good morning, sir," he said.

The deputy chief saw his scraper and didn't bother to return the greeting. "What's the idea—you like clean mudguards or something?"

The white-faced girl came up. "Can you help me start my car, sergeant?" she said.

"In a minute. In a minute." The deputy chief saw that Mills was pulling an envelope out of his pocket. "All right, give it here."

"It's empty."

"I gotta get on into town," the living death said. "I'm on my way to South America."

"Lady, get one of the boys to help you, will you please?" The deputy peered into the envelope. "There ain't nothin' in it."

"It's for the dirt," Mills said.

"I gotta make plans," the walking death said. "I'm meeting people."

Then Gates came up and said, "Good morning, sir."

"Look!" Mills said. "Oregon! Get that one, Pearly."

Gates darted off and Mills said, "Now, just watch what he does, sir, and you'll see there's no harm in it."

The deputy chief watched Gates closely. "That's all?"

"That's all."

"You got to be kidding!"

Mills explained that the dirt was for medical research. The chief said that he was sure they were crazy. The walking death told Derrick she had to be on her way to South America. The chief said he was considering sending them to Bellevue for observation. A moving van from Nebraska came along, and Derrick hopped over to get the dirt. The chief exploded. Mills looked anxiously at trucks going past to the right of them, trucks going past to the left of them.

"Look," he said. "Why don't you call our boss?"

"Oh, I don't know, Pat," Gates said, thinking of Dr. Morrissey.

"Who's your boss?" the chief said.

"Call the vice-president for research," Mills said. "His name is Mr. Caroline. Here. Here's his number. Look, you don't want it in all the papers that you sent three dedicated scientists to Bellevue, do you? You'll go down in history as the man who stood in the way of medical research. Radio commentators will make your name infamous—"

"All right, all right," the chief said. "You stay here. And no funny business until I talk to this fellow."

While the deputy chief was telephoning to Will Caroline, Mills eyed the walking death with interest. "She's going to South America, Charlie," he said.

"How's she going to get to South America," Gates said, "if she can't even get through the Lincoln Tunnel?"

"I mean I'm leaving for South America," the walking death said, seeing them looking at her, "and I gotta make plans."

"What are you goin' to South America for, ma'am?" Derrick said.

"We're looking for a lost treasure."

Gates looked pained, but Mills's interest was riding high. "Honey," he said, "you shouldn't go without medicines. You could pick up all sorts of diseases down there."

"Why should I pick up anything down there that I have not picked up, up here?"

"Honey, the air everywhere is full of diseases. Up here you've gotten used to our diseases so you don't get sick. But down there they've got a whole different class of diseases. Honey, believe me, you're taking a chance going without medicines."

"Red," she said, "you pulling my leg?"

"What you should take is penicillin," Mills said. He leaned closer. "Now, penicillin is pretty expensive, but if you'll keep quiet about it—" He looked at her soberly. "Are you a woman of honor?"

"Don't get fresh, Red."

"I mean will you keep your word? Because I know a fellow who will give you some penicillin—absolutely free—if you'll do something for him."

"What kind of something?"

"Every stop you make in South America, dig him a little dirt and send it back in one of these envelopes."

"You got quite a sense of humor, Red."

"I'm serious. This fellow needs the dirt. We're getting some for him right now. And, honey, you need the penicillin."

"I don't know—I gotta think about this," she said.

"Here." Mills handed her a slip of paper. "You can get in touch with me here if you decide to do it, and I'll take you to this fellow who's got the penicillin."

He looked at his watch and then, impatiently, over at the telephone booth where the chief was talking and gesturing. "What's taking that joker so long?"

The chief took off his hat and scratched the back of his head and put it on again, and after another few minutes he came out of the booth, shaking his head. "All right, all right," he said. "Go get your dirt. It's all right, Frank. I still can't believe it, but I guess it's all right," he muttered. "Now I've seen everything. Mudguards!" His voice rose. "Mudguards! I'll be glad when I start my vacation."

Mills turned around. "Where are you going on your vacation, chief?"

"I'm going to a nice lake way up north in Canada where there ain't anyone but me and the fish."

"Charlie," Mills murmured, "you had any from there?"

Derrick shook his head.

"Chief," Mills said. He walked back to him. "Chief, while you're up there—way up there—in Canada, how would you like to dig a little good Canadian dirt? Now—just let me give you a kit of these envelopes, and all you have to do . . ."

"Dr. Gates," Dr. Morrissey said, coming into Gates's office on Monday morning. "Now that the work on this antibiotic project is organized—" Nervously Morrissey glanced over his shoulder, as though someone were watching him. Earlier Gates had noticed him talking rather heatedly to Mr. Brainard, and he had seemed nervous then, too. "Now that it's organized, we ought to consider how we—you—are going to prepare your reports."

Gates regarded Dr. Morrissey with a certain coldness. After the deputy police chief of the Port of New York Authority, he no longer seemed such a formidable foe. "My reports are in order, Dr. Morrissey," he said.

Morrissey brushed at the pocket of his jacket. "As far as they go," he said. "But they don't go far enough."

"Why not?"

"I want a permanent detailed record for the department," Morrissey said. "Besides the reports to the biochemists and to Mr. Caroline, I want a day-by-day record of everything we do here—every culture you test, good or bad—and I want our department records numbered in simple numerical order, regardless of whatever strange numbers they get from Dr. Derrick or from Mr. Caroline. Our records will be in order—starting with Number One and going to—er—a million, if necessary. Now, I consider this particularly important. I want you to keep a copy here and I want a copy for myself just as complete and—" Dr. Morrissey looked over his shoulder again and his eye fell on Miss Potter. "Dr. Gates, what's she doing?"

"She's setting up turbidity tests," Gates said calmly. "On Dr. Cable's broths."

"But I told you," Morrissey said, sharply, "she's being transferred."

"She's still here, Dr. Morrissey," Gates said, amazed at his own firmness. "And she's my technician. And very good—look at her."

Without the slightest hesitation, Miss Potter was firing the mouths of test tubes, adding the cubic centimeters of broth, firing again and stuffing in the cotton, as though she had been doing this for months. Then suddenly, beyond Miss Potter, a wraithlike, white-haired, white-faced creature appeared in the corridor and came through the door into Gates's laboratory. It was the walking death.

When she saw Gates, her face lit up with recognition. "Hello-o," she said. "Where's Red?"

"Upstairs," Gates stammered. "One flight upstairs. He has the mice."

"Mice!" she said.

"Just go upstairs one flight," Gates said. "And go down the corridor. Third door on the left."

"That's Dr. Mills!" Morrissey said shrilly.

"Something wrong with him?" The wraith turned to Morrissey, and he backed away a little. Gates jerked his head and motioned for her to leave. "I mean I came for the penicillin, but if it's a gag, I'm leavin'. I don't want to get in any jam. I'm on my way to South America and I gotta meet people and make plans."

Even Miss Potter was watching, fascinated.

"It's all right," Gates said, feeling even more powerful than before. "Just go upstairs and he'll take care of everything. He's expecting you."

Rather uncertainly, the wraith wandered off.

"Who's that?" Morrissey said hoarsely.

"She's the daughter of a friend of his," Gates said. "The janitor of his building. We were in New York this weekend—in his folks' apartment—and she's the janitor's daughter. She's going away and he promised her some information, I think. You know, he's been everywhere."

Morrissey looked extremely doubtful. Then his eyes settled again on Miss Potter. Gates took a deep breath. Today he felt that he could handle anything. "Now—about the records, Dr. Morrissey," he said. "Naturally, I'll set them up and keep them any way you want."

"I would expect so, Dr. Gates," Morrissey said.

"I'll do it as soon as I get my new technician trained."

"What's that?"

"It'll take time to train a new technician in all these techniques that Miss Potter is doing now, but as soon as that's done, I'll get at those reports—without delay."

Morrissey thought about that for a minute. He frowned and tapped his pipe in his hands. He cleared his throat.

"On the other hand," Gates said, "if Miss Potter were to stay here —she's all trained—then I could get started on those records right away. Today, possibly."

Morrissey fussed with his pipe. "Well, Dr. Gates," he muttered, "perhaps it can be arranged. But you'll have to keep an eye on her —check her results carefully. This is serious business, you know."

"Yes, sir," Gates said respectfully. "You want that daily record in duplicate, you say?"

"Yes, duplicate," Morrissey snapped. "I want a copy and I want you to keep one for yourself—for constant reference."

Dr. Morrissey was vaguely aware that he had been had. Roughly speaking, he had been blackmailed. And by the most docile member of his staff! And for a woman! And with that female wandering in from the corridor, who obviously knew Gates and knew Mills and was, Morrissey suspected—although he couldn't be certain—a full-fledged, big-as-life whore. That woman wasn't the janitor's daughter!

In his own office, Morrissey shut the door and picked up the telephone. "Winifred," he said when she answered, "I'm worried about Dr. Gates. There are some awfully disturbing things going on around here lately." While Winifred cackled a bit on the other end of the line, Morrissey told himself that Gates never argued unless it was awfully important.

"It's Miss Potter," he said. "I tried to transfer her and he raised an awful fuss. I'd better watch that, Winifred. I wouldn't be surprised if there was something doing there. He fought awfully hard to keep her." Then he sighed. "I don't know, Winifred—things are getting out of hand here."

Just thinking about it, he got a sinking feeling. "You never know what's going to happen next," he said. "Everything's changing—it's not the way it used to be any more."

P UT EA 50 into solvent extraction to begin to purify it.

And throw out the second batch of cultures—except for the two you like—and with those two vary the broths and try again.

And test EA 50 and find that you hadn't accomplished much—the antibiotic went into the butyl alcohol and most of the impurities went right along with it—try amyl alcohol, it might be more selective. In Gates's laboratory, in serial dilution, it inhibited the germs in only sixteen test tubes.

And put the third batch of cultures into its second fermentation—all of them. And pick up a fourth batch. Add another broth at the start—that made eight.

And work a little later.

And a week passed.

And test EA 50 and find you'd gotten rid of a few impurities but not enough. It jumped from sixteen test tubes to twenty-five. Try another technique.

And vary the broths for the two from the second batch. And vary them again for the third batch. Come on—damn it—do something. And vary them for the fourth. One in the fourth hit five test tubes. Start another batch.

And work a little faster—there's too much work. You need more time—you need more hands.

And another week passed.

EA 50 was stubborn.

Vary the broths again—the third, the fourth, the fifth. The one in the fourth batch hit seven test tubes.

And new cultures keep coming—start some more—throw some out.

Work later—work faster. You need more time. You need more hands. Well, you don't have more time and you can't get more hands. *You need to find cuts.*

And another week went by, and the smell of bonfires was in the air.

EA 50 was a bitch.

Try another method.

"We'll try carbon adsorption, Moose," Tom said. "We'll line up ten beakers of EA 50 broth and toss in incremental amounts of this carbon. One gram in the first, two grams in the second, ten grams in the tenth."

"And what's it gonna do for us—this carbon?" Moose said, while he began to take out the beakers.

"Carbon's very porous. If we let it sit in the fermentation broth, it'll adsorb some of the stuff that's in the broth. Only some—not all. It'll be selective."

Moose was unimpressed. Moose, Tom had decided, was a creature of infinite logic, to whom nothing was more pleasing than a technique that he clearly saw made sense and had a chance of working. Then he embraced it wholeheartedly, and no matter how much work it involved, it was all right—as long as it was logical. But until he recognized the logic, his performance was perfunctory and unenthusiastic.

Now he jerked his big thumb toward the carbon. "So what's it gonna absorb?"

"Adsorb, Moose. Nothing's going to mix with that carbon. It's just going to collect in the pores and sit there. We hope it'll be the antibiotic."

"Yeah?"

"And we hope that not too many of the impurities will go along with it. We hope that carbon will be nice and selective."

"Yeah?" Moose was still reserving judgment. "Well—let's hope so."

It was dark now, and from his laboratory Tom could see the lights in the fermentation building as an attendant opened the door and stood outside for a minute. Over there, there were always men working—fermentation was a round-the-clock process—and the attendants, even though he didn't know them, were beginning to seem like friends in the night. Here in the research building, except for the nights when the janitor or Bessie Norowski, the cleaning woman, was on this floor, it was silent and empty. Bessie was here tonight. Tom could hear her working next door in George Weir's laboratory.

He was just finishing up, and he carried the equipment he'd been using over to the sink. Across the lighted yard he could see the twin towers silhouetted against the stars and against the lights across the bay. Once, he thought, he used to see these buildings every night from the other side, and they had been only a pattern of lights across the water—once when he used to go home every night at five o'clock, long ago, last month. Now he was usually still here when it grew dark and the pattern of lights was on the other side.

At the sink he picked up a flask, turned on the water and began to think about Diana. He had to laugh at himself—at the feelings that began to wind up inside him, as though on signal, every night when he started to rinse the equipment and knew that in a little while he would be with her. He put down the flask, reached for another and let the water run into it. When did a girl become special like this? he thought. When did she become different from the rest —from all the others you had known and held and thought briefly that maybe you loved? When did you begin to want her around—to wait for her those nights when she used to drop in, unexpectedly, unannounced—to miss her when she didn't come?

When did she become a part of you, so that you could have your mind completely on your work—and suddenly you thought of her and automatically you turned to look for the red sail on the bay? Or you saw her—and you knew that even when you were thinking about broths or about EA 50, part of you was always thinking about her. Or you just saw a head of short-cropped black hair, even when it wasn't hers, and something turned over inside you. Tom felt the water spilling over in the flask and poured it out. If anyone had told him two months ago that he would ever feel this way again, he would have laughed at the idea.

He turned off the water and, while he dried his hands, he let his eyes rest on the ten beakers of broth and carbon that Moose had left lined up on the counter. Maybe carbon adsorption would do it, he thought. Maybe it would get rid of a heap of junk. In Gates's last serial dilution tests EA 50 had been active in twenty-seven test tubes. When it was pure enough to be active in the sixtieth test tube, he decided, he would think about putting it into a mouse.

He tossed the towel back onto the rack, and then he heard Bessie coming down the corridor to his laboratory.

"Hey, boy, you here again?" Bessie said, setting down her pail.

Tom smiled. Bessie looked about a hundred years old and he guessed she'd earned the right to call him boy.

"How come every night you here, boy? You no like your wife, hey?"

"I don't have a wife, Bessie."

"You no got wife!" Bessie shook her head. "You better find one, boy! You getting pretty old fella not to have wife. So"—she jerked her head toward the counter while she began her cleaning—"how we comin'? You find out yet if any good with that stuff you're fussin' with?"

"Not yet." Tom took off his lab coat. "A little more work—then we'll find out."

"Then you give it to pretty sick fella, make him better, eh?"

"No, Bessie, we give it to a pretty sick mouse first. You can't give anything first to a pretty sick man."

Bessie cackled and poked her elbow into his side. "Hey, don't you think I know that? I tease you because you're such a serious fella. How long you think Bessie been here? Couple weeks? So when we gonna give it to a sick mouse—fix him up?"

"Pretty soon."

"I think you do pretty damn soon—you been working pretty damn long time."

She was right, Tom thought. It was a pretty damn long time. He lit a cigarette and leaned back on the windowsill, and Bessie looked at him shrewdly out of her faded blue eyes.

"I don' know," she said. "You listen to Bessie—you better marry girl from ole country. American girl no let you hang around here all night. You listen to Bessie—you find girl and marry her fast or be too late. You here all the time—can't find a girl at all—only Bessie be left."

"Well, now, Bessie"—Tom smiled—"maybe that wouldn't be so bad."

"I no marry you, by God. You give me hard time—stay out all night."

"Ah, Bessie, you know if I had you to come home to, I'd be there." Tom went into his office, hung his lab coat on a hook and took his tie and jacket off the hanger.

"How come you no got a girl, boy?"

"I've got a dozen of 'em, Bessie, and I love 'em all."

"Ah"—Bessie nodded toward the beakers on the counter—"them—there's your dozen girls. You watch out, boy. One other fella like you here before you came. He din't stay. I used to come in here, see him—I say, 'What you doin' just sittin' there, doctor?' He say, 'Just dreamin', Bessie.' He din't look good. I kill a pig one weekend, make good headcheese. The day I bring him that headcheese, he gone. 'Just dreamin',' he used to say. 'Bessie,' he used to say, 'this place ain't for me.' "

While he tied his tie, Tom glanced over at the beakers, too. Maybe this time it will work, he thought. Maybe this is the one that will do it. Carbon, he said to himself, I hope you're selective—I hope you're fussy as hell. If EA 50 would just take a good sharp jump, he'd feel better about it. Feel better—he'd feel great! Maybe even at fifty tubes, he thought, instead of sixty, he could talk to Mills about putting it into a mouse.

He put on his jacket and said good-night to Bessie and walked along the empty corridor and downstairs to the empty reception room. He wondered who the fellow was who used to stay late before he came and what it was that he had wanted to do and had not been able to, and where he had gone. He walked out to the parking lot that served the research building where his car stood alone.

Sitting with Diana in a corner of the pine-paneled cocktail lounge of the Tides Inn, Tom looked across the room and saw that there was an Enright party here tonight. The Gateses, the Weirs, the Derricks and the Millses were sitting together in front of one of the open fireplaces. Then Diana saw them too and said, "How can they bear it? They're together all day and their wives are together all day, and then at night, for a change, they all get together."

Tom smiled. "I don't think they think much about it. Anyway, if they've been here more than half an hour, they're talking shop by now."

"Oh, I doubt that."

"I'd bet on it. Why do you doubt it?"

"I just don't believe they care that much. You're the only one who cares—and you care too much. Well, that's the way it goes. Never any in-between."

"How can one care too much?"

"Oh, I think one can. It's like unrequited love. It can only hurt you in the end." She looked over at him. "And don't tell me it's better to have loved and lost than never to have loved at all. Please don't tell me that."

"No," he said. "I won't tell you that. I play to win."

The waiter brought their drinks. Tom handed Diana her drink and saw her studying him.

"And you," she said. "You go in early—you stay late. And even when you're with me, that's all that's on your mind."

"No," Tom said. "When I'm with you, you're all that's on my mind."

"And nobody at Enright thinks any more of you for it, you know. There are places where they might respect your dedication, but Enright is not one of them."

"And when I'm not with you, you're all that's on my mind."

"In the end, for all your extra work, they'll knock you down and tramp all over you, just as hard and just as fast."

Tom sipped his drink, feeling it relax him. "That's a pretty bloody future you're painting for me. Couldn't you do a little better —knocked down, maybe, but not tramped over?"

Diana laughed. "There are times I suspect you are quite mad, darling. And then other times I'm certain of it." She grew serious again and said pointedly, "For quite different reasons."

"Diana," Tom said, "you're bound and bedamned you're going to lecture me tonight—I can tell—and I don't want you to. Finish your drink and have several more quickly. I'm plying you with liquor."

Then he saw that Gates had seen them and he said, "In a minute Pearly Gates will be over to invite us to join them—so tell me now whether you want to or not."

"Of course I don't want to."

"They won't care if we don't. It's just Pearly's way. He feels it's the courteous thing to do."

Then a moment later Gates was there, inviting them, and Tom said, "Thanks, Pearly, but we only dropped in for a minute."

Gates sat on the edge of a chair. "I came up looking for you this afternoon, Tom. I wasn't entirely satisfied with the results of those last resistant-organism tests and I wanted to talk to you about repeating them. But I couldn't find you, so I did it anyway—repeated them."

"I was in the library."

Gates nodded. "I should have looked there. Anything new on EA 50, Tom?"

"We put it into carbon adsorption today."

Gates lit a cigarette and settled back in the chair. "God, she's kind of a stubborn one, isn't she, Tom?"

"What do you think, Pearly?" Tom said. "Could we do some more *in vitro* testing when it's pure enough to be active in the fiftieth test tube?"

"Golly, Tom, I don't know how much you'd find out—it'll still be pretty crude at only fifty."

"I'd like to try."

"I'd be glad to do it for you anytime, Tom," Pearly said. "I just don't know how reliable the information will be. I'd hate to give you a bum steer."

"I'm hoping you'll steer me right into testing it in a mouse."

"When it's still so crude! Golly, Tom, I don't know."

"Well, at least you can let me know whether it would be possible."

"Although"—Gates smiled—"I'd be mighty happy to see Mills get some work. God, I thought a minute ago we were going to have a little trouble here. Pat said, innocently enough, I thought, 'When are you fellows going to give me some work?' And George blew up like a dynamite arsenal. I don't know what's ailing George these days. Well, I'd better be getting back. Sure you won't join us?"

"We're going in a few minutes, Pearly. Thanks."

Gates stood up. "I hope that carbon will do great things, Tom. And I'll be glad to do that *in vitro* testing any time you want."

When Gates had gone, Diana said, "What's '*in vitro*'?"

"'*In vitro*' means testing in glass. '*In vivo*' means testing in life—anything from a mouse to a man. You test in a test tube first to get the information you need to go on to mice. Gates will test it against all kinds of disease germs—to find out what it might do as a drug—everything it will actually cure—how much it will take to do it—"

"You mean all this time you've been working on it, you don't know that?"

"I know it'll do something, or I wouldn't have been working on it."

"But what about the mouse? You said he'd tell you whether you could test it yet in a mouse."

"His tests show how much it will take to cure. You can only dilute a mouse's blood about twenty-five per cent. If the antibiotic isn't pure enough, you might have to give the mouse more stuff to cure him than his bloodstream can take. If that's the case, we can't give it to him yet—we'll have to wait until I get it purer."

203

Diana tossed her head impatiently. "I think it sounds horrible," she said. "Horrible and hopeless."

"No," Tom said, smiling at her. "EA 50's like a beautiful woman who's been good to you—and then suddenly gets contrary. I figure when I separate her from the bad company she's in, she'll behave better."

He handed Diana another drink that the waiter had brought. "Drink that down," he said, "and let's get out of here. I don't want to talk to you any more among dozens of people. I want you alone."

"But when will you do it?" she persisted, sipping her drink. "When will you test EA 50 in a mouse?"

"The minute I get it pure enough—you can bet on that."

"How pure is that?"

"I don't know."

"Well, how pure is it now?"

"I don't know that either."

"But that's terrible! How can you work on it so long and not know anything about it?"

"Because it's an unknown quantity."

"Why is it an unknown quantity?"

Tom looked at Diana, puzzled, wondering why she was so upset about this. "Because it's mixed up with a lot of junk, and I don't know how much is in there. If this thing has never been pure, then you've never been able to measure it pure and you don't know how far away from pure it is." He stood up. "Come on, Diana, let's go."

Diana put down her glass and stood up, too. But a moment later, as they walked to his car, she brought it up again. "Well, how do you measure it, then?" she said.

"You measure it at the start—at its worst—and then you measure how much better it is. Diana, why does this bother you so much?"

"Because it's so much worse even than I realized. So much more hopeless."

They reached the car, parked in the shadow of a row of pine trees, and as Tom opened her door he said, "Diana, why don't you let me worry about it? It doesn't bother me—and it bothers you too much."

"Well, it should bother you!" She got into the car and waited for him to walk around and get in, too, and then she said, "Every time I think of you going through all this at Enright—trying to do this at Enright—it's so hopeless—"

"It's not hopeless. Maybe EA 50 will be great and then I can retire." He drew her into his arms and kissed her and hoped she wouldn't bring it up again.

But then she said, "Tom, don't you understand why you say that?"

He laughed and touched her to draw her back into his arms. "Come back where you belong. It's not your problem."

"But don't you see that you just tell yourself that because you feel how terribly they're pressing you?"

"They're not pressing me—I'm pressing myself. Are you coming back where you belong, or do I get me another girl?"

Diana smiled and moved a little closer, but still she persisted. "If you were at all realistic, you'd admit it. But you don't because you're afraid to."

Tom sighed a little. "Diana, I like this antibiotic. It's by far the best I've had, and it's better than any George Weir has had and he's tried everything on them. And if I can just get her out of the bad company she's keeping, she might turn out to be quite a girl. And" —he smiled again and kissed her hand—"that goes for you, too— with some of your ideas, which are really terrible. You have quite a bit in common—you two."

"Darling, I'm serious about this."

He turned Diana's face to his and looked into the troubled blue eyes. "I know you are, darling," he said. "But I'm serious all day."

"And half the night."

"Yes." When did you realize that you wanted this girl so much that you felt a tenderness just in touching her that you hadn't felt in years—not since you were maybe fifteen, when you felt it and it got blocked inside you because you didn't know how to express it? "And so, when I'm with you, I just want to love you. I'm very serious about that."

"Darling, you're such an impractical optimist," she said.

"And you, my beautiful creature, are a pessimist, and if you're going to play on my team, I'm going to send you to spring training and get some changes made—teach you a few things."

In the dark of the pine trees he drew her close again, feeling her hold back at first because she wanted to talk some more, and then, slowly, the resistance left her and she came across the small space she had kept between them.

"Diana," he said when he looked up again, "all you have to do is love me and I'll do the rest. Remember that and it will be all right."

In the morning he told Moose to filter away the carbon from the fermentation broths, and he said to himself, Fifty—if it hits fifty, I'll talk to Mills. And if it doesn't hit fifty—if it doesn't miss by too much—I wonder if I could try it anyway. No, he thought, it's still too crude—much too crude.

He watched Moose set up the Büchner funnel and pour in the contents of the first beaker.

But penicillin was crude at first, he argued with himself. . . . Well, this is even cruder than that. . . . You don't know how crude it is—you have nothing to measure it against. . . . But unless it's very crude, it's not very good, because if there's a lot of antibiotic in there, it ought to do better, so you'd better hope it's crude. . . . It's crude, all right—but maybe this time you'll be lucky and get rid of a lot more junk, and then maybe it'll be O.K. to go into a mouse. . . .

"When it's filtered," Moose said, "everything to assay?"

"Only the broths," Tom said.

Moose looked puzzled. With solvent extraction, he had always taken everything.

"The carbon would be too hard to test to see if the antibiotic is there," Tom said, "so we test the broths to see if it's missing."

That pleased Moose and he nodded his approval. "Good idea!" he said. "And if it is?"

"If it's missing, we assume it's on the carbon. Then we have to get it off the carbon."

"Good idea!" Moose set up another Büchner funnel. Then he said, "How do you do it—get it off?"

"We replace it. We put the carbon into something that is even more strongly adsorbable than the antibiotic. Then that stuff goes into the pores and knocks the antibiotic out. Like getting a woman out of your system, Moose. The best way to do it is to find one you like even better."

"Good idea!" Moose, the man of logic, was warming up to this technique.

"We call it elution," Tom said. "The process of getting it off. We'll try half a dozen eluants at once and send them all to assay to see which one does the best job."

"Right!" Moose said happily. "This isn't such a bad idea!"

Tom smiled, and then suddenly he thought of Diana and turned automatically to the window, although it was too early for her to be out there, and he thought, When did you find you wanted a girl so much that you began to think about marrying her? And when did it begin to seem only natural to be thinking it—as though you had thought it many times before and this was not the first? And when that happened, what was it that held you back?

"Hell, I've quit worrying," George Weir said. Ever since yesterday morning's meeting, he had been thinking about this. Now, in the cafeteria with Gates, he leaned over his cup of coffee. "I figure this isn't going to be so bad for me if nobody else knows anything, either."

"Well—worrying won't help anything—you're right there," Gates said.

"Listen, for my money yesterday was the best meeting we ever had. And you know why? Because I don't know anything about this and I admit it. But yesterday I saw that nobody else knows any more than I do."

Weir gave a short laugh. He could still see their faces after Morrissey had stirred them up yesterday. Morrissey had touched off the fuse by complaining that Derrick wasn't supplying enough information about the microbe cultures. That, Morrissey said, placed an unfair burden on the other men in the department. It made it hard for the biochemists to select the right cultures to work on—and if they didn't pick the right cultures, how could they be expected to do anything with them? Then, after Morrissey had stirred them all up, everyone had begun to question Derrick, and after a little digging, it had become clear that Derrick wasn't offering much information because he didn't know much. He was running a lot of studies but he didn't have many facts.

"I suppose you mean Charlie," Gates said.

"Sure I mean Charlie! It's one hell of a specialist who doesn't know anything special."

"He's trying awfully hard. He's got five or six studies going, I know that."

"Anyone can do studies." Weir laughed. "Christ, even I'm doing studies, trying to pull a few lousy facts out of this mess. And I got sucked into it. That guy was hired as a specialist."

Gates looked uncomfortable and stirred his coffee that was almost gone.

"Until now," Weir said, "all this fumbling in the dark bothered me. I'm not like Cable. I don't go charging off half-cocked, just to look like I'm doing something. I want to know what I'm doing. So everything that comes up, I say to myself, Sure, it sounds O.K.—but the arguments against it sound O.K., too—so how do you know? Well, yesterday I sat listening to that crap, and all of a sudden it hit me. I can't make a mistake. It's impossible—because there are no criteria! No rules—no right way—no wrong way—no nothing! So why should I worry? Nobody knows any more than I do—"

Weir broke off because a new thought had just occurred to him. If nobody knew any more than he did, then he had as much chance as the next fellow of being the one. He had as much chance as anyone else of discovering an important new drug, if there really was such a thing. It was the first time this possibility had occurred to Weir, and he sat stunned into silence by the implications.

"I don't know about Morrissey these days," Gates was saying. "Sometimes I think he's getting old—the way he fusses over every little thing. Then I think maybe he's just still sore about the whole thing."

Weir snorted. Who wasn't? But his mind was working in another direction now. Wouldn't that be something—if he turned out to be the one! That would show them—that would show them all. Then Janet wouldn't look at him in that bored empty way. Then, when he called home, she'd be there, all right—because he'd raise forty kinds of hell if she wasn't and couldn't give a damn good accounting of where she'd been. And when he got her in bed, which would be as often or as little as he pleased, by God she'd act like she knew who she was with. And so, maybe, would a couple of other women. They'd consider it an honor and he'd let them know that it was.

"And sometimes I think he's so busy being important he never really thinks about it," Gates went on. "I don't know—maybe he's just worried like the rest of us and trying to do his best."

"Morrissey's beef yesterday was legitimate," Weir said, while his thoughts veered off in another direction. He guessed he'd hear from his mother then, too. She'd be sorry then about the stink she'd raised when he married Janet. She'd be pretty sorry about the whole damn thing, and she'd sit there in that dark living room with the dark red furniture, figuring out some way to make amends. He'd bet she hadn't changed a stick in that living room in the eleven years since he'd seen her last. It was probably as dark and gloomy as ever.

Probably she'd go next door, too, and tell the Marshes about it, because for once she'd have something to feel better than the Marshes about. Max Strong always reminded him of Henry Marsh with that superior manner of his. And Mills did too. They were all the same—that breed. They had a few ancestors and a little dough, and they figured they had a special berth a couple of steps away from God. Well, he just might show up the lot of them. Feeling new energy surging through him, Weir stood up and went for another cup of coffee. Well, why shouldn't he be the one? He knew as much as anyone else, didn't he?

When he came back to the table, Tom Cable was there talking to Gates, and as Weir sat down, Cable said, "Anything new that looks good, George?"

"A-ah—how do you find anything new?" Suddenly Weir felt let down and resentful again. "I'm still not satisfied with the results I'm getting. I want to try a few more things."

"Hell, George, dump 'em and move on."

Annoyed, Weir took a quick sip of coffee. It was too hot, and he set the cup down with a thud, spilling a little. "I don't want to dump them," he said. "I'm not dumping anything until I know for sure there's nothing there—not this boy."

He saw the way Cable was looking at him and the hell with him.

When Cable had gone, Gates said, "I think Tom's about ready to test EA 50 in a mouse."

Shocked, Weir looked up from his coffee. "What!"

"He got rid of a lot of junk with carbon adsorption," Gates said. "It's still pretty damned crude!"

"Yes, but it took a nice jump."

"He's got ants in his pants!"

"Well, he is impatient. But I did some broader *in vitro* testing for him, and it hit quite a few organisms very nicely. It looks even more exciting than we expected, and Tom wants to send it to mice right now to see what happens."

"Let him!" Weir looked down at his coffee. He'd put in too much cream. Now it had a thin milky look and he didn't want it. "You wouldn't catch me putting it into a mouse this crude."

"But won't it be great," Gates said, "if those mice live! By golly, it looked like a nice little drug, *in vitro*."

"Don't lose your head, Pearly," Weir advised. "*In vitro* isn't *in vivo*. Just because you work with test tubes, don't forget that's all they are—test tubes. They can't die."

"Well, of course, that's right," Gates agreed, "but still it was exciting to find an antibiotic that looked so good—"

"Maybe you won't be so excited after it goes into those mice. When did you say he was going to do it?"

"He's going up now to talk to Mills about it. By golly, won't it be something if those mice come through!"

"Ah-h—"

"Let that son of a bitch Cable do what he wants," Weir said to Janet that evening. "And I'm doing what I want—that's my attitude. I'm not sticking my neck out for something I don't believe in."

All day, ever since Gates had told him that Cable was going to test EA 50 in mice, his irritation had mounted, and when he came home he'd started to drink, walking around the house in sullen silence. Then all his problems and complaints began to go through his mind again, and now, sprawled in a chair, his third drink half gone, he was beginning to feel like talking. "'Dump 'em and move on,' Cable says to me today. Well, if you ask me, he just wants me to do what he's doing so I'll share the blame if they land on him for it. He's moving so fast you can't keep track of what he's doing."

Bored, Janet looked at her fingernails, which were coral today. Yesterday they had been pale pink. The day before bright red.

"That stuff is so crude," he said, "I'll bet those mice'll be dead in ten minutes."

"Can they die that fast?"

"Hell, they could die before Mills gets the needle out. Probably will. Jeez, that stuff is crude!"

Janet examined her fingernails again and he said, "That's a great little career you've got going—your damned fingernails!"

She gave him a long, totally undisturbed look and twisted the new bracelet she'd bought yesterday that, by God, really looked like a heavy solid gold. One thing you had to say for her—she knew how to shop. She had taste. She'd come a long way since he married her, the night of that football game, half out of infatuation and half to spite his mother. And she did well without spending much—looked a lot better than most wives—better than Madeline, who always looked frumpy and didn't give a damn—and better than Constance Strong, and Strong probably made double his own salary. And better than Sara Mills, too, and look at the dough her husband could spend on her. God, if he had Mills's money, what Janet would look like!

"I'll tell you a way you can play it safe," she said, bored, as though she didn't care but was saying it anyway, "and still do something that will put you ahead of all the rest."

"I can imagine," he said. What did she know?

"Suit yourself," she said. She twisted her bracelet again and uncurled her legs like a cat.

"All right—what?" he said.

"Drop dead," she said. She stood up. "Are you going to eat with us tonight?"

"All right, all right," he said. "What'd you have in mind?"

"Why not keep a record?" she said. "Why not keep a record of everything that happens—like a ship's log. . . ."

Later, after dark, Weir sat on the front steps, thinking.

At first he had just laughed at the idea, but now he was beginning to warm up to it. At first, when Janet had told him to keep a record of everything he did and everything Cable did and compare them and include anything else he knew about too, and write it all out and she would type it up, he had grown pretty disagreeable because it seemed stupid. But now he was beginning to change his mind.

After a while Weir got up and walked to the corner. Hell, he thought, when you came right down to it, wasn't that the way most people made it—on bluff? Wasn't everything about eighty per cent bluff? Look at Mills—everyone treated Mills so great and he wasn't such a great scientist. He hadn't ever done much. Everyone knew who his family was and he'd bought one of the big houses on the boardwalk and so he was a very popular guy. And look at Max Strong. Wasn't *he* all bluff? He was about one hundred and fifty-two per cent bluff. Who was he, anyway? He didn't have a thing to recommend him except that superior attitude of his—and everyone thought he was great.

Weir had walked another block and reached the boardwalk. Well, someday he'd live up here, and someday they'd think he was great too—Janet and his mother and Strong and Mills and Cable, who probably wouldn't even be here any more. Hell—he smiled—if anybody got canned, it was going to be Cable.

And if he should happen to discover that drug, he could still use that record—make it look as though all along he really knew what he was doing. Great show of superior dedication, application, reason. Well—nobody knew enough to say it wasn't so. He almost laughed out loud.

Cable! Cable staying late every night—kissing their asses, that's what he was doing. Look how hard I'm working, he was practically saying. Well, how did they know how late he worked? There wasn't anyone else around to prove it. Who were you going to ask—the mice? Maybe he just ducked out after everyone had gone—went over and laid Potter—or Brainard's daughter, maybe—everyone knew about Cable.

Well, you won't catch me working nights, Weir said to himself. How would he know what Janet was doing? Ho—he could just imagine what a picnic she'd have if he started working nights. But still, you had to hand it to her. She was smart enough to think of this. "I should think it would be important," she'd said. "No one else will think of it, and if the project fails, it'll show that you tried. And if the project succeeds, it could be a very important document."

And the thing of it was that she was right. How in hell had she thought of it?

"We've got some interestin' samples from the Mediterranean today, Nick," Derrick said to his assistant. "Dr. Mills's mother sent them. Ah hear she made friends with half the population of the islands—Capri, Corsica—"

"Dr. Derrick, didn't you hear the news?" Nick said. "Dr. Cable's going to test EA 50 in mice tomorrow."

"Ah heard, boy." Derrick put the samples on the counter. "Ah'm pretty excited about gettin' these—they're the first we've had from Italy. Ah believe ah'll give 'em special attention—work out a few more broths and see if we learn anything."

"Dr. Derrick," Nick said, "aren't you interested in Dr. Cable's EA 50?"

"Nick," Derrick said, "ah guess ah'm so interested ah'll probably be hangin' half out our door tomorrow for the news—but ah've been in research too long to stop workin'. When somethin' looks good, ah say that's the time to work twice as hard gettin' the next one ready —in case this one disappoints you. Now, this heah's one from Corsica—and ah never had one from there. . . ."

"Even if those mice live and recover and by nighttime are strutting around like prizefighters, it doesn't mean a thing, Ade," Will Caroline said. Hale had stopped in on his way home from work and they were sitting on the open deck, talking. "Because things can go wrong two or three days later."

"I know, Will," Hale said. "But your boy's pretty excited, too, about his drug. He likes it."

"A good research man is always excited, Ade. But you know that even if nothing goes wrong with these mice—now or later—we still shouldn't get too excited."

"Oh, Will!" Callie said. "We'll probably all be delirious!"

"We shouldn't," Will said. "There's many a slip between a mouse and the market—and an awful lot of work."

"Really, Will, you're such a prophet of doom. Do you want to call Helen to come over and stay to dinner, Ade?"

"We're going out, Cal. I'm late now."

"Maybe we can do it tomorrow night," Callie said, "to celebrate some healthy mice. Really, you know my whole attitude toward mice has changed."

When Hale had gone, Callie said, "This is so unlike you, Will. What's wrong? Do you know something you've been keeping from everyone?"

"Only maybe that the higher you go, the harder you fall."

"Darling," Callie said, "please don't make a sign out of that one."

"No, not that one," Will agreed.

Curious, Callie looked at him. "Why not that one?"

"Because, Cal, you don't put out the fire you need for heat—even though there's a chance, too, that it could burn down the house."

T

OM SAT on the wide weathered rail of the porch, his back against a post, and felt the chill of just before sunrise. In the distance the fall colors that laced the trees were muted in the soft early light, and a morning mist moved between the pale sky and the water. It had been a long time, Tom thought, since he had been up at this wet, white hour when the sky was just slipping off the night. It had been years. But today EA 50 was going into mice.

He sat still, too full of feelings he knew better than to feel, and listened to the first soft sounds of the day—the quiet water, the unhurried talk of birds, the tinkling of metal dogtags as two mongrels came trotting up the beach and stopped to sniff and pawed at the sand and moved around to sniff from the other side. At the water's edge a gull took off and he watched it, seeing the power in the broad, white, black-bordered wings that worked and then went taut, as it soared into the first streaks of sunlight. Up the road the brakes of a milk truck squeaked and the dogs cocked their heads and then came bounding up the steps and raced off.

This was the opiate hour, Tom thought, when everything seemed right—when a man's blood raced and he saw nothing but strength and he felt that nothing could go wrong.

Then the blurred shapes of the Enright towers began to show through the thinning mist, and he got up and went into the house. When he came out again to go to work, it was a brilliant fall day with the sun gleaming on the wet grass and pulling deep reds and golds out of the trees and shining white on the wide wings of gulls sailing over the water.

"Hello, fellas," Mills said, looking at a jar that contained six white mice. "Have a big night?"

Last night he had moved two jars of mice out of the storage laboratory, down the hall here to the testing laboratory. Because he used disease germs in testing, the two laboratories were kept separate and some distance apart.

"My men are set, Tom," he said cheerfully. "All weighed and marked—ready to go."

Looking into the jar, Tom saw that the six mice were awake and moving about, now that they had been disturbed. Each mouse had been marked with colored dye to identify it, three on their heads, three on their rumps. The colors were green, yellow and purple. There was sawdust on the bottom of the jars and water in bottles, inverted over the jars with drinking pipes extending down, and there were food pellets in small wire containers to one side.

Mills opened a notebook in which he had entered the identifying dye marks, the weight of each mouse, and the dose it would receive, determined by its weight. The doses were calculated and recorded in terms of milligrams of antibiotic per kilogram of body weight, and a mouse weighed about twenty grams, one-fiftieth of a kilogram. Mills would begin with 5 mg/kilo doses, which meant the mice would actually receive one-tenth of a milligram.

He took a minute to look at the mice and then lifted one out and stroked it, and put it back. "This is your day to be heroes, fellas," he said.

Then he settled down to work. He picked up the small bottle that contained the EA 50, which Tom had freeze-dried to a powder that resembled fine brown sand. He weighed out a small quantity and then measured out a very small quantity of sterile water in which to dissolve it.

Standing close by, Tom waited. Outside, the last of the fog was gone and the water sparkled silver and the sun struck a beam off a strip of metal on a truck backing up to dump waste into the barge. Mills worked at the EA 50 powder until it was completely dissolved and then set it aside.

He picked up a syringe and a cotton-corked test tube of disease germs.

"What are you using, Pat?" Tom said.

"Staph germs."

Slowly Mills drew a lethal dose of staphylococcus germs into the syringe. He took out the first mouse—the one with a green-spotted head—and holding it behind the ears, turned it over on his hand, and tucked under the tail. The pink legs stretched out and the pink body showed through the white fur, and the single tooth in the lower jaw was bared as the mouse opened its mouth. Mills plunged the syringe into the tail vein. The mouse squealed and urinated and Mills withdrew the syringe and put the mouse back into the jar.

Immediately the other five mice in the jar scurried over to it.

"They're looking him over," Mills said. "They'll smell him now from head to foot to try to find out what happened to him."

One by one, he injected lethal doses into the other five mice in the first jar and then into the six mice in the second jar. When he finished he looked at his watch and recorded the time. It was twenty minutes past nine.

He moved the second jar down the counter. "These are the controls," he said. "They get only the disease—no drug." He looked into the jar. "Sorry, fellas, no medicine for you. All we do with you is watch you die. But you're heroes, remember that."

He came back to the first jar, which held the mice that would receive the drug. "We'll give the staph germs half an hour to take hold," he said, "and then we'll get going."

Out in the corridor, people were going by and pausing to look in through the glass in the door. Outside, someone on the barge shouted to the driver in the truck. On the bay a boat whistle sounded.

Looking at the mice, Tom saw that they had finished commiserating with each other and settled down to sleep again—all but one. Five of them were huddled together the way they always slept, one's head against the other's rump—head, rump, head, rump, head. The mouse with the green-spotted rump stalked the jar.

"What's the matter with him?" Tom said.

"He's the sentry—out looking for trouble," Mills said. "If he finds anything to get excited about, he'll wake up the others. If not, after a while he'll settle down—or if they're still nervous, another one might take over the sentry duty." He looked into the jar and grinned. "They're nocturnal animals, you know. They're very quiet all day—but you ought to come over here some night and hear the racket."

Tom glanced at his watch, and Mills said, "You know, Tom, this might take some time. You don't have to stay. I'll let you know right away."

"No," Tom said. "I want to see what happens."

"O.K. Ah, here's Miss Watterling. Good morning, Miss Watterling."

"Good morning, Dr. Mills," Miss Watterling said coolly. She was a pale, serious-looking young woman. "Good morning, Dr. Cable."

"We have heroes this morning, Miss Watterling," Mills said, and Miss Watterling gave him a long-suffering look.

Mills checked the time. "Got some new white rats, Tom," he said. "Like to see them while we're waiting? They're down in the storage area with the mice. Miss Watterling and I have decided that rats have more character than mice, haven't we, Miss Watterling?"

"You've decided it, Dr. Mills."

"A mouse can be treacherous, Tom. He'll turn on you—give you a good nip just because he feels like it. But a rat will walk around on your hand for half an hour—mind his own business—won't bother you a bit. He'll only attack if you bother him. Giving the rat a bad reputation is a great miscarriage of justice. He's a splendid creature. Right, Miss Watterling?"

"I don't play with either the mice or the rats, Dr. Mills," Miss Watterling said.

"Just another few minutes, men," Mills said to the mice, and Miss Watterling winced, but she dutifully stationed herself nearby in case she was needed.

"You're right, of course, Miss Watterling," Mills said. "My wife agrees with you. She keeps saying, 'I don't know about this associating so much with rats—it doesn't seem the best company.'"

Mills checked his watch again and stopped talking. He picked up another syringe and referred to the notebook on the counter, and then he carefully drew up into the syringe the indicated dose of EA 50 solution. He reached into the jar and again took out the mouse with the green-spotted head. He turned it over on his palm, and while the mouse squealed and extended its pink legs and bared its tooth—Mills injected it with EA 50.

As soon as the mouse was back in the jar, the other five, awake and excited again, flocked around to examine it. Mills took out the one with the green-spotted rump and injected it with the same-sized dose. He wrote the time of injection in his notebook and quickly turned back to the jar to watch, very carefully, the two green-spotted mice.

"We'll wait a little while to see if anything happens to these two," he said, without taking his eyes off the mice, "and then we'll do two more."

"How long will you wait?" Tom said, watching from the other side.

"About twenty minutes—and if nothing happens—" Mills stopped and looked sharply at the mice. In the center of the jar the green-headed mouse stopped short. Its tail shot up stiff and the mouse began to shake. It dragged itself over to the side of the jar and shook harder, and then suddenly it rose up on its hind legs, eyes popping, and fell down again and lay where it fell and shook. By now the second mouse was following the same pattern. The first mouse tried to dig in the sawdust and gave up and trembled violently. Then the trembling stopped and the mouse was still. Mills took it out of the cage and flipped it over on the counter where it lay motionless, its four pink feet stretched out. There was no heartbeat.

"He's dead." Mills threw the mouse into a covered garbage can.

A minute later the second mouse stopped shaking and lay motionless, too. The whole thing had taken five minutes.

Stunned, Tom watched Mills put the cover on the garbage can for the second time. In the jar, the four remaining mice huddled together, their eyes open watchfully. One of them detached itself from the group and stalked the jar and returned. Tom looked at Mills.

"Maybe the dose was too much for them."

Mills shook his head. "I don't think so, Tom."

"Let's cut it. Let's cut it down and try again."

Mills didn't argue. "All right," he said. "We'll cut the dose in half."

In the syringe he measured a dose half as large as the first and injected it into the mouse with the yellow-spotted head and then measured again and plunged the syringe into the mouse with the yellow-spotted rump. It was five minutes past ten. A minute later, the yellow-spotted mice trembled—the tails went stiff and the mice reared up on their hind legs and shook and then fell down and began to dig and stopped digging and just shook harder. At ten minutes past ten they were dead.

The cover settled again over the garbage can. In the jar only the two purple-spotted mice remained.

"Was it any longer?" Tom said.

Mills shook his head. "Same time."

"Cut it again."

"I'll do it, Tom," Mills said, "but then it won't cure them. There won't be enough antibiotic in there to kill the germs."

"Let's try it anyway," Tom said. "That stuff is crude as hell now. Let's cut it way down and see if they live any longer."

218

Mills diluted the solution, and at a quarter past ten he completed the injections and they stood without speaking and looked at the last two mice. Miss Watterling stood behind them and watched, too, and when the mice died at twenty minutes past ten, Tom and Mills walked to the door. Miss Watterling picked up the dead mice and threw them away.

"It's toxic as hell, Tom," Mills said. "It's pure poison."

Tom nodded. "At least it is right now," he said. He motioned toward the other jar. "What about the controls?"

"They'll die sometime tomorrow," Mills said.

On his way back to his laboratory, Tom passed Gates and Weir going down for their morning coffee.

Upstairs Tom could hear Constance putting the children to bed while he and Max sat here in the living room going over what had happened. All day, once the shocked disbelief left him, Tom had been analyzing the significance of this first mouse test, and after work he had come over here to talk about it some more. Now it was past dinnertime and they were still talking.

"It comes down to this, Max," he said. "If you put a crude antibiotic into a mouse and the mouse dies, there can be four possible causes. One—the mouse died of the disease because the antibiotic didn't work at all in the mouse. Two—the stuff was so crude that there wasn't enough antibiotic in there to do the job. Three—the antibiotic was toxic and killed the mouse. Four—there were toxic impurities and they killed the mouse. In this case we know the first two reasons don't apply. The mice didn't die from the disease."

"Not with death in five minutes," Max said, "and the controls still alive."

"So it's one of the last two. Either that little bit of antibiotic killed them—or one of the impurities did. And there's no way of knowing which."

Max nodded and reached over and turned on a light, and then Constance came downstairs and went around and turned on some more lights.

"At that weight I'd guess it was still pretty crude," Max said.

"It was crude as hell! Probably a dozen different substances mixed in there—"

And any one of them, he thought—or any combination—could

have been toxic. Out of all that junk you can't assume that it was that little bit of antibiotic. Without the impurities, that antibiotic—alone—might be as nontoxic as penicillin.

"Tom, we both know that if a man eats a seven-course dinner and gets sick, you can't know which ingredient caused the trouble without further investigation."

Tom grinned. "I think we ought to get rid of a lot more junk in a hurry. You want to work on it, Max?"

"Of course," Max said. "Today doesn't mean a thing."

Constance stood up. "Well, that's settled. Will you stay to dinner, Tom?"

For the first time Tom saw how late it was—almost eight o'clock. "You should have thrown me out hours ago," he said and stood up.

"Fine chance I'd have had! Although I've known the answer all along. Obviously with all those unresolved questions, neither of you could resist it. What do you say, old dear? Are you staying?"

"Thanks, Constance," Tom said. "But I'll go home and leave you alone."

Feeling much better, Tom walked across the lawn to his own house. It didn't mean a thing that this first test had failed. It was entirely possible that a single impurity in there had killed the mice —an impurity that might be separated out tomorrow, on the very next try.

He ran up the steps to the porch, and then, as he opened the door, he saw Diana sitting in a corner of the sofa, waiting for him.

"Where've you been all this time?" The accusation in Diana's voice brought him up sharply. She looked angry and unhappy. Beside her there was an ashtray filled with cigarette butts. "What happened to the mice?"

He hadn't meant to dramatize the failure to her, but the strident edge in her voice goaded him and he said, "They died. They got the shakes and died in five minutes."

"I know," she said, her eyes accusing him, as though it were his fault. "I heard."

Well, he thought suddenly, in a way it was his fault. Maybe he had been overeager. Maybe he should have resisted the temptation to put EA 50 into mice until he had a purer antibiotic. Diana was watching him with the wounded look of a betrayed child, and Tom

220

conquered his first reaction of impatience and went over and sat beside her. "Diana, don't take it this way."

"How do you expect me to take it?"

"Well, it's not the end of everything—it's just one small setback!" Diana drew her hand away from his. "And what now?" she said.

Puzzled, Tom looked at her, realizing that she had never understood anything at all about the complexity of this project. "Now I'll work on it some more and try it again."

"Just like that!"

"Diana, the universal method of research is to try and try and try again."

"That's not the point."

"Well, what is the point, then?" She turned away, and when he tried to take her in his arms she drew off. "Come on, darling." He tried again. "Let's go out to dinner. This disappointment will wear off—I've forgotten it already."

"Yes, you probably have!" she said. "That's the trouble with you!"

"Damn it, Diana, you're making too much of this!" He stood up and walked away. "This was the first test on a crude product. We don't know anything about this antibiotic yet."

"All this time—weeks—months—and you still don't know anything about it! But that doesn't bother you—you've forgotten it. Well, other people aren't forgetting it!"

For the first time since he had known Diana, Tom was angry at her. He poured himself a drink and walked across the room to his desk, which was still covered with notes on broths and the accumulated notes on EA 50 and some journals he'd marked to read. In a corner he saw the card from Sam Lewis with the Boston postmark and the name of the nurse he ought to look up. Well, he thought, he ought to look her up. Whoever she was, at least maybe she had seen a little real trouble and wouldn't blow up when a couple of mice died. He drank the Scotch and picked up the card. Then he dropped it and turned and looked at Diana, standing small and bewildered in the dim light and he knew he was not going to call this nurse or anyone else.

It was just that she was young, he told himself. For everyone there had to be a first time for looking failure in the face and learning that it was only a transient and not a permanent resident—and for her the first time was late coming. And it was coming in a hard way because she wasn't a scientist, and even though she knew a few of the terms, to her this was a foreign language. He told himself that it was always harder to accept a failure that you couldn't understand—and he felt how much he loved her and he went back.

"Diana," he said patiently, drawing her down on the sofa again, "try to understand a little. This project is like an unmapped trail. We don't know how long it is—or where it's leading. We don't know whether the path we've chosen goes into new country or just around in a circle. When we come up against some woods—or a mountain —we try to go through or over, but we may have to back up and find another way. And even if we get through, we don't know what we'll find on the other side—an easy stretch or more trouble. We don't know anything about it until it's behind us. The only way you learn on this trail is by traveling it."

"What are you talking about?"

"I'm talking about us—because it's important to us that you understand this."

"I understand it very clearly! You're the one who's blind!"

"Diana, even if those mice had lived, there would still be a long road to travel. Mice are only the beginning. A drug has to be tested in rats and dogs too—for a long time—and at any point something could go wrong. And if it did, we'd have to start over."

"Why are you telling me this now—to make it even worse?"

"Diana—" Tom sighed and turned her face to his, and in the blue eyes he could see the barrier that had arisen between them. "Diana, I love you very much—but I'm involved in this, and if we're going to be together, you have to understand what we're in for. Every time we run into a little trouble, you can't go to pieces like this."

"Why can't you see it from my side?" she said. "Why can't you see that this is a signal of everything that's to come?"

"It's not a signal of anything!" Angrily, he stood up. "Diana, Constance Strong is sitting over there, and her husband just agreed to go to work on this—now, after these mice died—and she applauded!"

"Let her!"

Dumbfounded at the depth of her anger, Tom stared at Diana.

"Well, what else can she do if he's decided? She's a spineless housefrau with two children. She's practically a vassal! She has no choice but to agree."

Again Tom walked away—as far away as he could get. There

was nothing more to say, and he didn't want to look at her. With difficulty he restrained himself from walking out the door.

After a long silence Diana stood up again. He hoped she was leaving.

"It's not the failure, Tom," she said. "I'd suffer that with you. If you were a martyr in the name of decency, I'd be for it. I'd believe in you when no one else did. I'd take your side when everyone else had turned against you—"

"Don't dramatize this, Diana. No one has turned against me. And if I'm a martyr, I'm a very comfortable one."

"But I won't be dragged down with you—while you're used and degraded and disgraced by people I despise. It would be a violation of everything I believe."

At the door she stopped. "This isn't just a first little failure, as you call it," she said. "This is the first step down a ladder that you can never climb up again. And if you can't see that, there's nothing more I can say."

For a long time after Diana had gone, Tom stood on the porch thinking about her and about all the things she had said, in anger and in sorrow, but in earnest. There was a fog again, as there always was these late September evenings when the day had been warm and the night was cool, and he stood looking at it and thought that he didn't understand Diana's reasoning any more than she understood his work. She just didn't make sense. All this talk about martyrs and decency and degradation—it was a barrage of fine phrases without meaning. It wasn't logical and he couldn't understand what made her think this way. Like the drug, there was something else mixed in here, and he couldn't separate it from her and he didn't know what it was.

After working on it for two weeks with Max, Tom gave EA 50 to Mills again. And the mice, with their tails stiff, shook and rose up on their hind legs and fell over and dug in the sawdust and trembled violently and died.

"Cut it," Tom said.

Mills cut the dose in half and the tails went stiff and the mice were racked with the shakes and dug in the sawdust and died.

"Cut it again."

"It won't cure."

"Try it anyway."

The syringe with a diluted dose went into the tail veins, and within five minutes the mice reared and trembled and dug and died. Miss Watterling threw them into the covered garbage can.

Twelve days later EA 50 took a great jump in purity, and again Mills put it into six mice and, two at a time, after progressively reduced doses, six mice dug themselves into the sawdust and died, and Tom Cable poured EA 50 down the drain.

FIFTEEN

ETURNING HOME from work that evening, deeply preoccupied, Tom didn't notice Diana's car or the light burning in his house until he had turned into the driveway. Then when he saw them, his first impulse was to back out quickly and drive away.

For a week after their argument he had put off calling her. Then he learned from Callie that she had gone to New York, and she was still there when EA 50 went into mice for the second time. When she came home two days later, Tom told himself that if she hadn't cared, she wouldn't have returned—there was nothing else here to draw her back—and he went to her and for a little while everything was all right again. It was as though they understood that they had to be together and had tacitly agreed not to talk about the only thing that could come between them.

Now, sitting in his car, knowing it would not be that way tonight, he wished there were a way to avoid going in there. But she had heard him and had already come to the window. Very reluctantly, Tom got out of the car.

He could read in her face that she knew the answer, but she asked the question anyway. "What happened?"

"I threw it out." Tom poured himself a drink, not bothering to go for ice. He could see that she was about to explode and was only choosing her words, and he said, "Don't talk about it, Diana."

"You shouldn't be there! You should know by now that you can't do this at Enright!"

"Diana, mice don't die because they're at Enright."

He emptied his glass and poured himself another drink and then poured one for her. "I'll get you some ice," he said.

"I don't want a drink," she said, with false calm.

Taking the bottle with him, Tom went over and melted into a corner of the sofa.

"Are you just going to get drunk?"

"No," he said. "No." He put the bottle on the floor. He might as well get it over with. "Diana, it's not a disaster if the first one failed.

225

Things weren't meant to be that easy."

"That's not the way you talked before. Before you said, 'Why not? Why shouldn't it be this one? This one looks good!'"

Tom smiled. "I did say that, didn't I? Well, maybe it will be the next one."

She stared at him. "You talk like a child!"

"Well—maybe I do." He twisted the glass in his hand. "But this is the way I am. I worked that one as long as I believed in it. Now I'm thinking about the next one. There's another one growing nicely that I like."

"Just like that!"

"Just like that." Not quite like that, he thought. For a long time he would be thinking back to EA 50 to squeeze out of it every hint that he could. "Well, I guess I've learned a few things from it."

"And you don't care! You don't feel anything?"

"About the old one? Not a thing. I feel plenty about the new one."

"But that's crazy!" She stood in front of him. "It's unrealistic. That's what's the matter with you! You're not willing to face up to reality."

"Take your drink there on the table, Diana. You'll feel better."

"You run away from facts that are unpleasant." Her voice rose. "You sweep them under the rug and pretend they don't exist."

Who would have thought those eyes could hold such anger, he thought—those eyes that could go through him and stir up so much desire! He sighed. "Diana, what do you want of me?"

"I want you to leave here. I want you to go someplace where they won't destroy you if you fail—where they know that you'll fail and fail and fail—so you can admit it to yourself and stop running away from it."

Tom didn't answer, and Diana sat down beside him. "At Enright you can't admit that you've failed. You don't dare!"

"Diana, you're so mixed up. I admit I failed with EA 50. What do you expect me to do—lie down and die? Do penance the rest of my life over that first little failure?"

"And what about the next and the one after that?"

"Maybe the next one will work."

"There—you see! Everyone else knows that this is a million-to-one shot. Everyone else knows that Enright won't go to a million. They'll stop first. They'll destroy the project long before that, and you with it."

226

"How? You keep saying that like a broken record. How will they destroy me?"

"They'll push you and pressure you, and then when it fails they'll blame you and throw you out."

Tom felt on the floor for the bottle and poured himself another drink.

"Is that all you can do—escape into a drunken stupor?"

"I'm a heavy drinker. I have an enormous capacity." He settled back again on the sofa and looked at her. "Diana, what's the real reason behind all this?"

She sat straight on the sofa. "You mean you still don't understand?"

"I don't think you understand yourself." He looked over at her, feeling already a sadness at losing her. "But if what you want of me is to leave Enright because you hate it, I can't give you that. I talked them into this—I couldn't walk out if I wanted to. And I don't want to."

"Tom, you're blind!"

"It'd be different if I were the one to say I can't work here—or I can't work under pressure—or I can't work without more freedom. But I can work here. I'm getting my freedom—sometimes I have to fight for it, but I get it. And as for pressure—yes, you're right, there's pressure. It's there."

"You admit it now!"

"I admit it and I thrive on it. Quiet, scholarly, unhurried institutions are wonderful for some people. For some people it's the only way they can work, and they do great things and I don't belittle them. And maybe someday I'll want that, too. But I don't want it now. I love the pace here."

"Pressure—just for profit—and you love it!"

Tom stood up and picked up the bottle and walked over to the fireplace. "Pressure isn't all bad, Diana. It's like coal. It's dirty—and oil is greasy—but they both make heat."

Silently Diana watched him a minute and then she gave her head a sad, knowing nod. "People like you are unbalanced, Tom," she said. "Refusal to face reality is a form of insanity. It's just a question of degree."

Leaning against the fireplace, Tom smiled. "Oh, I don't know, Diana. Aren't most people like that to some degree? Think about it. Isn't it true that if the majority of people could foresee their destiny they'd give up?"

"That's different."

"No, it's not so different. In research we're constricting time to the short duration of our problem, but it's the same thing. Does the average clerk think he's going to be a clerk all his life? It may turn out that way, but he doesn't think it's going to be that way." He lifted his drink. "This is only in defense of my sanity, you understand."

"I'm not interested in clerks. I'm interested in you."

"Diana, I don't resent Enright and you do, and it's a hurdle we can't seem to get over. You resent the fact that they want results from my work and they want them as fast as possible. That doesn't bother me and it doesn't scare me. I'm not holding out a tin cup for charity."

"No! You're doing something much nobler—you're selling out, for money!"

Tom smiled. "They're betting my salary that I can produce, Diana," he said. "It's as simple as that."

"That is absolutely disgusting!"

"Not to me. I think they've got a good bet."

"It's not a good bet because they'll never back you long enough to win—even if you won't believe me now because you haven't the courage to admit the possibility of failure."

"No, I don't admit it!" Tom said, suddenly angry. "Why should I be preoccupied with failure?" He turned away from her and then, after a minute, looked back. "Diana, you talk so glibly of failure. You seem almost eager for it to happen. I wonder if you even know the meaning of the word. Have you ever seen a man who gave up —who gave in to failure? Do you know what a man is like who has been knocked down and won't get up again? Well, I've seen it. I saw my father—and it's not pretty. He simply resigned from life— he seceded from the world and set up a separate state in some static dreamworld where nothing touched him—and he just died. I don't even think he knew he was dying—he was dead already. Failure is a very serious thing, Diana. The simple failure of some little plan is nothing—but when a man regards himself as a failure, something has gone wrong with the machinery and it doesn't work right any more. So don't be in a hurry to convince a man that he's a failure—me or any other man."

Anger burned in Diana's face. She walked to the door and without turning around, she opened it and went out. Looking at the fireplace, Tom heard her footsteps going down the stairs. He let her go.

Until the sounds of her car were gone, Tom stood at the fireplace. Then he drained his glass and began to move about the room. All the women in this world, he said to himself, and you had to pick one who was hell-bent on fixing everything up—making everything over.

He looked at the bottle on the table. It had been more than a quarter full when he came home. Now it was almost empty. He went over and poured what remained into his glass, and then he emptied the glass he had poured for Diana into it, too. The world is jammed up with women, he said to himself, and you had to pick a reformer—a missionary to the dark continent of man's corruption —a happy little mender of everyone else's ways. He picked up the bottle cork and heaved it across the room, aiming at the waste-basket. It missed and he picked up the empty bottle, tempted to follow with that. He weighed it in his hand and then put it down and went back to drinking.

After a while he found himself at the desk, where there were still some broth notes and some EA 50 notes and the card from Sam Lewis. He picked up the card and thought why not—why the hell not—and threw it down again. He spread the pile of notes around on the desk and stood looking down at them. They looked dead now—they were like dry dead wreaths on tombstones, and there was a graveyard full of them, four months' accumulation. That damned EA 50 was in the first batch, he said to himself—and it was four months crawling to its death. That's slow dying. And some-thing's got to give. But what? What more could you have done?

He laughed without pleasure. The answer to that, my friend, is nothing, he told himself—because there isn't a damn thing you could have done to make it any good—nothing more with it and nothing more with her. With both of them you were on the wrong track from the start, and if you think otherwise you are kidding yourself—you're engaging in one of the great national pastimes, my friend—the warm, smothering art of self-delusion.

He dropped into the chair next to the desk. But maybe in another way you could have done more, he said to himself. Maybe you over-looked something that would have made a difference—not in the end, because whatever you did, it was no good, but in the beginning. A difference in time. Maybe you overlooked something that would have speeded things up and told you sooner that it was no good. That's the problem, he said to himself. You can't fix an egg when it's rotten—as the saying goes. But you don't have to eat the whole thing—as the saying goes on—to find it out. Why so many sayings about eggs? he thought. What's so basic about an egg? Hell, what's more basic than an egg? He was getting drunk.

And what about women, oh sage, oh wise one, as long as in your brilliant inebriated condition your machinery is clicking out great thoughts? How can you find out sooner about a woman?

That's your target for tonight, friend—how do you find out sooner? He slid down in the chair, considering this. What little thing that you don't know—or that you didn't do—would have told you faster that the damned antibiotic was no good?

Maybe—his thoughts wound up and shot off in another direction —maybe you're making a mistake somewhere. Maybe you're accepting something as basic—basic as an egg—and maybe that something is not basic. How about that? Talk about delusions! The world is cluttered with delusions! It's choking with delusions! Just consider the hallowed bloopers—the great delusions of history. The world is flat . . . and the sun moves around the earth . . . and bleeding is therapeutic. And Galileo was persecuted . . . and they burned witches in Salem . . . and they laughed at Columbus . . . and at Pasteur. And it wasn't so long ago that everyone knew that what was in the soil was harmful, and almost any great mind could have told you that it was the source of most epidemics. And the truth is that if those soil microbes died, that's when you'd get one hell of an epidemic.

So what about you? How many tidy little delusions are you buying? How many worlds are you calling flat? How many witches are you burning? Just because it's in the literature doesn't mean it's so. The sanctity of the printed page is a highly overtouted myth. Somebody makes a faulty deduction, based on incomplete evidence, and there you are—the sun swinging around the earth—a fact established—an error everyone has gotten so used to that the bastard becomes legitimate. *Never accept anything on superficial evidence without more questioning.*

And that goes for women, too. Especially women. In fact, with women, question them, and if they know the answer, forget them!

There was a little Scotch left in his glass. He finished it and sat still, deciding whether to take out another bottle. He looked over at the card on the desk and looked away, rejecting its suggestion. He thought of Midge Potter, and went to the telephone.

"You can't come over," Midge said. "I got a date."

"Break it." Propping the telephone against his shoulder, Tom reached into the cabinet for another bottle.

"Just like that?"

"Don't you start that," he said.

"Start what? Who's starting anything?"

"My coat is on—my tie is. tied, almost. I have a fresh bottle of Scotch precariously in my pocket and I'll be right there."

"I'm on my way out!"

"Turn around," he said. "I'm on my way over."

"Honest to God, I think you're crazy!" Midge said. She drew back the curtain and looked down at the street. "I told you—I got a date."

Tom opened the Scotch. "He's late—he's had his chance. We don't wait around here forever."

The big innocent-looking eyes examined him. "You're in good condition."

"The best."

Tom looked around the little apartment. In the weeks since he had been here nothing had changed. His eye took in the red slip-covered sofa that opened into a bed and the red curtains and the table with the little white radio next to the flowered lampshade. As always, the radio was playing a little too loud, and he went over and turned it off. He handed Midge a drink and started on his own.

Midge jerked her head at his glass. "You ain't exactly got much room for improvement."

"Don't complain," he said. "I can't stand a complaining-type woman. Why don't you come away from that window?"

Uneasily, Midge looked down at the street again. She was wearing a sheer, low-cut white blouse and a narrow black skirt that did little to conceal her natural assets. Her thick black hair brushed against her shoulders.

Tom refilled his glass and sprawled in a chair. "Midge, my beautiful, glamorous creature—you ever get it into your beautiful glamorous head that you have to fix things up—fix everything up?"

"All the time." She laughed. "I'm very neat."

"Good," he said. "That's what I like." A woman should never

know what you're talking about. The less the better. "Midge, my lovely creature—have you ever considered all the delusions from which the world has suffered?"

"I'm glad you asked," she said, "because that's something that bothers me all the time. What are you talking about?"

"That's a good question," he said. "That's basic—like an egg."

"Oh, boy," she said, "are you in good shape!"

"Will you come away from that damned window?"

Midge turned and settled her weight on one hip. "Look," she said. "I happen to have a date—which I'm not breaking."

"Then if you won't come away from the window, turn off the light."

"Honest to God, I think you're crazy!" she burst out again. "For more'n a month you play dead and all of a sudden, eight o'clock at night, you're on your way."

"You're right," he said. "I treat you very badly." He got up and turned off the light, and the red neon light from the corner drugstore threw a pink glow across her face and throat and the rise of her breasts over the low white blouse. "Don't have anything more to do with me."

"I'm thinking of it."

"Very sensible." He was like a man returning home after a long absence, he thought—leisurely savoring the almost forgotten pleasures and remembering how much he had enjoyed them once. Unhurriedly he moved his hand over Midge's face and her ear and her throat and along the frill of the low blouse. He drew her away from the window.

Outside a horn sounded and she moved her head. "That's my date," she whispered.

"You don't hear a thing!"

"Look, I gotta go!"

"You don't have to go."

The horn called again and she pulled away and he stopped her. "You don't have to go anywhere."

In the dark he saw her breasts rise and fall quickly, saw her lids close a little, saw her glance at the window and then at him and then again at him and he waited, letting his desire speak in its own language to hers, letting her desire speak to itself—and then the eyes changed and warmed and he saw that she would stay.

The horn sounded again, more insistent. "Maybe I should go down

232

and tell him."

"Will he come up if you don't?"

"No—he won't even stay out there long, when I don't come down."

He released her and dropped off his jacket and tie and moved over to the sofa that opened into a bed. When he turned, she was standing again at the window—barefoot, with her lacy blouse in her hand.

For a moment Tom stood quietly looking at her—at the broad bare back, at the fullness and firmness of the breasts. Waiting for her, he could feel his quickening stomach and inwardly he laughed at himself. What a deception is a man's desire, he thought. What a hoax! When one minute he can be ruled totally by a taste for the small and slender, the delicate-boned, the elegant-featured—and then an hour later by a different taste—and surely a more primitive one—and ruled again so completely that he could hardly recall the other, or hear the horn that sounded in the street.

A man is a creature of so many selves, he thought. And each self has its own desire—and each has a time when it rises up and struggles to rule. And the desire of one self is not necessarily compatible with the desire of another.

Midge dropped the curtain and turned from the window. "Well —he's gone."

She dropped her blouse on the chair and her skirt on top of it and came across the room, and he touched her warm shoulder, the self of this moment desiring totally, he knew, what the self of another time had not desired at all—the self of this moment desiring not at all what the other had desired totally. The I of now cares only for the I of now. Not Diana now—not knowledge now—no one else and nothing else and no other gain or goal or reason or desire of another self—this self had its own desire and this self commanded.

And then the desire was gained and gone—and another self took up the abandoned command. Satisfaction knows no urgency, and fulfillment fights no battles. Nothing conquers totally or reigns forever. He lay back with his head at the edge of the pillow and fell asleep.

In the morning Tom came awake slowly, feeling that overnight it had turned cold, and then he heard the traffic and a door slammed somewhere and he realized that he was not home, and in another instant he knew where he was and that he had stayed all night, which he had not done before.

In her sleep Midge moved, and he looked at her, turned to him now, her arm across the pillow. Turning on his side, Tom touched her and she awoke, smiling a little, as though even in sleep she had been waiting for him.

Then he was quiet again—and his thoughts, guided by his reasoning self again, turned in another direction, and he began to think about EA 50.

Warm in bed, relaxed, he began to build layer upon layer of reason. The natural function of an antibiotic, he told himself, is to protect the microbe—not man. If man can turn it to his own use, that's his good luck—but that is not its prime function in the scheme of things. In nature's design, antibiotics establish living space for the variety of existing species so that they can continue to exist— so that nothing conquers totally or reigns permanently.

That is a law, he thought suddenly. That is part of nature's code. Whether it is a microorganism or the most consuming of man's passions, nothing conquers totally.

And in nature's design, he thought, antibiotics enforce that law. They keep life in balance—all life. In nature's design the life of man is not the exclusive consideration. Nothing reigns totally.

And in that design the antibiotic has changed and developed and shaped itself to meet the life needs of the microbe, and there is no reason for it to be cooperative where man is concerned. It would be nice if it would be cooperative, but it does not necessarily follow that it must.

He looked at his watch and saw that it was time to get up. What does necessarily follow, he told himself, is that you can't keep taking four months with each one to get that piece of information. Somehow you have to get to it a lot sooner.

How could I have done it? he said to himself. What did I overlook? *What more could I have done?*

What more could I have done?

All day, while Tom worked at other things, the question kept coming back to bother him. All day the details of the past four months paraded through his mind, and he said to himself, Where did it start to look good? Where did my hopes begin to rise? And where did I go wrong? *What more could I have done?*

At the end of the day he sat in his office still thinking about it. How could I have gotten here faster—to the same place? What else could I have done—more than I did?

He stood up and moved to the window. It had been a cold gray day and now it was almost dark. Down below he could see people going home, walking across the yard with their collars turned up.

And then, suddenly, standing there at the window, looking out at the end of a gray cheerless day, Tom thought, No! Not what *more* could I have done! Not *more!* Less!

There it was.

What could I have done less?

For a minute he stared down at the dark moving shapes of people below. It was so simple—so logical—now that he had it. What could I have *left out?* How could I have arrived here with half the work —at the same place? And then he said to himself, What place? The place you've arrived at is that you poured the antibiotic down the drain because it was no good—and it was no good because the mice dropped dead.

All right, then, he said to himself, how could you have arrived there with half the work? Hell—how could you have gotten there with a quarter the work? A tenth? It's not necessary to do such a fancy job, he said to himself, of producing dead mice.

When he reached home and saw Diana's car in the driveway, Tom sat in his own car a minute wondering what she wanted now. Was it possible that she hoped to apply another splint, another bandage, to this shattered affair and try to heal it again? There was no light in the house and he wondered what that meant. Then he saw that she was sitting in her car.

"Hello," she said flatly, when he came up to her.

"What are you doing sitting out here?" he said.

She made no move to get out of the car. "Last night I came back," she said.

In the dark, with only the light from the streetlamp, Tom looked down at her.

"When I got home, he was gloating so—my father—saying it was all over. It was disgusting—so I came back. Where were you?"

"After you left, I went out."

"Where?"

"Diana, it's cold out here. Do you want to come inside?"

She didn't move. "I waited all night," she said.

"I stayed out all night."

She was silent, and accusation sat in her eyes.

"What did you come back for?" he said.

"To tell you—" she said and broke off and just looked at him.

He put a hand on the door handle. "Do you want to come in the house?" he said again.

"You stayed out all night last night."

"Diana, you knew before you came tonight that I stayed out all night last night. You were here."

With a quick movement, she started the car. "I only came tonight to say goodbye," she said. "When I was in New York I found a small gallery for sale. I've decided to buy it."

Around the fermentation building the tails of steam rose from the pipes against a gray sky, and the leaves were almost gone from the maple branch that reached across the window.

For the past month Derrick had been bringing data sheets on the cultures to the Monday morning meeting because someone, operating on the theory that if two heads are better than one, then ten must be better than two, had decided that if the group looked them over and discussed them, the chances of selecting the right ones would be improved. This morning everyone was discussing them more knowingly than usual because, for the third time since they had begun, Ade Hale was sitting in on the meeting.

With great care, George Weir was studying the data sheets, picking one here, one there, rejecting several in between. With an equally good show Metcalf, a third biochemist who had been assigned to the project, was choosing his. Metcalf was a crisp, efficient kind of man with an authoritative manner. At thirty-eight he still had the build of a football player, and looking at him, you had a feeling that his team would always win—even if he had to steal the signals.

"I like them with a good sharp-edged zone of inhibition," Weir was saying.

"Why?" Tom looked up. "What difference does it make?"

"I think a fuzzy edge is significant, Tom," Weir said, glancing up from the sheet. "I feel it indicates faulty activity. Now, here's one that seems fairly potent but I wouldn't touch it with that fuzzy edge."

Tom looked at it. "I'll take it."

He saw Hale watching him and he thought that it was too bad, in a way, that Hale had picked today to come, because there was probably going to be an argument here before this meeting was over.

"Haven't you ever noticed, Dr. Cable," Morrissey said with a patronizing smile, "that some areas of inhibition have this fuzzy edge while others are razor-sharp?"

"Of course I've noticed it. Only I don't know what it means."

"I agree with Dr. Weir," Metcalf said crisply. "I want a good clean edge."

For another few minutes they studied the sheets, and then Weir said he had enough. "I have some old ones I'm trying new variations on this week," he said.

Then Metcalf said he had enough, too.

"Tom?" Derrick said.

"Give me more. I'll take anything that's active and potent. Only give me a lot of them."

Morrissey jerked his head in sharp annoyance. "You've got more already than you can handle," he said, and then added, "if you're going to do any real work on them, that is."

"I'm not going to do so much work on them any more," Tom said.

"You're not doing enough work now," Morrissey said with quick anger. He was very nervous this morning. They were all nervous because Hale was here.

Tom could see the others beginning to look at him, with that damp look that he had come to recognize—that politely concealed disapproval of educated men.

"I've worked out ten broths that I like," he said evenly. "And from now on, I'm going to put every culture into all ten at once, right at the start. And that's all I'm going to do. It's got to work in one of the ten or I'm not going to bother with it."

"What do you mean, you're not going to bother with it?" Morrissey demanded.

"I mean that if the culture doesn't produce in one of the ten, I'm through with it. And if it does produce, I'm going to start getting

237

it out. I'm not wasting any more time fussing with broths for cultures that won't do anything—or growing a big supply of something that's no good."

Before Tom had finished speaking, Morrissey was on his feet. "I won't have it!" he gasped. "I won't tolerate it!"

Stubbornly, Tom shook his head. "From now on, with me, it's got to work in one shot."

"I'm shocked!"

"I know you're shocked, Dr. Morrissey." They were all shocked. "But for four months now we've been fooling around with broths —and what have we gained?"

"What have we gained! We've gained the certainty—"

Now suddenly they were all talking, all protesting, at once. Only Will Caroline seemed undisturbed—and, of course, Derrick. Tom glanced over at Hale, who seemed more watchful than upset.

"Not me!" Weir said. Disgusted, he sat back in his chair. "I won't do it."

"I can't say I care for that," Metcalf said.

Harrup was running his pencil point furiously along the seam of his briefcase. "If you're going to abandon this as an exact science," he said, "you might as well stop the whole thing right now—today." The corners of his mouth turned down. "If you're just going to look at it emotionally—"

"Well, look at it unemotionally, then!" Tom struggled to stay calm. All he wanted was to do it his way and not be delayed arguing about it. "Look at EA 50. I fooled around for weeks with those broths—and what did I accomplish? I grew a beautiful supply of a toxic drug."

"I won't sanction it!" Morrissey said to everyone at the table. "I won't tolerate it!"

"I don't know why we're even discussing it," Harrup said. "If you're standing over a precipice on only one solid board, you don't pull that board out from under you. Everyone knows the broth makes the difference."

"Until now we've accepted that fact," Tom said, "but we've made the wrong deduction from it. We've assumed that we had to fool around and fool around until we developed the right broth for each culture. This is a delusion—and it's caught us in a costly, time-consuming trap. Certainly if we fuss with the broths we get better yields. But the good ones look good from the start."

238

"I can't agree with that," Weir said.

"There's almost never a dark horse!"

For a moment there was silence, and he knew they were thinking it over, trying to remember, and then Hale said, a little impatiently, "Well, is it true or isn't it?"

"It's true. You can check the records," Tom said.

Hale leaned forward on the table. "You told me yourself about the precursor, Dr. Cable."

"In the ten broths a precursor will be there. Maybe not the best— but if the culture is any good, it will do something in one of them."

"We've improved penicillin yields considerably, experimenting with broths," Hale shot back. "Doubled and tripled it."

"I'm all for it—after the mouse lives!" Tom said. "The time to fuss with broths is when you know it's worth it."

"Well!" Morrissey said. "Just supposing penicillin had gone into one broth and it was the wrong one—"

"This is going into ten—not one."

"Just suppose that had happened, you'd have said, 'No good— out—down the drain!'"

"And that first penicillin wasn't in any special broth. It fell onto an ordinary agar plate—and the area of inhibition was enormous! Fleming couldn't help but notice that huge ring on the Petri dish!"

"I consider this the most dangerous statement that has ever been made in this room!" Harrup said flatly.

"Why? Why are you so sure it's necessary to work them so much at the start? How do you know?"

"You are talking emotions and I am talking about a proven fact," Harrup said.

"The proven fact is that you can increase yields—and I agree with that. But why do we need top yields of something that's no good?"

"This is a serious risk." Harrup turned to Hale. "This jeopardizes the whole program."

"A calculated risk!" Tom said. "But what about all those cultures in Dr. Derrick's laboratory? In the time I've wasted fooling around, trying to get cultures to produce that didn't want to produce—in the weeks I wasted growing a big supply of a toxic drug —how many more could I have worked through that are just lying around down there?"

"Of course, you're perfectly safe," Morrissey said. "We'll never know how many good ones you threw out unless we assign someone to pick up your work where you drop it."

"If you do that, I can't stop you," Tom said. "But this is how I'm going to work."

Later, back in his laboratory, he said, "Moose—from now on we're going to test these broths ourselves."

"Something wrong in assay?" Moose said.

"We can do it faster ourselves. We're going to keep it very simple. Nothing fancy with a series of test tubes. We're going to dip a paper disc into a broth, put it on an agar plate and the next day measure the clear area. Anything under twenty-two millimeters we're throwing out."

"After which incubation?" Moose said.

"After the first. Then, anything we like, we start to get out."

Moose reserved judgment for a moment while he thought that over. Then he jerked his head. "I like that," he said. "That's a good idea."

"I don't know, Will." Ade Hale shook his head as they walked back to his office. "Does he know what he's doing?"

"Leave him alone, Ade," Will Caroline said. "If he's wrong, he'll prove it to himself long before the others here will change his mind."

George Weir knew there was something womanish about disliking mice. It had to do with an atavistic fear of being violated, and he told himself as he stood in Mills's laboratory that it sure as hell wasn't anything like that with him. It was just that he hated things that crawled—snakes, caterpillars, worms. Without even thinking about it, when he came upon anything that crawled, he would put his heel on it and grind it into the ground until it had lost the shape of anything that could have had life.

In Mills's laboratory Weir looked at the six mice crawling around in the jar, and suddenly he remembered the garden snake he had killed last summer. He had come upon it in the back yard, in a patch of long grass, a thin brown snake about a foot and a half long, and he had beat it past recognition with an iron rake. And then he had thought about a time when he was a boy, when he

240

had found a rat near the cellar door and had knocked it senseless with a broom and then turned the broom around and beat it to a bloody mess with the handle. With him it wasn't anything womanish or squeamish or fearful. It was just that he hated things that crawled.

Now, as he watched Mills lift the mouse out of the jar, feet dangling, something turned over in Weir's stomach because he knew that mouse was going to die. He hadn't wanted to test this antibiotic yet, but it was a month since Cable had sent his first to mice and he was getting ready to send a second, and Metcalf, who had started later, was talking about sending one. Weir had decided that it wouldn't look good to wait much longer.

Mills flipped the mouse over on his palm and injected the tail vein while the mouse squealed and bared its hideous single tooth like a dirty old man and dripped urine, and Weir's hand closed into a fist around his key ring in his pocket. Mills put the mouse back, and the other little bastards crept over to it and began smelling around.

For a minute the mouse lay there on the sawdust, getting itself obscenely smelled. Then it jerked. It jerked and began to crawl. It crawled over to the side of the jar and started to shake. It pawed at the sawdust.

"Christ," Weir muttered. "Christ—look at him."

"That's a common pattern, George," Mills said. "They crawl and shake and start to dig and go into a convulsion and die."

Weir licked his lips.

Mills's hand went into the jar for another mouse, and Weir whipped around. "What're you doing another one for?" he demanded. "This one's dying already!"

Mills injected the second mouse. "One mouse isn't any kind of a test, George. You get individual differences and odd reactions with mice, the same as with people." Mills was watching the first mouse, and Weir looked back at it and saw it flop over against the side of the jar.

"A mouse could die of fright," Mills said. "Or you could get an old one dying of heart failure."

Now the mouse was all drawn in tight, legs pulled close to its body, and Weir knew it was having a convulsion.

Then it died.

And then the second one died. And the other mice were all crawling around looking and smelling. The key in Weir's fist was cutting into his flesh as he heard Mills say, "We'll cut it down."

Three days later Mills tested again for Tom Cable. This antibiotic was not as active as EA 50, but it was the best Tom had had for several weeks. It was gram-positive only and it didn't hit as many organisms as penicillin, but it was potent and easy to extract. It had separated nicely from a large quantity of impurities.

"All right, men," Mills said. He held the tail and found the vein.

"Oh—kee-rist!"

The syringe was still in the tail vein and the mouse was dead in his hand.

PART
THREE

DECEMBER 1946 –
APRIL 1947

Winifred was already at the table, drinking her coffee, when Morrissey came to breakfast—and the radio was playing and the announcer reminded his listeners that, including this gray day just beginning, there were eleven shopping days until Christmas. Ordinarily, Morrissey regarded himself as a fairly sophisticated man who could poke fun at this little commonplace, but this year it was nothing to joke about. At the end of the year people tended to appraise the work, and although in a way he wanted just that—wanted them to appraise this project and end it —still, when it happened it wasn't going to be pleasant.

He sat down and took out his pocket appointment book. "Full schedule today, Winifred," he said.

After a full minute, Winifred's eyes came away from her coffee, and if Morrissey hadn't known better, he might have thought that she had been considering his words. But Winifred was always like this at breakfast. Every morning you could read the hostility in her eyes, as though she had come awake considering the heavy load she carried, and every morning, wrapped in that dull flannel robe, she would sit there, concentrating on that mug of coffee as though it would vanish if she looked away. Between sips she would just hold it in front of her face and stare at it.

"What do you have to do?" she said finally.

"Well, you know Tony Vought is coming in today," he said. Vought was a biochemist at a Midwestern pharmaceutical house, a larger company than Enright, and over the years Morrissey had struck up a friendship with him at meetings and conferences. "I always enjoy a good discussion with Tony," he said. "He usually knows what he's talking about."

Winifred's eyes went back to the cup. "If he's on his way to Europe, why's he wasting a day coming to Enright?"

"Well, I invited him," Morrissey said. "When I heard he would be in the East, I asked him to come up for the day."

"His company sending him to Europe?"

"I believe they are. That's my impression, anyway."

The eyes stayed on the cup. "Why don't you get your company

to send you to Europe?"

Her day just wasn't right if she couldn't get it started with a few digs at him. Annoyed, Morrissey split the shell of his egg and changed the subject. "And it's Monday—there's always the meeting. And after lunch I've got to talk to some new technicians we're putting on."

Winifred looked up at that. "Who's getting new technicians?"

"Weir's technician is leaving—he's getting a replacement. And Derrick is getting another girl."

"He just got a girl! What—is everyone quitting over there?"

"No—no. His girl isn't leaving. He's getting another."

"Well." She bit into this news. "How does Derrick rate so much help?"

Morrissey shrugged. "I'm not sure I like it, I'll tell you that. And he didn't come to me about it. He went to Will Caroline and said, 'What I need is hands, not brains—don't hire me expensive college graduates—just get me some good girls—good hands.' He's a great one for speed. Speed—speed—speed."

"Now, what've you got against Derrick?" she said.

"Nothing," he said. It was true. Derrick was a likable enough fellow—easygoing, mild, unobtrusive. "He's pleasant enough—never argues—hasn't argued with anyone since the day he came." Morrissey fussed with his egg. "It's just that—well—I'm not sure that he knows very much."

Winifred looked at him hard and then she got up and went for more coffee, and Morrissey's thoughts worked around again to Tony Vought. The truth was that he'd wanted to get Tony Vought up here for several reasons. For one thing, a year ago Tony had mentioned an interest in streptomycin, and Morrissey hoped that maybe, by now, Tony knew something about it that nobody at Enright seemed to know, and if he did, he hoped he could pump it out of him. In Morrissey's mind, the biggest headache of this project was turning out to be streptomycin.

The trouble was that it was too common. They kept finding it over and over again—and streptothricin almost as much. And, worse still, it was tricky. It kept slipping past Gates and somebody would waste a lot of time working on it. And all that cost money—and it didn't look good—and it was a problem that no one at Enright seemed able to solve. But if Tony Vought had followed up his interest, he might have come across something special—and,

Morrissey thought, maybe Enright could pick up some useful information.

The second reason was that he would like to pick up Tony Vought himself. More than anything else Morrissey wanted to see the end of this. But he had just about decided that—if the work was to continue—he had to have an assistant director in whom he could have confidence and Vought was as good a man as he would find. He wondered what it would take to get him to come.

"What are you going to say to those technicians?" Winifred said from the kitchen.

"Oh, I usually tell them about the conduct that's expected of them—on and off the premises. And that we require good attendance, absolute accuracy—no sloppy jobs."

"Just let them know that whoever their boss is, you're his boss."

"Oh, I will—don't worry." Morrissey glanced out at the sky which was graying over heavily. It was going to rain—or, if it was cold enough, it might even snow. "Of course, they're all in my department—this new help," he said. "It gives me a pretty big staff. My department is much bigger than Neil Harrup's these days. Neil hasn't said anything, but I'm sure he's noticed."

Winifred snorted. "As long as they don't complicate Neil's life, he doesn't care who has a bigger department. Elaine cares—not Neil."

Well, she could make light of it, but it was a fact that his was the largest department in research now—and so far he was holding onto his control pretty well. If he could just keep it that way—keep them all proceeding logically from one step to the next instead of running wild—it would be all right. And if he could get a good assistant—someone he could depend on, someone who would back him up—he could probably do it.

"But then there's the other side of the coin," he said as she came back with the coffeepot and filled his cup. "When they look things over, they're going to find out that much more money went down my particular drain. Just streptomycin alone is costing a fortune. I've told you that."

"Regularly," she said. "With tears in your eyes."

"Well, I don't like these mistakes in my department," he snapped. "I've half a mind to order Gates to do each test twice, but repeating them probably wouldn't change anything—the tests just aren't good enough. And besides, then somebody would ask why my people can't do things right the first time."

Winifred carried the coffeepot back to the stove and came back. "Listen, Claude," she said. "Don't worry so much about your department. This is the whole company—not just your department."

"Well, it's my responsibility," Morrissey said irritably. "And now all this help for Derrick. I don't know whether he's going to turn out twice the work with it or just twice as many wrong cultures."

Suddenly Winifred jerked her head. "Say that today."

"Say what today?"

"Say that—at the meeting—that Derrick's giving you the wrong cultures."

"Well, he probably is—the way we keep getting streptomycin."

"Exactly." She jerked her head again. "Say it."

"I wouldn't be surprised if a great deal of our trouble is his fault," Morrissey said. "There are some areas in which his approach is shockingly unscientific. Take the soil samples, for instance. He takes them from anywhere—just anywhere. No system whatsoever. Most of them are still coming from around here, but he'd accept anything. He's probably not getting the right soil samples to begin with—so how can he possibly get the right cultures out of them?"

"Say that, too—and without the probably."

"I may—I just may. After all, this is Derrick's field. He should know enough to get the proper samples."

"If the samples aren't right," she coached him, "what's the point of the rest of it? That's what you say."

"Still—I don't know—I wanted to bring up something about Cable today."

Winifred plunked her elbows on the table. "Listen, Claude," she said. "You're worried sick about all these things going wrong in your department. All right, then—get yourself on record as objecting—"

"How can I know what's going wrong next?"

"Listen, Claude." She was like a bird dog—when she was hot on a trail, nothing could stop her. "Whenever anyone suggests something that's been proved, you be the first to agree. Leap to your feet and cheer."

"You know practically nothing ever comes up that's been proved."

"Anything else—anything new—object." She leaned forward on the table, the black eyes like beads. "Ninety-nine times out of a hundred you'll be right. And that's a pretty good average—even for you."

248

As much as Morrissey would permit himself to, he glared at her. You always have to get them in, don't you, you old bitch, he thought. You always have to get in your digs. "I do object," he said. "I object to all kinds of things. Winifred, if I do say so myself, I'm the man who's keeping this fire under control. In my department, it's logic above all—"

"Listen, Claude," she said. "For this project, if you're smart, you won't be so eager to have a department."

Dumbfounded, Morrissey just stared at Winifred. For eight years he'd had his department, and for fifteen years before that he'd worked for it.

"Every chance you get, you remind them that this is a *team effort*. Spread the blame. A team. No department."

"Winifred, it's *my department!*" He broke off because suddenly something told him she was right. He'd have to think about that. He felt in his pocket for his pipe, and after a moment he said, "Winifred—I've been thinking—what would you say to getting them to hire Tony Vought?"

"Is he good?"

"He's as good as any man in the field. Of course, it's a question whether he'd come."

"Ask him," she said.

Morrissey shot her a resentful look. She always oversimplified his problems—it was another way of ridiculing him. He got up to go to work, and she took her coffee and padded along behind him. In the living room, Morrissey picked up his briefcase and opened it to put in some journals. Every night now he brought home a few journals, and some nights he actually pushed himself through some articles he knew he ought to read. Other nights he couldn't even bring himself to open his briefcase. With distaste he looked at the journals he had tried to read last night. He saw Winifred watching him over her cup.

"Listen, Claude," she said. "Night and day you're worrying because you don't know enough about this. Let me tell you something. It doesn't matter. You don't have to *know*—you only have to *seem* as though you know."

He slid the journals into the briefcase.

"You don't have to *be* good," she said. "You only have to *look* good."

He took the briefcase and went to the door and she followed him.

"Listen, Claude," she said. "To come up with a new idea, you have to know something—but you don't have to know much to knock it. You do as I say. Object—attack—stir up trouble."

He opened the door and felt that it was cold. It was going to snow—he was sure of it. He put on a sweater and a scarf.

"What are you going to do with Tony while you're at the meeting?" she said.

"I've asked Brainard to take him around production for that hour or so."

Winifred shook her head. "Find something else for him to do."

"Why?" He found his rubbers and pulled one on. "It's all arranged."

"Claude," she said, "sometimes men are crazy enough to stay on a sinking ship—but did you ever hear of a man boarding one? If you want Tony, you find something else for him to do."

As he drove to work, Morrissey reflected on Winifred's advice. She was right, he thought. He should worry less and complain more. Winifred was always right. She had to get in her digs, but she was shrewd and her advice usually worked. Uneasily he wondered whether she was right about that department business, too.

He came into his office and put his briefcase on the desk. Then he saw suddenly that the barge was leaving the dock again and he stared at it. Only a few days ago it had pulled out—Morrissey brushed at his pocket—and now it was already filled and leaving again. He turned from the window and looked at the briefcase and moved it out of sight, unopened, down on the floor.

"You see, Tony, we have our problems," Morrissey said to Vought a little later as they were leaving Derrick's laboratory. "But—we try to solve them."

Tony Vought was a lean, good-looking man of about forty, who listened carefully when you spoke to him, and Morrissey was trying hard to be circumspect—to seem as though he were directing the project, but somehow not responsible—as though he were for it and yet recognized the folly of it.

"These new young fellows," Morrissey said. "Sometimes just keeping them in line makes me feel more like a top sergeant than a chemist. But I guess it's all part of the job."

250

"Oh, right," Vought said, with a bright smile.

"This fellow here—very peculiar personality." Morrissey nodded toward Derrick and then glanced resentfully through the glass panel at the rows of Petri dishes on the counter. Those dishes had caused him considerable embarrassment a moment ago—and all because Derrick had changed his testing technique without telling anyone. While they were in there Morrissey had picked up a dish and without looking at it he had said, "And this is where he tests them, Tony." Then he had looked at the dish and received quite a shock. Instead of the usual arrangement of a gram-positive line and a gram-negative line with an antibiotic line streaked across them, there were six small filter-paper discs arranged in a circle.

For one horrible moment Morrissey had stared at the Petri dish, not knowing what it was he was looking at—not even sure that this was a test plate. It could be something else entirely—one of those wild experiments Derrick was always running to try to learn something. Then Derrick moved up to the counter and said, "Now, here's a recent change we've made. We used to streak these test plates —ah know you've seen that technique, Dr. Vought. But now we incubate a whole plate with one gram-positive test organism, and we dip these filter discs into six different antibiotics and place them on it. Do the same on a gram-negative plate. That way we get to test them six at a time."

"Seems more efficient," Vought said.

"Yes, sir," Derrick said, "and it's faster to dip than it is to streak."

"Too bad you didn't know this at the start, Dr. Derrick," Morrissey had put in pointedly. "It would have saved a lot of man hours."

"Ah wish ah had," Derrick said pleasantly.

Now in the corridor Morrissey wondered uneasily whether Tony had noticed his confusion. "When he finally came up with this technique," he said, "I was pretty upset about the time he'd wasted with the old way. But then you can't do everything—you have to let them decide some things themselves."

"Oh, absolutely," Vought said.

"This fellow's been something of a problem," Morrissey said. "All speed—but like a football player racing toward the wrong goal. He's made some costly mistakes. Bungled the soil-sample collection program badly. We're having a meeting about that this morning.

I'll have to leave you for a few minutes, Tony—I hope you won't mind."

"Certainly not," Tony said. "I have some material with me to read on the plane. I'll get started on it."

"Oh, fine. I was going to give you a few interesting things I've come across lately—but then you've probably seen them."

They started back to the office. "Of course we're not without progress, Tony," Morrissey said. "Only thing is we'd like to see more. Sometimes I have the feeling that just a few good men in key spots would do it."

"Hmm," Vought said.

"We get nuisance problems—like streptomycin. This Derrick just plain can't recognize it. And Dr. Cable—that fellow you met earlier—I can't tell you how many times he's gone ahead and worked on a culture—put good time into it—before he realized he had streptomycin. Or streptothricin."

"They're pretty closely related," Vought said.

"Too damned close," Morrissey said, not entirely sure what he meant by that.

"That might be an interesting study—that relationship," Vought said. "I'm inclined to think that in evolution streptothricin is older. Predates streptomycin. I've had some thoughts about it—but I won't waste your time with them now."

Morrissey reflected on that a moment. "This something you've become interested in, Tony?" he said cautiously.

"Well—some," Tony said. "I got interested in t.b. a while ago and it led to this. But my company isn't doing much along these lines."

Morrissey looked up quickly, wondering if perhaps Vought was not entirely happy where he was. They came up to his office, and with a start Morrissey saw that Brainard was here, waiting to take Vought around production. With everything else on his mind, Morrissey had forgotten to cancel the appointment.

For a moment he groped for an excuse. Then he said smoothly, "Listen, Gil. Tony wants to take advantage of the few minutes I'm going to leave him alone today to catch up on some reading." Then, lest Tony protest or Brainard persuade him to change his mind, Morrissey added quickly, "I was thinking, Gil—there are some problems coming up at the meeting today that I think would interest you —I think you ought to come along to hear them."

While the others were still coming into the small conference room, Morrissey sat and thought about Vought, more convinced than ever that he was the man he needed. You could have confidence in Tony, he told himself. You could accept his word and rely on his opinions, which were never half-baked ideas, but sensible conclusions, coolly and logically determined. And who was there at Enright that he could count on? Not Cable, certainly—he was getting worse all the time. And not Weir. Weir was so sullen these days, you didn't know what to expect any more. And not Metcalf. Metcalf was a careful worker, but he didn't seem to produce much. And Tony was good. The fact is, Morrissey told himself, there isn't a man at Enright who can compare with Tony.

He saw that Will Caroline was ready to begin, and he spoke up because he wanted to register his complaint about the soil samples before they got off onto something else. "I have a few things to say, Will," he said.

"All right," Will Caroline said. "Let's hear them."

"The year's about over," Morrissey began. He wanted to get that in before someone else did. "And I've been evaluating the work for the last six months—and I don't think anyone's going to claim we've made much progress."

While he let that sink in, Morrissey looked around the little room, which was filled at meetings these days because now the chemists came, and the nut, Mills. Seated next to Mills, Derrick was listening patiently, totally unsuspecting of what was coming. It was almost a shame, Morrissey thought. But, after all, the man was doing everything wrong—it was his fault that things had bogged down like this, and he had to expect to be blamed.

"Now, I'm convinced the trouble is something pretty basic," Morrissey went on. "I think the weakness is at the very beginning. We're not being given the right cultures." He glanced around the table and saw that they were all paying attention. "I don't suppose you agree, Dr. Derrick?"

"Why, ah agree one hundred per cent," Derrick said good-naturedly. "We haven't turned up the right culture yet. We'll just keep looking."

"Well, it's my opinion that you're going about it all wrong," Morrissey said. "After all, Dr. Derrick, if you don't give us the right culture, there isn't much point to the rest of it."

"That's right, sir," Derrick said.

Next to Morrissey, Brainard chuckled. "Well, whatever you're doing wrong," he said, "you're certainly doing everything right for streptomycin. That's all you're finding."

"Oh, we find a couple of other things, too—now and then," Will Caroline said with a smile. Morrissey was surprised that Will Caroline hadn't asked what had brought Brainard to the meeting. Even though it would be awkward for him to object, you'd think he would exercise his authority enough to ask the question.

"Well, maybe you do," Brainard said, "but from what I hear it's getting to be a joke." He smiled. "Like finding the Pacific Ocean again every week. The thing's been found—you don't need an organized search to find it again. Right, Derrick?"

Derrick only smiled and Brainard said, "You ought to call this a streptomycin hunt. That's what you're finding. Might as well call it what it is."

Mills looked up. "Oh, I don't know, sir," he said soberly. "I had a great-grandfather who dug for gold, and for years all he found was rocks, but I don't think he'd have said he was digging for rocks. I think there's a fine distinction there, sir."

Well, obviously Mills was trying to take the heat off Derrick. He was a pretty sassy one and didn't care what he said or what you said to him.

"Maybe it's the solid medium," Metcalf put in suddenly. "Maybe you're plating them in a nutrient agar that brings out streptomycin." Then he added, "I've had a feeling all along that something's wrong somewhere."

"Ah don't believe it's that," Derrick said. "Ah keep changing the formulas but we still get an abundance of streptomycin."

"You keep changing them!" Harrup said.

"Yes, sir," Derrick said. "Ah use three different formulas at a time an' ah run tests and vary them—to try to get better results."

"Well, how do you know what you missed when you were using the wrong ones?" Harrup said.

"They weren't wrong," Cable said. "He's just trying to improve them."

"We can't get out what you don't give us, Dr. Derrick," Morrissey said testily, "You can't get orange juice from onions."

"Tell me something else, Derrick," Brainard said. "How much are you losing every day because you only pick forty cultures from a sample now, where you used to pick up to a hundred?"

"What do you mean, he only picks forty now?" Harrup said.

"His girls have orders to take forty from every sample of dirt, and that's it," Brainard said. "Throws the rest out."

"You throw them out—untested?" Harrup turned to Derrick.

"Ah look them over and satisfy myself that there's nothing more that interests me."

"It's nice to know somebody around here is satisfied with something," Brainard said.

Derrick only smiled. Morrissey could see that the smile irritated Brainard, but he wasn't sorry any more about the beating Derrick was taking. He deserved it. Why, he was no better than Cable. He did anything he pleased! Changed his nutrients, threw out half his cultures, varied his testing techniques—and never told you a word about any of it. He only appeared to be more agreeable—but he was really just like Cable!

"Ah did some tests," Derrick was saying, "and we consistently get between twenty-five and thirty-five interesting cultures from a sample—so I set the limit at forty."

"What do you call interesting?" Brainard laughed. "Streptomycin?"

"As long as you're not giving us the right cultures," Morrissey put in, "you should work everything."

"There are a million cultures in a sample," Cable said.

"I mean everything significant, of course," Morrissey said.

"That's what he's doing," Cable said.

"I still think it's the nutrients," Metcalf said.

"Maybe it's his testing methods," Weir said.

"We should be working more in depth all along the line," Harrup said.

"Just a minute," Morrissey said. "Just a minute—I think it's the soil samples. I think we're getting the wrong samples—the wrong kind—from the wrong places."

"How can we know that?" Mills said. "If anyone knew where the right one was, we'd go dig a bushel of it! Shoo, we'd get a boatload."

"All ah'd need would be a teaspoon, Pat," Derrick said soberly.

Mills grinned. Morrissey saw Will Caroline smile and Cable, too.

He burst out angrily, "Now, that's just the trouble!" His voice went shrill and he tried to lower it. "As long as we don't know, we—the team—should work out a plan and follow it. Dr. Derrick seems to be superbly organized in his laboratory. But with these soil samples, his attitude is just hit or miss. He just takes them from anywhere and everywhere."

"Ah'd like them even more from everywhere," Derrick said.

"I don't like that," Harrup said. "It's sloppy."

"I don't like it either," Morrissey said. "This team has got to work more systematically. You should start here—do this area thoroughly —and when you've eliminated it, move on."

"You're wrong there, Claude," Brainard said, interrupting him.

"What!"

"You're barking up the wrong tree," Brainard said. "You shouldn't take them from here at all. Look—why all the streptomycin? Maybe this is streptomycin country—you ever think of that?"

Resentfully, Morrissey turned to Brainard. When he invited him to the meeting, he certainly hadn't expected Brainard to oppose him.

"Maybe this is soil that produces a lot of streptomycin," Brainard said. "Waksman found it around here—in New Jersey—and strepto-thricin, too. Hell, maybe it's like black men turning up in Africa and white men turning up in Europe and yellow men turning up in Asia. And Scandinavians are blond and Italians and Spanish are dark. If it happens with people, why not with these bugs?"

"Now, just a minute, Gil," Morrissey said.

"You can look forever and you won't find a white man native to South Africa," Brainard said, "or blond Chinese."

"That's not the point, Gil—"

"The hell it's not!"

"The point is system—organization—"

"System, hell! Get 'em everywhere. Take anything you can get!"

Then they were all talking at once again and Morrissey couldn't get in another word and he couldn't follow half of it. What did Brainard know? he thought bitterly. Brainard didn't know and he didn't care. Morrissey knew why he was doing this, all right. And when the meeting was over he'd tell him so.

Then he tried to listen to what they were saying. But everybody had a different opinion and everyone had his reasons, and all the reasons sounded right and all the reasons sounded wrong and

Morrissey didn't know what he thought any more. But one thing he did know—they couldn't blame him. This was Derrick's fault. It was Derrick who was supposed to know these things. They couldn't expect him—they couldn't expect the team—to do the impossible —to get out something that Derrick didn't give them.

By the time he reached home that evening Morrissey was thoroughly wretched. It had snowed most of the day and he hated to drive in the snow, and in spite of the rubbers somehow his feet had gotten wet, and he felt damp and cold all over. He changed his shoes and socks and put on another sweater, and stood next to the fireplace where Winifred had a fire going.

"You were right, Winifred," he said. "It's Derrick's fault, all right."

"You discuss it today?"

"We had a very heated and thorough discussion—I saw to that." He sighed. "But it's discouraging. Nobody really knows where they should get the samples. I'd just finished telling them to narrow down the area—get the thing organized—and Brainard spoke up and told them to get even more disorganized—take samples from everywhere."

"Brainard said that?"

"Oh, I know why he did it—to add to the confusion so the project would seem even more hopeless. Then everybody began to argue about it—and Will Caroline doesn't stop them, he just lets them talk—and everyone has a different opinion. I don't know," he said miserably. "I just don't know anything any more."

"Listen to me, Claude," Winifred said firmly. "You stop fussing. You know more than Will Caroline and he's running it. I'll tell you all that Will Caroline knows—he knows people. Brainard doesn't know anything, but he knows enough to torpedo it all the way down the line."

"He certainly does!"

She touched his arm and shook her head. "You don't have to know," she said. "How did you make out with Tony?"

"Oh, yes—Tony. He seemed interested. He said we could talk more when he gets back. But what's the good of having even Tony here if that rotten Derrick doesn't give us the right stuff?"

Its number was EA 17, and at the broth stage it looked very

good—the best since EA 50. Tom had put it into solvent extraction, using butyl alcohol and sulphuric acid, and had re-extracted it into clear water and sent samples of everything to assay. Now, as Gates came into his laboratory, he asked about the volumes Tom had used and his face showed that something was wrong.

"You're losing it, Tom," Gates said.

"Losing it?"

"It doesn't add up. You don't have as much antibiotic as you had at the beginning."

Tom came over to look at Gates's report.

"Most of the junk stayed behind in the broth," Gates said. "And the antibiotic was mostly extracted into the butyl alcohol. But when you add them up—the amount of antibiotic in the alcohol and the little bit that stayed in the broth—you don't have as much in the two as you had at the start, in all the junk."

"How much are we losing?" Tom said.

"About half, Tom."

Moose looked up at that, his face protesting this violation of logic. Moose didn't expect things to be easy, but he expected them to make sense.

Tom's first thought was that someone in assay might have made a mistake. Then he realized that Pearly, finding this kind of discrepancy, would have repeated the tests immediately. Ever since streptomycin had begun slipping past him, Pearly had been agonizingly careful to recheck anything about which he had the slightest doubt.

"I tested it twice, Tom," Gates said. "At first I was afraid it was our mistake—but this is how it came out both times. It's great the way it separated from the impurities, Tom—but half of it has disappeared."

For Moose this was just too much. "So where'd it go?" he burst out.

"Someplace along the line, it's become unstable, Moose," Tom said. "The antibiotic is changing into something else." He finished studying the report. "Maybe it's a question of temperature, Pearly. Like penicillin."

In the early stages, the men working on penicillin had run into a similar problem. They had found that acidified penicillin was very unstable at room temperature. Then they had cooled it down and it was more stable and they had held onto it.

Tom put down the report. "It's probably no great problem," he said. "We'll cool it down and see what happens."

When Gates was gone, Moose said, "So how do we cool it down?"

"We'll need water, ice and salt. We make an ice bath and cool everything down in it."

"Jeez," Moose said cheerfully. "If it ain't one thing, it's another."

"Usually, Moose—usually," Tom said with a laugh. "But this probably isn't serious. Chances are when we cool it down, it'll add up."

But three days later, Gates was back with the same worried look. "You're still losing it, Tom," he said. "Not quite as much as before, but you're still losing it."

Frowning, Tom read the report. "Well, cooling did some good. There's more here than there was before. We'll grow a fresh batch and try cooling it down a little more."

But now he was not so confident. He was beginning to suspect that EA 17, which looked too good to ignore, was going to present a batch of troubles all its own.

O N THE SATURDAY before Christmas Tom
stood in a corner of Neil and Elaine Harrup's living room, looking
for a familiar face. Among some of the company executives there
was a notion that the Enright scientists and the other residents of
the town ought to know and understand each other better, and to
this end, now and then one of them would give a very large "mixed"
party. It usually turned out that there was very little mixing; the Enright people talked to each other and the town people talked to
each other and not much was done about mutual understanding.
Tom had never been sure what it was they were supposed to understand. After half an hour he usually wondered what he was
doing here, anyway.

Today he had just arrived, an hour and a half late. He had gone
over to Enright to transfer some fresh EA 17 broth from shake
flasks to stir pots, and then he had found a few other things to do.
Then he had spent a while puzzling over why EA 17 was behaving
as it was and had lost track of time. Now he stood alone, looking
around the room for someone he knew. He wanted a fixed target
before he fought his way through this mob.

On his left, two matrons were shredding the reputation of an
unnamed young lady. On his right a woman named Mona was
complaining to a man named Fred that too many people were getting into the club. "God knows what they'll let in next," Mona said.

"It's that or raising the dues," Fred said.

"Mary," the woman on the left said, "I know for a fact she's had
men in that house."

Tom shuddered and wondered where everyone from Enright was
hiding. Then he saw Natalie Brainard across the room, and all at
once he wondered whether Diana had come home for Christmas—
and then his eyes were sweeping the crowd too eagerly, looking for
her. He got hold of himself and finished his drink.

"Mona, look over there near the piano," Fred said. "Look at the
way Cliffie Brace is sucking up to Harry Pack."

Tom looked, too, and saw Harry Pack, red-faced and perspiring,
talking to a white-haired man, who kept nodding his head while

Pack talked. Pack was in better condition tonight, Tom thought, than the last time he'd seen him—that day on Tollie's dock.

"Fred, I can remember when Cliffie Brace wouldn't have given Harry Pack the time of day," Mona said.

"Mary, all that kind is interested in is you know what," the woman on the left said.

Tom thought maybe he would just go home.

Then somebody said, "Hello, Tom. My, you look as though you're having a fine time!"—and Madeline Gates squeezed in beside Mona.

Tom grinned. "I just got here," he said. "Where is everybody?"

"I would guess that they're either in the dining room or in the sun porch," Madeline said. "For the best of reasons. That's where the bars are set up."

"Mary, that's the worst kind," the woman on his left said. "These small-town girls who go to the big city. And she's not young any more, you know."

"Do you know who they're talking about?" Madeline said in a low voice.

"Now, how would I know who they're talking about?" Tom laughed.

"Your neighbor, Amity Welles. She came in with Will and Callie —looking extravagantly chic, and everyone has been buzzing. Gil Brainard told her that seeing her again was the best Christmas present yet. It was really a rather fulsome performance. He met her last summer when she was painting those Enright pictures. Then he whisked her off to meet some people—he said. There—now you're up to date on everything you missed."

"Good."

"My guess is that he wanted to get her off to himself to make a few exploratory forays—test existing defenses and all that." Madeline sipped her drink. "Don't quote me, of course. Woodrow keeps telling me that sort of talk will get him nowhere. Don't you know her, Tom? She lives so near you."

"By the end of the summer we reached a point where we said hello. I never see her around."

"She's just up for the holidays," Madeline said. "I'd tell you to take action there, young man, only Callie says she's engaged. Do you think I should tell these old crows that she's engaged so they'll feel better about her not getting any younger?"

"You'd spoil their fun."

"I'm sure you're right. Callie says the girl is quite a good artist. She also thinks she's rather lonely. It's too bad she's engaged, Tom. I thought she seemed quite straight—I liked her. On the other hand, if she's engaged, why is she here alone? And where is her fiancé and why is she lonely? Well, I guess that covers Amity Welles. Don't mind me, Tom. I'm a natural gossip and snoop—it's one of my great talents. And besides, I'm rather tight."

"Mary," the woman beside him said, "that family was always strange. Especially the father. You could never make any sense out of that man. Hope was sensible enough, but this one was always just like him."

"Fred," Mona whined, "Clifford Brace has gotten plenty just that way—knowing the right person at the right time."

"Oh, God," Madeline said. "I can't stand this any longer without another drink. What do you say we fight our way to the source?"

"Pearly seems more cheerful lately, Madeline," Tom said, as they made their way across the living room.

"He'll be fine now, Tom." They passed Janet Weir, a vision in green, her red hair fluffy, talking to a husky young man, and Madeline looked at her narrowly. "She is lovely-looking, isn't she?"

"Very."

"But, oh God, she's a fool! She'll be furious if she sees Brainard breathing heavily around Amity Welles." Then she said, "Woodrow has always been a slow starter, Tom. At the beginning he worries more than anyone I've ever known—except possibly Neil Harrup. But then he gets it out of his system and he settles down to work."

As they came up to the dining room, Tom saw that most of the Enright people were in here—the Millses, the Derricks, Max and Constance, and the rest of them—Morrissey, Harrup, Rosswell, Brainard with Amity Welles, and Callie. Brainard was doing the talking and some of the others looked rather upset.

"Let's go back to Fred and Mona," Tom said. "Brainard's sounding off and he's got them stirred up about something."

"An hour ago Gil Brainard was not in the best of condition—so don't be surprised at anything," Madeline said.

From the bar while he waited for their drinks, Tom looked at the little Enright group and wondered what was wrong. Max looked rather concerned and Callie, too—and Derrick's wife Kate looked very angry. Kate Derrick was a small, wide-eyed girl who, incongruously, smoked with a long black cigarette holder that dated back to her still-lamented acting career, and now she was flicking her fingernail impatiently against it while she stared at Brainard with obvious dislike.

Tom looked from Kate to Amity Welles and reflected on the difference between these two. While Kate was seething and making no effort to conceal it, Amity Welles was absolutely composed. As Madeline had said, she looked extravagantly chic in a black dress, with her heavy, honey-colored hair and her dark brown eyes, but there was something forbidding about her. She looked clever and aware—and aloof, as though she had withdrawn behind a shell that you could never completely chip away. Tom picked up drinks for Madeline and himself and they moved over to the Enright group.

"Hello, Tom—it's time you found us," Callie said, as he stepped up beside her. "You're missing a lovely philosophical discussion."

"About what?"

"About soil, darling. And about responsibility. Loosely translated —who can we hang if we need a hanging?"

Tom looked at Amity Welles. "Hello," he said.

"Hello," she said in that friendly way of hers, and Tom looked away.

Brainard was still talking. Now he waved his hand that held a glass and a cigar. "Rubbish!" he said. "Don't give me that. All of a sudden all I hear is teamwork. You fellows in research have a new theme song. All of a sudden you're a team. Boola-boola—fight, team, fight!"

"He's in good shape," Tom said to Callie.

"Splendid. Are you a teamer or a loner?"

Tom grinned. "Do you really care?"

Callie laughed, looked around at the Enright people and then beyond them. "Every time I come to one of these things I am reminded all over again that the desert covers a much larger proportion of the earth's surface than is reported in geography books."

Brainard thumped Morrissey's lapel. "You know why you're all suddenly so interested in being a team? Because you're passing the buck. You're all passing the good old buck—all the way down the line—to him." He jerked his head toward Derrick. "And he's an expert at passing it out into thin air. Nothing's his fault—eh, Derrick?"

Derrick wasn't paying much attention to Brainard, but Kate was flicking away at her cigarette holder. She drained her glass. A passing waiter took it and gave her another and she began to drink that.

Tom decided to get out of here. Then he saw that Harry Pack had come into the room, still with his friend Cliffie Brace. Pack was standing just a few feet away, staring at Amity Welles, obviously trying to place her. Tom glanced at Amity and saw that she had recognized Pack and had turned away.

Harrup was talking now. "That issue resolves itself down to one question," he said. "Does it make more sense to work with native soil or foreign soil? I say we should confine ourselves to this country—at least until we've screened it thoroughly."

"Sure," Brainard said. " 'Course that might take a few weeks. You've only got about two billion acres to cover. And nobody knows how to eliminate any of them." He looked pointedly at Derrick. Kate's eyes flashed at him as she finished this drink and began the tattoo again on the cigarette holder.

Then Rosswell spoke up, blinking behind his thick glasses. "It seems to me that this is getting expensive," he said. Rosswell went around these days like a mortgage holder and looked at the men involved in the project as though they were all six months in arrears. "We could waste a fortune on that foreign stuff. I say let's stay American."

"There's one to remember," Callie murmured. "There must be some patriotic group that could use that for a slogan. Keep our dirt American."

"There's no particular logic," Tom said to Rosswell, "in thinking that what we're looking for is going to be in the United States just because we're working here."

"Well, now, I don't know about that," Rosswell said. "Just the other day I was reading something—now, maybe some of you know about this, but then again maybe you don't. Anyway, it seems there was this nineteenth-century English parson—quite a devout fellow—"

Brainard gave Rosswell a pained look and wandered over to the bar.

"Lived in the English lowlands," Rosswell went on. "Now, of course, it's very damp there in that low country and the people suffered considerably from rheumatic pains—"

Then suddenly Harry Pack was beside them. "Sa-ay," he said to Amity Welles, "I remember you—you're that artist. I thought you was leaving town."

"I came back," Amity said evenly.

"Then you could paint my kid if you're back!"

"No. I'm only staying a few days."

Pack began to be annoyed. "Say—what've you got against my kid?"

But Amity only looked at him coldly. Rosswell showed that he was upset at the interruption and after a minute Pack wandered back to Clifford Brace.

"Now, as I was saying," Rosswell resumed, "this parson was a devout fellow and he believed that if the Lord permitted any suffering on earth, he would also provide a cure for that suffering close at hand—so—"

Brainard was back from the bar. "What's he talking about?" he said to Morrissey.

"This parson was sure he could find help for those rheumatic pains right there in the lowlands, so he prepared an extract from the willow tree because it was so plentiful in that damp area—and do you know something? It worked. It eased those rheumatic pains."

"What's he talking about?" Brainard said again. "John, what're you talking about?"

"You'll see my point in a minute, Gil, because do you know what that extract was? Well, it was aspirin. At least it was the forerunner of aspirin. At least the technical name for aspirin—what is the technical name for aspirin, Neil?"

"Acetylsalicylic acid," Harrup said.

"That's it. And one of those words is the Latin name for willow."

"Salix," Harrup said.

"Right! Now do you see my point? That's pretty pertinent to our problem. It may be that the Lord has placed the cure near the source of the illness and for American diseases we should get American dirt. Now, did anyone ever think of that?"

"John," Brainard said, "as far as the dirt's concerned, the problem is that the man who's supposed to know won't get off the fence. Ask him where you ought to get it and he says nobody knows. Not *he* doesn't know. No, sir. *Nobody* knows. Well, with that kind of information, nobody can decide much and nobody can limit much and that's your answer to that."

To Kate Derrick this last jibe at Charlie was the final straw. "Sir," she said, pointing her long cigarette holder at Brainard, "*some people* may be undecided—*you* may be undecided—but *Charlie* is not undecided."

Slowly, Brainard turned to stare at her. "Well, I'll be damned!"

"Me, I go for the esoteric approach," Mills spoke up quickly. "I'd like to see them from the Belgian Congo—the Taj Mahal—"

"Why should you expect to find a cure in the Belgian Congo for a disease in New York?" Harrup said.

"Why not?" Tom said.

"Good question," Mills said. "I'd like to get some from outside a couple of pyramids. Who knows what those Pharaohs got themselves buried with?"

But Brainard was not to be diverted. "If he knows so much," he said to Kate, looking amused, "why's he keeping it a secret? He's the only one here who hasn't said a word."

"Why should he?" Kate said. "This isn't a meeting."

"My mind's been made up all along," Derrick said easily, coming to his wife's rescue. "I want them from everywhere."

"Only you don't know for sure," Brainard said.

"As long as we work with soil, we'll probably collect it from everywhere," Derrick said.

"In my department," Brainard said, "what I have to know, I know for sure."

"'Man, proud man,'" Kate murmured, "'Drest in a little brief authority, Most ignorant of what he's most assured . . .'"

Kate looked at Brainard with steady eyes, and Brainard stared back at her, dumbfounded. A stunned silence fell over the little circle.

Then Mills murmured, "Charlie, you ought to make a lawyer out of Kate."

"Ah'm thinking of it," Derrick said. "Ah'll put her to work and ah'll retire."

"I'll retire with you," Mills said enthusiastically. "Let's retire to the South Seas. You go home and pack your bugs and I'll go home and pack my mice and we're off." He lowered his voice. "Kee-rist, Charlie, get her out of here!"

Then, before anyone could say any more, Harry Pack was back again. "Listen—what the hell—how long does it take to do a lousy ten-year-old kid?"

"To do him justice would take quite a while," Amity said.

Harry Pack considered that. "Helluva good-looking kid, ain't he?"

Callie took advantage of the interruption to coax Brainard away. Harrup and Rosswell drifted off, too.

"Smart, too," Pack said. "Teachers don't understand him, but what I say is, you don't live your life with teachers." He looked knowingly at Tom. "At least not if you got two eyes and a normal amount of manhood. They're mostly frigid— I got that straight from a fellow that knows. Ninety per cent of them frigid—other ten per cent—"

Then Clifford Brace came up with Fred and Mona. Fred slapped Pack on the back and Tom motioned to Amity Welles. "Shall we escape without learning the fate of the other ten per cent?"

He was surprised to see her smile.

"Lots of new faces over there at that place," Pack said behind them.

"What do they all do, Harry?" Fred said.

"Hell, they're scientists," Pack said. "Who knows what they do? They're a queer bunch—those birds."

"Well, they're different, all right," Clifford Brace said.

"Cliffie, they're not normal—if you know what I mean—I mean a normal man same as you and myself."

Mills, fascinated, moved closer. "What have we here?"

"Oh, that's a good friend of Max's," Tom said.

"I consider it a triumph," Max said.

"Listen, Cliffie," Pack said. "I'll tell you something that'll raise your hair. You know what I heard? They want to feed people dirt! Want us to eat it! Now, I'm not a sucker who believes every rumor he hears, but things like that don't get around about you and me."

"That's right, Harry."

"You know why these rumors get around? It's because they're so nutty. I heard they even plan to feed it to children! Cliffie, it's criminal. And I was just listening to them talking—and I think it's the truth!"

"Pat," Sara Mills said, "couldn't you find some nice friends like that?"

"Cliffie, when it stinks, it's rotten. Say there, girlie—" Pack turned to Amity again, but Max intercepted him.

"I didn't realize you were interested in soil microbes, Mr. Pack," he said.

"*Shoo*, Max, every normal man is interested in soil microbes," Mills said. "He knows a man's best friend isn't the dog, as is commonly supposed—but the microbe."

Pack looked bewildered.

"Don't you think, sir," Mills said to him, "that the way the microbe is ignored is damned upsetting? Damned unfair?"

"After all, sir," Max said, "consider what you owe to microbes— bread, wine, cheese, beer, sanitation—"

"You don't say!" Pack said.

"After you're dead, he'll decay your body for you."

"Cliffie—" A frantic note came into Pack's voice as he edged back a little. "Say, my hat's off to you boys—you got the right idea, all right—excuse me, young fella." Pack escaped to Cliffie and Mona and Fred. "Jesus Christ, Cliffie, you see what I mean!"

"Miss Welles," Tom said, "would you be interested in joining me in getting out of here while the getting is good?"

She laughed and said, "That interests me very much, Dr. Cable."

At the door, as they were saying goodbye, Neil Harrup brought up EA 17. "I understand you're having serious trouble with it."

"Well—a little," Tom said.

"I think you'll find you've got a real problem there."

"Now, Harrup, don't get started!" Elaine said sharply. "Just for once, don't get started." Her wide mouth set into a straight line, and then, as though to show she wasn't seriously annoyed, she gave Tom a knowing wink.

"Maybe it won't be so bad," Tom said. "We could stumble on what's causing the trouble anytime." He edged toward the door.

"If the trouble continues more than another few weeks," Harrup said, "you ought to set it aside for a while and go back to it later."

"Harrup, will you shut up about it!" Elaine said.

Tom looked at Harrup, surprised. "I'd hate to do that. It looks too good—before it starts to disappear, that is."

"Yes, but there's a board meeting coming up in February, you know." Harrup ran his finger back and forth along the table. "And that kind of trouble won't look good."

268

Tom reached for the door, wondering how a man could worry now about a meeting that was two months away. In two months so much could happen, but Harrup assumed that all of it would be bad. "Well, good night," he said, "and thanks."

"Aren't you going to put that on?" Harrup said, looking at Tom's coat.

"It's a mild night."

"You ought to put it on," Harrup said. "You'll catch cold."

Tom closed the door behind him. Harrup could worry about anything.

"What is EA 17?" Amity Welles said.

"It's the temporary number of a potential drug. At the start we just give it a number instead of a name—until we find out whether it's any good."

"Well," she said, "that's quite civilized."

In the dim light from Harrup's house, Tom glanced over at her. "Why civilized?"

"No name unless it's legitimate. Were there sixteen nameless bastards before this one?"

"No, we don't number them in order. And it's not quite that civilized, because if it lives long enough to go into advanced testing, it gets a name. And then sometimes it turns out to be no good after all."

"Well, that's civilized, too, isn't it?" She smiled. It was a perfectly acceptable smile—only not very warm. She stayed well behind that guarded wall.

In his car, Amity said, "Why don't you number them in order?"

"So the men won't get discouraged, always being reminded of the number of failures. It's Will Caroline's idea." He looked at her. "Does that bother you?"

"No—why should it bother me?"

"Well, you know, facing up to things is very popular these days." He smiled. "The world is full of realists running around looking everything squarely in the teeth."

For a moment Amity didn't answer. The bay was rough tonight, and from the shore road you could hear the waves hitting the beach. He looked over at her and saw that she was sitting with her head back against the seat, just looking ahead of her at nothing. He decided to take her home quickly.

Then, unexpectedly, she turned to him and smiled—a better smile than before. "Only not the good things," she said. "Just the ugly."

Surprised, Tom looked at Amity Welles with a new interest.

"They're really very uncomfortable, facing squarely up to anything beautiful." Then she said, "And what about you—do you face things squarely in the teeth?"

Tom smiled. "At heart, I'm an escapist," he said. "Show me trouble and I run."

"And do you get discouraged at the count of the failures?"

"No. But I'm kind of a fool. You might as well know it." He looked at her. A few layers of her shell had peeled away, and he wondered exactly when it had happened—and why. "Would you like to stop somewhere for a drink?"

"No," she said. "Thanks, but I think not." She was silent again.

"You getting married soon?" Tom said after a minute, more for something to say than because he cared.

"In May."

That surprised him a little. Why would she wait until May? "Are you here for long?" he said.

"Just over Christmas. I just wanted to get out of New York for Christmas."

"Don't you like New York at Christmas?"

"No, I don't."

Well, she'd found her shell again and tucked herself back inside it, and he was getting a little bored with trying to find something to talk about. They were almost home, anyway. Idly he wondered why she wasn't getting married until May. Certainly she couldn't be clinging to some girlish fantasy of a long romantic engagement. He tried to imagine what her reason might be for putting it off so long. Then they reached her house and he forgot about it.

"It's a rough night," he said, as they got out of the car and walked around the house to the boardwalk.

"I like it when it's rough," she said. "But then I grew up here."

"Did you always live here—summer and winter?"

"We were the first year-rounders here. In the winter we were the only people living on the boardwalk. In September everyone else would board up their houses—close the shutters and nail them down and draw all the curtains, turn off the water, disconnect the telephone—and then they would all be gone—and we would be alone."

"Were you lonely?"

"No," she said. "After a while Will Caroline came and then there were two of us. Then everyone else came. Have you ever noticed the way those rocks look bigger in winter?" She nodded toward the rocks that jutted out of the water beside Will's house. The humped outline was indistinct in the dim light.

"No," Tom said, "I've never noticed."

"My father always used to tell us that," Amity said. "Every winter just about this time of the year, he'd tell us to notice how bleak the water looked—and the beach—and how the rocks seemed bigger. Then, on what he thought must surely be the coldest day of the year, he would make a little speech that he had—that he saved for that day and made once every winter."

"The same speech?"

"He'd say we should remember that the good time always gives way to the hard—and that the hard time always softens again into the good—and that was something you could see anywhere, but that you saw it better if you lived by the sea. 'When you're up, remember that,' he would say, 'and it'll keep you steady—keep you from flying too high. And then when you're low, remember that spring and summer always show up again. Not too much self-praise—not too much self-pity.' That's what he used to say." She smiled. "I'm not sure it always works that way, but it's a good way to bring up children."

Astonished, Tom stood on the dark boardwalk and looked at Amity Welles. It was the longest speech she had made all evening, but it wasn't only the length of it that amazed him. It was the quality about her while she was speaking, a quality of . . . he searched for the word and thought, suddenly, a quality of grace—and then he was even more surprised at his own choice of a word.

Then, as though she realized that she had stepped too close to the fire, she withdrew a little.

"Amity," Tom said, "why'd you want to get out of New York for Christmas—and come up here all alone?"

"Oh—you know what New York is like at Christmas."

"No, I don't."

"Everyone in New York has problems—or at least all the people I know do."

"I suppose people have problems everywhere, don't they?"

"But there they seem to have more of them. Then at Christmas, suddenly they're trying so frantically to forget them. And it doesn't work. They can't forget them. And I think it's sad to watch them trying so hard. It depresses me."

At the steps she stopped. "Well—good night," she said. "And thanks for bringing me home."

She moved up the stairs without looking back and went into the house.

EIGHTEEN

PREPARE AN ICE BATH and fit in the separatory funnel used for solvent extraction. And take the fresh EA 17 broth and cool it down—more than before—cool it down to 0° C.

And cool the butyl alcohol, too, and add that and the sulphuric acid to the cold broth. And maintain the zero temperature while the broth and the alcohol gradually separate into two layers.

And drain off the broth, which was on the bottom, into one beaker. And drain the butyl alcohol, which was on the top, into another beaker and neutralize the acid immediately, in case the antibiotic was unstable in acid and that should be the cause of the trouble. Send everything to assay.

And you lost twenty-five per cent.

And a week passed and a new year began.

Grow some fresh broth. And test to see how stable the antibiotic is in the broth. That wasn't the problem. It was stable enough in the broth.

Try another technique. Try precipitation.

Set up a Büchner funnel and add a metal salt and hope that it will combine with the antibiotic to form a salt insoluble in the broth. Save time—set up four Büchner funnels and use four metal salts and hope that one of them will work.

Filter off the broths and send them to assay.

Dry out the damp solid materials—set them up overnight in a desiccator with calcium chloride on the bottom to draw the water out of them.

Send the dry solids to assay.

And the antibiotic stayed with the broth. No progress.

And another week passed.

"On the whole," Moose said, "this is one I could live without. She ain't friendly."

"On the whole," Tom said, "I agree with you. I'd like to chuck her myself, but she looks too good. Before she goes into her disappearing act, she's potent and she hits too many things to ignore."

"All the same, I don't go for her." Moose grinned. "She's bad medicine—if you'll excuse me bein' such a comic."

Tom laughed. "Moose, you're a great man. We'll try carbon adsorption."

And carbon adsorption was no better than precipitation.

You began to argue with yourself. Look at the time going into this, you said—look at the work going into it. If you knew that once you'd found a way to hold onto it, it would be good, you wouldn't complain. But you don't know that and you can't know it, because you can't put it into a mouse yet to find out. In the broth stage it's too impure, and after you get it out—in the only way that gets it out, which is solvent extraction—then there's not enough antibiotic left. So do you give it up? Or do you go on without knowing whether it's worth going on with?

"Go back to solvent extraction, Moose. Maybe it's the butyl alcohol. Try amyl alcohol. Try two other alcohols. Try amyl and try hexanol."

And you lost fifty per cent.

Cool them down to zero.

And you lost twenty-five per cent.

Test for acid stability. Set up some plain broth with acid and leave it at room temperature.

In the morning the broth hadn't lost its potency. It wasn't the acid.

"Golly, Tom," Gates said, "I hate to see this happening right at this time."

They were in Gates's laboratory, where Tom had come to see the results of the latest tests, partly because he was impatient and partly because, whenever possible, he liked to observe for himself. It wasn't that assay didn't report accurately. It was just that he believed in observation. He believed you could get a feeling about these bugs—much as with people—over and beyond what you could put on paper.

Gates motioned him to one side, where his technicians couldn't hear them. "Tom, you ought to put this aside until after the board meeting."

Tom smiled. "Harrup been talking to you, Pearly?"

"Well, he mentioned it. Tom, it's not going to look good. You've put almost ten weeks into this one—and you haven't gotten anywhere. I mean—don't misunderstand me—I know how stubborn it's been—and golly, I'm as discouraged as you are. Every time I do your tests I'm discouraged all over again."

Tom smiled. That was true. Pearly was bleeding right along with him on EA 17.

"You've got some others, Tom. Concentrate on them. Get them to a point where you could say something encouraging about them. I wouldn't put them into mice before the meeting," he added quickly. "But if you could say that they look promising—"

"This is the one that's promising, Pearly," Tom said. "This one—that I can't get out."

"The board meets the last Friday in February. It's only four weeks, Tom. Put it aside."

"I understand everything you're saying, Pearly," Tom said. "But I can't do it."

On Saturday Tom went into Enright to work on the other two. On Sunday he spent a restless day at home thinking about EA 17. Gates is right, he told himself—you're not getting anywhere. You might as well admit it. In ten weeks you haven't gotten anywhere. Maybe you should be sensible, for once in your life, and put it aside. Get it out of sight and out of mind and concentrate on the others. There's no law says you always have to be the company mule. The other two don't look as good—but at least you can hold onto them.

By late afternoon he was fidgety, and he tossed aside the journals he was reading and decided to get out of the house, even if only to go to Tollie's for dinner. Then as it grew dark, he saw a light in Amity Welles's cottage. To his surprise, he found the thought that she might be back rather pleasant. He walked out the door and up the boardwalk.

"How's your number?" Amity said. She put aside the book she had left open while she answered the door. There was a fire in the fireplace and two chairs were turned to it. "What was it—EA 17?"

"EA 17 is still the little man who isn't here," Tom said, trying to keep his feelings out of his voice.

"Not good?"

"I'm thinking of hanging a sign on the equipment, saying, 'EA 17 was here'—like Kilroy."

He looked at the fireplace, seeing the heavy andirons that were old and sturdy like the rest of the room. This was an old house with dark woodwork and wide floor boards, and the furnishings were old and faded and there was even an old sampler on the wall. Then, looking at Amity, Tom had to smile. She was wearing paint-stained blue jeans and a baggy sweater which, for her, were so out of character that his eyes kept going back to them. And yet, he thought, she looked good in them—in the same way that she looked good in this house, which was as unlike her as anything he could imagine.

Her dark eyes came over to him, and Tom thought that those would be damned beautiful eyes if they weren't so careful never to reveal anything.

"Do you believe in your EA 17 so much," she said, "to work on it all this time?"

"You're touching a sore spot." Maybe she didn't show much, he thought, but neither did she miss much. "All week I've been carrying on a private argument with myself about it. Do I want to give it up because it's stupid to waste any more time on it—or because it's too tough for me? Do I want to go on with it because I'm stubborn—or because I believe in it? I can argue it either way."

Amity drew her legs up under her, long and slim in the rolled-up jeans. "Has that ever happened to you before? Do you have anything to go on?"

"No—not in just this way."

"Could you give it up—now? Would you stop living with it?"

Tom smiled. "How'd you know I was living with it?"

"You just told me."

Thoughtfully, Tom looked at Amity. She had come very close to the mark, and he wondered whether it had been an accident. But he knew it wasn't—this was a very intuitive girl.

"You're right," he said. "If I give it up before it goes to mice, I won't stay away. I'll go back." It was one thing when he was convinced in his own mind that an antibiotic was no good. Then he tossed it out without bleeding, without looking back. But he wasn't convinced that EA 17 was no good.

276

Amity nodded and Tom thought that the eyes had softened a little. And then he thought, Pull yourself together, Cable. You were always a sucker for a pair of eyes. Look at what happened the last time you looked too deeply into a girl's eyes and forgot to look away. Besides—she isn't your type. Besides, she's engaged. "You still getting married in May?" he said.

"Yes."

"Why are you waiting till May? What's holding you up?" He saw at once that she didn't like the question.

"I just want to wait until May." Then she added, "I'm having a show in the spring. Not a large one—but I'm excited about it. I want to wait until that's over."

Tom bent over to put another log on the fire. He doubted that was the reason, but he knew that he wasn't going to hear the real one. He straightened up. "You like a drink?" he said. "I'll go home and get a bottle."

"Oh—I'm sorry. I have some." She took a bottle from an old sideboard and went into the kitchen, and Tom stood in the doorway talking to her.

"Doesn't he mind your leaving him like this—your fiancé?"

"He's away this weekend." She moved about the kitchen, getting ice and glasses. "He was married before. He has a little girl in Chicago and he's gone out to see her."

Maybe that was it, Tom thought—maybe the man wouldn't be free to marry again until May. Only he felt, somehow, that it wasn't that simple.

"He was going at Christmas," Amity said, coming back into the living room. "But then he had an important meeting scheduled for right after Christmas and he didn't want to be rattled—so he put it off."

"The little girl rattles him?"

"Of course not! His wife—his former wife—ex-wife—I never know what to call her"—she smiled—"I don't call her his first wife because I'm not his second wife yet—I don't like that term, do you? It sounds so sort of—you know—second-fiddle, second-string." She laughed. "Maybe at my age I'm getting sensitive."

The former marriage was not the reason. She talked about that freely. "Why does the lady rattle him?"

Amity shrugged. "She's pretty neurotic, I guess. She's done some

277

strange things. Not many people can rattle him—very few, in fact
—but she can. I suppose living with him, even for those few years,
she learned his sensitive areas."

It all sounded plausible enough, Tom thought—only it left him
with a feeling that it didn't ring quite true. On the other hand, it
wasn't any of his business. "What does he do?" he said. "What's his
job?"

"He's in advertising—he has the Enright account. That's how
I happened to come back here." She took her drink and stood by
the fireplace. "I told him about Enright and he went after the
account—and then he sent me here to do the paintings. It sounds
rather conniving, doesn't it? But you know"—she smiled—"what
can you do to advertise industrial chemicals?"

"I wouldn't know what to do to advertise soap. How do you
advertise industrial chemicals?"

"The idea of the paintings is to create a prestige image. For
that a painting is better than a photograph."

"If he has the account," Tom said, "does he come up here? Have
I seen him around without knowing it?"

"No—his assistant handles it. But the idea of the paintings was
his. I think it's quite a good one, don't you? He's very good at his
work, really."

Puzzled, Tom studied Amity. Where was the chill now? Where
was that icy wall that was the first thing he had noticed about her?
He was beginning to suspect that the wall was, in fact, nothing
but a thin coating, like an early morning frost on the grass that
vanished moments after the first light. He was beginning to think
Enright's advertising man was a lucky guy.

"Does he like New York better than you do?"

"He loves it!" She laughed. "For all he complains about it terribly sometimes. But he thinks I'm crazy to ever leave it to come up
here. I suppose after we're married, I won't." She looked around the
room that was so unlike her. "It's strange what time does to a place,
isn't it? Everything here is just the way it was when I left—eight
years ago. Only then it always seemed cheerful—everything was
bright and gay. And now things have faded and become old-looking.
It seems quite forlorn."

She moved a little into the room and stopped in front of the
faded sampler on the wall and turned on an old glass lamp. She

looked briefly at the sampler and turned back to Tom. "Well, if I keep coming here—afterwards—I'll have to do something about it. Do you want another drink?"

"Why don't we go out somewhere to eat?"

She hesitated and he thought she was going to refuse, but then, unexpectedly, she agreed, fixed him another drink and went upstairs to dress. He was almost tempted to tell her to stay in the blue jeans. He liked her this way.

For a few minutes, while he waited, Tom thought about Amity. She wasn't a simple person, he knew. She was complicated and temperamental, and she could probably be difficult. But the man who was letting her put him off until May had to be a fool.

Gradually his thoughts slipped off again to EA 17, and the all too familiar details pushed through his mind. Damn it, he told himself, there has to be an answer. There is always an answer.

He moved aimlessly about the drab little room and, failure by failure, he went over it all again. Nothing works but solvent extraction. Precipitation doesn't do a damn thing—carbon doesn't do a damn thing—the antibiotic just sits in the broth. And solvent extraction pulls it out of the broth like a charm—but then it vanishes. Butyl alcohol, amyl alchol, hexanol—all the same. Away from the impurities—and then it's gone.

He stopped in front of the old sampler. The faded crisscrossed stitches spelled out the words: TO THINE OWN SELF BE TRUE. He read it and looked away.

Butyl alcohol, amyl alcohol, hexyl alcohol. All alcohol—all fine, but . . . He stared at the sampler. *All alcohol!* Cable, you idiot—that's it! It's the alcohol! You pea-brain! It's unstable in alcohol! Use some other solvent that isn't an alcohol! Use chloroform.

"Amity," he called out. He rushed to the stairs. "Amity!"

She came out of her room, a brush in her hand. "What's the matter?"

"Ammie, would you come over to Enright with me for a few minutes—now—before dinner?"

She stood at the railing and looked at him, puzzled.

"I just thought of something—and I don't want to wait any longer than I have to—" Then he stood a minute considering whether he would save any time by going in tonight. If he was still worried about stability, he couldn't let it stand around overnight—

but it wasn't unstable in acid and it wasn't unstable in broth—and if he used chloroform . . . He decided to go in. "I don't want to wait to find out if I'm right."

Amity nodded. "All right."

"If you'd rather, I'll come back for you."

"No, I'll come. I'll be right there."

It didn't take long. The broth was in the refrigerator, already filtered. He took it out and measured some of it into a separatory funnel and added the sulphuric acid and the chloroform.

Glancing at Amity while he worked, Tom saw her looking around the laboratory, taking it all in, and the thought came to him that not once, in all those months, had he brought Diana here. Suddenly, with a little stab, he wondered whether it would have made a difference. Would Diana have looked at everything so carefully and seen that this was a good laboratory? And, if she had, would her respect for Enright have increased so that she might have thought him an honest man? Would a little thing like that have changed anything? The closest Diana had ever come to his laboratory was sailing past it in her boat.

Amity turned from the window where she had been looking out at the fermentation building. "When will you know if it works?" she said.

"It'll go to assay first thing in the morning. We'll have the answer early Tuesday morning."

"Will you come over and let me know?"

Tom looked around, surprised. "Will you still be here?"

"I'll probably stay another week."

He put the bottles of chloroform and of sulphuric acid back on the shelf. "Is he away all week, too?"

"No, he'll be back in a few days. I want to do some work up here."

He carried the two graduated cylinders that he'd used over to the sink and turned on the water. "Amity—is that show really the reason you're not getting married until May?"

"Yes," she said.

"How long have you been engaged?"

"Since last May."

Puzzled, he glanced around at her. "Do you believe in long engagements, or something?"

"Yes," she said rather emphatically. "I do." Then she laughed.

"Tom, don't worry about it so much. This is the way I want it."

He turned off the water and reached for a towel. "Aren't you in love with him, Am?"

"Of course," she said. "Very much."

And strangely enough, he thought—more puzzled than ever—she seemed to mean it.

On Monday morning, Tom sent the samples to assay. And on Tuesday EA 17 added up!

"Tom, for God's sake, don't send it to mice now!" Gates said. "Wait until after the board meeting."

Tom looked at Gates, dumbfounded. "That board meeting is still more than three weeks away!"

"But think of the time that's gone into this! Now you can say you had a serious problem but you've solved it! Leave it there!"

"I can't leave it there for more than three weeks!"

"Tom, use your head. This way you can hold out the possibility that this might be good. But if you put it into mice and the mice die—then what? Then they see three months' work that they can't understand—that failed."

"Maybe it won't fail."

"But what if it does? That board is made up of successful people, Tom. Palmerton is a very rich man—Bodenhof they call a wizard—Kaiser's an important lawyer. When these men invest three months' time and work in something, they're accustomed to seeing a substantial return." Gates made a hopeless little gesture. "Work on it a little longer, Tom. Get it purer. But don't test it yet."

"Pearly, it's pure enough now!"

Gates sighed and took the antibiotic to do the more extensive *in-vitro* testing that was necessary before it went into mice.

A week later Mills, cheerfully talking to his mice, which he had weighed and spotted, prepared to test EA 17.

"All right, men," he said, while Tom stood beside him and Miss Watterling stood back a few feet. "No conking out today. It's one thing to be heroes but there's a board meeting coming up. Everybody got the message?"

He reached into the cage for the white mouse with a green spot on its head and turned it over on his palm and tucked under the tail, and, while the mouse squealed and urinated and extended its legs and squealed again, he injected EA 17 into the tail vein and withdrew the syringe and returned the mouse to the jar. He reached for the mouse with the green-spotted rump and stopped.

"Pat—" Tom said, although he knew that Mills had seen it, too.

"Kee-rist!"

The mouse tried once to rear up and never made it. It keeled over and didn't move again. It made no effort to dig. It lay absolutely still.

"He's not dead." Mills watched carefully. "He's paralyzed."

The pink, watery eyes were popping and the mouth was open slightly, revealing the pink tongue and the single sharp tooth.

Mills bent over the jar. "It may be temporary—he may snap out of it."

He waited another few minutes, watching steadily, and then he took the mouse out of the jar and turned it over on its back on the counter. The mouse lay rigid—pink eyes popping, pink legs stuck out stiff—but its heart was still beating, slowly.

Mills pointed to the faint heart movement with a pencil. Then the heartbeat stopped. "Now he's dead."

Straightening up, Mills looked at the dead mouse for a minute without moving it. Then he said, "That was a quick death from paralysis. Not impossible—but quick."

Tom was still looking at the mouse, although there was no longer anything to watch. "What do you mean?"

"Death from paralysis doesn't usually come that fast. Oh, it can happen—it was probably brain damage, and it only takes three seconds for the stuff to reach the heart and another three seconds to reach the brain, so they can die that fast. But with paralysis, they usually go slower."

Tom looked at Mills. "Are you saying that something else caused death—not the paralysis?"

"It didn't die that fast *because* it was paralyzed. It could have been the same substance that caused paralysis and then this quick death." Mills looked up from the mouse. "Or could there be two unrelated effects here? One substance causing the paralysis— which we could see, and which they could have lived with for a few days, even—and something else causing death? I don't say that happened. I'm just asking."

282

"I suppose the antibiotic could have caused one and an impurity the other."

Mills nodded. "One impurity or several."

"Or impurities could have caused both, and the antibiotic could be O.K."

"If this is true, Tom—that there were two separate unrelated effects here—and if it turns out that an impurity is causing death, and the antibiotic is causing only paralysis but not death—well, I've seen many an animal recover from paralysis. I've gone home at night leaving them stiff as a board, certain they were dying, and come in the next morning and found them fine—roaming around good as new."

Mills moved back to his record book, and glanced around at Miss Watterling. "We'll leave this one a few minutes, Miss Watterling. Don't throw it out yet." He picked up the solution of EA 17. "We'll cut it way down, Tom—to see if either effect is altered."

He diluted the solution and prepared to inject the mouse with the yellow-spotted head. "All right, fella, let's see if you can behave better than your buddy."

But even before the mouse was out of Mills's hand, Tom could see the eyes popping and the paralysis starting to set in. From the time the mouse was returned to the jar, it never moved. When Mills turned it on its back on the counter, it lay, legs extended, as rigid as the first. For a while the heart continued to beat. Then it stopped.

"If you want, Tom, I'll do an autopsy," Mills said, "and see what I can find out. I can't promise to come up with a sure answer to whether there was one effect or separate effects—but I'll try."

"Well, see what you can find out," Tom said. "Maybe it will tell us something."

"We'll do the autopsy on the first one, Miss Watterling," Mills said. "The one that had the larger dose."

Tom lay on the sofa before the fireplace and thought that it was always the same old problem. He had had it with EA 50 and with three since EA 50 and now he had it again with EA 17.

Was it the antibiotic that was causing the damage or was it one of the impurities?

Only this time it was possible that the problem was more complex. If there was only one effect, he told himself—if the paralysis led to death—then it is the same as all the other times. Same old problem. No more complicated. And still not solved—because you still don't know whether death came from the little bit of antibiotic or from one of a couple of dozen impurities.

But what if there were two separate effects? One substance causing paralysis, and something else—an entirely different substance—causing death? Then—he thought carefully—then that means that two different toxic substances causing completely different effects were produced by the same microbe in the same broth. That means it would be possible for that to happen. Two different unrelated compounds made by the same microbe.

He shook his head. Well—why not? Why shouldn't it be possible? He sat up. For the first time he realized that somewhere in his thinking he had begun to suspect that this was not possible. Not in his thinking, actually—in that area that preceded thinking where your feelings were formed.

He got up and moved around the room, trying to sort out these new fragments of thoughts. If they are related—the paralysis and the death—then it is probably one substance. It could be the antibiotic—it could be an impurity—but, whichever it is, we can assume that it's one and the same thing.

He leaned over his desk, scratching out an irregular circle on a piece of paper and then a single line extending from it. But if death was not related to the paralysis, then the microbe has produced two toxic substances. He drew another line extending from the circle, below the first. He threw down the pencil and shook his head. It didn't seem—he just had a feeling about this—he struggled to define for himself exactly what it was he was trying to say—he just had a feeling that it wasn't right.

Then he realized that there had been a knock, and he went to the door and saw Amity there. He wrenched his thinking away from the mouse and asked himself what day it was, and then he remembered that he'd asked her out to dinner tonight. She was going back to New York tomorrow. He looked at his watch and saw that he was more than an hour late. He pushed open the storm door.

"Come on in, Am—I'm sorry, I forgot." Under the circumstances, what else could he say?

She wasn't dressed to go out to dinner—she was wearing slacks.

Maybe this wasn't the night. No—it was the night. "Did it let us down?" she said.

"Did what let us down?"

"EA 17—in the mice?"

"How'd you know?"

"You told me it would go into mice soon, and when you didn't turn up—" She slipped off her coat. "Did they die?"

Instinctively Tom turned away. This was all too reminiscent of other scenes in this room, and he had no taste for going through all that again. Then he thought, Oh, hell, she's not involved. She got in on this one by accident, so she's curious—it's not going to eat her up. And you're not in love with her, so if she's got a lot of damn fool advice, it's not going to tear you apart. When he turned around she was sitting in a chair, waiting.

"Yes," he said. "They died."

"Well," she said, "at least now you know."

For a minute he looked at her. He almost laughed out loud at the thought that he had dreaded a scene. Not her! This girl was all control—and it would take more than a few dead mice to blast it out of her. And why are you so surprised? he said to himself. This was the first thing you saw about her—before you ever spoke two words to her. But still, he *was* surprised. Since Sunday he had seen her twice. He'd been impatient, waiting for Gates to finish the *in-vitro* testing and he'd been glad for her company. She was intelligent and aware, and there was a quality of directness and honesty about her that he liked. Well, he said to himself, she's being honest now. She doesn't give a damn and she's not pretending that she does. You didn't want a scene and you didn't get one.

He poured her a drink from the bottle on the table and handed it to her and fixed one for himself. "I always leave this out on mice-testing days," he said. "Just in case."

"Only on mice-testing days?"

"Especially on mice days."

Only the other times, he thought, he'd come home and put it to good use. And tonight he had not. This was his first drink. That was something new. She didn't have much to say tonight, and he thought, She's probably thinking about going back tomorrow. After all, she's got a guy waiting on the other end.

"What happens now?" she said.

"I'll work on it some more. Max will come in on it. We'll get it purer to see if we can get rid of what caused the trouble. It doesn't have to be the antibiotic that killed the mouse." Or—he thought—that caused the paralysis. What was it about this that bothered him?

"Oh," she said. "I didn't know that."

He didn't answer. He didn't feel like explaining the whole thing to her—he didn't feel like talking about it at all.

"Then it still might be all right?"

"It could be."

"Only you don't expect it?" she said. "Not so much as before?"

"We'll get it purer and test it again. At this stage we don't know."

But she was right. He didn't expect it—his feelings about it had changed. Not his thoughts—his mind was going on with it, but his feelings were not—at least not so much. He looked at Amity, feeling a little better about her. "You're very perceptive, Am."

"You don't have the same head of steam," she said.

"I'm learning to tell myself not to be too excited when they look good and not to be too depressed when they fail." He smiled. "I haven't always been so intelligent. I used to fly—and then—pow!"

She laughed. "Well, you're getting older and wiser. I've flown a few times myself—and then pow. After a while you learn to avoid a few of the pows. It's part of your instinct for self-preservation."

Maybe so, Tom thought. Maybe that was why he hadn't bothered tonight with the Scotch. But it was partly, too, because he'd been trying to figure out that other thing—the one he couldn't quite give a form to, yet. It kept tugging at the fringe of conscious thought, but he couldn't get it out into the open. He sat down again on the sofa, more relaxed now.

"You still leaving tomorrow, Am?" he said.

"Yes."

"Is he back?"

"Yes," she said. "He's back."

"You still putting it off until May?"

"Yes."

"You going to tell me why before you go?"

"I told you why—my show."

"That's not all of it."

"No wonder you're a good scientist," she said. "You have an insatiable curiosity." But she didn't go into her shell any more. In a week they'd become good friends.

"It bothers me because it doesn't figure. Like it's bothering me tonight because I can't figure out something about these mice. That's why I forgot you, Am. I'm sorry."

"Well, concentrate on your mice and don't worry about me."

"If you say so—only I won't. It'll bother me."

She smiled and sat still in the chair and then she said, "Well, Tom, it has to do with those pows we were talking about."

"Do you mean that you're afraid that you'll fall in love with the man you're going to marry?"

"No. I'm afraid I'll fall out of love with him," she said. "I don't trust my own judgment. Well, don't look so astounded—it's happened before. You know—you soar, and then pow. You just described it very neatly."

"Well, you were probably young—that happens to all kids."

"Oh, Tom, honestly—don't look that way—I know what I'm doing." Then she said, "But it wasn't just when I was a kid. This is a regular pattern with me. I'm in love and then—boom—I'm out of love—just feeling sorry for him and his problems. But it's not love any more."

"Do they always have problems?"

"I am a magnet to people with problems."

"Am, if you can't love a man when he has problems, you don't love him."

"That's not it." She moved, a little impatiently, in her chair. "I don't know what it is. I just know that it happens. In the end I only see them as—well, just rather pathetic. Maybe I'm a sucker for weak men. And that's not what I really want. At least, I don't think so."

The way she referred to them—in the plural—Tom wondered how many times this had happened. "Were they all weak?" he said. "All of them?"

"They never seemed weak at the start. At the start, they seemed wonderful. And then, one day, would come the big awakening. My eyes would be open and I would see them as they were. And then I was only trying to help them—because they needed help—but I was out of love." She looked at him and smiled. "Once they were on their feet there was no problem ending it, because I was usually the first one they kicked over. But that's only natural, I suppose."

"What's natural?" he said. The whole thing was fantastic.

"Nobody likes to consider himself weak. In his reveries every man is a Hercules."

"Yes, that's natural, I guess."

"So when a man has cried on your shoulder, once the pain is gone, he doesn't like to be reminded of the tears. He wants to pretend they never happened and he tries to cut out the one thing that reminds him. In a roundabout way it's sort of like the best way to lose a friend is to lend him money—then he avoids you. Anyway, it never mattered. I was long since out of love. I had long since gone pow."

Tom tried to think of something intelligent to say, but this was so far from what he had expected. "What about this one—is he weak?"

"No. At least he doesn't seem to be."

"Is he loaded down with problems?"

"No more than anyone else—and he seems to handle them."

He was about to say, Then, hell, marry him—but he didn't. The words came to his lips and died and he remained silent.

"This one seems fine, and in May it'll be a year. If it can last a year, I think it can last. And that's enough of that. What about the mice? What did they die of?"

"They just died."

"Well, it wasn't old age!"

He laughed. "They were paralyzed—but I'm not sure that's what they died of."

If death is not related to the paralysis—he began to think about it again—then . . . There was still something about this idea he didn't like. "If it was an impurity that caused death, it can be separated out," he said.

"But you'd still have the paralysis."

"Yes."

"But would anyone use a drug that caused paralysis?"

"It's highly unlikely." But this wasn't what was bothering him. "Do you think maybe you can get rid of the paralysis, too?"

"If it's caused by an impurity, we can."

But what if it turns out that they're not separate? What if they're related? Then it's like all the other times—you're back to one toxic effect. In either case you've got to go on because you could get rid of the substance causing the trouble.

Still, he thought, if it's just one toxicity—if death *is* related to paralysis—I'll feel better. But why? He was groping through to something but he couldn't see it yet. And not even groping for an answer, he thought. He was still trying to ask the question.

A few days later Mills came into Tom's office.

"I can't be sure," he said, "but it looks as though they were related. I think death was from brain damage—the same as the paralysis. I don't find anything else."

Tom couldn't have said why this news should make him feel so good.

Frantically, for ten days he and Max worked on EA 17 and then gave a much purer powder to Mills. But as Tom stood beside him and watched Mills tuck under the tail of the first mouse, he realized that he was only watching to see how fast paralysis would set in and how fast the mouse would die.

When the heartbeat stopped, he knew that he had been expecting it.

NINETEEN

I HAVE a few questions I'd like to ask," Brainard said, glancing down at his note pad, "unless you've got some more yourself, Ade."

Exasperated, Tom braced his feet on the rung of his chair and thought, What's left? We've covered everything. For more than an hour now they had been sitting here in the conference room next to Hale's office, going over the whole thing from the beginning. It was a dark dreary morning late in February, and overhead the lights were turned on. Outside a lone gray plane drifted across the gray sky, the drone of the motor sounding hollow in the heavy air. Here in the conference room the dreary voices droned on. Behind Hale, May Nelson sat at her transcriber, taking it all down. What they were really scratching for, Tom knew, was a little good news to serve up next week to the board of directors. But good news was hard to find.

"Dr. Mills," Brainard said, "to date, as I figure it, you've tested eight antibiotics in mice. Any of them any good?"

"Mr. Brainard, you'd have heard about it if they were," Mills said.

"I hear about it when they aren't too," Brainard said. "Now—all eight were toxic—the mice died almost immediately—right?"

"Well—within fifteen minutes." Mills was wondering what Brainard was getting at—you could hear it in his voice.

"Now—Dr. Gates—" Brainard examined his dead cigar butt before looking at Gates. "How many times would you say you've found streptomycin and streptothricin, Dr. Gates—when they haven't slipped past you, that is?"

Gates shifted uneasily. "I haven't counted, sir."

"Every day of the week, practically?"

"I—well, yes."

Watching Brainard, Tom sat a little straighter and thought, He's working up to something—he's operated like this before. He's moving more carefully today because Hale is here—but his eye is on a target.

"And how many times in eight months have you found a broad-spectrum antibiotic?"

Gates fidgeted. "Well, some that were gram-positive have hit a few gram-negative, too—"

"Broad-spectrum, Dr. Gates. When we began, we were going to find a drug that would hit fifty or sixty different organisms—gram-positive and gram-negative both—a broad-spectrum antibiotic. Now —even if they were toxic as cyanide, Dr. Gates—how many like that have turned up?"

"If he'd found even one, Gil," Will Caroline said, "you'd have heard about that, too."

"Yes, I suppose I would have," Brainard said. "It'd be quite an event." He put his cigar butt into the ashtray where there were three other dead butts, lying side by side, and he took his pencil and moved the fourth one to line up precisely with the other three. "Now—Dr. Derrick—"

Tom looked up sharply. Something in Brainard's voice said that now he was on target.

"What do you make of all this, Dr. Derrick?"

"In what way, sir?" Derrick said.

"In eight months you've turned up a few unimpressive antibiotics that are instantly toxic, a lot of streptomycin—plenty of that —and not a single broad-spectrum antibiotic, toxic or otherwise. What does all this mean to you, Dr. Derrick?"

"What does it mean to you, Gil?" Hale said. "What's on your mind?"

"Just this, Ade. For an hour now, we've been listening to how Gates's tests don't work—and later he catches his mistakes—or somebody else does—and nobody knows what to do about that. And some of them don't like the way Cable is working and he doesn't like the way they're working. But the way I see it—and of course it's only my opinion, Ade—"

Brainard paused, giving Hale a chance to stop him, and Tom thought, He's very good at this. He's an expert at walking that fine line between kowtowing to Hale and seizing the reins just long enough to stir up trouble.

"In the end, none of it seems to matter," Brainard said. "Whatever they do—whatever they don't do—however they go about it— it all adds up to the same answer, which is zero."

"What's your point?" Hale said.

"The point is," Brainard said, "that with all this I don't hear anything about the dirt."

So that's it, Tom thought. He'd forgotten all about that little flurry of arguments, just before Christmas, about the soil samples. There were always so many new problems that you didn't think about the old ones when they didn't come up.

"That's right," Morrissey put in eagerly. "If he doesn't start with the right soil, whatever we do doesn't matter."

"This they don't talk about, Ade," Brainard said. "This they don't like the smell of—because obviously they're not getting the right dirt, and there isn't a man in the place who knows what to do about it. Not even our so-called specialist."

"Dr. Derrick has been perfectly clear about this," Will Caroline said.

"He's clear about his own confusion. Get them everywhere, he says. For an opinion like that you don't need a specialist. The fact is he didn't know where to get the dirt when he came here and he doesn't know now."

Narrowly Tom looked at Brainard and thought, What is it about this that attracts him? What is he trying to accomplish? If he wants to prove that we're still ignorant and terribly confused, we've proved it ourselves today in a dozen different ways—without this relatively minor issue that everyone else has forgotten. Is it because this one is less technical than some of the others—and easier for the board to understand? Or is there something else involved? Then he saw that Will Caroline was watching Brainard, too, in a way that said he was wondering the same thing.

Hale looked at Derrick questioningly, and Derrick said, "Ah believe, sir, that we ought to have the broadest possible variety of samples. We should get them from everywhere."

Brainard spread his hands on the table. "The world is my beat—that's his attitude."

"He's never pretended otherwise," Will Caroline said. "He's said this from the start."

"What he knew at the start hasn't produced much."

Brainard took out a fresh cigar, and Tom watched him clamp his teeth into it. Then he looked at Brainard's eyes, sharp and predatory, and he thought, He's doing this to show us up, all right, but apart from that, he enjoys it. He gets a charge out of needling Derrick. He enjoyed it at that other meeting—and that day at Harrup's—and he's enjoying it now.

"Of course," Brainard said, "everywhere covers a lot of ground.

When he doesn't come up with anything, he can always say we didn't dig him the right spoonful of dirt—eh, Derrick?"

"Mr. Brainard," Tom spoke up. "I thought that was what you wanted! Last time you kept saying we ought to spread out and get soil everywhere we could."

Brainard smiled, undisturbed, behind his cigar. "That's my point exactly, Ade," he said. "The ideal situation would be to have a man who could pinpoint a limited area and give some sound reasons for his choice. But Dr. Derrick can't do that—"

"Nobody could do that!" Will Caroline said.

"So what choice do we have?" Brainard went on. "Distasteful as it is, we've got to get dirt from everywhere. Now—my question is— why aren't we doing it? Why are we just talking about it?" He jerked his head toward Derrick. "He's playing one tune but he's dancing to another. The fact is—"

"Just a minute, Gil," Will Caroline said calmly. "If you're going to talk about getting the soil samples, talk to me."

"He's the specialist."

"It's my job."

"He's the man who's doing it, and he's working the same tired stuff from a limited area over and over, and he's pretending he's very busy doing a big job. Talks very big about getting soil from everywhere. All right, why aren't we getting it, then?"

"Now, just a minute," Morrissey put in. "I object. I think we should screen American soil first. This is where the germs are."

"Epidemics can spread anywhere," Tom said.

"I think we should absolutely stay American," Rosswell spoke up. To Rosswell any limitation would be cheaper than none. "I believe God places the cure near the ailment—"

For a minute Tom thought they were going to hear about the parson and his aspirin again, but Brainard cut Rosswell off.

"All right, here's your situation," Brainard said. "You've got a man who can't tell you what to do because he doesn't know. Right, Dr. Derrick? And neither can anyone else—so you've got two alternatives. Either you take the dirt from anyplace you can get it—no restrictions—and that opens up a lot of territory. Or else you do one area at a time. If you take it from everywhere, the odds against you are about a billion to one. But if you're not even in the right area, you're eliminating even those odds and your chances are zero. That's your choice. Right, Derrick?"

Derrick smiled. "Ah'm not much at figuring odds, sir," he said easily, "but ah'd be most reluctant to eliminate any area." Then he added, "Of course, sir, we're running studies all the time to narrow things down."

"It's time you had a few answers—not still be thinking up the questions."

"We're learning all the time," Derrick said. "We just keep trying to learn more."

"What?" Hale said. "What have you learned?"

"Well, sir—we've learned that fairly warm moist climates are best—and slightly alkaline soil, so we don't want too many from forests because forest soil is slightly acid. And we don't want sandy soil—and"—Derrick hesitated—"the other matters are pretty technical, sir."

"Dr. Derrick—have you had any samples from Africa?" Brainard said.

"No, sir."

"Asia?"

"Not yet, sir."

"Eastern Europe? How many from Eastern Europe, Dr. Derrick?"

"At the present time, the Eastern European countries are not easy to get into, sir."

"Then how can you say you've had enough dirt to draw even one conclusion, Dr. Derrick, if you're leaving out seventy-five per cent of the earth's surface?"

"Talk to me, Gil," Will Caroline said again. "Getting the samples is my job."

"It's Derrick's statement I'm questioning."

"It's my work you're questioning."

"Ah believe there was enough evidence to draw these particular conclusions, sir," Derrick said, patiently sticking to what he knew.

"Great conclusions—based on twenty-five per cent of the potential evidence."

Tom was beginning to get mad—at Brainard for what he was doing and at Derrick for letting him get away with it. And yet, he thought, that's why Brainard picks on Derrick instead of someone else—because he knows he can get away with it. He kowtows to Hale who is more powerful, and then he finds his own victim to balance his psychic accounts. Somebody that can't fight back—like Derrick—or like his wife.

294

Brainard struck a match and held it a minute before bringing it to his cigar. He looked at Derrick again. "Why only dirt?" he said.

"What's that, sir?" Derrick said.

"Why screen only dirt? Why not something else?"

"Ah believe the soil is the best source for microorganisms."

"Why not the air? The air's full of microbes, isn't it?"

"There are microorganisms everywhere," Derrick said.

"Penicillin flew into Fleming's laboratory through an open window. That wasn't in the soil, Dr. Derrick. That was in the air."

"Yes, sir."

"And my daughter told me a wild story about some British physicist who had penicillin a century ago and it fell into his test tube out of the air. Again not in the soil, Dr. Derrick. So—why aren't we screening the microbes in the air?"

"If anyone cares to bring me spores gathered in the air, ah'd be real pleased to work on them."

"And I understand you can get antibiotics out of plants. Why aren't we screening plants, Dr. Derrick?"

"Ah believe soil is the better source, sir."

"And the penicillin we're using most today came from a moldy cantaloupe. How about that, Dr. Derrick?"

"Yes, sir."

Disgusted and very angry, Tom began to shift about in his chair, silently urging Derrick to fight back. And yet he knew that Derrick could never fight on Brainard's level. He simply didn't have the vocabulary—or the malice—or the practice. Even to be effectively vicious takes practice, he thought, and Derrick had had none. He was just a patient steady man who liked his work, who by temperament could cope with failure—a gentle man, without rancor, who could never lash out at another man as Brainard could, or even effectively resist that kind of attack. It wasn't that Derrick was afraid of Brainard. It was just that what came easily to one man came with great difficulty to another—or not at all—and Derrick could not fight that way. It didn't make him more a coward or less a man.

"And what else are you overlooking, Dr. Derrick?"

Derrick looked puzzled.

"Where else are there microbes you're ignoring while you're playing around with your dirt? Where else could you find them if you took the trouble?"

But if fight did not come easily to Derrick, restraint did not come easily to Tom, and suddenly the lid blew off of his control. "Where else!" he cried. "Everywhere else! You can find microbes anywhere. A babbling brook, a stagnant pond—"

Brainard tried to ignore him. "No little man is going to turn up to spin flax into gold, Dr. Derrick."

"When you're looking for microbes"—Tom raised his voice over Brainard's—"you've got a big range! Rotting vegetation! A manure pile! The human gut! The vaginal vault! Any site of contamination develops a microbe community!"

"All right, Dr. Cable, we've got the picture," somebody said. That was Ade Hale.

"There's a big choice—you want some more?"

"You've made your point, Tom," somebody else said. That was Will Caroline.

Mills kicked him and Tom sat down. Brainard turned on him angrily. "Listen—you fellows get sore as hell when we criticize you, but the facts are you're not getting the right stuff—in the soil—or anywhere else. And until you do, nothing else matters. You start a race in the wrong direction and it doesn't matter how fast you run or what else you do—or don't do."

But a lot of the starch seemed to have gone out of Brainard, and a few minutes later the meeting ended.

"Kee-rist! Dirt! Cheapest thing in the world is dirt!" Mills looked around at the silent group sitting in the cafeteria where they had come after the meeting. "Whole thing falling apart on all sides because that son of a bitch doesn't like the dirt!"

But even Mills was lacking his usual exuberance, and when no one else spoke, he fell silent, too.

A few minutes later Gates looked up from his coffee and said, "Well, he showed us what we look like, all right. He made it pretty clear that in eight months we haven't accomplished anything."

"Too damn clear," Weir muttered. "And he's right."

At the end of the table Max crushed out a cigarette. "His eye was on the board meeting. He'll get a transcript of this meeting to them next week."

"What we needed was your wife, Charlie," Mills said, "to fire a few more volleys out of Shakespeare."

Derrick smiled. "At a time like this the only sensible thing to do is get drunk. Ah'd be mighty pleased to have you all as my guests right after work."

Weir stood up and went for more coffee, and the little group fell silent again. Outside the high narrow windows the sky was a dull gray patch. The lights were on and the room was still dark.

"It wouldn't be so bad," Gates said, "if there was a little good news, too. Just some ray of hope we could offer. But there's nothing."

"Hell, Pearly," Tom said, "all research goes like a sine wave. You always have your peaks and your low points."

But Gates was right. There was just nothing that Will Caroline could offer next week as a defense against Brainard. Tom had put aside EA 17 and nobody was working on anything else that seemed promising.

"All the same," Gates said, "sometimes it's the point you happen to be on when it comes up for revaluation that determines whether you go on. And right now things couldn't be worse."

"Well—shoo!" Mills said. "We've still got a whole week to turn up some good news!" Mills was trying hard to cheer up, but something was lacking. Weir snorted and Gates just looked at him without speaking.

"The board isn't going to drop this at eight months," Tom said. "There's a kind of timing about these things—and it's not time yet."

"Well—you may be right," Gates said. "But you can't count on it. If somebody comes up with an idea that looks good, they'll cut this way down. You know—they live by that opportunity-cost theory. Isn't that so, Max?"

"Well, it's true they've got more than enough places to put the money," Max said, "and they like to put it where it will do the most good." Then Max saw Harrup come in alone and he went over to sit with him.

"The trouble with Brainard is he's got too much time to think," Mills muttered. "Always snooping around. We ought to give him some trouble—take up his time. And Rosswell, too. We should go about it systematically—keep 'em all busy, so we can get some work done."

Derrick smiled. "Ah think that's a fine idea, Pat. Kind of a Committee for the Systematic Distraction of Management."

"I may never take another aspirin," Mills said.

But it wasn't in Mills's nature to remain silent or depressed for long, and after a moment he was talking again. "Dirt! Most plentiful commodity in the world is dirt. Whole damn project going down the drain for a lack of dirt. Kee-rist!" He looked over at the empty table where Will Caroline usually sat. "Mr. Caroline," he announced, "I quit. I quit, Mr. Caroline!"

"It's mighty nice of you to give us this performance, Pat," Derrick said. "Ah thought you saved this routine fo' the benefit of your technician."

"Ho, I'm pretty serious!" Mills said. "No—on second thought, I'd better ask my wife! If I tell my wife I quit because we have a dirt problem, she won't like it. 'I have dirt problems of my own,' she'll say. 'I'm getting dishpan hands and housemaid's knee, but I handle them—I don't quit.' Hold everything, Mr. Caroline! I don't quit. Changed my mind."

"Mills, you're crazy," Gates said, not very heartily.

But Mills's mind was working now. "We ought to attack Brainard with his own weapons. We ought to get him more dirt than he ever saw—or even heard of. We ought to bury the bastard in dirt."

"It's a tempting suggestion," Tom said.

Mills's face lit up. "Why not?" he said. "Now, why'n hell-damn not?"

"Why in hell-damn not what, Pat?" Derrick said.

"Listen," Mills said. "What do you do when you need a certain commodity? You go to the man who has access to it. Right?"

"Right," Derrick agreed.

"Supposing you need money, where do you go? You don't go to your friends and say, 'Scrounge around the house and try to dig up a few bucks, how about it?' No, sir, when you need money, you go to someone who has access to money. You go to a bank. You go to a guy who can get his hand in the till!"

"What do you know about needing money?" Weir said sullenly, and got up and left.

For a moment Mills looked after him, puzzled. But little remarks like that didn't bother Mills. Once he was wound up, he was irrepressible. "O.K., then, let's keep it on a simpler level," he said. "Take anything. Take girdles. Where's a woman go when she needs a girdle? She doesn't go to the A & P." He thought about that and turned to Tom, sitting beside him. "She doesn't, does she?"

298

"You're asking the right man," Tom said with a laugh.

"O.K., let's make it more specialized, because maybe you can buy the damn things in the A & P these days. I always think this is the age of specialization until I go to the A & P. Then my whole theory explodes. Now—supposing you don't have just any wife who can pick up a standard-size girdle in the A & P. Say you've got a big fat wife who needs a special-size girdle. Very fussy gal—but big. Needs them in all colors—blue, black, gold, lamé, painted with rosebuds. O.K., you got the picture?"

"Who wants a picture of a big fat fussy wife, Mills?" Gates said.

"Now, where does she go? She goes to a girdle shop. She goes to someone who's got access to a lot of girdles."

"Mills," Derrick said, "what in hell-damn are you driving at?"

"Well—shoo! We gotta go to people who have access to dirt."

"Like who?"

"Like, why don't we go to a mess of airplane pilots who go everywhere? Every place they stop they get out of the plane and walk around. Let's ask them to dig us some dirt."

It was so simple you wondered why no one had thought of it sooner!

"Shoo!" Mills said. "I'm gonna do that. I've got a friend with an airline that goes everywhere. I'm going down this weekend and ask him if he'll get all the pilots to dig dirt."

"Is he a pilot?" Gates said.

"Shoo! He couldn't fly a kite—he's the president," Mills said absently because already his mind was racing on. "Listen," he said slowly, after a minute. "Did you hear what I said?"

"Pat," Derrick said, "ain't nobody here been talkin' but you. You've got us spellbound, man."

"They get out and walk around." Mills waved his hand in a circle over the table. "Every time the plane lands, they *get out and walk around!*"

"Well, of course they walk around," Gates said. "The poor guys aren't going to sit in the plane all the time!"

"Then there's *dirt on their boots!*"

Immediately Derrick's face went into a broad smile. "Ah do believe they'd have some mighty dirty boots among them."

"Pilots coming into New York from all over the world," Mills said.

"It's as easy to scrape boots as mud flaps," Derrick said.

"Well—" Gates hesitated. He was looking from one to the other with a mixture of interest and doubt, and then he, too, capitulated. "Say—is that airport part of the Port of New York Authority?"

"Who knows? Why?"

"Well—hell!" Gates beamed. "We've got friends there!"

"What ho!" Mills cried. "The soil-sample brigade is on the move again. Boola boola—fight, team, fight! Mr. Brainard, you old bastard, sir—we're gonna pulverize you!"

"Mills," Derrick said amiably, "you're mad as a hatter."

"What do you say, Cal? Do you smell snow?" Will Caroline had finished his breakfast and stood at the window. Over the weekend the clouds had pushed apart a little, but this morning they were massed together again into a heavy gray blanket over the water.

Callie looked toward the window. "Are we for it or against it?"

"We hope it snows like hell," Will said.

"All right. Why?"

"I figure that an honest storm is good for at least three directors."

"Good?"

"Keep 'em away," he said. "Keep them away from the meeting."

Callie came over to the window, too. "Are things that bad, Will?"

"It's not that they're so bad. It's just a little harder to fight with no ammunition." Will smiled and shrugged. "The February meeting is always the worst of the year, anyway. Everyone's off his feed. They're irritable—they pick on little things—they've begun to worry about taxes. February's the bottom of the year." He looked out again at the heavy sky. "Come to think of it, I sort of hate it myself."

"I do think, darling," Callie said, "that in a thoroughly lousy spot the only answer is to attack."

"You're right, general." He reached over for another last drink of coffee. "And I would—if I had even a popgun."

Callie stood looking up at him. "What you gonna do, boy?"

Will Caroline smiled. "I'll bluff, Cal."

The snow began as he was driving over the bridge—big, heavy flakes that wouldn't last long. Will began to think about the board meeting coming up, and then about last Friday's company meeting in preparation for it, and about the fuss Brainard had raised. Will was beginning to see a pattern emerging—a certain design—and this fuss about soil samples was part of it. Morrissey had been the first to raise questions about the soil samples a few months ago, he remembered. And then Brainard had picked up the ball and run with it—only not in the direction Morrissey had intended. From the start they had worked together—at first to block the project and then to bring it to an early death, but on this question they separated. Because, Will thought, their positions are not identical. Brainard has only one thing on his mind, which is sabotage. But Morrissey has two. Morrissey wants a quick end to this, but he is worrying, too, about how he, personally, is going to look. He will have to wear at least some of the tattered rags of any failure, and they won't be becoming. And so he is building little defense walls and escape hatches all along the line.

And what about the motives behind those positions? Will thought. Approaching Enright, he stopped in the line of traffic waiting to turn into the lot. Of the two, Brainard's reasons were the more complicated. With Brainard, he said to himself, it's more than just the money—more than just wanting this allocation for his department—because if this works, production will triple, quadruple, and more—and he will be flying higher than ever. Brainard isn't a man who is afraid of a gamble—nor is he likely to be blind to one that could pay off in jackpot dividends. So it's more than the money.

The line of traffic moved and Will Caroline drove into the parking lot. With Morrissey, he thought, the reasons were easier to understand. With Morrissey from the start it had been fear—with all this blocking and feinting and defending, that was becoming quite clear—and whatever the fear was born of, it remained. Above all, Morrissey wanted to stay on the safe side of the fence because the other side looked like a jungle, full of unfamiliar dangers.

And it is, Will thought suddenly. It is a jungle. That is what has shown up so clearly in this soil question—and Brainard seized it because in it he saw the pattern of the whole project.

Here is a simple and completely understandable question, Will thought. And yet, to this one question alone there are dozens of possible answers. We can screen soil and we can collect it from around here or from all over the earth. We can proceed systematically or we can proceed at random. We can screen soil or we can screen air spores—or plants—or microbes from brooks or from stagnant ponds or animal or human waste or any of those other sources that Cable named. But you can't do them all—you have to make a choice. And Derrick has made one—but he knows he could be wrong. He's only playing the odds, and at best it's an educated guess.

And that was the pattern of the project and everything connected with it. There was that argument when Cable decided to put the cultures into ten broths for only one fermentation. Even now, the others were still fooling with broths for weeks. And who could say who was right? Nothing had come out of either side. And again last week, when Cable set aside EA 17, there had been a similar argument because the others said he was dropping it too soon and Cable held that he had worked it enough. And again, who could say? You made your decision and you told yourself that you backed it one hundred per cent—and you knew you could be wrong. At best, every decision was an educated guess. And that was the way it was going to be—right up to the end.

And that is what Brainard sees, Will Caroline told himself. He sees that the whole problem is represented right here in this one small and relatively unimportant decision. And every time we open our mouths to argue, we give him ammunition to use against us— and there is nothing we can do about it.

A little later, coming into the conference room for the Monday morning meeting, Will noticed that some of the men had recovered their spirits over the weekend. Gates and Cable seemed to be in a rather high mood. And Derrick, too, although Derrick was always on a pretty even keel. Looking around, Will saw that everyone was here except Mills. He waited a minute and then began without him. As always, Morrissey had some complaints, and Will decided to let him have his say for about five minutes if it would make him feel better.

A moment later there was a thud at the door, and Will looked around. There was another thud. Derrick stood up and started toward the door, but before he reached it, it squeaked open. Then, with boxes under his arms, boxes across his chest, boxes balanced precariously in front of his face, Mills came through the doorway and inched his way into the room. Once he stopped, boxes teetering, and cautiously peered around the pile to get his bearings. He took another step and slid the boxes onto the table.

"Dirt," he announced. Only then did Mills seem to notice that the meeting had begun. "Oh, excuse me," he said.

302

He sat down. His hand crept over and righted a box that had landed upside down. "African dirt," he explained to Morrissey, who had begun to talk again and then stopped again and was looking at him reprovingly. Mills lifted the lid and tilted the box to show Morrissey the envelopes inside. Then he seemed to notice that he was interrupting again and hastily put down the box. "Excuse me," he said again.

Incredulously, Will Caroline looked from Mills to the boxes.

"What do you mean, African dirt?" Morrissey said.

"I mean dirt from Africa," Mills said soberly.

Will restrained a smile, and Mills pulled out a few soil envelopes.

"Libya," he announced, reading the writing on the first envelope. "Algiers—Cairo—Morocco—Casablanca. Oh—just North African dirt in this box, I guess." He fished around in it for a minute and then pushed the box aside. "South African dirt must be in that one." He looked inside another box. "No, this is Asia. Singapore—Hongkong—"

Suspiciously, wondering whether this could be a gag, Will looked at the windfall on the table. No, he told himself, Mills wouldn't joke about this. But then, you never could tell.

Mills was poking around in still another box. "Europe—well, Southern Europe. Lisbon—Madrid—Rome—Athens. Oh, here we are. This one is South Africa. Johannesburg, Capetown—"

"Where did you get those?" Morrissey demanded.

"Sir," Mills said very seriously, "we got these from the pilots of six major airlines. It took a little footwork, but we managed."

Will Caroline looked around the table. They were all in on it—Derrick and Cable and Gates—that's why they were in such high spirits.

"And this is only the beginning," Mills said. "We have pilots armed to the teeth with envelopes who have already left for every corner of the globe and will bring back soil."

A little sheepishly, Will Caroline smiled. This was a good idea and he should have thought of it himself.

"Also, we've located a world traveler," Mills said, "whose stated aim is to shun the more civilized areas, where the pilots will go, and enter the hinterland—to see things as they really are."

"The fellow's going to bum his way around the world," Derrick explained. "We ran into him at the airport—promised him twenty-five cents a sample."

It wasn't a gag if Derrick was owning up to it, too. Mills might joke about it, but Derrick wouldn't.

"I hardly think that type of party would be reliable," Morrissey said. "He could dig one shovel of soil and put it into hundreds of envelopes."

"Charlie told him we could tell if the samples all came from the same place," Mills said. "In which case, no pay."

Harrup looked up at that. For several minutes he'd been staring at the pile of envelopes as though it were a snake and he was deciding whether to kill it or run. Now he said to Derrick, "Can you tell that?"

"Yes, sir," Derrick said. "Ah believe ah can."

Harrup's eyes went back to the envelopes, and then, to Will Caroline's surprise, he said, "It might be an interesting assortment."

Curiously Will looked over at him. He wasn't sure where Harrup fitted into the opposition alliance these days.

Back in his office, when the meeting was over, Will Caroline looked up from reading the list of countries Mills had given him and saw Morrissey and Brainard talking in the corridor, and he knew Morrissey was giving Brainard a full report.

Then his secretary came in and Will said, "Jeannie, do you remember what Lincoln said to his generals when they complained that Grant was drinking?"

"He said, 'Get that same brand to my other officers,'—or something like that."

Will laughed. "You're a smart girl, Jeannie. Someday I'm going to buy you a degree and put you to work." He handed her the list. "A dozen copies, Jeannie—before Friday."

Outside, he noticed, it had stopped snowing and there were patches of blue sky breaking through. With a smile Will told himself that it didn't matter any more. And then he thought, Well, now it's come full circle. Morrissey raised the issue as a defense maneuver—and we talked about it enough to give Brainard some ammunition against us—and then he blasted us with it and shook us up enough to get out and find some ammunition of our own. Will's smile broadened. It was nice to know it could work both ways.

He picked up the telephone to call Callie. This was too good to keep. "I've got ammunition, Cal," he said.

"Found yourself a popgun?"

Out in the corridor, Brainard's face said that he had the story now. Will Caroline grinned. "Cal," he said, "I've got a cannon."

Its number was EA 106, and it was one of the two that Tom had been working on at the same time as EA 17.

"Mouse," Mills said, as he injected the green-headed mouse, "you die and I quit."

He put the mouse back and then injected the one with the green-spotted rump. Tom bent over to watch as the two mice moved about the jar. The others gathered around to investigate, and five minutes passed and then ten, and they all began to settle down. Half an hour passed and a lone sentry stalked the jar.

"We'll double the dose," Mills said.

Then suddenly the green-headed mouse trembled and Mills paused. The mouse moved to the side of the jar and began to shake.

"Kee-rist!" Mills put down his syringe.

The mouse rolled over on its back and lay with its legs drawn up, clamped tight to its body. Then suddenly it shuddered and jerked, and the legs shot out straight and went rigid.

"He's having a convulsion," Mills said.

A few minutes passed and the tension went out of the mouse. It lay still, its pink tail stretched out straight, pink legs extended but not rigid, pink eyes open but not moving.

"Is it dead?" Tom said.

"No."

After several minutes the mouse moved. It made its way to the water pipe and with great difficulty heaved itself upright, one paw on the pipe, the other grasping at air. It drank and sank down to the sawdust again, and a few minutes later it went into another convulsion.

"This could go on for quite a while, Tom," Mills said as he cut the dose for the yellow-spotted mice, "before they either snap out of it or die."

Tom went back to his laboratory. When he checked again half an hour later, the yellow-headed mouse was having a convulsion. By lunchtime all six mice were having spasmodic convulsions, but all six were still alive. At about two-thirty, the green-spotted mice died.

By the end of the day all the mice were dead.

TWENTY

A LL RIGHT, fellas," Mills said. "Now is the time for all good mice to come to the aid of Enright—right, George?"

"Yeah—yeah!" George Weir muttered. He could live without the comedy every time he came in here. He looked toward the jar without looking at the mice. He could live without coming in here at all. There was no reason Mills couldn't do the tests and send up a report. But Cable came and watched—and if he stayed away, Weir told himself, someone would say he wasn't so interested, especially since Cable was turning out so many more antibiotics.

Then he realized that Mills had finished injecting the two green-spotted mice and he looked unenthusiastically into the jar, where the other mice were having a big time smelling them, and waited for them to start to die.

The green-headed mouse was crawling around, and then the one with the green butt began crawling, too, the rest following to nose them some more. Weir looked over at the flat-chested technician and then at Mills, who was watching the mice, probably hoping they'd die. Mills wouldn't want him to be the one to find a good drug. He'd want it to be Cable. Those two were great buddies. And why wouldn't they be? Cable was practically living down here.

Turning away, Weir moved over to the window. Outside a March wind was whipping around, stirring the spindly tops of trees and making the bay look mean. For a moment Weir stared at the angry water. He was fed up with this whole deal. You work your ass off, he said to himself, and finally you test because you don't dare hold off any longer, and you stand there watching the little bastards crawling around till they drop dead—and what for? And Mills—you'd think he had a woman in there, the way he stood watching.

Weir moved back to the counter. "Well, what's cooking?" he said.

"Nothing yet," Mills said.

Weir looked into the jar. The mice had quieted down some. One of them was moving around, not one of the green ones—and the rest were settled down—not sick-looking, just settled. Weir looked at the clock. For God's sake, he said to himself. It's almost half an hour. He looked back at the green-spotted mice. Those damned mice are all right, he said to himself. They're O.K., for God's sake!

"We'll double the dose," Mills said. "The green ones got a five-milligram dose. We'll give the yellow ones a ten-milligram dose."

Great, Weir thought—that'll finish them. But half an hour later the two yellow-spotted mice were snuggled up beside the two green-spotted mice. Jesus Christ, Weir said to himself. Those mice are in good shape!

"We'll double it again," Mills said. "Give the purple ones a twenty-milligram dose."

"What're you—in a hurry to kill them?" Weir snapped.

Mills laughed. "That's the life of a research mouse, George."

By lunchtime Weir knew that the word had gotten around that none of the mice were showing any ill effects, not even the purple ones that had received a twenty-milligram dose at eleven o'clock.

"You shouldn't get too excited too soon, George," Gates warned him.

With studied carelessness, Weir lit a cigarette. "Who's excited?" he said. "Damn mice'll probably go all at once this afternoon."

But after lunch the mice were still fine, and Weir spent a fidgety, agonizing afternoon, telling himself each time he checked that surely the next time they would be dead, and then when they were not, he would walk slowly back to his own laboratory, incredulous, thinking what a laugh it would be on the rest of them—on Cable and on Mills and on Strong—if this one turned out to be good.

When he checked for the last time at four-thirty, the mice were still fine—as good as the controls in the next cage that had received only the disease germs and no antibiotic.

"Good-looking mice, eh, Miss Watterling?" He beamed as he walked past her. He started to whack her bottom and caught himself. "Well, see you in the morning."

"It's wonderful, George," Gates said, turning out of the parking lot into the line of traffic heading home. "But don't let yourself count on it too much yet."

"Listen, Pearly," Weir said. "Who do you think you're talking to? I wasn't born yesterday. Overnight anything could happen."

"Even if the mice are fine in the morning," Gates said, "your antibiotic could still turn out to be streptomycin or streptothricin. I checked as carefully as I could—and I know you did, too, but—"

"It's not streptomycin or streptothricin," Weir snapped. "It's completely different."

But his spirits sagged a little. Of course that damned antibiotic could turn out to be streptomycin or streptothricin. It didn't look like either, but everyone knew the tests were so crude you couldn't be sure.

"Christ, I wish someone'd find some tests you could depend on," he said after a minute. "The tests we're using you can trust about as much as you can trust a woman."

Gates didn't answer. At first Gates used to tell him he trusted Madeline but lately he'd cut that out. Probably realized how asinine it sounded. Trusting Madeline was like trusting your grandmother. Who was offering anything?

"There are a couple of dozen things could happen to those mice," he remarked glumly. Overnight something would go wrong—he'd make book on it. He'd go in there in the morning and the little bastards would be dead. And Mills would be laughing himself sick.

"Mills!" he said. "You ever watch that bastard test his mice? You ever see him do it?"

"No," Gates said. "George, I don't know what you've got against Mills. He gets a little carried away, but he's a very nice guy."

"Listen, you've never seen him—Christ, he watches those mice like they were a bunch of whores in a floor show, peeling off their clothes. And when he's not watching, he's clowning around. Well, hell—why not? Nobody's going to blame him for anything. Big job he's got. Watches mice and tells you they died. He's nothing but a goddam reporter."

Gates stopped in front of Weir's house and Weir got out of the car. He knew that he'd riled Gates but he didn't care. What did Gates have to worry about? He was only a goddam reporter, too.

When he came into the house, he could see that Janet had heard the news—probably Pearly had called Madeline or Derrick had called Kate—everybody wanting to get into the act. And probably she had a lot of big ideas already. He walked past her and tossed down his briefcase.

"Oh, *jeez*, I'm getting sick of this deal," he said. "Going in there— watching those little bastards crawl around—"

"I thought the mice lived!" Janet said. "I thought they were fine!"

"Yeah, well, they'll probably all be dead in the morning." He took out a bottle and carried it to his chair.

"Maybe they won't be dead," she said. "Maybe they'll still be fine."

"I'm sorry the little bastards hung on at all!" he said. "I wish they'd dropped dead right away."

"Well, that's a marvelous attitude."

"Listen, when they drop dead right away, nobody notices. It's expected. If I worked for ten years and every one of my antibiotics killed the damn mice in five minutes, nobody would notice." He poured a drink. "I'm beginning to think Cable's got the right idea."

"Why?" she said. "Which idea?"

"All anyone notices is that he's grinding out about five times as many as anyone else. Nobody notices that the mice always die right away, because that's what they expect." He tossed down his drink and poured another. "I've got a good mind not to go and watch those damn mice any more. Mills can phone me. He has to write a report anyway—he can send me a copy."

"Don't you have to watch?"

"What for? A dead mouse is a dead mouse." He sat thinking. "And from now on I'm putting them through fast, like Cable. And I hope every one of the damned mice croaks. I get 'em purer and they live a little longer—so everyone gets stirred up. What'm I sticking my neck out for?"

"Is that why they live longer?"

"Who the hell knows?"

"Your others didn't live longer."

"Listen, you know so much—why don't you come in and we'll give you a job. You can be the one to find this antibiotic."

She went to the desk and took out the loose-leaf notebook in which she was keeping that crazy record. "Don't forget to write it up."

"I'll write it up when I get damned good and ready." He wasn't so wild about that idea any more either. Almost a year now and all he wrote about was failure. Cultures that didn't produce much antibiotic, antibiotics that didn't cure much, antibiotics that looked new and you worked them and they turned out to be knowns. Cable's failures, Metcalf's failures, his own failures. And even if you wanted to forget them, you couldn't—keeping that damned record book. He took another drink, and after a while he got up and slammed the notebook shut and shoved it into the drawer and slammed that shut, too. It was bad enough that he had to keep a notebook on his own work without doing it twice—and worrying about everyone else's work, too.

In the morning Weir looked at the jar and his stomach sank. There were only three mice in it—the two purple ones, who were moving around, and the one yellow one that lay off to one side, dying. "Well, that figures," he said sourly, turning away. "It's what I expected."

Mills looked around, surprised. "George, they didn't die of the antibiotic. They died of the disease!"

"Yeah," Weir said. "Well, they're just as dead, aren't they?"

"The purple ones aren't dead!" Mills said. "They had a lethal dose of disease, too, the same as the others—and they're fine. They were protected!"

For a moment Weir didn't understand, and then suddenly he understood very well. All the mice had had a lethal dose of the disease, the same as the controls. But the green mice had had only a five-milligram dose of antibiotic and the yellow ones had had only a ten-milligram dose, and that wasn't enough to protect them, so they had died of the disease. Not the antibiotic—the disease! Slowly, Weir walked back and looked at the two purple-spotted mice. Those damned purple mice were cured!

"You know, George," Mills said, "there could still be delayed toxicity—from the antibiotic. The purple ones could still die—today or tomorrow. We have to watch them for several days."

"Of course, Mills has to do an awful lot more work on it, George," Gates said. "You know that, don't you?"

"He's starting already," Weir said. "He's having a big time up there—got thirty mice lined up in jars on one counter. This damn thing doesn't protect at a ten-milligram dose and it does protect at twenty. He's going to start at ten milligrams and increase the doses by two milligrams all the way up to twenty. Using five mice for each dose. He's having a real big time."

Gates saw Miss Potter watching them and motioned Weir into his office. "George, he's got to find the minimum dose that cures."

"Yeah, well, he also has fifteen more mice in some other jars, and they're getting big doses of the antibiotic to see how much will kill them—find out how much they can take. They're getting twenty-, thirty- and forty-milligram doses—five at each dose. Ask me, he's awfully eager to kill them."

"George, he's got to find the lethal dose!"

"Listen, how do you know so much?"

"He told me."

"Yeah," Weir said resentfully. "Well, he never told me till he had to."

Just before lunch the five mice that had received forty-milligram doses of the antibiotic died. "That's not serious, George," Mills said, undisturbed. "They got a pretty big dose."

At two o'clock, the mice that had received thirty-milligram doses began to die. Mills was still undisturbed. "There's still leeway," he said. The mice that had received twenty-milligram doses were still fine. On the other counter all the mice that had received smaller doses looked healthy.

But suddenly, just before closing time, one of the mice that today had received a twenty-milligram dose died. Now Mills looked a little worried.

"Listen, what's going on here?" Weir said. "How come he died when the two that got twenty-milligram doses yesterday are still fine?"

Mills frowned and looked at the other four mice that he had injected today with twenty-milligram doses. "Mice are like people, George. What one can take, another can't."

Weir looked at him quickly, wondering whether he meant anything by that. He always suspected that Mills was thinking more than he said.

"This could be a fluke," Mills said. "Let's see what they look like in the morning."

When Weir came into the house, Janet wasn't home and he sat alone, drinking. It was nearly dinnertime when he heard her coming up the stairs. "Where've you been?" he demanded.

"Shopping."

"I don't see any packages."

"I didn't find what I was looking for."

She was wearing those damned gold bracelets, and they jingled every time she moved. He turned and walked away, back into the living room, and began to drink again.

"Don't you think you're hitting that bottle pretty hard, George? Even for you?"

"A-ah," he said. He tossed down the drink and stared at the ice in the bottom of the glass. "All the companies in the world that could have gone into this crazy deal," he muttered, "and it had to be the one I was with. All the jobs I could have had, I had to pick this one." He turned to her. "I think I'll quit."

She looked up quickly at that. "Don't be ridiculous."

"I'm thinking of it."

"You're not going to quit," she said. "You're going to stay right where you are. Where else are you going to get this much money?"

"Listen, there are plenty of jobs around." He began walking around again. "A-ah, with my kind of luck, I'd end up someplace doing something just as bad. The way I'm snake-bit, two weeks after I got there, they'd decide to work on something just as hopeless—like polio or cancer or something."

"What'd you go into research to find?" she said. "Rat poison?"

"That's what I need—a comedian around the house."

In the morning Mills looked up as Weir came through the door, and Weir knew there was trouble.

"Another one of the twenty died overnight, George," Mills said. "They're dying from the antibiotic—so a twenty-milligram dose is close to the maximum any of them can take."

Weir walked along the counter, looking into the jars. Some of them were empty, and in some he could see that the mice wouldn't last much longer, but in some jars the mice were fine.

"So?" Weir turned to Mills. "It's still protecting some of them."

Mills came over to the counter. "They've all died at ten milligrams and at twelve milligrams—or they're about to. And three out of five are dying at fourteen and one more doesn't look good. At the sixteen-milligram dose, they're all alive and healthy—so far—so that's the minimum that we can call the lowest protective dose—a sixteen-milligram dose." Mills looked up. "But they die at the twenty-milligram dose—from the antibiotic."

"So what? You've got sixteen and eighteen milligrams where it's O.K."

Mills shook his head. "It's too close, George."

"What do you mean, too close?" Weir shouted. "You've got a four-milligram difference! You've got ten protected mice there that aren't going to die."

"It's not enough—"

"What do you mean, it's not enough? What do you need? A hundred?"

"George, a mouse can tolerate much more per kilo of body weight than a dog can." Mills leaned on the counter. "And a dog can take much more than a man. With this it's taking almost as much to cure as it does to kill. We call this the therapeutic index, and it's just too low. Even twice as much to kill as to cure would be close, but we'd probably go on with it. This isn't even one and a half." Mills shook his head. "As it is now, it wouldn't even work in dogs—and it would never get to man. It's too dangerous. With the individual differences you get both in the amount people can tolerate and in the amount it takes to cure them, no doctor would use this."

Weir thumped Mills's notebook with his finger. "Listen, how do you know?" he said. "Yesterday none of them died at twenty. Look at them over there. They're still O.K. Today they're dying all over the place at twenty. What's going on here?"

"Work it some more, George. Maybe if it's purer, they'll tolerate a larger dose. It does protect them—it protects them fine. It's the best one we've had so far."

Weir wheeled around. "I should have got it purer before I gave it to you at all!" At the door he stopped. "One day you get one result and the next day another. Maybe today you'd get a couple more surprises—with your therapeutic index!"

"I'll test it again today, George, and see," Mills said.

Weir went upstairs. He didn't feel like working, and he shut himself up in his little office. Then he went up to the library and sat in a corner where it would be hard to find him if anyone came looking.

He ought to quit. He ought to get out of here and find something else. Then he remembered the fuss Janet had raised last night when he suggested it. Probably she had someone here she didn't want to leave. He'd never trusted her. Probably she'd been playing around since the day he married her. Probably before, even. Well, one of these days he'd show her.

Then his thoughts came around to his own predicament, and a

terrible despair swept over him. How can I quit? he said to himself. How can I get out? He was alone in this part of the library, and he put his face in his hands and thought, Where should I go? What should I do? Even if I find something, how do I know it will be any better?

"Mr. Caroline!" Mills said. "I quit!"

The antibiotic was EA 7, and all morning the mice had been fine.

But coming into the laboratory now, Tom had seen immediately, even before Mills spoke, that something was wrong. The mouse with the green rump was moving across the jar, and, almost imperceptibly, it was dragging one leg. Then the others moved and he saw that they were all dragging their hind legs. With some, the drag was only slight. With one—the purple-headed one—it was quite pronounced.

"Ataxia," Mills said. "They're losing muscular control. The hind legs usually go first."

By midafternoon when the purple-headed mouse dragged itself across the jar, its hind legs were stretched back almost flat. At the end of the day, Tom stood at the jar and watched the mouse with the yellow rump make a twisted effort to raise itself up to the water pipe. Its body sagged down to the sawdust and it lay there, one paw moving feebly, aimlessly, through the air. Tom turned away and went home.

But in the morning the mice were still alive. They lay around the jar, motionless and sick, and whenever one would try to move, its head would lop over crazily to one side. But all six mice lived through the day and all six mice lived through another night.

"Tom," Mills said on the following morning, "this EA 7 protects."

Frowning, Tom looked at the mice which had suffered an almost total loss of muscular control.

"These mice have already lived a day longer than the controls," Mills said. "They're an awful mess, but not one of them has developed the disease symptoms. Not even the ones that got the smallest dose."

Thoughtfully Tom walked back to his laboratory. That little bit of crude antibiotic had protected six mice against a powerful dose of disease germs—that much was certain. And whether the antibiotic or an impurity was producing ataxia was not certain. And so, he knew, he would have to work on EA 7 some more.

Its number was EA 202, and as Tom left Mills's laboratory that Monday evening, he told himself that he knew better than to feel so good because six mice had lived through the day. How many times, he said to himself, have there been six healthy mice at the end of the first day, that have died on the second day or the third? And yet, most of the time the mice died right away—within five minutes —and when they did not, for all you knew better, something began to happen inside you.

On Tuesday morning the controls died, but the mice that had received EA 202 did not. At closing time they were still in good condition, and, driving home, Tom reminded himself that he had been through all this before. And yet, he thought, no matter how much you warned yourself, when it looked good, you began to get excited.

On Wednesday morning he met Mills in the parking lot and went directly to the mouse laboratory with him. The mice were lying huddled together as always, but this morning they didn't respond, as they usually did, to a noise in the room. They stirred a bit but they were listless and obviously sick. Tom looked at them and turned away.

Mills continued to look at the mice in the jar. "They're sick, Tom. They've developed the disease. This is the way the controls looked yesterday."

"A day later?" Tom said. "The same disease?"

Mills nodded. "This EA 202 gives partial protection the way it is now. Not complete protection, because these mice are dying, but they've lived at least a day longer—all but one."

"All but one!" Tom looked back. Now that they had moved out of a huddle, he could see that there were only five mice in the jar. The mouse with the green rump was missing. Tom took a quick look around for Miss Watterling, thinking that she must have been here already and thrown the mouse away. But it was early and Miss Watterling had not yet arrived. "Where's the other one?" he said. "What happened to it?"

Mills looked up. "It died overnight."

"Who threw it out?"

"Nobody threw it out. Tom, this is the law of the jungle. They clean up their own mess. And when one dies, the others eat it. They eat it all. Sometimes the only sign is a small piece of skull—or like that." Mills pointed to a bit of fur, which was all that was left of the sixth mouse. "Sometimes there's no sign at all—just one less animal."

Slowly Tom walked downstairs to his own laboratory. No matter how much you warned yourself, when it looked good, something happened inside you. And no matter how much you steeled yourself against disappointment, you felt it when it came. But EA 202 protected partially, and he would have to work on it some more.

Then he thought of something and went back to Mills.

"Pat, when the others eat one that dies, does that affect their dosage?"

Mills shook his head. "No. By the time they eat it, it has excreted most of the dose."

TWENTY-ONE

THOUGHTFULLY, Gil Brainard closed his mouth around an unlit cigar while he considered this new development—hiring this new fellow, this Vought.

Standing in a corner of Morrissey's living room, off a little from the crowd that was here to meet Vought and his wife, Brainard was looking him over carefully, sizing him up. On the whole he didn't like this. It was one thing when they hired a jerk like Derrick or a nutty kid like Mills, but Vought was something else again. He was important and good and expensive. And—Brainard thought, watching him narrowly—he was a very smooth operator.

Next to Brainard, Neil Harrup said, "Have you met Dr. Vought yet, Gil?"

"I met him," Brainard said.

Harrup glanced over at Vought, as though he thought it his duty to discuss him, since the party was in his honor. "Claude's mighty glad to have him."

Brainard gave a short laugh. "Claude's like a kid with a new toy. Hasn't moved two feet from his elbow all night. Afraid somebody might steal him when he's not looking!"

Then Brainard looked back at Vought, too. He was a lean, fit-looking fellow with an important smile, who didn't drink much, Brainard had noticed, and who listened carefully when you spoke to him. He was listening carefully tonight, letting Morrissey do most of the talking, and all evening Morrissey had been walking a tight-rope, trying not to say too much and yet wanting to seem authoritative before his new assistant. And he might as well save his breath, Brainard thought—he's not fooling Vought for a minute.

"Claude says we're lucky to get him," Harrup said. "And I suppose we are. When you buy brains, you might as well buy the best."

Brainard grunted.

"Tony Vought does have a good reputation, Gil."

"Well, let him produce and he'll keep it."

Vought was leaning over a little now, smiling, giving Morrissey his rapt attention. Brainard didn't have to listen to know that Morrissey wasn't saying anything worth a damn. This Vought is a politician, he thought. This is a man who has known for a long time how to sell himself. Out of curiosity he moved closer to hear what they were talking about.

"It's not just having the facts," Morrissey was saying. "It's knowing how to use them."

"Oh, right," Vought said.

"You have to strip them down—get the significant ones away from all the excess baggage that obscures them. Like your thoughts about streptothricin, Tony. That's using significant facts in an original way."

Vought sipped his drink, not drinking very much. "Well, you know, Claude, I've thought all along that there could be a nontoxic streptothricin." Then he added with a smile, "But let's not talk about that now."

He doesn't say much and he doesn't drink much, Brainard thought—and he doesn't waste a muscle.

"Tony makes it a rule never to talk shop at parties," Vought's wife said. Her name was Vicki, and she was a sober skinny woman who wore glasses. Brainard had seen an hour ago that she was a bore.

But hell, all these wives were bores—Janet included, with that damned collection of gold bracelets she was squeezing out of him. If she added any more, she'd need a sling! The only one who wasn't a bore was Callie, and he didn't feel like tangling with Callie tonight.

"Of course, it's entirely possible," Morrissey said. "Although so far there hasn't been any evidence—at least we haven't found any."

Morrissey was trying hard but he was in over his head. Just to see whether he could shake him, Brainard said, "Those of us who don't go for this figured the board would give it six months. But it was so slow getting started that it's lasting a little longer. Now we figure a year. Kind of got a little bet going, eh, Claude?"

"Well, now, I don't know, Gil," Morrissey said brightly. "There've been some mighty interesting things turning up lately."

Then Winifred changed the subject, coming to Claude's rescue as she always did, and Brainard moved off to get another drink.

From the bar he saw that Hale and Helen had just arrived. He watched them come into the room and then stop to talk to Will Caroline. Brainard's hand tightened on his glass, and all the accumulated bitterness touched off by the addition of an expensive new man to the research staff raced through him. Damn it—sometimes he just didn't understand Hale. After all, Hale was a businessman. He should have seen long ago that this project was a loser

318

—and a serious drain on company funds. Sometimes you had to wonder whether Will Caroline had something on Hale, the way he'd been able to sell him this deal and keep on selling it to him.

Irritably, Brainard got another drink and wandered back to the group around Vought. Max Strong and his wife and Cable had arrived now and were standing around too, not saying much. Morrissey was still doing most of the talking.

Then Vought said, "With streptothricin, I can't help feeling it's so close. You have that delayed toxicity—and even that varies from three days to two weeks. I believe there could be a slightly different kind that would be nontoxic."

Brainard looked around and saw that Hale and Will Caroline were standing just a few feet away. Sharply he looked back at Vought. Vought was willing enough to talk now.

"And a nontoxic streptothricin might be effective against t.b. without the side effects of streptomycin—or without that quick resistance." Suddenly Vought was all business. "Of course, it could also have different side effects—it would have to be examined closely."

"It's good to have someone who recognizes that a few limitations are possible," Morrissey said.

"I believe in a little less motion until you know where you're going and why," Vought said and smiled that great smile. "Let's say a little more insight and a little less hysteria."

"That's what Claude always says," Winifred said. "There's no point in getting hysterical. The bugs won't hear you."

"That's very good, Claude." Vought smiled again. "These things are really perfectly predictable, you know, if only you're willing to think about them enough."

Brainard saw Cable turn and walk away. Suddenly, for the first time today, he felt better. These two aren't going to hit it off, he thought, because they're both prima donnas. And of the two, Vought is the cooler article, the better politician. He looked at Cable, who was far across the room now, talking to Callie, and then at Vought standing here, smiling, gathering all the attention, and he thought, This might turn out to be interesting yet.

"It's been my feeling for some time," Vought said, "that a careful examination of streptothricin would be rewarding."

"Well—it'd be interesting, all right," Morrissey said.

"I'm rather surprised your group hasn't done anything about that, Claude," Vought said. "It's not as though there were no clues. But then, I suppose you've been busy—well, maybe we can undertake it now."

Brainard grinned and turned away. Morrissey had hired himself a Judas! And I'll bet a barrel of pure penicillin, he thought, that he doesn't even suspect it!

A few days later Will Caroline sat in the New York office of the Society for the Propagation of the Faith, talking to Monsignor Joseph Harrington.

"Since there's no way of knowing," Will Caroline explained, "we're trying to collect these soil samples from all over the world."

Monsignor Harrington was a sympathetic listener. Half an hour later Will Caroline left him with a good supply of penicillin and a good supply of soil-sample kits for the missionary priests in China.

PART FOUR

MAY –

OCTOBER 1947

I T WAS a warm morning in May and tails of steam drifted off the pipes around the fermentation building, and copper buds peppered the lone tree outside the window, and the Monday morning meeting was running overtime because today for the first time since coming to Enright, Dr. Vought was speaking his mind.

Sitting in his usual corner, Tom tried to listen, but his thoughts kept slipping off—to his work and to himself and to this vague discontent he'd been feeling lately that had to do with both. Suddenly he was dissatisfied with everything—his work, the way he was doing it, the drudgery, the routine. He wanted to make changes. He wanted to do things differently. And yet, even to himself, he couldn't say what changes he wanted to make—or how he might make them—or give reasons for them. He only knew that suddenly everything he'd been doing seemed wrong, and he wanted to leave the old behind and get on with something new.

"I've been trying this month," Vought was saying, "to get the feeling of the operation as a whole rather than to observe closely any individual effort."

"Absolutely right, Tony," Morrissey said. "Above all this is a group project—not in any sense an individual undertaking."

Tom's thoughts wandered off again. He was still working on EA 7 and on EA 202, and now he thought about them—first one and then the other. How many times—he said to himself, while the discontent began to stir itself up again—have I worked them? How many times have they gone back to Gates? And how many times have they gone back to Mills? The same thing—over and over and over—and what have I accomplished? With EA 7 the mice still developed ataxia that began each time after lunch, the hind legs going first. And with EA 202 the mice still lived a day longer than the controls and then died of the disease. Tomorrow EA 202 would go to Gates again, and if it was purer than before, then it would go into mice again—probably on Thursday. And probably on the third day again the mice would die.

Then Tom heard Morrissey say, "It's too bad Dr. Cable couldn't be with us today. He might have wanted to discuss this point."

He looked up quickly and apologized. Morrissey chuckled good-naturedly, and Vought smiled that great smile of his.

"Dr. Vought was just saying, Tom," Will Caroline said, "that everyone ought to try to learn from everyone else's work as well as his own."

Tom looked at Vought, puzzled. "That's the idea of these meetings."

"My feeling is that there are too many independent decisions," Vought said, "without any evaluation of those decisions by the group. It creates a certain—well—confusion."

"Plenty of that." Morrissey puffed his pipe. "No argument there."

"What kind of decisions?" Tom said.

"This is just a suggestion, of course," Vought said, "but I feel that in these group discussions we might shift the emphasis a bit." He smiled at Will Caroline. "Just a slight change of focus. I don't mean this as a criticism, of course."

"How?" Will Caroline said. "What do you want to change?"

"Well—now at every meeting we get detailed reports so that we know very clearly what every man is doing, and that's very good—"

"But—?"

"But we don't hear much about why he's doing it. We don't hear the reasons." Subtly Vought's voice took on increased authority. "As it is now, every man is making all of his own decisions. I'd like to carry these group discussions a little further so that a man doesn't simply say, I'm doing thus and so. I want to hear him say, I'm doing thus and so *because*."

Carefully Tom looked at Vought. He was beginning to sense something here that he didn't like. He glanced at Max, beside him, and saw that he had caught it, too. "Do you mean," Tom said, "that the group should discuss—or that the group should decide?"

"I mean that the group as a whole must make the critical decisions."

"What do you call a critical decision?"

"Dr. Vought," Max said, "I don't believe you can invade a man's work to the extent of making his decisions for him."

Vought smiled, and Tom thought that for a man who smiled so much, the warmth never quite made it to his eyes. "I don't mean it as a rigid rule, of course," Vought said. "But on the whole, why not?"

"Because it's his work," Tom said. "You can't take over a man's decisions about his own work. He's the one who's close to it."

324

"No reason he can't tell us about it," Vought said. "We're prepared to listen."

"What if you don't agree?"

"The group would have the final responsibility—for every man's work."

"Not for my work!"

For a few seconds Vought's eyes rested on Tom, steady and sharp, the eyes of a strategist appraising enemy strength. Then he smiled over at Will Caroline. "According to my experience," he said, "—and of course it's by no means an absolute—it usually results in greater efficiency and coordination when the group is the responsible unit."

The group—Tom thought suddenly—under whose control?

"I'd like to say right now," Morrissey said, "that the first area where group approval must be established, absolutely, is when a man decides to stop working on a certain antibiotic."

"That was the area I had in mind, Claude," Vought said.

"I thought you did, Tony," Morrissey said.

I thought you did, too, Tom said to himself.

"After all, if a man stops short of the total job, we lose doubly," Vought said. "He doesn't learn anything from his work and neither do the rest of us. Nobody learns much from something that's down the drain."

Every group finds itself with a leader, Tom thought—and when Tony Vought spoke so piously about the inviolability of the group, his motives were not the same, he suspected, as Morrissey's, when he mouthed those same words.

"Another thing I've noticed," Vought said, "is that there's too much superfluous activity. Frankly, I see no point in chasing around to look at assay results—or to watch mice die. We have our reports—"

"I agree there," Weir put in heartily. "I've about decided to cut out all that stuff."

"I believe in observation," Tom said flatly. "I'll still go and take a look."

"Getting back to your first point, Dr. Vought," Will Caroline said, "I don't believe any man here would throw out something that he thought might be good—or that might give us valuable information."

Vought smiled and folded his arms. "According to my experience, a man can make a decision—believing that it's logical and based on scientific reasoning—and actually it's nothing more than a—well, a lack of stamina. He's run out of steam."

Now Tom looked at Vought sharply.

"I've had men work for me who would stick through anything," Vought went on. "Long after I expected them to give up they held on. And I've had other men who just don't have the endurance—the moral fiber—to sustain them through a prolonged piece of work. They're interested for a while—sometimes very excited about it—and then they cool fast." Vought turned to Morrissey. "You must have come across that, Claude."

"Absolutely," Morrissey said. "It's a problem that's always with us."

"We've all run into it," Harrup murmured.

"Surely you agree with that, Dr. Strong?" Vought turned to Max, as though testing to see how many sheep he could gather today. "They get a kind of—well, an itch to move on—play with something else—anything else, as long as it's new and different."

"Wanting to try something new doesn't always mean a loss of interest," Max said. "It may be a different kind of itch."

"Oh, absolutely," Vought agreed. "But on the other hand, it is a fact that in research, the same as in anything else, the grass can look greener on the other side. Naturally, I'm not implying that we've arrived at this condition here. I'm only suggesting that it might occur at some future date"—Vought smiled around the table—"and that we ought to set up some kind of check system to catch it when it happens—so that the company won't suffer, as of course it would, in the end."

Vought settled back and Tom thought, He's through for today. He's made his initial thrust and now he's easing off. He's a guerrilla fighter—the kind who wouldn't permit himself to be drawn into open battle, but who would end up with all the guns while he was still smiling and nobody even realized yet that there had been a raid. And this was his initial maneuver—to move the handle of power into position where he could grab it.

And yet, Tom knew, Vought wasn't only a manipulator, as Morrissey was, trying to compensate through strategy for what he lacked in knowledge. Vought was a skillful infighter but he was good at his work, too, and it would be a mistake to take him too lightly on either count.

. .

326

On Tuesday Tom had sent EA 202 to assay, and on Wednesday Gates had reported that it was purer, and on Thursday Mills had put it into mice for the fourth time.

Now it was Saturday, and Tom walked aimlessly along the boardwalk in front of his house. The sun was as warm today as a summer sun, and off somewhere, someone was pushing a lawn mower, and the smell of fresh-cut grass was in the air. It was the third day, and Tom had just come back from looking at the mice—and he knew they were going to die.

Idly he kicked at a pebble, watching it skip over the concrete and bounce off into the sand, and then he glanced over at Amity's cottage. Last night for the first time in months, he had seen her lights and had started over there and then stopped, realizing that it was May and that she might be married. Now he looked at the house again. You can't go over there, he said to himself. What if her husband comes to the door? What'll you say—can I borrow a cup of sugar?

He looked down at the beach—at the crusted sand and the ragged rows of seaweed left behind by winter tides—and his thoughts went back to EA 202 and to the nagging dissatisfaction that was always with him now, of which EA 202 was only a small coal in the fire. A man's so-called reasoning, he thought, could play him strange tricks. For months you went along, day after day, week after week, doing the same thing over and over and accepting it as the right way, seeing with a peculiarly myopic inner eye only the next step and then the one after that. And then, suddenly, one day you stopped accepting. It made you wonder how much of a man's thinking was his head and how much was what he ate or drank or the disposition of his girl of the moment or the feel of the sun warming into summer or new smells that came suddenly into the spring air and stirred your blood.

In front of Amity's house he stopped and looked at the closed door, and then he said to himself, "Oh, hell, go up and find out. If she's got a husband, you'll think of something."

He knocked and while he waited, his thoughts moved around to Vought. There were times when a man could get under your skin like a tick—and one seed of self-doubt that he sowed could take root and grow and eat into you so that it irritated you out of all proportion to its size. Why should Vought bother him when other men did not?

Then Amity stood in the doorway and he looked at her and past her into the house. "You married?" he said.

"No." She didn't seem particularly happy to see him—she was wearing her armor today—but that didn't bother him any more.

"Good. I figured if you were harboring a jealous husband, I'd say I was the Fuller Brush man."

She smiled a little and pushed open the screen door. "Come in."

"No—you come on out. It's too nice—and besides, I'm in a black mood. You want to come for a walk or something?"

She came out onto the porch. "What's wrong with you that you're in a black mood?"

"Probably that ancient malady—spring fever. Nothing pleases me. I'll be very bad company. Do you think you could stand it and come for a walk on the beach?"

The lawn mower had stopped, but the smell of cut grass lingered. On the beach he walked for a few minutes in silence, feeling the crust on the sand crumble under his feet, stepping around bits of debris that had accumulated over the winter—sticks and small rocks and broken glass. Now that he had company, he didn't have much to talk about.

"I think I'll go home later and rake my beach," he said after a while. "Everybody cuts his lawn and leaves raking the beach till last. All crusty and full of junk. I think I'll rake my beach and leave my lawn. I'll rake your beach, too."

"That'll be nice," she said. "What's chewing you up?"

He kicked at an empty Old Gold carton and bent over and picked up a yellowed newspaper. "Now, how would you say a Milwaukee newspaper got onto our beach?"

"Probably a ship from Milwaukee passed in the night."

"I doubt it. It's too logical." He dropped the paper. "Things are rarely what they seem to be. Things are rarely logical. The superior sense of inspired nonsense makes more sense most of the time."

"You are in a bad way."

"How was your show?" he said, suddenly remembering it. "How'd it go? Did you have it?"

"Yes, I had it."

"Well, how was it?"

"It was fine. On the whole the reaction wasn't bad, although some of the critics thought it was a little too bourgeois—too healthy."

"You—bourgeois!" He laughed. "Well, it's nice to know you're healthy. And it's all right with me if you're bourgeois. I'm not even sure what it means." He picked up a rusty can in the sand and tossed it aside. "What kind of a show was it? Did you use any of those paintings of Enright?"

"It was just portraits."

"I didn't know that. Is that what you do—portraits?"

"Only lately. But more and more I find that's what I want to do."

"Why?" he said. "Why portraits?"

"I like faces. I like to watch them." She bent over and picked up a stick. "At heart I'm a drugstore cowboy—I stand on corners, watching the faces go by."

Tom smiled. "Where are the corners you stand on?"

"Different corners. Sometimes down in the Village—that's where I live. Or I go over to the Astor Drugstore and sit and drink coffee and look at the faces—or over to the fifties at lunchtime. Those faces are different. They tell a different story."

He looked at her and thought that she was always surprising him. "Is there always a story?"

For a minute Amity just walked along, scuffing the sand. "I think that everything a man is—is in his face," she said slowly and then looked up at him. "The trick is in knowing how to read it. That's not so easy."

Tom smiled. "I'll have to take another look at some faces I've been looking at for a long time—that have been giving me trouble —and one new one, too. You think if I look carefully I'll find some helpful clues?"

Amity laughed. "The greatest artists in the world are men's souls —or their psyches—whichever you prefer to call it—depending on which fashion in thinking you're following these days."

"I'm not sure they conflict as much as the propaganda would have us believe—although I'm no philosopher. All I know these days is bugs." He kicked at a beer can—Rheingold—and walked on in silence for a minute. "And I'm not even sure how much I know about them. Suddenly everything I'm doing seems wrong. You ever feel that way?"

"Of course. Everyone feels that way sometimes."

He kicked at another Rheingold can. "This place is lousy with beer cans. Where do they come from? I never see anyone out here drinking beer. You ever seen anyone here in winter, drinking beer?"

"No." She smiled. "What seems so wrong to you?"

"I don't know what—or why." He shrugged. "I've got these two antibiotics, and one of them—EA 7—protects the mice, but it's toxic. The other one—EA 202—doesn't protect them entirely, but they live a day longer. A year ago either one of them would have had me flying. I'd have worked on them night and day. Now I work on them, too—only it's not the same."

He kicked the can again, and it skipped over the sand and settled beside a red pencil. He picked up the pencil. It read, CASEY FOR COUNCIL. "Vote for Casey for Council," he said. "I'm a scavenger today." He tossed away the pencil. "Maybe that's what I ought to be in my work. More a scavenger." He thought about that for a minute. "And less a mechanic."

"If you think so, you're probably right," she said, "although I've no idea what you're talking about."

"Why, that's a nice faith! I should talk to you more often. Nobody else has that kind of faith in me. You're unique. We have a new man—Dr. Vought—who is supposed to be very good. Dr. Vought hints that I'm lacking in mental stamina, moral fiber—all that stuff."

"You! You're joking!"

"He doesn't come right out with it, but in a veiled kind of way he suggests that as a biochemist, I'm sort of a slob. Maybe I am."

"Well, it seems rather out of character."

"You know, I should hire you to give me a lift when I'm down. It's too bad you're getting married. I'd consult you regularly. You going to let me dance at your wedding?"

"No," she said. "Why a mechanic—and why a scavenger?"

"Well—I take an antibiotic and get rid of some of the junk, and it goes to mice. And the mice die. And I take it back because it's still pretty crude, and I try one thing and another to get it purer. And each time it goes to assay for a test. And when it's purer, it goes to mice again. And the mice die. And I try again—and back again—over and over and over. That's being a mechanic. I don't know—I'm beginning to have doubts about all this."

"Is that so bad—to have doubts?"

"No—except that I don't know what I do want—only what I don't want. I feel it in my blood—something is rejecting all this. I still do it—only I don't still believe in it. Every time this feeling has set in, I've worked them longer—long after I've wanted to give them up —and every time in the end it's been the same. They were no good anyway."

330

They came up to a six-pack carton. "Something's wrong—the cans are Rheingold and the carton is Schlitz." He kicked the carton and looked out at the bay. "Lots of boats in the water already. I ought to do something about mine. I never get anything done any more."

"Why a scavenger?" she said.

"Because none of these have been what we really want. We've been hoping to find an antibiotic that will cure a large number of diseases—but they're not so easy to find. They don't come along. So when we don't find what we want, we work on what we have."

"That seems reasonable," she said. "What's wrong with that?"

"Because while you're working on what you have, you're not looking as hard for what you want." They reached the rocks beside Tollie's, and Tom paused a minute and put his foot against a low niche. "Lately I've been saying to myself, You're giving everything you've got to something you only half want—to a compromise. Maybe you should be giving it to finding what you really want. I keep saying to myself, You may not pass this way again—don't compromise." He moved away from the rock and smiled at her. "Actually I haven't been thinking that all along. I just thought it now—for the first time. But I think maybe I've been feeling it all along."

They walked out onto the dock, and Tom looked at Amity and grinned. "None of this makes sense, really. It's just a lot of talk because suddenly I'm all wound up with the idea that something's wrong. Let's talk about something else. How come you won't let me dance at your wedding?"

"You didn't tell me you could dance. Maybe you have to know what you don't want, Tom—before you can know what you do."

"Maybe," he said. "Tell me some more about the faces. I've never thought about that—that a man's soul is an artist."

Amity smiled. "It's a slow artist," she said. "It takes a long time—but sooner or later everything gets drawn there on the canvas. The artist is that thing deep down inside—that inner something that is integrity or expediency—that is grasping or openhanded—that fights or gives up—that stays clean or gets dirty. And if you look, it's all there—sort of like Dorian Gray at the end. Although sometimes people surprise you."

"Yes," he said, looking at her. "Sometimes people do."

"People you didn't expect to like, you find you do—and people you liked turn out to be—well, not what you thought. But the trouble isn't with the artist—it's with you—you're not reading it right."

They reached the end of the dock and Tom leaned on a pole and looked down at the water. Maybe, he thought suddenly, that was what was happening to him with these bugs. What you knew about them wasn't only scientific—it was intuitive, too, but it was intuition based on observation. He picked up a shell and ran it along a crack in the top of the pole. Maybe after watching these bugs for a year he was seeing more than he realized. Maybe with these bugs, too, the information was all there and you had only to know how to read it.

He tossed the shell into the water, out toward his own empty mooring, and his gaze drifted across the smaller boats just off the end of the dock and came back to Amity. And then something turned over inside him and his eyes went back to the boats. But he didn't have to look again to know what he had seen. He didn't need a second look to be certain. There was no one in it, and the red sail was down and covered, but he would know that boat anywhere. When at last he looked away, he saw that Amity was watching him and that she, too, knew it was Diana's boat.

For another minute his hand gripped the post, and then he moved away, forcing himself not to look again. "Let's go," he said. "Let's go up to Tollie's for a drink." He took her arm. "How come you won't let me come to your wedding?"

"Think about your bugs, Tom, and stop worrying about my wedding. Think about all those changes you want to make."

"I'm beginning to think," he said, "that something has changed already. You've got me wondering whether I've been reading faces, in a way, without knowing it."

"You mean you've changed—without realizing it?"

"I don't know—you've started me thinking, Am." He paused, still turning this over in his mind. "At first when the mice died, I used to say to myself, What's causing that? Is it that little bit of antibiotic or is it one of a hundred impurities? Now I don't say that any more. Now I stand there in that mouse laboratory, and when the first mouse begins to fall around or go into a convulsion, I say to myself, It's no good. The antibiotic is no good. I never think any more, What's causing that? Something in me always says the damn thing is poison. It's a feeling I get—but I always get

332

it. And I take the antibiotic back and get it purer—but the feeling doesn't leave me."

"If it's that strong, maybe you should trust it."

"Maybe I should." He shrugged. And then suddenly he stopped and looked at Amity. "When's it going to be, Am? You set a date?"

She didn't answer.

"Am," he said. "Are you still getting married?"

"No," she said evenly. "No—I'm not."

"Why not?" He stared at her, and suddenly he wondered whether it was by watching all those other faces and studying what was drawn there that she had taught herself the trick of revealing nothing. "What happened?"

Amity smiled a meaningless smile. "Well," she said calmly, "to plagiarize the poets—the deal's off."

They passed some kids balancing on a side rail, and then Harry Pack's boat and then the steps to the lower landing.

"Did you change your mind again?" Tom said. "Like before?"

"No—not this time."

"Then what happened?"

"Don't keep saying that," she said coolly. "Do you mind not keeping on asking that question?"

He walked on beside her in silence. The sun was lower now and beginning to slice a white path across the water.

Then, without his asking again, Amity said, "He found somebody else. I was busy with my show—and I had some other work to get out, and for a while I didn't have much time for him—so—" She shrugged. "When people get lonely, they find someone—that's what life is all about."

"Did he tell you that?"

"Actually nobody told anybody much of anything. I saw them together—one of those happy coincidences that happen in New York. And once I'd seen them, he told me she understood him better than I did."

A chill was coming into the air, and the bay was growing choppy as the tide came in. Through the spaces between the boards of the dock, Tom could see the foam churning up on the dark water below. After a moment he looked at her again. "He wasn't for you anyway, Am."

"You've never even seen him!"

"I sensed it. It was all wrong."

Amity laughed. "Like you sense something is wrong with your bugs?"

"Just like that." Tom smiled. "Only I'm even more sure of this."

On Monday morning, Gates came into Tom's laboratory.

"Tom," he said in a queer voice that made Tom look up quickly. "This one here"—Gates held out the report on a batch of new cultures Tom had sent him—"this EA 10—"

Tom tilted his head to read the sheet. "What about it?"

"Tom," Gates said in the same queer strained voice, "EA 10 is broad-spectrum."

TWENTY-THREE

BY NOON on that Monday in May the news had shot through a stunned company that, after all the arguments, after all the speculation about whether such a phenomenon could exist, a broad-spectrum antibiotic had actually turned up at Enright. By evening a feverish excitement had erupted. Enright spirits soared like a balloon—higher than ever before.

By mid-June the balloon had deflated.

The bug turned out to be a miser and stubbornly resisted all Tom's efforts to coax it into producing more antibiotic. No matter what he did to it, it just didn't make much, and fermentation after fermentation resulted in large quantities of material and very little active substance. This, in turn, complicated the already complicated problem of separating out that active substance. As Tom had described such a situation hypothetically several months ago, it was like Madame Curie working through tons of pitch for that little bit of radium.

Even that would not have been so discouraging if they could have found a technique that worked. But the antibiotic itself was as uncooperative as the microbe. When the antibiotic stayed in the broth, the impurities stayed in the broth. When the antibiotic was extracted into a solvent or precipitated as a metal salt, most of the impurities went right along with it.

For six weeks EA 10 had remained bogged down in Tom's laboratory, and he had not been able to send it for even a first tentative inconclusive trial in mice.

On a hot day late in June, Ade Hale sat in his office talking to a young account executive from the advertising agency, whose name was Lawrence Croft. Croft had requested the appointment, and now, while he listened to him, Hale thought that his timing was remarkably good—so good, in fact, that he wondered whether it was just a coincidence that he had turned up at this time with this suggestion.

"For some time now, sir, I've felt that we could do so much more for Enright than we're doing," Lawrence Croft said. He was a polished young man in his early thirties, with dark hair and clear dark eyes, and he took advertising very seriously, which was all right, Hale supposed, as long as that was his business. "I'd like to show you—just in a general way, sir—some of the possibilities."

Hale toyed with his glasses that lay on top of a report on EA 10 that he'd been reading when Croft arrived. "I'm willing to listen, Mr. Croft," he said. "But it's only fair to warn you that there's nothing in the budget this year for additional advertising."

"This would be a long-range plan, sir—and very flexible. It would be as useful next year—or the year after."

Hale warned himself against judging this Croft too quickly. He was prejudiced against these overpersonable young men, and he knew it. Probably he'd have felt better about Croft if he'd had a bump on his nose or if his suit were not quite so conservative, his tie and cuff links in such good taste. Everything about him was perfect and perfectly understated. And yet, Hale had to admit, he seemed to know his business.

"All right, Mr. Croft," he said, "what do you have in mind? And how do you want to go about it?"

"The first thing I'd like to do, sir," Lawrence Croft said, "is spend some time here to get to know the company better."

Hale looked up, surprised.

"If I wouldn't be in the way, of course. I do have some ideas now, sir—but I hope I'll be forced to discard them."

Hale smiled. "That bad?"

"No, sir, they're not bad at all," Croft said pleasantly. "But I don't want this to be a run-of-the-mill, synthetic job. I want to learn the things that are special about Enright. It would be easy to take accepted ideas with perhaps a new twist to adapt them to your products. I don't want to do that. I want to develop the ideas from an understanding of the company."

Even his answers were perfect, Hale thought. He wondered what kind of image a man like Croft had of a chemical and pharmaceutical company. The few times that Hale had explored this question with men who dealt in public opinion—newspapermen, public relations men—he'd found that their knowledge of the facts seldom went deeper than the label on the bottle.

"What is it you want to understand about us, Mr. Croft?"

"I believe I'm up to date on your products—your bulk products, of course—and your vitamins and penicillin." Croft sat quietly in

336

his seat, all business. "I don't mean to be presumptuous, sir, but I was very much pleased the day that first package of Enright vitamin capsules came to my desk. And the penicillin tablets, too, even though that's a prescription drug. In shaping a public image we can do many more exciting things with a finished product."

"If you know the products, Mr. Croft, what is it you want to see about us?"

"I want to know how they get that way, sir. I want to see production. I want to see research—talk to your scientists. With production I have some idea from Miss Welles's pictures. . . . By the way, sir, did you see those pictures? I'll be glad to bring them to you—"

"I saw them," Hale said. "I liked them."

"She's a good artist." Croft hesitated just a moment. "I—hope—there was no trouble while Miss Welles was with you?"

"Certainly not."

"We're always a little uneasy sending an artist on a job. They can be temperamental."

"We found her very pleasant."

"I'm relieved to hear that." Croft dropped it. "What I hope to do, sir, is to come here a few times to learn what Enright is all about. And then hear what products particularly interest you, something about the direction the company is heading—so I'll know where to concentrate."

Hale's eyes went again to the report on his desk. It wasn't only EA 10 that was troubling him. It was the whole project. In a year they had put down what was getting to be quite a large number of dry shafts. A lot of soil had been screened, a lot of antibiotics had been fermented, and a lot of mice had died. There were other places that Enright could be putting this money, and, knowingly or not, Lawrence Croft was here to talk about the most logical alternative.

"And then I'd like to draw up a long-range plan," Croft went on, "showing several ways we might go—and discuss them with you."

"It might be some time before we're ready for any of them."

"You may want to put off even discussing them until later. If you do, the plan will be available whenever you're ready for it."

Actually, Hale thought, there was nothing wrong with this young man. He was intelligent and businesslike. And certainly his request

337

made sense—to spend some time here. For a few minutes Hale debated with himself. On the one hand he was tempted to tell Croft that it was a good idea but he wasn't ready for it. Let him wait a few months—until they'd made up their minds about the antibiotic project.

On the other hand, with EA 10 at a standstill, why not let him go ahead? Let him make his study and organize his ideas— be ready to talk when they were ready for him. If the antibiotic program didn't pick up soon, this was the direction to go—expand the finished-products line and push it.

Thoughtfully Hale tapped his glasses on the EA 10 report. Then he stood up.

"All right, Mr. Croft," he said. "Let's go down to Mr. Brainard's office. You can arrange with him to see production. And after lunch you can talk to Mr. Caroline about meeting the research staff—although appointments with them might be hard to plan. If they're excited about something, they probably won't stop to talk to you."

"I'd like to see that, too, sir," Croft said.

Hale restrained a smile. This young man had the right answers for everything. He'd even bet, he thought suddenly, that next time Lawrence Croft came to Enright, he wouldn't look quite so perfect. He'd be just a little bit mussed up.

"And thank you, sir," Lawrence Croft said. "This is something I've wanted to do for a long time."

"What about EA 10, Will?" Hale said a few minutes later to Will Caroline. "You think you should put a few more men on it—along with Cable?"

"Strong's working on it, too, getting it out. It's only a little over a month, Ade."

"Getting it out isn't his only problem. He can't grow it."

"So far the bug doesn't seem to make much," Will admitted. "Although Cable tested a broth yesterday that looked good."

"How good?"

"In that rough test he does in his own lab, it more than doubled. He sent it to Gates to check it."

"What about Cable, Will?" Hale came out with it. "There's some feeling that he can't grow EA 10 because all this time he's refused to fuss enough with broths. He's insisted on this one-shot-in-ten-broths notion of his, while the others have really worked on them."

338

"He's discussed it with the others, Ade. They haven't come up with much."

"It's been a lean six weeks."

"Ade, you're bound to run into these things," Will Caroline said. "If it were easy—"

"I know—if it were easy, everyone would be doing it. Will"— Hale leaned over the EA 10 report—"when Claude Morrissey doesn't agree with Cable, it's one thing. Claude's getting to be an old lady—and he hasn't warmed up to this idea from the start—so I tend to discount his complaints. And Harrup, too, in a way—although he does more questioning than complaining. And even when the other biochemists didn't agree, I figured there was no reason to think they knew any more than Cable did. But now Vought comes along—here we have a high-priced man who's supposed to be one of the best—and he doesn't agree with him either."

"No," Will said. "They don't often see eye to eye."

"Vought's had a lot of experience. He's supposed to be good. He was supposed to beef up that department."

"He is good," Will Caroline said. "He's a top-notch biochemist. But he hasn't proved himself here yet—in this special field. He hasn't had time. When he does—if he does—I think Cable will be the first to admit it. Meanwhile Cable's turning out more antibiotics."

"More antibiotics—and more toxic antibiotics."

"Most antibiotics are toxic."

Hale frowned, unconvinced. He was beginning to wonder a little about Cable. "I don't know, Will. I've seen a lot of smoke and not much heat before."

"A broad-spectrum antibiotic has turned up. He was right about that."

Well, that was true. Hale stood up and began to pace around the office, and Will picked up the EA 10 report and glanced through it. "You know, Ade, the only reason everyone is watching this so closely is that EA 10 is broad-spectrum. Otherwise no one would notice."

"That's reason enough."

"Yes and no. Don't you think the others—Weir and Metcalf, and Vought, too—have worked six weeks on an antibiotic before sending it to mice? They do it all the time. But this one is important— this one could be a bull's eye—so every day seems a week."

Hale walked to the window. He had a feeling that this bothered

Will more than he showed. Where this project was concerned, Will Caroline was losing his objectivity. It was his baby, and he could no longer stand outside it and appraise it to see if it still made sense. And as far as the research staff's arguments were concerned, for all he scrupulously let every man have his say, he wasn't impartial there either. Privately he had taken sides. He was for Cable.

Will Caroline put the report back on the desk. "What about when this finally does go to mice, Ade?" he said. "What then?"

Hale looked around.

"Most of the time the mice die right away—within five minutes," Will said. "Because EA 10 is broad-spectrum, it doesn't change the odds."

"Is Cable afraid of that?"

"I'm sure he's thought of it." Will folded his arms and sat quietly in his chair. "Until the antibiotic goes to mice, nobody has a right to assume that it's good. All that early excitement was excessive and premature—and because of it, now that EA 10 has run into trouble, there's a serious reaction. You feel it too, Ade. It's one reason you're receptive to this advertising man you just told me about—this Croft."

"Is that why Cable hasn't sent it to mice? Is he afraid to? Is he suddenly cautious because it's broad-spectrum?"

"He's more impatient than you are, Ade. I'm worried that he'll send it too soon—and there'll be an even greater letdown."

Hale walked over to the door. "Let's get over there and talk to him, Will—see how his new broth made out. Maybe if they had more of it, they'd find a way to get it out."

When they came into the laboratory, Cable was over in a corner with his technician, in front of a tall glass column called an ion-exchange column. Obviously he still had had no luck with EA 10, and he was switching to another technique.

"How'd that broth work, Tom?" Will said, as Cable came over to them. "The one that seemed to produce better."

"When I checked last, Gates hadn't finished. I'm going back in a few minutes."

Cable glanced around at his technician, who had gone over to mix a broth while he waited. Hale looked around the laboratory. Cable was a worker, he'd say that for him. This wasn't the most orderly lab he'd ever seen, but it looked as though the man in it meant business. "What are you doing over there?" He nodded toward the area where Cable had been working.

"We're going to try resins," Cable said. "Ion exchange. See if we can get it out that way."

Then, before Hale could say more, the door opened and Gates came in. "Tom—this new broth—" Gates started and then saw that Cable was not alone and stopped. "Oh, excuse me—I didn't mean to interrupt. I'll come back later, Tom."

"No—come in, Dr. Gates," Hale said.

Gates hesitated and Cable said, "What's the matter, Pearly? Isn't that broth as good as I thought?"

"Well—yes and no. There's more antibiotic now—much more—"

"Good," Hale said. "That's something, anyway."

Gates looked miserably toward the door.

"What's wrong, Dr. Gates?" Will Caroline said.

"Well, there's more of it—there's more antibiotic, that is," Gates said unhappily. "Only—it's not the same antibiotic any more."

Across the room, the technician, his back turned, grunted audibly.

"In this broth," Gates said, "the microbe has pulled a switch—and it's making something different. It's entirely different, Tom. It's not EA 10."

"Is the new one any good?" Cable said. "Is it still broad-spectrum?"

"No, it's not," Gates said. "It's not much good at all. It's very, very narrow!"

"Well," Hale said, in the corridor outside Cable's laboratory, "what now?"

"Now he'll backtrack and try something else," Will said.

Hale was silent for a minute. It didn't bother him to back a man who stood alone—for a while, anyway. He had stood alone a few times himself. But when nobody ever agreed with your man, sooner or later you had to consider the possibility that he might be wrong—that he just plain might not know what he was talking about—or what he was doing. It was a fact that now, when it counted—with EA 10—Cable wasn't producing. And it was a fact, too, that this project was a year old and it wasn't producing either.

"I told Croft that you'd see him this afternoon, Will," Hale said. "What time can you make it?"

"I'll see him after lunch," Will said. "I'll be glad to talk to him then."

When he left Will Caroline, Hale walked across the yard, feeling that the weather was turning hot and humid. The yard was almost deserted, and the kind of quiet hung over it that settled in before noon on these sultry summer days. For a while Hale just walked, toward the fermentation building and past it and down to the water.

Will would talk to Lawrence Croft, and give him the information and arrange the interviews that Croft wanted, but he was opposed to bringing in an advertising man now. Will had definitely lost his objectivity. And yet, Hale thought—that was all right, too. A man didn't do a good job unless he cared. And, he supposed, it had been inevitable. Living so close to the work for a whole year, Will would have had to develop feelings about it.

It was all right if they were all emotionally involved, Hale thought, as long as he himself remained detached—as he was now and as he would continue to be, to the end. However long this project went on—or however soon he cut it off—Hale intended to stay outside it and be able to take that long hard look to see whether it still made sense. And when it did not, he would end it.

After a while he headed for the production building and went inside. He walked through the first-floor packaging room, stepping around the men washing the floor, watching the women filling and capping tubes, and then he left by the other door and walked down the corridor of a small testing area. Here, through the glass partitions on either side, he could see the women spot-checking bottles —the first woman checking for size with a projector that threw the dimensions of the bottle against a small screen where the proper dimensions were outlined; the next woman using a small hammer to test the impact that the bottle could withstand; the next cutting a bottle in half with a diamond wheel in order to measure the thickness; and then a woman testing the tightness of the lid—how much of a twirk it would take to open it; and, next to her, another testing whether vibration would loosen it in transport; and then a woman testing the rubber stoppers for leakage; and another testing the silicon-lined bottles used for liquid injections to see whether they drained empty in the prescribed length of time.

Watching these minor tests that had become routine, but which were all part of turning out a consistently reliable product, Hale thought that here everything was in order. Here everything progressed as it should—at a known rate, with certain expected results —and you always knew what was happening and the reasons for it.

As he went up the stairs, Hale's thoughts moved to Lawrence Croft, and he told himself again that actually there was nothing wrong with the man. He was businesslike and he knew what he wanted to do and talked to the point. Maybe, Hale decided, before Croft left, he'd talk to him again and find out when he planned to have a program ready.

On the second floor he stopped outside the solid windowless wall of the sterile area where penicillin went through the final stage of recovery—where it was put into solution and filtered and crystallized under sterile conditions. While Hale stood there, a man opened a door and went inside. Before he came near the penicillin, Hale knew, that man would walk down a corridor and go through three more rooms. In the first room he would disrobe. In the second room he would take a disinfectant shower. In the third room he would put on previously sterilized clothing, including a mask and rubber gloves. And only then would he be permitted to enter the work area.

And these were not the only precautions taken to guarantee sterility. Every piece of equipment was sterilized. Pieces that could not go into the autoclave were exposed for two hours to ultraviolet rays so intense that if a man were exposed to them unclothed for even a few minutes, he would die.

Even the air was sterilized. Every room in that special area was supplied with sterile air, and pressure was maintained at six different levels—the highest pressure in the workroom where the penicillin was being handled, the lowest pressure in the first corridor by which the man entered the area—so that, as he opened each door to proceed toward the work area, the airflow was always away from the penicillin. No contamination could slip into the workroom through an open door; only sterile air, blown in, could enter that room. And since men leaving the work area could have developed contamination through perspiration, they were not permitted to leave through the sterile dressing room. They left through a special egress corridor, again with the air pressure going from high to low, away from the penicillin, when the door opened.

Here in production, Hale thought, they knew exactly what they were doing. Here every detail had been worked out, every step

343

was under control, everything worked as you knew it would. Where efficiency was required, efficiency was excellent. Where sterility was required, sterility was absolute.

And over in research, nothing behaved as it should and nobody agreed with anyone else, and nobody, except Cable, had found anything very much. And Cable couldn't seem to handle what he had found.

A man came out of the egress corridor and Hale watched him walk away. And yet, he thought, it hadn't always been this way here. Production had had its problems in the past—nobody knew that better than he did—and now the wheels ran smoothly because the problems had been solved. He could remember more than one batch of valuable penicillin that Enright had lost to contamination —both in the fermentation tanks and here in recovery—and at a time when penicillin was scarce and expensive and a contaminated batch was a disaster.

Thoughtfully, Hale stood another minute and let his eyes travel down the corridor. From here he could see the rows of cans packed with finished penicillin, each can containing twenty thousand grams sealed in a polyethylene bag—rows and rows of cans of pure white sterile penicillin. And four years ago, he thought—in 1943—finished penicillin, as pure as we could get it, looked like dried mud.

And one gram of that terribly impure, brown penicillin had cost two hundred dollars. And today a gram costs about seven cents.

And—then—a bag this size, twenty-thousand grams—if there had been twenty-thousand grams—would have been worth four million dollars. Today it costs a hundred and forty dollars.

And at the beginning—in 1943—the total world supply of penicillin was seventeen grams. And today we could supply the world.

Hale walked alongside the wall of the sterile area and looked at the bags of white penicillin. The path from seventeen grams of mud to a world supply had not been easy. He could remember how new problems had turned up every day—and for every one you solved, there were two in its place. He could remember how they couldn't grow it—and when they did grow it on milk bottles, there weren't enough milk bottles. He could remember how they had argued and how nobody had agreed with anyone else. And when they finally managed to grow it in deep tank fermentation, the chemists couldn't get it out—and when they found a way to get it out, then the penicillin wasn't stable. And still, they had shipped it off, brown, muddy, less than fifteen per cent pure, to the army in time for the European invasion, and it had saved lives and they had felt damned good about it. And, Hale thought, it still felt good, remembering.

Maybe, he decided, he wouldn't talk to Lawrence Croft again today. Let him do his homework if he wanted to—but the talking could keep until next time.

"This heah's our first package from the Far East, Nick," Derrick said. "Ah believe we'll do these right away."

Nick took the package. "I'll start them this morning."

"Be interesting to see what they turn up," Derrick said.

Nick nodded. "Is there anything new on EA 10, Dr. Derrick?"

"Ah believe they've made a little progress gettin' it out, but there's so little of it, they've still got a long way to go. It's like havin' about four specks of gold dust in a gallon of vegetable soup. If you've got to concentrate those four specks into a thimble, you've got to get rid of an awful lot of celery an' onions an' broth—an' whatever all else they put into vegetable soup, which isn't a subject on which ah'm highly informed."

Nick smiled and went over to the refrigerator.

"Course, it'd be easier if you could increase the four specks to forty or four hundred—but they can't seem to do that either."

"I thought I'd take these new broths to assay," Nick said, "since Miss Buxton's on vacation." He took out a rack of test tubes and looked a minute into the refrigerator. "We're sure piling up a lot of cultures here," he said, "because of EA 10."

"That's the time to keep turnin' 'em out, Nick," Derrick said. "The bigger the pile-up, the more you'd like to see one that looks head an' shoulders above the crowd."

"EA 10's head and shoulders above the crowd—and look at the trouble it's causing."

"Well, now—that's another reason for us to keep turnin' 'em out," Derrick said. "When you've got one that's makin' more'n its share of trouble, you'd like to be able to turn up another one that's just as good—an' more cooperative."

Nick grinned. "And when you've got one that looks great, that's the time to keep turning them out in case it lets you down—so you can have another one ready."

"Ah expect that's what we're here for, Nick—to keep turnin' 'em out."

Nick laughed and told himself there was something about working for Dr. Derrick that made you feel more a man yourself. It took more than a little bad news to shake up Dr. Derrick, which was more than you could say about some of them around here. In the year he'd worked for Dr. Derrick, Nick figured he'd grown up about five years. He didn't even blush any more—except maybe now and then.

A few minutes later he looked into the assay laboratory and thought that this was his lucky day—neither Dr. Gates nor Dr. Morrissey was here.

"Can I leave these with you, Miss Potter?" he said, setting the rack of test tubes on the counter.

"What—have they got you delivering again?" Miss Potter said.

"Miss Buxton's on vacation," Nick said and blushed. Well—hell— he'd bet he wasn't the only man around here who blushed when he talked to Miss Potter. "Well—there they are."

"Ask me, you ought to all take a vacation down there," Miss Potter said.

"Well—" Nick said and cleared his throat.

"Give them about a year to catch up with you—then you can come back and get going again."

"Well"—Nick jerked his head toward the rack of test tubes he'd brought—"shall I put those into the refrigerator for you?"

"Ah—I can manage."

Well, he guessed he ought to get back to work. "You know, Miss Potter," he said, "actually at a time like this we should be working harder than ever in the mycology lab."

Miss Potter laughed.

"When we have so many, we should be trying to turn up some that are head and shoulders above the rest."

Miss Potter thought about that for a minute. "Maybe you've got something there," she said.

Nick leaned against the counter, and Miss Potter reached over and turned off her Bunsen burner.

"It's the only thing that makes sense," he said. "And when we've got one that's causing so much trouble, like EA 10, I think that's the time we should be working harder than ever—looking for a better one."

Miss Potter settled a hand on one hip. "Well, I gotta say this for you," she said. "At least you're not cryin'—like half the people around here."

"Well—you know—every time there's a little bad news, some people start shouting the sky is falling." Nick drew a deep breath. "It's hot, isn't it?"

"Mmm," Miss Potter said.

"It's supposed to get hotter still. Well—can I help you put those into the refrigerator?"

Miss Potter looked at the rack and smiled. "Why not?"

"Miss Potter—"

"Mmm?" Miss Potter opened the refrigerator door and Nick slid in the rack of test tubes.

"Miss Potter, do you think sometime you could have dinner with me—or go to the beach—or something?"

"Why not?"

Nick blushed and grinned. "Well—how about tonight?"

"Why not?" Miss Potter said.

It was a day when everything seemed a problem and nothing got done. All day the heat and the humidity had climbed steadily, and now, in the later afternoon, the sun burned through a haze that hung like settled steam, damp and hot and still. Sitting at his desk, Tom shook his head to clear it. His eyes burned and his neck ached, and after a minute he dropped his pencil and just looked across the desk at his briefcase that was filled with literature on ion exchange, which for three nights now he had stayed up very late reading. You could never really win, he thought with sudden despair. You waited a year for a broad-spectrum antibiotic, and when you found one, you couldn't grow it. And when you could grow them, you couldn't get them out—and when you could get them out, they were toxic. *Nature always evens things up.* It was one of his favorite sayings. He was sorry he'd ever said it.

Outside the screen a bee hovered aimlessly, and he watched it and stood up and moved to the window. The water was smooth as oil, the boats barely moving. He looked along the bay as far as he could see in either direction and then looked down and rested his head on his hands. He ought to get out of here. You got these days when you couldn't do much, and this was one of them. Tomorrow would be better. It was an old law of physics, he told himself, that

347

everything pushed against exerted a counterpressure, and this afternoon something in him was having its day pushing back after weeks of being pushed against, and his brain refused to function. He looked at his watch and told himself that he would get going again in a minute and finish up the work he'd started. Then he would leave.

Out on the bay the boats had found a thread of wind, and he watched until the sail he was looking for came into sight, as he had known it would about now. All day she had been out there. Other days she had been out there and he had seen her and it hadn't bothered him. He had told himself that he didn't care so much any more, and he had believed it. Now he dropped his head on his hands again. Damn it—today he cared. And maybe this was some kind of counterpressure too—although he guessed he wouldn't waste time thinking about that one. Get to work, he said to himself. Get to work and get out of here.

He left the window and went over to the refrigerator. Behind the flasks of EA 10 broth, there were several test tubes of cultures that he was holding to work on, that he had put off while he concentrated on EA 10, and, in a rack at the back, some that he had already worked on and put aside. Now he stood and looked at those old cultures—a few powdery white ones, a few yellow ones, two pink ones, all on neat agar slants. He knew every one of them as well as his own face, he thought. He knew how much he had worked them and why he had stopped and why they still interested him. With each, he had poured the broth down the drain. But he had saved the culture, thinking that he might go back to it someday. You never knew when you might learn something that would solve the problem that had made you give it up. Someday, he had told himself, these might be interesting. Past history didn't always stay in the past.

Now, looking at them, he wondered what he was saving them for. Right now he didn't seem to be learning much about anything. For nearly two months he'd worked late every night and then gone home and combed the literature until he fell asleep reading it, trying to find some clue on how to grow EA 10 and get it out, and the results showed he hadn't learned a damn thing. And he hadn't learned anything to send him back to one of these other cultures either. With them, past history was staying very much in the past.

He closed the refrigerator door and turned away. Across the room, Moose was finishing up for the day.

"On the whole this dame makes me lonesome for all our old girls that only gave us a little trouble," Moose said. "This one has practically nothing to recommend her."

"Only that she's talented, Moose. She can do things the others could never do. She's broad-spectrum."

She was so beautifully broad-spectrum that if she worked she would be worth all the trouble.

Now the red sail was just opposite the window, and he watched it go by. Past history, he thought, doesn't always stay in the past. And not with people either.

It was dark when he left Enright. He'd gone up to the library and found some new material and had settled down to read it. Finally, hearing Bessie come onto the floor, he saw that it was nearly nine o'clock. He put the material into his briefcase.

"Pretty goddam hot night," Bessie greeted him.

"Go home, Bessie," Tom said. "It's too hot to clean. No one will know the difference."

"Go home yourself," Bessie said. "You look pretty damn good— like maybe gettin' ready to die."

On River Street people were standing around on the sidewalk or sitting on front steps or on fire escapes. In the city the streets were almost deserted. Turning into the shore road, Tom thought of stopping at Tollie's for dinner, but he was hot and tired and he decided to go home and have a drink and go for a swim and then come back.

A fog was rolling in, and there were little pockets reaching out onto the road. As Tom rounded the curve, he turned on his windshield wiper. Then, abruptly, he stopped the car. Ahead of him through the thin fog, he could see a light in his cottage. The motor died and he sat perfectly still in the car, stopped in the middle of the road, and felt his pulse pounding. There was only one person who had ever gone into his house when he was not there and turned on the lights and waited for him—no matter how late he came.

Slowly he opened and closed his hands on the wheel, and for one wild moment he told himself that he didn't want to see her. He

349

thought of going back to Tollie's and staying there until she left. He saw that Amity was here tonight, and he thought that he could go in there. Maybe, he thought suddenly, it was Amity down there waiting for him. But he knew better. Amity had never gone into his house to wait for him. She never even stopped in when he was there. Unless he watched for her lights, he never even knew when Amity was in town or when she left. It wasn't Amity waiting for him.

He started the car again and turned into his driveway.

She was sitting curled up in a corner of the sofa, where she had always waited for him, and the same lamp beside the sofa was turned on, shining down on her short black hair, and she looked just the same. She was very tan, and the blue eyes were the same—and her smile.

"Hello, Tom."

He came in and closed the door and stood looking at her. "What brings you here, Diana?" The words came out at last, and after he had spoken them, they seemed to hang hollow in the hot humid air. He could feel perspiration rising on his temples and at the back of his neck.

"Why—the best reason in the world," she said and smiled. "I wanted to come."

The blue eyes followed him as he walked across the room and dropped his briefcase on the table. He picked up the bottle of Scotch and poured himself a drink, and then he motioned to her with the bottle and she shook her head.

He drank down the Scotch and felt it hit his stomach. He looked over at her, where she sat straight and elegant in the corner of the sofa, looking as cool and clean as he felt hot and dirty. He filled his glass again. She was handling this much better than he was, he thought, but then she had known it was going to happen. Then he laughed at himself. You knew it was going to happen, too, my boy, he said to himself. Day after day when you saw her sailing back and forth past the lab, you knew that some night you'd come home and find her here. And who are you kidding? You've been waiting for it.

He went over and sat in the other corner of the sofa, feeling the blue eyes watching him steadily. "How've you been, Diana?"

"You look awful, Tom," she said.

"Well—" He shrugged. He got up and opened the front door that in his confusion he had closed. "It's hot—and I worked late."

"You work late every night."

So this was not the first time. She had been here other nights. A halfhearted little breeze drifted in from the quiet water, and he went back to the sofa.

"Tom," she said, "there's no reason we can't be friends."

That—he thought—was one of the silliest statements of all time. Friends! "No," he said aloud. "No reason."

He doubted that Diana had come here to be friends. On the other hand, why had she come? A month ago it might have been because he'd found EA 10 and everyone had gone crazy with excitement— but that wasn't the reason now, when nothing was going right and everything was at rock bottom.

"Except for a few small points on which we disagree," she said, "we have a great deal in common—you and I."

Even the way she sat, straight and small in the corner, even that stray lock of hair that fell over her face was enough to bring it all back.

"Would you have let the whole summer go by, Tom—seeing me almost every day—without coming to me?"

"Well," he said, "it's only June, Diana."

"I think my competition is just too rough."

"What competition?" Tom laughed. He couldn't remember when he'd last seen a girl, except for Midge—and Amity now and then. And neither of them counted.

"I mean your work," Diana said. She moved over to him. "Tom— could you have stayed away?"

The blue eyes were very close now and he moved his hand to her face, and just touching her—the face, the hair—started an aching loneliness in him, felt suddenly and sharply now that she was here, that he had denied while she was not here—and believed the denial.

He stood up and went back to the table and poured himself another drink that he didn't want. He hadn't eaten since noon and he was hot and sticky, and the Scotch was only making him boil over. Well, it wasn't only the Scotch.

"Why don't I go get cleaned up, Diana?" he said. "And we'll go out somewhere."

"If that's what you'd like to do."

He stood looking at her and thought that that was not at all what he would like to do. And then she was standing in front of him and he put down the glass, and she was in his arms and all the hunger of the eight months without her welled up in him—sharper now than without her. He held her close and kissed her mouth and her hair and her throat where her pulse pounded as fast as his own. He felt for the light and turned it off and closed his arms about Diana again—and there was no failure in him now and no tiredness and no despair—and all he felt was the inexpressible joy of having in his arms what he had been so long without, what for so long he had needed. After a long moment he lifted his head and looked down at her and touched her face.

"Darling," she said. "I waited such a long time for you."

"Tonight?"

"No. Since then."

He touched her hair, and her hands tightened on his shoulder. Her eyes were dark in the dark room.

"I couldn't live through it again," she said.

"No."

"There's no one for me like you. I can't pretend there is. Other people can pretend things—I can't."

He drew her over to the sofa and she moved again into his arms, but even while he kissed her, a traitor deep inside him found a voice and told him that she was pretending now—and so was he.

"Diana—" he started, and stopped.

"Don't talk about it, darling," she said. "All I know is that I've missed you every day since EA 50 failed."

EA 50! He hardly remembered it. How many more had failed since EA 50? Dozens. And soon there would be another. Pale light slanted across the room, across the table, across his bulging battered briefcase—bulging with his latest—the word was back—his latest failure.

He turned on the light and stood up. He found a cigarette that he didn't want and drank part of the drink that he didn't want either. "Diana, this will never work—you know that."

"I don't know it." Her eyes laughed at his foolish protest.

"We tried last year. We tried everything."

"We were fools last year! All I know is that I missed you. And you missed me."

"Yes," he said. "I missed you."

She was standing close to him again.

"Diana, sit down and wait for me. I'll go change and we'll go somewhere."

She touched his face and moved her hand to his open collar, and her fingers felt cool at his throat. Cable, you think too much—he said to himself—and not too well.

He took her hand away and kissed her fingers. "Diana, I'll be right back."

In the bedroom Tom closed the door and stood in the dark, looking out the window. The moon was still low and there was a haze across it, and the foghorn sounded. Slowly he unbuttoned his shirt and took it off and tossed it onto a chair and moved about in the dark.

And then the door opened and Diana came in, and he saw that she had left a darkened room behind her. She closed the door and stood against it. The moon slanted a path across the floor to her, and the foghorn sounded, and it was the hottest night of the year. And Tom thought that a man could be starving and not know it—a man could go dry, slowly, and not know it, the way earth could go dry, a little more each day—and you could go a long time without seeing how dry it had become—and then you could pour water on the earth and watch the dryness suck it up and the water sink down into deep places that thirsted for it and took it naturally as part of life.

He moved around the bed and stood beside it and held out a hand to her.

"Miss Watterling," Mills said. "Have you been inoculated against t.b.?"

"No, I haven't," Miss Watterling said. "Why?"

"If we ever get to test EA 10, and if it should be any good, it's one of the things we'll test for," Mills said. "And I was reading the other day about a culture somebody in Texas has been working on, that showed activity against t.b. Tilotoxin. It's available to anyone who wants it. I may write for a sample."

"Do you want me to get inoculated, Dr. Mills?" Miss Watterling said.

"Not if you're reluctant to, but I can't let you work with t.b.-infected mice unless you've been inoculated."

"Then I'll get inoculated."

Mills thought that he had known she would. "We're testing today for Dr. Vought," he said. "He won't be with us. He's sent us a detailed report form instead that we're to fill out."

He took out the form that Vought had given him, and Miss Watterling came over to look at it.

"Forty questions," Mills said. "Did you know there were forty ways to say the mouse died?"

Miss Watterling read the sheet and gave it back. "Mr. Caroline," she said, "I quit."

Mills grinned. Miss Watterling, he thought, I wish this project had come half as far as you have since those early dark days.

About a week later, Gates reported for the first time that EA 10 had taken a considerable jump in purity and that a test in mice was in sight at last.

TWENTY-FOUR

M

OUSE," Mills said, "you die and you're the last damned mouse I'm gonna test. Now—do you want that distinction?"

The green-headed mouse looked at him out of empty beady eyes, and Mills injected it with EA 10 and then injected the second green-spotted mouse, and Tom saw that it was nine-thirty.

"If they live, they deserve a medal," he said. "That has got to be the crudest stuff that ever went into a mouse's tail." He looked into the jar, watching for the first signs of convulsions. The other mice gathered around, smelling the two green-spotted mice from end to end, and the green-headed mouse flicked its pink tail and made its way across the jar. Five minutes passed.

"If that mess doesn't kill them," Tom said, "they'll probably die of the disease. That stuff is still so crude there's probably not enough antibiotic in there to protect against anything."

"The in vitro tests showed enough," Mills said.

"The bug is a bastard of a miser—that stuff is crude as hell," Tom said.

Ten minutes had passed and the mice were beginning to settle down. The green-headed mouse nuzzled in between two others, and the yellow-headed mouse took up sentry duty and stalked the jar.

"I won't even mind too much if they die of the disease," Tom said, "as long as the antibiotic doesn't kill them. I know how little active stuff is in there."

Now fifteen minutes had passed, and everything in the jar was quiet. The two green-spotted mice looked as healthy as the other four, and Tom thought, It's always the same—when they don't die right away, something begins to happen inside you.

At ten o'clock Mills doubled the dose and picked up the yellow-headed mouse, and the needle plunged into the tail vein and the mouse squealed and the knot in Tom's stomach pulled a little tighter.

Now that they had been disturbed, the mice were all moving again. The green-rumped mouse headed for the water pipe, and Tom watched, wondering whether this was the first sign of trouble.

But the mouse just hoisted itself up to the pipe and drank and eased down again and wandered off. Tom watched to see whether the green-headed mouse would go for a drink, too, but it only gathered with the others around the yellow-spotted mice. And the yellow-spotted mice looked as good as the green-spotted mice, and so far there was no hint of stiffening—there was not a single tremor.

"So far, so good, Tom," Mills said cautiously. Tom looked up at the clock. It was twelve minutes past ten, and the mice were quiet and lying close together. He told himself this still didn't mean a thing.

"We tested for Vought last week," Mills said, making conversation.

"He come in to watch?"

"No. Sent enough instructions to launch a large-scale invasion. Didn't use any of 'em. Damn mice died in my hand." Mills grinned. "I think he was kind of sore. Probably figured they wouldn't dare—with him."

The second hand swept around the clock, and the minute hand crawled from sixteen to seventeen minutes past the hour.

"You ever hear of tilotoxin, Tom?" Mills said.

"I've seen the name in the literature. Somebody out West wrote about it, I think."

"Texas. He gave it up—but it showed activity against t.b., so I sent for the culture. You like to look into it when it comes?"

"Sure. Why'd he give it up?"

"It's unreliable—never seems to behave the same way twice. But it can be given orally." Mills glanced up from the jar. "That'd be important for t.b.—as long as streptomycin has to be injected. There isn't anything yet for t.b. that can be given orally."

At ten-thirty Mills doubled the dose again and injected the purple-spotted mice.

The other mice sniffed and roamed and settled down again, and the purple mice huddled in with the rest, and still there was no evidence of any reaction to EA 10. This was nothing yet, Tom told himself—but still it was more already than he had dared hope for.

"That last was a good-sized dose," he said. "We've seen them go into convulsions on a lot less."

"They've died in my hand on a tenth of what the purple ones had," Mills said. "A twentieth. Of course they could still go any minute."

356

At quarter to eleven Tom took a last incredulous look at the six healthy mice, and he left for the Monday morning meeting that was already in session.

For an hour that seemed like a day, he sat at the meeting and fidgeted.

Will Caroline told them that somebody named Croft from the advertising agency wanted to talk to them on Wednesday, and Tom wondered what an advertising man could have to say to research men or they to him. He propped his feet on the rung of his chair and wondered whether, by now, there were six dead mice.

Then Vought began to talk about streptothricin. Vought was convinced that there could be a nontoxic streptothricin. Tom told himself that the last thing he would put money on was finding a nontoxic streptothricin. He looked at his watch. It was eleven-fifteen. Probably by now the purple mice are dead, he said to himself. That was a lot of junk Mills shot into them.

Vought was still talking, and Tom wondered whether he really believed all this or whether he just liked the sound of it. Vought always managed to sound good—he was great on theory, and his talk was scholarly and erudite. And he always managed to look good, too—his lab was a model of tidiness, his notebooks were beautifully organized records. But so far he'd only turned out two antibiotics. It was eleven-thirty. Maybe this fuss about streptothricin was a red herring Vought was dragging across the trail of a damn low production rate, he thought. It's two full hours since the green mice got those injections—I wonder if they're dead, he said to himself.

At last the meeting was over, and Tom raced up the stairs to Mills's laboratory.

"What's happened?" he said. Mills and Miss Watterling were standing over the jar.

"Nothing's happened."

"Nothing? No tremors? No convulsions?"

"Nothing," Mills said. "Not a thing."

Tom came around the counter and saw that all six mice were alive—and all six mice were healthy.

The six mice lived all afternoon, and when Tom looked at them at

357

four o'clock they still seemed fine. "What about the disease?" he said to Mills.

"It's too early to tell." Mills nodded toward the controls. "No symptoms there yet either."

Tom worked until six o'clock, and when he left, the mice were alive. He came back at ten o'clock and they were alive, and Mills was there, with his wife, checking on them, too.

"The controls are beginning to wheeze," Mills said. "They've developed the disease."

But the six mice that had received EA 10 were fine.

The next morning the controls died, and the mice that had received the antibiotic lived. Even the green-spotted mice, which had received the smallest doses of that exceedingly dilute solution, lived.

Tom reminded himself of what had become the first rule of survival with this project: Not too pessimistic when it looks bad—not too optimistic when it looks good.

"We've had an awful lot of mice keel over on the second day," he said to Mills.

"We've had them live through the second day and die on the third."

During the morning he checked every hour, and the mice showed no change. While he was in Mills's laboratory after lunch, Ade Hale came in with Will Caroline.

"How are they this afternoon?" Hale said before he reached the counter.

"So far they're in good shape," Mills said. "Very good."

"It's only the second day, Ade," Will Caroline said.

Hale looked into the jar. "Is there anything here that I don't see?" he said to Mills. "Any symptoms or side effects that you pick up with a trained eye—that I don't, with an untrained eye?"

"No, sir," Mills said. "Nothing yet. Of course, there could be some internal damage—something developing slowly that doesn't show yet."

"Dr. Mills," Will Caroline said, leaning back against the counter, "how many times would you say we've been this far? Six healthy mice on the second day."

"At least a dozen—maybe more. Anything could still happen—and until now it always has."

358

Will Caroline nodded without saying any more, and Tom thought, They're all talking about toxicity—delayed toxicity, now—but these mice could still die from the disease, too, the way the EA 202 mice did. EA 202 protected partially, and the mice lived two full days—twenty-four hours longer than the controls. These controls died only five hours ago.

Working late that night, Tom found himself counting the hours until the mice would have lived longer than the EA 202 mice had lived. When he left, after midnight, there was still eight hours to go, but the mice had eaten their pellets and had drunk normally and there had been no wheezing, no listlessness, no symptoms of the infection developing—and although he tried to rein it in, a strong feeling was rising up in him that these mice were going to make it. They were going to live.

At one o'clock, he passed Brainard's house and saw a light in Diana's room. With a little stab of guilt, he stopped the car, knowing that she must have waited for him tonight. While he sat there, she came to the window as though she had heard him, and he was tempted to call to her. But he didn't want to see Diana tonight. That was one of the reasons he had stayed at Enright—because something in him shied away from talking to Diana about this, at least until three full days had passed. He knew that she had heard about EA 10 from Brainard—he knew that if it failed, she would hear that, too—but still, he felt that if they didn't wait it out together, he and she, if they didn't discuss it, her hopes would not rise so high—and if the mice died tonight or tomorrow, the fall would not be so hard.

He started the car and drove home.

On Wednesday morning the mice still lived, and the time was longer than EA 202.

Now Tom developed a new worry—that EA 10 might be streptomycin. He asked Gates to repeat his tests, and then in his own laboratory he set up every test he knew for a double check. A year of failures had made him suspicious that anything that protected and was nontoxic was going to turn out to be streptomycin that was behaving just strangely enough to avoid detection.

In the middle of the morning when he went back to Mills's laboratory, he found Hale and Will Caroline there again, and today Brainard was with them.

"It's only the third day," Will Caroline said. "They could still go."

"I know—I know," Hale said. "You've been this far before."

"The third day has been the critical one with a few others."

"All the same, Will—they look mighty good." Hale nodded toward a row of jars on the opposite counter. "You going on today?" he said to Mills.

"I thought I'd start to find the therapeutic index—begin to work up to the largest tolerated dose—and find the lowest that protects."

"Getting a little tired of sitting on your hands after a whole year, eh, Dr. Mills?" Brainard put in.

"I can wait out this third day if you'd rather, sir." Mills looked at Hale. "Start it tomorrow—if the mice live."

"No—no," Hale said. "Go on—go on as much as you can."

"Is anybody sure this isn't streptomycin?" Brainard said.

"It doesn't look like it," Tom said. "Dr. Gates and I both set up confirmatory tests this morning."

Brainard shook his head. "Beats me how they can do all kinds of marvelous things around here but they can't solve the most expensive problem we've got—is it or isn't it streptomycin." He jerked his head toward the mice. "Well, let's hope this one isn't—but those mice look too healthy to me for it to be anything else."

Hale moved over to a jar of mice on the other side of the room. "What are you doing here?"

"Tomorrow I want to test whether it can be given orally," Mills said. "Those are set aside so they won't be fed tonight."

"Need an empty stomach for oral administration?"

"It's better," Mills said. "No competition in the stomach from the food."

Hale started to leave. "We'll be back this afternoon," he said to Mills. "If there are any changes before then, let me know."

Brainard and Will Caroline left, too, and Mills picked up the small bottle of brown EA 10 powder. "All morning," he muttered, "whole damn company parading through here. I think we'll start to sell popcorn, Miss Watterling."

By lunchtime anyone could have walked into the Enright dining room and sensed that something out of the ordinary was happening.

360

As Tom entered the dining room, Gates stopped him to say that he'd set up the tests for streptomycin. "I went up to see your mice, Tom, and—I know it's only the third day and there's enough excitement already"—Gates glanced around the dining room—"but, golly, they do look good."

"Listen," Weir said. "You know how long it'll be before you really know whether this is good? A couple of months. You know how many things can go wrong in a couple of months?"

Gates got a worried look on his face. "Once this passes acute toxicity, I may need more help," he said. "We'll have an awful lot more to do—and I wouldn't want my people to hurry and make mistakes. I think I'll have to ask for another technician."

"Listen," Weir said. "Don't go rushing up yet to ask for anything."

Tom went over to sit with Max and Brewer Wentner, and they began to talk about the next steps to take to get EA 10 purer, not noticing who took the remaining seats at the table until Harrup interrupted them.

"Max," Harrup said. "I say, Max—have you all met Mr. Croft?"

Morrissey and Vought were at the table, too, and as Harrup introduced Lawrence Croft, Tom remembered that Will Caroline had said the advertising man would be here today.

"I hope I can talk to you later, Dr. Cable," Croft said, "although I realize that I've caught you at a bad time. These mice—I confess I don't understand a thing about them, except that they're alive—which seems to be cause for general rejoicing."

"Well," Tom said, "it's a little early for rejoicing."

"This is really nothing yet, Mr. Croft," Morrissey said. "We've had mice live until the third day before. I'm afraid this isn't a simple problem."

Vought smiled his best smile. "There's more to it than these few mice, Lawrence. Although if they're still alive at this time tomorrow—why, then we might begin to prick up our ears a bit."

"Awful lot of work ahead if they do live," Harrup said. "This one is presenting strange problems."

"Still—there seems to be a very real excitement," Croft said. His dark eyes were bright and interested. "It's a marvelous thing to watch. You know, among my associates, I see so much of the opposite—the blasé attitude—this is refreshing. But then, this is so much more worth while."

"Let's eat and get out of here," Max muttered.

"Now, Mr. Croft," Morrissey said. "Don't tear down your own work. Personally, I feel the company image is very important."

"But your goals are so much loftier," Croft said. "I consider it a privilege to be associated with this work even if only as an interpreter to the layman. Tell me—don't you ever feel just a little—well—overawed at your tremendous responsibility?"

"That's very well put, Lawrence," Vought said and smiled. "And sometimes frustrated, too, because we know we can't work miracles. I think we'll feel a little of that tomorrow—if our mice pull through."

"I'm going to have to stay an extra day," Croft said. "They'll crucify me in New York. You know what competition is down there. But how can I tear myself away? I want to know what happens."

"We all do," Morrissey said. "We've been at this a long time. My department has worked hard—and been discouraged more than once, I confess."

Harrup traced a line on the table with his knife and leaned over to Max. "I think we'd better have a talk this afternoon, Max, just in case," he said. "I think we're in for some serious problems here."

"I know better than to try to move you two into the dining room," Constance said, bringing a platter of sandwiches into the living room, where Tom and Max were still talking about EA 10, deciding what to do next. Without looking, Max reached for a sandwich, and Constance said, "I suspect you wouldn't notice if it were rat poison."

Max smiled. "We sent some of our particularly toxic antibiotics to the University of Wisconsin testing lab to see what they were good for, and two were very good for rat poison. Another was good for black carpet beetles."

"Your lights went on half an hour ago, Tom," Constance said. "Shall I ask her to come over?"

Tom hesitated and saw Max frown, and he knew it was because Max didn't particularly like Diana. He also knew that the reasons for his dislike were something Max would probably never discuss.

"Why don't you do that, Constance?" Max said. "We'll be at this a while yet."

"What a coward you've become in a year!" Diana said, as soon as they were outside Max's house. "Hiding out from me like this—for two days."

362

"Yes," Tom said, "I did."

"But why?"

It was a bright night, the moon lighting the boardwalk brighter than the streetlamps, and they walked slowly back toward his house. "In a way, I guess I'm like the fellow who has something he can't afford," Tom said. "He knows it has to go back, but he'd like to enjoy it a little first."

"Afford!"

"I've just gotten you back, Diana. I didn't want to lose you again so soon."

"But your mice are alive tonight," she said. Tom looked down at her, puzzled. Diana's attitude was different this time. She was detached. She talked about EA 10 and about the mice, but she didn't really seem to be interested.

"Yes, they're alive—but what if they had died today?"

"Then they'd have died."

"Would you be here now?"

"Darling, did you suppose I was so naïve as to think the mice would live because I had decided to accept them? At a distance, of course, you understand—not too close."

"Would you like to go over and see them?" he said. "Very healthy-looking mice—at least when I left, they were."

"No—no, thanks."

He told himself that he shouldn't feel this disappointment that she didn't care. Last time she had cared too much. It was better this way. Across the water he could pick out the lights of the mouse laboratory on the fourth floor.

"Maybe if you'd come over there, you'd feel different about everything, Diana."

"Darling, I know what it's like."

Tom told himself to drop it. This could lead to the kind of argument he'd been trying to avoid. And yet, he thought, even though they didn't talk about it, the friction between them remained intact, just as it had been from the start, lying just below the surface, and it wouldn't stay buried forever. And it was friction based on a misunderstanding, he thought. And tonight there was a reason for going.

"How long has it been, Diana," he said, "since you've been over there?"

"Really, Tom, I learned all about Enright at a very early age."

"From your grandmother."

"Yes, from my grandmother." She looked across the water. "I haven't been over there in years. Why would I go now?"

For the best reason in the world, Tom thought—because over there in that lighted room on the fourth floor there are six mice halfway through the third day. "How long?" he said again. "When were you last over there?"

"Well—" she said. "Well, darling, I've never been over there." And then, seeing his look, "Well, I didn't want to go—I knew all about it."

"You've *never* been over there!"

"Well, what difference would it make if I went over and looked at a few offices—or a few laboratories—or a few mice? I grew up on Enright. My whole life I looked at it across the bay. My whole life I've heard about them—my father, Ade Hale, Will Caroline—Morrissey, Harrup—Rosswell—and that board of directors—Mr. Palmerton, Mr. Kaiser—all of them."

She broke off and looked at him. "Tom, don't say another word about it. This is our own private no-man's-land, and we have to learn not to talk about it."

For a moment Tom just stared at her.

"I don't ask you why you stay," she said. "Don't ask me why I won't go over there."

Still he stood there, asking himself whether to insist that she come with him now, tonight, when there was a reason to go. And then he thought maybe she was right. If she couldn't be for it, it was better for her to be out of it altogether.

He slipped an arm around her and led her up the steps and into the house.

The next morning, very early, Tom stood alone in Mills's laboratory. The mice were still alive, and now it was three full days and he knew they were going to be all right. He stood at the window, looking out at the bay where an early mist moved over the glassy water, and all the restraints that all week he had kept tightly clamped on his feelings blew away.

He knew this was only the beginning. He knew clearly that this three-day acute-toxicity test in mice proved nothing except that the antibiotic was not pure poison. He knew that a long period of chronic-toxicity testing lay ahead, during which Mills would administer daily doses of EA 10 to rats and to dogs and then perform autopsies on them in order to examine the effect of the drug on every part of the body. In acute toxicity the question was simple—and the answer was simple. It was easy to tell the living from the dead. But in chronic toxicity the questions became more complex—what about the heart, the lungs, the liver, the kidneys—what about stomach, colon, intestines, glands—brain and bone and blood?

He told himself that chronic-toxicity testing could reveal that EA 10 was a slow poison instead of a fast one.

He told himself that still, very far in the future, lay the final and all-important question—the only one in the end that mattered: What does it do in man?

He told himself that there was still so much that could go wrong.

It didn't help. He turned and looked again at the six mice, sleeping in a huddle in the jar—six mice that had received enough disease germs to kill them—six mice that had received injections of a very crude EA 10 and so had not died.

For a year you kept insisting it could happen. And then, when it did, you could hardly believe it—especially that it had happened to you.

A little later Gates came in to say that EA 10 did not seem at all to be streptomycin.

"Babette, I'm still at Enright," Lawrence Croft said over the telephone to his secretary. "I'm caught here, dear. I walked into a madhouse. . . .

"Well—a week ago it *was* a sleepy little company—but since then a half-dozen mice had some new drug and lived, and all hell's broken loose. . . .

"But it's important to these people, dear. Last night was the critical period. I told them I couldn't think of leaving, and I believe they were impressed with my interest—I think they were grateful. . . .

"I wish you could see this place. Everyone who can walk is trying to do something with this new thing, and there isn't even enough of it to go around. This morning they're setting up some new operation to make more—a pilot plant, they call it—makes little tankfuls instead of potfuls or something like that. It's all pretty confused. I'm beginning to think it's a miracle we ever get any medicines at all, Babette. I'm developing a whole new respect for my pills. . . .

"I'm going over now to watch a test for something they call oral administration—that's a test on mice, dear—giving them a drug by mouth. Last Monday they injected it—now they're going to give it orally—to see if it works that way, too. . . .

"I thought so, too, dear. A drug is a drug—like a rose is a rose—if it would work one way, it would work the other. But it seems it ain't necessarily so. . . .

"I don't know how you get the mouse to take it orally—that's what I'm going over to see. . . . No, I don't think they flavor it with cheese, darling, but that's very good. . . .

"Well—hold the fort, dear—don't let them steal our accounts before I get back. . . ."

"You always lose some efficiency in oral administration," Mills said. "The question is how much." He measured out a brown powder that Croft was shocked to learn was the antibiotic. "With any drug you give a bigger dose orally than by injection to get the same results."

Mills began to mix the powder with water, measuring everything carefully, and Croft's eyes went over to the mice. "Cute little buggers, aren't they?" he said.

"They just had a lethal dose of disease germs."

Croft edged away. He was beginning to find all this rather depressing. The room was as aseptic-looking as a hospital, and the technician wore that dismal white laboratory coat, and everywhere you looked there were mice. Croft waited until Mills put down the bottle of brown powder, and then he said, "I realize it's just my ignorance, Dr. Mills—but why shouldn't it work orally if it works by injection? I mean—why such a difference just because of the way they get it?"

"The drug doesn't work unless it gets into the bloodstream," Mills said.

"Oh?" Croft said, still confused.

"When you give it to them orally, it's got a long way to go. Down the esophagus—into the stomach—and then absorbed into the bloodstream. It doesn't always make it."

"But why not?" Croft said. "What happens to it?"

Mills shrugged. "Could be inactivated by gastric juices. Could be something else. Sometimes it just passes into the intestines and out. We don't usually ask why. We just say it's not absorbed—we can't give the drug orally."

Mills picked up an odd-looking blunt syringe, and Croft stared at it. The equipment was almost as depressing as the mice. "Well," he said, trying to be cheerful, "I suppose if you can't, it's no great tragedy. Doctors always seem to have plenty of needles."

"It's better if you can give it orally."

"Oh, I agree with you there." Croft smiled brightly. "I swallow pills all day long—you know what the pressure is in the city—but it's better than being stabbed in the arm."

"Or the butt."

Croft looked up at Mills quickly. He had a feeling that Mills didn't like him, and he told himself to be more careful—one man in a company talking around about you and finding fault could ruin you. And Mills was sharp—he wasn't just a country boy like some of them. "Well, naturally, I can see that it'd be better," he said. "Anyone would prefer it orally, of course."

"Mmm," Mills said. He was figuring and writing in a notebook, and Croft thought he probably hadn't heard a word he'd said. Then Mills looked up and said, "Mr. Croft, if a drug can be given orally, a doctor prescribes a dozen pills with instructions to take them every four hours or every six hours, and he can check his patient once a day. If the drug has to be injected, the doctor has to keep going back or send his patient to a hospital. Now, if he has a choice between two drugs that are equally good, and one has to be injected and one can be taken orally, which is he going to use?"

Something clicked in Croft's mind, and he understood why this was important. It was important, not only medically, but financially. This was business. This would interest Hale—it would probably interest Hale a hell of a lot more than that fuss going on downstairs where Cable and Strong were trying to clean the drug up a bit and Gates was trying to find out what minor diseases it would cure. Discuss this with Hale, Croft said to himself—remember that.

Now Mills was drawing that muddy mess up into the syringe, measuring again, and Croft knew that he was getting ready to put it into the mice and got a sick feeling in his stomach. He looked away, across the room, and saw the technician take some mice out of one jar and put them into another. Fascinated and repelled, Croft watched, wondering how it would be to sleep with a woman who handled mice all day—would you be able to do anything, or would you be utterly defeated by the knowledge that the hand touching you had, only a few hours ago, been touching mice?

Then he saw Mills looking at him, and he said, "Well, I can certainly see why you're anxious to know—why this is the first test you do."

"We do it because we want to know—and because it's something we have to know—before we go on to chronic toxicity."

"Chronic toxicity?" Croft said. "What's that?"

"Mr. Croft," Mills said and turned to him, holding the syringe in midair. Then, as though he'd decided he might as well get it over with, he said, "Mr. Croft—before a drug is ever given to a human patient, it goes through a long intensive study in animals, during which we try to find out every kind of trouble that drug could conceivably cause. Anything—anything at all—that enters the human or animal body is toxic if you give enough of it. Even water. Did you know you could die of too much water, Mr. Croft? And I don't mean drowning. Even aspirin, which is the most harmless of drugs. Even coffee. A shot of caffeine would send one of those mice into convulsions."

Croft's eyes slid over to the mice again and then to the muddy liquid in the syringe, and he wondered what the mice would do when Mills put that mess into them.

"And a drug isn't water or coffee, Mr. Croft. A drug is powerful stuff that can do a lot of good or a lot of damage—and you have to study it damned carefully to find out whether you can give it to a human patient at all. And if you're going to give it to him, you'd better be damn sure you know how big a dose he'll need to cure him—or he's going to die on you. And you'd better know how much it's safe to give him—or he's going to die on you for another reason. And the only way you can find out what you have to know is by testing it for a long time in animals, and that's what we call chronic-toxicity testing. And we have to give it to animals the same way it's going to be used later in people, because the route of administration can make one hell of a difference. So I do this test now to learn right away whether it can be given orally. After today, I'll be doing a lot more work to pin down the exact dosages—because if I want a doctor, a few months from now, to give a man a pill, I'm not going to give the drug to rats and dogs by injection. I'm going to shoot it down their throats."

Mills consulted his notebook and then relaxed a little and grinned.

"It'd be like testing a girl for the Aquacade on dry land, Mr. Croft. She might be gorgeous, but what happens when she hits the water?"

He picked up his syringe again, and Croft said, "Dr. Mills, isn't that an odd-looking syringe—with that blunt end? Aren't they usually pointed?"

"Christ, man—it's going down its throat!"

Croft looked at the syringe and at the mice, and he wished Mills would get it over with. There was something horrible and fascinating in thinking about that instrument sinking deep into a mouse's throat. He folded his arms and tried to appear calm. "It'll never be quite the same casual thing taking a pill again," he said. "People all over the world would probably be amazed—if they knew what you go through so they can take their pills."

"People all over the world don't take pills."

"Oh—now—I thought that was one thing we all had in common —our pills."

"Hundreds of places a doctor wouldn't think of prescribing pills. Parts of South America—Asia—Africa—even some parts of Europe —a doctor never sends a patient home with a dozen pills."

"Why not?" Croft said. He was certain now that Mills didn't like him, and he suspected that he was pulling his leg.

"Because the people don't understand pills and would probably louse things up." Suddenly Mills was ready and he reached into the mouse jar, and Croft shuddered—you'd think he would wear gloves to handle those mice!

"How?" Croft said. "How would they louse things up?"

"Half of them wouldn't take them at all, because they wouldn't believe a little thing like that could help what ailed them. The other half would take them all at once—figure if one would work, twelve would work faster. Where people aren't used to taking pills, you can't trust them to follow the instructions. In those places the doctor wants injections—not pills."

Now Mills had the mouse out of the jar, and the little bastard looked terrified. It stuck out its pink paws and its pink eyes popped and it opened its mouth, and Croft saw it had only one tooth—one sharp gnawer in its bottom jaw. Mills thrust the blunt syringe into its mouth—deep into its mouth, past the single sharp tooth—and shot the muddy liquid down its throat.

Mills put back the mouse and Croft unfolded his arms.

"Mr. Caroline gives penicillin to missionaries working in Asia and Africa in return for their sending us soil samples," Mills said, while he refilled his syringe. "They always want injections—never pills."

Croft made a mental note to talk about that to Mr. Caroline. He had a feeling Mr. Caroline didn't like him either.

This was the pilot plant where all equipment was an exact replica of commercial production equipment, scaled down so that it filled a large two-story room instead of a whole building. Here were the same graduated fermentation tanks, the same maze of pipes, the same recovery equipment to separate that little bit of antibiotic, by whatever techniques were required, from the great quantities of broth that would be pumped out of the tanks. It was all here— filters, extraction tanks, precipitation tanks, ion-exchange columns —and, with push-button repiping, it could be adapted in a few hours to the requirements of any product.

Standing just inside the door of the huge room, Ade Hale watched the men preparing the equipment to produce EA 10. Already a man was sterilizing the smallest fermentation tank, and Hale let his eyes go over the maze of pipes around it. He could pick out the pipe through which sterilized mash would be fed in, the pipe through which sterilized air would be blown in, the pipe through which waste gases would escape, the pipes through which cooling water would be pumped to maintain exactly the temperature best suited to this microbe.

Hale's eyes moved across the room. Off to one side, next to a mixing tank where they would prepare the mash, he could see a few bags of soy flour and corn meal and bone meal. He stepped closer and spotted the Chilean nitrate and cane sugar.

This production in the pilot plant—larger than laboratory production, smaller than commercial production—was the bridge between: taking direction from one and providing a guide to the other. Here larger quantities of EA 10 would be produced, now that larger quantities were needed, and here, if there were going to be any production problems, they would be discovered and ironed out.

And here, Hale thought, he understood what was happening. Now that an antibiotic had reached this stage, he felt better.

On the weekend Will Caroline went to Boston for a meeting with Dr. R. E. Loedick, to whom he had spoken on the telephone several times during the past year. Dr. Loedick was a professor of internal medicine at Harvard Medical School, a physician experienced in the clinical testing of new drugs. He had agreed to supervise the clinical testing of the antibiotic if and when Enright discovered one.

"The drug must meet with my approval, you understand," Dr. Loedick said, tapping his fingers on his cluttered rolltop desk. "If I don't like it, I won't touch it. I'm not a patient man—you should know that before we begin."

He was a tall, deceptively rakish-looking man, who seemed younger than his sixty-four years, but when he talked about his work, his features sharpened, and when he grew excited, his dentures rattled. He spoke in short declarative sentences, the thought of one sentence not necessarily related to the one immediately preceding it. The impression he gave was that when he had covered a subject to his own satisfaction he jumped to another, feeling no obligation to bother with transitions.

"I'll talk to your pharmacologist," he said. "I have no time to do all the work I have to do. No time for fools. Let them waste each other's time—they enjoy it—not mine."

"Dr. Mills is a good man," Will Caroline said. "You won't have any trouble with him."

"Good. I'll come and talk to him. This interests me. If I like your drug, I'll do it—but it has to be done my way. I require more testing than some clinicians do. You can hire someone else if you like."

Will Caroline smiled. "We'll probably ask your reasons."

"I want more testing to get more information. What else?" He shuffled through the papers on his desk and turned up a pipe which he pushed aside impatiently, and then picked up and held by its stem. "A colleague gave this to me. He thought I might be less disagreeable if I smoked." Loedick's blue eyes were gay for a moment. "I didn't throw it out right away. It got lost in the papers on my desk. Then one day when I was in a particular rage, unusual even for me, I found myself banging the desk with it. Since then that's been its function. Who has time to smoke?"

He tossed aside the pipe and searched about on his desk some more. "I'm looking for an article I wrote explaining my requirements in animal testing. I can't find it. I'll send it to you. If I can work with your pharmacologist and if your company gives me my own way, we'll get along all right. We need more antibiotics. Let's hope you've got one."

On Monday Mills reported that EA 10 was absorbed into a mouse's bloodstream and could be given orally.

Two days later EA 10 received a name. The soil sample from which the culture was picked had come from Barbados, and the antibiotic was named Baramycin.

TWENTY-FIVE

Natalie Brainard hoped it would succeed. She knew nothing about this antibiotic project—she cared nothing about it except that its success would be a painful blow to Gil —and the thought of Gil's being thoroughly beaten provided Natalie with as sweet a pleasure as the contemplation of taking a new lover. Like notching a gun, long after their names and faces were dim memories, Natalie kept a count of the number of lovers she had had because to her each one represented another secret triumph in cheating him—another cherished act of revenge.

Tonight Gil had invited Lawrence Croft to dinner, and Natalie looked into her empty glass, where the ice had melted to twin marbles, and wondered whether to try to get another drink now or wait until Mr. Croft arrived.

"If I'd been handling this, I'd have had those dogs ready," Brainard said. "If I were in charge, they'd have started that testing the next day. The way they're horsing around, they'll be almost a month just working up the dogs."

"A month?"

"Worming them—giving them shots—examining them. They've got a vet who's practically moved in."

He was drinking straight whiskey in short gulps, as he did when he was irritated, and she saw his neck getting red and thought how coarse it looked. Her eyes went to the bottle at his elbow.

"I couldn't get a checkup like that if I paid for it—blood counts, kidney tests, hearing, skin, urinalysis. Ask me, that vet's making a good thing out of it. Knows he's got a live one in Will Caroline." He poured himself another drink, spilling a little on the bar. "I don't know why Ade puts up with it."

"Here is your Mr. Croft," Natalie said.

While he went to the door, she poured a drink quickly and drank it and poured another. Then she looked up and saw Lawrence Croft, and a little flicker of interest stirred inside her. She watched him as he came across the room.

"How's Baramycin coming along?" Lawrence Croft said.

"They don't know any more than they knew two weeks ago," Brainard said. "They're working up the dogs."

"Oh? Why do they do that?"

"Make sure there's nothing wrong with the damned mutts to begin with. Anything shows up later, it'll be from the drug."

"I'm certainly impressed with all this," Croft said.

He was probably five years younger than she was, Natalie thought—no more. She waited until his eyes came over to her, and smiled at him over her glass.

After a minute Croft's eyes moved back to Brainard. "And what does everyone do in the meantime—just wait?"

"Wait!" Brainard snorted. "Croft, these scientists can think of more tests than anyone'd bother to do on you and me if we were dying. Gates is playing with his test tubes—testing and retesting against every disease he can lay his hands on—Cable and Strong running around like a couple of nuts, still trying to get it purer—in and out of the pilot plant every time there's trouble there. Mills is testing and retesting his doses—curing mice and checking and rechecking—curing rats and checking and rechecking."

"Still?"

"These scientists are test-happy. Stop in and see for yourself tomorrow. Just the fuss they're making over those dogs is enough to make you sick—examining—testing. The way they're going, they'll probably put on a full-time vet. But then, why not? They're hiring everyone else in sight—might as well hire a vet, too. I tell you, Croft, the cost of this thing is brutal."

Croft looked sober and sympathetic.

Natalie picked up a cigarette, and as Croft stepped over to her, his lighter in his hand, she let her eyes talk to him. Croft's eyes lingered a second after the flame was out.

"Had two new men here last week," Brainard said. "Fellow named Loedick from Harvard—he's going to test the thing on people if this Baramycin ever gets that far. Big-time clinician—very big wheel. Now, a fellow like that doesn't work for peanuts."

"I should think not."

"He'll probably be hanging around from now on, just looking around—and getting paid for it. Paid plenty. Let's have your glass, Croft."

Brainard motioned with the bottle, and Croft took his glass and stepped up to the bar.

"Loedick spent the whole day here when he came—jawing first with Mills and then with the pharmaceutical chemist, Jaxman—

that's the other fellow they've hired. He's a pillmaker—he doesn't even come into the picture until they've got a product, and they've hired him already. Croft, the waste on this thing is appalling."

"And they say advertising is expensive," Croft murmured, his dark eyes thoughtful. "At least it pays to advertise."

"Advertising is good business," Brainard said.

Croft crossed his leg over his knee, and Brainard picked up the bottle again. He saw that it was empty and bent down behind the bar to get another from the cabinet. His keys jingled as he picked out the one to the liquor cabinet. Natalie looked again at Croft, and now his eyes were waiting for hers.

"I'll tell you one thing, Croft," Brainard said, as he relocked the cabinet. "Production at Enright is a damned sight more efficient than research."

"I'm looking forward to seeing it tomorrow," Croft said to Brainard while his eyes stayed on Natalie. "It's something I've wanted to do for a long time."

Perhaps seven years younger, Natalie thought. Eight at the most —no more. She looked at Gil as he straightened up. She burned with the hope that Baramycin would be a great success so he would be thoroughly licked.

Dr. Loedick and Mills had worked out a program for chronic-toxicity testing which called for twenty-four dogs and one hundred rats, and now, in an executive meeting, Mills was explaining it. Listening, Will Caroline wondered whether he should have brought Dr. Loedick in today to do this. Not that Mills wasn't doing a good job. He was. But as Dr. Loedick had warned, his standards were high, and Will could see opposition developing. He wondered whether Mills would be able to handle the barrage of questions that would follow. Already Brainard had held a whispered conference with Rosswell and another with Kaiser, the company lawyer, who was here, too. And Mills had barely begun—he still had a lot of ground to cover.

Mills was working at the blackboard, charting the program as he described it.

The dogs, Mills explained, would be divided into four groups with six dogs to a group—three male and three female—so that one male and one female would be available at each of three autopsy periods. One group would be the controls, and instead of Baramycin they would receive daily doses of sugar or cornstarch. All the other groups would receive the drug daily over an extended period but in different-sized doses. The first group would get a therapeutic dose—the dose corresponding to that which would cure a man. The second group would get a medium dose—about five times as large as the therapeutic dose. The third group would get a toxic dose— about four times as large as the medium—and these dogs would get sick from the drug and eventually die.

On the blackboard the outline read:

Level of dose	Number of dogs
Controls	6
Therapeutic dose	6
Medium dose	6
Toxic dose	6
	24

"One male and one female dog from each group will be sacrificed at the end of one month," Mills said, "and at the end of two months —and at the end of three—"

"Three months!" Brainard interrupted. "You expect us to sit on our hands—waiting—for three months?"

But Hale waved his hand and said, "Let's get the whole picture first."

"The rats will be similarly divided into four groups." Mills wrote on the blackboard. "Twenty-four to a group—eight from each group at each autopsy period—four male and four female. There will be four rats left over, which we would like to carry for longer than three months. The rats will receive corresponding doses—therapeutic, medium, toxic—and of course there will be a group of controls. The rats will be sacrificed at the same times as the dogs."

"How are you figuring these doses?" Hale said.

"The therapeutic dose is the dose that would cure a man—scaled down for the dog's body weight and for the rat's. A rat's weight is about one-eighth of a dog's."

"And the others?"

"The medium dose will be five times the amount needed to cure. We've tested to determine the toxic dose and in this case—with Baramycin—it's about twenty times the therapeutic dose." Mills hurried on. "And before anyone asks me why we have to give animals twenty times the amount that will cure them, that's one of the things I'm going to explain."

Mills moved to the next panel of blackboard and wrote, in large letters:

DELAYED
CUMULATIVE
SENSITIVITY

"These are three things to remember in setting up this program," he said. "First, that toxicity can be delayed. It doesn't always show up right away—it doesn't always happen right away. Even with very serious side effects, sometimes there's no immediate evidence, even under the microscope. That's one reason for running the tests over an extended period of time. An example of this is streptomycin. Streptomycin can cause deafness, but it doesn't happen within a day or two or even a week or a month after the patient begins to get the drug."

"And plenty of times it doesn't happen at all," Brainard put in.

"That's right," Mills said, "which brings me to—"

"Keep it straight, Mills," Brainard said. "Don't try to peddle your program by coloring the facts. Three months!" He shot a look at Rosswell.

"This brings me to Point Number Two," Mills said, undisturbed, "which is that toxicity can not only be delayed but can be cumulative. Sometimes it occurs right away—after the first dose or the first few doses—but other times it occurs only after *repeated* doses. This has happened in certain cases with penicillin. There are histories of people who have tolerated penicillin through two or three illnesses, showing no unusual side effects, and then, suddenly, they do not tolerate it. The same dose—that was previously tolerated—will send them into shock. Because"—Mills tapped the blackboard—"the effects have built up. They were cumulative."

Mills left the blackboard and came back to the table, leaning over his chair. "The third reason is that people are different. They react differently to situations and they react differently to drugs. They're unpredictable. They don't always recover when the book says they should—they don't always die when the book says they should—and they don't always react to drugs as they are supposed to. There's a very wide range in sensitivity to drugs. A dose that one man tolerates easily will produce side effects in another. One man will show trouble at a low-level dose—another man won't show it until a much higher level. It is the most sensitive person, not the least, that we must bear in mind."

Mills paused and Brainard spoke up again.

"Mills, we produced penicillin here—and we did it without all these fancy ideas. With penicillin we stuck it in animals and it didn't kill them. We infected animals and it cured them. We produced."

"With penicillin nobody knew anything about antibiotics."

"Penicillin is a damn good drug."

"Penicillin is a great drug. And, normally, a very nontoxic one. But you know, Mr. Brainard, that when penicillin got into broad general use, you began to hear unexpected things. That was when you began to hear about people going into shock—some people even died, they were so sensitive to it. It was a question of numbers. When the drug was used on a large enough number of people, some very sensitive ones were bound to be included—"

"Mills, you know how many people had these reactions you're getting hysterical over? Less than one-half of one per cent."

"Mr. Brainard, do you know how many people one-half of one per cent is?"

Will Caroline listened uneasily. He liked to let a man take care of himself as long as he could—but Brainard wanted a fight, and Mills was getting a look on his face that Will didn't like. He decided to put the discussion back on the track. "Dr. Mills still has a lot of ground to cover," he said, nodding toward the blackboard. "This is just background information. The whole purpose of the program is to get information about this drug, and if you'll let him, he'll tell you how and why."

Arms folded, Mills studied Brainard another minute without speaking.

"Go on, Pat," Will said.

Mills turned and stepped back to the blackboard. "I'm adding another word," he said. Across the blackboard, in larger letters still, he scrawled:

POISON

Looking steadily at Brainard, he said, "Every drug is a poison."

"Dr. Mills, what do you mean by that?" Kaiser said unhappily.

"I mean that every drug, if you give enough of it, will do some damage. Every drug, at some point, is poison. There is no drug that, at some dose, is not poison. There is no drug you can give me that I can't kill an animal with—using enough of it. That's what I mean."

"Mills, you're distorting the facts!" Brainard said.

"The only questions are: *How* is it poisonous, and how poisonous *is* it?" Mills said.

"Listen, Mills. You may test this thing—this Baramycin—and find it's too toxic to use as a drug—and that wouldn't surprise me at all —but every drug is not a poison."

"Right," Morrissey said. "That's going too far. There are some very fine drugs."

"You care to clarify your statement, Dr. Mills?" Hale said.

"When you produce drugs," Mills said, "you will never, at any time, have a product that you can give to a doctor and say, 'This is absolutely harmless—use it indiscriminately.' The best you will ever be able to say is 'We've tested it and it seems to be safe at the level that cures. Use it when you have to.'"

"There's one hell of a sales pitch," Brainard said to Rosswell.

"And we can't say that yet about Baramycin," Mills said. "All we know about Baramycin is that it cures simple infections in mice and in rats—and that it doesn't kill them instantly. With these few facts you can't put a potentially dangerous substance into man."

Brainard had leaned behind Rosswell to hold another whispered conference with Kaiser, and now he sat up again.

"Mills," he said, "you know the law on this?"

"The law isn't good enough."

"Tell him." Brainard looked at Kaiser.

"You can get past the Food and Drug Administration with three weeks in rabbits."

"You can't get past Dr. Loedick with three weeks in rabbits," Mills said. "He won't put it into the clinics."

"Find someone who will," Brainard snapped.

"No, sir," Will Caroline said. "Dr. Loedick is one of the most respected clinicians in the country. On his word other doctors doing clinical testing will be willing to try an experimental drug. It's Dr. Loedick's opinion that any less testing would be unsafe."

"The law's good enough for me," Brainard said.

"The law will change," Mills said.

"You a lawyer too now, Mills?"

"The law is tighter now, because of penicillin and streptomycin, than it was three years ago—and in another few years, as evidence piles up from other antibiotics, it will be tighter still."

"You're a talented boy, Mills. We're glad to have you aboard."

"Dr. Mills," Hale cut in, motioning toward the blackboard, "let's get back to your program. Have you established your doses yet—and if so, what are they?"

"For a dog the therapeutic dose with Baramycin is three hundred milligrams or three-tenths of a gram. Five times that is one-point-five grams for the medium dose. The toxic dose is four times that—six grams. The dogs will get sick at six grams."

Hale wrote down the doses and Brainard did, too. Rosswell, who was already figuring, squinted at the blackboard, figured some more and looked up, disturbed.

"Dr. Mills, this is an awful lot of material! An experimental drug that isn't in commercial production is very, very expensive." Rosswell looked at his pad again. "Now, as long as the law permits it, it seems that rabbits would use far less material than dogs."

"A dog has a digestive system very close to a man's. You wouldn't get as accurate information from rabbits."

"There's no question about the dogs," Will Caroline said. "We're using as few as possible."

"The law is satisfied with rabbits," Brainard said.

"Dr. Loedick won't go from a rabbit to a man. It's too dangerous."

"Well, then," Rosswell said, still examining his figures, "why must you use such large doses? Six grams a day to each dog at the toxic level—that's thirty-six grams every day right there. And the other dogs besides—and all those rats, too. It seems there could be a saving there. That's twenty times the therapeutic dose."

"All right," Will said, "now we're getting to the crux of the problem. This is what Dr. Mills is trying to explain—if you'll let him."

"The point of this program is not to get away with as little as possible, but to learn as much as possible," Mills said. "And we use large doses to learn things that with small doses we wouldn't learn for years. We deliberately push doses to the danger points—with animals, in the laboratory—so we can learn all the potential damage that this drug could do. We must use six grams of Baramycin in dogs because with this drug this is the toxic dose. This will make them sick. We want the dogs to get sick so we can find out *how* they get sick. We want to know how much of this drug an organism can take. When they die we want to know what they died from."

"Nobody's ever going to give a man twenty times what he needs," Brainard said.

"You never give a man any more than he needs. With human patients in clinics you never push dosages beyond the minimum that will cure, even if you feel the patient could tolerate more. You do not experiment with human beings. This is a moral question."

The whole thing was a moral question, Will Caroline thought, and he was beginning to wonder whether Brainard could even understand that. Thoughtfully he studied him across the table. There are men, he reflected, who cling to a precious image of self-importance and must prance a little and hold the limelight before they will give in and agree to what must be done. And if it was that, it was something Will could understand. He couldn't respect it, but he could understand it. Or if Brainard was doing this to play both sides —to be on record as having objected to costs if the drug failed and to be on the bandwagon, urging quick production, if it succeeded— that was still something Will could understand. But if Brainard was seriously bargaining with lives for dollars and for power, that was something else again.

"You experiment with animals," Mills went on, "to get every scrap of information you can about the drug—so you'll be better equipped to treat human beings. If you limit yourself to small doses and if there were side effects only in very sensitive animals, you might complete your testing and miss that effect altogether. If it turns up in only one-half of one per cent—like sensitivity to penicillin—you could test a thousand animals and still miss it."

"That's true," Harrup spoke up suddenly. "I came across some statistics on that once."

"A drug could look almost perfect," Mills said. "It would be produced. It would be used in people. And then suddenly you'd run into trouble—trouble that could be painful and tragic. Then what? To a large extent that kind of surprise—that unexpected disaster— can be avoided by testing long enough in animals, and using enough animals and high enough doses to force the trouble and get the information."

Brainard was having a whispered conversation with Rosswell now, and Rosswell began to figure again on his pad. Brainard said,

"Mills, nobody's agreed to your three months, and I, for one, don't intend to. And as for your doses, if trouble is only going to turn up at twenty times what you need, it's an academic question. You and your Loedick are being a couple of professors with Enright money—that's all this amounts to."

For a long moment Mills looked at Brainard without answering, and Will Caroline wondered what was wrong. Certainly Mills was not suddenly intimidated or at a loss for words—not Mills. Then Will saw a light come into Mills's eyes that he could recognize now, and he thought, Oh, no! And then, Why not? He was tired of Brainard and his arrogance—he was tired of the penurious Rosswell—and if Mills wanted to explode some fireworks around them, Will thought, he wasn't going to stop him.

"Mr. Brainard," Mills said, "let me illustrate this to you in terms of a product with which we're all familiar." He leaned over his chair and smiled innocently. "Alcohol. The drinking variety. Whiskey."

Brainard laughed.

"If a man is nervous and tense," Mills said, "you might give him a drink—one drink—and that drink might relax him, and you'd say, 'This is very good for this purpose. It relaxed the man, brought relief from nervous tension—showed no visible ill effects.' So far so good—with one drink. And if the dose were doubled, the side effects that you would see would probably not be very different. It might even relax him a little more. And you might say, 'One is good, two is better.' But what if you doubled it again—four times the original dose—or increased it to six or eight times? Now you would begin to see some different side effects. Alcohol pushed to high doses doesn't just relax a man. At high doses it can cause loss of balance, loss of ability to focus the eyes. It can slow a man's reaction, impair his power to think, cause vomiting, loss of consciousness, severe headache—immediate or delayed. It can upset his gastrointestinal system. It can produce psychological changes—such as making him mean or happy, loquacious or silent. It can increase sexual desire. And the side effects would not be the same with every man. And none of this would be obvious at the one-drink level—only at higher levels. And even then, because some people are more sensitive to alcohol, certain side effects will appear in some people at the two-drink level or the three-drink level which, in other people, may not appear until the six-drink level.

"Now, carrying this a step farther—all these side effects might be produced every day for a month. But each time, after the administration of the alcohol was stopped, the effects would disappear in due time, and if, after a month or two, administration were stopped altogether, there would probably be no lingering ill effects—except possibly that alcohol is habit-forming and there might be a craving for it.

"But if the administration of alcohol were continued for a long time—not just one month—there would be permanent ill effects: bloodshot eyes, bulbous nose, fatty tissue around the stomach—and, more serious—cirrhosis of the liver, which would be fatal. Now there, in simple terms, are all the reasons for this program—for the high doses and for continuing the tests for at least three months. As a matter of fact, we want to carry four rats for six months or a year just to see whether we learn anything more."

"Boy," Brainard said with a laugh, "we'll all give up drinking."

"Dr. Mills," Hale said. "The fact remains that an antibiotic is rarely given for more than three or four days—five at the most. This isn't a drug for a chronic disease—like diabetes or arthritis—that a man would take every day of his life."

"If it were for a chronic disease," Mills said, "it should probably be tested for a year—or longer."

Brainard threw up his hands and looked at Rosswell, who was still figuring on the pad. "You through?"

"In a minute."

"I'd like to make it clear," Will Caroline said, "that forcing the trouble doesn't necessarily mean that Baramycin would be considered a dangerous drug. But when we give it to the doctor, we'll say, in effect, 'At very high levels this kind of side effect occurred. Be aware of it—know about it. If you run into the exception—that extremely sensitive patient who defies all testing and has an adverse reaction—know what to look for. If anything goes wrong, it will probably be this.' We wouldn't know that to tell him without this testing and—"

"Will," Brainard said, "with doses like that, your boy is going to find something a lot faster than three months."

"But after one month the damage might show up only at toxic levels," Mills said. "In three months we might find it at therapeutic levels. That changes things. That's what happened with penicillin.

383

And with penicillin there was some excuse. Nobody knew anything about antibiotics—there had never been any antibiotics—and nobody knew that it might happen."

"There was a better excuse than that," Brainard said. He shot an impatient glance at Rosswell, who was still figuring, and Rosswell, annoyed, jerked his head and kept figuring.

"There can't be a better excuse," Mills said. "The doctor is entitled to know about the drug. If damage appeared at the therapeutic level after extended use, we would have to say, 'Use it if you must, but use it sparingly.'"

"You'd make one hell of a businessman, Mills—putting out a product and saying, 'Don't use it.'"

"Aside from the moral implication," Mills shot back at him, "it's better business to tell the doctor everything. This isn't killing your drug. It's helping it. Some side effects can be reversed. If the doctor knows about them, he'll watch for them and be ready for them. There are side effects that he can be prepared for with an antidote —provided he's been warned. But he wants to know and *he* wants to decide."

"The standards for accepting or rejecting a drug aren't absolute," Will Caroline said. "Give a doctor a drug that will cure cancer and it can have quite a bit wrong with it and he'll still use it eagerly. Today there would be leeway on antibiotics."

"Then use it!" Brainard said.

"If a patient is dying of pneumonia," Will went on, "and he doesn't respond to penicillin, there's nothing else to give him. If a doctor is standing there with a drug that will give him a rash or—say—impair his hearing, as streptomycin can, he'll use it. The man is dying. It's all that he has, and he uses it. But the day he has a second antibiotic that will cure without producing those side effects, he's through with the first one. And there are other kinds of leeway. There are drugs that are so dangerous that they can be used only in hospitals where there is equipment to follow the patient's reactions very carefully and stop the drugs when it becomes necessary. They're used. They save lives and there's no other drug available. But the doctor doesn't want any surprises. If he decides to use such a drug on a patient, he wants to do it with full knowledge of the dangers—because it's a risk he has to take—and with emergency measures ready as much as possible—"

"All right," Brainard cut in as Rosswell finished figuring. "Let me remind you of a few figures—all of you." He looked around the table. "With the exception of our eager beaver, Mills, you were all here then, so this is just to refresh your memories. Our earnest young man here—"

"Don't needle him, Gil," Will Caroline said and Mills grinned and Will smiled, too, knowing that Mills didn't need defending.

"Our pious moralist here says we didn't do this with penicillin because we didn't suspect the possible dangers. No other excuse, he tells us. Now, look at that program he's got outlined there, and I'll tell you what it would have cost to do that with penicillin." He looked at Rosswell, and Rosswell handed him a few sheets of paper.

"Now, in the first place we couldn't have done this with two dozen dogs and a hundred rats for three months. We couldn't have tested even one dog this way for three months—with six grams a day—because in 1943 the entire world supply of penicillin was seventeen grams. So much for that. Now, according to Mills, he's going to give a dog in the therapeutic group three-tenths of a gram every day, a dog in the medium group five times that much—that's one-point-five grams—a dog in the toxic group six grams. Every day. That's seven-point-eight grams a day, times six dogs in each group. That's roughly forty-seven grams. For one month that adds up to about fifteen hundred grams. And back in 1943 penicillin was worth two hundred dollars a gram. At that rate, with penicillin, it would have cost us three hundred thousand dollars for one month for the dogs alone. To say nothing of the rats—which are one-eighth the weight and four times as many, so that makes it half as much again. Four hundred and fifty thousand dollars for the month for the program. Some are going to be sacrificed after a month—some after two months. The entire program, just as he's drawn it up, would have cost over a million dollars."

"Let's keep this realistic, Gil," Hale said. "Baramycin is costing us about twenty dollars a gram—not two hundred."

"That still makes for a damned expensive testing program. And that doesn't include the half-million dollars we poured into the research program before we even found Baramycin. And you've got no guarantee it's any good. It could still fail. And I say we've got no business throwing away money on it—testing it any more than we have to. What do you say now, Mills? You still think we should have done this with penicillin?"

"It's an academic question, Mr. Brainard," Mills said. "Penicillin

385

is behind us. Baramycin is here, and you can't cut this program without sacrificing safety."

"Safety! Safety is a word with a hundred meanings. Like a politician jawing about 'the general good.'" Brainard thumped his finger on the table. "I say do what the law says to do—test it three weeks in rabbits—that's safety according to the law. And don't throw away a fortune on it when we don't even know whether we've got anything—looking for some long-shot trouble that might never happen."

"Cutting into this program is deliberately denying knowledge that it's within our power to give!" Mills said.

"Rot! Do you know how many different ways a man could die in a car? They don't keep cars off the market."

"Gil," Will Caroline said, "you keep talking about how expensive it will be to test this way. Have you considered how expensive it might be not to?"

"Have you thought how expensive it will be if it fails?"

"Maybe it'd be good business for us to know how good an antibiotic we've got," Will said. "It's not cheap to bring a drug onto the market—producing it, promoting it. If we invest a lot of money in Baramycin and then it develops that it has serious side effects, two things are going to happen. First, the day another antibiotic comes onto the market that cures what ours will cure without the side effects, that's the end of ours. If that's going to happen, we ought to know it."

"Worry about that when the time comes. These things aren't turning up so fast."

"And besides that," Will said, "the doctor won't be eager to use our products again if he can't depend on our information."

"Enright has a damn good reputation," Brainard said.

"Let's think a little about keeping it that way," Hale said.

"Test as much as the law says to test," Brainard said. "You'll be giving him as much information as anyone else will. And let's not be conned into pouring money down a drain just because some doctor had a nightmare—saw a couple of patients that didn't do what they were supposed to. The law is the law, and I'm opposed to setting yourself above it—either way—doing less or doing more. Meet the law and produce."

"Even if people are seriously damaged?" Mills said. "Or die?"

"They were going to die anyway."

Now Will Caroline saw Brainard as he had never seen him before. "We're liable, Gil," he warned.

Brainard snapped around and looked at Kaiser. Kaiser nodded. "You're liable—you could be sued," he said.

Brainard snorted. "It'll never happen!"

"How do you know it won't happen?" Harrup said.

"What doctor is going to admit he gave a patient a bad drug? He gave the drug—he's involved. If the patient dies, he'll say, 'We couldn't save him—we tried.' Or if the patient goes suddenly, he'll say it was a coronary. He's not going to admit to anything—say he gave him an untested drug—he'll get sued for malpractice. Look, you've got everything going for you on this—the less they know about your commodity, the safer you are. You said yourself that people are unpredictable—sometimes they die when they're not supposed to. Of course they do. Everyone knows it. The patient died —he shouldn't have—he wasn't supposed to have died. Too bad. And in this case he was dying anyway, so the thing is even more confused. Most of the time the doctor won't be sure himself what happened. We probably won't ever hear about it. What are we going to do—go around and ask the families of everyone who died whether by any chance he had our drug?"

Will Caroline stared at Brainard. Here, he thought, was all the evil of all time—all the men since the beginning of time who had found excuses for immorality where there were no excuses. Here was a man gone blind with his own greed and his own lust for power—the petty power over a limited little band of men in a limited company—and, for that, selling out principle and morality. The petty tryant, centered in self, and so walled in that he had come to believe this meager little acre was all. Here was Judas, and this petty domain was his twenty pieces.

Shaking with anger, Will stood up. "The subject is closed," he said. "The discussion is over."

"What do you mean—over? It's only over if you're conceding on your fancy program."

"I am conceding nothing. There is not one point in this program on which I will concede—not one point on which I will compromise." Will thrust his notes into his briefcase and zipped it shut. "I'm directing this program," he said, "and no antibiotic will leave Enright that has been tested one day less than it should be tested. I have a hundred rats and twenty-four dogs for this drug, and I will use a hundred rats and twenty-four dogs—and I will test it for three months. I will not permit anything to reduce this program. I will not discuss it. I will not compromise on it. The argument is over."

Later, sitting out on the deck long after dark, Will thought that there was a difference between the time you called a man the opposition and the time you knew he was the enemy.

On a morning in late July, Morrissey walked down the first-floor corridor toward the elevator. Behind the closed door of the dog laboratory a few dogs were barking, and inwardly Morrissey tensed and walked a little faster. He knew it was only two weeks since the dogs had arrived, but it seemed to him that they had been here forever. It seemed that he had been waiting for months for the testing on them to begin—dreading the outcome, worrying about what would happen if the drug failed and how a failure would affect him personally. He worried about it steadily, unrelentingly. He discussed it with Winifred. He dreamed about it.

A man came up the corridor, and he saw that it was Dr. Bent, the veterinarian. Morrissey knew Dr. Bent because for years Winifred had had an ugly dachshund which he had been forced on several occasions to accompany to Bent's office. Bent was a big honest fellow who looked, Morrissey thought, as though he'd first learned about animals on his father's farm. Now he was sorry to see that Dr. Bent was going to speak.

"Come in and see the dogs," Bent said, after he had greeted Morrissey.

"I'm just hurrying up to the assay lab," Morrissey said. "They're so busy in there with Baramycin—I don't like to take my eyes off them too long."

"Only take a minute," Bent said. He pushed open the door, and the dogs stepped up their barking.

The dog laboratory was cool and smelled of antiseptic and washed-down concrete. Off to the right, in a glass-paneled examination room, Mills was talking to an animal attendant in a white lab suit and a black rubber apron. Looking around, Morrissey saw that someone had tacked pictures of animals on the walls—several breeds of dogs, a few cats and even a monkey—and he wondered, annoyed, whether it was Mills or the animal keeper who hoped to extend his activities to other animals. Now the rest of the dogs had taken up the barking and yelping, and Morrissey decided that the racket made any effort at conversation unnecessary. He followed Dr. Bent to the kennel and dutifully looked in at the dogs. He supposed he ought to say something.

"Are you almost through here?" he shouted over the din.

"Winding up this week," Bent shouted back. He closed the kennel door and it was a little quieter.

"Seems to be taking a long time," Morrissey said.

"There's a lot to do." Bent pointed to a calendar where Monday, July 29, was circled in red pencil. "One week from today is our launching date."

Morrissey moved toward the door to escape. "Well—keep up the good work," he said. "We're all anxious about this, you know."

Out in the corridor he could still hear the barking and he hurried away.

At least they were getting started soon, he thought, and the waiting was one step closer to an end. But, on the other hand, it could be one step closer, too, to possible disaster. My God, he thought, while panic stabbed through him, what if it fails!

But now at least they couldn't put all the blame on him. Now at least others would have to share it. Harrup's department was involved, too. And plenty of money was going into Mills's department and Mills was only beginning. Still—Morrissey pressed the button for the elevator and brushed at his pocket—there was always the hideous inescapable fact that if anybody added it all up, the largest sums had been poured into his department.

On the other hand, he told himself, if it did work—if it actually, by some miracle, did succeed—think of the glory. His name would be on the patent—high on the list because most of the work had been done in his department—and he could claim a lion's share of the credit. After all, he had carried most of the responsibility, hadn't he? It would be almost like achieving immortality!

The elevator came and Morrissey decided not to go to the assay laboratory right now. He hated assay these days. They were so busy in there it made him nervous. It reminded him of how this project had mushroomed and of how much he was involved, however unwillingly. And even if Baramycin did succeed, it could still spell trouble for him, personally. With a good antibiotic, Enright would become more and more a producer of drugs—and, in proportion, less a producer of industrial chemicals—and the problems would become more complex—and he just didn't like the drug field. Sometimes he wasn't sure which would be worse for him—failure or success.

Entering his office, Morrissey looked out at the barge and looked away. He might as well call Winifred to tell her the animals would be getting the first doses next week. At least that was something—although it would still be a month until the first autopsy.

"So what's the story around here?" Weir said, sitting down to lunch. "You still in business for the rest of us or not?"

"Of course we're in business, George," Gates said. "If you've got something, send it down. Miss Potter's doing that work now."

"I'm only asking," Weir said. "What about you, Mills? You still testing for us common people?"

Mills looked up. "Bring it in, George. If I'm not there, give it to Miss Watterling. She's doing acute toxicity these days."

Weir gave an unpleasant laugh. "The rest of us don't go first class any more, eh?"

"George, we've all got an awful lot to do," Gates said irritably. Right now he was hurrying through lunch to get back to check on some cultures that Miss Potter was supposed to have done for Vought. Vought was coming in for the report after lunch, and Gates had forgotten to ask Miss Potter whether it was ready. This had been a particularly hectic morning with Baramycin. They were testing for the pilot plant, they were testing for the chemists, Gates himself was doing closer work on the bacterial spectrum. And besides that, there was still the routine work coming in at the usual rate—work like this batch of cultures Vought had sent down. With so much on his mind, Gates couldn't remember whether he'd mentioned it to Miss Potter at all. Then he saw Weir looking at him resentfully and he said, "Well, Miss Potter's done the tests as much as I have—and she never makes a mistake."

"Okay—okay," Weir said. "I guess we'll live."

Gates put down his fork. He knew that his anger was rising out of all proportion, but he felt so harassed these days—so driven by the endless stream of work pouring into his laboratory. "All right, George," he said. "If it matters so much to you, I'll do yours myself. I'll be glad to."

"Don't strain yourself, Pearly," Weir said, and turned his attention

390

to the menu and Gates, for no real reason, lost his temper completely and left the table.

Going upstairs, Gates thought that sometimes George could be the most upsetting man he knew. With everyone working so hard, it just wasn't right for George to be that way. Then his thoughts came back to everything he had to do, and the feeling of harassment settled over him again and he hurried along.

Walking into the laboratory, he saw gratefully that Miss Potter was back from lunch and working already. When she saw him, she set the test tube she was holding into a rack and came toward him.

"Come here," she said. "I got something to show you."

She walked toward his office, and Gates walked a little behind her because walking behind Miss Potter was almost as tantalizing an experience as facing her.

"What's the matter, Miss Potter?"

"Come look at this." She reached across his desk for a report she had left there. "Dr. Vought's," she said. "Look at that—EA 44."

With experienced eyes Gates read quickly down the sheet, and then his eyes froze. He read it again. He looked up at Miss Potter and Miss Potter nodded. Gates read down the sheet a third time, although he knew now what was on it. For the second time in two months, he was looking at a report of a broad-spectrum antibiotic! EA 44 was as broad-spectrum as Baramycin and much more potent.

TWENTY-SIX

O N THE LAST MONDAY of July, Mills guided
a blunt syringe down the throats of the white rats and then
threaded a stomach tube down the throats of the dogs and administered the first doses. Chronic-toxicity testing of Baramycin had begun.

Each morning thereafter, doses of Baramycin were administered
to all the animals except the controls, which received sugar and
cornstarch, and every day Mills observed the animals closely, looking for alterations in appearance or behavior, especially in the dogs.
There were none. The dogs were alert. Their behavior was normal
—they were not overstimulated or depressed or disoriented. There
were no physical disturbances, such as vomiting, diarrhea or bleeding. Their appearance remained good.

When a week had passed, Mills and Dr. Bent examined the
dogs and found no problems. Skin, eyes, lining of the mouth, behavior, reflexes, balance, hearing—everything was normal. Nor had any
visible side effects developed in the rats.

Meanwhile a great deal of work on Baramycin was going on in
parallel. The chemists were still improving purity. The pilot plant
was perfecting production techniques. Gates was continuing a close
study of the drug's spectrum. Mills was training new technicians to
perform autopsies on rats and to prepare the tissue slides for microscopic examination.

And Vought was working on EA 44.

After two weeks Mills and Dr. Bent examined the dogs again and
took blood and urine samples for analysis.

Half an hour after he had completed the second weekly examination of the dogs, Mills came into his office and picked up his schedule for the next week. He was still training his new technicians to
perform autopsies, and Miss Watterling had just told him that
Vought's EA 44 was coming in tomorrow for testing. If the mice
lived, he would have to rearrange his training schedule to allow
time to work on it.

Sitting down, Mills put his feet up on the desk and considered
the schedule, noting the changes he could make, and then took a

minute just to think. Another examination and another week were behind them, and the news was still good. And yet, Mills knew, it couldn't continue that way. Eight dogs were receiving toxic doses, and they had to get sick and eventually die, and even though that was expected, he wondered what the reactions around Enright would be when the first symptoms appeared.

There was a knock on the door, and Mills got his feet off the desk. Then Derrick came in and he put them back.

"Charlie," Mills said, after he had answered his question about the condition of the dogs, "what's going to happen around here when the first ones get sick?"

Derrick smiled. "Ah expect everyone'll run true to form, Pat. Some won't react much at all. An' some'll start up a period of mournin'."

"Even though they know it has to happen?"

"Knowin' won't get in the way of worryin'," Derrick said. "Some men are just made that way, Pat. Give 'em a bite of bad news and they really chew on it. You know that."

Yes, he knew, Mills thought—probably better than any man here, because he was always around when it happened. He saw the good news first and he saw the bad news first—and he knew how every man in research reacted to both. He knew which ones could take failure in stride and which ones were plunged into gloom—and he knew how much or how little they showed of their feelings. Whether they watched with him or he brought the news to them afterwards, he was always there when they heard it.

Mills crossed his feet on the desk. Sometimes he wondered whether he was hard on them—whether he was wrong not to cushion the blows. But Mills had no patience with quick quitters or instant despair. The few times he had tried to break the news gently he'd made a poor job of it, and in the end it was all the same.

"It has to be soon," he said.

There was another knock on the door, and he took his feet off the desk again. He saw that it was Gates and put them back again.

"It certainly is encouraging," Gates said, when Mills told him the dogs were still fine. "It really looks good, doesn't it?"

"So far," Mills said.

"Pat, about EA 44," Gates said. "Has Vought said anything yet about testing it?"

"We just heard—we're getting it tomorrow. That's fast for Vought."

Gates nodded and looked as though he had more to say and wasn't sure he ought to say it. "Either Vought is a genius," he said finally, "or that EA 44 is the sweetest-handling antibiotic around. He's brought it along faster than anything we've ever had—his or Cable's or anyone's."

"That one looked good from the start," Derrick said. "Even on my plates."

"How pure is it?" Mills said.

"It's at least as pure as Baramycin," Gates said a little reluctantly. "And in my tests it's awfully, awfully good."

"How?"

"It handles easily—it's stable—and the bug makes a lot of it, which the Baramycin microbe doesn't. And, *in vitro*, it's terrifically potent."

"More potent than Baramycin?"

"Much more potent—and broader spectrum, too." Gates hesitated. "Of course, we don't know anything yet about toxicity—but in my tests EA 44 is just about the best antibiotic we've ever had."

Gates lowered his voice although the door was closed and there was no one here but Derrick. "In my tests, EA 44 makes Baramycin look sick!"

The next day Mills injected EA 44 into six mice. They lived through the critical first five minutes. They were fine at lunchtime, and a ripple of excitement and disbelief could be sensed in the dining room. They lived through the day.

In the morning they were dying.

They were going to die at the same time as the controls, and they appeared to be dying in the same way—of the disease. Mills was almost certain that EA 44 was not protecting.

"With this one we'd better be sure," he said to Miss Watterling. "Let's put it into six uninfected mice. No disease. Just the antibiotic." He wrote down the doses. "See what this does to them."

The next morning the six uninfected mice were alive and healthy.

When Mills returned from the dog laboratory, Hale and Caroline and even Vought were waiting for him. A quick look told him that the mice still showed no toxic effects. "We could still get delayed toxicity," he warned. "A second or third day development that didn't show in the others because the infection killed them first."

"I don't believe there will be," Vought said.

"Why not?" Hale said.

"I've observed mice before," Vought said. "I'll have this ready for another test next week."

"That soon?" Hale said.

"Oh, yes," Vought said. "This EA 44 handles well. It's already as pure as the Baramycin that you're putting into animals. Personally, I'd prefer to wait until it's absolutely pure before testing it again—but that doesn't seem to be company policy, I'm sorry to say."

"Don't be too fussy," Hale said. "You've got a broad-spectrum antibiotic there. If you get a good jump in purity, test it."

Vought wouldn't wait until it was pure, Mills thought. He was too much of a prima donna. In his own eyes Vought was a golden boy and success was his due. If Baramycin weren't around, Vought might have waited—but with Baramycin two weeks into chronic-toxicity testing, he would be back with EA 44 as soon as it was purer.

The first dog was sick.

On Friday of the third week, when Tom stopped at the kennel as he did every morning, Mills and Plesch, the animal attendant, were bending over one of the dogs.

"First one," Plesch said, nodding toward the ailing dog.

Mills glanced up. "You know this isn't cause for alarm, Tom. This whole group will get sick and eventually die."

Tom bent down beside Mills. The dog—a male of the toxic-level group—was lying listlessly on the floor. He seemed to be aware and in no particular pain, but unquestionably he was getting sick.

"We'll examine him and see if we can find anything," Mills said. He patted the dog and stood up. "If he dies, we'll do an autopsy immediately—otherwise we'll wait until the month is up."

Upstairs, Tom stood at the office window and thought about the dog. It was a hot muggy day in August with a nervous kind of wind that stirred without cooling, and a white moth was buzzing around outside the screen. The dog didn't seem to be seriously ill yet, Tom thought, and it probably would live until the first autopsy. On the whole that was good—but still it was hard to know that the evidence on which everything hung was there now, concealed in the body of at least one dog and probably more than one—and to have to wait a week or longer until it was unveiled.

He turned to his desk and picked up the reports on some new cultures he was bringing along in a routine way. Compared to Baramycin, they were all uninteresting. He scanned the reports and put them down. Then the door opened and Brewer Wentner came in.

Walking quickly, as he always did, bouncing a little on the balls of his feet, Wentner came across the room, perspiring profusely in the damp heat. He was carrying a piece of glass about six inches wide and eighteen inches long. "Can I prevail upon you to do me a small favor, Tom?" he said. "One that won't take a great deal of your time?"

"What've you got there, Brew?" Tom said, seeing that the glass was actually a shallow receptable with thin pieces of glass glued on all around to form the sides.

"Consider this a large rectangular Petri dish, Tom," Wentner said. "I have to get a few of these seeded with test organisms in nutrient agar. Over in chemistry we don't have the equipment or the organisms. Could I prevail upon you to do it for me, my boy?"

"I guess you can prevail, Brew. What's up?"

"I'm working on a production problem with streptomycin," Wentner said. "Potency has been inconsistent, and I suspect the trouble is that they've got both kinds in there—streptomycin A and streptomycin B. As you know, A is far more potent, and if B is in there too, that would affect potency. So we'd like to find out."

Tom nodded toward the plate. "You going to do it with that?"

"Right." Wentner moved to the counter, and little beads of perspiration rolled off his layered chin. "With paper chromatography. Have you read about paper chromatography, Tom?"

"Some—not too long ago, I think."

"Developed in England by two men named Synge and Martin," Wentner said. "Used first on amino acids. Then to separate the three different kinds of penicillin appearing in one broth. Now it's being used to separate the two kinds of streptomycin."

"I remember now."

Wentner unrolled a sheet of paper about the same size as the glass plate. At the top and bottom, the paper had been hemmed with crudely sewn seams. Wentner slipped a pencil into each hem, letting the sheet hang from one pencil, weighted by the other. "This is the paper we use. Absorbent, you see." He tapped the bottom of the sheet. "Put a drop of streptomycin at the bottom and

396

hang the sheet in a jar—hangs into a solution in a tray on the bottom. Piperidine solution. Stinks to high heaven—good thing the jar has to be covered—but that's beside the point."

Now Moose had become interested and came over to listen. "So what then?" he said.

"It's like this, my boy." Wentner rocked a little on the balls of his feet and looked up at Moose who towered above him. "That stinking piperidine solution—terrible stink, really—whew!—gags you! —that solution travels up this sheet of paper by capillary action, like water moving up blotting paper. Travels up until it reaches the top. And the penicillin or streptomycin goes traveling up too, but —now, here's the beautiful part of this—really this is beautiful— pay attention now—"

"I'm listening," Moose said. "Everything's moving up the sheet of paper—"

"But," Wentner said, "not at the same rate."

"What not at the same rate?" Moose said.

"The streptomycin doesn't travel at the same rate as the solvent. It goes at its own pace. But what's even more beautiful—the two kinds of streptomycin—A and B—travel at different rates from each other."

"How come?"

"Just a physical fact, my boy, like two people don't move at the same speed," Wentner said. "Now, I personally move very quickly. Very few people can keep up with me and that's a fact. Now— when the solvent reaches the top of the paper, you take the paper out of the jar, and someplace on that paper is streptomycin A and someplace on that paper is streptomycin B—only they're not in the same place. In that piperidine solution, A moves just a little farther than B. And to make it even more beautiful, they take slightly different shapes on the paper. Describing them roughly, A ends up as a blob shaped like an ice-cream cone and B ends up shaped like a milk bottle. Ho—what do you think we could do to the Rorschach tests with this, Tom? Could confuse all hell out of a psychologist, couldn't we?" He turned back to Moose. "So you see, my boy, on the paper they are quite different from each other—decidedly individual."

Tom smiled. Actually it was very simple—and, as Wentner said, it was beautiful.

"And that's how you tell," Wentner said to Moose, "whether you've got both kinds in the broth."

"The plates," Moose said. "Where do we come in—makin' the agar plates?"

"Because you can't see anything on the sheet of paper. It's there but you can't see it. We dry it and then put it on the plate for half an hour."

"So?" Moose said.

"You got streptomycin there, my boy," Wentner said. "The moist agar leaches that streptomycin from the paper, and wherever it stopped in its travels, streptomycin is going to inhibit the test germs at that spot on the plate. If you've got two kinds in there, you're going to have two different spots. Incubate the plate and it'll be cloudy, except where streptomycin A or B is working, and there you'll have clear spots—areas of inhibition. Then you can see it— on the plate—whereas you couldn't see it on the paper."

"Say!" Moose's face lit up with comprehension and admiration. "That's all right. I like that!"

Tom laughed. "Your paper chromatography has passed the test, Brew. If Moose approves of it, it's good."

"Good?" Wentner said. "It's beautiful!"

Looking at the sheet of paper on the plate where Wentner had placed it, Tom thought that once the hard ground had been broken, progress almost forced itself on you. It was only a short time since Waksman, after agonizing years of work, had discovered streptomycin and since it had first been produced, about fifteen per cent pure. And now the men working on it were involved in such subtleties as two different kinds with different potencies, that in solution would travel up a sheet of paper at different rates of flow. Always, Tom thought, the first steps were slow and painful—and months and even years seemed unproductive. Always at the beginning, it seemed that you worked forever to turn up even the smallest scrap of information. But once you broke through and you began to put those scraps together into something meaningful, information snowballed—and at a constantly accelerated rate. Once you had the core for the bits of information to adhere to, then knowledge almost forced itself on you—knowledge like this—a different rate of flow of two kinds of streptomycin. And it always turned out, too, he thought, that nature was full of clues—you only had to find them—

398

and that once you knew what to look for, you found them everywhere. And how many clues, he wondered, were lying around that might help them with Baramycin or with some other antibiotic, that they didn't even know enough yet to stumble over?

After Wentner left, Tom went down to the dog laboratory where Mills and Dr. Bent had finished examining the dog without determining what was wrong. The other seven dogs that were receiving toxic-level doses of Baramycin still seemed healthy, and the ailing dog appeared to be about the same as before—no worse.

At closing time Tom stopped in again and still saw no changes, either in the ailing dog or in the other seven.

While the sun dropped low and sank behind the houses silhouetted against the last purple band of daylight and a warm evening breeze skipped over the water, Tom lay on the deck of his boat and watched Diana without speaking. They had gone for a late sail to escape the humid heat, and now, back at the mooring, they lingered another few minutes. Diana was restless tonight. Even before she'd brought it up, Tom knew that she had heard about the dog and that the news had stirred up all those barely buried feelings.

"But they must have found something when they examined it," she said.

"No—nothing that told them anything."

"But the dog is dying," she persisted. "What's it dying from?"

He didn't answer. He was irritable himself tonight, partly because of the weather and partly because—well, when it was your problem, you could work on it; when it was out of your hands, you could only sit around and wait. Then he said, "Diana, seven more dogs are going to get sick, too—and die. Please let me worry about it. We can't go through this with each one."

"Tom," she said, her eyes suddenly bright, "how do you feel about it? Tell me exactly how you feel."

"I knew it was planned to happen this way—and I know we have to wait for the autopsy."

"Tom, what if Baramycin fails?"

Now a strange kind of excitement was running through her, and Tom stirred uneasily. He had seen Diana like this before—when any answer was the wrong answer and either irritated her or invited other questions until the answers to them irritated her. Last year she had been this way often—although not so much lately. Or maybe she had—maybe he had been too preoccupied with Baramycin to notice.

"How would you feel then?" she said. "What would you do?"

"I don't think of it in terms of failure, Diana." He held out an arm. "Come on over here. It's getting dark."

Usually she came willingly. Tonight she didn't move. "But what would you do then?"

"I'd look for something else to come along. Vought has a good one —maybe his will work. Come here."

"Vought's! But then it wouldn't be your success! It would be his!" She stared at him, incredulous. "Do you mean to say you wouldn't care if yours failed?"

Inwardly Tom winced, just thinking how much he would care. "Diana, every day I go in to look at the rats. Every day I go in to visit the dogs. I'm as bad as Mills, the way I talk to them. 'How's your heart today, old boy?' I say to them. 'How's your liver?' When that dog got sick today, I got sick right along with him. Of course I care."

Diana turned away and Tom looked at her fine profile etched against the last low flame of daylight, and a melancholy feeling went through him. Nearby a gull was busy, dropping swiftly to the water, rising sharply upward again, and Diana watched it. When she turned back to him, there was a glow in her eyes and again that sense of restrained excitement. "Tom, what if Enright were to decide not to go on—and you saw it coming—saw very clearly, that it was just a matter of time—*then* would you leave?"

"Then I probably wouldn't be thinking about leaving. I'd be fighting to get it extended."

Suddenly she came over to him, her eyes very blue and intense. "Darling, I want you to understand—it isn't that I don't believe in you—it's that I believe in you so much more than anyone else does."

The restrained diffused excitement was almost sexual. He drew her down beside him, but she propped herself up instantly on one elbow. She wanted to talk. "Tom, don't you see? They'll never realize over there how great you are—but even if they don't, I do." The blue eyes blazed. "That's the fate of all great men."

"What's the fate of all great men?" He moved his hand along her throat and across her collarbone and down over the rises and hollows of her warm slender body and felt how much he wanted her and felt, too, that she hardly noticed.

400

"All through history no great man has had more than one or two people who absolutely believed in him—and I am yours—I am your *believer*."

He smiled at her and felt how much he didn't want to argue with her. Below the water lapped the boat, and overhead the sky was all dark now. "I'll be satisfied for now if you'll just be quiet and let me love you."

"Some day you'll do something brilliant"—she plunged on with her fantasy—"utterly brilliant—and I alone will have appreciated you. Enright could never appreciate you—society could never appreciate you—as I do."

Tenderly Tom reached up and touched her face, but when he spoke, his voice was firm. "Diana, save those feelings for your artist friend—that's the way you used to talk about him. I don't want you to feel that way about me."

Immediately she was very angry. This was a sore point with her. "I'm not ashamed of giving Adam money," she said. "I'll be very proud when his work is recognized—to know that I saw his worth when no one else did. I was the only one."

"Diana, I don't think Adam is ever going to do very much, but if it gives you pleasure to support him, that's your business."

"Are you jealous of Adam?"

"No, I'm not jealous of Adam—I just think he's a leech."

There it was—a chasm as wide as the Grand Canyon opening up between them again—and he was letting it happen, over something as unimportant as that stupid "beard." Only he knew better than that. This wasn't about Adam—it was about them.

But as quickly as it had flared up, Diana's anger subsided and suddenly she was quiet and tender. "Darling, when they fail you— over there—you'll want me to believe in you—then, when nobody else does. That's when it will be important. And it's important to Adam, too. And I will believe in you"—she bent over and touched his face—"even if not another soul does, in the whole world."

It was a condition devoutly to be desired, Tom thought—only he didn't believe it.

"And then someday when you do something great, even if it takes years, we will laugh at them all and say, 'See? You fools!'"

Disturbed now and deeply puzzled, Tom looked at Diana in silence. Nothing, he thought, could ever bring the kind of fire to those eyes that burned when she talked this way. It was her favorite reverie, and when she lapsed into it, it was as though she had found the mainstream of her being.

"Darling," she said softly. She bent down and kissed him, and his arms closed around her. "Will you promise me that if this fails, you'll go to the kind of place you should be at? A place where you won't have to prostitute your genius under pressure for profit—someplace very, very good—and even if they don't pay you much for a while, it won't matter because I can be your patron, the same as Adam's—"

He let her go. There was something very deep-seated here that they didn't understand about each other, and he couldn't even say what it was. Maybe it was his fault, he thought—maybe he'd never really tried to understand her or what she wanted. He had resisted her ideas—he had told himself she was chasing moonbeams—but he hadn't ever asked her what she hoped to have when she caught one. And he had never been able to make her understand how he felt about these few things that were important to him. Maybe he hadn't tried hard enough there either.

He sat up on the deck of the gently rocking boat. "Diana, there are two things you must try to understand if we're ever to be happy together. For a research man, 'good' doesn't lie in a name or in a label. A good place is where he can do the work he wants—the way he thinks it should be done—without too many people getting in his way too often. Having to work hard under pressure is no punishment. The only punishments are being blocked and frustrated and having to waste time playing politics and wanting to do it one way and having some fool tell you that you have to do it another. If you can't work freely in a place, that place is bad. If you can work there freely, that place is good. That's all that matters—not some label or name or fashionable opinion or anything else. Can you understand that?"

"Of course, darling," she said. "I'm only talking about if the time should come when you find you can't work there."

He wondered, but he didn't argue. "Now, let me tell you one more thing, and then I want you to tell me exactly what you really want—if you know."

She laughed. "What is your one more thing?"

"What you have with Adam—you can't have that with me, ever."

She looked puzzled.

"I'm delighted that you believe in me, although I'm not sure that you really do—at least I think sometimes you find it very hard. But you can't ever give me money."

"I don't mean just give it to you. I mean if there was something you really wanted to do—"

"No, Diana—"

"But, darling, I want to!"

Suddenly he thought that he didn't have to ask what she hoped to hold in her hand when she caught those moonbeams.

"But *why?*" she said.

"Because I won't let you, Diana. Because it's a very bad thing for a marriage. Diana, I love you—but not enough to let you make an Adam out of me."

He had expected her to be angry again and she wasn't—not at all. She moved close to him again and said, "Darling, I don't want to make an Adam out of you. I love you—not Adam. I only meant that if there was something you were just burning to work on—and there was no other way—"

She moved into his arms. Her reverie was over and now she wanted him, too. And yet he felt that she hadn't understood at all—anything that he had said. Or was it, he thought, that she understood too well—and was confident that eventually necessity would resolve their differences—that the time would come when he would not be able to work at Enright—that the time would come when he would need her—and not as he needed her now?

By Monday all but one of the other dogs receiving toxic-level doses were sick, and a day later the last one succumbed and a few rats began to show the symptoms.

As Mills came into his office after examining the newly affected dog, Miss Watterling came in behind him. "Dr. Vought's technician called," she said. She sat down and lit a cigarette. "EA 44 comes in again tomorrow."

Mills checked his calendar. "Well—we'll have two days to work on it if the mice live, before we start the Baramycin autopsies on Monday. Shoo—we can do it, although the pace may be a little rough."

"I guess we'll survive," Miss Watterling said. She leaned back and smoked her cigarette.

Mills thought for a minute. "To save time, I think we'll do six extra mice with EA 44," he said. "Six mice to get no infection—only the drug."

Miss Watterling nodded and then a messenger appeared in the open doorway, knocking as he came in, with a small package.

"What have we here?" Mills said. Then he realized what it was. "Oh, kee-rist! It's that damned delinquent culture from Texas—tilotoxin!"

Miss Watterling raised her head from the back of the chair. "Oh, God!"

"At a time like this," Mills muttered. "What in hell am I going to do with this thing?"

"Dr. Mills," Miss Watterling said firmly, "give me that immediately. I'll give it to Dr. Derrick until this deluge we're caught in is over. Just forget that you ever heard of tilotoxin, Dr. Mills."

Mills handed her the package willingly. "Miss Watterling," he said as she was leaving, "let's make that twelve extra mice tomorrow for EA 44."

He had a feeling about EA 44, and with twelve mice he could push the doses up progressively to a high level.

The next day EA 44 was injected into twenty-four mice. On the following morning the six mice that had been infected and treated were dying at the same time and in the same way as the six controls. The twelve uninfected mice that had received only EA 44 appeared to be fine.

"These over here," Mills said as Hale and Caroline and Vought looked at the dying mice, "these twelve weren't infected. But they received large doses of EA 44—some of them very large indeed."

The others came over to look at the twelve healthy mice.

"Obviously the antibiotic isn't protecting, but it seems to be very nontoxic," Mills said. "Probably something in the mouse's body is inactivating it—converting it to something else before it can be effective."

"In my opinion any evidence based on testing before the drug is pure is inconclusive," Vought said.

Mills hesitated a moment. Since the last test on EA 44, something had been going through his mind, but he was still very uncertain about it. "I've been wondering," he said, "whether we should try this for a while in rats."

Hale looked at him, puzzled. "You mean put it into chronic toxicity, even though it isn't working?"

"I thought maybe large doses in a limited number," Mills said, "for a month or so—"

"What for?"

"It appears to be one of the most nontoxic drugs I've ever seen."

"But it won't even protect a mouse!" Hale said.

Even now Miss Watterling was removing two dead mice from the jar and throwing them into the garbage container.

"I know," Mills said thoughtfully, "but a mouse isn't a man. A mouse isn't a dog."

"What are you driving at?" Hale said.

"This is so potent in a test tube, but it does absolutely nothing in a mouse. I just wonder if it might be a freak—if it might fail in a mouse and still work in a man."

"Do you have any basis for this kind of thinking?" Hale said.

"Only that you can't find out everything that will happen in a man by testing in a mouse or a rat, because they're enough alike to learn a great deal, but not enough alike to learn everything. There are important differences. Maybe those differences could also affect whether a drug protects—the same as we know they influence toxicity." Mills hesitated. He was just examining this idea as a possibility, by no means convinced himself. "We know it's possible for a drug to work in animals and not work in man—so it seems that the reverse could be true, too."

"Do you know any instance where it's happened, Pat?" Will Caroline said.

"No, sir, I don't," Mills admitted. "It just seems that it would not be impossible."

"Well, I certainly don't think it should go into chronic toxicity until it's pure." Vought shot Mills a look that said he was half grateful for the suggestion and half resentful that he hadn't thought of it himself.

"Maybe you should try to cure a few rats," Will Caroline said.

"I'll try," Mills said. "But if it doesn't work in a mouse, I don't think it will work in a rat."

"Dr. Mills, I follow your reasoning," Hale said, "but I can't say it appeals to me."

"It doesn't appeal to me either," Mills admitted. "But this antibiotic is very broad-spectrum and very potent, and it appears, now at least, to be very nontoxic. Some of these mice had huge doses. It just seems that we shouldn't throw it out too quickly."

"Let me get this straight, Pat," Will Caroline said. "In putting this into chronic toxicity in rats, is your purpose to eventually put it into man—even if it doesn't protect?"

"Yes, sir," Mills said. "If high doses in rats for a few weeks or a month show it to be as nontoxic as I think it is, then you'd have to decide whether you want to put it through the regular chronic-toxicity program with rats and dogs. You'd have to do that to be certain that whether it would cure a man or not, at least it wouldn't harm him."

"It's not encouraging," Hale said, "if a mouse getting huge doses doesn't even live a few hours longer."

"No, sir, it's not," Mills agreed. "But in the test tube it's quite a remarkable drug."

Nobody was really for it, and nobody was turning it down either.

"This is something we ought to think about, Ade," Will Caroline said. "Talk it over very carefully."

As soon as the others left, Mills infected six rats and tried to protect them with large doses of EA 44.

The next morning three of the rats were dead when he arrived. The other three died before ten o'clock.

Six rats that had received only EA 44 and no infection were fine.

But to Mills's surprise, at the end of the day Will Caroline told him, rather unenthusiastically, to put EA 44 into a few dozen rats in large doses.

"Dr. Vought will make it up for you," Will Caroline said. "We won't send it to the pilot plant yet—until we see what happens." He started to leave. "Oh, yes—and it will get a name."

Over the weekend EA 44 was named Illiomycin.

TWENTY-SEVEN

MILLS REMOVED the rat from the ether chamber and cut the arteries. He was beginning the first Baramycin autopsy—on a male rat from the toxic-level group. The small immaculate room smelled of ether, and a soft morning sun, filtering through an early haze, sparkled off the scissors on the table and sliced across the white page of the record book. Mills motioned to the laboratory assistant standing beside him, a small serious young man named Frank Clarke. Mills would do the first autopsies himself, and then Clarke and the two other assistants, Mrs. Painter and Miss O'Neil, would continue the work on rats while Mills performed the autopsies on the dogs.

"The rat is dead now," Mills said. "It dies when the arteries are cut."

Placing the rat on its back, Mills took a sharp scissors and cut the body open lengthwise, cutting from tail to head. Then he cut the *vena cava*—the blood vessel returning blood to the heart—and held the opened rat under running water, letting the blood wash out into the sink. "Move quickly and get it clean," he said to Clarke. "We don't want any blood in the organs getting in the way of our examining them."

"Do you think we'll see the damage today?" Clarke said.

"We'll know in a minute. If we can't, we'll see it next week under the microscope."

The blood was washing out from red to pink under the running water. Mills glanced at Mrs. Painter and Miss O'Neil, who were sitting at a table near the window. "Before you touch the rat, check its number, Miss O'Neil—in the record book and on both jars." He was reviewing, step by step, what he had said a dozen times while he trained them. "Remember—in this work there's no margin for error. A single mix-up—calling a control a rat that received a dose, or vice versa—can throw the whole thing off."

Mills turned the rat under the water and saw that it was bled out now and washed clean. He laid it open on the counter so that its whole orderly intricate system was revealed. The heart, moistly smooth and a dark red, was still pumping. A narrow leg muscle twitched.

And instantly, in the midst of the pink, moist, orderly system that he knew so well, Mills saw the disorder.

Beside the still-pumping heart, below the deflated lungs, close to the small curved brownish-red kidney, lay the liver—grossly damaged—looking, in the rest of the body, like a hideous sore. The normally deep red color had turned a grayish-yellow. The surface, usually shiny smooth, was crusted and scarred. Normally the size of a chicken liver, it was half again as large.

With a stab of alarm, Mills viewed the scarred, discolored organ. He had known that trouble existed at the toxic level—he had known that the evidence might be visible in gross pathology, but the condition of this liver was very serious. He motioned to Frank Clarke. "Do you see it?"

Clarke nodded.

"Do you see anything else?"

Clarke looked carefully. "No—everything else looks all right."

"Everything else seems normal—at least to the naked eye," Mills agreed. "At this point in any autopsy, if you see anything that you even suspect isn't right, stop and call me. I want to see it in the body—before dissection."

Clarke looked at Mills to see how serious this liver damage was to be considered.

"This is a toxic-level rat," Mills said. "And, so far, only one."

He carried the rat to the table where Mrs. Painter would dissect it and where Miss O'Neil would weigh each organ and record the weight and slice sections. The sun had moved higher, and now it traced a narrow path into the next room, where Miss Watterling would direct two more technicians in the preparation of the microscopic slides.

Mrs. Painter picked up a scissors. Starting at the top, she cut out the thyroid gland, washed it in a saline solution and passed it to Miss O'Neil, who weighed it and wrote the weight into the record book. Then, with a razor, Miss O'Neil sliced off a thin section and dropped it into a jar. The jar contained Bouin's fluid, a fixative that would prevent deterioration of the tissue. The second jar contained formalin and was for nervous-system tissue only.

Continuing downward, Mrs. Painter cut out, in order, the thymus, the heart, the lungs, the damaged liver—which cracked a little as she lifted it out—the kidney, the spleen. As she began to cut around

408

the gastrointestinal tract, Mills saw that Miss O'Neil was slicing off a lung section and he stepped over behind her. Miss O'Neil dropped the lung section into the Bouin's fluid and picked up the yellowed cracked liver. Mills looked at the scale. The liver was almost one and a half times its normal weight, and the damage, now that the organ had been separated from the surrounding tissue, seemed even more severe. In the sunlight drenching the room, the color was a hideous bilious yellow and the surface was heavily crusted with scars.

Without speaking, Mills watched Miss O'Neil slice off a section and drop it into the Bouin's fluid. Then he looked over at Frank Clarke and said, "We'll do a toxic-level female next."

Mrs. Painter was almost finished. She had cut out the adrenals and the male reproductive organs, and now she was removing the bladder. Mills watched while she took a one-half-inch piece from the leg muscle. Then she opened another one-half-inch piece of femur and scraped out the marrow—the soft red center of bone—and cut out the femoral nerve. Working back upward, she cut out the breast bone, the epiphyses of the ribs, and then the eyes. Mills would section the brain later. To cut a fresh brain was to damage it completely.

Mills went back to the sink where Clarke waited with the female rat. He nodded to him to do this one himself. Clarke put the rat into the ether chamber for one minute. Then he cut the arteries, opened the rat, cut the *vena cava* and bled out the rat under running water, spreading the cleaned severed body out on the counter.

Mills bent over the rat and looked at the liver, enlarged and yellow and scarred, the same as the other. He examined the other organs carefully and saw no other damage. Clarke carried the rat over to Mrs. Painter. Miss O'Neil had set out fresh jars of Bouin's fluid and formalin for the second rat and checked the numbers. Mrs. Painter began to dissect the rat.

"Bring me a medium-level," Mills said. "A male."

The rat lay open on the counter, bled out and washed, clean and orderly—and damaged. Mills took a single look and his heart sank. In spite of the severe damage at the toxic level, those rats had, after all, received doses intended to damage and, finally, to kill. At the medium level he had hoped he would see nothing. In one month, at the medium level, he had hoped there would be no toxicity at all—or, if there was toxicity, that it would be so slight it would be invisible in gross pathology and might be detected only under the microscope. But in this liver there were unmistakable alterations. Mills could see the off color—not yellow-gray as in the toxic level, but not right—and he could see the texture beginning to roughen—not scabby and scarred as in the toxic level, but not soft and smooth and shiny either. This liver was not enlarged one and a half times, but he could detect a slight distention, as if it were just beginning to swell.

Mills was worried now and trying not to show it—although he had trained these people and they knew this was not good. He finished examining the medium-level male rat and carried it over to Mrs. Painter. He looked at the yellow scabby liver from the female toxic-level rat that was still in front of Miss O'Neil, still to be weighed, and then at the liver in the medium-level rat in front of Mrs. Painter and compared the color and texture. It was true that the medium-level was much better. The damage was not nearly so extreme. An untrained eye might not have noticed. Still, at the medium level, after only one month, this was disturbing and he knew it.

Clarke brought a female rat from the medium level, and opened it and bled it out. Examining it, Mills saw the same slight alterations, the barely distinguishable signs of damage.

He ordered a male rat from the therapeutic level. He put the rat into the ether chamber and waited a very long minute. He prepared it for examination, working quickly, and laid it open on the counter. He studied it carefully. Slowly his hand that gripped the counter eased open. This liver seemed undamaged. The color was right, the surface was moist and shiny, the size was normal. He took the scissors and very carefully cut out the liver and placed it on the counter. It was a deep red, smooth, healthy-looking liver.

He bled out a control and examined it, comparing the liver of the therapeutic-level rat with the liver of the control rat. They seemed identical.

Relief rushed through him, in spite of his knowing that relief was not warranted when he could see the damage at the medium level. He examined a second rat from the therapeutic level.

The sun was high and the path of light on the floor had shortened to a square patch when Mills left Clarke to continue with the rats and went downstairs to begin the autopsy on the first dog.

It was late when Mills reached home. He let the screen door slam behind him and dropped his jacket and his tie on a chair. He led Sara over to the sofa and sat in silence with his head back and his eyes closed. With the dogs, it had been the same as with the rats. He had opened the first dog and bled it out, and he had found a yellow crusted liver about eleven inches in diameter where it should have been seven or eight inches. Then instead of continuing the autopsy, he had put the dog into the refrigerator to prevent deterioration of the tissue and had proceeded to the female dog at the toxic level and then to the two at the medium level and then the two at the therapeutic level, examining only the livers. Then he had resumed the complete autopsy. Now in his mind's eye, he could still see those yellowed, scarred enlarged livers.

He opened his eyes and looked at Sara. "There was liver damage—at the medium level."

"Serious damage?"

"I could see it in gross pathology. If you can see it at the medium level after only one month, that's not good."

"Could you see it at the therapeutic level?"

"No—they looked like the controls. But damage could still show up—under the microscope."

"How long until you see the slides?"

"About a week." It would take that long for Miss Watterling to prepare them. "But even if there's no damage at the therapeutic level, this changes things. It becomes a borderline drug. Damage at the medium level in one month makes it a risk—so it will have a short and limited life. It'll be used only when nothing else will work. And soon someone will come out with a safer drug that won't involve a risk of liver damage, and then it won't be used at all."

"Yes," she said. "I can see that."

Sara sat quietly and Mills was grateful that she was not the kind of woman who enjoyed being sympathetic, who would wring her hands or mouth idiotic remarks, because any comment now would be inadequate.

He smiled at her—a disheartened smile—and said, "Woman, you're going to drive me to drink with that chilly calm."

"I know," she said. "I'm trying."

"They'll find me rolling in the gutters and they'll say, 'Why did this splendid upstanding fellow come to this sad end?'" The sun was almost gone now, and dim shadows slanted along the floor. For the first time in his life Mills felt totally drained of energy. "And I'll tell them you drove me to it with that terrible imperturbable icy calm."

"That'll be fine," she said.

He leaned back and closed his eyes again. They had worked such a long time, he thought, and the bottom could fall out so fast.

Without opening his eyes, Mills drew his wife over to him. "It's going to fail," he said. "If you can see damage at the medium level, the chances are there'll be cell damage under the microscope at the therapeutic level—and then—"

Then it would be finished.

TWENTY-EIGHT

THE LIGHTS along the dock were still turned up bright, and the night was warm and boats still rode at their moorings, but it was September now and summer was over. The dock was deserted and Tom walked aimlessly to the end and over to a corner where three posts stood, roped together. Today Mills had looked at the slides under the microscope and had found cell damage at the therapeutic level, and Tom knew that Baramycin was all over.

Its death, he thought now, had been like any other slow death that you did not accept until it happened. During the past week the toxic-level dogs had died and the first of the medium-level dogs had gotten sick—and still they had waited for the slides with a small and diminished hope, adjusted and readjusted downward, that they might have a limited drug if no longer the queen they had hoped for. Now they had seen the slides.

Tom moved up next to the post and stood with his foot on the low rail. In the bright moonlight he could see the movement of the water and the foam that washed back from the post and the yellow-white barnacles on the post below the surface of the water.

He was never good at burials. He could never find, as some people could, the words properly fitted to the shape of an ending—to make it look any better than it was or any worse. Soon enough, he knew, there would be too much talk. Every step would be reviewed—the corpse would be circled with a strong light and re-examined from every angle in a ritualistic tribute to the loss. And soon enough, too, he knew, there would be too much talk with Diana.

He turned and looked at the lighted houses along the beach and wondered whether she had come tonight for the final showdown. Or had she stayed away to let her absence argue for her—and the emptiness of his house and the emptiness of his bed? He had not gone home—something in him wanted to be alone, for a while anyway—maybe to make friends with one death at a time. His eyes went again to the lights far down the boardwalk. He might as well have gone home—she was with him here. One loss mixed with the other, and his thoughts moved back to Baramycin.

It was just after lunch today when Will Caroline and Mills had come in to tell him. He had been working in the laboratory, helping Moose prepare some plates for Wentner's paper chromatography, and he had just inoculated the warm agar, he remembered, when the door opened. He looked around and knew at once why they had come. In his office they talked about it for a few minutes—briefly enough, but still more than was necessary. At the beginning there was always too much to talk about—but what was there to say at the end?

Then Mills left and Will Caroline stayed a little longer. For a minute Will just looked through the glass at Moose, who was beginning to pour the liquid agar into Wentner's plates lined up on the counter. Then, in a matter-of-fact voice, he said, "Have you anything else coming along, Tom?"

"Nothing unusual," Tom said. "Only tilotoxin—that culture that Mills ordered from Texas."

"Is it any good?"

"Mills is interested in an oral drug for t.b.—that's why he wrote for it—but I don't think it's much. It's very erratic. Sometimes it tests out more active than other times, but never as active as that Texan reported it. I'm beginning to wonder about it a little."

"Wonder—how?"

"I think there might be more than one antibiotic in there. No one ever got it pure enough to find out."

In the laboratory Moose tilted a plate, gingerly, to spread the agar without sending it slopping over the edge, and Will Caroline watched him, curious. "What's he doing there—with those plates? What are they for?"

"Those are for Wentner's paper chromatography."

Then, as though Baramycin had not just died, Tom explained paper chromatography—that different kinds of penicillin or streptomycin traveled at different rates up the paper and so stopped at different places and took different shapes—and Will listened, interested.

"Kind of like a fingerprint, isn't it?" he said.

"I hadn't thought of it that way," Tom said. "I suppose you could say that."

"Each one just a little different," Will said. "That's like a fingerprint." He started to leave. "Try to bring tilotoxin along if you don't turn up something better, Tom. It'd be a good idea, if we can arrange it, to have something promising soon."

Tom walked out to the laboratory with him, and as they passed Moose, Will stopped to watch again. "I don't know why this idea appeals to me," he said. "I guess it amuses me that these antibiotics have their chemical fingerprints. I'm always amused to find our so-called human laws are not exclusively ours."

Then he left, and Tom realized that not a word of regret over Baramycin had passed between them. Not once had Will spoken of their hopes that only a week ago had been so high.

Now, standing here on the empty dock, Tom thought that probably their hopes would never fly quite so high again. Always now there would be Baramycin to remember—the work, the struggle, the wildfire kind of hope—and then the abrupt and total failure.

He looked at the lights of Enright, bright across the bay on this sharply clear, calm night, and sat on the low rail and picked up a piece of rope. He looked at the softer lights from the houses along the shore.

Then suddenly, for the first time in months, memories of his father came vividly into his mind. He saw him as he always saw him —an empty-eyed, motionless figure, sitting in his tall chair. He remembered the way his father had sat out his life in that chair, after he had let failure crush him. He remembered, too, the way his mother would look at him, with guarded eyes, concealing emotions she chose not to show. Tonight Tom understood what years ago he had not—that for his father there had been only one failure, but that for his mother there had been two, and that it was not the first that had troubled her. At his father's financial failure she had gathered her wits and her resources, and she had intended to survive— and she had expected his father to do the same—and his father had not. Under fire he had not stood—he had turned and run, not to fight another day but not to fight at all.

Why does it hurt so, Tom thought, when someone you love fails you in just that way? Is it because you want so much to be able to go on loving them? Or because they are so much a part of you that you feel diminished by their lack? Or because at their failure something goes out of you and you are empty? Why? In the dark he leaned back against the post and felt emptiness run through him. Why does a boy hurt when his dog turns tail and runs?

Tonight, Tom thought, because he loved Diana, for the first time he could feel a small sympathy for his father's anguish. But much more, because of Diana, he could understand his mother's.

And yet, with Diana, he had known from the start that it would be like this. All the time that he had evaded it, had not talked about it or thought about it, he had known that for Diana there was no going forward from failure. And whatever else we felt, he thought, that had to come between us.

He picked up the rope again and tied a knot in it while his mind worked back to Baramycin. Baramycin—that took four and a half months of our time, four and a half months we couldn't afford to give. Time is important, he thought. Every day you read more and more about antibiotics. Every day more people are becoming aware of them, more people are working on them and time is running out. And we wasted too much on Baramycin—which was never any good. It's true, he said to himself. It was a dud from the first day I touched it. Nothing about it came easily. It never grew as it should —the microbe was a miser, and it stayed that way to the end. It never handled as it should. From the start it was tough to get out —and it stayed that way to the end, too.

And yet Illiomycin grows like a dream—handles like a charm— protects nothing.

He untied the knot and started another. We never ring the bell, he thought—there's never one that's everything it should be. Always there is something that says no, this is not the one. Baramycin didn't say it just once—it said it a dozen times, in a dozen different ways. It fought us every inch of the way. And maybe—Tom tugged at the rope until it dug into his hands—maybe we shouldn't have argued with it so much. Maybe we should have taken no for an answer sooner.

He dropped the rope and it fell to the water and he got up to go home. We're doing it wrong, he said to himself as he walked down the dock. We're not getting anywhere. Nothing has come out of this yet—not even understanding—and by now it should have. We have to change things, do it differently. Only what should we change —and how?

He reached the steps and didn't see Diana in the dark until she spoke.

"Hello," she said. She looked up at him from the first step where she was waiting—sitting straight with her legs tucked under her. "I've been looking for you."

She stood up and touched his hand and moved into his arms, and all the feelings that he had held so tightly controlled rushed through him and he felt unbelievable gratitude and love because he needed her tonight and she was here, not with demands, but with love and with silence. His arms closed about her, and he knew that he had never loved her so much as now.

"Sweetheart," Wentner said to the waitress, "I'll have pot roast, mashed potatoes, gravy, peas—"

At the end of the table Metcalf and Weir had been talking soberly. Now Weir looked around. "What are you celebrating, Wentner?"

"George, my boy," Wentner said, "in times of trial, look to the small comforts. Remember that."

Weir snorted, and seeing Tom smile, he said, "What's so funny, Cable?"

Tom looked at Weir without answering and then let his eyes travel around the dining room. Defeat was everywhere today. You could hear it in the silence so that every clink of a dish sounded across the room. You could see it in Morrissey's nervous eyes and in the drained, greenish color of Harrup's face and, here at this table, in Gates's own special brand of depression as he toyed with his food. Weir and Metcalf were talking again.

"The way I see it," Metcalf said, "you play on the losing team long enough, you get the label."

"Christ, you don't have to convince me," Weir said.

"You get known as a loser and nobody wants you—you know what I mean?"

Impatiently Tom looked away.

"A little thing like this doesn't bother you, eh, Cable?" Weir said.

Picking up the menu, Tom glanced at Wentner beside him. "Did something happen here before I sat down?" he said in a low voice, "or are these happy faces in honor of the occasion?"

"Right-o," Wentner said. "The latter—obviously."

"Ah'd like to take this opportunity to remind you gentlemen," Derrick said, "that our department is still in business. We've been the fo'gotten men these last few months an' in our own admirable quiet manner we've developed some mighty interestin' cultures."

Gates looked at Derrick and sighed.

"Ah'm gettin' such a pileup, if you fellows don't take 'em off my hands, ah'm goin' to have to request larger quarters."

"That's a riot, Derrick," Weir said.

Then Mills came to the table and said cheerfully, "Tom, where's my tilotoxin? We're waiting for you, man. We've got a special t.b. area set up—Miss Watterling had herself inoculated—and no tilotoxin. What're you doing, there, boy—leaning on your shovel?"

Tom laughed. "Your tilotoxin is nothing but a sinister plot to confuse my addled brain."

"Miss Watterling was pretty damned gallant about it, Tom. Hell, man, you owe it to Miss Watterling to see that her inoculation wasn't in vain."

"You're a riot today, Mills," Weir said.

"I'm even thinking of inoculating Freddie so he can join us when the time comes. Old Fred likes to be where the action is."

"Who's Freddie?" Weir said.

Tom suppressed a smile, and because he knew who Freddie was, he changed the subject. "I don't think tilotoxin is just a single antibiotic, Pat," he said. "It's so erratic I think it's a couple of antibiotics, and at least one of them is pretty temperamental. And neither is much good."

Mills thought a minute. "That would explain a lot, Tom."

"Or at least two different kinds of the same antibiotic—like streptomycin—one more active and potent than the other."

"Ho—I could tell you a few things about that," Wentner said and returned his attention to his lunch which he was enjoying enormously.

"Christ, Wentner," Weir said, with the same dark inarticulate anger, "you're eating that as though it was your last meal."

"George, for God's sake!" Gates spoke for the first time.

"Well, listen to them," Weir burst out. Angrily he looked around the table. "What's the matter with you guys? Who do you think you're kidding? 'Where's my tilotoxin?' Your tilotoxin'll be a bust just like Baramycin—and like Illiomycin—and like all the others."

"Illiomycin isn't over yet," Mills reminded him.

"Only for you, Mills," Weir said. "Christ, you guys kill me! You're dead and you don't know it. Don't you see what's happened here?"

"George, everyone knows what happened," Gates said wearily. "They've got a right to feel as they please about it."

418

"All right—" Weir turned on him—"do you still think this can be done?"

Gates sighed. "No—I don't think it can be done."

"All right, then." Weir looked angrily around the table. "Listen —you know how long this thing has to live? Until the next meeting—that's how long. Because at the next meeting, when Brainard gets through with us, we're going to look like a pack of jackasses. So you can save your breath, Cable. And you, too, Mills."

Mills took a long look at Weir as though he were a species of animal he'd never seen before and didn't expect to identify. Then he turned back to Tom. "Are you going to drop it, Tom—tilotoxin?"

"I don't think it's much," Tom said, "but if you want, I'll fool around with it a little longer. I'm curious myself whether one antibiotic could be so erratic. I think it has to be two—at least two."

"Good," Mills said, with a fresh burst of exuberance. "I'll tell Miss Watterling to be patient. Her inoculation has not been for naught. I'll tell Freddie to be patient, too."

"Who in hell is Freddie?" Weir said.

"Freddie's his pet mouse," Gates said. "He has a pet black mouse who sits on the counter near him while he works. He calls him Freddie."

"Short for Frederick the Great," Mills said. "There's something regal about Freddie."

Weir's face went a dark red, and he scraped back his chair and stood up.

"Sit down, George," Gates said. "George, sit down."

"Listen, Mills, you bastard—"

"George, Mr. Caroline's coming."

Weir whipped around as Will Caroline came up behind him.

"Excuse me, George. Are you coming or going?" Will Caroline said.

Weir sank down again, and Will Caroline took a chair for himself from the next table. "Tom—that problem you were telling me about yesterday, with tilotoxin—"

"Which one?" Tom said. "With tilotoxin, we've got a million."

"That you think it's two antibiotics. Well, I was thinking about those plates you were preparing yesterday for Wentner here—for paper chromatography—and I was wondering—couldn't you use that to find out?"

"Oh, good Lord!" Wentner put down his fork.

"Wouldn't it work?"

"I've lost my appetite." Wentner pushed away his plate. "You can send me to a home for deteriorating chemists. I've been listening to them chewing around this problem for half an hour and I didn't think of it!"

"Then it might work?"

"Why not?" Wentner said. "We might have to fool around to get the right solvent system—my God, I must be slipping more than I thought possible."

"You can move over, Brew," Tom said. "I didn't think of it either."

"Let's try it," Will said. He stood up and moved back his chair. "How long before we'll have an autopsy on an Illiomycin rat?" he said to Mills.

"About two more weeks," Mills said.

Weir jerked his head as Will Caroline left. "And he's another," he said. "Brainard'll make such a jackass out of him."

Mills looked up and grinned. "Shoo, George," he said. "There's an old saying among my bandit ancestors. He who would make a jackass out of his fellow man often gets kicked in the teeth."

"Hah," Weir said.

"A-ah, there's nothing in it any more," Metcalf said. "There's nothing in it for any of us. . . ."

Its number was EA 28, and it was Cable's. Mills injected it into six mice and they lived through the first five minutes. After ten minutes they began to lacrimate and salivate, and in an hour their white fur was drenched and matted from head to foot, and they were trembling. By midafternoon they were dead.

The number was EA 53, and it was Metcalf's. The mice developed diarrhea and died.

The number was EA 109, and Weir had been working on it for nearly two months before he discovered that it was streptomycin.

The number was EA 46, and it was Cable's, and the mice died in Mills's hand.

It was like a merry-go-round that had gone full circle and stopped, Will Caroline thought, and they could see that they were back where they started—and that was what was wrong with them. A merry-go-round with horses that went up and down and they had been riding high with the music blaring, and they had reached for the brass ring and missed. Now the ride was over, and they could look around and see that they had gotten nowhere—that nothing had changed.

And some of them were on horses that were way down and they wanted to get off. The music had stopped and the motion had stopped and the horses were low on the ground, and they wanted to step off and walk away.

And some horses had stopped higher.

And some had been low and were starting to go up again.

And some clamored on their horses and said, Pay another dime and start it going again!

And some said, in the fashion of a frugal woman, If you had saved the dime, you would have it still—I told you so, but you insisted—or if you had spent it sensibly, you would have something to show for it, but you wasted it and now you have nothing.

And some said, I wasn't eager to try it at first. I didn't think I'd like it, but now I want another ride.

And some had been frightened from the start and had needed someone to stand beside them.

And on some merry-go-rounds, between every five or six horses, there are benches that stay on the floor, so that you can ride without going up and down—and there are some who prefer that.

And there are some who don't like merry-go-rounds unless they can run them.

And some who just don't like merry-go-rounds.

"Charlie, do you think we'll be able to go back soon?" Kate said.

Derrick looked up from his dinner. "As a winner or a loser?"

"You know nothing good has happened—to make any winners."

For a long moment Derrick looked at the tablecloth and straightened his knife and lined up the spoon next to it. "I couldn't quit, sugah," he said, and looked up.

Her disappointment showed and Derrick felt the twist of remorse, as he always did, whenever this came up.

"Kate, ah'd like to explain how ah feel about times like this," he said at last, "times when everything's gone wrong. In our lab we turn out thousands of cultures, and ah don't work any harder on one than on another—ah don't develop any more feelin' for one than for another, except maybe if one comes along that looks really good, even on our plates, then ah'm interested in it. But ah don't invest the agony in them, tryin' to make them grow or get them out. Ah don't have any sleepless nights worryin' about them, the way Cable does—or the chemists. Ah don't have to tell anyone things aren't getting any better, the way Pearly does—or tell a man who's invested months of work that the mice just die an' die an' still die. By the time an antibiotic gets to mice, it's just a stepchild to me— ah've almost forgotten it. So ah feel that when things take a downward turn—as they've done right now—an' they're not pickin' up—"

Derrick paused. This was something that had been on his mind a great deal lately. At odd moments he would catch himself thinking about it—in the dining room, at the Monday morning meeting, or just looking up from his work and seeing someone walking down the corridor a little slower than usual, looking discouraged.

"Ah feel the least ah can do is to be optimistic—tell them ah have lots more interestin' cultures—urge them to get busy on them because maybe there'll be something excitin' in these. An' why not?" He looked up. "Out of hundreds of cultures why couldn't there be a good one—why not more than one? You know, sugah, sometimes all it takes to get an engine runnin' again is just gettin' it turned over and started. All it takes to start walkin' again is that first step —an' then the second comes easier. An'—well—everything with this work starts with me. Ah have the supply. An' ah'm the one who was spared—an' ah figure ah have no right to complain an' be depressed. Ah'm the one who should be pushin' an' urgin' an' coaxin' them to take that first step."

Derrick paused again. There was more that he wanted to say— not to reprove her but because he felt it would help her. He fooled a minute with his fork and put it down again.

"An' in a way you're spared, too, sugah," he said. "Ah don't mean to criticize—but you know Pearly sees an awful lot of disappointments an' Madeline has to hear about them. An' Pat sees the mice die an' Sara's bound to hear about some of that. An' all the others have their bad times an' they're bound to bring some of it home. But ah don't have those bad times—you an' I don't have sleepless nights—an' ah feel that maybe when you're talkin' to the others, you ought to try to be optimistic, too—"

He broke off. She was looking at him now with that special wideeyed look of hers and he knew that to her he had become a hero again, and his speech, which was something he felt deeply, had become a soliloquy.

"Charlie," she said emphatically, "I think they're terribly lucky to have you over there, and I think someone should tell them so!"

Derrick grinned. "Ah'll do that, sugah," he said. "The next time there's a pause at the Monday mornin' meetin' ah'll tell them."

Wentner put a drop of tilotoxin on the bottom margin of a piece of filter paper. An inch away along the margin he put a drop of streptomycin as a control—to be sure that everything was working properly, that the organisms on the test plate were growing, that they had not become resistant. He hung the paper into the piperidine solution in a jar. When the solution had climbed to the top, he took the paper out and dried it and placed it for half an hour on a seeded agar plate and incubated the plate overnight. In the morning he held the plate up to the north window, directing it against the dark background of a brick ledge of the building to see it better. The streptomycin had moved a few inches up the sheet, and there was a large slightly elongated spot where it had stopped. The other spot, which was tilotoxin, was smaller, and it was still at the bottom margin—still at the starting point. Tilotoxin had not moved.

"If it didn't work, it's because the solvent system is wrong for this antibiotic," Wentner said to Will Caroline. "I'll try again."

"What does that involve?"

"It could be just a simple variation of this system, or it could require something altogether different that will take a little time to work out. It's trial and error—this is pretty new and there's not much yet to guide us."

Wentner tried two other systems. Then two more. Each time streptomycin moved up the paper. In the different systems it moved at different rates and the spots took different shapes, but each time streptomycin moved. And each time tilotoxin stayed stubbornly at the starting point, refusing to budge.

Mills took a rat that for a month had received very large daily doses of Illiomycin, and put it into the ether chamber. Then he opened it, cut the *vena cava*, and bled it out.

The rat lay open before him, moist and clean, heart beating, leg muscle twitching. He examined it carefully from head to tail—

liver, heart, kidneys, gastrointestinal tract, reproductive organs, bone structure. He stepped aside to let Frank Clarke examine it and then looked again himself.

After a month of extremely high doses, this rat showed not the slightest evidence of damage from Illiomycin.

Mills carried the rat over to Mrs. Painter to begin dissection for the preparation of the slides. But already he realized that Illiomycin, which was potent and stable and broad-spectrum, also appeared to be one of the most nontoxic antibiotics he had ever seen.

Its number was EA 117 and Cable sent it to Mills and the mice died in the classic style. Within a minute they developed convulsions and rose up on their hind legs and then began to dig, and in four minutes they were dead.

September slipped into October, and the merry-go-round was not moving. The music was not even starting up.

PART FIVE

OCTOBER –

DECEMBER 1947

I T WAS a hussy of a day, startlingly clear, with a bold blue sky and flaming orange and gold trees and those that had not yet turned still a flashy green in the brilliant sunlight, and Brewer Wentner was in a very bad mood. He had been up most of the night because four of his six children were sick and now this morning, with a dull tired ache behind his eyes, he looked at the paper chromatography plate, holding it up to the north light. He was puzzled and disheartened and beginning to feel ornery. Six times now he had tried to make tilotoxin move, and today's results were like all the rest. The streptomycin control had moved up the sheet—in this last solvent system it had moved just above the center of the sheet and had taken a narrow elongated shape—but tilotoxin had stayed at the bottom.

Wentner wondered why he was still bothering. It was only an academic interest now. Cable had given up working on tilotoxin, convinced that it wasn't much good, and nobody else had picked it up. Nobody cared about it any more. For that matter, Wentner thought, nobody seemed to care much about anything any more. Dr. Harrup was worried about his ulcers and today he was out sick. Dr. Morrissey was practically having a nervous breakdown. Wherever Wentner went in the building, it seemed—to the cafeteria, to the assay laboratory, over to Max's laboratory, to the men's room—he would run into Morrissey hurrying down a corridor. The two biochemists that Wentner usually worked with, Metcalf and Weir, had become extra meticulous, but not because they cared. And Cable was pushing his cultures through so much faster—doing less work on each, giving them up sooner—that Wentner wondered whether even he still cared as much.

He put down the plate and decided to go over and talk to Max. In the corridor he passed Morrissey moving along at a steady clip.

"The guy's turned into a track man, for God's sake," Wentner said to Max. "He's become a compulsive walker."

"When he's not walking, he's asking questions," Max said. "His department hopes he'll keep walking."

"What kind of questions?" Wentner looked out the window. He

wasn't going to get a damn thing done today, he could tell.

"Tom says he's in there ten times a day asking questions. Tom's technician is mixing a broth—Morrissey says, What's he doing? Tom throws one out—Morrissey says, Why are you throwing it out? Tom says, It's no good. Morrissey says, Why is it no good? Tom says, It's poison. Morrissey says, Oh, and takes off on the next lap."

Wentner looked at the bright sunlight drenching the brilliant fall colors. "It's a hell of a day, isn't it, for everything to be so lousy?"

Max laughed.

"It's like a gorgeous and not too well-bred beauty with blue eyes and red hair and orange lipstick and gold bracelets, dressed in shimmering green chiffon—and she has a sassy walk, you can be sure of that." He turned away from the window. "It's a tantalizing thought but not today."

"Go take a walk in the corridor," Max said.

Wentner went downstairs for coffee and found Mills and Derrick there.

"You get your tilotoxin traveling yet?" Mills said.

"Tilotoxin's a home girl. She doesn't travel."

"Dr. Harrup has a fine suggestion," Derrick said. "He wants us to screen all the cultures over again, now that we know more. He has a feeling we might have missed something last time around."

"Good," Wentner said unenthusiastically.

"Ah told him to wait until we knew still more. Ah said we don't really know much now, an' he agreed with that—just a bit too quickly, ah thought."

"I've been thinking of hiring a plane," Mills said.

"Take Morrissey for a ride—get him out of the corridors."

"We're not finding it in the ground. Why not try the air? We could put a vaseline slide over the vent—collect spores that way." He brightened. "I think I'll do that. You like that idea, Charlie?"

"It's one of the better ones around here lately," Derrick said.

"How about plants?" Mills said. "I have a friend who collects rare imported shrubs. Maybe we should pay him a visit."

Wentner went back to his laboratory, and his wife called to say that the doctor had been there and the four children had chicken pox. He picked up the paper chromatography plate and looked at the tilotoxin spot right down on the starting line. "Why in hell don't you move?" he muttered.

His technician looked around.

"Four of my kids have chicken pox, Miss Eberle," he said. "I may get it."

"Haven't you had it?"

"Oh, probably. But everything considered, I'd just as soon get it again." He ought to give up on tilotoxin. But it bothered him because somewhere, he knew, there was a system to make tilotoxin or anything else move.

After a while he wandered over to Max's laboratory again and found Cable there, too.

"You still roaming around?" Max said.

Wentner shrugged. "I'm thinking of doing a few laps with Morrissey." He leaned on the windowsill and stared at the bank of flaming trees. "The truth is I'm thinking of getting chicken pox— just to get away from tilotoxin." He glanced around. "I interrupt something here?"

"No—I just came across a kind of far-out new technique." Cable held out a journal. "You want to see it?"

"Some other time. Today I wouldn't understand it." His thoughts went back to his own problem. "Streptomycin climbs like a rose. Six different systems, and every time streptomycin moved. It moved a different distance in each system, but in every one of them it moved. And tilotoxin sits there like a clod." Wentner shrugged. "Anyway, one thing is certain. Nobody will ever work on tilotoxin a couple of months and suddenly come up against the good news that it's streptomycin. I'll guarantee that."

Cable laughed and bent over the journal again.

"If anybody wants a written guarantee that tilotoxin definitely, positively, beyond any doubt, is *not* streptomycin, I'll give it to him. If you run into anybody who happens to want that particular guarantee, I'll sign it. Tilotoxin is not streptomycin. There is positively not one drop of streptomycin—"

He stopped. A small shock skittered through him. For a moment Wentner just stood there with his mouth open. "Oh, *no!*"

Cable and Max glanced up from the journal.

"Did you hear what I said?"

"I'm sorry, Brew," Max said.

"Tilotoxin is positively *not streptomycin.*"

Max and Cable looked up, puzzled.

"Tilotoxin is *not streptomycin, and I can guarantee it,*" Wentner said. "*With paper chromatograms!*"

429

Slowly Max and Cable straightened up.

"Paper chromatography could tell you that with *any culture*—that it *is not streptomycin,* or that it *is streptomycin!*"

Cable closed the journal.

"Think!" Wentner said. "Think what we can do with this! How many times has streptomycin slipped past us? How many hours have we wasted fooling around with it? How many times has that son of a bitch Brainard put the needle into us because of it? Well—why not test your cultures with paper chromatography—test them before you waste time on them?"

Wentner rocked with excitement, and his chins rippled against his collar. "Oh-ho! I knew this was a beautiful tool—I fell in love with it from the start. Now I know why! My God, when I think that this has been lying around under my nose!"

"Don't go away," Cable said, hurrying toward the door. "Don't get chicken pox."

"Where are you going?"

"I'm going to get some broths. We're wasting time."

"We'll need plates, Tom," Wentner called after him.

"They'll be ready." Cable stopped in the doorway. "How in hell did we go all this time without seeing this?"

"And, Tom"—Wentner rocked and chuckled—"if you run into old Brainard, give him the good news. Tell him the party's over."

Wentner prepared the piperidine solution, and Miss Eberle sewed the hems in the filter papers. Moose put the plates into the autoclave, and Tom hurried down to assay to borrow some agar. He selected fifteen cultures and brought the broths down to Wentner. Putting five broths and a streptomycin control onto each sheet, Wentner put them into the piperidine solution. Then, so that all results could be double-checked, he prepared a second system that he had developed while he was working on tilotoxin and put all fifteen broths into that, too.

It was late afternoon when Wentner took the papers that were hanging on glass rods between chairs in his office, where he had left them to dry, and placed them on the seeded agar plates for half an hour. It was six o'clock when, at last, he put the plates into a constant-temperature oven to incubate overnight.

Then he remembered that his children had chicken pox and that

430

his wife was probably tired, and that he had slept only an hour and a half last night and probably would not sleep much tonight.

The sun was down and daylight was nearly gone as he walked to his car, and he looked at the muted colors of the distant trees, soft burnished golds against the pale sky, and he thought, What a hell of a day this turned out to be!

In the morning Wentner held the plates up to the north light with the ledge of the building for a dark background.

Of the fifteen broths, six appeared to be streptomycin. Three others had not moved in the first system, but in the second system they had climbed far up the sheet and the spots stretched from the center, almost to the top. They were not streptomycin, but whatever they were, they were the same.

"You sure it's not streptomycin B?" Tom said.

"It didn't move in System One," Wentner said. "Any streptomycin would have moved. And in System Two it moved faster than streptomycin. The spots are higher."

"Maybe it's streptothricin," Cable said. "That's the second most common culture—and there are three of these out of fifteen."

"Right!" Wentner said. "Probably just what it is! I'll get streptothricin from Gates and run these three again to find out. We should do this to eliminate streptothricin, too. We should have thought of that."

"If they are streptothricin," Tom said, "you've eliminated nine out of fifteen cultures. That's pretty fancy cutting."

"Ho-ho, this is beautiful!" Wentner said. "Isn't it beautiful?"

By the end of the first week they were thinking of paper chromatography as a tool to eliminate both streptomycin and streptothricin. During the second week Wentner began to test several other "knowns"—including penicillin, actinomycin, Baramycin—running them in the two systems he was already using, working out still other systems, making copies of all his results and comparing them.

"We're getting better all the time!" he said one morning. "I've been working with six other knowns besides streptomycin and streptothricin—and as of today every one of them has moved."

Beaming, he held up his latest plates to the north light, and Max and Cable came over to the window. Derrick and Weir were here, too, and Derrick looked over Cable's shoulder.

"Jeez, Wentner," Weir said, "I think you've flipped your lid over this thing."

"Listen—I've been thinking." Wentner rocked with excitement. Wentner was continually excited these days. "Why not apply this technique to all active cultures before you work them up—shoot the works—take 'em all—run 'em all through? What do you think?"

"Man," Derrick said, "if you can make it work, you'll be breaking one of the biggest bottlenecks of all time!"

"Ho—it'll work, all right!" Wentner said. "We're learning more every day. Another month and we'll have a nice little business going here!"

"You're dreaming!" Weir said. "You're not going to break any bottleneck with this thing!"

"Yes, we will, George. We'll eliminate all the knowns at the start."

Weir snorted. "Don't make book on it."

"I'll give odds!"

"Wentner, you're drunk!"

"Oh, George, boy, talk about glass houses—" Wentner murmured.

Weir flushed angrily and looked over at Cable, who was still examining the plates. "Christ, Cable," he burst out, "what do you think you're going to see there looking so long—dirty pictures?"

There was a gasp from the doorway and they turned to see Morrissey advancing into the room. "What's going on here?"

"We're making such great progress with this paper chromatography," Wentner said. "We're just considering how we can work it into the program."

"Are you referring to paper-*partition* chromatography?" Morrissey said.

"Yes, sir," Wentner said.

"Then use the correct name," Morrissey said. Then, suspicious, "What do you think you're going to do with it?"

"We could test for all knowns with this," Wentner said, "and eliminate them at the start. Incorporate this into the program as a regular step."

Morrissey was shocked. "In the field of antibiotics," he said, "paper-partition chromatography has been proved effective *only* in separating different kinds of the same antibiotic—different kinds of penicillin, different kinds of streptomycin. Nothing else."

"Yes, sir," Cable said. "This is a great find."

Morrissey stared and then turned and darted to the door.

432

Puzzled, Wentner looked after Morrissey a minute and then he said, "Why don't we try it with another dozen or so broths? See how many knowns we can identify—see if any of them are together in one system and apart in another—find out our margin of error?"

"I'll get them," Derrick said.

"Miss Eberle," Wentner said, "can you sew us a few hems?"

At the door Derrick stopped as Harrup came in, obviously agitated, and then, behind him, came Vought and Morrissey. Then Mills passed the door and saw the crowd and came in, too, to find out what was happening.

By the time Will Caroline arrived at Wentner's laboratory, in answer to Morrissey's urgent call, nine men were there, arguing heatedly, and Will could see that a fair-sized storm had blown up.

"I've seen these crackpot schemes before," Morrissey was saying as Will came into the room. "Whenever the going gets rough, someone always comes up with a half-baked idea to cut corners—something wild like this."

"Absolutely right," Vought said. Then he saw Will Caroline. "We'd better stop this little adventure right away. This is hardly the time for jokes."

"Jokes!" Cable said. "This works!"

"Ho—you bet it does!" Wentner said. "Every time we run these chromatograms, we find plenty of streptomycin and plenty of streptothricin. And when we really get rolling, you'll be able to send us anything and say, 'Is this a new substance?' and we'll be able to answer the question for you—yes or no."

"Never," Vought said. "It'll never work."

On the counter Will noticed several empty paper-chromatography jars and a few stacks of plates. In Wentner's office, the door closed against the smell, he could see a few chromatography sheets hanging from the glass rods between two chairs to dry. In a far corner of the room, Wentner's technician was sewing. Gradually the group edged over to Will.

"It's too unreliable," Harrup said. "I don't trust it!"

"Exactly—I don't trust it either," Morrissey said. "That's just the way I feel."

"It all depends on the solvent system," Wentner explained. "If the antibiotic is soluble in the system, it will move."

"You couldn't move tilotoxin," Weir put in.

433

"Oh, yes, we did! We finally moved it. It wasn't two antibiotics, it was three. All very weak!"

"All right, then—it took you a month to do it. You going to spend a month on every culture?"

"Not at all!" Wentner said. "We learned from tilotoxin. Why, we could write a book on what we learned from tilotoxin! We should be grateful to it for being so tough."

"Right!" Mills said. "Shoo—when I look at what came out of tilotoxin, I think I should send for a few more cultures I've been reading about. Who knows what might come out of them?"

"Mills, you read too much," Weir said.

"There's more to read lately," Mills said. "Haven't you noticed?"

"That's true." Cable looked up, as though Mills had touched a nerve.

"Don't change the subject." Vought said impatiently.

Will Caroline smiled to himself. It was always the same. Whenever something new came up, two teams formed, always with the same men on either side. And always one side said it would never work and the other side said it was great. The truth, Will thought, was usually somewhere between the two. Well, he'd better listen to the arguments, although he was certain that he was not going to stop these experiments—not yet, anyway.

"There are two very serious faults with this technique," Vought said. "First, it's not one hundred per cent reliable—you don't even claim that it works every time."

"What technique does?" Cable said.

Vought ignored him. "Second, for this purpose, it's unproven—and therefore can't be taken seriously by anyone with respect for scientific attitudes and for his work."

"You see, I told you," Morrissey said. "Nobody has proved it works."

"*We're* proving it!" Wentner said.

"Not to me," Vought said.

"Here—look at these plates."

But Vought never engaged in lengthy arguments. He liked to issue final statements and preferred to deal only with the top. Now he turned to Will Caroline. "This is dangerous," he warned. "This could threaten the entire program."

Wentner was perplexed because Vought refused to understand,

434

but Cable's temper was rising fast. "The only threat around here is the threat to stop this," he said. "For more than a year we've been wrestling with this bottleneck. This will open everything up."

"It can't be that good," Harrup said.

"It's the best thing that's happened to us," Cable said. "We're in a race, and every hour that we waste working on a known puts us farther behind. And this race is getting tighter every day. Mills is right when he says there's more in the literature. There's a lot more. A year ago you had to comb the journals to find anything at all about antibiotics. Now suddenly they're full of it. And that means that more people are working on them."

"Then at least we might get some reliable information," Morrissey said.

"But everyone else is getting that information, too," Cable reminded him. "And everyone is getting approximately the same soil samples. We don't have a single edge over the others in this race. This is the greatest advantage we've had yet."

"Disadvantage," Vought said. Vought was getting mad. Tempers ran short these days when nothing went right. "You could have a great antibiotic in the palm of your hand, and if two spots happened to be in the same place, you'd throw it away!"

"If you have a great antibiotic, you'll be trying everything you can think of," Cable said. "The great ones don't turn up so often."

"It's just possible, Dr. Cable, that you won't know it right away."

"Oh, hell—if it's great, you know it!"

"Oh, do you? How? Tell me—how does that happen? Do your bones twitch or something?"

Cable grinned and nodded. "Or something."

"Ah'd just like to say," Derrick put in, "that ah'm gettin' quite a pileup of cultures, an' if this could be worked out to eliminate even the streptomycin and streptothricin, ah believe it'd be mighty helpful."

"Derrick," Weir said, "if they try to use this, there'll be a pileup here in Wentner's lab that'll make yours look like an ant heap. The mechanics of this alone will tie them up in knots. First his technician has to sew the papers—look over there—and then—"

"Tailors aren't hard to find," Derrick said.

"Then she has to wrap up every plate before it's autoclaved—"

"Why do you wrap your plates?" Derrick said.

435

"The air around here is full of penicillin dust," Wentner said. "We'd get spots all over them. We wrap them before the autoclave so they'll stay sterile after they're out."

"Find something easy—and reusable," Derrick advised.

"That's still only the beginning," Weir said. "We'll have to prepare all those plates in biochemistry—and where are we going to find the room? We don't have enough room now. And after Wentner does the papers, they have to hang around to dry. Look at them there in his office, with the door shut because of the stink. And every plate has to be incubated—where are you going to find all that incubator space? Derrick's turning out hundreds of cultures a week. You'll have a bottleneck that'll stretch from here to New York!"

"Right," Morrissey said. "Absolutely right."

"As a man accustomed to working with mass production techniques," Derrick said, "ah believe those problems can be overcome."

Happily Will Caroline folded his arms, careful not to reveal how pleased he was. This was the first time since Baramycin had failed that they'd argued like this—that anyone had cared this much about anything.

Morrissey waved a hand around the laboratory. "Dr. Weir is absolutely right," he said. "It's in the way already. All those jars—and papers and plates all over—cluttering up the labs."

"Cluttering up the labs!" Cable said. "To find out at the start whether a culture is new, I'd hang the equipment from the ceiling —I'd take it home!"

"It's taking time and space away from other things, and it's scientifically inacceptable," Vought said, as though that ended it. "It's too new."

"Yes, it's new!" Cable burst out. "And with anything new, it's always the same—there's always this inertia to overcome."

"All right, Dr. Cable!" Vought lashed back at him, very angry now. "That's an old trick—resorting to name-calling when you lack sound arguments. Only I won't let you get away with it. What you call inertia, I call keeping our heads. While you're running around like schoolboys with a new toy, some of us are managing to exercise better control. In my opinion this is part of an hysterical reaction to the failure of your Baramycin—nothing more. And if you'll pardon me, I will not be guided in identifying my cultures by this exquisitely precise technique of holding a piece of glass up against the ledge of the building between the hours of nine-thirty

436

and twelve o'clock. If you didn't have that ledge, you'd be out of business."

"Oh, I don't know," Mills said cheerfully. "We'd find something else—we're getting pretty ingenious around here."

But Vought was wound up now, and other pent-up grievances began to pour out. "I'll tell you something else, Dr. Cable," he said. "Do you know what's wrong with your work—basically? Your premise is wrong. You're always trying to assume that this can be done with less work—less information—less digging into each one. I say it needs more and more and more again." He turned to Will Caroline. "This foolish plaything won't solve our troubles. We're in trouble all right, and I'll tell you why. Because we're too limited. Because we need more of everything. More space, more help." Vought brought his fist down on the counter with each demand. "More work, more digging, more knowledge."

He looked at Cable, expecting a rebuttal, but Cable only screwed up his face into a puzzled frown. "I'm not sure," he said. "I don't know."

"Not sure of what?" Will Caroline said, and the look left Cable's face.

"No-no," he said quickly. "I was thinking about something else. With paper chromatography, I'm sure. Paper chromatography will work."

"Mr. Caroline," Vought demanded, "are you going to permit this to continue?"

"Oh, I think we have to!" Will said. "I respect your right to doubt it, Dr. Vought, but Dr. Wentner's entitled to a fair chance to prove that it works. Any man's entitled to that. And besides," he said with a smile, "I'm curious about this myself. If it does work, it'll be great."

Without a word Vought walked out of the room, and Morrissey followed.

Watching them go, Will Caroline thought that maybe they were right—maybe this would turn out to be unreliable—more a toy than a technique. Maybe Vought was right when he called it an emotional reaction to the Baramycin failure and maybe he was even right when he said that they needed more men and more space. Or maybe not. Whenever things bogged down, everyone wanted to make changes, and everyone had a different idea about what those changes ought to be, and everyone was sure he was right.

But they couldn't get more men and more space—at least not right now. And paper chromatography was here, and they were stirred up about it. For the first time in a long time, the merry-go-round was beginning to move. Maybe paper chromatography would turn out to be a great tool, or maybe it would turn out to be nothing. But this much Will Caroline knew—without movement, you didn't build up momentum, and without momentum, you didn't get far, and right now he wouldn't trade that head of steam for all the scientific attitudes in the world.

M THIRTY

ORRISSEY LAY AWAKE in bed, examining over and over again this utterly hopeless situation. His mind, like a determined rat, gnawed systematically at every detail of his problems, lest one be overlooked and rise up later to undo him. Lying still, he could feel the pressure starting again that made his head feel like a balloon inflating, ready to burst. He turned over and pressed his face into the hot pillow, and the pressure went away. In the distance a church clock chimed and he counted that it was midnight.

To Morrissey it was inconceivable that he had ever dared to hope—that once he had actually anticipated a modest glory, had imagined himself reading a paper, perhaps before an international meeting of biochemists in London or Geneva. Now he could only foresee disaster. His mind catalogued all the past problems for which he might be blamed, came up to date, and plunged on. Tomorrow—today, now—there would be a meeting about Illiomycin, to decide whether to drop it or go on. Illiomycin was out of his department now, he thought, and maybe if they went on and spent more money in another department, it would look better for him. But how could any sane man advocate spending more money on a drug that didn't protect animals?

And then there was the other problem—paper chromatography. Paper chromatography was like a monster you couldn't kill. Every day it grew bigger and they talked of nothing else, and sometimes it seemed that they were doing nothing else.

And there was a board meeting less than two weeks away.

His head was blowing up again and he turned over and it didn't help. He sat up in bed. The church clock chimed once, and Morrissey wondered whether it was twelve-thirty or whether he had fallen asleep for a while and it was one o'clock or half past some later hour. For a moment he stared at the objects on his dresser, distinct in the moonlight—his brush, his wallet, his key ring—and then he got out of bed and went downstairs.

The kitchen clock read twenty minutes to one. He rummaged in the refrigerator and spooned out a dish of applesauce and poured cream over it, and took it to the kitchen table. Then he heard Winifred padding down the stairs, and a moment later she stood in the doorway, her dull brown hair like a round mop, her dull flannel robe tied around her. Still half asleep, she moved to the sink and drew water into her coffeepot, and Morrissey knew she was going to sit up with him. He smelled the coffee as she measured it, and then she put the pot on the stove and sat down.

"Couldn't you sleep?" she said.

Morrissey shook his head. He looked at the little furrows the cream was making in the applesauce. He didn't really want the applesauce—he ate poorly these days, as poorly as he slept.

"I have to decide about Illiomycin," he said after a while. "There's a meeting tomorrow—today, now. They'll ask me for an opinion." He waited for her to tell him to decide then—but she only looked at him and waited. "I suppose I ought to stand by Tony—although I'm not sure that Tony would stand by me."

"Don't worry about Tony," she said. "Worry about yourself."

"I'd rather spend money on Tony's work than Cable's." But he couldn't think of Tony now. He couldn't afford to. He was responsible for too much money already, and his only hope was to play it safe. "I think Cable tries deliberately to upset me," he said. "I think he takes a sinister pleasure in it. Like that paper chromatography—that isn't science. It's like some fraternity prank."

"I thought that was Wentner."

"It is—and that's Harrup's department, and they're not going to unload that blame on me, I'll tell you that."

"How could they?"

"Well, Cable's involved. I questioned him about it, and he pretended to explain, but it was just a lot of double-talk to mix me up. And I'm supposed to know what he's doing—I'm the one who'll be blamed. I hate that man, Winifred. I feel I was cursed the day he walked in, and as long as he stays, it'll never be the same. He's out to get me—I know it."

"Control yourself, Claude," she said sharply. "Talk about one thing at a time. Now—what about Tony's?"

"What about it?" He sighed. "With Tony's, the question is, if it doesn't work in animals, will it work in man? I don't see why it should! But some of them are actually discussing it seriously—as though it might." He hated Mills almost as much as Cable. They were both troublemakers.

In the silence he heard the rapid *plop-plop* of her coffee in the percolator. She went over and lowered the flame. "What does Neil think about paper chromatography?" she said.

"He doesn't trust it. But I haven't really talked to Neil since then —since Baramycin failed."

"Why not?"

"I don't know, Winifred. Things aren't the same with Neil any more. I feel—well—he's sort of the enemy."

"Neil! Why?"

"Well, if it comes down to who gets blamed for what, well, I just feel that Neil is plotting against me—and it may turn out to be a matter of survival. When the board meets, there'll be a costly failure for them to look at, and they like to pin down the responsibility."

The strong smell of her coffee was beginning to fill the room. He didn't know how she could drink it at this hour—even the smell bothered him. He took out his pipe and opened his tobacco pouch and the pouch slipped out of his hand, and the tobacco spilled. He stared at it—everything went against him these days.

"Give me that," Winifred said.

While she filled the pipe, he said, "I've tried to study, Winifred —to form sensible opinions, about Illiomycin and that other thing. But there's so much—I just can't keep up any more."

"You only think you can't, Claude."

"I've tried! I don't absorb it."

"You don't absorb it because you're blocked by fear. If you'd get over the fear that you can't learn, you could keep up."

She was right about the fear. The fear was part of him now, like a parasite that had invaded his body and was feeding off him. He shuddered at the horrible thought.

"It's no harder than what you know now, Claude," she said firmly. "It's different—it's new—but it's no harder."

"I don't know—" He shook his head. "There are no facts on Illiomycin—there's no sense to paper chromatography. With paper chromatography, half the problems aren't even scientific. For instance, the glass plates—the sides fall off in the autoclave because the glue won't hold. Last week I found them in a huddle with a roofing cement salesman! Not a laboratory supply representative—a roofing cement man!"

"Maybe he had the product they needed," Winifred said.

"And there's always such confusion! One day"—he paused and drew a deep breath—"just to show you—one day I went into Ca-

441

ble's laboratory, a little before closing time—I have to keep tabs on him, he never tells you anything—and there was no one there. He and his technician were both off somewhere. And on the counter there was a note propped up so someone would see it. A note to a woman. Well, naturally, I thought—you know how he is—he's really a very low type—"

"What'd it say?" Winifred said.

"It said, 'Bessie, you beautiful creature—do you have a sewing machine?' Well, naturally, I thought there was more to this than I could see. Do you know what it turned out to be?"

"Who's Bessie?"

"Well, that's the story. Bessie is some old hag who comes in nights to clean. If she had a sewing machine, he wanted her to sew the hems on the paper chromatography papers! That's what it was all about."

Winifred went over and poured her coffee and came back with it. "Claude, there's nothing wrong with that."

"But it isn't just that! It's everything. I just feel—" He took a paper napkin and began to sweep the spilled tobacco together into a little pile. "I just feel as though the walls of Enright have fallen down and the corridors are filled with the enemy—like some medieval fortress that has fallen and the enemy rushes in and swarms all over the place. Everything is being ruined and I don't know what to do. I don't know what to do about anything—Illiomycin—paper chromatography—"

"Claude, it doesn't matter any more," she said sharply. "Don't you see—neither decision matters any more."

"It does matter."

"It doesn't, I tell you. It's almost over. As soon as the board meets, they'll end it. Use your head, Claude. The whole project has bogged down. Nothing has come out of it. That board isn't going to dump money into Illiomycin when it doesn't work. And they're not going to prolong a total failure because of paper chromatography. Even if it were a great tool, which you say it isn't, they wouldn't extend a dying project for one new technique."

He hardly heard. "Winifred, how did we let this happen? Once everything was so right. And now—"

"You couldn't have stopped it then. Now it's finished."

"Our research used to be scientific. It was systematic and predicated on reason, and the problems were problems you could solve, and you could prove that you were right. And *this*—" His voice rose. "No facts—no proof—it's nothing but guesswork. Even when they say they understand, I know they're lying. There's nothing to base understanding on—and they're liars."

"Claude, get hold of yourself!"

He sagged a little in his chair. "We had progress before—we didn't just stand still—but it was calm and orderly progress. It didn't upset anything. Now everything is in a frantic upheaval—and I don't know what lies ahead any more or where I fit into it. Winifred, what could I have done? Why did this have to happen to me?"

"Claude, will you listen? You're not listening. At the next board meeting they'll cut off the funds, and it will die. You just have to hold on a little longer. Do you hear me?"

He nodded and moved his pipe and meticulously swept up the last shred of tobacco. "Brainard feels that too," he said, a little calmer. "He's in touch with some of them, but that's confidential, Winifred. He's talked with Mr. Palmerton and with Mr. Kaiser. Kaiser was in on some of our meetings, you know, and he's quite concerned. And Mr. Palmerton didn't like it from the start."

"Good!" she said. "You see. Now—let's go back to bed."

He went upstairs and lay down again. Presently he heard the clock chime three times.

"After one month," Mills said, "if there's no damage in dogs, we could give a dose to a man—a single dose—and do blood tests to see if it's working." For half an hour they had been talking about Illiomycin, and Morrissey knew they were going to put it on the shelf. Nobody except Mills had argued for it—not even Tony, who obviously realized that there was no scientific reason for going on with it.

"Before we could give repeated doses to a human patient, we'd have to put it through the regular chronic-toxicity program," Mills said, "but it would be safe after one month in dogs to give a single dose."

"Nobody's going to give a sick man a drug that won't cure anything," Harrup said.

"I don't mean a sick patient," Mills said. "I mean give a single

443

dose to somebody who is perfectly well—then do blood tests to see whether the antibiotic is being absorbed. If it's absorbed, it will work."

"Where are you going to find a well man to take an experimental drug?" Harrup said. "Especially one acting as strangely as this?"

"You only need one dose," Mills said. "It won't be untested. We'll be putting large doses into dogs for a month. We'll do autopsies and examine the slides. There wouldn't be any danger in one dose after all that."

"How do you know?" Harrup said.

"One small dose! Shoo—I'll take it myself!"

Harrup stared as though he knew Mills had lost his mind.

"I'll take it," Mills said again. "You let me put it into dogs for a month and I'll take it."

But the truth was that nobody really believed in it. Illiomycin was quietly dying and would be quietly buried, and they would hear no more about it. This was something Morrissey understood—he had seen it before and he knew the pattern.

But then the discussion moved on to paper chromatography. This month Wentner had tested a hundred broths. He had put each one into at least two entirely different solvent systems and sometimes a third and even a fourth. Next month, he said, they would double the number of broths tested. Morrissey felt himself breaking out in a clammy sweat.

He was working out mass-production techniques, Wentner said—crowding more broths onto each sheet, more sheets into each jar.

"We want to bring this to a point where we can get the samples when Dr. Gates does and have our answer ready at almost the same time. There'll only be a delay when we have to use additional solvent systems to be sure."

More broths meant more jars, Morrissey told himself. More systems meant more jars. And more plates. More of everything—cluttering up the labs. He spoke up, interrupting Wentner. "I'm opposed to letting this go any further. It's in the way already—and now you want to do twice as much. Rushing like that, you'll make mistakes—a hundred broths—two hundred broths a month—there won't be room for anything else. I want to be on record as opposed."

He looked around the table for someone to back him up.

"Whether you look at a hundred spots a month or a thousand spots a month is of no interest to me," Vought said coldly. "I don't intend to be guided by your spots. I will continue to depend on tested scientific methods."

"Exactly," Morrissey said. "The tested proven techniques are good enough for me."

"They're not good enough!" Cable objected. "They've failed us over and over again."

"Of course, you realize," Vought said to Will Caroline, "we'll never be able to measure the loss—in time or in space—where other work could be done—or in good cultures thrown away out of ignorance."

"I won't use it," Metcalf said. "Take a chance on throwing out something good. No, sir—not me!"

"This is a comedy of errors," Morrissey said, "and it's getting worse every day—jars everywhere, papers drying all over the place —there's no room in the constant-temperature ovens because they're always full of those plates."

"They even stole the janitor's broom closet for their paper sheets," Harrup complained.

"That's next to the pipes," Cable said, and grinned. "They dry so well in there."

"All the same—the janitor couldn't get his brooms. And then they cluttered up the other pipe closet, and the fire inspector made them take them out. Then when he'd gone, they put them back."

"What!" Morrissey said.

"We figured the firemen could ax their way through those papers if they had to," Mills said.

"That's not the point," Morrissey said. He turned to Will Caroline. "You see—nothing but problems, wherever you look."

"We're solving them fast," Max Strong said.

"It does seem they're getting on top of them," Will Caroline agreed.

Morrissey's heart sank. As long as Will Caroline stood behind them, they would have their way and the confusion would continue and the clutter would increase.

"I will not accept chromatograms," Vought said firmly.

"I will not begin without them," Cable said.

The meeting was over and Morrissey stood in his office, feeling as though the trap in which he was caught had pulled tighter. Outside the sky was a heavy gray and the water looked cold, and it depressed him further to think that winter was coming and four or five dreary months lay ahead. Then an awful thought crossed his mind. What if the directors should decide to tour the laboratories while they were here? Half those labs were his responsibility, and if they questioned the disorder, what would he say?

He hurried out of his office, walked down one corridor and up another, and spied Wentner and Cable in the assay laboratory in front of the constant-temperature oven. Wentner was holding one of the chromatography agar plates carefully horizontal, and Cable was underneath it, marking the bottom with a red crayon. Miss Potter was standing nearby.

When Morrissey demanded an explanation, Gates told him that a whole batch of agar had melted in the oven and that Cable was marking the spots on the plates. Morrissey looked at the plate in Wentner's hand. The agar looked like sloppy jello, to which someone had added too much water. A large crack ran down the middle and smaller ones branched out from it.

"Okay?" Miss Potter said, as Cable stood up. "Can we get in there now?"

"It's all yours, Miss Potter," Cable said.

"You like a couple of lessons in fixing agar?" Miss Potter said.

Cable grinned. "Name the hour, Miss Potter."

By the time Morrissey left the assay laboratory, Wentner and Cable had walked down to the far end of the corridor. Morrissey saw them stop and look into the all-purpose refrigerator there and he knew immediately what they were after. Wentner had to store his samples until he used them and then hold them until all his results were in, and he was running out of refrigerator space.

Morrissey hurried up to them. "Don't think you can take this over," he said sharply. "Other people use this, and the space is carefully allotted."

Cable nodded, but Morrissey knew he would ignore the order completely. Cable ignored all authority. Basically he was an anarchist. And if he stole somebody else's refrigerator space, Morrissey would get the complaints.

After lunch, when he walked down the corridor again, Morrissey saw a porter pushing something into Cable's laboratory. It turned out to be a crude-looking metal cabinet—about three feet wide and thirty inches high and a foot deep—obviously a homemade job, made up in the shop. Inside the laboratory Morrissey saw Cable and his technician trying to fit another cabinet, just like the first, into a corner. He went inside and learned that they were going to substitute these cabinets for the paper-chromatography jars.

"We can do three or four times as many cultures in these cabinets," Cable said. "Dr. Wentner has a couple in his lab already, and we took these in here until he can make room for them."

It was too much. At last Morrissey went to Will Caroline.

"Just let me ask you something, Will," he said. "We've been friends—you and I—for a long time. I've always respected you, Will —you know that."

Will Caroline smiled and folded his arms. "What's the trouble, Claude?"

Morrissey struggled to remain calm. Never had he felt more that everything was falling apart than at this moment. "Tell me the truth, Will," he said. "Can't you see what a madhouse this has become?"

"Yes, I can see it."

"Well, aren't you discouraged?"

"No—not particularly."

Morrissey took out his handkerchief and wiped his hands. "But can't you see that in a year and a half there's been no progress?"

"Sometimes progress is hard to define," Will said. "I think there's been progress. I think paper chromatography is progress."

"Progress! Paper chromatography is chaos! It's disorderly and unscientific! This whole project is disorderly and unscientific!"

"This is a frontier, Claude. One characteristic of any frontier is disorder—a certain violence. Law and order come later."

"I don't think these men believe in paper chromatography. I think it's a trick—to look as though they're accomplishing something, now that Baramycin has failed and nothing else has come along. This whole project has been like that—tricks and chaos and failure."

Will Caroline leaned back, and Morrissey saw his long fingers tapping the desk. "Claude, a lot of what you say is true." The fingers stopped tapping. "But everything has to have a beginning, and beginnings are usually disorderly. Most of what we accept now as order, because it's been proved and organized, began with disorder. Gradually mistakes are ironed out and facts are brought together into some kind of system, and meaning comes out of the experience. Then you have order. If you could see that, this would be easier for you to understand—and to put up with."

"I don't want to put up with disorder, Will. I hope I'll never be weak enough to accept that kind of compromise. As long as I run it, my department will be orderly. I pride myself that I'm as broadminded as the next man—but this is too important. The whole meaning of Enright research is involved. I intend to fight for system and sound techniques wherever I can. Anything less will always bother me, I'm afraid."

"I know it bothers you, Claude. But out of all these new and rather bizarre ideas, one might work. And sometimes all it takes is one."

"You don't build a sound house with sloppy methods, Will. That's as old as the Bible."

Will Caroline smiled and tilted back his chair. "Claude, I don't think they're sloppy. New, yes—sloppy, no. Oh, I know—you think they are, and you're an experienced man and entitled to your opinion. You don't think these men are making progress. I do. I think they're beginning to see meaning in all this experience, and, gradually, to bring order out of chaos."

After Morrissey had gone, Will Caroline thought it was true that this project was chaotic, but it was no different from everything else. Life was chaotic—and a man had to find in it some kind of order. And he could do that in one of two ways. He could try and fail, explore and reject, question and discard, and at last forge a meaning for himself out of his own experience. Or he could accept an established order intact, complete with ideas, rules, rituals—an order already formed and approved, where nothing was questionable and nothing questioned so long as you followed the prescribed and tested rules.

These are two completely different kinds of men, Will Caroline thought, and when they are scientists, they are two completely different kinds of scientists. They have turned to science for diametrically opposite reasons. To one kind, science spells adventure—there is always something new to try—always something around the next corner to discover. And that is Tom Cable.

And to the other kind, science spells certainty because it can be tested and proved. And that is Claude Morrissey. And these are not small differences. These are entirely different kinds of people, and they are never going to get along together. In all history these two people have never gotten along. Morrissey must have his security, his absolutes, his proof—and in Morrissey's eyes, Cable is a revolutionary who threatens his whole traditional way of life. For Morrissey this is a fight for self-preservation. And it always was, Will Caroline thought. Right from the start.

Toward evening it started to rain, a cold steady rain that leaned toward winter, and Morrissey stood at the streaked window. "At first I thought I was losing my mind," he said. "Then I realized that I'm not the one who's crazy. He is."

Winifred sighed and said nothing.

"After all, everyone reliable agrees with me—not with Will Caroline," he said. "I really do think he's crazy, in a way, Winifred. There must be a name for people like that."

He looked at her for support, and she said, "He's divorced from reality. The hospitals are full of people like that."

The rain streamed relentlessly down the window and Morrissey dropped the curtain and went over and sat in his chair. "If only we'd had a few hints," he said. "Some better tests—so that it wouldn't have been such a costly failure." Fear swept over him—the fear that was a part of him now—and pushed so close to panic that he felt he could not live with it another night. He dreaded going to bed.

"They'll say we should have known—they'll say we should have found a way to know." He couldn't sit still, and he got up and began to walk around. "Of course, *they* don't know either, but they'll say it anyway. *They* don't have to know. They're free to criticize and blame and accuse without knowing. They can say, 'We don't have to know—we pay *you* to know.'"

"Claude," Winifred said, "who is *they?*"

"*They* is the company. *They* is the board. Hale—Rosswell—Palmerton. *They* is anyone who can sit back and say, 'We're paying *you* —*you* do it.'" He sat on the edge of a chair. "Winifred, it's hopeless, and I'll be blamed. In two weeks they're going to meet—and they'll examine the whole thing and—oh, my God!"

"Claude, listen to me." She came over and shook him roughly. "Listen to me, I say. Everything will be all right."

"Everything won't be all right."

"Yes, it will. You just wait this out. You won't be blamed. There are too many other people to blame."

449

She touched his shoulder, more gently now. "Claude, you only have to hold on two more weeks, and it will be all over—and everything will be all right again."

If only he could believe it. If only he could feel that things would ever be as they had been—that he would ever again be in control of his department—that his life would ever again be orderly and rational and serene. He had hoped to have these golden years of dignity and authority—in charge of an efficiently functioning unit—years that might reach a climax in a single nice piece of work for which he would be quietly respected. Now all the things he had valued and dreamed of had vanished, and he had no real hope for their return. Whatever Winifred said, he felt it would never be the same again. All the things he had hoped for and failed to get would never be.

THIRTY-ONE

I T'D STILL BE a great thing if we could do it, Ade,"
Will Caroline said. "Aside from business, it'd make us feel pretty
good."

Hale glanced up from the fireplace where he was poking at an
unburned log, moving it into the fire. Here in his den he and Will
had gone over everything that would come up tomorrow at the
board meeting. Now it was past midnight, and they were just talking. "Lots of things would be great if we could do them," he said.
"It'd be great to find a cure for cancer—schizophrenia—arthritis."

He knew what Will meant, though. This was a business problem,
but if you'd let it, it could get a hold on you, as it had on Will, and become something else—something that had nothing to do with business. "Science is today's frontier, and drugs are a part of it. On any
frontier there's plenty to be done."

"You're beginning to talk like a good research man."

"No. It's a condition I can't afford. The first rule of the frontier is
to stay alive. And not to lose your head."

Hale fussed with the fire another minute, thinking about Will. A
man could go along on a steady keel for twenty-five years and be as
sane and rational as any man alive—and then something fired his
blood like an infection, and suddenly he became a crusader.

But this was a business decision, and you couldn't let other things
mix into it. You could be interested—hell, you couldn't help being
interested—but when the time came for decisions, you stood apart.
You gave a business question a business answer. And the question
tomorrow would be: When a million dollars has produced nothing, is it sound business to go on? Or do you put your next million
where you know it will pay off?

Hale gave the fire a final poke and straightened up, and Will said,
"There's more than one way a man can lose his head, Ade. When
luck goes against him, a man can retreat from ground he's won that
he could have held."

"We haven't won much."

"I'm not so sure."

"Will! You put the reasons for staying with this on one side and
the reasons for dropping it on the other—it's a hell of an imbalance."

451

"But the worst is behind us," Will said easily. "They're not floundering so much—they've become pros. It'll make a difference."

It would be nice to think so, Hale thought. And if it was true, they had become pros at Enright's expense—a million dollars' worth of it. But was that reason enough to send another million after it?

He saw that Will was ready to leave, and he moved away from the fireplace.

"I don't suppose that with everything else tomorrow," Will said, as they walked out to the hall, "we could get out of hearing that idiot, Croft?"

Hale looked up. "You think Croft's an idiot?"

"No." Will smiled. "He's not an idiot. He's a smart boy. And very smooth."

"That bother you?"

"He gets on my nerves. Probably, I suppose, because he's my natural enemy. Whenever I look at his earnest handsome face, I have a mental picture of him parading before the board like a busty female in a bathing suit—all curls and curves—with a banner across her chest saying TRY ME!"

Hale laughed. But Will was right—that was the way it was shaping up. Aloud he said, "Everyone knows what's in that report, anyway—Brainard's been leaking it like a bad faucet."

He opened the door and stepped outside with Will. It was a clear November night, sharp and cold, and the faint smell of the fire inside hung in the air. From the porch Hale could see a light in his bedroom, and he knew that Helen was waiting up for him.

"Ade, it's worth sweating out a little longer," Will said. "It's picking up." In the dim light he turned to look at Hale. "I believe that, Ade."

Hands in his pockets, Hale nodded and hunched his shoulders. "Only we're still a business. We don't have benefactors like a foundation. We don't have rich alumni like a university. We don't have Congress to vote us another million like a government laboratory." Unhurriedly, they walked down the steps to Will's car. "Nobody helps a business that's in a jam. It's kind of like the nice girl who gets into trouble. Everyone says, 'Too bad, but she should have known better.'"

"It hasn't come to that yet."

"No. But it's not simple, either."

It wasn't simple, because as a businessman you didn't think only about the million you'd lost. You had to figure that you could have been doing something else with that time and money that would have produced a profit.

"You know—they always say research goes like a sine wave," Will said, "but that's a bad description." He stopped beside his car. "A sine wave is regular—evenly rising and falling curves. And research is full of bumps and jerks. Research blows sky-high—and then the bottom falls out and it hits the ground and drags along at rock bottom, jerking forward one step and slipping back two. Then suddenly you get hold of something and you're sky-high again."

"The decision tomorrow would be easier if they were on the way up."

"The decision won't be made tomorrow," Will said with a smile. "The decision is yours—tonight. Tomorrow depends on you." He got into his car. "I'm not thinking of financial suicide either, Ade. I think we can do this far short of that kind of trouble."

Hale hunched his shoulders again. "You're eternally optimistic, Will. I'm not sure I think we can do it at all."

Hale stood in the driveway while Will Caroline drove out to the road. He could feel that the temperature had dropped since early evening, but the cold never bothered him. Dressed in a wool shirt and a sweater, he was quite warm enough, and he stayed outside a few minutes longer.

Will was right when he said the decision would be made tonight and not tomorrow, he told himself. And then he thought that wasn't entirely accurate either. He hadn't stayed up tonight until after midnight, talking the thing out with Will and with himself, in order to reach a decision. He was still up, still outside here on this cold winter night, because he was trying to make friends with the decision already reached—reached some time ago.

Out on the water a lone lighted ship made its way slowly toward the bend in the bay, and Hale watched it and thought about the way the arguments would line up tomorrow when the board heard the research department report and then heard Croft's.

On one side there would be a split group, disagreeing among themselves about everything. And the best that their most confident and articulate champions could say would be "We're trying and we're learning—we have nothing to show yet—we can't promise anything—we can't predict the cost—we think we can do it."

And on the other side there would be a young man who obviously knew his business, who would support every statement and every suggestion with facts, figures, details, statistics and projected results. Croft was going to present those directors with one of the best-prepared reports they had ever heard. If he stressed what he could do with finished products, you couldn't blame him. That was where he could do the best job—with mass-consumption products—toothpaste, shaving cream, deodorants. Hale began to pace the driveway. That report was going to dangle very attractive bait, and a lot of the directors were going to want to change direction and go after it.

And maybe we should change, he thought. Maybe we should have gone the other way in the first place. We're a business and we have to show a profit. If a man puts his money into our company, he has a right to expect a return. And where else do we get the money to pay salaries—keep up the plant—pay for research? This million came from profit—nothing else.

He glanced up and saw the light in the bedroom, and he walked around the house to the woodpile at the side door and he brought in a few slabs to leave in the log basket and went upstairs.

A few minutes later he stood at the bedroom window, talking to Helen, while inside him the two sides still argued.

"A good line of finished products makes sense," he said. "As a matter of business, it's the saner alternative."

Helen remained silent, letting him think out loud.

Hale watched the lighted ship making its slow progress across the water. "Only we came so close."

After a minute he went over and sat on the bed. "Sometimes I think it's all those damned mice I'm always looking at. All those dogs and rats I went over to see every day during Baramycin. I should have stayed in my office—let them send me reports."

"I can imagine that!" Helen said.

Hale smiled and then, abruptly, he stood up and went back to the window. "All the same—if you go and look, you get too close to it. You get the taste of it and the feel of it. You begin to care. You can still be objective—only it's harder." He leaned a hand on the middle windowsill and fell silent.

After a while Helen said, "Ade, is the board going to decide against this tomorrow?"

"They will if I keep quiet." He saw her watching him. "The board won't decide—I'll decide."

454

"You've decided."

Out on the bay the lighted ship was just rounding the bend, and Hale saw from the pattern of the lights that it was a tanker—probably coming into the harbor with its heavy cargo at high tide.

"For the first time in my life," he said, "I'm adding up the facts—and with my eyes wide open, I'm taking the wrong answer." He turned from the window and gave a puzzled half-smile. He didn't understand it himself.

The six former presidents looked down from the walnut-paneled walls and the black ashtrays and the white pads and the yellow pencils were on the table.

The research men had already reported, and now Croft was speaking. Croft had already spread out three or four folders of plans, costs and statistics on the table. The research group had remained in the room because Mr. Palmerton had suggested that, after hearing Mr. Croft's report, the directors might want to question them.

"If Enright continues primarily as a production company," Croft said in a serious, businesslike voice, "the area in which it has been so impressive, we will continue, as we have been doing, to create a prestige image. I've prepared a study of the various media, together with costs, that would lend themselves to this approach." Croft put another folder on the table.

Hale had read this report, and while Croft talked, he let his eyes travel around the table, watching the reactions. Palmerton, tapping the eraser end of his pencil, probably knew everything that Croft was going to say. Palmerton was Brainard's strongest connection on the board. Hale's eyes moved on. Cortland, the Wall Street man, was listening carefully and seemed to like what he was hearing. Bodenhof was relatively unimpressed. Bodenhof was Will Caroline's man on the board.

"And now I'd like to examine the possibilities of a different kind of promotion," Croft said. "On a different kind of product. Finished products—products sold over the counter for mass consumption."

Croft's businesslike voice took on a little sparkle. "This is an area in which we in advertising can do much for you. With low-cost necessities that a man can walk up to the counter and buy—just pick up off the shelf and pay for—products like toothpaste, shaving cream, deodorants, laxatives, aspirin, nose drops—with these, there is almost no limit to promotion possibilities. I know this is a course you've considered. If you ever decide to go into this market, we will make Enright a name known everywhere."

Hale's eyes moved on around the table. Kaiser liked it very much. Mentally Kaiser was already putting the plan into operation. Hale looked at Admiral Sutherland and wondered, as he had at times in the past, whether the admiral was thinking as little as his face revealed.

"In this case, we would consider all the mass media," Croft said, "—all the varied and exciting ways of reaching different segments of the population—radio, television, which is coming up fast, newspapers, magazines, billboards—I've prepared a detailed study of this—the costs of all the various media, statistics on the number of people reached with each."

Croft was picking up recruits like the marines on the day war was declared. These directors came to a meeting with one thought above all others—to make money for the company. And Croft was showing them a way to do it.

"Also a special study which would interest me for Enright—a program designed to appeal to young adults who are just forming buying habits. Statistics show—"

Hale looked briefly at the research group, sitting together at the end of the table—Vought looking calm and cool, Cable fidgeting as he did at every meeting, the others just looking bored or unhappy. Hale's eyes moved along to Brainard, took in the fingers clamped around the burned-out cigar butt that he would presently line up with the other two butts in the ashtray, and then traveled up to Brainard's face. Brainard was gauging the directors' reactions too, and for a minute Hale watched him.

This whole business with Brainard puzzled Hale these days. He had known Gil Brainard and worked with him a long time. He had always considered Brainard a first-rate production man and a good company man, and he had never looked beyond that. And Brainard was still a good production man—he was good at organization, he was good at detail—he got along reasonably well with people who worked with him. And maybe he was still a good company man too, Hale thought. Maybe he was only doing what, in his own judgment, was right. Hale had no quarrel with an honest difference of opinion.

Croft was making his final speech. "With the right kind of campaign," he said, "we can give new meaning to the name Enright.

Dynamically, imaginatively handled, we can make the name Enright a household word."

Quietly Croft placed his last folder on top of the pile. It had been a long time since anyone had painted so rosy a picture in this room.

Immediately Palmerton stopped tapping his eraser. "Sounds attractive," he said. "I like it."

Hale sat up in his chair. "We'll have copies of Mr. Croft's report for you. Meanwhile does anyone want to question him further?"

"I was wondering, Mr. Croft," Kaiser said, "what about vitamins—in addition to these other things? We make money on our vitamins."

"Wonderful!" Croft said. "Vitamins are hot right now. We could really do something for you there. Not too many buying habits formed yet."

Palmerton's eraser was busy again. "Mr. Croft, what about our veterinary supplies? Mrs. Palmerton is very much interested—she has considerable to do with a cat and dog hospital, and she'd like to see us do more with that."

"Marvelous," Croft said. "People will go all out on pets—pets and children. In addition to a regular line, you might consider a whole line of preparations for children—aspirin, mild laxatives, something for when they get the sniffles—but pets are marvelous, too. We could make Enright a name for the whole family."

Hale settled back and half closed his eyes. He'd give them about ten minutes and then get rid of Croft and let them question the research group again, if they wanted to, and then dismiss them too, and get down to business.

When Croft had left the meeting, Will Caroline motioned toward the research group. "Are there any more questions for these men—or can we send them back to work?"

Bodenhof leaned forward. "I'd like to know what's happening in other places with antibiotics. What kind of progress is being made in the field?"

"René Dubos at the Rockefeller Institute found tyrothricin," Cable said. "Waksman has found others, besides streptomycin."

"They find 'em but they can't use 'em," Brainard said. "They're all toxic."

"We don't hear everything, but the whole field is picking up momentum," Will Caroline said.

457

"Melanie at Columbia discovered one," Cable said. "Bacitracin."

"I've heard about that one, too," Brainard said. "It's good for leg ulcers. How many people get leg ulcers?"

"What about some of these other products?" Palmerton said. "Would they present a problem? Could your department prepare a good toothpaste?"

"Oh, yes," Harrup said.

"Cough drops, laxatives—all these things?"

"Certainly. No problem."

"It's no problem and it's no drug," Cable said. "It's nothing."

"Well, it's certain that more people use toothpaste than get leg sores," Admiral Sutherland said. The admiral didn't like insubordination.

"I like the idea of products people use," Palmerton said. "Products people need. With this population boom, there's going to be quite a demand."

"We should remember that there's a good supply, too," Hale said.

"Mr. Palmerton," Will Caroline said, "can you imagine what the demand would be for a good broad-spectrum antibiotic?"

"There's a demand for gold, too," Palmerton said. "But it's mighty scarce."

"But the people who found it got rich," Bodenhof said.

Brainard unwrapped a fresh cigar, tapped it on the table. "Before we send these boys out," he said, "I've got something to say, and let them see if they can answer it. I like what Croft said, and I like the way he backed himself up with facts and figures. These boys never come up with a fact or figure in connection with their work. So I've collected a few myself." He took out a piece of paper. "You've all heard the streptomycin story. They're always telling us Waksman did this, Waksman did that—so I did a little checking into exactly what happened there."

Brainard took a minute to light his cigar. "Now—Waksman had a little laboratory and a small staff at Rutgers. They were all earning their keep, teaching classes, so nobody cared too much if they worked on this, too. They got out and dug their dirt themselves. There was no balance sheet involved."

"Merck was backing them, Gil," Will Caroline said. "And besides, men like Waksman have their own kind of balance sheet."

Brainard stood up and went to the blackboard. "Now, this was no operation on a grand scale, gentlemen. These were a few men

458

off in a farming college—and altogether they looked at about ten thousand cultures, over God knows how many years."

On the blackboard, Brainard wrote:

10,000 CULTURES

And then, under it:

1,000
100
10

He tapped the blackboard, his cigar angling out from the chalk. "Out of the ten thousand, one thousand looked good enough to work on a little more." Next to the 1,000 Brainard wrote: INTERESTING. "Out of the one thousand, about a hundred grew well enough and produced enough antibiotic substance to actually inhibit the growth of microorganisms in a test tube." Next to the 100, Brainard wrote: ANTIBIOTICS.

"Out of that hundred, Waksman took serious steps to isolate only ten. And that's because isolation techniques were primitive then—and nobody knows much more today. Today, gentlemen, this group into whose sievelike hands you have already poured over a million dollars and which now wants more—these geniuses not only do not know how to find what they're looking for—if, indeed, it can be found—but they don't know how to handle the prize even if they should find it. That's where you're putting your money. Now—" He thumped the blackboard, which read:

10,000 CULTURES
1,000 INTERESTING
100 ANTIBIOTICS
10 ISOLATED

He drew a huge figure 1, which trailed all the way down to the chalk tray, and the chalk fell out of his hand to the floor. He seized another piece and circled the figure 1.

"Out of the ten that Waksman isolated, one was good! One was streptomycin. These were the odds, gentlemen: one in ten thousand. Is there any man here who would seriously think of playing against that kind of odds?"

The men around the table looked sober.

459

"Now, by comparison—what have we done?" Brainard went on. "We've had more men working and we've had them doing nothing else. Dr. Derrick isn't looking at ten thousand cultures a year, but about fifteen hundred a week, which is seventy-five thousand a year. And he's been at it for a year and a half. It took him time to get going, so we'll say he's looked at a hundred thousand cultures."

Brainard scrawled a large 100,000 on the blackboard. "Our odds are worse already—ten times worse—and we haven't found our one."

"We've found streptomycin, too, Gil," Will Caroline said.

"I'll say you have. Too much."

"We found it long before ten thousand," Will said.

But Brainard was making his point. "For Derrick to look at these —and for the others to work the few that they do work—and less than one per cent are getting to mice, so we don't know what's being overlooked in there—"

Hale sat up and looked at Brainard sharply. Brainard was keeping an even closer eye on this project than he had realized. These figures were remarkably accurate.

"For them to do this much has cost us more than a million dollars," Brainard said. "And they've turned up two broad-spectrum antibiotics—two out of one hundred thousand chances. One of them won't cure any living thing of any disease—and the other will cure the disease and kill the patient."

Brainard put down the chalk and looked at the research group as he walked past them back to his chair. "What do you boys have to say to that?"

"In something like this you don't stand around figuring the odds!" Cable answered. "You say I think this *can be done*."

"And you think so," Brainard snorted.

"Yes!"

Brainard threw up his hands and Will Caroline broke in. "After those figures," he said with a smile, "maybe we'd better let these men go back and examine a few more cultures—if there are no other questions."

As the research men filed out, Bodenhof said, "What's happening in other companies working on this, Will?"

"We don't hear too much about them," Will Caroline said. "They keep quiet, just as we do. But we know there are several in the race."

"In that case," Kaiser spoke up, "have we got any business being involved at all? The bigger companies must be working on a larger scale—and size is against us. A lightweight in the ring can't be a heavyweight contender. He has to stay in his own division."

"That bothers me, too," the admiral said. "You know—whatever the wind, sails can't compete with power. Power tells."

Hale looked at his watch and decided to speak his piece soon and then break for lunch.

"We took a crack at this and we didn't make it," Brainard said. "Let's get back where we belong—to what we've always been—a production company."

"And a good one," Palmerton agreed.

"In production we've always been the best," Kaiser said.

"It's not just a question of what we've been." Hale spoke up, and then waited while the others turned to look at him. "It's a question of what lies ahead, too. And not just for Enright—but for this whole industry."

"What do you mean, Ade?" Palmerton said.

"I mean that we can't just sit here and look backward. Science everywhere is breaking out of the old boxes, and we are in a scientific industry. These past few years men have pointed to the atom bomb—to radar—to aircraft—and they've said that each one has opened the door to a new age. Well, I say—what about penicillin?" Hale leaned forward and looked around the group of men who, a moment ago, had thought their minds were made up. "Penicillin was the beginning of an age in medicine—as much a beginning as Columbus, as much as Kitty Hawk, as much as the atom bomb."

The others were silent, thinking this over, but Brainard had an answer. "Now, Ade, I don't say you're not right about that," he said agreeably. "Maybe medicine is entering a new age—I'm not a doctor and I don't know—but Enright isn't primarily a drug company. Enright is a chemical production company."

"And a good one," Palmerton said again quickly, as though that settled it and he was glad to be rid of the problem.

"Another year and you're out another million dollars," Brainard pointed out, looking at Palmerton.

"It's a lot of money," Palmerton said.

"We tried and failed," Brainard said, picking up courage as Palmerton agreed with him. "I say it's time to quit!"

"Quit!" Hale hitched up his chair and prepared to fight. He

461

wasn't ready to quit, and he wasn't going to get pushed out of this race—not yet, and not by his own vice-president. "This is no time to quit!" he said. "This is the time to move! It's now or never. There's no trick to recognizing a new age when you're waist-deep in it and every preacher and newspaper columnist and Monday-morning quarterback is shouting that this is a new age! The time to recognize a new age is when that first shadow crosses your path—when that first thread of evidence shows up. And we're already beyond that—penicillin was more than a shadow. Penicillin was a beginning and drugs are already in a new age. If we hadn't started when we did, it would already be too late!"

"I agree!" Bodenhof put in suddenly.

"I was wondering," Palmerton said unhappily. "What about some kind of a compromise? Cut back on these heavy expenses, but still keep a small group working on antibiotics—just in case something happens."

"Do it right or not at all," Bodenhof said.

Hale smiled. Success could have different effects on different men, he thought. With one man it made him a property owner and he became cautious, playing it safe, protecting what he had. And with another it gave him confidence and he took chances. "We knew when we began that this would be expensive," he said. "We never expected it to pay our dividends the first year."

Brainard started to protest and thought better of it and clamped his mouth over his cigar.

"Of course this is a risk," Hale said. "We all know it's a risk. We knew it then. And we have obligations—to the company and to the stockholders—and we're all aware of them. But if we do this—if we can pull this off—it will be a greater thing than any man here today can imagine." His eyes moved around the full circle of the table. "It will be great for the company—it will be great for the stockholders—" He glanced at Will Caroline and smiled in spite of himself. "—And it will be great for humanity."

Hale pushed back his chair. "We'll break for lunch."

It was enough to make you wonder, he thought. A man could go along for years—unemotional, objective, as rational as any businessman alive—and suddenly, if he wasn't careful, he could turn into a damned crusader.

RY SOLVENT EXTRACTION. Try six solvents simultaneously to save time.

And send it to Gates.

And if it's pure enough, send it to Mills.

And the mice died.

And get it purer.

And back to Gates.

And back to Mills.

And the mice died.

And it could be the antibiotic that was toxic, or it could be the impurities.

Get it purer.

Back to Gates.

Back to Mills.

And . . .

Late in the afternoon Tom stood at his desk and thought, Today we had a reprieve—but there will not be many more reprieves. Time is running out. And we're doing this wrong.

He looked down at his notebook, opened to the notes on the latest of his half-promising antibiotics that was not quite good enough—EA 4. With EA 4 the mice had lived for about six hours and then gone into convulsions and died. Three times now Gates had reported that EA 4 was purer. Three times Mills had put the improved EA 4 into mice. Three times the mice had died late in the day.

"Moose," he said, "we're still doing too damn much work."

Moose grunted. "I can't argue."

Tom moved to the window. Down in the yard a truck passed, its headlights already turned on, carrying containers of penicillin, each container labeled ENRIGHT in large square letters—ENRIGHT, that Lawrence Croft wanted to make a household word. Time, Tom thought—time is the most important thing we've got, and we're wasting it. While we do these things over and over—back to Gates, back to Mills, back to me—time is running through our fingers like sand. Somehow we have to make some changes to speed everything up. Impatiently he turned away. For a long time now he had felt this dissatisfaction and had been telling himself to make changes. But the changes that ought to be made refused to show themselves and he only continued the same routine, and the dissatisfaction pressed harder.

He walked through the laboratory and out into the corridor. Max was working on EA 4 too now, and he supposed he might as well go find him and decide about their next moves. He passed the constant-temperature room and went in to look at the new batch of cultures. Sometimes by Friday afternoon he could see one or two that were growing particularly well. Of course they could still be toxic—and probably were. Weren't they all? He walked along the rows of stir pots, looking at one average-looking muddy broth after another, and saw nothing exciting and left.

As he passed Derrick's laboratory, he could see the girls picking cultures, flaming their needles, transferring the cultures to agar slants, and then Nick walked past the window carrying a rack of test tubes. Tom kept walking, but his eyes went to the refrigerator where Derrick stored the cultures and then to the smaller refrigerator where he stored the unopened envelopes of soil samples. He looked back at Nick. Each of those racks, he thought, holds ninety-six broths—and the girls average four racks a day—four days a week. More than once Derrick had said that he had a serious pileup, and during Baramycin it had grown worse. And since Baramycin, nobody had reduced it much.

He found Max upstairs in his office, packing his briefcase to go home. Mills was with him, and Tom went in and sat against the desk. "That pileup of Derrick's," he said. "How much do you think he's got down there?"

"Too much," Max said.

"A hundred soil samples at forty cultures each would be four thousand."

"They're not all active," Mills said.

"No. But there's an endless supply. Two hundred envelopes would be eight thousand."

Down the corridor he noticed Brainard and Croft in Morrissey's office. Brainard was talking, gesturing with his cigar. In his mind's eye Tom saw him again, standing at the blackboard, reciting his facts and figures, his sharp blue eyes seeming, while he presented his case, to grow more predatory. Next time that case will be even

464

stronger, Tom thought—and unless we can do something, ours will be automatically weaker.

He remembered EA 4 and started to speak to Max and then turned to Mills instead. "Pat—how are you going to feel about EA 4 when you get it again—if you do?"

Mills showed mild surprise. "You thinking of giving it up already?"

"You've had it three times."

"Shoo—I've had them a lot more than three times."

"All the same—how do you feel when you get them again and again? Do you feel just the same on the fourth trial as you do on the first? With EA 4 the mice live about six hours. Next time will you expect them to live through the day—and be alive the next morning—and live through the next day?"

Mills thought a minute. "No—I guess not," he said. "I sort of stop saying, 'Fellows, you're heroes.' I just say, 'O.K., you poor bastards, let's go.'"

Tom nodded. The answer fit his own feelings.

Brainard and Croft left Morrissey's office, and Mills looked after them. "You know," he said wistfully, "sometimes when I'm sitting around with nothing to do—the way we research fellows do at Enright—I say to myself, How in hell did that bastard Brainard manage to live this long?"

Tom laughed, but then he said, "The hell of it is he's on strong ground. We won today, but it was only a minor skirmish. The shaving cream and deodorant brigade will be back."

"We didn't win any battle today," Max said. "Hale handed it to us—God knows why. And he won't do it forever." He stood up. "Let's clear out of here. Let's stop at the Inn and have a couple of drinks."

Back in his own office Tom snapped on the light and stood a while at the window, feeling the nagging dissatisfaction churning up again, knotting his stomach because he knew something was wrong and he couldn't say what it was. All right, we have a reprieve, he said to himself. We have another six months. But what if it had ended now? In a year and a half what would we have done? We'd have gotten an unimpressive number of antibiotics almost pure and learned that they were toxic.

And what would we have left undone? How much would we have left lying around in Derrick's lab—in refrigerators—in test tubes—on plates—or in envelopes that nobody even opened?

Moose looked in and said, "You decide anything about EA 4?"

"Let it sit over the weekend, Moose."

Moose jerked his head as though to say that made sense.

"It wouldn't break my heart to chuck it altogether," Tom said, and Moose grunted as though to say that made sense too.

Max and Mills were already at the Inn, sitting at the bar, and when Tom came in he was surprised to see Max talking to Lawrence Croft. Then as he came up to them, he understood.

"I can't understand this eagerness of thinking people to affiliate," Max was saying. "You'd think they'd want to establish the differences between themselves and so-called mankind, rather than the similarities. After all, it's the thinking people who classify things."

Tom estimated that Max was on his third drink. Marco, the bartender, held up a bottle of Scotch and Tom nodded.

"Max," Mills said, "this is a pretty damned remarkable hypothesis. Whole damned virgin territory here." Mills was feeling no pain either.

"They don't do it with animals," Max said. "Animals are neatly subdivided. No confusion. But with people the classifications are plain sloppy. Now, why call everyone a human? Why not some subdivisions? Hu-pigs, hu-weasels—"

Croft sipped his martini and smiled uncertainly at Tom. "Max has quite a sense of humor."

"He's serious," Tom said. Then he stopped listening, and his mind worked back to the questions that had been bothering him all day. It's like trying to find a crack in a stout wall, he thought—circling round and round, tapping every inch, looking for a weak spot where you can break through, and not finding any.

"Naturally, the classifying would be absolutely democratic," Max said. "No rigidity of class—no inheriting of labels—every man establishes his own. But the label—human—by God, should have to be earned."

"Max," Mills said, "you should publish this."

Max reflected a moment. "It would never work," he said. "In time the word human would become the least respected. It would be too hard to be human. One of the hyphenated humans would realize that it was easier to laugh at the quality than to achieve it. Then all the others—the hu-pigs and the hu-sheep, the hu-cats and the hu-rats—would all join in the laughter. And after they had laughed long enough, the humans would begin to feel there was something faintly disreputable about being human—although they couldn't say what or why—and they would try to pretend that they weren't really humans. And then, of course, they wouldn't be any more. They'd have changed. They would be hu-weasels or hu-pack dogs— and some would be hu-hyenas, laughing loudest of all at what used to be their own kind."

Croft smiled but not as though he meant it. "Those ideas are hardly representative of the company, Max," he said. "You ought to keep them to yourself."

"On the contrary," Max protested. "In this age of sentimental slop, when everyone is understood and any slob can be a hero, someone, by God, has to express the minority point of view."

Tom saw that Croft just didn't understand, and he thought that of course he could not. How could Croft know that this was Max's way of weathering an unpleasant crisis? With Morrissey, a crisis edged his nerves—and with Harrup, it stirred up his ulcers—and with Brainard, it brought out the killer. With Max, it reminded him that men are as they are, and he considered the human frailties, one by one, that were responsible for the unpleasantness, and mourned them and then rose above them.

Mills stood up to leave and Croft got up too, as though glad to escape. "I'll walk out with you," he said. "I want to phone a girl I used to know who lives around here."

Tom moved over to the empty stool, and Max said, "Another six months isn't going to make a hell of a lot of difference, Tom."

Tom fiddled with a swizzle stick. "Max, the way we're going about this now, if we find anything, it'll just be a lucky accident— a whole series of lucky accidents. Derrick's got that pileup, and we're working less than ten per cent of the possibilities. It'll be pure luck if he opens the right envelope, luck if I pick the right culture —or Vought does or Weir or Metcalf. That's just too much luck to count on. When you work less than a tenth of the possibilities, your chances are ten times worse than the normal odds, which are bad enough."

"You're right," Max agreed. "I can't argue with you."

"There's got to be a way to work them faster—so we can work through more of them."

"Getting an antibiotic reasonably pure is work, Tom. It'll never be anything but work."

And until it was reasonably pure, you couldn't be sure. You circled and circled, tapping for the weak spot where you could break through, and each time you came back to the starting point without finding it. And yet the weak spot had to be somewhere. There is always an answer.

A little later Max left too, and Tom sat alone, finishing his drink, still bothered about Derrick's pileup. Suddenly he thought, What if the good one is in there already—that one good one that is everything we want? What if someone has already sent it in?

Croft was back, and said that he hadn't reached his girl. "Just as well, probably," he said. "We used to be close—but the truth is she's kind of a bitch."

Tom didn't answer and Croft said, "We did a little work together once. My analyst felt this girl was very bad for me."

Supposing some pilot has already dug it up—somewhere in Africa, Tom thought—or a missionary priest in China, or an Enright salesman in California—dug it, sealed it in an envelope, mailed it in, and then—end of story because we didn't get to it. We were too busy working on one that wasn't any good—that was no better at the end than at the beginning!

"Still, in a way I owe this girl something—she told me about Enright," Croft said. "Of course, I got the account myself and I kept it. In my business that's not easy—someone's always trying to steal your accounts."

Isn't there at least as good a chance, Tom thought, that the answer is in one of the hundreds still on the shelf as in one of the dozen I'm working—over and over? Why not?

"On the whole these business dames are lousy, Cable," Croft said. "This girl put me through hell. She was frigid—and in the end I made her a whore in bed."

Why not one on the shelf as easily as the one in the lab? But why not the one in the lab as easily as one on the shelf? No reason. Take your pick. Toss a coin. But his stomach knotted, and he thought, Is it that simple? Is it that even a choice—as even as the toss of a coin? Or is there an answer that we're not seeing?

"And the hell of it is I've still got a yen for her. I'd like to see her. It's one of the reasons I stayed over tonight."

But if there is an answer, we haven't found it, Tom thought. If there is a reason, we don't know it. And you can argue logically either way. You're at least as well off with the one in your lab as with the one on the shelf. But still—there were all those cultures that nobody had touched, that nobody had worked on at all.

He finished his drink and stood up.

"Leaving already?" Croft said.

"Early date."

"She hasn't got a friend?"

"No, she hasn't."

Halfway to his car Tom stopped. For a minute he just stood there in the middle of the driveway, asking himself whether he really had heard, only half listening, what his mind now told him he had heard. Had Croft really said that the girl he was talking about had told him about Enright? Slowly Tom walked back and went inside.

"Croft—" He just couldn't believe it. "Croft, you're not—you can't be the guy she almost married!"

Croft looked up. "Who's that?"

"You know who. The girl you've been shooting off your mouth about—Amity Welles."

Croft's eyes brightened. "You know her!" Then he said, "Married! Hell—Am and I weren't about to get married! We were just —hell—we were just *playmates!*" The dark eyes gleamed as though Croft were telling a dirty joke. "Cable, don't believe a thing she told you about me. It's probably a lie."

Staring at Croft, Tom told himself that this rage he felt was beyond all reason. And yet he felt it.

Suspicion came into Croft's eyes. "What'd she say about me, anyway?"

"She didn't say a damn thing—she hasn't even been here for a hell of a long time."

"Cable, you're crazy. She comes here every weekend. She'll probably show up yet tonight."

"That's impossible. She lives two doors away from me. If she'd been here, I'd have seen her. Or she'd have stopped in."

And then he realized that it was possible. The little he was home, he was with Diana—and when he was with Diana, he wasn't looking.

Croft laughed. "Cable, Amity Welles wouldn't stop in if you were dying."

How could it have happened? Furious, Tom strode back across the parking lot. How and why and by what deceptions could Amity have ever thought she loved a man like Croft? By what means could he have been transformed, in her eyes, from a facile manipulator to the man she must have thought he was—for a while anyway —for as long as the illusion lasted?

Then sadness mixed into Tom's anger, and he thought what a rotten time Croft must have given her, and how let down she must have felt at the end, when—too suddenly, probably—the illusion had been shattered and she had seen him for what he was.

He reached his car and tossed in his briefcase. A night wind had come up and the lower branches of trees dipped, and in the brush an animal moved—a cat or a skunk prowling for food. Illusions are always the same, he thought. They are blinding and hard-shelled. Nothing is seen clearly so long as they endure. No evidence gets through the shell until it cracks. What a waste, he thought—Amity and Lawrence Croft.

He drove out of the parking lot. Then he said to himself, Talking about illusions, what about you? What illusions are you laboring under? What are you doing that you think is right—that is not right? That you think is necessary—that is not necessary? How much are you calling right that is wrong? And if you could answer those questions, how much could you speed up?

Now, pulled by that relentless magnet, his mind was back where it had been all day, and he said to himself, Your problem is not really that complicated, my friend. You know you have to work through more cultures. And there is only one way to do that—which is to do less work on each. So the question is: What can you eliminate without feeling you might be throwing away something good? That's your question, old boy. Now answer it.

Think about that, he said to himself. All that grind—back to Gates, back to Mills—is just to answer one question: Is this a toxic antibiotic? All that endless repetition is only to get rid of enough impurities to be able to say: The *antibiotic* is toxic. All right, then —how could you get that answer sooner?

As he turned into the shore road, his thoughts moved on to EA 4, and immediately that needling irritation began stirring around inside him again. Why go on with it? he said to himself, knowing that the words came not so much out of reason as out of his feelings. Why go on with any of them? They're toxic and they're not getting any better—so it's probably the antibiotic. And if it is, how could I

470

have found that out earlier? Much earlier. That the *antibiotic* is toxic?

He rounded the curve in the shore road and saw a light in Amity's house and remembered that Croft had said she would probably be here later. He knew that Croft would try to call her again, and the thought bothered him. The whole idea of Amity and Croft bothered him.

Then he saw a light in his own house, and he slowed down and forgot about Amity. A light meant that Diana was there waiting. He wondered what was wrong and then, uneasily, whether this was going to turn out to be a bad night.

A few minutes later he stood at the fireplace, his back to Diana, trying not to listen to the words that poured out of her.

"Darling, what can you do in six months?" she said. "In six months you won't do anything—you won't make a dent! Tom, don't you see? You're so sheltered—so isolated here—you never talk to anyone about this, except the other people at Enright, who don't dare admit the truth, even to themselves—and you've convinced yourself that there's going to be a miracle." Her voice changed and she sounded close to tears. "Darling, there's not going to be a miracle."

For a moment Tom didn't answer. The dreary day had given way to a damp night, and the foghorn sounded hollow in the heavy air.

"Six months will pass, and then what? Then do you wait for the master to say, 'All right, you're trying, I'll think about letting you live another six months'?"

Wearily, Tom thought that there had never been a night when he felt less like talking. The whole day had been hectic and disturbing—the meeting—the directors, Brainard, Croft—Croft this morning and tonight, too—and all day that other problem had been nagging him, was nagging him still—and he thought that all he would like to do tonight was to have Diana in his arms and about four more shots of good Scotch inside him and, just for a few hours, forget about everything. But she was all wound up and at the edge of tears, and it wasn't going to be that kind of a night. He went over and sat beside her. "All right, darling," he said, "if you're that unhappy, let's talk it out."

"Don't you see, Tom?" She brightened as she turned to him. "You just don't realize how insulated you are here, but I've talked to all kinds of people about this—very famous people—biologists, chemists, doctors—and everyone says this is a lifetime undertaking. You'll be lucky if you can make a single interesting contribution. And the contribution will probably be that penicillin is the exception—a mutation that will never happen again."

"Well—that mutation will never happen again," he said. He put his arm around her and dropped his head back and closed his eyes. "An identical mutation doesn't happen twice."

"Like man," she said. "Nothing else developed into man—only man. Only man stands on his two feet."

"Only some men," he said, and smiled. "Darling—"

"Only man is capable of reason."

"Only some—"

"And just as man is the highest form of mutation among animals, penicillin is the result of the best mutation among microbes, and there will never be another."

Tom gave a little sigh. She was so fascinated with these scraps of information she had picked up—and she thought they were all. "Max was talking about that tonight," he said, teasing her. "Max believes there are several species of man that resemble each other only superficially."

"Max!" she said. "Max is a cynical egomaniac."

Surprised, Tom opened his eyes.

"Max hasn't the slightest desire to do anything for mankind. He has no ideals whatever."

"Diana," Tom said, sitting up a little, "Max is the greatest idealist I have ever known."

"Max!" Her eyes went to the glass in his hand. "How long have you been drinking?"

Silently Tom looked at her—at the eyes that could change so when she was angry. He stood up and walked back to the fireplace and then bent down and began, slowly, to build a fire, snapping a piece of kindling across his knee to break it, laying the pieces across the andirons and snapping another. He would never understand her, he thought. After Baramycin, which had been a failure, she had been everything a man could want—serene, warm, sympathetic. And now—

"Tom—" she said.

He turned around, torn between rising impatience and his desire to coax her back to tenderness.

"Don't even go in tomorrow," she said. "Leave now."

"Diana, I won't even talk about that."

"Well, I want to talk about it!" she said.

The foghorn called out with its hollow sound in the damp night. He could hear the angry edge in her voice.

"Why should you be a martyr?" she said. "And sacrifice your whole future for a wild-goose chase? There's something queer about martyrs—everyone knows that."

Slowly Tom turned and stared at her. "Diana, this is quite a different tune you're whistling!"

"Well, if you're going to be a martyr, be one in a way that will do you some good!"

Tom stared at the crossed sticks of kindling in the fireplace and then slowly added a log and then another and struck a match. He told himself not to listen to her. Something had upset her even if he didn't understand what it was, and when she was upset she said anything—things she didn't mean. Then she got over it and she was all right again. He told himself that it had been a long time since she had done this, that she had been trying, that in the real crisis, after Baramycin, when he had needed her, she had been wonderful. He watched the paper go into flames and begin to lick at the kindling.

"Diana," he said, "couldn't we talk about this some other time?"

"You only stay there for the money," she burst out, as though he hadn't spoken. "Oh, you're so false!"

He reached for the Japanese sword to poke the fire.

"Even that thing is false! It's not a battle trophy. You won it in a poker game!"

Tom sighed. "You're against so many things, Diana."

"There are so many things to be against!"

He poked at the logs. "Diana, what are you for?"

"You know what I'm for. I'm for freedom. Absolute freedom."

Freedom. She didn't understand the word any more than she understood the scientific terms she used. Freedom had to be freedom her way. He couldn't even be a martyr his way—only her way. He stared at the orange flames running along the thin dry sticks of wood and thought, What's happened to us? What brought this on? Why now—tonight? After Baramycin I expected it—Baramycin was a serious failure, and everyone knew it could mean the end. But that danger is past, for a while, anyway, and now—

And then—all at once—he understood. After Baramycin she had thought what everyone else had thought—that now it would end, and she would have her way at last!

"Diana"—he turned sharply to look at her—"did you expect this to die today?"

Her chin tilted.

Slowly Tom put down the poker and stood up. "You thought—" He had trouble speaking the words. "You thought that by tonight it would all be over and then you would be able to have it your way!"

"Everyone expected it to die today!"

Silently Tom looked at her—at the blue eyes that were so altered, so sharp and—he felt a little shock as the word flashed across his mind—vicious. He looked at the chin that he used to call elegant, that now seemed hard. He looked at the eyes again. He turned back to the fireplace where a log snapped.

"Yes, I thought so!" she said. "And I hoped so—for your sake."

Sadly Tom shook his head. "No, Diana—not for my sake."

She was talking again. Listing her cherished hatreds, he thought —those prejudices that are so important to her, that she feeds off of, that give her a sense of special wisdom and of superiority over ordinary mortals, and maybe even a sharper sense of being alive. He didn't want to hear them. He walked past her to the farthest window and looked out at nothing in the darkness. All these weeks she has been waiting, he thought—like a hawk hovering over prey she need not bother to kill. Only a little longer—and other natural enemies would do the killing for her—and she would move in and take what she wanted. And today she had been expecting the kill —and the other natural enemies had let her down.

"Will you do it, Tom?" she said. She came up behind him.

"Will I do what?"

"Leave," she said impatiently. "Will you leave?"

He stared out the window. "Diana," he said dully, "even if I did leave for you, you'd never be satisfied. After a while you'd find something else to be against, and you'd want me to move again."

"That's not so."

"Wherever I went, you'd be against the people who were running things—the way you're against Ade Hale and Will Caroline. You don't want me to go to a foundation because it's any cleaner or nobler—and it's not any nobler. Wherever you go where there are

474

people, you'll find jealousy and politics and men fighting to corner the power and grab the credit and take the bows. You want me to go because—" he broke off.

"Because *why?*"

He moved closer to the window. He didn't want to look at her. He didn't want to go on.

"Tom," she said, "*answer* me!"

He turned.

The blue eyes were sharp, and he stared at them with nothing to say, and all at once he understood how much he read in them now. Earlier today he had looked at those eyes, he thought—those same eyes, sharp as these were sharp, presiding over facts and figures—the eyes of a man just as certain he was right, the eyes of a man to whom his own power was first and last and all!

"Well?" she said.

"Because you want power, Diana. You want me to go because I'd earn less—and if we were married, eventually, you believe, I would be at least partially dependent on you—and to that extent you would have your little power."

"You're mad!" she said. "You've gone mad!"

"What about Adam, Diana?"

"Adam!"

When Adam is appreciated, I'll be through with him, because I'll know he has sold out, she had said. But meanwhile he was not appreciated and nobody cared and nobody supported him and he was all hers.

When Adam is recognized, I'll be proud to know that I alone saw his genius . . .

When you are recognized . . .

Someday you'll do something brilliant and I alone will have appreciated you—we will laugh at them all and say, See, you fools . . .

"What has Adam to do with this?" she said. The blue eyes burned into his.

"Nothing," he said. "Nothing."

He looked at a face he had never seen before and turned away.

Long after Diana had gone, Tom stood on the porch. You gained one thing and lost another, he thought. And yet he knew this feeling of loss was a sentimental one. The girl that he had lost he had never wanted and the girl he missed now had never existed.

The moon was a blurred sliver tonight, already lowering, and out past the bulb of the streetlamp the lighthouse blinked. How could he have gone all this time—and have seen her and talked to her and loved her every day—and still not have seen her at all until tonight? Although others had, he thought. Max had. And Callie. *Life to Diana is a spectator sport,* Callie had said.

And then as memories crowded back, he knew that he had seen it too. *When Adam is recognized . . . When you are recognized . . .*

And—*Diana, you can't ever give me money. . . . But, darling, I want to. . . .*

The clues had been there, all along the way, and he hadn't seen them because he had been blind—hard-shelled—and no evidence had gotten through.

After a while he walked out to the boardwalk where the dim bulb etched a small circle of light. He could smell the dampness in the air. Far out on the bay a ship's lights moved downstream. He looked over at Amity's house and walked slowly toward it. She was the only one on the boardwalk who didn't draw the front curtains in winter, and he could see her in there. Then he saw she was talking to someone, and he knew that it must be Croft. He watched a minute and walked on.

A man could lose what he didn't want, Tom thought, and still be miserable. He kicked at a stone and watched it skip over the boardwalk that was wet and gray in the damp night. The sense of loss might be a sentimental one, but the feeling of emptiness was real enough. And then he thought, Oh, hell—you don't break up with the girl you were in love with for two years and feel nothing!

A man could get what he did want and be miserable too—as he had been miserable all day with the questions that were needling him. The picture returned of Derrick's technicians, picking, picking —of nearly a hundred test tubes in each rack—of countless racks on shelves—of dozens of envelopes of soil samples, unopened. And he thought, It is certainly possible that the good one is in there now. It's possible that it has been there for months—untouched on a shelf—while we've been doing these others, over and over. Back to me—back to Gates—back to Mills. He jammed his hands into his pockets. Every day for more than a year he had looked at Diana without ever really seeing her—without seeing the evidence that had been there. And he was beginning to feel that for more than a year he had been looking at this problem too—looking probably at just as much evidence—and not seeing that either.

He turned and walked back and came up to Amity's house again. He was certain that Croft was in there. Who else could it be? Croft had said he had stayed over to see her. After a while Tom turned into the walk and went up the steps.

Amity opened the door, and then Croft came into the hall and said, "Hello, Cable—I thought you had a date tonight."

"Come in, Tom," Amity said. "Lawrence is an old friend. We haven't seen each other for a long time."

"Now, Am, dear," Croft said, "don't say just an old friend. Am and I were very close once, Cable. We were just talking about it."

"What are you drinking, Tom?" Amity said.

"Nothing, thanks." He looked at Amity. Her hair was pulled back, and she was wearing a sweater and the rolled-up paint-stained dungarees, and he thought that she wasn't trying very hard, anyway, to please Croft.

"Lawrence?" Amity said.

"I'll get it, dear," Croft said and went over to a side table where there was a bottle and some ice. "Am and I meant everything to each other once, Tom."

Tom watched Amity's face. She didn't care much about Croft any more.

"This is a marvelous girl," Croft said. "Helped me in my darkest hour. My first wife ran out on me—I'll tell you about my wife some-time, Cable. Terrible woman—nearly destroyed me." He looked at Amity with a sad, tender smile. "And then after Ammie saved me, she walked out on me, too—over a trivial misunderstanding."

"Well, let's not go into that now, Lawrence," Amity said.

"Darling, you knew that Lucille meant nothing to me."

Unhappily, Tom stood in the middle of the room, sorry he'd come in here.

"You were busy, darling—you had that damned show. And what was I to do? You know the tension I work under." Croft sighed. "Sometimes I wonder whether it's worth it, Am. You have to bow and scrape—kiss their asses. And they're all ready to knife you. First I have to do my work and then work to get the credit for it. And then somebody else who hasn't done half as much tells the right lies and gets moved up over me."

477

Bored, Tom looked around and saw that Amity had made some changes. The faded wallpaper was gone, and the walls had been painted white. On one wall there were several paintings hung in three horizontal rows—two scenes of the bay, another vivid landscape and some portraits.

"You been here every weekend, Am?" he said.

"No. Only now and then."

Tom looked at Croft, but Croft apparently had no recollection of his earlier statement. He was looking at Amity.

"You weren't fair to me, Am," he said. "You know the pressure I'm under—my analyst says relief from all that tension is important. And when I was free to play, you were busy. My God, you were so busy. I needed someone and you didn't have time for me. So I found Lucille—I admit it—and I played with her awhile and then it was over. I've forgotten her—like last year's tie."

What am I doing here? Tom thought. Why am I staying, listening to this egocentric idiot unburdening his psychic garbage? He stood up. "I guess I'll be going, Am," he said.

Amity's eyes came over to him. "Why don't you stay a few minutes, Tom?"

He hesitated and reluctantly sat on the arm of the chair. Croft went over and mixed himself another drink. "All the fuss you made over that show, Am. Everything was fine with us until then—and it wasn't worth it."

Amity's armor held firm. Only her chin angled a little higher. "You didn't go to it, Lawrence, so you can't say."

"I didn't want to go, darling. I didn't want to see how bad it was. A friend of mine had to review it. He said you were still screaming about the individual, and that's a bore these days. Am, dear, you're out of step with the times, and you won't admit it. You were out of step about Lucille." Croft sat down and leaned his head back. "Although in retrospect I don't know how good Lucille was for me. Actually she was a bitch. I hated her. I only stayed because the sex was good."

"Please don't tell me about it," Amity said.

Croft looked up. "Why not?"

"Because I'm not interested. And because it's a private matter—between you and the lady."

"Darling, you're joking!"

With remarkable restraint, Amity got up and moved about the room.

"Darling," Croft said, "sex is normal—natural."

"And private."

"Darling, you don't believe that! Am, dear, if you believe that, you're sick—you need help."

"I'll try to find it, Lawrence," Amity said.

"I don't know," Amity said, coming back into the room after seeing Croft to the door. "Maybe he's right and I'm wrong."

Tom laughed. "Don't be silly. He couldn't be right about anything."

"You know—in all the months I knew him, I never saw him like that," she said. "It's a completely different side of him coming out. Oh, he had problems and he talked about them—sometimes too much—and about the tension he was under and his analyst—"

She broke off, and Tom smiled, a little halfheartedly. The clues had been there—the clues are always there, only you don't see them —and then you begin to see them and you deny that you are seeing them—and then comes the rude awakening—the grand disillusioning—and you see them all too clearly.

Amity looked at him. "What's wrong with you tonight, Tom?"

"Nothing. Well—nothing."

"You looked pretty wild when you came in"

"I'd had a falling-out with Diana." With Diana, who was not Diana. "I guess I don't feel like talking about it, Am." He stretched out his legs and began to relax a little. "It's been a good night for both of us."

"Oh, it wasn't so bad for me. With me the end came long ago."

Tom nodded toward the paintings on the opposite wall. "Those all yours, Am?"

Her eyes went to the paintings. "All but one. The Swiss farmer in the second row."

Tom looked at the portrait of a rough peasant face.

"I bought that one," she said. "I'd only been in New York a little while and I went to an exhibit—it was supposed to be an important exhibit of modern painters. It was quite large and I can still remember how I felt as I went through it, looking so carefully at every painting. I went on and on, and I was feeling more and more let down—and then I came to this one. In the whole exhibit there was only one strong face—this man's. For days afterward I thought about it. And then I went back and looked at it again, and finally I bought it. It wasn't expensive. And since then I've seen others that are as good—or better—but this one had a special meaning because that day it was the only one. And looking all that time before I came to it—I sort of fell in love with it." She smiled. "Look at him. You see —he has a face of iron. He might not have won every battle—but you know he fought them."

Then she said, "Lawrence is right, really. I'm out of tune with the times. I don't express the mood of our age. Other artists show that man is fragmented—or depraved—or that life is meaningless. A friend of mine did a group of paintings that was considered very exciting—men and women at work or at play or engaged in the simple business of living—all without faces. He feels that is the essence of our civilization—the faceless ones. And I understand what he's saying—and others like him—but it's not what I want to say. This is the age of the group, and a single face doesn't mean much any more. Only to me it does. I'm still the 'civilization is one man at a time' school. I argue—" She paused and didn't go on.

The room was very quiet. Tom looked at the painting on the opposite wall and then at Amity beside him, and he thought that this was the first time all day he had felt really clean.

After a minute he said, "You argue what?"

She laughed. "Nothing so fascinating. It's just that—to me, anyway—one wonderful face is proof that everyone hasn't become one of the faceless ones. That some rare and lovely individuals still have the courage to *be*—against the odds. So I go on—looking for my faces. But Lawrence is right. I'm out of step. And I'm not going to change anything, single-handed." She smiled at him. "You never do, you know. You never really change anything. Single-handed or any other way."

"No," Tom said. "You don't change anything." Then Diana crept back into his thoughts. "And you don't change people, either. No matter what you do, you can never change the deep hard core of a person. I know that now."

"Did you try to change her so much?" Amity said.

He smiled. "It was hopeless from the start. I understand that now. A person does what he does because he must—because for him it's inevitable. Or for her. You don't change the inherent nature of any-

480

thing."

He fell silent, still remembering. From the start, he thought, he and Diana had seen only what they had wanted to see and had ignored the rest—and so had let themselves believe that the unchangeable would change, that the inflexible would yield—that the unadmitted would dissolve—vanish—bury itself. And yet the evidence had always been there. The clues are always there. You have only to see them—only sometimes a man doesn't want to.

And sometimes, he thought sharply, not thinking about Diana now —sometimes he doesn't see them for other reasons. Because his vision is focused wrong. Or because it is cluttered or because he is prejudiced. The eye is a prejudiced organ—it sees selectively. And the eye of the mind is more prejudiced still.

He sat up. You cannot change the inherent nature of anything, he thought. That is a law. He was beginning to feel something—and his mind struggled to pull this sudden intuitive feeling into a clear and exact thought. You cannot change in people—you cannot change in anything—what will not be changed.

I've thought this before, he said to himself. He got up and began to walk around the room. I thought it with the broths. With the broths I said, If it won't grow well in one of the ten, it won't grow well. It's not its nature to grow well. Forget it. And all this time the only exception I ever made was Baramycin. And with Baramycin we tried everything—and it never grew well. And when it was all over, the first thing I said was, I shouldn't have fussed so much!

And if an antibiotic is toxic . . . hell, almost every antibiotic is toxic! Except for a handful that didn't protect, every one has been toxic. You expect them to be toxic. You practically *assume* now that they will be toxic. The antibiotic that is not toxic is a rarity! He went to the window, and for a long time he stood there, not moving or noticing where he was.

You've undergone a change, my friend, he said to himself. A subtle change. Or maybe not so subtle. You used to assume that an antibiotic was innocent until proven guilty. Now you are thinking something quite different. Now you're thinking, It's guilty—until proven innocent.

Think about that.

He looked out at the dark bay where the only light now was that of the lighthouse, shrouded in fog.

If they are guilty until proven innocent, he thought, that changes everything. Then you will say, It doesn't grow well. Guilty. Next. It doesn't handle well. Don't bleed over it. It's guilty. Next. It's toxic. Guilty. How do you *know?*

This doesn't hold, he said to himself. It doesn't make sense. It's not logical. He shook his head impatiently. He knew it wasn't logical —and yet in his feelings, it made sense. He couldn't say why—he couldn't give the reason—he only knew the feeling that it was right and that somewhere, even though he couldn't find it now, there was a logical answer.

THIRTY-THREE

I F THEY ARE GUILTY until proven innocent, then . . .

It's not logical—it doesn't make sense. Still—if they *are guilty* until proven innocent . . .

All weekend Tom had thought about it. All weekend one part of him had argued against it while another part had searched for reasons to support it, without finding any. And still the feeling grew stronger. Now he sat in the Monday morning meeting, still thinking about it—although, he told himself, you couldn't really call it thinking. Something inside you decided, and then the so-called rational mind thrashed about trying to catch up—to find a way to make it sound plausible to others. He wondered whether he ought to bring it up today or put it off a week and think about it some more.

There was never any trouble rejecting ideas of that rational mind, he thought. Those rose up in endless supply—like ducks in a shooting gallery. The wheel turned and they were up for a minute and down and forgotten. But let that other, nonrational, intuitive part—that indolent, uncooperative partner of your thinking (that for months could stay idle, giving no hints and no help, as though it had retired from the enterprise—had, in fact, never joined it)—just let that other part begin to stir around and tell you something—and try to get rid of that. Just try. Argue against it, and it answered: Do you have all the facts? Half the truth is not truth. Argue that there was no reason to it, it answered: Is this all the evidence—or is there evidence that you don't see—or that you see and don't understand? Argue that there was nothing to support it, and it answered: Look again.

It was a nervous meeting this morning because Hale was here. It was always a nervous meeting when Hale sat in, but this morning they interpreted his presence as a warning that he was in this now and that if they didn't produce, he would know why. Choosing their words carefully in order to sound the right note between caution and perseverance, to say enough but not a word more than was necessary, Vought and Metcalf had reported and now Weir was talking.

Across the table, halfway down, Vought was taking notes as Weir spoke. Beside him, Morrissey sat quietly drawing on a pipe that had gone out five minutes ago. Lately Morrissey had been strangely silent at meetings, hardly speaking at all any more. Next to Morrissey, Harrup was making notes too. Hale was sitting back a little from the table, behind Morrissey and Harrup.

"Nothing awfully exciting in those yet, Dr. Weir," Vought said, when Weir finished. "Although, of course, they could shape up."

"Oh, yes," Weir said. He didn't believe they were going to shape up.

Tom looked down at the data sheets of the cultures he had taken this morning. Because he had decided to work faster, he had taken more than twice his usual number, and Vought had noticed but hadn't questioned him. Vought was a planner. With Hale here, he would want to know the reasons in advance to be sure he had the answers. Idly Tom flipped through the data sheets. Maybe in a week those reasons he'd been chasing would stop slipping away. Now it's still only a feeling, he said to himself—you can't support it with anything. The best you can offer is the practical argument that Derrick has a serious pileup, which is a logical reason for a manager, perhaps, but is not a logical reason for a biochemist.

"Your EA 4 is still the best we have at the moment," Harrup said to Tom.

All right, Tom said to himself—decide.

"With that one the mice lived six hours last week," Vought said to Hale. He turned to Tom. "What's happened to it since?"

"It went to mice again and they still only lived six hours." Whether you tell them this week or next, they're not going to accept it, Tom said to himself—you might as well get it over with and get to work. "I'm giving it up," he said.

"Giving up what?" Harrup said, not comprehending.

But Vought was quicker. "You can't!" he said. "Those mice lived for six hours."

"They never live any longer than six hours," Tom said. "It isn't getting any better."

"That doesn't prove a thing," Vought said. "It could still be good."

"It's had three chances—it's toxic."

"It may not stay toxic."

Tom looked at Vought and saw that anger ran close to the surface in him today. "But it may," he said.

"That doesn't make sense!"

"It does to me." They were all looking at him now, with the look he was beginning to recognize—that said he was stirring up trouble again. "I'm beginning to think it's a mistake to work these things over and over," he said, "for weeks and months, even—when they stay toxic. Dr. Derrick has that enormous pileup—"

"What are you doing—giving him storage space?" Vought said, looking pointedly at Tom's pile of data sheets.

"At the rate we're going," Tom said, "we're never going to even get to most of those cultures. We ought to be working through that pileup—we don't know what's in there. And the only way we can do it is by working less on each one."

Vought turned with an indulgent smile to Hale. It was not Vought's policy to become embroiled in arguments. "Dr. Cable has a remarkable faculty for seeing the problem," he said, "and then consistently coming up with the wrong solution. The pileup is disturbing. This is not the answer."

Thoughtfully, Tom turned a few pages of his record book. He didn't want to lose his temper now. Now he wanted to say this as clearly as he could, which was not so easy in view of the fact that he was not backing it up with anything very convincing.

"We should throw them out much sooner—" he started again.

"We can't!" Weir said. "It's too much of a risk."

"I think we have two factors to consider here," Tom went on doggedly. "First, Derrick's pileup—we don't know what's in there and we're not finding out—and second, the fact that most antibiotics are toxic."

"You don't know that!" Harrup said.

Tom looked up. "We do know that!"

Morrissey's eyes darted back and forth and his lips moved. Tom thought he wanted to speak and he waited, but Morrissey said nothing and after a moment Tom went on. "In a year and a half we've thrown out a lot of antibiotics around here, and except for a few that didn't protect, every one that was good enough to work on was discarded in the end because it was toxic. Now, with this evidence—"

"That's not evidence," Vought said.

"Considering this non-evidence," Tom said, "I can reach only one decision. If they stay toxic and don't improve, after a few trials in mice, we should throw them out. We should move on to others and get some idea of what we've got. It's a risk—I admit it—but it seems a reasonable risk because all the work we do never seems to change anything."

Hale was leaning forward, listening, and now he pulled his chair closer. Harrup and Morrissey hastened to move their chairs to make room for him.

"I think we should get rid of some of the junk as fast as we can," Tom said, "and test a few times. If the mice still die, we should assume that it's the antibiotic that's toxic and move on. There are a hundred more waiting for us. Three times in mice is enough."

Vought turned to Hale again. "Dr. Cable has never done enough work on his," he said. "We're never sure, when he throws one out, whether it might not have been good. I've always suspected that this was a problem of personal endurance—a lack of stamina. Now, it seems, he's collapsed altogether!"

"Look!" Tom exploded. "Derrick's got a mountain of cultures there. We ought to be examining them!"

"What Dr. Cable is saying," Vought said, "is that since he has failed and failed and failed in the past, the solution is to do even less work in the future!" He smiled. "I'm sure the exquisite logic of this argument is apparent to everyone. If you can't do everything right, do everything wrong."

"It's not that simple," Tom said. "What's the point of doing a great job on something that's no good? What's the point of working on it for months if it stays toxic?"

Vought sat back and looked at Tom, not smiling now. "Give me one reason," he challenged, "why, if a mouse dies from a crude injection containing fifty unknown substances, it is logical to assume that it was one thing—the antibiotic—that killed it, and not the other forty-nine. Why?"

Why indeed? You don't know why, Tom said to himself. You're buying this blind—on a hunch—because for weeks you've been telling yourself that somewhere there's a missing piece to this puzzle. And now you're saying maybe this is it. Aloud, he said, "Only that it seems to work that way."

"That's not a reason."

"No, it's not," he agreed. "But it's the only one I have right now." And yet there *was* a missing piece—he was sure of it.

Vought was a man who knew when he had gained an advantage, and moving quickly to consolidate it, he turned back to Hale. "This is an old argument," he said. "It's one we always run into when the going gets rough. Quantity versus quality."

Harrup smiled, too. "I always call it width versus depth. You know—do you work in width or do you work in depth?"

"Same thing," Vought agreed. "In the end there's no substitute for the quality job. Quantity doesn't accomplish a thing—scratches a lot of surface and nothing more. In this business it's knowledge, not activity, that turns the trick. What we need is the man who will work and work and work again—not the one who will half try and then lose heart and run off to the next."

These little barbs were beginning to get to him, and Tom took out a package of cigarettes and concentrated on opening it. Then he told himself that it wasn't Vought who mattered—it was Hale and Caroline, and they were still listening. He calmed down.

"It sounds fine to say we should work and work and work," he said quietly. "But what have we accomplished with all this work? We've satisfied ourselves that the antibiotics we threw away were toxic."

"That's hardly a statement of our objective," Vought said.

"I know it's not our objective—but it's what we've done. Whether we like it or not, what we've done is *prove* that a lot of antibiotics were toxic. When we poured the stuff down the drain, we were satisfied that we were throwing away a toxic antibiotic. Fine—that's a reasonable thing to want to prove; nobody wants to throw out a good one—but at what cost? Do we buy absolute assurance at the price of all hope? Someplace we have to draw the line—someplace we must yield on this demand for absolute proof and take a calculated risk."

"We have never been closer to losing all hope than at this moment," Vought said coldly. "To accept this hysterical suggestion would mark the end of any hope for success. To abandon a promising antibiotic—like your EA 4—after only three trials in mice is as discouraging a step in the wrong direction as I, personally, have ever witnessed."

"EA 4 is toxic," Tom said flatly.

"But it wasn't even close to pure!" Harrup turned to Gates. "Was it?"

Gates looked miserable. "No," he said, "it wasn't very pure."

"Unquestionably it could still be good," Vought said.

"You want it?" Tom said. "I'll give it to you."

"I don't want your cast-offs! I want you to work on them a reasonable time."

"That's what I'm going to do—a reasonable time."

"In my opinion," Vought said, "the work's too hard for you. It's a question of knowledge and endurance—nothing more."

"What knowledge? What endurance?" Tom demanded angrily. "Don't get philosophical about a very practical matter. What does all your so-called endurance produce? What good is a pileup? What good is a lot of stuff in a notebook? Why work a bad one to death in the hope that it will be good? I'm more interested in one that's new and might work than in one that has already failed—for any reason."

Vought looked at the power group at the end of the table, waiting for the reprimand, and none came.

Instead Will Caroline said, "The argument is not without merit, Dr. Vought."

"Totally!" Vought cried. "Totally without merit!" The imperturbable Vought was losing his famous control, and at his tone Morrissey turned to him, startled. "It's illogical and unscientific!" Vought said. "It's purely arbitrary. Why three times? Why not four or seven—or one? Why not just once, Dr. Cable?"

He was right there. It was arbitrary. But you had to be arbitrary —and that was what bothered them. They didn't want to be arbitrary. They wanted to be sure.

Now suddenly they were all talking at once, all objecting—Harrup, Morrissey, Weir, Metcalf—and Tom shoved back his chair and stopped listening. What was the point in arguing? he thought. They would never accept this approach. It violated everything that was holy to them as scientists. For years they had put a halo of superior knowledge around themselves, and now they were caught in it— and acted in this as though they actually had the superior knowledge. To them this Edisonian approach—try this one and if it doesn't work, try another—was too gross, even if that was what it took to win. They had to be elegant—they had to give off an aura of being logical—predictable—of knowing exactly why they went from step to step. Well—he would like to know, too. He would like to be sure, too, and have a reason for everything before he did it. But for this job, in the early stages, there was a lot to be said for the Edisonian approach—and he intended to use it.

They were still buzzing, everyone getting in his protest, and Tom swung around a little and stared out the window. A stiff wind rustled the dry leaves still hanging onto the maple tree and lifted the tails of steam off the pipes beyond. It was the kind of wind that could bring snow—the first of the winter. He swung back to the table. He didn't need snow to remind him that time was passing.

Then he saw that Vought had brought his briefcase up to the table. Vought had regained his great control and was putting it on display, as though to convince them that it had never really left him. Unhurriedly, he opened the briefcase and took out some notes.

"We're wasting time arguing about a minor point," he said to Hale, as though only the two of them were in the room. "This is just a small part of a major problem that I've been considering for a long time—our single most serious problem. I'd intended to discuss it privately first—but now I think I should bring it into the open where we can all face up to it candidly and realistically."

Vought smiled the smile that never quite made it to his eyes, and Tom wondered what he was getting at. He sounded like a politician making a speech, and, Tom thought, in a way he was. Vought was playing politics most of the time.

"First let me say that this is neither a sudden decision nor an emotional one," Vought said. "It hasn't been made in anger or in panic. I've been thinking about it for a long time."

He paused, and Hale said, "All right, Dr. Vought, what's the problem?"

"In all our discussions," Vought said, "we've always asked two questions. First, can this ultimately be done?—and we all know we're divided on that. And second, can *we* do it? To the first question my answer is yes—ultimately it can be done." Vought paused and straightened his pencil and the others looked at him, waiting. Vought let them wait a minute. He was a good actor and his sense of timing was sharp. "To the second question—can *we* do it?—" he said, "the answer is *no.*"

Tom looked up. "Why not?"

Vought ignored him. This production was for an audience of one —Hale. "You've all heard the old axiom: 'There are no impregnable fortresses—there are only badly executed attacks.' Well, this is a bad attack."

"That's right," Tom said. "You're trying to be subtle when you should be storming the gates."

"Our facilities are inadequate. We should have at least twice as

489

much of everything—space, equipment, personnel."

"It's a great idea!" Tom muttered. "Why don't you ask for the facilities of Harvard while you're at it—or the Rockefeller Institute?"

Mills and Derrick grinned, but Vought gave no indication that he had heard.

"Unless we can increase our facilities immediately," Vought said to Hale, "so we can work on more cultures and still cling to standards of excellence—unless we can double everything—the undertaking is impossible. I've been reluctant to say this, but in good conscience I can't put it off any longer. With our present facilities, the job is too big for us."

"I agree!" Morrissey burst out. "I agree—one hundred per cent."

"I do not!" Will Caroline said.

"This is a waste of the time and money going into it," Vought said. "The resources might as well be used for something else."

Tom looked at Vought sharply. Is it possible, he said to himself, that he really thinks he can wheedle double of everything? Or, he thought suddenly, is he scared and using this as a way out—to sabotage the whole project and end up a hero for doing it—the only one with the courage to face this so-called truth and tell it to Hale?

"Dr. Vought," Hale said, "are you saying that you must have double of everything?"

"At least double."

"And otherwise—" Hale leaned forward. "Do I understand you correctly? Otherwise you are saying we should quit?"

Vought waited until the room was quiet. He straightened his pencil beside his briefcase. He looked at Hale. "I am saying we should quit, sir!"

Instantly Tom was on his feet. "Don't give me double facilities to do a more thorough job," he said. "Don't give me double anything. I don't want them."

"No, you couldn't handle them," Vought said. "You wouldn't—"

But Hale interrupted. "Why not?"

"Because I still won't do a more thorough job. With double or with triple. Because it's a waste of time to do such a thorough job. I don't want to do five at a time and do them beautifully. I want to do twenty-five at a time and do them my way." He could hear himself shouting, and he told himself to calm down. Then he thought, hell, he was mad—why should he calm down? "I don't want to do ten a month and do them beautifully. I want to do a hundred and fifty a month—my way. And if I have double facilities, I still won't do a more elegant job! I'll do three hundred a month—my way. And get through them and get on. Because there's an endless supply, and when they're toxic, they stay toxic, and all our beautiful work can't change that!"

"All right," Vought said very coldly. "All right. Stop right there. What would you say—now, listen carefully, Dr. Cable—what would you say if one of us did exactly that—tomorrow? If one of us purified one that has been toxic—and when it was pure, it was nontoxic?"

"Then I'd admit I was wrong."

"And if it happened two months from now—or six months from now?"

Then I would be dead, Tom thought. Then I could never win another argument when the majority was against me. He looked at the solid block of hostile faces turned to him, and he thought that it would have been smarter to keep quiet and work on EA 4 a little longer and quietly drop it. On the other hand, how many future battles would there be if they didn't do something soon? And then he thought, Now who's thinking like a politician? Fight this battle now, the way it has to be fought, and worry about the future battles when they come.

"And in those six months," Vought said, "how many would you have thrown out?"

At the new pace he hoped to set, it would be hundreds—perhaps even a few thousand.

"All right, then!" Harrup broke in, understanding what Vought was saying. "How will you know, your way, that you're not pouring a five-million-dollar antibiotic down the drain?"

"How do you know that there isn't a five-million-dollar antibiotic lying around on a shelf?"

"That's not the question."

"How do you know there isn't a five-million-dollar antibiotic sitting in a package of dirt that you're never going to get to?" Tom said. "Or that's in somebody else's package of dirt, too—that they'll get to first, while we're working them so beautifully?"

"Get it through your head," Vought said impatiently, "that this is not a race!"

491

"This *is* a race! And the idea is to win!"

Vought stared, and a muscle fluttered in his temple.

"This is a race, and the prize is to the first—not to the most elegant."

Vought threw down his pencil. "To me this marks the end of any logical scientific approach to this problem."

"Sometimes you can make too much of a logical scientific approach—"

"Madness!" Morrissey burst out. His voice rose. "I think you're crazy!"

"This is a race," Tom repeated, "and we must have the courage to run it! We must have the courage to throw things out—to take that risk." But this was where they parted company. The others didn't want to assume risks. They debated. They wanted to be safe. Risks tortured them. "We must have the capacity to make this decision," he said, "or we'll be bound by a horrible inertia—as we are now—plodding along, playing it safe. We're bogging down in our own terrifying caution and elegance. All we're looking for is a simple answer: Is this a toxic antibiotic? Yes or no. We can't afford to go down too many blind alleys because they're scientifically interesting. You know as well as I do the result we're after. Let's get there and not be so concerned with the steps along the way. Otherwise we're going to have a nice case of the operation was a success but the patient died."

"The steps are just as important," Vought said firmly.

"The steps are not important."

"Every single step is important—or you won't know what you're doing. If you should happen to get there, you won't know where you are."

"I'll know where I am!"

"Or how you got there—or why."

"Get there! Find out why later!" Tom gripped the back of his chair. "For this job one thing is important. For this job we have one measure of success—and it's not beautiful notebooks or beautiful work."

Vought smiled, totally without humor. "Dr. Cable, I very much doubt that you have many serious thoughts on the measure of any scientific success."

"Oh, I do!" Tom said. But he had glanced down the table and had seen Will Caroline restrain a smile, and he realized that nobody had told him that he couldn't have his way. Suddenly he grinned. "My measure of success is simple," he said to Vought. "It's something in a bottle."

Vought looked so shocked that Tom wondered what he had expected him to say.

"Something in a capsule—" Tom said—"in a bottle." He smiled and sat down and added, "In a drugstore."

After the meeting Hale said, "Give him a second technician, Will."

Will Caroline looked around, surprised and then amused.

"I've backed him this far," Hale said and shrugged. "I might as well go the whole way with him."

T

HE MEETING had just ended. Morrissey rushed into his office and closed the door and dropped his briefcase on the desk. It fell to the floor and he left it there.

This was the end. Now they had reached a state of absolute chaos —now all reason had been abandoned, all logic had been totally suspended, and they had entered a no-man's-land where nothing made sense. Now all hope was gone.

Desperately—a little wildly—he whipped about in a complete circle, as though looking here, behind the closed door, for a better place to hide. His glance flicked past the window. He knew what was out there today. He didn't want to look at it. Compulsively his eye went back and froze on it. How hideous it was—a floating garbage dump! And with every month that passed it seemed to be filling up more quickly—it was no sooner back than it was leaving again. At this rate, soon they would need two. Morrissey lowered the shade and sat at his desk. He had even dreamed about that barge—twice now. In his dream he had been on it, trying desperately to get off. The barge had been full—full to the brim with the dingy, brownish waste—and it had been racing across the bay at an impossible speed, out to the open water, the muddy waste undulating in the bins. He had stared at the waste with a horrible revulsion and stared too long, and then he had fallen, had half stepped into it —stepped into it compulsively, fighting not to and then sinking, like a man in quicksand. Then, even while he was sinking, he had seen the barge back at the dock and leaving again, starting out on the trip down the bay to open water all over again—and he was buried deep in the brown mud and crying out, "It's a mistake—it shouldn't be me—I don't even work on them—penicillin or streptomycin, either—I don't touch antibiotics—I'm in industrial chemicals."

Morrissey put his head in his hands. He could feel his face wet with perspiration. He couldn't fool himself any longer—this was the handwriting on the wall. They had turned away from a defeat that should have been the final blow and had gone on, and now they had made no move to chain a man running wild—had flatly refused to stop him—and now Morrissey knew this was a roller coaster to disaster, with no brakes, and that there was no end in sight.

He hated them—he hated them all. They had cheated him. His life had been orderly and arranged, and his department had been his—and rightfully his, a reward he had earned—and they had stolen it all away from him. And what could he do? They were just hoodlums—they defied all authority and laughed while they did it. There was nothing he could do now, but someday he would get even with them, if it took a lifetime—all of them—Cable and Mills and Derrick—and Will Caroline, too—yes, and Ade Hale, too. They were all to blame.

He'd show them. And he'd show her, too—Winifred. She wasn't entirely blameless—not by any means. If she hadn't been so social-minded, he could have studied more. She had made her demands—and always with her digs ready to be sure she got them. Well, she'd had her way, and now she'd have to pay for it. Now she would have to suffer, and it served her right.

Still, she was smart. He ought to call her and tell her about this. Maybe she could think of something to do. He picked up the telephone and then put it down again as Brainard came in. He blamed Brainard, too, he thought—and he hated him. Brainard had promised him that it wouldn't come to this, just as Winifred had, and they had both lied.

"How about your reports, Claude?" Brainard said. "You're a couple weeks behind."

Morrissey knew he was behind. He hadn't done them because he couldn't bear to look at the reports. "I haven't had time," he said. Why should he torture himself preparing them when Brainard wasn't using them as he had promised?

"What the hell, Claude?" Brainard said angrily. "You make time."

Morrissey could feel himself perspiring again. "I've had a lot of reading to do," he said. "I have a lot to keep up with." He waved a hand toward his desk where his briefcase should be and remembered that it was on the floor. He bent down to pick it up. When he straightened up again, Brainard was laughing.

"Why don't you go back to school, Claude?" Brainard said. "Why don't you get a leave of absence and go back to school?"

Morrissey felt the color draining from his face. "Get out!" he whispered.

Brainard's smile died.

"Get out—get out!"

Brainard looked startled, but he left and hurried down the corridor, looking back a few times, until he reached the end.

Morrissey's heart pounded, and a pain stabbed down the center of his head as though splitting it in two. He seized his briefcase and rushed out of his office and went home.

In the living room he sat on the sofa, still wearing his overcoat, and stared at Winifred, unable to speak. Then he jerked his head and burst into tears.

"I'm going to kill him, Winifred," he said hoarsely. "Cable—he's trying to kill me—I'm going to get him first."

For a long time Winifred stood looking at him in silence. Morrissey slipped off his coat and let it drop behind him on the sofa. Exhausted, he leaned back and closed his eyes.

When he opened them again, Winifred was standing in the same spot, studying him like a thoughtful bird. Then he began to talk and couldn't stop. He told her about the meeting and about the barge and that Brainard had harassed him and that the others were deliberately persecuting him—and that he would have his revenge on all of them if it took forever.

Winifred waited until he had finished and then, without a word, she walked to her desk and took out a large envelope and opened it. She held out a letter to him. "Sign it," she said.

Morrissey looked up. "What is it?"

"It's an application for a teaching position. It's all arranged, Claude—a small new college in upper New York State. They're just starting, and they want people with doctor's degrees. You'll be the head of your department."

Morrissey tried to focus on the application and could not. "How," he said, "how is it all arranged?"

"I've been in touch with them. I told them that all your life you've wanted to teach and that you're torn between the thing you want to do and loyalty to Enright because they need you. I told them that if you didn't move soon you never would, and I didn't want you to go your whole life without doing the one thing you wanted to do most, which was to teach."

With a trembling hand, Morrissey took the application. He still could not read it. "It's true, Winifred—you know I've always wanted to teach."

496

"I know," she said.

He looked up. "Winifred, I've been at Enright my whole life."

"What Enright is doing now isn't for you, Claude. When it seemed that this would be just a brief experiment, I felt you should try to weather it, out of loyalty to the company. I don't feel that any more. Enright has changed. It takes a certain brute-type, thick-skinned man to endure this kind of rough climate. After all, it wasn't the sensitive men who were pioneers—it was the brutes. The sensitive men stayed home and went later. Enright has moved away from you, Claude, not you from it."

"That's right, Winifred," he said. "You're right."

"These people are very excited about getting you, Claude." She touched his arm gently, almost lovingly. "Someone with a doctor's degree who is experienced at running a department. They want you very much."

"Listen, he's been out almost two weeks now," George Weir said. "Ask me, something funny's going on."

"The first day he was out, Winifred told Neil he had a cold," Gates said, glancing toward Harrup's house next door.

"I think he's got a cold like I've got a cold," Weir said.

"Why doesn't somebody just phone and find out?" Janet said.

"I did," Gates said. "Not to snoop. I thought I ought to ask how he was feeling. I've phoned him every day. There hasn't been any answer." He sighed. "Things are getting awfully discouraging."

"Frankly, I think things have been discouraging for a long time," Janet said.

Weir looked sullenly at his drink. "Ask me, what gave Morrissey a cold is that bastard Cable."

"Well, for heaven's sake," Madeline said. "Can't you let the man indulge in a miserable cold without all these wild ideas?"

"Have you *seen* Morrissey lately?" Weir said. He turned back to Gates. "What about Cable? He really going through with it—doing what he said?"

Gates nodded.

"He working any old ones at all?"

"He had two that had only been to mice twice. He sent each of those once more. The mice died and he gave them up."

Weir finished his drink. "You know, he's got a hell of a nerve—Cable has—doing this to us."

Gates shook his head, worried, without answering.

"Well—I should think you two would be ecstatic at the possibility of breaking this wide open," Madeline said.

Gates looked at her. "You don't understand, Madeline. When you feel that a man doesn't know what he's doing, you don't work with the same confidence."

"Maybe he does know what he's doing!"

"Stopping like that without half doing them—how could he?"

"Why should *we* bother?" Weir said. "Why should *we* knock ourselves out, when maybe every week he's pouring a good one down the drain?"

"Well, then—why doesn't somebody take them after he's through?" Madeline said. "Just keep your eye peeled, and as soon as he lets go, grab 'em!"

Weir didn't think it was funny. "Oh, sure—just put the extra work on us! As though we didn't have enough."

"I don't think anyone should do any extra work around there unless they get paid for it." Janet flicked her cigarette, and her gold bracelets jingled. "I tell George if they want him to work harder, let them pay him. There haven't been any raises over there for a long time."

Weir turned on her angrily. "Will you get off my back about a raise!"

"They've got plenty of money," Janet said.

"They don't pass around raises when you're failing," Weir said. "You don't like what you got, you get out and do something about it. Or have you had a couple ideas about that already?"

Undisturbed, Janet examined her long purple fingernails. "Did anyone ever tell you you're very crude when you're drinking?"

"It seems to me," Madeline said cheerfully, "that if anyone has assumed an extra burden, it's Tom. He's the one who's working twice as many as anyone else."

"Twice as many!" Weir said. "He's working five times as many—if you'd call that working." He turned to Gates. "Those two that he sent once more—and then dropped—were they anywhere near pure?"

"God, no. They were still crude as hell."

"Did the mice live any longer?"

Gates shook his head, dispirited.

"Really, George," Madeline said briskly, "I think you're in quite a choice spot. If you just watch Tom's and after he's through, you pick up the ones that still look good—why, look at the work that's already been done on them. You're starting out way ahead."

"Listen, if they still looked good, he wouldn't part with them," Weir said. "When he dumps them, they've killed the mice three times!"

Madeline smiled and said nothing and Weir, understanding the meaning of the smile, turned away. "A-ah—you're a great back-seat driver, Madeline. Only you don't know what it's all about." He turned back to Gates. "Listen," he said, and spoke the awful word. "You think Morrissey's quit?"

Gates deflated a little more. "I don't know. Maybe he has." He sighed. "And maybe he has the right idea."

"Woodrow, don't be ridiculous!"

But Gates was in one of those moods when all the spirit had gone out of him. He seemed to just draw a protective curtain around himself and retreat behind it.

"You're joking, of course!" Madeline said. "How could you even think of leaving anything as exciting as this?"

Gates didn't answer, and Weir looked at her sourly. "What's exciting about failing and failing and failing?" he muttered. "What's exciting about having every goddam thing you do go wrong—and knowing that no matter what you do, it's still going to go wrong? What's exciting about knocking yourself out to do the job right when you're working with a guy who gets one crazy goddam idea after another and louses everything up—turns the whole thing on its ear?" Weir's face flushed with anger. "He doesn't know what he's doing—he can't back it up with anything."

"That's right, Madeline," Gates said. "He can't."

"He can't prove anything. He doesn't have any reason for what he's doing. He could be so wrong it's not even funny—and everyone else is pretty discouraged about him, too. *Nobody* is with him—not even Strong, even though he won't come out against him—not even Wentner, although Wentner won't say so because Cable backed him. Mills says maybe—Derrick says maybe."

Then, all at once, there was a sharp knock on the door, and Madeline went to answer it. Neil Harrup came in and, without a word, hurried past her and into the living room, where he stood looking at Gates and Weir.

"Dr. Morrissey—" Harrup said, and stopped. He was pale and

visibly upset.

"My God, what's happened to him?" Gates said.

"Dr. Morrissey just phoned me—from somewhere in New York." Harrup shook his head. "Dr. Morrissey has resigned!"

For a minute there was silence. Then George Weir wheeled about and began slapping the table, almost hysterically. "I told you!" he shouted. "I told you—I told you—I told you!"

"George," Janet said, and her bracelets rattled. "Calm down."

"I told you!" Weir shouted. "I told you!"

When at last they had all gone, Madeline closed the door and came back into the living room. "Now, Woodrow, I don't want you to let this get you down," she said. "Morrissey has been bitching since the day you began, and in my opinion it's no loss."

But Gates was very low. "Madeline—I don't see any future in this."

Madeline picked up the bottle to fix him another drink. "Woodrow, I want you to listen to me—carefully. This is a small crisis. It will pass. In any crisis—Woodrow, are you listening?"

He looked at her balefully.

"When there's a crisis, the patient recovers more often than he dies—remember that."

"It's not just this, Madeline." Gates leaned his head back. "For a long time I've been thinking of asking to be let out of the project."

She stared at him. "Woodrow, I won't hear of it!"

"It's different with the others," Gates said. "They couldn't all be reassigned. For most of them, it's this or nothing. But I could be reassigned. There's enough assay work just for production."

Madeline came over to him. "Drink your drink," she said. "And then I'm going to give you a sleeping pill. I think you need a good night's sleep." She put the bottles into the cabinet. "Frankly, Woodrow," she said casually, while she picked up the ashtrays, "I simply could not bear it if you were to quit. It's just not like you." She started for the kitchen. "It's so—so unmanly!"

Brainard swiveled around in the chair and reached for a cigar, glancing at Vought across the desk. Vought was thinking it over, but he was a fast thinker and it wouldn't take him long.

On the clock beside the humidor Brainard noticed that it was

500

after three o'clock. Janet would be at the cabin by now, waiting. Undisturbed, he looked away. Let her wait.

"It's an interesting suggestion, Gil," Vought said. "It's worth thinking about."

Brainard nodded and took his time unwrapping his cigar. Morale, it's wonderful, he thought. When it's high, you can hit them with everything you've got and they hardly feel the punch—but take it away, and you don't even have to push. You can just sit and wait for things to fall apart. Now that this project had started to slide, it was going downhill fast.

He lit his cigar. Down in the yard, he could see two men hurrying as if they were cold, and he thought that maybe he wouldn't bother to go out there at all today. After a while, if he didn't show up, Janet would leave.

"On the whole it seems a constructive idea, Gil," Vought said. "Perhaps we should think about it and then get together and work out the details."

"Whatever you say, Tony," Brainard said. "You're closer to it than I am."

"Well, I'd like to think so," Vought said. "Although you have a remarkable grasp of the essentials. Much better than some men who are closer."

Well, he was making up his mind, Brainard thought. He was coming around. Vought wasn't a man that you had to spell things out for —the way you did with Morrissey. When you told Vought that it might be a good idea to have a record in addition to Will Caroline's, Vought understood that the record already existed. When you just happened to mention it a week after Morrissey resigned, Vought understood that Morrissey had been supplying the information and that now he was being offered the job. And he wasn't still deciding. He was only figuring the angles, considering how he could best turn it to his own advantage. Vought was a sharp dealer, and he wanted to establish the best possible terms before he came in.

Brainard said, "Well, I try to keep an eye on things, but I've got my own job to do. I can't see everything. You're the man who'll be in touch now."

Vought examined his cigarette. "Of course, I haven't been formally appointed to Claude's position," he said.

"What the hell, Tony—who else is there?"

Vought smiled and smoked and said nothing.

"Will Caroline's not a fast mover," Brainard said. "It takes him time to get around to doing anything."

Hell, Will Caroline wasn't going to appoint Vought director, now or ever. He was protecting his baby, Cable. Will was going to run the show himself. And that suited Brainard fine, because he didn't want any second-string patsies. He wanted to pin the blame squarely where it belonged—on Will Caroline—and get rid of him. And then it would be a long time before anyone around Enright thought of dumping a couple of million dollars into research again. Research would be back where it belonged—a small untroublesome group that they kept around to smooth out production problems, increase yields and stay out of the way. Follow orders and not be seen much—or heard either.

"Tell me something, Tony," Brainard said. "What's your opinion of this new tack of Cable's—privately, that is?"

"You don't have to ask me, Gil," Vought snapped. "Claude resigned because of it. And you can just look at the other men and see that they haven't given him a vote of confidence."

"You don't go along with it at all?"

"Gil, if I had the authority, I wouldn't keep Cable working for me for five minutes. He's had a continually destructive effect, and this is the worst yet. My men feel that chances of success have been cut down to practically zero. If a good one comes to them, they'll follow through with it, but if it goes to him, chances are fifty to one it'll go down the drain."

Personally, Brainard would not have gone along with those odds, but he hoped Vought was right.

Vought stood up to leave. "Let's think about this record, Gil, and get together in a few days."

When Vought had gone, Brainard leaned back and butted his shoulders against the chair. This thing was going to fall apart all at once. Cable had rocked the structure, and Morrissey's resignation was the first crack in the plaster. Brainard had to smile. The whole time Morrissey had fought against this project, he hadn't done it as much damage as he had by the simple act of leaving it. Now suddenly Morrissey was credited with clairvoyance and decisive action —he was the man who had anticipated disaster and had the sense to leave the sinking ship. Well, if they wanted to make a prophet out of Claude Morrissey, Brainard wasn't going to stop them. He puffed contentedly on his cigar. That resignation couldn't have come at a better time. Another year was dragging to an end, and there would be the year-end reports—and that would send them into an even worse tailspin. When a man was licked, there was nothing like making him report and remind himself exactly how bad things were. Brainard was almost looking forward to watching them crack, one by one. Almost—hell, he intended to enjoy every minute of it. Some of them were beginning to crack already.

Then he remembered Janet and decided he'd just stay right here today, where he was comfortable and warm and feeling pretty good about things. What the hell—he didn't need her reports any more. He had Vought now. And she was getting expensive. Besides, he was sick of her.

Four o'clock passed, and he lit another cigar and leaned back to enjoy it, still turning the situation over in his mind. Let them go on a little longer, he said to himself. That's all right. Pretty soon another six months will be gone—and nothing will have happened. And another half-million will be gone, with nothing to show for it. And then who will those directors wish they had listened to?

And then—slowly Brainard sat forward in his chair—then who are they *going* to listen to? This time they listened to Hale because they've been under his thumb so long, it's practically a habit. But let him try that six months from now and see if they fall down again like tin soldiers.

It was growing dark already, and Brainard got up and switched on a light. And now Hale has stuck his neck out, he said to himself. He's taken a stand.

Thoughtfully Brainard began to walk around the room. He would win in the end, all right, because this would fail. But suddenly a whole new idea had come to him. He had been thinking only of getting rid of Will Caroline. Now he was beginning to wonder whether he couldn't do better than that. Let this go on long enough and it was possible that he could squeeze out Ade Hale, too.

THIRTY-FIVE

I N THE WEST, if he looked, Tom could see the moon, still high above the skeletons of trees, and over the water the first light of day was beginning to sift into the sky.

He poured a cup of coffee and stood at the stove, thinking that a man could insulate himself against all questions except his own. Against the doubts of others you could erect a buffer so that they couldn't touch you if you wouldn't let them—at least not often and not for long—but there was no defense against yourself, no way to fence off your own questions into some separate area where they wouldn't trouble you. Every day these past few weeks—while he did what he believed had to be done—he had said to himself, What if I am wrong? What if Lilly comes up with one that I have thrown away—or Lederle—or Merck? There has to be a reason for what I am doing.

Now, in the cold pale edge of daylight, he thought that there was an agony far worse than that of a failure like Baramycin. A failure didn't pull you out of bed before dawn, demanding to be settled. A failure was settled. It was a fact, and you knew there was nothing more you could do, and you put it behind you. But your own unanswered question didn't leave you alone—especially when you knew there was an answer. (There is always an answer.) Especially when you felt that you were very close to it and that you had been very close to it before and it still eluded you.

It was a cold morning, and he carried the coffee into the living room and piled some wood into the fireplace and lit a fire. On his desk were his record books, spread out as he had left them, from which, all weekend, he had tried to wrench that extra fragment of meaning that would furnish the missing piece and give him the answer he was groping for. He turned away from them. He knew those records practically by heart. He could probably recite them verbatim, cover to cover, and not make a single mistake. Like some idiot whiz, he thought, who could recite whole pages and not understand anything he was saying.

And that's not such a bad analogy, he said to himself. That's you, all right. You could recite the facts from beginning to end, and you don't know what you're doing, either. At least you don't know *why*,

which amounts to the same thing. . . . Not at all the same thing.
. . . The hell it isn't!

The sky was whitening now, and he could see long fingers of clouds beginning to pick up color from the sun. All the same, he said to himself, it is true that there has not been a single time when one of us took a crude antibiotic that was toxic and purified it and found then that it was nontoxic. Maybe it could happen. Maybe it has happened somewhere else. But it has not happened to us—not once.

He felt the little indefinable quickening in his stomach that was becoming familiar to him—the recurrent symptom of this struggle to bring to the surface the buried, half-formed thought that his feelings refused to yield up. Come on—come on—he pressed himself. His eyes went back to the record books. The story was always the same. The antibiotic was toxic and it stayed toxic. The *antibiotic* was toxic . . . His mind balked. The more you struggled, the more you forced it, the tighter your mind closed up. He put down the coffee cup and took a jacket and went outside.

The sun was firing the sky now, and a single gull was up looking around, diving to the water. Tom watched it and thought that the pickings must be lean this time of the year. He walked up the boardwalk, moving quickly to keep warm. In Amity's yard he saw two small brown birds, pecking at strips of suet she had hung for them on the branch of a tree, and he walked idly across the frozen ground for a closer look. The strings were weathered gray, and the suet had been eaten down to the shreds. Amity had been here since the ground hardened, he decided, if she had hung out food for the birds, but you couldn't tell from the pecked shreds how long ago.

It was very cold. He slipped his hands into his pockets and looked at her house with the shades drawn and the look about it of no one home. He was beginning to wonder a little about himself. He missed Diana, even though he didn't want her. He wanted a girl and yet there was no girl he wanted. He was waiting for a girl that he had never wanted—and yet it was true that he was waiting for her, and not only because something in him was trying to fill the empty place left by Diana, although that was probably part of it. He shrugged. He didn't pretend to understand it, and he didn't have time to think about it. Maybe it was just the old story—a man was a creature of many selves and each self had its demand and the demands were not necessarily in harmony.

In the same way that one part of him was certain he was right, and another part of him said, Why?

He looked back at the small birds pecking diligently at the shreds of suet. These were the early birds—the small ones. In another hour they would be driven off by big loudmouthed starlings. That was a useless piece of information which he had observed these past mornings when he was up early and out pacing the boardwalk. Now, with the pickings scarce, this was how the small ones survived—by getting busy more than an hour ahead of their tougher competition. One way or another, the species survives, Tom thought—one way or another it finds a means that will work. Just as a microorganism produces an antibiotic to kill another and the second develops resistance in order to live—and the first then effects subtle changes in its lethal ammunition. All to survive, he thought. Just to get a fair share of food and living space. Grub and lebensraum and another fellow's poison. And these small birds were up and busy by six-thirty, and the starlings didn't show up until eight o'clock. Standing here on the hard frost-covered ground, Tom grinned. He liked that—something about that pleased him.

And then suddenly something stirred in him, and he felt again that indefinable quickening in his stomach. Your stomach is getting to be like a hound dog's nose, he told himself—twitching every time it gets a whiff of the scent. Only you are not much of a hound dog, personally, because you get the scent but never the fox. His stomach stirred again. I never say, This crude stuff is toxic, he thought—I always say, This *antibiotic* is toxic.

And there wasn't a single time, he told himself, when getting rid of some of the impurities—or getting rid of damned near *all* of the impurities—changed anything. Take EA 7, he thought. With EA 7, the mice had developed ataxia but they had been protected. They had lived a day longer than the controls and died on the third day— from the antibiotic. And after I dropped EA 7, Max went on with it —because it protected, and the mice lived for two days and everyone else was excited about it. And he took that one all the way. He got it pure. And it was still toxic—same way—same time. The mice still died on the third day.

And some of them, he said to himself, we threw out because they didn't protect. Like EA 202 and like Illiomycin. The mice died from the disease but the antibiotics were nontoxic—and *right at the start they were nontoxic. At the very first test, when they were loaded with impurities, they were nontoxic!*

When they're toxic, they stay toxic. Get rid of the impurities and they're still toxic.

And when they're nontoxic, they're nontoxic—right at the start. And when that happens, it can only mean that the antibiotic is nontoxic and since it's loaded with impurities, they are nontoxic, too.

Take penicillin, he thought. That first penicillin was like brown mud—everyone who saw it describes it the same way. That first penicillin that went to the army was about ten per cent pure. But it saved lives. And it didn't do any harm. I saw men who got that crude penicillin—I saw hundreds of men who got it—and it cured them. It saved their lives. And that means the penicillin was nontoxic—and the impurities were nontoxic, too.

And the same with streptomycin! Streptomycin was even less pure than penicillin when they first used it. And people got up and walked around because of it who would otherwise have died. It was loaded with impurities—it was more than ninety per cent impurities —but those impurities didn't do any harm! The streptomycin was nontoxic and the impurities were nontoxic!

All right, then, he said to himself, what does this tell you? What are you trying to say? That only the antibiotic is toxic and never the impurities? No—not that. That isn't logical. And yet it seems to happen that way. Toxic stays toxic—no matter how much junk you get rid of. Nontoxic is nontoxic right at the start—no matter how much junk is still there.

And then he thought, *maybe together!*

Until now, we have said, Here is a bug making fifty to a hundred different substances, and some of those substances are toxic and some are not. Until now we have said, We can't know which are toxic —so we must get rid of the impurities, and then perhaps the antibiotic, by itself, will be all right. From the start, that is what we have said—and that is what we have done. And maybe that is wrong!

Maybe, he said to himself, the emphasis should be on the *producer* rather than on the *product*—on the bug rather than on the stuff it turns out. Maybe one bug turns out a product that is toxic and another bug turns out a product that is nontoxic. Not good *antibiotic* —bad *impurities*—or vice versa. But good *bug*—bad *bug!*

507

And if that is true, he thought, then it all falls into place. Toxic antibiotic—toxic impurities. Nontoxic antibiotic—nontoxic impurities. And that is what seems to happen. That is what the evidence seems to say has happened—and that is what can be expected to happen in the future.

He felt it. He felt that it was right. Deep inside him something was released, and he felt the answer that he had been struggling for. He felt the rightness of it in his blood and in his bones. He felt it in a way that was more than reason. He felt it in a way that was visceral.

Then a starling screeched, and he saw that it was time to go in and get ready to go to work.

When he arrived at the Monday meeting, the other biochemists were already there, all sitting together, lined up beside Vought.

As soon as Hale and Will Caroline entered the room and the meeting began, Vought spoke up for them. "The rest of us," he said, waving a hand in the direction of his followers, "have been discussing this radical departure from all accepted procedure, which, I am told, Dr. Cable has now put into practice."

Tom smiled. He guessed they had—every time you saw them, they had their heads together, and it didn't take much imagination to figure out what they were talking about.

"Frankly, I didn't think Dr. Cable would go through with it," Vought said. "I thought his integrity as a scientist would assert itself, and that when he considered that incredibly impure antibiotic after the third trial in mice, his conscience would force him to work on it further. Now I understand that he is indeed throwing them out after three trials in mice."

Tom looked up and started to speak, but Vought held up a hand. "Please let me finish," he said. "The rest of us have consulted together, and we wish to register a formal protest against this reckless action. We feel that it is pure defection—an open refusal to do the work—and we want it so understood."

The others hastened to concur.

"We feel," Vought went on, "that while we have persisted and done a thorough job—because we know we should—one man has compromised our standards of excellence. One man—completely alone, without the support of even one of his colleagues, without a

508

shred of scientific evidence, with no logical scientific reason—has made a decision to abandon the work at a stage at which the rest of us feel we have hardly begun. The antibiotic is no purer at his third trial than at our first, and yet, at that point, he stops working on it. It's our opinion that this man, with this action, jeopardizes the entire combined effort of the rest of the staff, and we wish to so state in this formal protest."

Tom waited a minute. "Are you through?" he said to Vought.

"I have finished my statement," Vought said. "Now our group would like to have it discussed."

"O.K.," Tom said. "Today I have the reason."

Vought looked at him. "What reason?"

"First let me ask you whether anyone has re-examined his records and found a single instance of an antibiotic that was toxic the first time it went into mice that, later, after it was purer, was nontoxic."

There was no answer. But Tom was certain that they had looked and looked hard.

"Second—is there any man here who has not had a nontoxic antibiotic—one that he threw out because it didn't protect?"

"Dr. Cable, our concern today is not with our work but with yours," Vought said.

"Well—we all at least know of antibiotics that have gone into mice and the mice died the next day—from the infection—"

"Dr. Cable, if you're referring to Illiomycin—" Vought said sharply.

"I'm not referring to Illiomycin—but we can use it as an example. Illiomycin—or my EA 202. You got Illiomycin pure—but the first time it went into mice, it wasn't pure. It was loaded with impurities —it was mostly impurities. Why didn't the impurities kill the mice?"

"This is irrelevant to our discussion," Vought said.

"This is not irrelevant!" Tom said. "The impurities didn't kill the mice, because from the start the antibiotic was nontoxic and the impurities were nontoxic."

"Well, what does that prove?" Weir muttered. "It was still no good!"

"And when they *are* toxic at the start, they stay toxic—no matter how many impurities we get rid of."

"That is not a proven rule," Vought said.

"You can't disprove it!"

509

"The burden of proof is not on me!" Vought said.

"Give me one instance," Tom pressed him, "one instance in which getting rid of the impurities changed anything."

The others sat silent.

"Well, is there?" Hale said.

"I don't know of one, Ade," Will Caroline said. "That's why this interests me." He nodded to Tom. "Go on."

"From these two facts, we can draw one of two conclusions," Tom said. "Either we can say only the antibiotic is toxic and never the impurities—"

"That's totally illogical," Vought said. "That doesn't make sense."

"You're right—that doesn't make sense," Tom said. "And so we take the only conclusion left to us." He paused and leaned forward. "If a microorganism makes a toxic antibiotic, it tends to make toxic impurities. If it makes a nontoxic antibiotic, it tends to make nontoxic impurities. The same. They go together."

"Oh, this is unbelievable!" Vought said.

"Think about it!"

"Oh, I can't believe it!" Vought sat back and shook his head. "Really, Dr. Cable—when a microorganism turns out fifty to a hundred different substances, what is the rationale of supposing that one substance is toxic just because another is?"

"What is the rationale," Tom countered, "of one little bug turning out a hundred things so different that they are totally unrelated to each other? These are busy but fairly simple little bugs—and they'll change like foxes to respond to conditions—but what they produce tends to be chemically related. And so, whether antibiotic or impurity, the stuff that one bug turns out is a man's meat and the stuff that another bug turns out is a man's poison. Or a mouse's. Or a rat's."

A silence settled over the table while they turned this over in their minds. "For this program now," Tom said, "we have one critical question—can a microorganism make toxic impurities in the presence of a nontoxic antibiotic? And the answer is no—it cannot! If the crude antibiotic is toxic, we don't have to say it may be only the impurities—get rid of the impurities and we may have a nontoxic antibiotic. Because we won't have a nontoxic antibiotic. If it's toxic at the start, whatever we get rid of, it will stay toxic, because toxic impurities go with a toxic antibiotic—the product of this microbe is toxic. This microbe is an enemy. Throw the stuff out. And if a microbe is turning out a product that is all right, everything is going to be all right. The mice will live the first time—which they do."

"This is your reason!" Vought said. "This is the reason you've brought us to justify quitting after three times in mice?"

"You don't need three times!" Tom said. "Once!"

"Once!" Harrup gasped. "Last time you said three—"

"Now I say once!"

"You can't be serious!"

"Now we can really fly! We only have to get that antibiotic pure enough to be able to put enough into the mouse to cure it. We know that a mouse can take about one cubic centimeter of stuff. Once Dr. Gates tells us how much of this antibiotic is required to protect, we only have to get it pure enough so that there will be that much antibiotic in one cubic centimeter. As soon as it's that pure we can test it, and we only have to test it once. If the mice die, it's toxic. It's not going to get any better."

"Oh—this is just fantasy!" Vought said.

"There is no instance when this has not been so."

"It can't be true," Harrup said. "There must be an exception!"

Tom smiled. "Probably there is. Knowing how diabolically clever these bugs are, I think that somewhere, someday, there will probably be an exception—but I don't know of any, and at Enright we have not had any."

"Nature always has its exception," Will Caroline put in. "A tornado is an exception—an earthquake is an exception."

"And they can destroy you," Vought said.

"But you don't live in fear of them," Will said. "You don't build your life around that remote possibility of calamity—and make every moment of every day a precaution against it."

"But this would be suicide," Harrup said.

"Dr. Harrup," Tom said, "you're always saying, 'How do you know?' Now I say it to you. How do you know?"

But he could read the hostility in their faces, and he knew they were unconvinced.

Then Mills spoke up. "It's true that they don't seem to get any better," he said. "So maybe Tom is right."

"And if he is not?" Vought said. He turned to Tom. "If you are wrong, what then?"

"I don't think I'm wrong."

"But if you are wrong," Vought persisted, "who suffers the loss?

Not you. You come in here, breathing fire—telling us to find the courage to take risks. But are you talking about courage or panic? You're ready to gamble everything on a hunch. And that's all this is —intuition—nothing more. Totally unverified—totally unproven in any controlled way. It's about as reliable as a hayseed farmer saying, 'I just kinda got a feelin' it's going to blow!'"

He was right there, Tom knew. It hadn't been proved. But in his own mind there was no doubt.

"And yet you are taking fifty per cent of the best cultures!" Vought hammered on. "Dr. Derrick only brings in the best, and with this obsession for speed, you are taking half of them. We've built up an elaborate system for getting cultures from all over the world—we've worked out carefully organized procedures for screening them—and now fifty per cent of the best are going to be haphazardly grown, slightly purified, tested once while they're still unbelievably crude—and then thrown down the drain."

With a final gesture of disgust, Vought zipped shut his briefcase. "Well—that's not for me! Why should this company waste another dime on this project when one man is throwing out fifty per cent of the best possibilities—on a hunch? One test indeed! And that one coming much too soon—on material much too crude—to be conclusive. If you talk forever, Dr. Cable, you can't say enough to convince me. There is no argument that can persuade me to concede one inch to your intuition. At Enright's expense I will not be so generous."

The room was silent. Tom knew that most of them were thinking that Vought was right. He could read the accusations in their eyes. They felt that he was failing them when they needed him most—not only failing them but turning on them, sabotaging their own last desperate efforts.

"Well, Dr. Cable?" Hale said.

For the first time Tom felt himself waver. Vought's figures were accurate. It was true that he was taking fifty per cent of the best. And it was true, too, that he wasn't getting them very pure—that he was sending them, still very crude, to mice. And now he was saying that the first test would be the last. And do I have the right, he thought, to take this chance?

"The only thing to do is to set up a check system on his work," Harrup said to Vought. "Examine everything before he throws it out, and see that the best of them go to someone else."

512

"It's not fair to the other men," Vought said.

"You can't let him go on like this without doing it," Harrup said. "With no proof whatsoever—"

For a moment the old doubts flooded back. What if I am wrong? Tom thought. What if I throw out a good one—a great one—that actually did have only a toxic impurity?

Vought caught the first flash of doubt in Tom's eyes, and he knew that his words had found their mark. A little disdainful smile came to his lips. "We can't burden every other man," he said, "because the work is too hard for one man—because he is cracking under the pressure of our standards."

Suddenly Tom wondered whether Vought could be right. Is it too hard for me? he said to himself. Am I giving up and then finding reasons to justify it? Have I dreamed up this convenient theory as an excuse not to do what I am no longer able to do?

"The rest of us don't like it, either," Vought said. "It's work—it's frustrating—we're understaffed—but we know our job and we do it. We—shall we say—resist the urge to fly." He smiled.

It was true, Tom thought, that he hated that grind. But the others hated it, too—and yet they did it, day in and day out, week after week. Even Weir, for all he complained, did it—he worked on them and he sent them to mice and he took them back and tried again— over and over. And always the easiest person for a man to delude is himself, he thought. Always some faithful inner ally supplies reasons for doing what he wants to do and keeps him from seeing his own weaknesses and failures.

"There's a lesson here for us," Vought said, "and we should profit from it. The whole project must have stricter central control —it must be guided absolutely by carefully considered group decisions."

Tom looked up and suddenly he grinned. Vought just couldn't resist trying to squeeze out a dividend for himself. Always the politician, he had to use it to seize a little more power. And then Tom laughed at himself, too. What are you getting so cautious about? he said to himself. You know you believe this—you know you think it's right. Just because Vought has to have it proved a dozen different ways doesn't mean you have to catch the disease, too. Then suddenly his thought veered off in another direction, and his hound dog of a stomach turned over.

"Well, Dr. Cable?" Vought said. "Is the discussion closed?"

"Wait a minute," Tom said. He held up a hand, trying to think something through. Maybe, he told himself—maybe you can give them what they want.

"Wait a minute for what?" Vought said.

Tom looked up at all the accusing faces across the table. He looked at Hale, who was showing his growing doubts. He looked at Will Caroline, who was wondering why Tom had backed off so suddenly. He looked back at Vought.

"You're right," he said. "Don't agree with just a hunch. Don't concede anything. Don't be generous."

Vought smiled. "I'm glad you've come to your senses."

"Test me."

Vought stared. "Test you!"

"How are we going to test you?" Harrup said.

"There's no established test for your theory," Vought said. "If there were a test for it, we'd have used it months ago."

"This didn't come up months ago," Will Caroline reminded him.

"Take the two antibiotics that we know are good," Tom said. "The only two that we know are nontoxic. Penicillin and streptomycin." The more he thought about this, the better he liked it. "With these two, we know positively that the pure antibiotic given in the proper dosage will not kill the mice—or send them into convulsions—or paralyze them. Right?"

"Obviously," Vought said.

"Only I won't get them pure. I'll treat them exactly as I want to treat the unknowns—and get them only pure enough to test. So when they go into mice, they will be loaded with impurities. I'll take penicillin and put it into my ten standard broths, just as I do the unknowns, and in each of those ten broths the microbe will make different things, so we're going to get all different kinds of impurities. Do you agree?"

"Of course," Vought said impatiently.

"Same thing for streptomycin?"

"That's right."

"And in each case, if it were pure, it would be nontoxic."

"Yes."

"So if anything happens—if there's any toxicity—it will be in the impurities?"

"That's fairly obvious."

"And if nothing happens?"

514

"That's a test," Will Caroline said.

Hale nodded. "That's a test."

"Take it one step further," Tom said. He turned to Derrick. "Give them to me in blank."

Derrick looked up. "What do you mean, Tom?"

Tom picked up the culture reports in front of him. "These are the ones I'm taking today. Take out two and put in penicillin and streptomycin. Don't tell me which ones they are—just give them a number like the others. See if I miss them. Let's find out how soon I would know that they're good, how soon they will interest me, how much I would have to purify them, how many times I would have to send them to mice before I got excited about them. After all"— he grinned—"if I threw out penicillin or streptomycin, I'd be throwing a five-million-dollar antibiotic down the drain."

Their faces said they knew it wouldn't work.

After the meeting Tom dropped his briefcase on his desk and stood at the window. It was a brilliant winter day, and outside a lone gull skimmed over the water—just one, where in summer there were dozens—and Tom wondered whether it was the same one he had seen this morning and then where the others had gone and why this one had stayed behind. Every winter when the rest went off—to where things were more comfortable, probably—a few stayed behind. The odd ones, he thought—the irregulars, the loners. He looked at the gull and said, "Hello, friend," and it dropped into the water and rose again. Tom smiled and turned away and walked out into the laboratory.

Will Caroline heard the occasional sounds of the cook in the kitchen fixing dinner, and he hoped she would be slow tonight. He was in a mood to just drink his bourbon and talk a little with Callie. He didn't know why today's meeting should have started him thinking this way. He'd known these men long enough, and he knew, probably, most of what was good or bad about them and just about what could be expected of each one. There wasn't any reason for today's argument to set him off any more than some of the others had. Maybe, he thought, it was because the city, when he came through it tonight, had been jammed with Christmas shoppers and there had been colored lights everywhere and a Salvation Army Santa Claus on every block, reminding him that another year was almost gone. Or maybe it was just the mood he was in. Maybe every man, now and then, had to ask questions he already knew the answers to, just because he wished he could change them.

After the meeting he had walked back to the office with Hale, and Hale had said, "How about it—you think he's right?"

Will had taken a minute to answer, and then he hadn't really answered. "We'll find out, anyway," he had said.

At his voice, Hale had looked at him. "You only back him because he was the underdog?"

"He's no underdog."

"What's the matter, Will? Don't you like it?" Hale said.

"I like it very much," Will said. "I was just thinking about it, Ade —that if he's right, this is new and it's his own. He didn't read this in a book. He didn't come across it—or a part of it—in a journal. He thought of this himself—alone."

"If he's right—" Hale said.

"If he's right, it's the best thing that's happened yet."

And the others knew that, too, Will thought—and that was what was bothering him. Vought—and the others who had objected— all knew that if there was anything to it, it could break this wide open—and they should have been more willing to listen before trying so hard to bury it. And—he thought—if they had read it somewhere, they would have. If they had found it in a journal, even offered as a suggestion rather than as a fact, they would have at least examined it. But coming as it had from one of their own, it was too close. It didn't have the authority of the printed page, and they couldn't accept it. And what makes them like that? he wondered. Is it personal animosity? Is it an extension of self-belittlement? Is it that a man is never a prophet in his own home town? He shrugged. Maybe Tom would be wrong and it would turn out to be just good sound sense.

Only, he thought now, sitting here with Callie, they still should not have backed away so fast—faster than they could have thought about it. Nothing could change that. Backed away as fast as they could—all of them together—like a circus troop trained to jump at the shot of a gun. Well, that shouldn't bother him—they had always stuck together. They were all for teamwork. He was used to that.

Still, after a minute, he said aloud, "Cal, what makes a man make a cult out of teamwork?"

Callie smiled. "Different reasons, I suppose. Misery loves company, for one."

That was part of it. He thought about Vought and said, "Vought talks about the group and about teamwork as if they were just coming into fashion and you had to pump for them—to be sure they caught on."

He heard the sounds in the kitchen again and glanced in that direction. Callie looked at him and then got up and went out there, and he knew she would put dinner off awhile.

But when wasn't man part of a team? he thought. When did he ever live or work in a vacuum? Man has always been part of a team. And he has always been alone.

"All science is teamwork," he said, when Callie came back, "one way or another—and always has been. One man contributes one scrap—another man adds another scrap. If you're going to be absolutely literal about it, Cal, the minute a man opens a book, he stops working alone. In fact, he stops before he begins. By definition, his degree means he's absorbed vast quantities of information contributed by other individuals. What difference does it make if he reads it in a journal or gets it from another man sitting in the same room with him?"

Callie laughed. "Will, that's not the kind of teamwork they mean!"

"I know that," he said and smiled, "I'm sorry to say."

"Their team is a kind of robot battalion," Callie said, taking his glass to refill it, "in which no man thinks alone or acts alone and no man can be blamed alone."

That was it. He knew it too. And he wouldn't even mind so much, he told himself, if they would just act together with a little more courage. Although the idea of no man thinking alone was silly. How else did a man think, except alone?

"How do the others feel about this team propaganda?" Callie said. "The mavericks? Does it bother Tom, for instance, to always be called part of the team?"

Will laughed. "I don't think he cares what they call him, Cal—including a few pet names—as long as they don't get in his way."

Then his thoughts moved back to the theory that Tom had come up with, which was new and his own, and he said, "I suppose they really believe that there could be such a phenomenon as a team thought—a team mind."

"They believe it because they want to."

"It can't happen, Cal. Once the idea is born, men working together can do wonders with it—prove it, adapt it, develop it, apply it—but no idea ever had a miraculous multiple birth. The seed has to be born alone."

He drank the bourbon, beginning to feel better for it, and for getting this damned team foolishness out of his system. They talked about teamwork as though it were the noblest end man could achieve. But which was the greater miracle? he thought. The working together? Or the thinking, which had to happen alone?

"When will you know if Tom's right?" Callie said.

"It depends on how much he has to purify them—how long it takes. Probably not until after the first of the year."

"What if it works, Will?"

"If he's right, I think it will break things wide open."

"And if he's wrong?"

He shrugged. "The man who has never been wrong has never tried much." Then he said, "But they can talk team till they're hoarse, Cal. In the end—or in the beginning—every idea has to originate in one man's mind."

Tom grew the cultures for a week and filtered off the mycelium. He set up assay tests with paper discs on Petri dishes and sent samples for other tests to Gates. Overnight one of the cultures left huge rings of inhibition on the Petri dishes, and Tom knew it had to be penicillin or else the most potent antibiotic that anyone had ever had around here.

He went down to Derrick's laboratory.

"I'm interested," he said. "I'm interested in EA 117 right now."

"How'd you work it so fast?" Derrick said.

"I haven't worked it. I'm interested without doing a thing. Is it penicillin?"

"It's penicillin," Derrick said.

Back in his laboratory, Tom selected the best of the penicillin broths and was about to put it into solvent extraction when he stopped. This was a very potent broth. He looked again at the huge clear zone it had left on the Petri dish and he thought, What if I did nothing to this? What if I didn't purify it at all? Would it protect an animal?

He measured the zone of inhibition and figured. It seemed possible.

He took it to Gates for a double check.

"Pearly, tell me whether this is pure enough to go into mice."

Gates looked at the number. "Tom, you just started this yesterday."

"This is penicillin, Pearly. It hasn't been purified at all. Only filtered and dried. Check it and see whether, in this crude state, we can get enough antibiotic into a mouse to cure it."

"But, Tom, you haven't done anything to it!"

"Not a thing. Just tell me whether it's possible, Pearly," Tom said.

He left Gates and went upstairs and told Mills that he expected to bring in an antibiotic tomorrow.

The next morning Gates looked up when Tom came into his office.

"Not enough?" Tom said, at the expression on his face.

"Yes—there's enough," Gates said unhappily. "But, Tom, it's so crude. I mean—my God, Tom—don't you think, for your own sake, you ought to get rid of some of the junk?"

But the idea was to purify it only to the point at which Mills could get enough antibiotic into a mouse to protect it. And this was pure enough.

At ten o'clock Mills took out the first mouse and began the test. At eleven o'clock he injected the last mouse and put it back. At noon the mice were still fine. And they were fine at closing time. And at ten o'clock. And at midnight.

During the following morning, the controls died but the treated mice lived. And that night they were still alive. And they were alive the next morning. And the next.

He had done nothing to it. He had injected penicillin, with every impurity the microbe had made, into mice. And the mice lived.

PART SIX

MARCH –
SEPTEMBER 1948

I T WAS THREE MONTHS now since Claude had resigned, but Neil Harrup still caught himself looking into the next office, expecting to see him there. As long as he had been at Enright, Claude had been in that office. Now no one else had moved in and it was empty. Just as Morrissey's house was empty. A few weeks ago Winifred had come with the movers, and yesterday Harrup had seen an agent showing the house to strangers.

Standing at the glass panel, he looked at the bare desktop, with the two faint marks where Claude's heavy bookends had stood, and at the empty chair and at the file drawers, neatly closed. It was all so unnecessary, he thought. Claude would have been kept. Whatever happened to this ill-starred project, Enright would always need a small research staff, and Claude had seniority and he would have been kept.

Harrup turned away from the empty office. Three months. They had been the most depressing three months he had ever known. Not because of any specific reversal. Not because something had raised their hopes and then let them down—but because hope had not stirred at all. Nothing had happened. The days had dragged into weeks and the weeks into months that stretched into a dreary monotonous pattern of failure. The biochemists took their cultures and found nothing exciting. They worked the best they had and sent them to mice, and the mice died. Cable threw them out; the others worked them longer. Either way, it didn't seem to matter. With the others, ten a month were failing; with Cable, hundreds a month were failing. It was still failure.

Harrup moved to his desk and tried to get to work, even though the day was almost over. Then he saw Vought approaching, probably coming to talk about Cable's latest discards. As Vought came in, Harrup saw that he had the reports with him.

"He's getting worse all the time," Vought said. "Every week less and less work on each."

"Yes, I suppose he is," Harrup said.

"Just look at the number he's going through. What else can you think?"

Harrup took the reports, and the melancholy feeling that hung over him deepened. When he looked at these discards, he didn't think, as Vought did, that Cable was getting worse. He thought that here was another pile of failures. Another few hundred added to the thousands that had already failed. He thought that out of another whole batch, nothing had happened. "He doesn't seem to get discouraged—at not finding anything in all these, does he?" he said.

"He doesn't know enough to get discouraged."

Harrup's stomach was beginning to hurt. "Have you ever thought, Tony—the rate of failure in this kind of research is incredible."

"The rate of failure is increased," Vought said, "in direct ratio to the lack of organization."

Harrup looked at Vought and thought that he really believed that. In his own mind Vought had fastened the blame on a few men—Cable for his lack of discipline, Will Caroline for condoning it—and he really believed that was all that was wrong. Well—maybe for him it was a good thing. It was easier to go on if you thought the trouble was something you could correct and that then everything would be all right.

Harrup put the reports next to his briefcase. "I'll look them over tonight at home," he said.

After Vought had gone, Harrup picked up a journal that he wanted to take home, too. Then he found himself staring again into the next office. If only Claude had held on a little longer, he thought. But he couldn't have held on longer or he would have. And Claude could never have endured these last three months.

And yet, Harrup thought, it took a certain courage, too, at Claude's age, to quit. To just pull up stakes and leave everything behind—your home, the position you'd held for years, your own department, a good salary, a good retirement fund. Leave it all behind and go to something new. In some ways it took more courage to quit than to stay.

It was growing dark now, and Harrup put the reports into his briefcase. He was glad the day was over.

"They showed the house again today," Elaine said when he came in. "Twice."

Harrup's stomach twinged.

"Somebody's going to get a real steal there, you wait and see." The wide mouth smirked. "Claude Morrissey was a damn fool."

524

Harrup stood at the window, looking out at Gates's house. "In a way it took courage." He said what was on his mind, without thinking. "Picking up like that—leaving everything."

"Harrup," she said, "don't get any ideas about that kind of courage."

He didn't answer. There was so much she didn't understand about him. And, in a way, much that he didn't understand about himself. Like his feelings about this project. He was discouraged and dispirited—and he was not the only one—and he would still have opposed starting it. But now that so much had gone into it, if anyone asked him whether to stop or go on, he wasn't sure what he would say. Probably it was the practical streak in him—partly, anyway. He still hoped there might be some return on their investment. And it was partly something more. Pride, he guessed—for want of a better word.

"What are you thinking, Harrup?" Elaine said sharply. "Just standing there like that."

He glanced around. "I don't feel well," he said, because he didn't want to explain. His work was his own—the one area she couldn't invade. "Maybe I ought to see the doctor."

"Now, what's the doctor going to do? Harrup, that doctor knows your belly like his own face. He's told you what to do. Stop stewing."

"Maybe I should quit, too—for my health." He was only talking —saying it because he felt depressed and perverse and slightly ill.

"Don't be an ass! Now, who do you think would hire you if you quit?"

He didn't answer. He was sorry he'd said it.

"Harrup, you're forty-eight years old—and you look ten years older. Who would want you? After forty you're on the dark side of the labor market. I used to work with people with this problem. I know."

If she lived to be ninety, he thought, she would still have an answer for everything because for three years, as a social worker, she had worked with people with problems. Sometimes when he thought of all those poor people with all those problems that she had tried to manage, he shuddered. "Claude is fifty-four," he said.

"Claude Morrissey got a job as a teacher in a small college," she said. "Well, I am not settling down on any teacher's salary. And I'm not teaching my kid to pinch pennies—to live on any teacher's salary. Let somebody else's kid develop that little talent—not mine. So just you listen to me, Harrup—"

"Don't worry," he said. "I'm not going to quit."

"Why not?" she said, immediately suspicious that there was something she didn't know.

Harrup turned away. It was pointless to try to tell this woman anything. Long ago he had given it up. His thoughts went back to Claude and he wondered whether, now that he was up there at that college, he regretted his move. He'd like to drive up there someday to see how he was getting along. Maybe he would phone him tomorrow from the office—just to say hello.

A few minutes later Gates came home, and Harrup watched him walk dejectedly up his front steps. Sometimes he wondered how much longer Gates could hold on. Sometimes he even wondered about himself.

It took a certain talent to live with failure—day after day, month after month—and some men had it more than others.

"Every day Morrissey looks more and more like the guy who used his head," George Weir said. He gulped his drink and felt it harsh in his stomach. "And I just may decide to wise up and pull out too."

Janet shrugged. "Maybe you should start looking around."

"Well, what happened to you?" Weir looked up. "Last time I said that, you damn near busted a gut!"

Janet studied her hair in the living room mirror. "Why sit around waiting to be blown up? Morrissey's quit already. Find something with a decent salary and take it."

"Decent salary—decent salary! That all you married me for—a decent salary?"

"What else did I get?"

He picked up the bottle and looked at her, hoping she'd object.

"Don't look at me!" she said. "You buy the liquor. You know how much you're hitting the bottle."

She walked out of the room and he looked after her. She'd probably broken up with some guy she had somewhere. Give her time to find another and she'd be telling him not to quit. "What's the matter?" he called after her. "You got no one around here who interests you any more?"

There was no answer. She was in the kitchen.

"You figure there's more in it for you somewhere else?" he shouted.

She came out of the kitchen. "George, get this through your sotted head. I don't give a damn whether you stay or quit. Suit yourself. Only shut up. And quit pulling this every night in front of the kids."

He sat down and put the glass on the table. He felt rotten. Everything was rotten. Nothing ever went right for him, and she was no help and he didn't know what to do. He jerked his head at the record book on the desk. "And that was another hot idea. Why should I keep writing that damn record? Nothing ever happens but failure."

"I don't give a damn whether you do that, either," she said.

The soft hazy light of a March thaw cast blurred shadows on the snow left by a late storm, and little rivers ran across the paved yard, forming black puddles that glinted in the sun. At his office window, Tom stood and looked out at the signs of the end of winter and thought that a man could be certain within himself that he was right and tell it to himself again and again—and yet, when nothing happened, old doubts came creeping back. And this had been a winter of feverish activity that had produced nothing.

Since the first of the year he had had a second technician, a wiry girl named Nancy Blye, who was quick and smart. By the middle of January he had had twenty-five cultures going at once. Shoot for thirty-five, he had said to himself. Look them over and move on—assume that most of them are no good. If they're only grampositive, they had better be very good, because with penicillin around, you are trying to beat something that is very good. Better to look for something unusual, he had said to himself.

By February he was working thirty-five at a time. Shoot for fifty, he had said to himself. If there is a reason to drop it, drop it. And look for the reason. If it doesn't grow well, that's a reason. If it's unstable, that's a reason. If it's toxic, that's the best reason of all. Don't bleed over it. If it's good you'll know it, he had said to himself—everything about you will know it.

Now it was March. It was the seventeenth of March and he had raced through hundreds of cultures—and he had found nothing. There had been no broad-spectrum antibiotics and very few that were even interesting. It was hard to find new ones, and when you did, they were toxic. Once, he remembered, he had described himself to Amity as a scavenger. Now it was like scavenging on an endless beach that yielded no treasure. It was just a fruitless search, day after day. He was geared to rejection. And he was rejecting.

For a moment he thought about Amity and wondered what had happened to her. She didn't answer her telephone in New York— she hadn't answered his letters—and she never came here any more.

A blob of snow slushed off the roof and down the window and Tom turned away. In the laboratory he could see Moose and Nancy Blye beginning to work on the cultures he had selected out of this week's batch. Once again there had been nothing very exciting. On his desk were Derrick's data sheets. All gram-positive. Nothing unusual. On the counter under the window he could see the rows of Petri dishes where each week they set up their own quick tests on the new cultures. Nothing very potent. A few decent-sized rings of inhibition, made by antibiotics he would work on if everything else was all right—the best of a dull lot. He looked at another stack of reports—the ones he was rejecting—and the doubts began to sift back, as they did every week now when he looked over the new cultures and found nothing—each week a little stronger than the week before. What if I am wrong? he said to himself. What if I'm going too fast and throwing away something good?

The door opened and he saw that it was Gates, bringing his reports on this latest batch. He would compare Gates's findings with his own, Tom thought, and he still would find nothing. Then he saw that on Gates's face as he hurried into the room, there was a look that no one had worn around here in a long time.

"Tom, you've got one!" Gates called out before he had the door closed. "You've got one, Tom! It's broad-spectrum!"

Gates thrust a report at him, and Tom looked at him and thought that there must be a mistake. Somebody in Gates's laboratory must have mixed up his samples with somebody else's.

"Well, look at it, Tom—for God's sake!" Gates tapped the report. "Right there. EA 77."

Puzzled, Tom read the report. This was his culture, all right. He looked up at Gates. "There must be some mistake—"

"Why?" Gates said. "There's no mistake! EA 77 is broad-spectrum!"

"But it's not." Tom went into his office and found Derrick's data sheet. EA 77 hit gram-positive only. "Pearly—something's wrong."

"Wrong! After all these terrible months—it's great! I mean, I know it isn't awfully potent, Tom—but my God, it is broad-spectrum!"

Moose came over and handed Tom two of their own test plates for EA 77 broths which showed average-sized zones of inhibition. "It's not bad, Pearly," Tom said.

Gates looked at the test plates. "Tom—we didn't get that big a zone."

Something inside Tom sounded a warning. Something that had learned to suspect every trick these bugs could play told him that there was something strange here.

Now Gates was becoming puzzled, too. "It is strange, isn't it?" he said. "This potency difference—and the way it didn't hit gram-negative on Charlie's plates."

Why not? Tom thought sharply. What happened? What's the matter with it? "Pearly," he said suddenly, "when did you set this up?" Gates looked puzzled, and Tom said, "We sent you the samples in the morning. What time did you get to work on them?"

"Let's see." Gates thought a minute. "Your Miss Blye brought them in—and Miss Potter took them—and then Vought came in and insisted we do his first. He always pushes us, Tom," Gates said apologetically. "It's almost easier to agree than to argue."

"Pearly, what time? What time did she get to them?"

"It was late afternoon—I think about four o'clock."

Tom closed his eyes and thought, It's unstable. "We did ours in the morning—as soon as we filtered them. It's unstable enough to change between ten o'clock in the morning and four in the afternoon."

Now a disturbed look spread over Gates's face, too. "Golly, Tom, that's a tough break." Then the look changed to one of alarm. "But, Tom—you're not—I mean, I know you don't work on them if there are things wrong—and I respect your right to feel that way—but, Tom, you're not going to reject this one? I mean it is *broad-spectrum*."

Unhappily, Tom looked at the report in his hand. You no sooner made yourself a rule, he thought, than you had to break it. If it has one defect, that's one defect too many, he had said. If anything will stop you, let it, he had said. And here was EA 77. Not very potent. Not much of it. Obviously unstable. Everything wrong. But it was a broad-spectrum antibiotic, and it had been a long time since they had had one. And what could he do?

He told Nancy Blye to grow some more. He had a feeling he was going to need it.

He put EA 77 into solvent extraction with acid and butyl alcohol, and because it was unstable he re-extracted it immediately into a basic solution. He did the work himself—he wanted to watch this one—and when he was through, he took the samples himself to Gates.

The next morning when he came into the assay laboratory, Gates and Midge Potter were in a huddle over a report sheet. One look at Gates's face told Tom that something had gone wrong, and he thought, So it wasn't extracted and that means it's not going to handle easily—and will be more trouble still.

"Didn't work?" he said.

"We don't know, Tom," Gates said in a disturbed voice.

"Not through yet?" Tom said.

"Yes, we're through." Gates's eyes went to Midge and then to the report.

"All right, then, where's the antibiotic?" Tom said. Sometimes you had to work awfully hard to get the story out of Gates. "Is it still in the broth? Did we get it out? Did we re-extract it? Where is it?"

"It's nowhere, Tom."

"Nowhere!"

"It's disappeared," Gates said unhappily. "It's not in anything. You've lost it completely."

Midge Potter handed Tom the report.

"Send us some more, Tom, and we'll do it over," Gates said.

But Tom knew there was no mistake. He would send another sample and Gates would do it over, but he knew that the trouble was with EA 77. It was so unstable it had just decomposed. It had changed completely into something else and was no longer an antibiotic.

Already beginning to argue with himself, Tom walked back to his own laboratory. If it has one defect, that's one too many. If there's a reason to drop it, drop it. If it's unstable, that's a reason.

But not if it's broad-spectrum. If it's broad-spectrum, you find out why it's unstable. And then you try again.

Beating a nervous tattoo on his desk, Brainard looked at Vought impatiently. "Are you watching it?"

"I'm watching it carefully," Vought said. "And it's good. It's very

530

broad-spectrum. It's also very unstable."

Brainard fidgeted. He knew all that. He knew it was broad-spectrum and unstable. Who didn't? Even the janitor, probably, knew it was broad-spectrum and unstable. Irritated, at Vought and at everything, Brainard let his eyes go over to his humidor, and the tapping began again. Lately Brainard had been having headaches, and his doctor had cut him down to two cigars a day. It was only ten o'clock, and he had already smoked two cigars today. He looked back at Vought. "Why?" he said. "Why is it unstable?"

Vought smiled. "He can't find out why. He's tested with acid and it's not the acid. He's tested with alcohol and it's not the alcohol. It was unstable before he tried to extract it—but for some reason that our Dr. Cable hasn't been able to come up with, it was much worse afterward." Vought said it with a certain relish. Then he shrugged. "This week he's been working in an ice bath at five degrees, and he's had some luck. He's held onto it."

"It's no great achievement," Brainard said flatly. "Cool any antibiotic down—and it's more stable."

"Of course. Although I've heard there's still trouble. Gates is repeating some tests right now."

"All they do with this is to do it over," Brainard snapped. "First they do it—then everything stops and they do it over."

His eyes went to the cigar box. He would feel better if he got up and walked around, but he didn't want Vought to think he was unduly nervous about this EA 77. He didn't want Vought to start thinking anything, because he didn't trust him from here to the door. But with EA 77 turning up, Brainard had to reconsider his strategy. While he sat here trying to pull the story out of Vought, another part of him was already considering what this could do to his plans.

"What's your opinion, Tony?" he said. "Could it straighten out?"

"You know it could, Gil—as well as I do. It could straighten out overnight."

That was the trouble, damn it. "You think it's going to?"

"That's any man's guess."

"You're the man who's watching it, Tony."

"Gil, we both know an antibiotic always becomes more stable as you get it purer. Always."

Brainard moved his hand to the cigar box and hesitated, fingers tapping, and finally he took a cigar, telling himself it was just to fool with. With a cigar in his hand, he could think better. He said, "What I know right now, Tony, is that it's stalled dead."

The question was, would it stay that way? The May meeting was more than a month away. If EA 77 was still a problem then, still unstable, still crude, still untested in mice, then—Brainard's mind worked ahead while he thought this out carefully—then, with the right groundwork laid ahead of time, he could probably kill the project at that meeting. The board was growing impatient. Several directors were worried—he was in touch with enough of them to know that. But if he was going to do it, he would have to move soon.

Only Brainard didn't want to kill this project next month. He wanted it to go on. He wanted it to get worse. He wanted the situation at Enright to get bad enough to get rid of Will Caroline—bad enough to get rid of Ade Hale. Bad enough so that he would be damned certain he could do it—and not the hard way, with a lot of rough, behind-the-scenes spadework. When the time came, he wanted to slide this past the board as easily as a knife through butter. And that time wasn't here yet. Now he could probably kill the project—maybe even squeeze out Will Caroline—but that was all. And that wasn't enough any more. Why settle for half when, if he waited a little longer, he could get the whole pot?

Narrowly Brainard looked at Vought, sitting there, calmly smoking a cigarette, smiling—and saying next to nothing. He suspected that Vought was holding out on him. "All right, Tony," he said. "A man like you doesn't stand around watching a thing like this with no opinions. What do you think is causing it?"

Vought crushed out his cigarette before he spoke. "Of course, it could be a contaminant, Gil," he said. "Something in the broth that the microbe is making, along with the antibiotic."

That wasn't anything Brainard didn't know, either. And he knew, too, that if Cable could hold onto the antibiotic, working in that ice bath, until he got rid of the contaminant, then he was in business. Brainard fiddled with the cigar. Maybe he ought to move at the May meeting, after all—settle for what he could get, even if it wasn't everything he wanted. But on the other hand—supposing he made his move and lined up enough votes to kill the project—actually had a majority of directors walking into that meeting, expecting to drop the ax—and supposing a few days before the meeting they got this EA 77 into mice and the mice lived? Then what?

Ground lost that way could be hard to recover. And he'd have stuck his neck out—farther than ever before. Maybe he'd better wait.

"If he can hold onto it until he gets it relatively pure," Vought said, "it could steady up and be quite stable."

Nervously Brainard sniffed the still-wrapped cigar. "It'll take time," he said. A throb of pain shot through his head, and he yanked off the cigar wrapper. The hell with it. If his head was going to ache anyway, he might as well smoke. He put the cigar into his mouth without lighting it.

"Yes, it'll take time," Vought agreed. "But it could still be very good."

Brainard clamped his teeth into the cigar and struck a match. It broke in his fingers and he threw it down and struck another.

"If it's just some little fluke causing the trouble," Vought said, "you find it and get rid of it—and the company has a great broad-spectrum antibiotic."

The suspicion came to Brainard that Vought was needling him, that he knew more than he ought to—and he looked at him sharply. "Let me tell you something, Tony," he said. "No man in the company is more anxious than I am to see a really sweet broad-spectrum antibiotic in the palm of our hand. Something tried and tested—that I can produce. But I'm an officer of this company, and I've got an obligation and a responsibility." He pointed the cigar at Vought. "As long as I'm at Enright, to me one thing comes first—the good of the company."

"Oh, right," Vought said. "Absolutely."

"All right, then. When can we expect to hear something worth hearing about this fool thing? How close is it to mice?"

"Gil, it's very, very far from mice. This is still grossly impure."

"Likely to take a sudden jump?"

"Not that kind of jump."

Brainard waited, and when Vought didn't go on, he said, "Cable going to be able to handle it, Tony?" That would bring a reaction—and it did.

"Cable's not much at handling anything," Vought snapped. "You know how he works. Well—now he's stuck with his sloppy methods. This is one he can't throw out. Of course, he's not the only man in the company."

"You be interested in working on it, Tony?"

"I'm interested in anything promising," Vought said smoothly. "Naturally, if I worked on it, I'd expect authority and I'd assume the responsibility."

The bastard is worrying about how he can grab the credit if it's good, Brainard thought.

"With this one, it won't be a matter of a couple of purifications and off to mice," Vought said. "The microbe doesn't produce much —he'll have to really concentrate the antibiotic before he can send it to mice. This one won't be simple or easy."

Brainard smiled and thought that hatred was a beautiful weapon when you knew how to use it. He was getting his information now, all right.

"And Cable isn't that good," Vought told him. "He's very cocky with his radical theories—he's an arrogant personality—but when the going gets tough, he doesn't measure up."

"You're probably right," Brainard said.

He stood up to get rid of Vought. He had all the information he was going to get out of him today, and he wanted to think about it. "Let me know what the new trouble is, Tony," he said.

Brainard closed the door after Vought and walked around his office, thinking. He could wait. He didn't have to do a quick emergency job of trying to torpedo the project next month. This EA 77 wasn't going to straighten out in a hurry. And if it did, there would be something else wrong with it—like all the rest.

Everything was going to be all right, he told himself. Just give this project six more months and the directors would be asking themselves questions, without his telling them to, and getting the right answers. Questions like who had been smart about this from the start—Hale or Brainard? Who had been the realist? Who had been the businessman? Who had given them the right steer about its chances and its costs? . . . And who had been a damned fool?

With a new flow of confidence, Brainard puffed his cigar. Well, Hale was a fool. What else could you call him? And when he thought of the way he used to jump when Hale said jump—the way he used to keep his mouth shut if Hale wore a certain look! It made him sick to remember it. Why, today he didn't even respect the man. Today he saw him for what he was—a gullible fool—a tin god, still hoping to be restored to his former glory by a miracle that wasn't going to happen. Maybe Ade Hale had been a big man around here once, but that time was past. Every day Hale's stock was going down—and it wasn't going back up, either. And when the right time came, Ade Hale was going to be out in the cold with the door of Enright slammed in his face.

Brainard broke off the ash and looked at his cigar. His head felt better. Hell, these cigars didn't cause his headaches. That fool doctor probably couldn't think of anything else—so he'd told him to cut out the cigars. Then he was thinking about Hale again, and he shook his head at the memory of what used to be. Ade Hale. Brainard hated him now. He hated him for all the times he had kowtowed to him. He hated him for the runaround Hale had given him all those years. But mostly he hated him for a fool.

Working in an ice bath at five degrees, Tom tried once to purify EA 77 and made some progress.

He tried again and failed.

He did all the work himself—he kept it in the refrigerator every minute that he was not working on it—he took it to Gates himself. He tried a third time and there was a small improvement—too small to be encouraging.

He tried a fourth time. And he lost it.

"Lost it!" He seized the report from Gates. "Didn't you keep it cold?"

"Of course we kept it cold," Gates said miserably. "We didn't leave it out for a minute."

"You got a real Houdini there," Midge said. Midge wasn't trying to be funny. She was puzzled, too.

Tom read the report again. It just didn't make sense. He had done all the work himself, and he was certain that he had used nothing in which the antibiotic was unstable. He had kept the temperature at five degrees—and he believed that Gates had, too— and now, for no reason, EA 77 had disappeared again—completely!

"Tom," Gates said, very much disturbed, "that antibiotic decomposed after you got it purer."

"After?"

Gates nodded. "You got rid of a lot of junk, Tom. You concentrated it—quite a bit."

That made even less sense. An antibiotic always became more

535

stable when you got it purer. Never less. If he had really gotten this purer, there was even less reason for it to decompose. Only there was a reason—because it had happened.

George Weir was sitting at a corner table at the far end of the cafeteria with his back to the room and when Gates came in, he wondered what he was doing way down there all alone, just staring across the table at the green wall. Derrick and Mills were at a nearer table, and Gates got his coffee and sat down with them, and glanced over, uneasily, at George's back.

"Ah've seen 'em before where you had to keep 'em cold," Derrick was saying, and Gates knew they were talking about EA 77. "But ah never heard of one like this. Did you, Pearly?"

Gates stirred his coffee. He had worried so much about EA 77 he hated to even talk about it. "Keeping it cold helps," he said. "But apparently not enough. When Tom lost it at five degrees, he cooled it down to zero and held onto it again. Then he got it purer—and then yesterday he lost it again."

"At zero?" Derrick said.

Gates nodded. "He got it purer and it just decomposed."

"If it weren't so damned critical," Mills said, and grinned, "and taking so much time with no time to spare, I'd be all for this EA 77. At least it's got everyone out of that rut."

"It's got everyone miserable," Gates said.

Weir walked past on his way for more coffee, and Gates looked up and said, "Get your coffee and sit down, George."

"No, thanks," Weir said. "I'm reading something down there."

Gates watched Weir go down and sit alone again in the corner, and then, reluctantly, he took his coffee and went down there, too, noticing as he sat down that Weir was not reading anything. "That report I sent you this morning on your EA 103 was encouraging, George," he said. "That took a good jump."

Weir took out a small pill bottle. "I haven't seen it yet."

"But, George, I sent it up two hours ago. Didn't you get it?"

"I got it. I just didn't get around to reading it yet."

"But that one looks good, George. You could send it to mice—" Gates broke off. Weir had unscrewed the top of the pill bottle and he was pouring a liquid into his coffee. "George, what's that?"

"That?" Weir said. "That's a tonic, Pearly."

"George, what's the matter with you!" Quickly Gates looked to see whether anyone was watching. If George were seen drinking on the job, he would surely be fired. "For God's sake, George!"

Weir sipped his coffee, and Gates looked at his eyes and wondered how many cups he had had already.

"So what's the scoop today on EA 77?" Weir said.

Gates hesitated. For weeks George had been disagreeable and hard to get along with, but now all his hatred seemed to have focused on EA 77, and Gates didn't know why he should feel that way when it wasn't even his antibiotic, but he hated to discuss it with him.

"Well, what's it doing?" Weir said.

"There's nothing new, George. Max is working on it, too, now."

"How cold was it when they lost it this time?"

"Around zero."

"A-ah—it couldn't happen. Last week you said they held onto it at zero."

"It is happening, George. The more you concentrate it, the more unstable it gets."

"It can't! It doesn't make sense!"

"It's happened twice now. They lower the temperature and they hold onto it. Then they get it purer and they lose it and they have to lower the temperature again."

"It's something else," Weir insisted. "They're lousing it up some other way."

Gates kept quiet. There was no point in arguing. Weir drank his coffee, which must be lukewarm by now, and lifted heavy eyes to Gates. Gates thought that he must have had quite a few cups before he came in.

"Pearly—you can't depend on anything around here, any more," Weir said. Gates could hear the discouragement in his voice and felt some of it stirring in himself, too. "You can't trust anyone. Just like a goddamned female. You can't trust anything."

Gates just sat without answering, and Weir leaned forward on the table. "Not that I mind things changing. Now, I always kept up with new stuff as much as any man. You know that, Pearly."

"Of course you did, George. George, let's get back to work."

"Now, wait a minute and let me finish! Now you know I always kept up. But, Christ, the bottom is falling out of every goddam thing we ever learned. Everything we used to count on has turned to dirt. You got nothing solid, any more."

"Oh, I wouldn't say that," Gates said.

"What? What you got that you were once sure of, Pearly, that you're still sure of today?"

"Well—not as much, it's true."

"You got nothing!"

Weir lit a cigarette and flicked the match toward the ashtray and missed. Gates picked it up and put it in.

"Pearly," Weir said suddenly, his eyes narrow and mean, "maybe it's your fault. Maybe you're the one who's lousing it up."

"My fault!"

"Maybe they aren't losing that Number 77 at all. Maybe you are, Pearly. Maybe you're pulling one hell of a boner somewhere—you ever think of that, hey?"

Shocked and hurt, Gates stared at Weir. "I watch that from the minute it arrives," he said. "I've done every bit of the work on it myself."

"You can make mistakes, Pearly."

Resentfully Gates stood up. "George, I'm going back to work. And you should, too." He waited a minute. "George?"

But Weir was wound up now, and already he was talking about something else. "Pearly, we got skinned, you and me—you know that?" he said bitterly. "We got degrees. Degrees! It was nothing but a gyp. Those professors—acting holier than anyone—and they didn't know a goddam thing—the sons of bitches!"

Weir drained his coffee cup and plunged on. "It's not going to be that, Pearly," he burst out, and Gates realized that his mind had gone back to EA 77. "It's something else lousing it up—not that it's more unstable because it's getting purer. That couldn't happen. Everything gets more stable when you get it purer. That holds. That's always been."

"George, why don't you stop worrying about EA 77 and think about the good one you've got in EA 103? Why don't you go up and read that report that's been sitting on your desk all morning?"

Weir laughed. "What for? What's the rush?"

"Because it can go to mice, George."

"All right, so it can go to mice!" Weir shouted. "So I'll send it to mice, and the mice'll get the shakes and drop dead. Listen, Pearly —that bastard Cable is right about one thing. When he says, 'Why bother? They're all lousy anyway.' Then he's right."

Gates stood another moment at the table, and then Weir got up and followed him out of the cafeteria, still talking. "If I look at your report today or tomorrow or next week, what difference does it make? What difference does any of it make? Everything we ever counted on is wrong. We don't know anything. We can't trust anything."

By the time Gates got back to his own laboratory, he was thoroughly depressed.

The next day Tom lowered the temperature of the ice bath to five degrees below zero and he held onto EA 77.

He got it purer at five below—and he lost it.

"What's wrong, Will?" Ade Hale said. "What's he leaving undone?"

"He's not leaving anything undone, Ade. He's working day and night, literally—trying everything—reading everything. And Max Strong is, too. There's just never been anything like this one—anywhere—and the clues are scarce. All they can do is keep lowering the temperature until they can find out what's causing the trouble."

"Then tell them to push it down and get on with it."

Will Caroline was silent, and Hale began pacing the floor of his office. "Will, we both know this can't go on much longer. The board won't sit still for it, even if I would. And I'm not sure I want to."

"Broad-spectrum antibiotics do exist, Ade. We've found them."

"The moon exists, but we can't reach it. And Enright can't afford to try."

Ade was having a bad day, and Will Caroline thought that this frustration was taking hold of everyone. If they could even define the problem, they would feel better, no matter how difficult it might be to solve. But this was like shadowboxing. They were trying to explain the behavior of a vanishing antibiotic when that behavior defied all past experience and every law they knew. And they were getting nowhere.

"Will, there isn't a man on the board today who sees any sense in going on."

"Most of them didn't think it made sense two years ago."

"And maybe they were right," Hale said. "We've put a fortune into this—and there's no return and not much promise of any. Those men are adding up the figures—they're thinking about what they could have done with that money and the return it would have brought." He looked around. "And if they overlook anything, Brainard will remind them."

"The two years haven't been altogether a waste," Will said. "We've come a long way."

"The board isn't thinking about how far we've come. They're thinking about profits that weren't made—and about extra dividends that might have been paid." Hale stopped at the window and looked out at the fermentation building. "And they don't like it. They can't turn back the clock and undo the damage, but they can say enough. And they're saying it. And I'm about ready to say it, too. We took the chance and it didn't work. We'll write it off because there's nothing else we can do—but let's get back on the track and start to make some money."

Hale began walking back and forth across the room again, stepping over his long telephone cord every time he came up to it. Will watched him a moment and then said, "We've solved a lot of problems since we started, Ade."

Hale threw him a doubtful look and stepped over the telephone cord and kept walking.

"Things that were problems in the beginning have become routine in these two years," Will said. "Do you remember the arguments they had over where to get the soil? And how many to pick from each sample? We never hear about those things any more. And not so long ago they were arguing about paper chromatography—and now they've accepted it. Whether they admit it or not, they all look at those chromatograms—and nobody works streptomycin or streptothricin any more."

"It's not enough, Will."

"Those are the things that slowed us down, Ade. It was only a few months ago that they were arguing about whether to work in width or in depth—and when Cable said he would test only once in mice, that was going to be the end of everything. Well, nobody sends them to mice six or eight times any more—not even Vought, for all his speeches. Everyone is working them less. We have more to show for those two years than the board realizes—more, I think, than we realize ourselves, sometimes."

Hale shook his head. "You're an incurable optimist, Will."

Will Caroline stretched out his long legs. "We've learned a lot."

"Will, all that we've got to show for the two years right now—all that we've got to report to the board—is a wild story about a vanishing antibiotic that nobody can hold onto—that nobody can understand—that nobody can get into any kind of shape to test in mice to see whether it even promises to be good. And the board isn't going to cough up another half-million dollars for that. And I'm not sure I want them to."

Will stood up too now and looked at Hale, wondering whether this was only a bad day or whether he was serious. A coolness on the part of the board was regrettable, but not fatal. Not yet, anyway. But when Hale was finished, that would be the end.

"Ade, we've solved the problems that slowed us down. And we've paid high for those solutions. But now we know what we're doing."

Hale came back to the desk. "As things stand now," he said, "the board isn't going on. They want out. If they do go on, it will be for one of two reasons. Either there's going to be an antibiotic on the fire—that's been tested and looks so good that a blind man could see that we have to go on. Or else I'm going to beat them into it. Not coax them or bait them or humor them this time, Will. Beat them. Force them. And I'm not going to do it on nothing."

"It could still be a contaminant causing the trouble, Ade. It's far from pure."

"If it is, it's getting stronger all the time."

"It's possible that they're concentrating the contaminant even more than the antibiotic—so that every time the antibiotic gets purer there's even more of the contaminant to knock it out. And if that's it, they could separate it out anytime—today—tomorrow—and EA 77 could shape up and be very good. Then they might not even have to work it cold."

Hale turned and looked at him. "Do you think it's that?" He said it as though he didn't believe it, and Will thought that he didn't, himself, really.

"I don't know," he said. "They don't know, either—and they're living with it."

"I'm not going to the board with a story about a contaminant that we're working night and day to get rid of and getting more of instead," Hale said. He pulled the telephone cord out of the way. "Get that antibiotic into mice, Will. I want it tested."

For a long moment Will was silent. Then he said, "You might as well know—we're in for a delay."

Hale looked around sharply. "We've had nothing but delays."

"They've gone beyond their equipment."

"What do you mean, they've gone beyond their equipment?"

"You can't get an ice bath much colder than five below. And they lost it yesterday at five below. They can't go much colder with their present equipment."

"Then get them other equipment."

"There's nothing available."

"What do you mean, nothing available?"

"Working at low temperatures is a special field," Will said. "It requires special equipment—that isn't available in the supply houses anywhere."

"Then how do they think they're going on?"

"They'll design it themselves," Will said. "We'll have it made up in the shop."

For a long time after Will had gone, Ade Hale paced his office. He ought to call a halt. Everything that was logical, everything that was sensible, everything that was prudent and practical and businesslike—and everything in him, too, that was self-protective—told him it was time to stop. He didn't honestly believe any more that they were going to succeed. There were times when he wondered whether he had ever believed it. And still, even now, a stubborn streak in him held out. Sooner or later someone was going to do this. Sometime, somewhere, it was going to happen.

At the window he looked out at the fermentation building, seeing the tails of steam slanting off the pipes in the wind. He couldn't argue with Will, he thought, when he said they had come a long way. They had started in the dark—not even certain that their objective could exist—and now at least they knew it could. At the beginning they had known nothing; now they were beginning to know—a little, anyway. Only if they had known then how much they didn't know—if they had known then what they were getting into—would they have begun at all? He wondered. Now, after two years, they probably knew as much as any group in the field today—which still was not saying much.

Hale turned away from the fermentation building, about which he knew everything, and went back to his desk and resumed what he had been doing before Will Caroline came in. There were places in this organization where they could drive for greater efficiency— where savings could be made. This thing had to be paid for and a profit still had to be shown. Since he had been president, there had never been a year when Enright had failed to show a profit or missed a dividend, and as long as he remained president there would not be.

THIRTY-SEVEN

TOM WALKED around Tollie's and stopped a few minutes at the rail before going inside. It was Friday evening, and he had nowhere to go but home and nothing to do when he got there except think about this vanishing EA 77. He would think about it, and first he would torture himself about why it was disappearing, and then he would think about all the time that had gone into it—and would have to go into it still—and then he would begin to ask himself whether it was worth it. There was little doubt now that EA 77 was growing more unstable as it became purer. Maybe it had never happened before, but this one was different and it was happening now. And it was different, too, Tom thought, because it was broad-spectrum and it had not been to mice yet—and he was thinking about dropping it.

Idly he looked along the gray dock and out over the bay. This had been a spring when nature seemed to stand still—a raw damp season with little sun and a poor show of new green on distant trees. The water was choppy and a stiff wind was blowing, snapping the flag against its pole at the end of the dock and whipping against a boat already in the water. The boat, with its sails down and covered, had an abandoned look about it, alone at its mooring.

But the lights that had come on across the water at Enright were dim in the lingering daylight, and the smell in the air was different from a month ago and stirred a different restlessness in your blood, and whatever it looked like or felt like, you knew it was spring. It was almost May. And May would be two years.

And after two years, how much time do you have left? he said to himself. After two years, it's possible that these next few months will be your last. And if they are—then what should you be doing with them? He walked down the steps to the dock. After two years, he said to himself, should you be spending your last chance on EA 77, which makes less sense the more you work on it, or using the time, instead, to race through as many as possible to try to find a better one?

He tossed a pebble into the water and watched it hit the foam while a familiar argument ran a familiar course inside him. If we go on with it, our troubles are just beginning, he said to himself. We'll have to design that equipment—and that will take time—and then have it built, and that will take more time—and then working at low temperatures will be slow work, and that will take a lot more time still. And is it worth it?

It's broad-spectrum, he argued back.

But in the time that this one is taking, you could go through hundreds, he said to himself. How do you know what else you might find—in the time you're giving to this one, that you can't figure out and can't control and can't hold onto?

It could still be a contaminant, he argued back. It could straighten out all at once. It's possible.

It was possible—but he didn't believe it. It was just a damned peculiar antibiotic and nothing else.

Maybe it's peculiar, he argued back, but it's broad-spectrum. And how many of them have you had?

He gathered up a few more pebbles off a pole and pitched them one at a time across the water. It was growing dark now and the Enright lights were brighter, and the string of dock lights had come on. The lone boat had an unreal quality about it, and its rope squeaked with the rhythm of the tide. Could you really do it? he said to himself. Could you really turn your back on a broad-spectrum antibiotic before it has gone to mice? He threw the rest of the pebbles into the dark water and walked back along the dim string of lights to the steps.

And then, he thought, there was another thread, too, woven into this fabric of mixed feelings—a thread that he told himself he had no place for at a time like this. But when something was happening in your laboratory that had never happened before, anywhere, you couldn't just forget it. You wanted to stay with it until you found out why. And you could tell yourself it had no purpose, and that there was no time and you couldn't stop for it now. But there still remained something inside you that burned to solve the riddle— for the simplest and most pressing reason a scientist could know. Just to solve it.

He walked up the steps and thought again that he didn't feel like going home, and he went into Tollie's for a drink.

The place was empty except for three men and a girl in a corner booth. Tom sat on a stool and ordered a drink and glanced at a newspaper lying on the bar. There had been a plane crash in Brazil, and somebody had said business would be better, and the weather report predicted rain. He put aside the newspaper and began to think about the equipment for EA 77. They would need an insulated box that they could keep very cold, and they would have to anticipate all the laboratory equipment they would require and plan the box big enough to hold it and still leave room in which to work. And they would have to use a cooling method that could produce extremely low temperatures if that should become necessary.

Necessary, he thought. He looked into his empty glass. Was any of it necessary—or even desirable—at this stage of a dying project? If anything will stop you . . .

In the corner booth the three men were trying to get the girl drunk and the one beside her was running his hand up her back. She wasn't a very good-looking girl. Tom looked away. A few more drinks and he wouldn't notice what she looked like. Maybe he'd get out of here—go over and see Midge. Only it was Friday night, and Midge wouldn't be sitting home on a Friday night. He toyed with the empty glass and signaled to Tollie for another drink that he didn't want. He was restless tonight. He wanted something he couldn't give a name to. He didn't know what he longed for—he only felt the longing.

Tollie brought the drink and stayed a minute to talk. "Season's almost here again," he said, leaning on the bar. "First thing you know I'll be full of boats out there. An' everyone wanting service at the same time—and it'll be hot as blazes."

Tom nodded and didn't answer.

"All the same," Tollie said. "You know—time flies."

"You're touching a sore spot, Tollie," Tom said. "Talk about something else."

In the corner booth the girl laughed a little too loud, and Tom looked at her. He didn't want that either. He finished his drink and went to the telephone to call Midge. Then, instead, he dialed the operator and gave her Amity's number in New York. He knew it by heart. He had called it often enough, although she never answered. Probably she wouldn't answer now. The telephone rang twice and a voice said, "Hello?"

"Am—" he shouted.

"Miss Welles ain't here," the voice said. "I'm the lady who cleans. I'm just leavin'. You're lucky you caught me."

"Where is Miss Welles?" he said.

"I'm gonna miss my bus," the voice warned.

"Where is she? Where'd she go?"

"She's out'n the country. If I miss my bus I gotta wait a half hour and it's rainin'." The voice was silent.

Tom hung up. He dialed Midge's number and there was no answer. He tried to think of someone else he could call. There was no one. When you worked this way, you gradually cut everything out of your life—and then when you wanted somebody, there was no one. From the telephone booth Tom saw that Harry Pack had come in and was talking to Tollie, probably about his boat. He went back to the bar, and his mind began to talk shop again.

That box would have to be designed so that all work could be done inside it—everything. It would have to be a miniature laboratory in a refrigerator. Mentally he began to list the equipment that would have to go into the box—in addition to the equipment that would be necessary just to keep it cold. That was going to have to be one hell of a big box. If anything will stop you, let it. . . . If it's good, you'll know it—everything about you will know it. . . .

Then Harry Pack was standing beside him. "Hello there, young fella!" Pack slapped him on the back. "How's it going? You still trying to feed people dirt—kids and all?"

"I was just thinking about going into the box business," Tom said. He looked down at the newspaper. The columns weren't entirely steady—he'd better get out of here.

"I'll tell ya, young fella, you ought to do it. Get away from that dirt. Be the luckiest day of your life."

"Today is my lucky day all around," Tom said.

"Well—I always say—luck is what you make it," Pack said.

"I always say luck is organized chance," Tom said soberly. Pack looked confused and Tom added, "Only something is always coming along to upset the odds."

Then all at once it occurred to him that the lady who was missing her bus might have meant that Amity had come here this weekend. He rushed back to the telephone and dialed, and this time it was Amity who answered.

"This place is crawling with Enright people tonight," Amity said.

"Always on Friday night. They pile out and come here as though someone played reveille and everyone had to report." Tom looked around the lounge of the Inn. The Gateses and the Derricks and the Millses were across the room. The Brainards and the Voughts were near the bar. Brainard kept looking at Amity, and Tom thought that tonight he didn't blame him. Amity had spent the winter in Mexico and in the Caribbean, painting, and she was very brown, and there were sun-bleached streaks in her hair, and she looked marvelous.

"I know of a great place about forty miles out of town," he said. "If I were in focus, I'd take you there—if I hadn't been drowning myself for a couple of hours at Tollie's." He smiled at her. "I missed you, Am."

"That's good," she said.

"I did. I've been waiting for you. I've been watching your house. I even watched your damned bird food until it all disappeared— nothing left but the dirty chewed-up string. Didn't you get all my letters?"

"They were great letters, Tom."

The letters had been all the same. They had all read, "Where in hell are you? Tom." He laughed. "Well, some were better than others, but that's the way it goes. Some days are better than others."

"You are in fine shape."

"I am that." He watched Vought look at him and lean over to speak to Brainard, and he knew that now they were talking about EA 77. He downed his drink and saw Amity watching him.

"Think you can walk out of here when the time comes?" she said.

"Just watch me."

"I intend to."

Tom laughed. He signaled the waiter for another round and caught the look in her eyes. "Don't preach at me, Am—I couldn't stand it tonight."

"Why should I preach at you?" she said.

He leaned back in the chair and grinned at her. "My God, you're wonderful. I love you, Am."

"That's good," she said again.

Tom looked at the waiter standing at the service bar beside the bar stools and at Marco measuring out two jiggers of Scotch. "I haven't seen you since that wonderful night when your ex-fiancé became my favorite villain," he said.

She smiled. "It was a nice evening, wasn't it?"

"I'd been talking to him earlier. I'd had a drink with him—there —at the bar."

"Well," she said, "bars are great levelers."

The Enright representation was increasing. The Harrups and the Rosswells had joined the Brainards and the Voughts. From the meaningful looks coming his way, Tom knew that now they were all talking about EA 77.

"We should have gone to Tollie's," he said. "There I was alone—except for three fellows getting a girl drunk. And your friend Harry Pack. I had a fine talk with him."

He slid lower on his spine and fell silent. He was sobering up fast, and the great debate was coming back.

"Am," he said, "suppose there were a man—a hypothetical man—and he had to make a choice." He shifted his legs alongside the table. "Suppose this man had something of a fortune which he had been spending without replenishing, so that one day he discovered it was almost gone. He was down to his last few dollars. But he did still have those few dollars—so he felt that he still had a last chance—but just one—one last chance that he could live or die with. Are you following me?"

"Perfectly."

"Back to our hero. If he uses this last chance right—wisely, judiciously—then he could still come out on top. He could build himself another fortune. But if he muffs it—then the last of his fortune goes down the drain with the rest. So he's playing for keeps."

"Obviously," she said. "Serious business."

Tom smiled and thought that he had forgotten how good it could be just to sit and talk to her. "Now—the decision is further complicated by the fact that our man is living in pretty barren territory. The pickings are lean—any opportunity is rare. Now, here is his choice. Right at hand—here and now—he has an opportunity that could work. He knows it could work. It's possible that it could be a huge success. But it has enough things wrong with it so that he honestly doesn't believe in it. Only remember—opportunities in this never-never land are very scarce, and here he's got one, big as life. Now—what should he do? Should he take that last chunk of money and put it into this opportunity that he doesn't really believe in? Or should he pass this one up and wait for a better one—even though he can't be sure that any other opportunity will come along, better or worse, before his money runs out? Now, what do you say? If you were the man, what would you do?"

"Is that the problem, Tom?" Amity said.

He nodded and then, although he had not intended to, he was telling her all about EA 77 and the way he felt and the argument he had been having with himself about it.

"I've had times like that," she said. "It's always easier if you believe very much or not at all. It's that no-man's-land in the middle —where your feelings are mixed—that can be hell."

Tom smiled. He felt better already for having talked about it, even though he was no closer to a decision. "You can argue it either way," he said. "You tell yourself that you could go through thousands in the time you're spending on this—and maybe find a better one. But you know, too, that you could go through thousands and not find another one at all that's broad-spectrum. Then you tell yourself you'd better work on this."

"Only you don't really think so," she said.

Tom thought that he had forgotten, too, how perceptive she could be. "I've had the feeling before that time was running out," he said. "But now I feel that it's nearly gone. If we work on this one, it will be our last—we won't have time for another. And this isn't the one to end with."

"It's this weighing the pros and cons that can drive you crazy," Amity said. "But then, of course, when you really believe in something, there are no cons."

She was right about that, too, he thought.

"How rare is the opportunity, really, Tom?" she said. "Those broad-spectrum antibiotics—how many are there now?"

"There aren't any."

"I don't mean yours. I mean—you know—anywhere."

"There aren't any, Am."

"None!" She turned to him, amazed, and he realized that of course there was no reason for her to know. Even when he used to talk to her for hours, he hadn't explained everything to her, the way he used to explain to Diana. And, he thought suddenly—she used to listen, anyway, because she had understood that he wanted someone to talk to—as he had wanted someone tonight—and all those times she hadn't understood half of what he was talking about! Tom sat up and stared at the bar where he had sat with Lawrence Croft, who had come to her with his troubles, too. "A marvelous girl —helped me in my darkest hour," Croft had said. And how is this any different? Tom said to himself. He sat perfectly still with the shock of the question.

"What's the matter, Tom?" Amity said.

Slowly he turned to her. "Am, are you sure you want to hear this?"

"Of course I want to hear it. I had no idea there weren't any at all."

"No, there aren't any at all," he said slowly, still wondering about himself. "At Enright we've been looking for two years. And a lot of other people have been looking, too—but still nothing has reached the drugstore. That means that very few are turning up, anywhere— and that the few that have been found are toxic."

"How many have you found at Enright?" Amity said. "Even though they were toxic?"

Tom's eyes went across to Derrick. "In two years," he said, "Derrick has probably looked at about two million cultures. And picked about a hundred and fifty thousand—"

"Two million!"

Tom nodded. "Obviously we haven't worked on two million—or even a hundred and fifty thousand. Plenty of microbes don't make any antibiotic—and most don't make anything very interesting. But Derrick has looked at that many. He just brings us the best. And out of the hundred and fifty thousand, we've had three broad-spectrum antibiotics."

"Three! Out of two million!"

"Baramycin turned up last March and it was toxic. Illiomycin turned up last May and it was good in a test tube but wouldn't protect an animal. It just did nothing in animals at all. Although it wasn't toxic. And this one—"

Uneasily Tom glanced over at the bar and then, very thoughtfully, back at Amity. "So when you say to yourself that in the time that this one is burning up you could look at thousands, you have to argue back that this one is here and it is broad-spectrum—and there may not be another."

Amity smiled. "This is the bird in the hand—and you don't know what's in the bush."

Tom nodded and his eyes went again to the bar. "Am, you feel like getting out of here?" he said.

The air was chilly but the night smelled of spring and a half-moon came and went between the houses as they drove home along the shore road.

"Did you ever see Croft again, Am?" Tom said. "After that night?"

"Just once. He came to see me in New York. One night I came home and he was waiting for me." Amity put her head back on the seat. "You know, Tom, I sat there, looking at him, talking to him—the same as that other time when you stopped in—and all I could think was that I almost married this man and—well, it was shattering."

Tom smiled. "Just be more careful next time." Then he had a terrible thought. "Next time hasn't already happened, has it? There isn't somebody else?"

"No," she said, "that's not my game. I know it now."

A light fog was beginning to roll in and the foghorn was talking. "What do you mean, it's not your game?"

"I just don't really understand it."

"What is there to understand?"

"Oh—you know, some people are very good at that sort of thing —they're always in love—they thrive on it. And some people make all the wrong moves."

Tom looked at Amity, sitting beside him with her head back and her heavy hair spilling along the seat. "Am," he said after a minute, "did one guy do all this to you?"

"You know there was more than one!" she said. "There was a long line—a long line of faceless wonders—gods that turned to straw under my magic touch."

"Why faceless wonders?"

"Because I can hardly remember what they looked like. And you know—faces are important to me. And yet I hardly remember theirs—these people who, for a little while, anyway, meant so much to me."

Amity fell silent and Tom waited for her to go on. Once, he thought, she would have pulled her defenses around her while she talked like this. Once she would not have talked like this at all—but now she was quite relaxed. She really didn't care, which was probably good in a way—but not altogether. Little threads of fog were sifting out onto the road and settling into pockets in the hollows. "Am—I think the trouble is that you've never had a real man."

She laughed. "Oh, don't be silly. That's not the trouble at all."

"You've had a bunch of weaklings, who brought you their troubles." Tom paused. That uneasy feeling nudged him again and he put it aside. "They cried on your shoulder and took your sympathy because they needed it—and they conned you into thinking sympathy was love."

"No," she said. "It's not as simple as that. The whole thing is a foreign language in which other people can talk to each other and understand each other, and I can't."

Well, it was still a defense, Tom thought—only a different kind. He pulled up in front of her house. Thin layers of fog hovered in the beams of the headlights and piled beads on the windshield. Tom put out the lights and turned a little in the seat to look at Amity. "You've been talking to the wrong people, Am," he said.

"Yes," she said. "But I'm old enough to know better." She settled back against the seat again. "Nobody can have everything, Tom. I have my work—I'm good at it—I'm a success. I'll settle for it. It's quite a good life—better than most."

His hand moved across the back of the seat and found a strand of her hair. "That's nonsense, Am."

She was silent and he looked at her, with her sun-streaked hair back against the seat, pale in the dim light. Once he had called this girl cold and aloof. Now he wondered how he could ever have thought it.

Amity turned her head to him and her hair brushed his hand. "Have you ever considered, Tom," she said in a calm, detached voice, "that man gives himself freely to almost everything today except love?"

"No," he smiled. "I haven't considered it. But I will if you want."

"Don't bother—it's not worth it."

"Oh, it's probably worth it, Am. What does he give himself to so freely?"

"All kinds of things." She spoke as though she were only making conversation—talking about something that didn't really concern her. "His job, his bank account, his causes—the most spurious causes—other people's opinions of him. Everywhere you look, he's in there—giving his all. Except with love. There he's a miser. There he expects the most—and gives the least. Why?"

"I don't know." He twisted the strand of hair. "Why?"

"I don't know why, either. But when I asked Lawrence that, he said I was the one who was wrong—not the other people—that I wanted to use love as a ball and chain. We had quite an argument about it. I don't know what I was arguing about. I didn't care any more. Not at all."

"He was never in your class, Am. It was doomed from the start."

Through little beads of fog, Tom could see the light she had left burning in her house and, down the road, his own house which was dark, and he thought that they ought to go into one or the other instead of just sitting here. In the near dark he looked at the smooth line of her throat and her chin and the high bones of her cheek as she sat with her head back against the seat. Tonight she was not erecting those barriers she was so good at, he thought—tonight she was warm and desirable and setting up no defenses. His hand moved to her face. And then, almost involuntarily, he stopped— and felt his desire leap with the stopping.

He stopped and wound his fingers into her hair and told himself that desire like this was not meant to be questioned. He told himself that she was not a child and that she could say no. And then he thought of the others who had come to her with their troubles—as he had come tonight—because she was warm and intuitive and because she had so much love to give—and slowly his hand came back to his lap, and he closed it over the steering wheel.

After a little while he looked at her again and thought that of course the love she had known had been a foreign language to her. When someone like Lawrence Croft spoke of love and when someone like Amity spoke of love, they were talking about two different things—so different in quality and in intensity that there couldn't possibly be any understanding between them—and the words of one had to be foreign to the other.

Sitting a little away from her now, looking at her across the width of the car, Tom thought that it was inevitable that the others had failed her. They had sought her out for her strength—because they were weak—and in the end they had failed her for that reason— because they were what they were—weaklings. And it was inevitable, too, he thought, that she should have been hurt so deeply because the same fine grain, that felt so completely another person's pain, felt her own.

"—Büchner funnel—hose—vacuum—filter," Tom said, listing the equipment that would have to go inside the box, "and the usual stuff—flasks, scrapers, bottles, test tubes." He tapped his pencil on the rough sketch of the box. "How cold you figure we'll have to go, Max?"

"Depends on how close it is to pure," Max said. "It's falling into a regular pattern. Every time we get it purer, we lower the temperature."

Tom bent over the sketch again. "We'll plan to work from the front," he said, pointing with his pencil. "A glass wall with two holes in it—large enough for hands to fit through. Keep the cooling apparatus up and back—out of the way of the work area."

One side would have to open up, he thought, so they could get the stuff in and out. And they couldn't plan to use any technique requiring water, because at these temperatures water would freeze. They would have to use organic solvents. And what else do we have to plan for? He studied the sketch. "This box is going to be at least five feet long. And complicated."

Max nodded. "Let's be sure we haven't overlooked anything. We want it right the first time."

Tom went over the list of equipment, indicating a place for everything, blocking in the cooling apparatus at the top. He put down his pencil. "Max, we ought to try to test this in mice—now."

Max laughed. "How can we test it? We don't even know what shape it's in. We won't know how much antibiotic is getting into the mice."

"We should go back to the point where we last held onto it," Tom said. "Tell Mills to have his mice all set to go. Then we'll freeze-dry it—get it to him and into the mice right away." He tapped the design on the table. "We're getting into pretty extreme conditions here, Max. We ought to at least try to test in mice first."

Max shrugged. "Why not?" he said. "What have we got to lose but a few mice?"

The mice were ready. They had been weighed and spotted and infected and had only to be injected with the antibiotic—and now for the time EA 77 was freeze-dried and showed itself to be a white powder.

"I'll take it right up," Max said, scraping it into a bottle. "Call Mills and tell him to be in the mouse lab."

In his office, Tom picked up the telephone and dialed, and then he noticed that out in the laboratory, Max had not moved. He was standing perfectly still, staring down at the counter.

"Oh, God!" Max said.

Tom put down the telephone and hurried back, and then he stared, too. In the bottle on the counter the EA 77 powder was no

555

longer white. It was changing color, taking on a brownish tint, and even while they watched, the brown was deepening—like iron rusting, but rusting very quickly—so that you could see the change from minute to minute.

"It's unstable in air!" Max muttered. "On top of everything else, it's unstable in oxygen!" The color was still changing, still darkening. "We can't test this, Tom. It's gone already."

For another ten minutes they watched the color change, and then it stopped changing. All together, twenty minutes had passed since the antibiotic was freeze-dried. The white powder that had been EA 77 was dark brown.

"Well," Max said, "we might as well tell Mills the test is off."

Looking at the dry brown powder, Tom thought that now there was one more thing to consider. If EA 77 was unstable in oxygen, that box couldn't contain air. It would have to be filled with an inert gas. "We've got to try again, Max," he said. "We have to try to get this into mice—before we go on."

"What kind of a test would it be?" Max said. "The way this thing disappears we couldn't be sure there was any antibiotic left when the needle went into the first mouse."

"We know now that we can't dry it—we'll have to keep it in dilute solution." Tom fiddled with a pencil while he thought. "But we could put the solution right into a deepfreeze to keep it and give it to Mills frozen. Let him thaw it out one minute before he's ready to use it. Maybe that way we could hold onto enough to learn something."

"Tom—the way we're losing this, we wouldn't know what we were shooting into the mice—whether there was any antibiotic there at all."

It was true and Tom knew it—but he still felt they had to try. "If the mice die of the infection, we won't have learned anything—because we won't be sure that they actually received any antibiotic. But if they die of the antibiotic—"

Max gave a little smile.

"Then it's toxic and we're rid of one big headache."

Max leaned against the counter. "I'm not sure I want to be rid of it," he said. "This is breaking all the rules—I want to know why."

For a moment Tom didn't answer. He knew how Max felt because he felt it too. Whatever happened to the mice, Tom knew, Max would go on with EA 77, in his spare time, at least, until he solved the riddle. And Tom knew, too, that he would not—however much he might want to. As long as there was hope that EA 77 would be a good, if difficult, antibiotic, he would stick to it. When that hope ended, he would stop. He had decided.

It was done. They had frozen EA 77 and given it, frozen, to Mills, and Mills had thawed it out one minute ago. He was using ten mice instead of six, administering the usual doses to the green-spotted mice and the yellow-spotted mice and the purple-spotted mice, and then giving two larger doses besides.

"I'm giving a good stiff dose to the two orange-spotted ones," Mills said, and an even stiffer dose to the two red ones. If the antibiotic does start disappearing, maybe with big enough doses something will still get into the bloodstream."

"I'm not even sure there's anything left right now," Max said.

"It just might work, Max," Mills said cheerfully. "It's more stable in dilute solution. And in the bloodstream any antibiotic is in very dilute solution."

Mills injected the last red-spotted mouse and leaned over the jar. "All right, men," he said. "Hang in there, now."

The mice were crawling and sniffing. So far, they showed no ill effects.

Back in his own office, Tom stood at the window, thinking that, as always after the mice had lived through the first hour, there was nothing to do but wait. Wait and try to keep busy between the trips you made up that flight of stairs to see whether the mice were starting to shake—to see whether they were crawling around or becoming paralyzed—to see whether they were sleeping wedged together or lying around in convulsions or hemorrhaging or trying to drink too much, trying to hoist themselves up to the water pipe and not able to make it. Back at noon—and back after lunch—and again at midafternoon and again at closing time. How many times have I walked up that flight of stairs in two years? he thought. How many mice have I watched shake and stiffen and fall over and die? And if they were alive at closing time, back at midnight to see whether they had begun to wheeze, along with the controls.

He leaned on the windowsill. Spring had come all at once this week, and he looked at the bay, still and sparkling in the sunlight, and thought that the water always seemed to glint and shine and bounce off brighter lights in spring than later in hotter months under a stronger sun. Or maybe it was the fires spring stirred in a man that brightened the sparkle and made him see it that way.

Then, in the yard, Tom saw Ade Hale and Will Caroline walking toward the research building—probably coming to look at the mice —and he thought that everyone was watching this one—hanging on this one—and, damn it, this wasn't the one for everything to depend on. Then Brainard showed up in the yard, caught up to Hale and Caroline and walked the rest of the way with them. Watching him, Tom wondered whether Brainard was hoping these mice would live or die. Below, the three men disappeared into the building and Tom turned from the window. He wasn't sure which way he was rooting, himself.

At closing time when Tom looked into the mouse laboratory, Hale and Will Caroline were there again, and Mills was saying, "Either it's doing nothing at all—or—so far, it's very nontoxic."

Tom came in and looked at the ten mice. They still appeared to be totally unaffected by the injections they had received. Even the orange mice and the red mice which had received huge doses looked unbelievably healthy.

"It probably never got into them," Tom said and left.

Those mice are going to die, he said to himself as he drove home. And they're not going to die now from the antibiotic. They're going to die from the disease, like the controls—and you're not going to know anything more tomorrow than you do today. Not whether it's toxic and not whether it cures—because you don't know whether any antibiotic ever got into them.

Even if it doesn't kill these mice, it could still be toxic, he said to himself—because it could have changed into something else before they ever got it. And if these mice should die of the disease, you won't know whether or not it could protect them—for the same reason. So what are you going to do?

He walked around his house and stopped on the porch and automatically looked over at Amity's house. It was a warm evening and there was still light over the water and the smell of lilac was in the air. For a few minutes Tom watched the colors change and blend over the water. Then he looked again at Amity's empty house and went inside to telephone her.

"They're going to die," he said. He carried the telephone over to the sofa and sprawled out on it. "I know it."

"Well," she said, "is that good or bad?"

"I don't know. If it had been toxic, there wouldn't have been any problem. I could have junked it."

"What if they live?" she said.

He drew his arm across his eyes. "You mean altogether?"

"That's right."

"They won't."

"You are in fine spirits," she said.

"Oh, hell," he said.

"What if they do live?" she said again.

"They won't live."

"Well, then—what if they die?"

"If they die from the antibiotic, I'll stop. If they die from the disease, I'll have to go on. Either way, Max will go on."

"Why will Max go on?"

"Max has been bit. He can't stand to think this is breaking the rules and he doesn't know why."

"And what about you—don't you want to know why?"

Tom was silent for a moment. "Yes—I want to know why."

Now Amity was silent, waiting.

"I'm dying to know why." But he wanted something else more, and he couldn't have both. "No one can have everything, Am. You said it yourself. Are you coming up this weekend?"

She hesitated. "No—not this weekend."

"Next?"

"Maybe next."

After he hung up, he went outside again and watched until daylight died over the water. Then he went to Tollie's for dinner. And then he did what he did every night now. He went back to work.

When he went upstairs to the mouse laboratory at midnight, Max and Mills were there already. The controls were beginning to wheeze, and he looked into the other jar and saw that some of these mice were wheezing, too. "Well, we don't know any more than before," he said.

"Look at the purple ones," Mills said. "And the red and the orange. They haven't developed symptoms yet."

In the morning the controls died. And the green-spotted mice died. And the yellow-spotted mice died. And one purple-spotted mouse died and one did not. And the red-spotted mice and the orange-spotted mice lived. They lived all that day and all the next day. It had taken larger doses to do it, but the mice had been protected.

On the fourth day Tom stood at the jar with Hale and Will Caroline, looking at the five healthy mice.

"What if EA 77 doesn't straighten out?" he said. "What if we have to go very cold and stay very cold?"

"Then we'll sell it frozen," Hale said.

"It might have an early obsolescence," Tom said.

"We'll work for it ourselves," Will Caroline said. He smiled. "It may have a pretty long life."

There was nothing more to argue about. "What's its name?" Tom said.

"How about Arctimycin?"

Tom sighed. "We'll get started on the box."

A week later Mills infected rats and attempted to protect them with Arctimycin. When he arrived at the laboratory the following morning, the controls were dying. Of the treated rats the two at the smallest dose level died during the morning. One rat that had received a medium-sized dose died a few hours later. The other three rats lived and remained healthy and showed no ill effects from the large doses they had received.

"Something is happening to part of it," Mills said, "because it's taking larger doses than it should to protect—but it is protecting. And it seems to be very nontoxic."

A few days later he infected rabbits. The rabbits that received the smallest doses of Arctimycin died. The ones that received larger doses lived.

THIRTY-EIGHT

G ATES AWOKE that morning with a severe headache and just lay still in bed, certain that he was too ill to go to work. He opened his eyes and saw the brilliant June sunlight and closed them again. He wondered whether George would go in today. Something strange was happening to George—something not very pleasant. He seemed to have withdrawn from the project completely and at the same time to be daring everyone to say so. George had stayed home two days last week and one already this week. Thinking about George's absences, Gates stirred in bed and decided that he had better go to work.

In the next room he could hear his two girls chatting, and then their door slammed and the noise slammed through Gates's aching head. George was the only man in the company, he thought, who still had not seen that box—the only one who had not gone in to look at it where it stood on a counter in Max Strong's laboratory, nearly five feet long and about a yard wide and a yard high. The "hope chest," some of them called it. To Gates it was more like a coffin. It was a metal box with asbestos insulation on the outside and one glass wall with two holes in it for the hands to pass through. Running across the top was a pipe containing nitrogen. They were cooling the box by pumping nitrogen over dry ice until it was cooled to the desired low temperature. During the first week that temperature had been ten degrees below zero. Then they had lowered it to fifteen below. Now they had lowered it to twenty below.

To George Weir the box had become the target of all his hatred, the symbol of all his frustration. Gates understood that it wasn't only the box—nor even the fact that Arctimycin was breaking all the rules, although that was part of it. George had lost faith in everything—in the project, in the tools available to him to use, in himself. Gates understood that, but it didn't make George any easier to get along with. And when George said there was nothing left to depend on and that everything just ended in failure anyway, Gates knew he wasn't entirely wrong. To see that it was true, Gates had only to look at that daily record—that depressing special record that he'd had to keep for Morrissey and that now he had to keep for Vought—that showed the fantastic number of cultures they had worked and reworked, tested and retested, that had come to nothing.

After another few minutes he got out of bed. While he shaved, he considered again the possibility of not going to work and decided against it. He dressed slowly and went downstairs. The children had already left for school, and he thought that in another week they would be out for the summer. The awareness of the passing days both depressed and cheered him. Like a man awaiting execution, he dreaded the terrible end and yet he would think, too, that soon it would all be over. He stared at his scrambled eggs and raised heavy eyes to Madeline. "George didn't call?"

"No," she said, in the tone she always used when she spoke of George. "George didn't call."

"I guess he's going in today, then."

"I'm rather sorry to hear that," Madeline said.

Gates moved a piece of bacon with his fork. "They've lowered that temperature again," he said, "to twenty below. Every time they push it lower, George seems to take it as a personal affront."

"Well—I don't know why George is making such a thing of this," Madeline said. "It isn't his problem."

"It's upsetting, Madeline. This was an accepted fact—that if you got an antibiotic purer, it became more stable—and now here's this one doing exactly the opposite. When that happens, it shakes your faith—not only in this piece of information that has failed you, but in everything. You have to ask yourself what else you've been accepting that's wrong—how many other mistakes you've made that you don't even know about."

"You do not have to ask yourself how many other mistakes you've made. Furthermore, don't you dare ask it! There's nothing to be gained from such a question. Well, you can't eat this now." She took his plate and coffee cup. "I'll fix you some more. Do you want eggs or something else?"

"I'm not hungry, Madeline—George will be here in a minute."

"Then take the car yourself. I don't need it today. I'll call George and tell him not to stop."

Gates only gestured unhappily. "Did I tell you they're starting to work up the dogs?" he said. "For chronic toxicity."

"Yes, you told me." Madeline came back to the table and looked at him. "Woodrow, for God's sake, take the car yourself. Take it every day and stay away from George. George is three-quarters of what's wrong with you. You leave here fine, and you ride with George and you eat with George, and by the time you come home you're a wreck."

"George isn't himself these days, Madeline."

"Personally I think he's himself—only more so."

"He spends half his time in the cafeteria drinking coffee. He's drinking gallons of coffee."

"Then he must be spending the other half in the men's room. When is he working?"

Gates looked up. He could never quite get used to Madeline's earthy remarks. "He's not working. He doesn't seem to care very much."

"Exactly. If it weren't Arctimycin, it would be something else. You stay away from him, Woodrow."

He would like to. He dreaded being with George, who was always at one extreme or the other—either sunk in a depressed silence or else talking compulsively, which was worse because then he grew bitter and vicious. Gates sighed. "If I won't put up with him, who will? I'm his closest friend."

"It's a questionable honor," Madeline said. "He's drinking, you know."

"Yes, I know." Then a horn sounded and George was outside. "I'd better go with him," Gates said. "It'll only upset him more if I don't."

"So what's the latest bulletin?" George said as Gates stepped into the car. "What'd I miss?"

"I don't know, George," Gates said, reluctant to talk about it.

"They still at fifteen below?"

Gates didn't answer, and George just stared ahead at the road for a while. Then he said, "They find out yet—about what's causing it?"

"They don't know, George. They don't really believe it's a contaminant any more. It just seems to be something about the antibiotic."

"That's crazy—it can't be."

"Well, maybe not, George."

"Just because those stupid bastards can't find out what they're doing wrong. Well, if they ever get it figured out, they'll see it's something else. You take my word for it, Pearly."

Gates put his hand over his eyes. It would be nice if George could be right, but it didn't seem to be working that way.

George was silent until they reached Enright and silent while they went into the building and upstairs. As they walked past Max Strong's laboratory, they could see him already at the box and hear the pump working, circulating the nitrogen over the dry ice. Then Cable came along, heading for Max's laboratory. Only one man at a time could work at the box, and Max and Cable were taking turns, changing every half hour, which was as long as their hands, protected only by thin rubber gloves, could tolerate the extreme cold.

"So what's the patient's temperature today?" Weir said to Cable.

"Twenty below," Tom said. "We'll probably go down to twenty-five soon." Then he added, "Mills and Bent are getting started today, working up the dogs."

Gates's stomach tightened, and Weir slammed into his own laboratory without another word.

Gates spent a miserable hour and a half trying to work while his headache grew worse. Finally at ten-thirty he went downstairs for coffee. George was not in his laboratory when he stopped for him, and Gates was surprised to see that he was not in the cafeteria either. On the way back he stopped again at George's laboratory, and when he still could not find him, he began to worry. He looked in the library, although he didn't really expect to find him there, and then went again to George's laboratory where his technician said he still had not returned. Gates started back to his own laboratory. Then he remembered Madeline's remark about the men's room.

As soon as he opened the door, Gates caught the smell of whiskey and saw pill bottles strewn about the floor. Then he saw Weir sitting on a chair, tilted back against the washbasin, reading a magazine with a picture of a scantily clad girl on the cover. On Weir's lap were two more magazines. "George!" Quickly Gates closed the door. "For God's sake, George!"

Weir held out the magazine, opened to a picture of a nude girl wearing a cowboy hat and twirling a rope. "How do you like that, Woodrow?"

"George, are you out of your mind?"

Shaking off Gates's hand, Weir studied the picture. "I had a hundred like that," he said. "And it wasn't hard, either."

He turned the pages to a picture of a girl wearing only a sailor

564

hat and a blue scarf and carrying a life preserver. "Ah—we're too good to 'em," he muttered. "We should keep 'em in the kitchen—takin' care of kids. Then they'd keep their pants on. Then when they climbed in bed, it'd be 'cause they were tired."

Gates felt disgust rising up in him. He never knew what to say when George talked this way. "Come on, George," he coaxed. "Get to your feet."

For another minute Weir sat, shuffling through the magazines, and then he spilled them onto the floor and pulled himself to his feet, supporting himself on the washbasin. Then, as though he had just caught sight of his face for the first time, Weir stared at himself in the mirror. After a long moment, he said, "You know something, Pearly? In high school I was voted the best-looking guy in the class. And the most likely to succeed—you know that?"

"You have been successful, George. I think you've been very successful."

Weir leaned close to the mirror, as though examining every separate blemish on his face, and Gates, looking too, thought that George did look terrible these days—with those heavy eyes and the bags under them and the flushed face that was getting flabby and coarse. He saw that George had nicked himself twice shaving this morning and that he had a sore at the corner of his lower lip which could have come from too much whiskey.

Weir examined the nick in his chin and the sore. Then he gave a short bitter laugh that sounded more like a sob.

"George, you shouldn't have come in today if you felt like this," Gates said. He noticed the pill bottles again, strewn about the floor, and was just bending down to pick them up when suddenly Weir turned on him, so violently that Gates almost lost his balance.

"Well, what am I supposed to feel—good or something—after two years of nothing?" Weir advanced on Gates and thumped his shoulder with hard fingers. "Only I know it wasn't two years of nothing, Pearly, boy. I had good ones in that time—I know it—and you loused me up. Like you've loused up everything else. This whole stinking failure is mostly your fault—more than anyone else's. You made the mistakes, boy."

"George, you know that isn't true!"

"You know it is true!" Weir's hand closed over the loose sleeve of Gates's lab coat. "Like how much time did we waste working on streptomycin and streptothricin that you didn't catch?"

"That wasn't my fault."

"And how many could we have found in that time? Out of all the lousy tests around here, whose broke down the most, Pearly, boy? Not mine." Weir pushed his forefinger into Gates's chest. "Your tests, Pearly. Yours."

Deeply hurt, Gates backed away from Weir's pounding finger, and Weir moved after him. "I took your word! Christ, I ought to have my head examined—when I think of it—depending on *you!* How do I know how many I threw out that you said were no good —how many times you crossed me up—you and your lousy tests? I had one—I had more than one. I could have been the guy—and I threw them out because of you."

Gates told himself that George didn't know what he was saying.

"Well, it's the goddam truth!" Weir was shouting now. "And if you don't like it, go cry to Madeline. What would you do without Madeline?" He seized a magazine and held out a picture of a girl wearing only a gold chain, lying on a bunny rug. "You wouldn't know what to do with a woman like that, Pearly. That's not your type. What you need is a wet nurse—Woodrow—and that's what you've got. A mother!"

With a quick jerking motion, Weir pulled out another pill bottle and tossed the contents into his mouth. "She mothers you—and she looks like your mother, too. People look like what they are, Pearly. It's no accident. You ever think of that?"

Gates bit back a retort about Janet. George was miserable enough already—and suspicious enough, too.

"She's built like a cow. And she's two years older than you—and she looks ten years older. And that doesn't bother you—and you know why? Because that's what you want—a mother."

"Stop it, George!"

"You'd love to have a wife that looks like mine—you probably lie in bed nights thinking about it—only you gotta have a mama more."

Gates was shaking with rage. Fists clenched, unable to speak, he stared at Weir—at the flushed face, at the weak mouth with the sore at one corner—and all he could think was that he was going to hit him. He was going to hit him until he fell, and then he was going to pound that flabby face against the floor until it no longer looked as it did now—until it had stopped smirking and stopped sneering —until the mouth had stopped talking. Terrified at his own thoughts, Gates fled into the corridor, rushed down to his laboratory and into his office.

He sat at his desk and felt his head pounding and tears rising in his eyes. In the laboratory Miss Potter was a blurred double image, and Gates held up a journal as though he were reading it. The lines swam around, and he took out his handkerchief and went to the window. After a while his eyes were better. Miss Potter was a single image again. He sat down. He felt that he ought to call Madeline just to talk to her—as though somehow he owed her this gesture. He picked up the telephone and put it down. He couldn't do it. He would start to cry at the sound of her voice.

He thought of George and of how he hated him—he had never felt this kind of hatred toward a man before. He wondered whether he was still down there in the men's room—in that condition—and who else had gone in and seen him.

And then, uneasily, Gates thought that he couldn't just leave him there. He hated him, but still—someone would see him and he would be fired. Perhaps someone had seen him already.

With no real idea of what he was going to do, Gates made himself start back down the corridor, expecting every minute to see someone come out the door at the other end—someone who had seen George—or, worse still, George himself, roaring drunk. The corridor was silent. The door did not open. When he reached the men's room, Gates stopped and listened and heard nothing. He cracked open the door. George was still there, leaning on the windowsill now, his back to the door. Quietly, Gates closed the door. He wondered whom he could ask for help. Cable, maybe—Cable would keep his mouth shut. Then he thought of Derrick. Derrick's laboratory was closer.

"Ah be damned!" Derrick said, when Gates motioned him out into the corridor and told him.

"Charlie, we can't leave him there," Gates said.

"Where are we going to take him?" Derrick asked, logically enough. "Can't take him to his lab—his technician's there. An' he's sure to raise a fuss. Ah mean—he's not exactly a happy drunk."

Gates nodded again. He agreed. He more than agreed.

"Ah suppose we could try the dispensary—say he was sick—"

"Charlie, he's reeking. The nurse would smell it. And he's ugly."

Derrick thought a minute and then Gates's stomach sank as Vought appeared in the corridor. Gates and Derrick stepped back into Derrick's laboratory and watched Vought walk the length of the corridor toward the men's room and then past it and out to the stairs.

"How about if we stink him up?" Derrick said suddenly. "Put something on him that'll outstink the booze?"

"Good! Do you have anything in there?"

Derrick shook his head.

"I'll get something from Tom. Charlie, you go in there with him. If anyone comes in—well, do what you can."

When he was halfway to Cable's laboratory, Gates remembered the magazines. He couldn't leave them in the men's room. He couldn't even throw them into the wastebasket—someone like Vought might see them and ask questions. And he couldn't walk through the corridors with them. He rushed down to his own office for his briefcase and then hurried back to Cable's laboratory.

With a bottle of benzyl mercaptan that Tom had given him in his briefcase, Gates rushed back to the men's room. Derrick was standing, uncertainly holding the magazines, and George was sitting with his face in his hands, crying.

"What are we goin' to do with these?" Derrick said.

"Snakebit—that's what I am," Weir sobbed. "Nothing ever goes right for me."

Gates stuffed the magazines into his briefcase. He handed Derrick the bottle of benzyl mercaptan and then hastily began to pick up the empty pill bottles, jamming them into his briefcase, too.

"Anything I do, it turns against me," Weir moaned. "Turns sour. Here I was the guy supposed to succeed—you know that, Charlie? I was the guy supposed to amount to something. A-ah—what's the use?"

Derrick uncorked the bottle, and immediately a smell like the violent smell of a scared skunk on a hot night filled the room. Weir's face turned green, and he rushed across the room and threw up violently.

"We won't be lyin'," Derrick said, tight-lipped. "He's real sick now."

"Come on, George," Gates said. "Come on down to the dispensary. You can lie down there."

With a surprising lack of protest Weir allowed himself to be led to the elevator and out onto the second floor to the dispensary.

Later, when everyone was at lunch, Gates took him home.

That evening before dinner, Gates sat alone in the little upstairs den, thinking that never in his life had he felt so completely let down. He had come home early, and then, to keep his mind off George, he had come up here to try to catch up on some work. He had taken out the record book on which he was always falling behind because he hated it so. Now he sat here, staring at it and at his briefcase, which held the filled notebooks, and at the laboratory reports of the latest failures that still had to be entered—and he felt that he simply could not write another word. He was still sitting there with his pen across the empty page when Madeline came upstairs.

"Woodrow, what on earth is wrong with you?" she demanded. "What happened today to set you off?"

Gates only gave a disheartened shrug and stared at his desk. How could he tell her?

"Well, something must have happened to make you feel this way." Her eyes went to the record book. "What's that?"

"Nothing much—just a daily record I have to keep—something Dr. Morrissey started."

Madeline picked up the record book.

"I was hoping when Morrissey left I could stop—I really hate keeping it. It just reminds me of the thousands and thousands of cultures I've tested—that have all ended in failure. I'm doing nothing but describing failure."

"Do you mean you've been keeping a running record—of everything that's happened—for two years?"

Gates nodded and sighed, thinking about the other notebooks that he had already filled. He glanced at his briefcase.

"Woodrow," Madeline said, "do you mind telling me why?"

At the edge in her voice, Gates looked up. "I told you—Dr. Morrissey wanted it. He thought it was more systematic—you know how fussy he was. And then Vought heard about it somehow and he wanted it, too. These notebooks are a daily record—numbered in order—so they always tell exactly how much has been done. Only— they tell how much has failed, too."

"*They?* You mean there are others?" Madeline snatched up his briefcase and pulled out a few journals and dropped them on the desk and pulled it open wider. Suddenly Gates remembered the magazines—and just at that instant Madeline found them. She pulled one out and glanced at the cover, and then, to his amazement, she tossed it onto the desk as though it were only a journal and pulled out another. The first one slipped to the floor and fell open to the picture of the girl dressed in a cowboy hat. Gates froze. Madeline glanced down at it and back into the briefcase. At last she pulled out the record books.

She opened the notebooks one at a time. "Every day?" she said in a sharper tone than he had ever heard her use. "Every day—for two years?"

He nodded.

"In addition to your regular reports?"

Gates nodded again. He had never seen Madeline so angry.

"Woodrow, do you learn anything from this? Do you do any better testing? Do you run a better lab?"

"No."

She picked up the current notebook off the desk and flung it into the wastebasket and threw the others in after it. "You have written your last entry in that abominable thing!"

"Madeline! Vought wants this information!" He bent to retrieve the notebooks, and she snatched them out of his hand.

"Then let him get it himself—out of the files."

"Madeline, why are you so upset about this?"

"Why!" she said, bristling. "You said yourself that it reminds you of all the other failures. Every time you open it to write the next number, you're reminded all over again. And then what do you do? You don't just worry about the current ones—you worry about all those others, too—that have already failed. That's not part of your job. Your job is to run the assay lab—not to do the company worrying. The men who are supposed to do the worrying don't have to do the work. If you try to do both, you are going to crack—not out of weakness, but from trying to carry a double load. That's one of the first rules of survival, Woodrow. Ration your strength—use it where it's needed and don't waste it. Woodrow, do you understand what I'm saying?"

Gates nodded. He felt as though a heavy burden had been lifted off him.

"All right, then. Don't let me hear of your doing this—even once more." Madeline walked out of the room, and Gates heard her go downstairs and tell the children, sharply, to come into the kitchen to help her. From the sounds downstairs, he knew she was still very angry.

He bent down and picked up the magazine that was still open to the picture of the girl with the cowboy hat, and put it with the other one on the desk. He wondered whether he should try to explain the magazines to Madeline and whether she would believe him. Maybe he should just throw them into the wastebasket—but then she might think he had done that because she had found them. He could put them back into the briefcase—but that would look as though he wanted them. And besides, then where would he throw them out?

"Woodrow—"

Gates started and hurried toward the stairs. Now she was going to ask him about the magazines. "Yes, Madeline?"

"Come down here and get into your chair this minute and have your martini. I won't have you up there all by yourself, working up another case of the creeping blues. Peter, get the ice for your father's martini. He's had a hard day."

By the time Gates got downstairs, Madeline was back in the kitchen. He mixed a martini and sat in his chair and drank it and had another. Then, all at once, he started to laugh.

Startled, Madeline hurried in from the kitchen. "What's the matter?"

Peter came in behind her and then the girls, and Gates just laughed and shook his head and poured himself another martini. "I'll tell you afterwards," he said.

Later in bed he looked at her, propped against her pillows, reading.

"Madeline," he said, "didn't you notice those magazines—what kind they were?"

"Of course I noticed them."

"Well—didn't you wonder—"

"Woodrow, there was nothing in those magazines that I haven't seen before."

Gates shook his head. "But didn't you wonder what I was doing with them?"

"Woodrow, if I thought it would keep you from getting so depressed, I'd tell you to subscribe to the foolish things. Or go find the models and woo them like Don Juan. I'd give you money out of the household account to have yourself a high, wide and handsome time!" Madeline turned back to her reading. "However, since you would turn absolutely scarlet even going into a store to buy one of those magazines, I can only assume that your good friend and mine, George Weir, was the donor."

Gates smiled and turned over in bed, away from the light. "Madeline, I'll never get used to you. I don't know where I ever found you."

"You found me in the hospital when you had your tonsils out."

"I ought to grow them back," he said sleepily. "Who knows what kind of luck I might fall over the next time?"

"Perhaps we ought to try your appendix. That might produce a blonde."

"I don't mean that kind of luck."

"I know you don't, Woodrow. Good night."

He was glad for the look on her face that said she was pleased.

For the rest of the week Weir was absent. Then the news came that he had resigned. Gates didn't learn exactly how George had quit. He went once to his house and rang the bell. He suspected that George was in there, but there was no answer. He tried the door and found it locked. There was no sign of Janet or the children and he left—not entirely unhappy that he didn't have to see George—or that he had quit, either.

Tom drew his hands out of the cold box and signaled to Max's technician for more dry ice. Standing behind him, watching, Lawrence Croft said, "You stopping?"

"Max takes over for half an hour now."

"What do you do—take turns?" Croft looked amused.

"Half an hour at a time." Tom felt the tingle in his hands as they began to warm up. He peeled off his rubber gloves. He hated to work with rubber gloves—they slowed you down—but at these extreme temperatures, you needed the little protection they gave.

"Why turns?" Croft said. "Just to keep everything even?"

"Croft, it's thirty below in there." It was a hot sleepy July day with no breeze stirring, and Tom thought how incongruous it was to be working in this heat with your hands freezing.

Croft peered into the box through the glass wall and said, "I hear it's going into chronic toxicity—quite soon now."

Tom nodded without answering. Arctimycin was going into chronic toxicity on Monday, and Croft knew it as well as everyone else. That was why he was hanging around asking questions. Croft was a planner and he wanted to know what to expect.

"Will it be the same as last time—dogs and rats?" Croft said. "Same number and everything?"

"Twenty-four dogs and a hundred rats."

"I suppose there'll be the same autopsies, too?"

Tom nodded.

Croft lowered his voice a little. "What kind of trouble do you suppose it'll be this time?" he said.

"No reason to think there'll be trouble," Tom said, with an optimism he didn't feel. Then the technician was back, and Tom turned off the pump that circulated the nitrogen and opened the box to put in a fresh supply of dry ice. He closed the box and started the pump again and saw that Croft was still here.

"Cable—" Croft started. Then he stopped as Max came in and drew on his rubber gloves. Tom spoke a minute to Max and then left. Croft followed him to the door.

"Cable, tell me something," Croft said in a confidential tone. "What's your opinion of this one? I mean, you know you can depend on me not to talk. What do you honestly think is going to happen with it? You know—it's a month or six weeks until we'll have any inkling—and hell, man, I'm curious."

It was more than curiosity, Tom thought. "I'll tell you what you do, Croft," he said. "I only see a small part of the work. Mr. Caroline is the man you should ask. He sees the whole picture."

Walking down the corridor to his own laboratory, listening to the sound of the pump until he couldn't hear it any more, Tom thought about Croft's question and about his own feelings about Arctimycin. It's four months now that we've worked on it, he thought, and it's almost pure and going into chronic toxicity. And we've learned a lot about it—only not why it behaves as it does. And he could not have answered Croft's question if he'd wanted to. He had no idea what to expect of Arctimycin in chronic toxicity.

After four months, even though all the tests had been encouraging, even though Arctimycin had protected mice and rats and rabbits, he still had no faith in it—and he could not have said why.

On Monday, thawing out each dose one minute before he used it, Mills injected Arctimycin into dogs and rats, and chronic-toxicity testing began. There were no immediately visible alterations in the animals. None had been expected.

At the end of the first week Mills and Dr. Bent conducted routine examinations on the dogs and found nothing irregular.

At the end of the second week, they examined the dogs again, and this time did blood and urine tests. There was no evidence of toxicity, not even in the dogs receiving very large doses.

Everything was routine, except the mounting excitement. When things looked good, no matter how much men cautioned themselves against too much optimism, their spirits broke out of those careful bonds and soared, and they couldn't hold them down.

THIRTY-NINE

ALL WEEK the fishing boats had been in the late summer places, far out on the water—the places where the fish ran in August, that were different from the places where they ran in July. Now that the day was over, the boats were beginning to move, heading home. But all day, Tom thought, they had been out there in the same place, and the fishermen just sat and waited. Walking up the beach with Amity, he looked out at them. He knew something about that—about waiting. He was very bad at it. It was three weeks now that Arctimycin had been going into dogs and rats, and to him it seemed three months. There were many things he did badly, he thought—but none of them so badly as waiting. He looked back at Amity. With her he was waiting, too.

All summer she had been putting him off. At first he had told himself that there were other girls—and that it didn't matter. Then it did matter—and he had told himself that there were other girls, and that he could wait. Now, glancing over at her as they walked idly up the beach, a little apart, without speaking, Tom wondered whether for him there could be other girls any more. Tonight it was not so easy to tell himself he could wait.

"Those boats are always out there," he said, nodding toward the line of boats moving homeward. "Whenever you look, they're out there—all day in the same place."

"They've been there for years," Amity said.

"You wonder how the men can sit still like that—just waiting."

She looked at him and smiled and walked on without answering. The shadows on the cool sand were stretching long, and the gulls were drifting in, white against the white sky, as dusk settled over the water. These were the first hints of summer pushing past, Tom thought—the dark settling in earlier, the gulls coming earlier to the beach. This had been a summer of waiting, and it was almost gone.

After a minute Amity said, "Stop fretting, Tom. Three weeks are behind you, and you just have to live through one more now."

He smiled. She was beginning to know him too well.

"It's only one more week if the news is bad." One week until the first autopsy, he thought—and with Baramycin that had been it. "It takes longer to find out that it's good."

"And if it is good?" she said.

"Then we wait a week for the slides—and if the news is still good, we wait through two more autopsies—at two months and at three months—and even then we won't really know. The test that counts is when it cures a man—and doesn't harm him."

She nodded and they were silent again, and Tom thought that he had never known anyone with whom he had spent such long periods of silence and still felt that so much was being said. The water was warm tonight and he walked along at the edge, looking up at Amity now and then, seeing her slender ankles and her long brown legs and her long hands swinging easily at her sides. She was long and slender-boned, and it gave her a young look—like a racehorse, he thought. Not like a colt still romping in a pasture, but a beautiful spirited mare. To him she always seemed young, he thought—maybe because life was always fresh to her. Or maybe because love is always young, he thought. What else can love be—except young? He smiled a little to himself. It was the first time he had used the word love, thinking about her—and yet, he knew, she was a part of him now—a part of his deepest self and of his private talking—and he had loved her for a long time.

After a while he said, "Last time—with Baramycin—at the end of three weeks the dogs at the highest dose level had started to get sick. This time that hasn't happened yet. These dogs are fine."

"Then why are you so pessimistic?" she said.

"I don't know," Tom said. "I wish I did. Maybe it's only this waiting."

"Is it harder this time—the waiting?"

"It's different." It was better and it was worse, he thought. It was better because of her—because every weekend she came here, and she filled his life in a way that was different from anything he had known before. It was worse because of his own lingering skepticism that hadn't changed. He still didn't really believe that Arctimycin might be the one.

Aloud he said, "Actually there's no reason to be pessimistic. They're resigned to selling it frozen if they have to—and, aside from that, there's every reason to think it might be good. The dogs aren't sick—the rats aren't sick. It protected mice—rats—rabbits. Mills had to use large doses, but the animals were protected."

576

"Is that bad—that it took large doses?"

"If it would save a man's life, you'd give him as much as you had to—and as often—provided the large doses didn't do too much harm. Am, I don't have any reason to feel as I do. I just don't believe in it. Every time they tell me something else good about it— like it actually worked in those animals and protected them—well, I'm surprised all over again."

Amity thought a minute and said, "Still there must be some reason."

"Maybe not. Maybe only the letdown. It's moved away from me now. When the antibiotic goes into animals and when Mills's people do autopsies and prepare slides, I'm not involved." He slushed along at the edge of the beach, listening to the soft splash of the water. "I'm not even working on it much any more. It's almost pure, and Max is finishing up."

"What are you doing?"

"Me?" He came up out of the water and walked beside her. "I'm working through new cultures again—hundreds of them—looking for something else. And I'm not finding anything."

They reached the end of the beach where the land curved away at Ade Hale's house, and turned and started back. Looking along the shoreline, Tom thought that it, too, even in the fading daylight, had the look of late summer. The trees were a darker green, and he could see patches of lawn burned brown and low clusters of early-turning sumac already gone bright red. His mind came back to Arctimycin.

"Maybe it's only disappointment," he said, "because it's not the kind of broad-spectrum antibiotic I anticipated—because it's not perfect—and I was always looking for one that was—or that was nearly so."

Tom walked on, silent, remembering the arguments he had had about that. Over the water the sky was almost dark now, and behind the houses the reflected rays of the sun flashed a red streak across the treetops.

"I'd arrived at a feeling," he said after a few minutes, "that everything about them had to be right—that if they were good they would be naturals. I had decided that you didn't have to reach for them—that the good ones would almost find you. Like people, in a way—if they were right, you wouldn't have to think about it. You would know it. Now, if Arctimycin is good—and God knows I hope

577

it is—that explodes my theory. Maybe that's all that's the matter with me." He smiled. "Vanity. Nothing more."

"It's possible—but I doubt it's that."

"A pet theory can be like a baby—you can become very vain about it," he said. "Fight like a tiger for it—be blind to its faults. That can happen."

She laughed. "Well, maybe it is that, then."

For a long time he fell silent again. He joked about it, he thought, but still, sometimes he wondered whether it could be only that—only vanity—only that Arctimycin disproved the theory in which, for some reason that he couldn't explain, he still believed.

It was almost dark when they came up to the rocks beside Will Caroline's house. A full moon hung low over the water—big and yellow, like a harvest moon—and Tom thought that even the moon was wearing the look of late summer. He stepped on a low rock and Amity came up on the rock too, and stood a minute beside him and then began to climb higher and farther out. She was restless tonight too, he thought. He watched her while she moved from place to place, stepping with the sureness of having climbed here often. She stopped before a high boulder, her arms crossed on it, facing the water, and Tom went out and stood beside her.

In the clear night the Enright lights seemed very close, and Amity looked at them and said, "My whole life those lights have been there—across the bay—but before this they never really meant anything. If I thought about them at all, it was only, That's Enright over there—or the Enright lights are on already, or you can't see the Enright lights tonight because of the fog."

"And now?" Tom said.

"Now—I look over there and I say, How are your dogs tonight? How are your one hundred white rats tonight? What's going on there—inside them—that nobody knows about?" She laughed. "You see—this summer Enright has taken on a whole new meaning."

The moon sliced a wiggling path across the water, and the surfaces of the rocks glinted in the soft light. He looked at Amity and touched her hair, and she looked up at him and then, quickly, away. Tom thought again that tonight something was reaching between them that had not been there before. He could feel it in this sudden silence and see it in the stillness of her hand on the rock and in the quick turning of her eyes away from him, not to look at him, looking instead at her hand on the rock. He saw that she knew it, too—that she felt it as much as he did.

He looked back across the bay at the Enright lights, and after a minute, in his mind, he was seeing the dogs, too—he always pictured the dogs, not the rats—and he thought, Well, what is going on inside you that we don't know about? What's happening in your stomachs—or your livers or your kidneys? Or your blood or your nervous systems? Impatiently he looked away, down at the rock. Just one more week and you'll know something, he said to himself —and if it's bad enough, you'll know it all. And if not, you'll wait some more—and then some more—and more again. And after all the waiting, maybe this will be the one. And after the waiting, if this is not the one, then what? Maybe this one is not what you had in mind, he said to himself—but you had better hope it works.

It's more than two years now, he thought—it's almost two and a half years. His memory began to work back through time to the beginning. My God, I was excited then, he thought—and young and naïve! Then he saw Amity looking at him. "I was just thinking how long it's been," he said. "More than two years. In some ways it seems like only a few months—and in some ways it seems it's been going on forever."

Did I ever think even once, he said to himself—then, when we began—that it might be two and a half years—or longer? Or that it might not be at all? Did I ever think even once that it might fail?

"We've changed in two years," he said thoughtfully. "It's funny what something like this does to you. You don't see it while it's happening—only in retrospect when you realize how you've changed."

"I don't find you so changed."

"We've all changed. We began to change almost from the start, I think."

"Oh—starts are always flashy," she said. "That doesn't count as such a great change."

"Our start was flashy—for those of us who cared, anyway. At first whenever something looked good, we flew sky-high—as though anything could be that easy. Then we learned better."

"Well," she said, "you probably had to learn that—or die."

Parts of it were so vivid, he thought, remembering—and parts so vague. "Then I think there was a point—after three or four failures —when we realized that failure was part of the deal. That was the first change. That early excitement changed to something that had to be able to go the distance. We learned to protect ourselves a little." He thought about that and said, "Some of them began to protect themselves by drawing away from the work—by finding little ways to keep it at a distance. And the rest of us—well, I guess we learned how to fall. We learned to steel ourselves against too much hope and to brace ourselves against too much disappointment, because we knew we had to last."

Looking out at the lights, Tom thought that these emotions seemed far in the past now. "And then I think we changed again. Failure became part of our lives. We knew better than to believe anything until we saw it—or to hope at all until all the evidence was in. We expected failure. I guess we all had to grow up a little, and that was when it happened."

Then abruptly he turned away, and took Amity's arm and led her down off the rocks. Walking up the beach again, he reached for her hand and felt her quick response to his touch. Then he felt her hand go tense in his, and he thought that what existed between them tonight was stronger than any reasons that had held them apart—whatever they were. His own reasons were simple enough. His own reasons were the dozens of little ways in which she had told him not to love her. His reasons were that he couldn't force her or press himself on her, and so he had been waiting for her to want him—waiting unwillingly, feeling the pressure of the waiting, but waiting all the same. Her reason was something he only sensed was there. He didn't know what it was. And whatever it was, tonight it was in the past.

They walked across the beach to the steps, and in the black shadow of the wall he stopped and drew her to him and closed his arms around her. He could feel her warmth against him and her breasts against him and the bones of her back through the thin shirt as she tried once to draw away and he held her firm. He could feel her resistance as she waged an inner struggle to hold onto that small separation between them. He felt her tense—he felt her long slender body hold back—clinging to that thread of her separate self while he insisted against it. Then the resistance ended. He held his arm around her and they walked to the steps.

Reasons, he thought as they moved along the walk to her house —of everything a man knows with any part of him—out of all the knowledge of blood or bone or brain, reasons are the least. Who cares for reasons except as excuses when he doesn't know anything else—what to do—what not to do? Reasons are not-knowing.

In the dark house, the moon streaked a white path across the room, across the low sofa, and across her hair and her face and her throat and her breast. Tell her, he said to himself—tell her it is love. Tell her that it is not like the others—that she is different from all the rest—say it—tell her and it will be better, tell her because she has to know it, because she needs it as much as she needs you, because she needs it more—tell her because she has to know—tell her, tell her, tell her, tell her, tell . . .

The light was on. The hard glaring light was on, and Amity moved about, turning on the others—turning on all the lights—until the room was very bright. Then she came back to the sofa, where he lay watching her, and sat a little away from him.

"Go home now, Tom," she said.

He drew her hand to his lips. "I love you, Am."

She smiled a disbelieving little smile—disbelieving him—or herself—or this moment. "Go now," she said again.

"Why?"

"I don't want to talk about it. Just go. Just leave me."

"Am—I've never said it so easily, so willingly. I love you in a way different from everyone else I've known."

"I don't want you to love me."

"How can I not love you? I do love you. It's there." He smiled and then he grew serious and sat up beside her. "I've loved you for longer than you can imagine. You've held me off and I've let you hold me off—because I didn't know what was wrong—and because I thought maybe the old scars still hurt—and because you're the best thing that's ever happened to me, and I didn't want to lose you."

For an instant the dark eyes were warm and unguarded, and then they grew defensive again. "It didn't matter that much—you were too busy."

Tom smiled. "There are some things you find time for."

She stood up and began to move about the room again. He watched her, seeing the glare of the bright lights on the white walls, seeing on the opposite wall her paintings that were so varied

581

and showed, he thought suddenly, how different her moods could be. She walked past the paintings and stopped at the fireplace. After a moment Tom stood up and went to her.

"Tell me what's wrong, Am."

"Tom, can't you see I don't want to talk about it? I just want you to go."

He tried to hold her and she drew away. "*Why?*" he said.

"Because," she said angrily. "Because you're the last man in the world I want to get mixed up with—in some sordid little romance."

"Would it have to be sordid?"

"They usually are, aren't they?"

"No." He smiled. "Sometimes they can be very good."

"Tom, there isn't really anything between us yet."

"There is quite a bit between us, Am."

"Let's just keep it simple. We live two doors apart—we're both alone—and you're too busy to go looking for someone else—so we've drifted together. That's all it is. Let's not tell ourselves it's something more. The only reason you and I have ever spent ten minutes together is that we live a hundred feet apart."

"That's what's known as the most fortuitous kind of luck, Am."

She walked away, back to the sofa, and he followed her. She gestured impatiently. "Tom—I love it here at the beach."

"All right," he said. "What does that have to do with it?"

"I don't want to spoil it. I don't want to have to stop coming—because of you."

"Would you stop because of me?"

"Don't you see? Now it's all so simple. Now when I come here everything is relaxed and there are no problems. I don't want to complicate it. You're only a hundred feet away—and now that's all right because we're only friends. If you feel like coming over to see me, fine. If you don't feel like coming over, that's fine too. Now I can go out on my beach or take a walk—walk in front of your house—and you can walk in front of my house—and we don't either of us think anything of it. We're both perfectly relaxed. But once we become involved—to a greater or even a lesser degree—that's the end of a lovely casual relationship."

He touched her hair. "I was thinking of something better than a casual relationship."

"And when it's over, then what?"

"This is the shortest romance I was ever involved in. Why end it before we even begin?" He smiled at her. "Am, I don't want to end it. I love you."

"But *think*," she said. "Think how it will be then—when it's over. Then all that will change. We'll avoid each other—try to be casual when we see each other. Then I won't want to come here any more, and I'll stay away. And I don't want to stay away."

"How do you think of all these things?" he said. "I never think of these things."

"What if Diana lived a hundred feet away from you, Tom? Could you just wander out on the beach and stretch out there—as carefree as an old cat—or wander past her house five or six times, just taking a walk—and think nothing of it?"

Tom frowned. She was right about that.

"Think how it was last summer. I was with you when you were dodging Diana. I saw your face when you saw her—when you even saw her boat—seeing her and pretending not to see her and then wanting to see her and pretending you didn't want to see her. Well, I don't want that to happen to me—not here. I don't want to have to stop coming here. Where else would I go? Now if you come over, I'm glad to see you. If you don't come over for months, no damage done."

"It'll never happen. I'll be sitting on your doorstep."

"I don't want you sitting on my doorstep."

Thoughtfully Tom looked at her as he realized that this was the reason she had been putting between them. "Am, you must have been thinking about it—if you've thought of all this."

"Yes," she said. "I thought about you—and gave you up—months ago."

For a long moment Tom sat perfectly still. "Am, this is nonsense. If you don't love me—and can't love me—that's one thing. But if you do—then you are keeping us both from something very good."

"I'm keeping us from something very painful."

"Am, I don't want to hurt you. I love you."

"That will change."

"No, it won't change."

"Yes, it will change!" she cried. "You thought you loved Diana, and you changed. Other men have thought they loved me, and they changed. And I thought I loved them—and I changed."

"With Diana—" Tom hesitated. "She was very young and I was busy and—well, we made a mistake. We were together so much—

583

and we thought it was love." He stopped. He didn't want to talk about Diana. "I never really saw Diana. I guess I was too busy to really see her."

"You're busy now."

"This is different."

"No, it's not different. You're busier now—and you're too busy to see me, too. But when you aren't too busy and you do see me, then what? Is there any reason to think it won't end? Of course it will end. They always end." She stood up and walked away. "If there were a man a hundred feet away on the other side, I wouldn't get involved with him either."

There was something final in her tone, and he looked up quickly and said, "Will you come next week?"

"No," she said. "I thought I'd stay away for a while."

He put his head back against the sofa, feeling very tired now and let down. "No," he said. "You want to be able to come here. Then come. And if we're together, fine—and if not, no damage done—if that's the way you want it. Don't stay away because of me, Am."

He stood up and walked out the door. He told himself to forget her—that he could get along without her. But he couldn't forget her. She was the best thing that had ever happened to him. He would get along without her, he knew—only right now, tonight, he wasn't sure how.

"Well?" Brainard said.

"Well—what?" Vought's irritation showed through his smile.

"Do you know anything yet? Do they know anything yet?"

"They still don't know why it's unstable," Vought said, "if that's what you mean. And it's still not pure."

"It's damned close," Brainard snapped. "You said they couldn't do it. Well, they're doing it."

Vought shrugged and Brainard swung around. Today he was too nervous to sit still, whatever Vought might think. "You got any ideas on the subject?"

"I am not doing the work."

Brainard came back to his desk. He threw his burned-out cigar into the cluttered ashtray and automatically pulled out another. "Do you know that Mills repeated and repeated those tests on mice?" he said. "And protected them every time?"

"I've heard about it."

"And rats, too—and rabbits, too? The ones that got the smallest doses died, and the others, that got bigger doses, were fine—absolutely healthy—nothing wrong with them. And do you know that this is the fourth week and not one animal has begun to get sick?"

Vought looked at Brainard with disdain. "I am not the pharmacologist, but I do know it, yes."

"And do you know what all that means?"

"Certainly," Vought said calmly. "It means that Arctimycin looks very promising."

A week later Mills began the autopsies. He sacrificed the first rat from the group that had received the largest doses and bled it out and examined it carefully. In the opened body lying before him he could find no damage, see nothing wrong. He watched while Mrs. Painter dissected the animal, and he examined each organ as she removed it from the body. Still he found no affected part.

An hour later he began the autopsy on the first dog from the high-dose group. With growing amazement he examined the body as it lay open on the autopsy table and then examined each separate part while the dissection continued. Nowhere in this dog's body could he see any alteration caused by Arctimycin.

By the end of the day it had become apparent that in gross pathology he could see nothing wrong. Even huge doses of Arctimycin, given daily for a month, had caused no damage to these animals that could be seen with the naked eye.

They began the preparation of the slides. Everything was routine except the excitement, and for a week, somehow, they would have to live with that.

"Someday I will write a primer for scientists' wives," Madeline Gates announced. "I expect it will become a classic."

Smiling halfheartedly while everyone else laughed, Tom moved away from the table and leaned against a stool at Tollie's bar. A sudden storm had blown up in the middle of the afternoon, sending them all hurrying back to the dock, and now a party was getting started in Tollie's.

"This book," Madeline said, "will contain not only philosophical

585

advice but invaluable instructions—explicit directions for coping with all the coping areas that a research man's wife faces in her checkered career. I mean the important things—like how to put up the storm sash, how to unplug the sink—"

"Don't forget the plumbing," Kate Derrick chimed in. "And how to fix the washing machine—"

"And what to tell your children," Madeline said, "when they say, 'Mummy, do I have a daddy—like sometimes other children do—sometimes?'"

"'Yes, you do, honey—in a way,'" Kate Derrick said. "'It's just that Daddy forgets sometimes where he lives because he has these here bugs, dear.'"

Everyone shrieked with laughter and started on another round of drinks that Tollie brought. Sitting on the fringe of the party, Tom looked across at Amity. Last week she hadn't come to the beach. Now she was here, and they were together and trying to pretend that there had never been anything between them—that there was nothing between them now. Out in the boat they had tried to make small talk for a while and then had given it up and lapsed into silence. Tom had been almost relieved when the black clouds began piling up and they had to come in.

"Ah believe we could collaborate with you and turn out a great epic, Madeline," Derrick said. "We should do a picture story on life at Enright—how the modern scientist spends his day while he's researchin' and discoverin' and all."

"Call it 'Modern Science—His and Hers.'"

"The first picture will be of you, Charlie," Gates said, "stooped under huge sacks of dirt."

"I think he should have a cigar in his mouth. That'd make him look real important," Kate said.

"Will you smoke a cigar to have your picture taken, Charlie?"

They're all high as the sky, Tom thought—all except me. And it's only half booze. The other half is hope. It was less than a week since Mills had completed those first autopsies, and he still had not looked at a single slide—but when there was nothing wrong in gross pathology, even at very high dose levels, a drug looked good. Hope was spilling out all over the place—as hard as the rain outside.

"I'm thinking of new chapters all the time," Madeline said. "You'll have to get your own book—you can't share mine. Mine will have so much advice it will be enormous—all by itself. I think I should give a complete chapter to 'How to Hold Your Own Against the Bugs.'"

"'How to Keep a Savory Dinner for Nineteen Hours on the Back Burner,'" Sara Mills said.

"But don't worry—don't fret. He's only out for a drink with the boys—talking things over. He'll be home by two A.M.—starved."

"We ought to have a picture of Vought smoking a cigar, too."

"And his feet on the desk."

"Reading the *Police Gazette*."

"In depth."

They shouted with laughter again and Tom laughed too, but he thought that he ought to get out of here because he was going to be a wet blanket. He tried to catch Amity's eye to ask if she was willing to leave, and couldn't. He looked out the window and saw that it was still raining very hard.

"I think 'How to Compete With a Bug' has to be more than one chapter," Madeline said. Madeline was feeling no pain. "It has to be explored on several levels—'Bugs Are Romantic but Do They Wear Well?'—'A Bug at Best Is Only an Office Wife.'"

"'Bugs Are Fascinating but Are They Deductible?'"

"'Can You Curl Up With a Bug on a Cold Winter Night?'"

"Sex should have a whole separate chapter, Madeline."

"Now, there's a challenge," Madeline agreed.

"I think we should have a picture of Mr. Caroline chasing the mice or the mice chasing Mr. Caroline," somebody said. "Mr. Caroline—can we take your picture, with the mice?"

"And a cigar in your mouth?"

Will Caroline laughed. He was standing with Callie, off a little, too, and Tom heard Callie say, "I've never seen them like this!"

"They're under a strain," Will said. "And there's nothing they can do about it—except wait."

Tom moved to the window and looked out at the rain peppering the gray water and beating on the dock where people were still tying their boats and hurrying in. When he looked around, Amity was watching him. He signaled to her, asking whether she would leave, and she nodded. A few minutes later she stood up and came toward the door.

Now, in Tom's living room, it was the way it had been earlier on the boat. Suddenly there was nothing to say. Amity asked about the autopsies and he told her about them. She tried to make other small talk and he did, too, but long silences stretched out between the brief snatches of conversation. Not the relaxed, easy kind of silences they had known before, in which they simply had not felt like speaking. Not the kind of silences in which he had felt so much was being said. These were silences in which they didn't speak because there was nothing to say. When you couldn't say the things you wanted to say, nothing else came to mind.

Outside it was still raining steadily, slanting against the house from the direction of the water, and Tom moved restlessly about the room, glancing at her now and then where she sat in a corner of the sofa.

"Everyone seems to be terribly excited about Arctimycin now," Amity said after a while.

"They're trying not to be," he said. "Today it came busting out all over. Tomorrow they'll all be sober and anxious again—and settled down to the waiting."

She didn't say any more, and after a while Tom went over and sat in the chair next to the fireplace. "Did you get very wet?"

"Not very."

She had taken off her sneakers and left them beside her on the floor. He got up and moved them to the hearth, even though there was no fire, and then, with a little start, he realized that he had done that because Diana had always put her shoes there to dry. Standing at the fireplace, he saw that her hair was still damp and that there were little wet patches on her red shirt—and that she kept her eyes from meeting his too directly or too meaningfully.

He looked away and thought, This is ridiculous. How much can have happened to her that she doesn't talk about, to have made her feel this way? She is full of love that slips out in so many ways because it's there and she can't keep it bottled up.

In dozens of little ways she seemed to affirm all that was good about love—while she denied that it could exist for them. He told himself not to bring it up again—not yet. It wasn't time. But neither could they go on like this.

"Are you still looking at cultures?" she said, after a minute.

"Yes," he said. "Hundreds of them."

"Have you found anything interesting?"

"No—I haven't."

The rain sounded like a river rushing down the side of the house,

588

and he walked over and stared through a streaked window at the waves climbing up onto the beach.

"Maybe I'd better go, Tom," Amity said.

"You can't go out in this—it's pouring." Then he said, "No—don't go."

She went to the fireplace and looked at her sneakers and then back at him. The rain, coming harder now, began to spatter into the house from the porch, and he went over to close the door. Outside the low branches of trees moved up and down as regularly as breathing, while the upper branches stirred in the wind and then were quiet and then stirred again. He heard Amity open a window across the room.

"It's not coming from this side," she said. She stood at the open window. "Isn't that a wonderful smell—that smell of wet leaves and wet earth and warm rain!"

Tom winced and thought, This is impossible. He moved back to the fireplace and stood with his hand braced against the fieldstones. He looked down at her wet shoes on the hearth. He looked at the Japanese sword lying lopsided in the log basket. He looked at Amity, sitting uncertainly on an arm of the sofa, and thought that there had to be a way to reach her. After a minute he said, "Am—do you remember when you were a kid, you used to bring dying fish to Will Caroline and he used to give you pills for them?"

She looked at him, surprised, and then she smiled. "Now, how did you know about that?"

"He told me once—a long time ago—before I knew you."

"Imagine him remembering that!" she said. "I haven't thought about that for years!"

Tom ran a finger along the seams of the stones in the fireplace. "Has it ever occurred to you, Am, that you never stopped carrying fish?"

She was still smiling, remembering. "What do you mean?"

"That's what you were doing with those guys who let you down—Croft and the others. They came to you with their troubles—they were people who needed help, who had to be taken care of—and you tried to give them that help. You didn't love them and then stop loving them. You didn't change—your love didn't end. You never loved them at all. You were just carrying fish all over again."

The smile stayed on her lips. "You're probably right," she said.

But he knew he hadn't reached her. He turned back to the fire-place and traced his finger back and forth over the outline of the stones. He noticed the poker again, lying lopsided in the log basket, and bent down to straighten it.

Behind him, she said, "That's an odd poker."

His hand stopped on the handle.

"I've noticed it before," she said. "I meant to ask you what it is."

Tom hesitated. He hated to tell her—he had been through this before. "It's a Japanese sword," he said, not looking at her. He took his hand away without straightening it.

"Oh," she said. "Is it some kind of trophy?"

He sighed. "I hate to disillusion you, but it's not. I didn't get this in any bloody battle. I won it in an all-night poker game in Hongkong."

She laughed and he looked around quickly. "I rather like that," she said.

"Why?"

"Better off a live gambler than a dead man."

He looked at her and slowly he straightened up and he went over and sat beside her on the sofa. "Am, I can't go on like this—I love you too much."

Even while he said it, he knew it was no use.

"Am, you can't go on like this either!" He turned her face to make her look at him. "You won't live your life alone. You can't."

"No, I can't!" she said. "You're right. I wish I could. I wish I even thought I could—but I know myself and I know that I can't."

Her face flushed and her eyes were bright, and Tom knew that she had been as miserable all day as he had. "Then don't turn me away, Am. I love you."

"You're right!" she said. "I'll make mistakes again—more than one! I'll fall in love again—or I'll think it's love again—and I'll make a mistake again. But I'm not going to make it here."

"Don't think of it as a place. It's not here we're talking about. It's us—you and me. We're in love and we're both miserable this way."

"That's it. That's it exactly!" she said. "To you it's just a place. To me it's not just a place. To me it's home. This is where I grew up. This place has meaning for me—more all the time. Here I can al-ways come back—always come home. Maybe that sounds sentimen-tal to you, but I need that. I need this place to come to. This house is the only permanent thing in my life—and that's something I won't gamble with, so don't ask me to."

Once again he tried to take her in his arms—one last time he tried to reach her to make her understand. "Am"—he touched her hair and buried his face in it—"I need you."

She looked at him and smiled, a little sadly. "You don't really, you know. If you're in love with anything, it's with your work. And when you need diversion, it doesn't really matter whether it's me or somebody else who is with you. Anyone would do. Anyone who would be untroublesome—just someone to talk to now and then, when you're feeling low or when you're temporarily out of steam."

He raised his head. "It matters because I love you."

"No," she said. She shook her head. "Don't. Don't love me. I don't want your love. I don't want to be in love with you. All of it—any of it—I don't want it."

She broke away and rushed out the door, and he watched her run barefoot through the rain across the lawns to her house.

In the morning before he went over there, he knew she would be gone.

"Sara," Mills said, "I want to take a dose of Arctimycin."

Across the table Sara stared at him. "What do you want to do that for?"

"Well—you remember the way it was with Baramycin," he said. "As soon as I opened up the animals, I saw those lousy-looking livers. I didn't even have to wait for the slides."

She nodded.

"And this time in gross pathology I didn't see a thing—not even at the toxic level. Well, late today—just a little while ago—I looked at the slides."

Sara's fork stopped over her plate. "Well, why didn't you say something? What did you find?"

"Almost nothing," he said. "A little kidney damage at the toxic level."

"But you expected something at that level," she said, puzzled. "Didn't you?"

"They were toxic doses—there had to be something," he said. "They were enormous doses and there was relatively little damage."

"Well, that's marvelous, then! It must be very nontoxic."

"It's one of the most nontoxic drugs I've ever seen."

Sara's voice changed. "What's worrying you, Pat?"

"Those enormous doses." Mills fooled with his dinner. "Sara, you remember when I infected the rats? I told you it took larger doses to protect them than I'd expected?"

"I remember."

"Those rats weren't protected at anywhere near the dose that should have done the job. I'd calculated the dose from Gates's work in test tubes and from my own in mice. And the two that got that dose died. The ones that lived got much larger doses."

"But you've always said that a body isn't a test tube—that there's always some loss of efficiency."

"I allowed for that," Mills said. "But this loss was enormous. Even with the mice it took much more to protect than it should have. And the loss in rats was greater still. That was why I went on to rabbits, and it happened with rabbits, too. Arctimycin cured them —but those animals got huge doses. I'm getting suspicious about it. With man it might be even worse—so much might be lost that the drug would be worthless."

"Is that why you want to take it?"

He nodded. "A single dose. And have Gates test to find out how much of it gets into my bloodstream—and how long it stays there." He looked at her. "It's perfectly safe."

Sara toyed with her water goblet, and Mills knew she was thinking it over. He knew, too, that she could understand why he wanted to take it—why he didn't want to let the testing and the hope drag on another two months with these doubts nagging him. She understood him very well—probably because she'd had him hanging around her for practically her whole life. At one age or another, in one way or another—teasing her, tormenting her, elaborately avoiding her and then courting her—he had always been there.

She looked up and said, "How much would you learn by taking it?"

"We'd learn whether it stands a chance of working in man. We can't learn yes, definitely. But we could learn no, definitely. I hope we won't."

"Why not yes?"

"I won't be sick—and the crucial test is still whether it cures

592

somebody. But we can find out whether the human body will absorb it—whether enough will get into the system to do any good."

She was looking at her water glass again, and, watching her, Mills thought that he understood her, too. He understood that she wouldn't have hysterics or make a fuss as some women might. If he had thought she would, he wouldn't have said anything. He would have just gone ahead and done it.

"Pat," she said, "you're not doing this to be some kind of a hero?"

"It's not heroic. It's perfectly safe. Shoo—the day will come when they'll do this with all drugs. After a month of chronic-toxicity testing—if a drug looks as harmless as this one does—it'll be routine to find a couple of well people to take a single dose and do blood tests. There's no harm in it. Nothing is going to happen from a single dose—especially with anything as nontoxic as Arctimycin. Only that day hasn't come yet because the whole field of drugs is just waking up. Officially the company still frowns on this. They'll ask Kaiser, and Kaiser will have a big time worrying about law suits. When I offered to take Illiomycin—that one of Vought's that didn't protect animals—Kaiser practically went into shock. And—oh, hell—why should we go three months if it isn't going to work?"

"No reason at all," she agreed.

"Okay, then?"

She looked up. "Pat—I wouldn't be happy to see anything happen to you."

"Sara, this is as nontoxic as penicillin. You're not taking somebody else's word for it. You're taking mine."

"When are you going to take it?"

"Tomorrow morning. I'll take it early and then take blood samples every hour during the day and have Gates set up assay tests on them—the same as on an antibiotic in any ordinary solution—to find out how much Arctimycin they contain. The next morning he'll have his results—and then we'll know."

"All right," Sara said. She smiled, as though at her own foolish fears. "How would you like to call me—just now and then—during the day?"

"Dr. Gates," Miss Watterling said, "Dr. Mills sent this to be assayed for the amount of Arctimycin it contains."

Surprised, Gates looked at the sample of blood. "More blood-level tests?" he said.

"I believe so," Miss Watterling said.

"I wonder why—I thought we'd done those pretty thoroughly on mice." Gates took the sample. "Has anything happened, Miss Watterling? Anything wrong?"

"I don't think so," Miss Watterling said.

"Maybe it's a different animal," Gates said. "What animal is it, Miss Watterling?"

"I don't know, Dr. Gates."

Gates smiled, puzzled. "Where did you get it?"

"Dr. Mills gave it to me," she said. "Dr. Mills administered the drug at eight o'clock. This is the sample taken after one hour—at nine o'clock. I'll bring the two-hour sample as soon as we take it."

"What's the mystery, Miss Watterling?" Gates said.

"I don't think there's any mystery, Dr. Gates. Dr. Mills just wants another series of blood-level tests on Arctimycin—that's all."

After Miss Watterling left, Gates tried to telephone to Mills to ask what it was all about, but Mills didn't answer the telephone, either in his office or in any of the animal laboratories. Gates went out to the laboratory and set up the test.

At ten o'clock and at one-hour intervals for the rest of the day Miss Watterling brought the blood samples.

"How much, Pearly?" Mills said the next morning. "How much was in there?"

Gates was wearing one of his very unhappy looks. "I tried to find you all day yesterday, Pat. What kind of test was that supposed to be, anyway?"

"It was an ordinary blood-level test, for God's sake," Mills said. "How much antibiotic did you find in the samples? How much got into the bloodstream and how long did it last?"

"Pat, what animal was that?"

Mills gestured impatiently. "Well, Pearly, that animal was me—now get to the point."

"You!"

"Yes—me! That was my blood. How much antibiotic did you find in it?"

"Pat, there wasn't any!"

"None!"

"None," Gates said.

"Not even the first hour," Mills said, "or the second?"

"There wasn't any antibiotic in those blood samples at all," Gates said.

Mills left Gates and walked down to Cable's laboratory to ask him to repeat the test—to take a single dose of Arctimycin and let him draw a sample of blood every hour all day. You couldn't rule out a drug on evidence from only one man. Or even two men. He would have to get a few other people to take it, too.

But what had happened was about what he had expected to happen—a little more extreme, maybe. He had thought there might be traces of the antibiotic in the blood, during the first few hours, anyway. He would get Cable to take it, he thought—and a few other people, too, but the results would be the same. Arctimycin was reacting with so many things in the body that it wasn't lasting long enough to have effect on the bacteria it was designed for.

He spoke to Cable and went upstairs to his own laboratory to prepare the dose. But even before he began, Mills knew that Arctimycin was finished. From the day they found it, it had created a stir, he thought, as he took the solution out of the freezer—and now it had come to a quiet, sudden death.

Two weeks later Max Strong got Arctimycin pure—at forty degrees below zero—and solved the problem of its strange behavior. The answer was no longer of practical value—it had no use whatsoever. To everyone else at Enright it was an anticlimax. To Max it was a triumph.

At forty degrees below zero and pure, Arctimycin was still unstable. It could be kept only in a dilute solution.

"We should have known," Metcalf said bitterly, at lunch. "Right at the start, when it was so queer, we should have known."

"So even pure, it's unstable," Vought said, leaning over from the next table where he was sitting with Harrup and Brainard.

"What about it, Max?" Mills said. "What causes it?"

"The molecules are combining to form something else," Max said.

"Combining with what? It's pure now."

"With each other. When the molecules get close together, they combine with each other and form something different. It's a phenomenon called polymerization."

"Then it wasn't a contaminant after all," Mills said.

No, Tom thought, it wasn't a contaminant after all.

"The more we concentrated it, the closer together we brought the molecules," Max said. "Then, as they moved around—with the normal amount of motion—they would bump into each other and combine. And when they combined, they became a different substance—with different properties. Every time that happened, we would lower the temperature, and that would slow down the motion of the molecules so that they didn't bump into each other. Then we would concentrate it some more and that would bring the molecules still closer together, and they would start to combine again—and then we'd have to get it colder to slow down the motion even more. That's why, even pure, it's more stable in a dilute solution."

"So that's the story!" Mills said. "I've never heard of that happening before."

"I don't believe it has happened before with any other antibiotics," Max said. "But it's the explanation with this one. I'm sure of it."

"Max." Brainard broke in from the next table. "Let me ask you something. You came over nights for this. You came over weekends. Even after everyone knew it was no damn good, you were playing with it. What in hell for?"

Max smiled without answering, and Tom thought that this was something you could never explain to a man like Brainard.

"Gil, there's just something about a problem like that," Harrup said. "It gets you and you have to follow through on it. You can't stand not to know the answer."

Brainard snorted. "Well, I suppose that's what they call a nice piece of work."

"It is," Harrup said. "It's a brilliant piece of work."

"It doesn't make for anything in a capsule," Brainard said, "in a bottle in a drugstore."

Tom winced as he recognized his own words coming back at him.

Two days later Will Caroline watched while Tom read the paper he had handed him. When he had finished the first part, Will gave him an Enright record and watched while Tom read that and compared the two. Even before Tom spoke, Will knew the answer.

"Where'd you get it?" Tom said.

"Dr. Loedick sent it to me. Is it familiar to you?"

"It's Illiomycin!"

Will nodded. A company in California had just patented it. The name was different but the product was the same. There was no mistaking it. Tom was flipping quickly through the rest of the literature. "Didn't they get the same failure in animals?"

"Yes," Will said, "it's all there. They had complete failure in animals, just as we did. It was so nontoxic they decided to take a chance and test it in man. And it worked. It cured a man."

He waited while Tom read parts of the paper again. "There's no question in your mind, Tom?"

"None." Tom shook his head. "It's Illiomycin."

Will Caroline stood up. He might as well go down and tell Ade. And then find Vought and tell him, too.

Three days later Vought's resignation arrived by telegram.

"Listen," Metcalf said, "Vought knew what he was doing."

"That's just a myth," Mills said. "He worked at it."

"He stayed until now, didn't he?" Metcalf said.

"I'll have the roast turkey, sweetheart," Wentner said to the waitress, "with all the trimmings. Pumpkin pie for dessert."

"Listen, Morrissey quit almost a year ago. Weir threw in the towel three months ago. Vought stayed. What do you say to that?"

Mills shrugged. "I say the rats are quitting the ship."

"Listen, Mills, this is no time for comedy."

"I'm glad to see the last of him," Mills said. "The guy was a cold-blooded, arrogant son of a bitch."

"But he stuck until now," Metcalf said. "Now he's quit—and I say that means something."

"It means he's a son of a bitch," Mills said cheerfully.

"Ah believe ah liked that better the first time," Derrick said soberly. "Ah think a cold-blooded, arrogant son of a bitch describes it better."

Metcalf exploded. "Vought was no fool!"

"That's true," Gates said. "He was hard to get along with, but he was no fool."

Mills ordered his lunch from the waitress and opened a journal he had brought with him. "I found the damnedest machine," he said cheerfully. "You give an animal a drug—like an antibiotic— and you make the drug radioactive—and then when you've got slides, this little old machine tells you exactly where most of that drug went. I think I'll ask Mr. Caroline if I can't have that machine."

"Mills, are you crazy or something?" Metcalf burst out.

Mills was reading the journal again. "Shoo," he said, "I like that machine."

Metcalf pushed back his chair and left the table.

An hour later, in Gates's office, Metcalf said, "Three months from now you know what we're going to be? We're going to be two dozen scientists out of a job."

Gates nodded, worried.

"Vought was smart. He found something." Metcalf lowered his voice although there was no one around to hear. "If you ask me, we'd be smart to get out now too," he said. "Get ahead of the mob."

Two weeks later, Metcalf's resignation arrived in the interoffice mail. When he quit, nobody really noticed. Nobody had known Metcalf very well. But his resignation meant that one more man had left the sinking ship.

PART
SEVEN

NOVEMBER 1948 –
MARCH 1949

TWO HUNDRED THOUSAND," Brainard said. "Dr. Derrick's laboratory has now tested two hundred thousand broths."

For more than half an hour at the November board meeting Brainard had been talking, and Ade Hale watched him covertly, wondering how far he intended to go. It was beginning to look as though he might have a showdown on his hands before the day was over.

"Two hundred thousand shots at the target—at a cost of three million dollars," Brainard said. "And I don't have to tell you what we've hit. Now, what kind of game are we playing here? What odds are we waiting for? One in three hundred thousand—one in four hundred thousand? How high do we go?"

The late morning sun sliced across the walnut-paneled wall— across the portraits of three of the six former presidents. Palmerton was tapping the eraser end of his pencil on his white pad. Kaiser was wiping his glasses for the third time. Several times Will Caroline had interrupted to argue or to object; twice Bodenhof had interrupted with questions. Otherwise Brainard had done the talking, and he was mounting a strong attack with a remarkably full and accurate mass of figures and details.

"Two and a half years—and three million dollars," Brainard said. "It's enough."

"It's enough for me," Palmerton said.

"This has been a dynamic period in business," Brainard said. "In all business—and in this industry in particular—"

"That's true!" Palmerton put in. He looked around the table. "It's true," he said to Kaiser who was sitting beside him.

"I know it's true," Kaiser said irritably. "Business has boomed."

"If we had expanded, we could have kept pace," Brainard said. "We have not kept pace."

"You can't deny that!" Palmerton said across the table to Bodenhof.

"I don't deny it," Bodenhof said.

"If we had invested in production instead," Brainard hammered on, "Enright would be a front-line company today—solid as the Rock of Gibraltar."

"Let's get something straight," Hale said calmly. "Enright is a solid company now."

"We could have become rich," Brainard shot back. "If you had let me earn the money first for you to play with—"

"We earned the money," Hale said. "We didn't borrow it or steal it."

"If we'd gone into finished products, we'd be a front-line competitor. You heard Croft's report—more than a year ago."

Narrowly, Hale looked at Brainard. Brainard's confidence had soared—you could tell from the way he talked. Hale wondered how much of it was certainty and how much was bluff. And how much was miscalculation.

"About the course we took and where it has brought us, the facts and figures speak for themselves." Brainard looked around the table. "For the good of the company," he said, "for the sake of its future, I propose that this project be terminated—now—today!"

"Just a minute!" Will Caroline broke in.

"I'm proposing termination of your project, Mr. Caroline. Immediate termination."

"I have funds until the end of the year."

"We'll change that."

"Oh, no, you won't!"

Angrily Will Caroline and Brainard faced each other across the table. Then, slowly, Will scraped back his chair. By the time he got to his feet and walked around behind the chair and leaned over it, he was smiling.

"Well, now," he said, "that's a pretty serious proposal."

"It's serious, all right."

"And a pretty reckless one."

Brainard snorted.

"It's reckless and very shortsighted!" Will said. "You're proposing to write off an enormous investment just when it stands a chance of paying off."

"Rubbish!" Brainard said.

Will looked around the table, talking to the directors. "In two and a half years, gentlemen, you've paid for a lot of experience."

"That we know!" Brainard put in. "That we all know."

Will continued to talk to the others. "Do you have any idea how far these men have come in that time?" he said. "Do you know how much they've learned?"

"They should have done their learning somewhere else."

"There wasn't anywhere else! That was the only reason we ever had a chance."

"Great chance! Zero in two hundred thousand shots."

"These men learned what they know in our laboratories. They patched it together out of the failures—out of a scrap they found here and a scrap they stumbled over there. We paid for that."

"You've spent three million dollars running a school," Brainard said to Palmerton.

Palmerton tapped his pencil eraser nervously.

"If these men had known at the start what they know now, they'd have given you an antibiotic a year ago!"

Palmerton's eraser stopped on the pad. "Do I understand," he said to Will Caroline, "that you are suggesting—that you are still suggesting—that this can be done?"

Will looked at Palmerton as though he couldn't believe the question, and in spite of himself Hale had to smile.

"Mr. Palmerton," Will said, drawing himself up to the full height of his rangy form and taking a long look at Palmerton. "Make no mistake about this. I am not *suggesting* that this can still be done. Not *suggesting*. It is my absolute conviction that this can be done."

Ade Hale shook his head. It was hard not to admire this show of bravado. Not that he blamed Will, he thought, for wearing a good front to the end. You might as well hang for a lion as a dog. And then he thought that even now it probably wasn't all bravado. From the start Will had been the only one who had never wavered, who had never seemed discouraged. From the start Will had believed in it, and maybe he believed in it still. And maybe he was right. Or maybe he was just blind to the facts—like a punchy fighter who kept getting up off the floor and saying, "Next round I'll kill him."

"These men are trained now," Will said. "They're hardened. They know what they're doing. They can do this—"

"Oh, rot!" Brainard yanked open his briefcase and pulled out some papers.

"Gentlemen," Will persisted, "you have a heavy investment here —of hard-earned, hard-learned knowledge. Don't turn your back on it just at the moment it is about to pay a return—"

"All right!" Brainard interrupted. "So you think it can still be done? All right, then—listen to this!"

"You finished, Will?" Hale said.

"I don't mind being finished for the moment," Will said.

"Now, listen to this," Brainard said. "This is the report of a symposium of the nation's top research men—held less than a year ago."

"What kind of research?" Bodenhof said.

"Medicine. What else are we talking about? Less than one year ago. It's a long report—I'll just read you the high spots.

" '*One*,' " Brainard read, holding up one finger. "Now, this isn't me talking—I'm reading this. 'All over the world, *thousands* of types of bacteria, molds, fungi, algae, and plants have been screened. There has been *frantic activity*, but nothing comparable to penicillin has been discovered.'

" '*Two*.' " Brainard held up a second finger. " 'Thousands of new substances have been found, capable of killing bacteria in *test tubes*.' " Brainard looked up. "And we've found our share of those thousands right here at Enright." He read on. " 'But among the thousands which kill in test tubes, only very few are proving useful in the *treatment of disease—because* (a) they lose activity in the presence of animal tissues'—and we've had plenty like that, too, gentlemen, including Arctimycin which cost us a half-million dollars." He resumed reading. " 'And (b) practically all are toxic. *It is unlikely that many other miraculous penicillin-like substances will be found in nature.*'

" '*Three*.' " A third finger went up. " 'The biologist extracting microbial cultures proceeds *blindly, by hit or miss*, spurred on by the hope that he will again find on his way some other penicillin-like wonder drug.' " Again Brainard looked up. "Blindly, hit or miss. That's what your money's going for. Blind hope. Now—here's the conclusion—listen to this.

" 'The discovery of a new agent which exhibits antibacterial effect in the test tube has only little significance. Of the many "miracle" germ-killing substances announced in papers, very few will cure a mouse of an experimental infection. Still fewer will reach the physician. *For a long time to come—*' " Brainard looked all around the table. " '*For a long time to come, penicillin will remain the glamour girl among anti-infectious agents of microbial origin.*' "

Brainard finished. The room was very quiet, while the directors, disturbed and thoughtful, looked at each other and at their white pads and yellow pencils on the table. Palmerton's eraser was busy again, and Kaiser was wiping his glasses very clean.

"All right," Brainard said. "That's not me arguing. That's a national symposium—better brains than ours—less than a year ago. Now, what do you say to that?"

"Why—that just proves how far ahead we are!" Will Caroline said. "Miles ahead of the field!"

Brainard threw down the paper in disgust. "If you can twist this report to mean that, you can twist anything."

"That report proves that the accumulated knowledge in the field is still very small," Will insisted, "and that ours is special—and valuable. Gentlemen, you paid for that knowledge. If you don't use it— if you let it go—these men will take it somewhere else. And somebody else will grab it. And profit from it. And somebody else will get the dividends from your investment. That's something to think about —very carefully."

"There's nothing to think about," Brainard said. "Let 'em go."

"I want to think about it," Bodenhof said.

"Let 'em go and good riddance. Let's get back to where we were before we made this colossal blunder—back to making some money."

"This wasn't a colossal blunder! This has never been more promising!"

"Any other direction would have been better. And every day we go on is only extending the blunder that much longer. I say stop— stop today."

Hale looked sharply at Brainard. "As long as Enright is in good shape," he said, "this isn't a blunder of the dimension you're trying to make it. As to other directions we might have taken, none of us is clairvoyant. It's one thing to talk about what might have happened. It's another thing to make it happen."

"With this, nothing has happened," Brainard argued.

"The alternatives were not without competition—the cost of entering new markets wouldn't have been small. Maybe they would have been profitable—maybe not."

"Could it have been worse? Almost three years and we're at rock bottom. We've just spent a half-million dollars on one that failed, and a week later we found out that another one that we spent a quarter-million on—and didn't work long enough—looks like it might be good. Our best men are quitting—those who know."

"Oh, no," Will Caroline said. "Not those who know!"

"They're quitting in droves. We've had three major failures. And not one man today even claims to be working on anything that looks good."

"That could change overnight."

"It's rock bottom." Brainard thumped the table. "It's time to quit."

Hale leaned forward. "Rock bottom is not the time to quit!"

Brainard swung around from Caroline to Hale. "I say it's time—" He broke off, and his head thrust forward as though from the momentum of a checked swing.

"Rock bottom is never the time to quit," Hale said. "There's too much emotion involved."

He stopped and waited for Brainard to answer. For a long, silent moment Brainard looked at him, leaning heavily on the table. The retort was ready. It was at the edge of his teeth. Brainard hesitated and Hale waited. Brainard took a fleeting look around the table, counting his strength. He doesn't know, Hale thought—he's not sure. This is his chance and he knows it, and if he were sure, he would take it. Still he waited. Brainard remained silent and the moment was past.

Hale sat back. "There are funds until the end of the year," he said, "with a reserve to go two weeks into January. We'll go that time. If the situation doesn't change by then, I'll be in favor of bringing this, systematically, to an end. But when we decide, we'll decide out of reason. Not out of hysteria and despair." He pushed back his chair and stood up. "We'll take a break."

"Just one thing," Bodenhof said. "If it comes to that, I want a special meeting in January to vote on it. If I'm selling out at a heavy loss, I want another look at the prospects. I've seen too many times when you'd have gotten your money back if you'd held on a little longer."

For the first time since he had been at Enright, Hale went home early. By four o'clock the directors had all left and Hale left, too. Today he had won a round, he thought, as he drove over the bridge —but today was not the end. He might still have to put up a fight for his job. And in a showdown, he knew, it wasn't past profits that counted. A man could spend twenty years building up a company, but memories could be short, and if you had made a decision that resulted in a three- or four-million-dollar loss, you could find yourself out of a job. And then what? He turned into the traffic and headed for the shore drive. Then they hung your picture next to the pictures of the other men who had become only a few square feet on a walnut wall, whose words and acts and policies had been long since forgotten. The world of business was like a sponge, he thought—you pushed at it and made a little dent, and then you removed the pressure and the surface smoothed out again as though you had never been there.

And what if you had a young wife to whom you were an idol? What if you had a wife twenty years younger—and you failed? Then what? Were you still an idol, or just an irascible old man? He turned into his driveway and gave his head an impatient little shake. This was silly—all of it. He was getting morbid. Still—twenty-two years older . . .

Helen wasn't home yet and he went upstairs to change, but she hadn't laid out his things before she went out, and he didn't know where to find them. He went back downstairs and lay on the leather sofa in his den. He should have ended it today, he told himself. He should have taken the initiative while he was still in control—he should have moved first, without giving Brainard the chance, and told the board that it wasn't working out and that it was time to stop. All the things that he had let Brainard say were the things he should have said himself. And he knew it—he knew it then.

Then why didn't you? he said to himself. You could have and you should have—and you didn't end it today, because you didn't want to.

Then Helen came in, alarmed because she had seen his car.

"What's the matter?" she said, hurrying into the den without taking off her coat. Her hair was a little blown, and the cold had brought color to her face. "Ade, what's wrong?"

"Nothing's wrong," he said. "The meeting was over and I just came home early. That's all."

She sat on the edge of the sofa and looked at him carefully because she didn't believe that was all. She began to pull off a glove, and he watched her a minute.

"I gave them two more months," he said. "Don't ask me why. I should have ended it today."

She smiled and drew off her other glove.

"Your man may be out of a job, Helen," he said.

She stood up and put her coat on a chair and came back.

"What would you do then?" he said.

"Well," she said, "I probably wouldn't do much of anything then. I'd probably leave the doing up to you, Ade."

He smiled. "Do you remember I used to say, Helen, that I was the one who was objective about this? I'm afraid that cold-blooded objectivity got lost somewhere."

"A long time ago, Ade."

"You saw that?"

"As early as Baramycin—that first day Croft came to see you and you talked half the night about the early penicillin."

"It might have been better for both of us if you'd pointed it out —right then and there."

"I'd have bit out my tongue first," she said. "Ade, you know you're never happier than when you're in a fight. You've enjoyed this one."

"I'd have enjoyed it more if we'd won."

"It's not over."

"Damn near, I'm afraid."

And yet, he knew, if he had it to do over, he would probably have decided the same way. He wasn't sure that he had ever believed they would succeed, but he had thought the effort should be made—and he would think that again.

There is a tide in the affairs of men, Will Caroline thought—and this was a long low tide. There are times when everything goes sour, when nothing is with you, and this was one of those times. And when that happens, there is nothing to do but wait it out—wait until this stretch of bad luck has had its turn and run itself out.

The meeting was over and it had been no worse than he had expected. Brainard had scored his points, but nobody had fought very hard when Ade had insisted on two more months. Remembering his own words, Will Caroline shrugged a little. He had said what had to be said—but that had become his role now. He was the fool in this little drama, he thought—the court jester, who watches and listens to the whole comic-tragic spectacle, who sees and hears the tale of defeat and despair, and clutches at one small, insignificant straw and sings about it merrily.

And yet, he thought, in spite of all that, what I said was the truth. If we can last, we can do it. It's there to be done. If someone else gets there first, that will be one of the tricks of fate—in every game someone wins and someone loses—but it's going to happen. Some-one will do it.

He stood up. He might as well go over and tell the men they had two months. They would be waiting to hear. He wasn't sure how they would feel about the news. It was half reprieve, half ultimatum. And if the project ended two months from now, he wasn't sure how they would feel about that either. Just relieved, maybe. They were all discouraged. You only had to walk down the research corridors to see it.

A few minutes later, in Cable's laboratory, he said, "It's not final —there'll be a meeting in January—but then I think it'll be final, unless we have something promising."

Cable nodded, and Will saw that his eyes were tired and inflamed. "You ever sleep?" he said.

Cable nodded. "I sleep."

"When?"

"What do you mean, when? At night."

Will Caroline smiled and started to leave. "Where?"

Tom shrugged and turned away.

He slept anywhere, Will knew. He fell asleep on his own sofa, and many times his lights burned all night. Twice he had slept here on the cot in the dispensary. But it wasn't just lack of sleep that produced that look. It was lack of hope. He walked out of Cable's laboratory and glanced at him again through the glass panel. Like everyone else involved, Cable had changed. His spirits were down —his buoyancy was gone. He was working very long hours, but he wasn't working eagerly any more. He was working compulsively. Will walked down the corridor. When hope is strong, he thought, nothing can touch you—but when hope is low, everything hurts. The smallest intruder becomes an invader, and an ant is an army.

He had made the rounds and told the others, and then, walking back across the yard to his office, he thought about them—about those who were still here for him to tell—those who hadn't quit. Once, he remembered, Callie had said that love was an ingredient of genius. Now, he thought, he knew there was another one just as important: the capacity to endure—the ability to survive.

It was dark already, and the lights were on in all the buildings and the smell of a winter night was in the air. Once he used to wonder what made them quit. Once, whenever a man quit, he used to ask himself what had happened inside him, so that this moment—no worse than others he had lived through—had become the moment when the man couldn't go on. Now he didn't ask it any more. Now he asked what made a man stick.

And yet, he thought, there were some that you knew wouldn't quit. They were discouraged too. Right now they were very low—but you knew that somehow they would hold on. He went into the administration building where people were already leaving to go home. It was the difference between one man and another, he thought—between the first-rate and the rest.

An hour later, at home, Will poured his bourbon and drank it. He needed this drink tonight. He refilled the glass and stood at the window that faced the bay. Across the water, the Enright lights shone with a hard bright look of permanence.

"Isn't it remarkable, Cal?" he said. "From the beginning of time the world has owed all its progress—all its good things—to a handful of men, a precious handful of geniuses—and yet it's always against them."

Right from the start, he thought. It laughs at them when they begin, it thwarts them along the way, it ridicules them when they fail. He finished his drink and turned to see Callie watching him, troubled because he was troubled.

"And yet somehow that genius survives," he said. "Exists on its own nourishment—resists the attacks and the ridicule. It fails often and has to pick itself up—by itself—if it's going to get up. And somehow it gets through it all—in spite of the mob."

And when it finally produces something, he thought, the mob is always there to seize the product as its due, with hardly a backward glance of thanks. The mob is always there—upper mob or middle mob or lower mob, it's all the same. The mob is the mob. Will gave himself a little shake and went over and sat on the sofa and put his feet up on the table. "It's been a long time since I've felt this way," he said.

Callie came over and sat beside him. "It's infuriating, Will," she said. "Of course it is. But you know—there's something rather wonderful about it."

"About the mob?"

"No, darling—about the surviving in spite of it."

"Well—"

"Think, Will," Callie said. "In the midst of all the mediocrity, all the ignorance, all the self-satisfaction and the utter lack of imagination—there, in that barren desert, somehow genius settles. And—you just said it—it thrives. It feeds on nothing but its own spirit, and it produces the only progress man ever makes. And somehow I feel that is quite marvelous. It's like a childhood fairy tale. It's the gallant old story of the daisy growing out of a rock or a crack in the pavement. No sustenance—no encouragement—trampled on by every kind of thing—and yet, there it is. It's one of the few modern miracles."

Will smiled. But he thought that they were going to need that kind of miracle and another, more specific one too, if they were going to keep this project alive, now.

FORTY-ONE

IT SEEMED now that the days were all the same.

On Monday you took the new cultures and you grew them for six days—three days in shake flasks, three days in stir pots.

On Friday you went into the fermentation room to look at them, although there was never anything unusual to see—and if there had been, you would have told yourself that it didn't mean anything.

On the following Monday the broths came out of the fermentation room, and you filtered off the mycelium and sent samples to Gates and set up your own tests, too, on agar plates.

On Tuesday you checked the results. (If there is one thing wrong, that is one thing too many.) On Tuesday you threw out most of them.

And you began to work on the rest and found other things wrong —and you threw out a few more.

Out of the whole batch there might be one or two that you purified enough to send to mice. And the mice died and then you threw those out too.

Earlier or later they all ended up the same way. You threw them out.

On a Friday afternoon late in November Tom stopped outside the fermentation room and told himself that he ought to go in and look at the broths—sometimes by Friday afternoon you could see something. Then he thought, What for? Even if a broth looked interesting, it didn't mean anything. Even if it looked great—even if next Monday it looked great—it would still end up down the drain. After you'd poured out about a hundred thousand of them, you knew that whatever they looked like—on Friday or on Monday or a couple of weeks later when the antibiotic went to mice—that's where they were going to end up. Down the drain. For a full minute he stood at the fermentation room door. Then he turned his back on it and moved on.

"Anything look good today?" Moose said, when he came into the laboratory.

"I haven't gone in yet." Tom went into his office.

It had been a cheerless day, and now the water was a gray blanket against a gray curtain of sky. He began to read his notes on his latest antibiotics. Two were unstable. Throw them out, he said to himself—if anything will stop you, let it.

Two others were fighting back. They couldn't be extracted with solvents, and they weren't good enough to be interesting. They're never good enough to be interesting—how long since you've had one that was really interesting? He laughed without humor. He couldn't remember. Throw them out, he said to himself.

That leaves three to work on awhile and send to mice—and then you can throw those out too. He studied the three. They didn't interest him either. He probably wouldn't even go to watch the mice—just send the stuff upstairs and let Mills tell him when the mice died. In the time he'd waste watching these kill the mice, he could throw out a dozen more. He dropped the pencil on the desk and covered his eyes. Maybe he'd get started on these three tonight and work on them over the weekend. Then around Tuesday they could go into mice, and he'd be rid of them. They were no good—he knew they were no good.

After a while he opened his eyes and saw Moose looking at him. "You want something?"

"No."

He saw that it was dark outside. "You leaving now?"

Moose nodded and still stood there, and Tom knew he was trying to tell him to go home. "Stop in the fermentation room, Moose," he said, "and take a look at those broths."

"O.K.," Moose said. And then, "Well, good night."

Tom looked at his notebook again without reading it. He told himself he might as well get started on the work and get out of here—go home. Go home for what? Hell, go home and get some sleep, for God's sake. He told himself he would get started in a minute.

Then he put his head down on his arm on the desk and gave himself up to the fatigue and despair that he was beginning to know too well—that came over him often now and settled in. There were times when he felt that he couldn't look at another culture, that he couldn't grow another culture, that he couldn't begin one more time to get an antibiotic out and send it to mice. Now you know, he thought—now you know what it is to fail. Now you know what it is to be wrong—not in a small or a simple way, not in a way that you can straighten out, but to be terribly wrong in a way from which there is no going back and for which there is no help.

He began to think about Amity, and tried to make himself stop, and for a while it didn't work. Usually he could make himself stop, and lately he didn't think about her so much any more. Then suddenly—like now—the feeling of loneliness and of wanting her would rush over him, worse than before. Stop thinking about her, he said to himself. Think about something else. He wondered where she was—and when she would come here again. It'll be a long time, he thought. Maybe not—maybe not such a long time—because you'll be out of here soon, and then she'll come again. It'll be quite a day for everyone around here when you finally clear out—for Amity, so she can come home again—for Enright, so they can try to get back in business again. They'll probably hang out the flag. You're in good shape tonight, he said to himself.

Moose was back. "There's only one," he said.

"One what?"

"One broth in the new batch that looks like anything."

"Well, that's about par for the course."

Moose nodded. "Looks thicker than the rest."

"Fine," Tom said.

Moose stayed. "You want to come look at it?"

"I'll go down later. Go home, Moose."

"Listen, Dr. Cable—" Moose began.

"I know, Moose. I look like hell. Go home."

By nine o'clock he had finished the work on two of the antibiotics, and he felt that he couldn't do the third one tonight. He went into his office and took off his lab coat. Across the yard in the fermentation building the door was open a little, and in the block of yellow light he could see the attendant moving among the tanks. He stayed a minute, watching, and then looked away. Beside the sink were the pieces of equipment he had used. Down the corridor Bessie was beginning to clean this floor. Out there was the fermentation building attendant. It was always the same. The days were all the same and the nights were all the same. He took his coat off the hook and started home.

On his way out, Tom passed the fermentation room again and slowed down. He ought to go in and look at that one. And then he thought, The hell with it. What are you going to see? A broth that's

614

a little thicker. How many broths have you seen that were a little thicker? And where are they today? He walked on to the stairs and stopped. For the first time he admitted to himself that he didn't want to go in there. He was sick of going into that room. He was sick of looking at the same unpromising results of another week's work. He was sick of the whole thing.

He forced himself to go back and push open the door and go in. Quickly, mechanically, he walked along the row of stir pots, looking at them, seeing nothing. They were all the same—always all the same—week after week the same muddy broths. He came to the end of the row and turned the corner and looked mechanically along the second row.

His eye stopped. In the fourth pot in the row, the broth was different. This was the one that was thicker than the rest. Much thicker—and it was getting yellow—yellower than any broth he had seen before.

He stood and looked at the thick yellow broth, swirling in the stir pot. Something in him that had looked at a hundred thousand broths told him that this one was different. And then something in him that had poured a hundred thousand broths into the sink warned him that it didn't mean a thing. A broth could be thick and be toxic—it could be yellow and be unstable—it could be different and be worse, not better.

And yet for a long time he stood there, looking at it, because after weeks of monotony, after thousands of broths that looked alike, when you saw one that was different, a small, almost played-out thread of hope inside you tightened and vibrated again—not as strong as once it had, but still, something began to stir and you were curious.

He went back to his office to check on it. On Derrick's plates it had hit gram-positive and gram-negative organisms, but that didn't mean much. It could be streptomycin, streptothricin, Illiomycin, Baramycin, Arctimycin—they all turned up regularly, streptomycin and streptothricin every day. Baramycin in cycles every couple of months. He checked Wentner's reports and his spirits sank. Wentner had reported that it was Baramycin. He might have known.

Still—something in him protested. That broth didn't look like Baramycin. He went back to the fermentation room. Baramycin never got that yellow, he thought—not in any broth. Although that didn't prove anything. The color could just be some quirk—from a change in the nutrients, even. All the same—I know Baramycin, he thought—and I put it into a lot of broths—and it never looked like that. It never got that yellow and it never got that thick. Not even after a week—and this is only Friday. He didn't believe it was Baramycin.

He went out again into the silent corridor. Bessie had finished and gone by now and on the whole corridor there wasn't a sound, other than the muffled noise from the fermentation room. Tom walked down the stairs and across the silent parking lot and sat in his car, alone in the lot. Gradually the melancholy feeling of hopelessness settled over him again. So you've got a thick yellow broth that may or may not be Baramycin, he said to himself. Well—you've had thick broths before. And there is no reason to believe that a yellow broth will be any more potent, any more stable, any less toxic than a dirty brown broth. The odds are that this yellow broth will never get to mice—and if it does reach mice, then the odds are heavier that those mice will die in five minutes. Those are odds you know, he said to himself. Those are odds you know too damned well. So go home and go to bed—you need the sleep. He started the car. But he didn't want to go home, because it was Friday night—one more Friday night when Amity wouldn't come, when her house would be dark to remind him. He drove out of the parking lot and headed for the bridge.

The trouble is there's no one else, he told himself—and you don't have time to find someone else. If you would find a replacement, you would forget her fast enough. It's not her so much, he said to himself. The hell it isn't, he said to himself.

He stopped at Tollie's and looked inside. There was a crowd tonight. He closed the door and went down to the dock. It was too cold to stay here long, but he turned up his collar and walked to the end. In the black night he felt achingly lonely.

He leaned on a post and stared at the black water. Suddenly he began to think about his father—seeing him again in his mind's eye as he always did—a faded man in a straight-backed chair—and he thought wearily, I used to hate him for admitting that he was a failure. I used to hate him for just giving up and dying. Now I know how he felt—and what he felt—because now I know what it is to fail. Below, the water spanked the post and threw up an icy spray, and he moved back a little. He was tired, he thought, and he was without hope. He wasn't even sure when hope had died—he just knew that it was gone and he didn't hope for anything any more. They would go to the end and stop, and he would leave here —he would have to leave here because he was responsible for this failure, more than anyone else—and there was no way to make amends except to succeed. And that was the one thing he couldn't do.

Once he had been so sure, he thought—so certain he was right— as his father, too, must have been certain once. And now he was backed into a corner from which there was no out. Now he had failed. For the first time in his life he thought of his father with compassion. The wind blew across the dock, and he walked back to his car and drove home.

He saw that he had left his lights on again. He walked around the house, thinking that once that would have meant Diana was here waiting. At least then he had come home to someone—not just an empty house. Now the lights only meant that last night he had fallen asleep on the sofa and left them burning and then hadn't noticed them this morning. The wind was colder here than on the dock, and he moved quickly up the steps. He opened the screen door, still hanging in November, and let it pull shut behind him. For several minutes longer the house door stayed open.

She was sitting on the arm of the sofa, with the light falling on her hair and one hand flat, her arm straight, bracing herself. She was sitting very straight and her chin was tilted—in a way that could have been defensive or defiant, or carefully cold.

He stood in the doorway, staring at her. "Am—" he said.

"I thought—" Amity said, and stopped. Her eyes, unguarded and direct, met his.

Tom dropped his coat on a chair and came over to her. He wasn't sure whether, tonight, he was glad to see her or not. It was the same as with the yellow broth. He was at a low ebb. He had tortured himself over her as much as he could bear.

"You thought what?"

Amity's chin went a little higher. "I have been thinking," she said, "that if I gave you up to keep a house, I would begin—I have already begun—to hate the house."

"Am," he murmured sleepily.

"Mmm—?"

"I love you, Am."

617

She stirred beside him. "That's good," she said.

"You'd better think so, because I haven't time for any more problems."

"Tom," she said. She turned her head to look at him. "You did look awful, you know."

He ran his hand under her hair, spread across the bed to his shoulder, and grinned. "I'll look great in the morning."

"Tonight you looked miserable."

"I can't think why."

"Just tired, maybe?"

"Mm—"

"What is it they say—courage is a child of the morning—"

"Mm—?"

"Nothing—"

He turned over. "Courage isn't a child of the morning, Am." In another minute he would be asleep. He touched her and felt her warmth and her smooth skin and her long wonderful bones. "Courage is a child of love."

She stirred again beside him.

"Am—"

"Mmm—?"

"I love you, Am."

He moved his face against her hair on the bed and fell asleep.

FORTY-TWO

BY MONDAY MORNING the broth had gotten very yellow and very thick. Four times over the weekend Tom had come here to look at it and had seen it thickening and the color deepening. Now, on Monday morning, it was startling and striking.

He filtered off the mycelium and looked at the clear, deep-yellow broth. *Once I said these things would almost discover you,* he thought. *Once I said the good ones would force themselves on you. And this one would have forced itself on anyone—anyone* would have noticed it. *Once I said, If it's good, you'll know it—everything about you will know it.* Everything about him was talking to him now. Insistently. Passionately.

He sent a sample of the broth to Gates and a sample to Wentner for another chromatogram, and he set up his own potency tests on gram-positive and gram-negative test plates.

Its number was EA 39.

And then he decided that he couldn't wait a whole day for the results of all the tests, and as soon as he had sent out the samples, he put EA 39 into solvent extraction. He used six different solvents at once and re-extracted, and before noon he carried all the samples down to the assay laboratory—six samples of broth from which he hoped the antibiotic was missing, six samples of solvent into which he hoped it had been extracted, six samples of solvent from which he hoped it had been re-extracted, and six samples of water into which, if he was lucky, he had re-extracted it.

"But, Tom—this is EA 39," Gates said. "I just got the broth samples this morning."

Tom nodded.

Gates looked at him, puzzled. "What happened, Tom? What's up?"

"I like this one, Pearly. I didn't want to wait."

"But how do you know?" Gates said. "I mean, what makes you like it already?"

Tom tried not to show his feelings. "I like the looks of the broth, Pearly," he said.

Gates turned away, disappointed and a little annoyed, and Tom thought that he couldn't blame him. Nobody expected anything any more, not even when an antibiotic had gone pretty far. Certainly nobody was going to let himself begin to hope again because of the appearance of a broth. Nobody except a fool like me, Tom thought.

On Tuesday morning a huge clear area covered half of Tom's gram-positive test plate; a huge clear area spread over half of his gram-negative test plate. On both dishes EA 39 had left zones of inhibition as large as those left by penicillin.

An hour later in the assay laboratory a bewildered Gates, who had been trying very hard never to hope too much again, reported that EA 39 was very potent, EA 39 was broad-spectrum, EA 39 was stable, EA 39 could be extracted with solvents.

Tom walked out of Gates's laboratory and over to the administration building to talk to Will Caroline.

Coming up to Will Caroline's desk, Tom saw that Will had been going through the latest reports—on cultures discarded, on antibiotics worked a while and then discarded, on antibiotics sent to mice. He noticed that outside a few snowflakes were falling. He noticed that the day calendar on the desk read November 30.

"I want help," he said. "I want some help right away. I've got one that shouldn't wait."

Will Caroline's face brightened. "Well, that's good news! Which one?"

"EA 39. I want Max right away and more help still—as soon as I can have it."

"I didn't know you had one that good, Tom!" Will Caroline flipped through his reports, looking for the one on EA 39. "Where've you been hiding it?"

"I just got it. It's from last week's batch." Tom saw surprise chase the pleasure from Will Caroline's face, and he said quickly, "But this one is different—this one is important."

"It just came out of the fermentation room yesterday?"

"I knew it was good yesterday! I knew while it was still in there —I knew last Friday when I saw the broth!"

"You knew it from the *appearance?*"

Tom knew that Will was thinking that a man who had poured out as many antibiotics as he had should know better. He told him-

620

self to calm down—to try to be at least a little rational. How could he expect anyone—even Will Caroline—to understand how he felt, or why? Why? He didn't even know, himself, why.

"It's broad-spectrum, Will," he said. "It's as potent as penicillin—it's stable—it can be extracted with solvents. Will, this one is different from anything we've ever had."

Now, in the batch of reports, Will had found the one on EA 39. "Tom, no wonder it's broad-spectrum. It's Baramycin again."

"It's not Baramycin."

"But Wentner's chromatogram—" Will Caroline pulled out the report.

"I know Baramycin," Tom said. "This is too potent—too good. It's not Baramycin. Wentner's doing another chromatogram now."

Still puzzled, but beginning to listen, beginning to wonder, Will Caroline stopped reading the report. "Sit down, Tom."

"Will, don't waste time," Tom pleaded. "Don't waste a day. Give me some help on it to rush it through!"

"Tom, you've had it only two days, and you're asking me to pull men off other work?" Will Caroline stopped and just looked at him, not really arguing, even—just deeply puzzled.

"Right away. Max right away, anyway."

"But you don't know anything about it. Everything could be wrong with it."

"Everything is right with it!"

"Tom, it could be as toxic as hell."

Tom knew that everything Will Caroline said made sense—but to him today, none of it made sense. "Will, I know these bugs," he said. "I *know* them. And I know this one is important."

For a long moment Will Caroline didn't answer. He just sat leaning back in his chair, his fingers pressed together in a cone under his chin. He sat perfectly still, without speaking, just looking at Tom and studying him and thinking.

"Will"—Tom gripped the edge of the desk—"*this one is it!*"

For only another second Will Caroline hesitated, looking at Tom over his arched fingers. Then he dropped his hands to the desk. "All right, Tom."

Tom let go of the desk and straightened up.

"I'll get you help. You tell Max and I'll talk to Harrup. I'll get you whatever help you need."

Brainard headed for the research building. Morrissey was gone, Vought was gone, Weir was gone—and now if he wanted to know anything, he had to find it out for himself. He had to get around and ask questions. He had no choice—he got around and asked them.

On Wednesday, the first of December, Wentner reported that EA 39 still appeared to be Baramycin, and Brainard felt better. Then, that same afternoon, he walked into Wentner's laboratory and found him running more chromatograms.

"Why?" Brainard said. "How come?"

"Cable doesn't believe it," Wentner said.

"Well, what the hell—your tin can there says so, doesn't it?"

Wentner nodded. "I've only run it in four systems. I'm trying some variations now."

"Hell," Brainard said. "What are you letting him push you around for? Four systems should be enough for any man."

Wentner rocked a little on the balls of his feet and grinned. "I never argue with a man with a bug in his pants!" he said.

By Friday, December third, Wentner had run chromatograms of EA 39 and Baramycin in every system he had ever used. In some systems neither antibiotic moved. In three systems they both traveled at the same rate up the paper and stopped in the same place.

Brainard felt as though a weight had been lifted off his shoulders. An hour later he found Wentner in his office working out new systems. "What for?" Brainard demanded.

"To try to pull them apart," Wentner said.

"You're wasting your time," Brainard said. "You've found six different ways that EA 39 is Baramycin."

"We think that in the fourth system we can detect a slight difference," Wentner said. "Of course it could be some impurity causing it, but then again—I'll work out other systems over the weekend and see what happens."

Brainard strode out of Wentner's office and went down to the assay laboratory and walked into some more bad news. Twice Cable had gotten EA 39 purer, and now Strong was working too—and had gotten it purer still.

"They're going crazy," Brainard said at dinner that night. "They're all going stark raving crazy."

"Why?" Diana said. "What do you mean?"

"Because EA 39 is Baramycin all over again, and the chromatograms have told them so six times—and still they all go on working on it, night and day."

"Why are they bothering," Diana said, "if it's Baramycin?"

"Because Cable doesn't think it's Baramycin. He's decided. He tells them it isn't Baramycin, and they all fall in line and go to work."

"I remember that one," Diana said. "I remember Baramycin."

"Who doesn't remember Baramycin?" Brainard pointed his fork at her. "You're well rid of that nut, I can tell you. You thought he was crazy then. Now he's lost his senses completely. He's working on this like a maniac."

"But why?"

"He's got a feeling about it! He believes in it!"

Diana put down her fork.

"What's the matter with you?" Brainard said.

"He never believed that much in Baramycin."

For some reason Brainard found that disturbing. Then he said, "You haven't seen him in a year. He's crazier now. He's a hell of a lot crazier now. Where you going?"

Diana had left the table, and now she was walking quickly out of the room and up the stairs.

On Tuesday, December seventh, Wentner announced gleefully that EA 39 was not Baramycin.

"Six inches apart!" he said, holding the plate up to the north light. "Look at that—six inches apart!"

"What kind of a tin can is that?" Brainard exploded. "A halfdozen times it came out Baramycin!"

"Not this time!" Wentner said. He rocked on the balls of his feet in that idiot way he had. "Ho-ho!" he shouted. "Never argue with a man with a bug in his pants, Mr. Brainard!"

The next day, December eighth, Gates reported that the antibiotic was pure enough to test. On Thursday, the ninth—ten days after the yellow broth came out of the fermentation room—Mills prepared to put EA 39 into mice.

At nine o'clock the green-spotted mice . . .

And the half-hour wait . . .

Max was here, Will Caroline was here. Hale had been in and gone and would be back. Will Caroline and Max were leaning against the side counter, talking in low voices. Miss Watterling was finding things to do until the time was up.

At nine-thirty the yellow-spotted mice . . .

And the half-hour wait . . .

Max and Will Caroline came back to the jar. Tom watched the mice and walked away, walked around the room, stopped at the window and looked out at nothing, came back and looked at the mice again.

At ten o'clock the purple-spotted mice . . .

Hale was back. The sniffing and the crawling around were over, and the mice were huddled together in the usual wedge formation. There were no signs of tremors or of convulsions or of paralysis.

It was eleven o'clock. A green-headed sentry stalked the jar.

The long wait began.

Up the stairs before lunch, and after lunch, and throughout the afternoon, and again at closing time, and hang around until six o'clock, and back at nine o'clock, and back again at midnight, when they would be starting to wheeze if they were going to.

At a little past midnight Tom stood with Amity in front of the jar where it wasn't even necessary to look carefully—because when there was anything wrong, you saw it right away, and when the mice were all right, you saw that right away too. In the other jar the controls were already wheezing.

"Did you come a day early because of them, Am?" Tom said. He had been surprised to find her there when he came home tonight.

Amity didn't answer. She bent down and looked at the jar of treated mice and then at the controls.

"Did you, Am?"

"Of course," she said, without looking up. "You know that."

"In case they died?"

"Well—you know me," she said with a laugh. "I'm the possessive type. If you were going to hang one on or something, it was going to be with me." She glanced up at him and back at the mice. "You know these are really very attractive mice. Very neat and white—with those pink eyes and pink paws."

"Am, those are the most beautiful mice in the world—as long as they stay alive."

She smiled.

"Look at me, Am," he said. He drew her back from the jar. "Am, I found EA 39 eleven days ago, and you've been with me for seven of them."

She smiled. "I'm hooked—like the rest of you."

"You're carrying fish again. You know that, don't you?"

"Yes, I know that."

"Is that all it is, Am?"

"No—that's not all it is."

"That's all it was with the others—with Croft—and you didn't know it."

"You're so much like Croft," she said. "I'm always remarking on how you're just like him. I think of it often."

He laughed.

"Don't bother me with this nonsense," she said. "I know I'm carrying fish again. What can I do? I'm in love."

She looked away, into the jar again, and he turned her face back to him. "Then why won't you marry me, Am?"

"Because you don't have time to get married."

"It doesn't take long."

"Because I have two other husbands who are hoping to make me their sole means of support."

"Am, I want to get married."

"Well, I don't want to get married," she said. "I'm ridiculously in love—like an adolescent. It's as though I had lived my whole life in a cave and suddenly someone opened the door and let in the sunlight—that's the way I feel with you. So leave me alone and let me enjoy it while it lasts and stop bothering me about getting married. I'm an old hand at patching up a battered heart—that I know I can live through. I don't want to have to get out of a marriage that has gone bad."

"I think you just won't marry me"—he bent over to kiss her—"because I keep asking you in all the wrong places—in the middle of a mess of test tubes, or with a lot of mice running around."

"That's it—now you know." She looked back at the mice. "You can't be very worried about them if you're talking all this nonsense."

He looked at the mice too now. "I should be worried. I should worry for three days—and for weeks of testing after that—and for months of chronic-toxicity testing after that. I should worry right up until the time it cures a sick patient."

625

"Then why aren't you?"

"I am." He bent over to kiss her again. "If I ask you again in bed tonight, how about then, Am?"

"You're getting very fresh."

"Will you marry me if I ask you then?"

"Don't keep saying that," she said. "Keep your mind on your business."

On Friday morning the controls were dying, and the treated mice were fine.

"Don't wait," Tom said, as soon as Mills came through the door of the mouse laboratory. "Don't wait three days. Keep going."

"They sure do look good," Mills said.

"Keep going, Pat," Tom said again. "Find out if they can take it orally."

An hour later, when the mice treated by injection had lived only one full day, Mills infected two more jars of mice and then, using a blunt syringe, he shot doses of EA 39 down the throats of the six mice in one of the jars.

He placed the two jars on the counter beside the other two, the one containing the controls infected the day before, that were dying —the other containing the six mice treated by injection that had remained healthy now for one day.

By noon the controls infected on Thursday had died, and Miss Watterling removed them and there were three jars left.

On Saturday morning, in one of the three jars, there were six dead mice—the second set of controls. There were six live mice that had been treated by injection. There were six live mice that had been treated orally.

On Sunday morning the six mice treated by injection were fine and the six mice treated orally were fine.

On Monday, the thirteenth of December, EA 39 became Ambermycin.

FORTY-THREE

I T WAS LIKE A RIVER, Will Caroline thought.

It was like a river that had gone almost dry—that had fallen so low, it had bared every rock and stump and broken branch in its muddy bottom—and then had filled up again.

It was like a river built up out of hundreds of streams, and it rushed on, swelling larger, driving faster, adding new streams every day.

The chemists took back the crude Ambermycin to get it purer.

Gates tested it against every pathogenic organism he had and found it effective against fifty-two disease germs. He checked and rechecked and wrote to the office of the American Type Culture Collection for more organisms.

The chemists got it purer.

Mills began work to determine the therapeutic index—the ratio of the amount that killed to the amount that cured. The minimum dose that cured, given orally, was five milligrams per kilogram of body weight—and a mouse weighed about twenty grams, one-fiftieth of a kilogram. Figuring accordingly, Mills weighed thirty mice and gave them graduated doses to find the size of the dose that would kill. He gave:

15 mg/kilo to ten mice (three times the therapeutic dose)
25 mg/kilo to ten mice (five times the therapeutic dose)
50 mg/kilo to ten mice (ten times the therapeutic dose)

A therapeutic index of ten was considered not only safe but exciting. The thirty mice lived.

Resuming where he had left off, Mills gave:

50 mg/kilo to ten mice (ten times the therapeutic dose)
75 mg/kilo to ten mice (fifteen times the therapeutic dose)
100 mg/kilo to ten mice (twenty times the therapeutic dose)
150 mg/kilo to ten mice (thirty times the therapeutic dose)
200 mg/kilo to ten mice (forty times the therapeutic dose)

A therapeutic index of twenty was considered not only exciting but amazing. The fifty mice lived!

He watched all the mice for a week, looking for delayed toxicity.

After a week eighty mice lived, eighty mice ate and slept and moved normally. Eighty mice showed no effects from their doses of Ambermycin.

Cable went into the pilot plant to work with the engineers on the fermentation problems that always arose in scaling up production from a few grams in a flask to a thousand gallons in a tank.

The chemists got it purer.

Christmas came and went, and hardly anyone noticed. The river rushed on, picking up new streams and new force every day.

Mills weighed forty more mice and resumed where he had left off. He gave:

200 mg/kilo to ten mice (forty times the therapeutic dose)
300 mg/kilo to ten mice (sixty times the therapeutic dose)
400 mg/kilo to ten mice (eighty times the therapeutic dose)
500 mg/kilo to ten mice (one hundred times the therapeutic dose)

And forty mice lived!

Max Strong went to work in the isolation pilot plant where there were problems resulting from differences in timing. In the laboratory it took about three hours to isolate a few grams of Ambermycin. In the pilot plant it took three days to get the antibiotic out of a thousand gallons of broth.

The chemists got it purer, and the new year began.

Mills weighed thirty mice and gave:

500 mg/kilo to ten mice (one hundred times the therapeutic dose). Ten mice lived.

750 mg/kilo to ten mice (a hundred and fifty times the therapeutic dose). Six mice lived and four mice died.

1,000 mg/kilo to ten mice (two hundred times the therapeutic dose). Ten mice died.

At last he established the therapeutic index at more than a hundred to one. Ten to one had been exciting. Twenty to one had been amazing. A hundred to one was almost an anticlimax.

Gates found that Ambermycin was effective against seventy-four organisms. And checked and rechecked.

Mills cured mice of twenty diseases. And checked and rechecked.

And worked up the dogs.

And cured rats. And checked and rechecked.

And the chemists got it purer.

Dr. Jaxman, the pharmaceutical chemist, began to work on a capsule dosage form.

Dr. Loedick came to talk to Mills.

It was a river now, Will Caroline thought, from which men would live or in which they would drown.

On January 10, 1949, chronic-toxicity testing of Ambermycin began on rats and dogs.

And the longer wait began.

On the seventh of February Mills stood at the autopsy table and examined the stomach of a dog that had received the toxic-level dose of Ambermycin for a month. In the rats from the toxic-level group he had seen nothing. In this dog's stomach there were several sores half the size of a dime and one sore that was larger—the size of a quarter.

He motioned to Will Caroline who stood quietly to one side, waiting.

"Ulcers," he said. He pointed to the dog's stomach—to the area where it curved down to the intestine. "These sores—here in the duodenum, just above the intestine—do you see them?"

Will Caroline nodded. "You didn't see them in the rats?"

"Only the slightest inflammation—so slight I couldn't be sure. Dogs can't tolerate as much as rats."

"Do you see anything else?" Will Caroline said.

Mills shook his head. "We didn't find anything else in rats, either." He straightened up. "There had to be something—this was a toxic dose—a hundred times the therapeutic dose." He smiled. "At a hundred times the dose that cures, who's going to worry?"

He examined another dog from the toxic level and again found ulcers in the area of the duodenum and nothing else.

"Just ulcers," he said. "And you don't get ulcers in the few days that you take an antibiotic. And ulcers have to be pretty bad before anyone dies from them."

He examined a dog from the medium-dose level and found nothing.

Under the microscope, at the medium level, he still found nothing. "Only at the toxic level," he said. "And it takes a hundred times the therapeutic dose to do it."

Dr. Loedick was examining the evidence as Mills gave it to him. "A hundred to one?" he said.

"A hundred to one."

Loedick looked from Mills to Will Caroline. "That was your toxic dose that you gave to the animals—a hundred times the therapeutic dose?"

"That was the toxic dose. At that level I found ulcers in dogs. No other toxicity at that level. Nothing at all at the medium level, under the microscope."

Loedick closed the record book. "I'd like to give a single dose of this to a man—to a few men—as soon as possible."

"Dr. Cable will take it," Mills said. "I'll take it. Dr. Cable's technician wants to take it."

"Tomorrow morning," Loedick said. "Let's not waste time. I'll stay over. I want to see this myself."

At nine o'clock in the morning Tom swallowed a capsule of Ambermycin, and Dr. Loedick took a blood sample every hour for six hours until three o'clock and then one at six o'clock and one at nine o'clock. Gates set up the test on each sample to measure the amount of antibiotic it contained.

The next morning Loedick sat at Will Caroline's desk, studying the results.

"Six hours," he said. "At least six hours it stayed above the therapeutic level—probably longer."

"Well—at least it's being absorbed," Will Caroline said.

"Oh, it's getting into the system, all right!" Even Loedick was beginning to show excitement. He tapped his pipe on the table. "Reached its peak in two hours—fell gradually after that—still above the therapeutic level at six hours—traces of it in the bloodstream all day. I want to repeat the test today on Dr. Mills and the other fellow."

Mills took a capsule of Ambermycin and Moose Daniels took a capsule, and all day Loedick took the blood samples and Gates set up the tests.

"Give me some capsules," Loedick said a day later to Will Caroline. "I'll take them with me. If there is an opportunity—if there is a patient with a disease that penicillin won't cure—I'll try it. I can't make the opportunity—you know that. I have to wait for it. I don't know when it will be—I'll let you know."

The daily doses to dogs and rats went on.
Production went on.
The waiting went on.

On the afternoon of March third, Will Caroline's telephone rang.
"I have a patient."
It was Loedick, and Will Caroline sat up sharply.
"I have a woman who is dying," Loedick said. "She is dying of pneumonia and she is violently allergic to penicillin. If she gets penicillin she will probably die. If she gets nothing she will almost certainly die."
Loedick paused, and Will Caroline waited for him to go on.
"Are you there?" Loedick said.
"I'm here, sir," Will Caroline said.
"This woman is in very bad condition. Her general condition was poor to begin with. I was not her doctor. I was just called in on the case—less than an hour ago. Her condition is so low that it's possible she is past saving with anything—that she will die anyway—that this will not be a fair test. Her doctor and I decided we should take the chance. She is very far gone, Mr. Caroline—you understand that?"
"I understand it."
"She had a dose of Ambermycin five minutes ago."
Will Caroline looked at the clock. It was five minutes after three.

FORTY-FOUR

WHEN WILL CAROLINE and Callie arrived at the hospital in Boston, the woman was in an oxygen tent and her temperature was 104 degrees.

"She's low," Loedick said. "Very low."

Will looked around the lobby. "I'd like to wait here."

"This could go on for some time," Loedick said.

"I know. Where can we wait?"

"There's a room at the end of her corridor. You can wait there. Or if you go to a hotel where you can be comfortable, I'll call you."

"We'll wait here," Will said.

Loedick accompanied them to the waiting room on the woman's corridor. Leaving, he said, "Of course, she's only had one dose—at three o'clock. The drug hasn't had time to work."

Tom's house was filling up fast. Mills and Sara came in immediately after work, and then Max came over and went home again, and Derrick and Kate and Gates and Madeline came together, and Max came back with Constance. At a little past six Amity arrived, and a few minutes later Wentner came in.

"What've we heard?" Wentner said, rocking excitedly on the balls of his feet.

"Not much," Tom said. "Will called as soon as he got there. The woman was hanging on—with a temperature of a hundred and four."

"How long since she got that dose?" Wentner said. "Four hours?"

"They began at three," Tom said. "She's only had that one dose."

Wentner looked at Mills, who was pacing about the room. "What do you think, Pat? Should something have happened by now?"

"I'd feel better about the whole thing if Loedick had gotten to her with it sooner," Mills said.

"Why'd he wait?"

"Loedick didn't wait. He saw her at two-thirty and she had the capsule by three o'clock."

"She'd been sick for two days before they called him in," Gates said.

"But now she's had it for four hours. Should it have started to work?"

"It's working if it's going to—but her condition wouldn't change this fast."

"When, then?"

"It's hard to say. Maybe not until morning," Mills said.

"If she lives until morning," Gates said.

"Take a drink and sit down, Brew," Tom said. "There's nothing to do but wait."

At a few minutes past seven the telephone rang, and Tom rushed across the room to answer it.

"I can't say that it looks good," Will Caroline said, and his voice sounded worried. "Her temperature's up to a hundred and five."

"They haven't given up!" Tom said.

"She's still alive," Will said. "She'll get the second dose in two hours."

Tom hung up and passed on the report.

"A hundred and five!" Gates moaned. "She'll never make it."

"The woman's only had one dose, for heaven's sake," Madeline said.

"Well, why don't they give her more, then?"

"It wouldn't help," Mills said. "She's getting enough to cure her if it's going to. She'll get another dose at nine o'clock."

"She'll be dead by nine o'clock," Gates said.

"Well, just don't be so sure of that!" Madeline said. "People don't die so fast."

"This won't be fast," Gates said. "She's been dying for two days!"

"All the same," Madeline said, "people are always surprising you. Sometimes they don't even die when they ought to. Sometimes," she added, "they don't live when they ought to, either—although that's probably not the thing to say tonight."

"Not tonight," Gates said.

At eight o'clock the woman's temperature was 105.4.

"How long can this go on, Madeline?" Derrick said.

"This should be the peak. You usually get your peak temperature around seven or eight o'clock."

"It'd better be the peak," Gates said. "Or she's dead."

"How long before it might break?" Derrick said.

"That's hard to say. It'll be a while."

"She gets the second dose in an hour," Mills said.

At eight-twenty the telephone rang again.

"She's dead," Gates said.

She could be dead, Tom thought as he picked up the telephone. It was Moose.

"Jeez, haven't you heard anything?" Moose said.

"No change yet, Moose," Tom said, and he saw ten people in the room breathe with relief in the same instant. "I'll call you as soon as there's anything definite—good or bad."

At five minutes past nine, Ade Hale answered his telephone.

"She's had her second dose, Ade," Will Caroline said. "A few minutes ago."

"How is she?"

"Her temperature at nine o'clock was a hundred and five."

"Down four-tenths?"

"It's not significant."

"You see her, Will?"

"Nobody can see her. I'm in a waiting room on her corridor. Two doors away. I come out to talk to Loedick and to telephone."

"How does it look, Will?"

"Not good," Will Caroline said. "This is a very sick woman. And the family are emotional as hell, which doesn't help. Half an hour ago Loedick barred them from her room, and they made a hell of a fuss outside the door—yelled they knew she was gone. Loedick said he'd throw them out if they pulled it again. They're down in the waiting room now, still carrying on."

"Do they know she's getting a new drug?"

"This isn't a family you could tell. Even though there was nothing else to give her, they wouldn't understand."

"What do they think you're doing there?"

"They haven't asked. I'll call you in an hour, Ade, but Loedick doesn't expect much either way before midnight."

"You plan to stay there all night, Will?"

"I'll stay here."

"Where's Cal?"

"Cal's in the waiting room with her back against the door—keeping the family inside. I'll call you at ten, Ade."

634

"Are you going to quit?" Natalie said. "If that woman lives, are you going to quit?"

Brainard turned from the telephone. Rosswell was calling him every hour, as soon as he had a report from Hale. Now it was a few minutes past ten and the woman's temperature was 104.6. She wasn't any better—but still, neither had she died.

"Are you?" Natalie said again, and Brainard stared at her, astonished at her temerity in asking the question. Then he saw that she had gotten a drink while he was talking on the telephone.

"This isn't over yet," he said.

"But if that woman lives, Gil—are you going to quit?"

"No," he said. "I'm not going to quit. And get rid of that."

"Certainly," she said. She drained the glass.

Brainard's stomach was bothering him badly now, but he needed a drink himself. From across the bar Natalie watched him, smiling.

"*You* bet on the wrong horse, Gil!"

Brainard looked up and stared. "I did what I thought was best for the company."

Natalie shook her head, still smiling. "You did what you thought was best for you, Gil."

"Listen." Brainard lowered his glass. "I may still be the one who was right."

"But you may not be right, Gil." The vapid smile lingered.

Brainard turned away.

"You may be wrong—and then what are you going to do?"

Brainard sat down and put his head in his hands. He would beat them yet, he told himself. That woman wasn't getting any better. He thought of her with hatred, lying there, refusing to die. And what if she didn't die! Panic flashed through him. His stomach contracted violently and he crouched forward. Then he became aware of Natalie standing in front of him. She had taken another drink, and she was just standing there at an uncertain angle, her face flushed and her eyes unnaturally bright.

He stared at her, and she began to smile again. Then suddenly she started to laugh hysterically. She finished her drink and went back and poured another, spilling a little on the bar, and drank part of that, all the time laughing very hard.

"Shut up!" Brainard yelled.

Abruptly Natalie stopped laughing and leaned over the bar,

grasping it with both hands. "You were so brilliant!" she screamed. "You were so sure!"

"Shut up!" he yelled again. "Go sit down!"

"You and your power grab!"

"Go on. Go sit down before you fall down."

"You were the one man in the company who didn't have to stick his neck out—and you didn't see that. In the whole place—the only one who could have played it safe!" She held on to the bar, rocking a little. "You weren't involved! They find a drug—wonderful—you produce it! On the bandwagon! They don't find a drug—who'd have been clean? You! The only man not involved in the mess! You couldn't lose!" She began to laugh again. "You couldn't lose—and all this time you didn't see it!"

Slowly Brainard got to his feet. "You saw that!"

She tossed her head.

"All this time! And you didn't say something!"

"Say something!" she screamed. "When did you ever let me say something?"

"You should have said something!"

"When did you ever let me say something? When? Name me one time in twenty-five years when you ever let me say something! When did you ever let me say something?"

"Shut up, Natalie," Brainard warned. He advanced toward her.

"You see! When did you ever let me say something?"

Brainard raised his hand.

"You could have done nothing—absolutely nothing—and you bet your whole stake on the wrong horse!"

Brainard brought his hand hard across her face, and Natalie reeled back and stared at him, stunned, and then turned away.

"I wouldn't have told you anyway," she said. She walked uncertainly across the room and sank into a chair.

Brainard buried his face in his hands again. The cramps in his stomach were growing worse, and he was getting nauseated. He looked at Natalie, sitting a little crooked in the chair, and saw the red blotch that his hand had brought to her face. But she was right, he thought—he could have done nothing. And now—in the whole company he alone had to hope for failure. How could he have let himself get into this position? What could he have been thinking of? He must have been mad!

Natalie moved in the chair. "Why don't you quit?" she said dully.

He didn't want to quit. He didn't want to leave this company—this town—this house, even. He was too old for change. He was sick. He didn't want to leave the routine he knew and was used to.

"You'll never quit," Natalie said dully. She had another drink that he hadn't seen her take. She was going to pass out soon. Let her, he thought. He'd leave her there. He'd like to hit her again and help her along.

But she was right about that, too. He wouldn't quit.

At eleven o'clock Tom hung up the telephone. For the fifth time Will Caroline had reported that there was still no change in the woman's condition.

"That second dose hasn't done much," Gates said.

"She's still alive," Madeline said. "She's hanging on."

"It's eight hours now since the first dose, and there's still no change. It doesn't seem very hopeful."

"Woodrow, that patient is alive," Madeline said firmly. "Just don't you forget that."

Tom motioned to Amity and stepped out on the porch, leaving the door open a crack so he could hear the telephone if it rang. He stood beside the door, leaning against the wall of the house. Inside he could hear the weary idle talk that had been going on now for six hours. Along the boardwalk you could pick out the Enright houses where the lights still burned. Max came out and walked down to the boardwalk and came back and went into the house.

"What will happen to it now, Tom?" Amity said after a while.

"If she dies, Loedick will probably test it again sometime—when there's another chance—because this woman was so far gone—"

"I mean if she lives."

"You think she's going to live, Am?"

"As Madeline keeps saying, that patient is alive. Don't you forget that."

Tom smiled and reached for her hand. "Well, if she lives, there'll have to be a lot more testing—a lot more work. But not for me. It's moved away from me now."

"Whose work now?"

"Mills still has to take it through three full months of animal testing—to be sure there are no hidden problems we haven't found yet—no delayed reaction that hasn't showed up."

"But they gave it to this woman—"

"This woman was going to die without it." He paused and thought that she was still dying—with it. "This woman was almost certainly going to die, so you take a chance. Every patient who will eventually get this—if it becomes a drug—is not certainly going to die without it. So with them you don't take a chance. You do the testing in animals for the full three months. You do more testing in clinics." He smiled at her. "Only none of it," he said again, "is mine any more."

It was midnight, and Callie had gone out for sandwiches and coffee. Across the room the woman's husband had fallen asleep and was snoring. Her daughters and their husbands had gone off somewhere. Loedick came out of the patient's room, and Will Caroline got up and went out to talk to him.

"At midnight the temperature was a hundred and three," Loedick said.

Will looked up hopefully.

"It's a normal drop from the early evening peak, and it could be only temporary. You get these swinging temperatures."

"It could go up again?"

"It could. This can't be considered a change in her condition—it's not a significant break in temperature. But if there's going to be a break, it should happen soon."

"Will you be back soon?" Will said as Loedick turned to go.

"I'm not leaving," Loedick said. "I'm only going to look at another patient. I'll be back."

Will Caroline made his telephone calls to Hale and to Cable's house and then walked down the long corridor to stretch his legs. Then he saw that Callie had returned, and he went back to the waiting room and stood at the window looking out at the lights of cars moving along the street and at a few people walking on the sidewalk in front of the hospital. Callie held out a sandwich, and he shook his head. Then she handed him a container of coffee. He drank it standing up. An ambulance passed below the window and disappeared around the corner of the hospital. He could hear the woman's husband snoring. He finished the coffee and put down the paper container and looked back out the window. Across the street a clock in the window of a restaurant said twenty minutes to one.

"Will—" Callie said.

He looked around and saw Loedick walking toward the waiting

638

room, and he hurried out to meet him, alarmed because it was early for the hourly report, and all he could think was that the woman had died.

Then he saw Loedick's face and he knew that the woman had not died. Loedick stood in the corridor, just outside the waiting room door, and nodded his head several times.

"The temperature is ninety-nine-point-five," he said.

At five minutes past one, Brainard stood with his hand on the telephone, asking himself whether he could quit and knowing that he could not. He almost wished they would fire him—he would be better off. But they wouldn't do that either. They would just push him to the rear—force him to take a back seat. And whatever he did, he would never push his way to the front again. He would stay here, he knew, and go on—but it would never be the same again.

He moved away from the telephone. His stomach contracted violently, and he went into the bathroom and threw up.

At two o'clock the woman's temperature was normal.
At three o'clock she received the third dose of Ambermycin.
In the morning she was alive.

"Am," Tom said. It was light over the water, and the others had gone home and they were alone. "I won't wait, Am."

Amity came over to the sofa where he was lying and turned off the light beside it. "It's morning," she said. "Go to bed and get some sleep."

He reached up to her. "I won't wait any longer, Am."

"Go to bed," she said. "The woman lived. You don't have to sleep on sofas any more. I don't want to wait either."

He looked at her, surprised. "What changed your mind?"

"The woman lived."

Tom smiled, puzzled. He knew her too well to believe that it was the difference between success and failure.

"The woman lived," she said, bending over him, "and the mistress who has had the best part of you for three years left you last night and moved into the clinics. If I don't take you now, somebody else will."

She stood up. "And now I'm going home," she said. "Good night."